JONATHAN C. BLAZER

Out of the Night

First edition

ISBN: 13: 978-0-578-40071-6

This book was professionally typeset on Reedsy.
Find out more at reedsy.com

Acknowledgement

To everyone that helped; I don't have enough space to thank you all. Just thank you, this story wouldn't exist without the help of so many hands.

I

Part One

"But I am a blasted tree; the bolt has entered my soul; and I felt then that I should survive to exhibit, what I shall soon cease to be - a miserable spectacle of wrecked humanity, pitiable to others, and intolerable to myself."

— Mary Shelley, Frankenstein

Chapter 1

"I've come to believe there are things that cannot be changed, like air is needed to make fire. I cannot leave this place any more than the moths can leave a flame once they see its light. I can have no more blood on my hands. My memories of this place keep me here," I said, facing the balcony.

"What a shame, James—you would have been magnificent at this job," the man in shadows said.

I waved him on, still facing forward, knowing what I had to do to set things right. I waited a long time, in the silence of the room. It was oddly peaceful; everything felt right at that moment. I stood up, taking the rope with me to the balcony overlooking the ruins of my city.

Down below me were memories, memories that had taken the shape of every form there is. Tall, broad, short, black, white, male, female, the young, and the old. All were fragments of a bigger picture than they realized; all were searching for the meaning of what was in their heads, unable to move on from this place; ghosts of the mind, ghosts of everything I could remember.

I tied the rope to the railing on the balcony; I hoped I had gotten the knot tight enough. I stepped up onto the railing, and thousands of eyes looked upon me: Center stage at the end of the world. I was the final punchline of the entirety of the human race; the last man on Earth would die without anyone to watch.

To my wife, thank you for the joy you gave me in our union. I am truly sorry for the way it became. To my daughters, Daddy is the one to be blamed, not you kiddos. *I guess there is a heart after all in this ugly armadillo,* I joked to myself. Facing my demise would be grossly mundane if I ended it on a sad note.

Might as well go out with my head held high. "My name is James, and I was a computer guy all my life. I was the best in the world at solving problems. I had a loving wife and a beautiful daughter in every sense of the word. They were mine, and I was theirs. My name is James. I don't want to remember anymore. I am a ghost of the man I used to be. I—we—are the ghosts of what we used to be."

I looked over the edge. Seeing all the ghosts below me, I had hoped I wouldn't become one—but I had. I lifted my right leg and let it hang over the railing. The ledge no longer felt so wide.

Chapter 2

"Foul, on number eight blue!" The referee blew into his whistle and the game came to an abrupt halt—the reason being because my daughter had been thrown to the ground by a much bigger kid.

"Watch where you're going, nerd!" said the bigger girl to my daughter. My daughter lay on the ground, tucking in her bottom lip from tears already forming. A moment later, the referee blew his whistle, signaling the end of the game.

I wasn't one of those fathers with a complex for always worrying about his child being hurt; I simply didn't want her to be hurt, ever, if I could help it. So I ran out onto the field and gently picked up my daughter Molly, by the arm, brushing dirt out of her long auburn-blonde hair in the process. "Are you okay, kiddo?" I asked her. Molly was already showing the puffy red cheeks of a child, and I could tell they were about to spill over with tears.

I knew Molly would be embarrassed if she cried in front of all the other girls—she is a very sensitive girl, after all. I could see them start to water up; I bent down to tell her a joke in hopes of distracting her from her pain. "Hey. What do you get from a pampered cow?" I asked her.

Molly looked at me, confused, her pain momentarily forgotten.

"I don't—know," she said between choked hiccups.

"It's an easy one, kiddo, it's spoiled milk! Get it?" I told her, smiling the best dad smile I could muster.

Molly's joke standards were thankfully as low as her old man's. She started to giggle until her small tears began to go away, like rain drying on a hot summer's day. I was thankful for that—crisis adverted.

"Come on, Molly, let's go get some ice cream, get you cleaned up, honey," I stated, taking her hand. Molly just nodded her head, not talking.

As we walked past the bigger girl from earlier, Molly spoke to her: "Sorry." Molly has always been a sweet kid, you couldn't ask for a better child. That is something she took from me, but when it came for standing up for herself... Well, my wife and I are still working on it.

The girl looked like she had been slapped in the face, clearly taken off balance by Molly's comment. She scoffed and walked away, staring long and hard at both Molly and me. I looked at the girl's face a moment longer before she turned away—she was clearly dumbfounded, though I was more concerned about the purple bruise at the top of her head. She definitely didn't get that from an eight-year-old girls' soccer game. The shape was too round, and the size was too big to be anything else. I shook my head at the sight. Some parents do sick things, and I was one of those parents who wouldn't let them get away with that. You just aren't supposed to hit a child.

I gripped Molly's hand a little tighter and started walking off the field; the sun was still high in the North Carolina summer. It would stay like this for a few more hours yet. As we started to walk away, a heavy-set woman had pulled aside the big girl and was yelling up a decent storm for an after-school soccer game. They both had broad shoulders and long black hair, leading me to assume they were related somehow.

Must be the mother, I thought, as we walked towards them on the way to the main road. *Look at you; you can't even take out a kid half your size. Pathetic, really. When I was your age, I could do a hip fake like no one's business.* The woman yelled at the poor girl, turning her head like a righteous preacher amongst the heathens.

It wasn't my place, I knew that, but I just had to say something as we were walking by. I made sure to get her attention with a long stare of my own. The woman made eye contact with me as I spoke. "To be fair, lady, I am sure that was a very long time ago for you."

I just never could imagine saying something like that to Molly, being that mean for no reason. Not waiting for her rebuttal, I dropped down on one knee and looked at the girl. Her mom recovered quickly from her moment of lapse in intelligence. "Excuse me—who do you think you are?" she shouted.

I ignored her; instead, I focused on the girl. "You did well out there; you have some real fast legs. Keep playing and you will go pro someday, I bet!" I gave her thumbs up and a big smile.

The girl just kept her head pointed towards the ground (the tough girl act from before was gone now), and mumbled, "Thanks." I stood back up, taking Holly's hand, and nodded to the girl. As I was turning away, I made sure to make eye contact with the lady. Her eyes fumed with fire, and I could only imagine what she might have actually been wishing upon me.

Hideous and troll-like indentations formed almost rock-like cheekbones, and fat rolled on her face as she grew angrier at my comment. The troll (as I was now viewing her inside my mind) spat in my direction, yet I simply smiled. Growing up, my mother had always told me to kill people with kindness. It always worked, though personally, I am a fan of the "confident smile" trick, and generally the result caused people like this woman to go insane with anger, which was fine by me.

"Let's go, Molly," I said as the two of us started walking away faster from the soccer field, heading into the rest of the park. Molly kept her eyes pinned on the girl behind us. I looked down at her, noticing she was still looking back; I knew she would have questions about the girl. I just had to be a good father and come up with the right lesson from all of this.

As we walked, and as our journey moved from simple woods to high structured city, a rusting red truck pulled up to the edge of the park. Inside the truck were two men. The larger one had a grizzly beard, and an old hat with popped-out strings all set in place by a fishing hook. I recognized the younger, slim man with wild hair as Benny, who I had gone to school with, once upon a time. Every class had a druggie, and Benny had been ours. There were very few days he didn't have puffy red eyes from drugs, or he would reek of something awful. It had been years since we last seen each other, but it was hard to forget a face like that. It came with the territory when you stayed in your childhood hometown. That is, running into people you would never want your children to see.

They both looked pissed, as Benny rolled down the window speaking to me. "Hey, I know you. You're James. Yeah, I know that face... We went to school once... Yeah, I know we sure did," he said with a mischievous smile forming over his face, showing ghastly yellow teeth.

I really didn't want to talk with Benny. To best of my ability, I wanted to shield Molly away from people like him for as long as possible. "How's it going, Benny? Long time no see," I responded with a wave of my free hand, trying to tuck Molly behind me with my other.

"Long time no talk, is more like it. Why don't you come with us? We can get us some beers and catch up for a bit," Benny told me, rather than asking me.

I gestured to Molly behind me. "Have to take a rain-check, Benny. Need to get the kiddo home. Goodbye Benny, take it easy," I said, turning with Molly and moving quicker out into the city before Benny could respond. "Kill them with kindness," I whispered as my heart thumped in my chest.

While we were still within hearing distance, Benny mumbled, "Rich prick."

We moved a little quicker, and before we left the view of the park altogether, I turned back seeing the troll lady and the girl getting into the truck. The silent passenger with the beard and fishhook turned towards the girl, and in that moment, something bad kicked me in the stomach. Looking at him, he just felt wrong like I could tell he was something bad. In real life, monsters don't just show themselves. They don't just present themselves and say, "Hey I'm a monster." However, something about him felt inhuman. I turned back around and moved us quicker, out of the park. *Maybe I should call the police,* I thought, but it probably wouldn't have done any good—I just had a hunch something was wrong. *Molly is my priority; just keep walking away and don't expose her to such things.*

Staying true to my word, I got Molly ice cream on our walk home. I was savoring the cold chocolate of my cone when Molly finally spoke up for the first time since leaving the field. "Daddy, why were you nice to that girl? I mean, I said sorry only because I didn't want her to hit me again," she stated.

I sighed, trying to form what my old man would have told me if I asked that question. My father had lived his life as a righteous person, something I aspired to be every day. My parents were now a few years gone and for all it was worth, my wife and I were on our own with raising Molly. I always worried; I always worried about saying the right thing to Molly. "Well, its simple, Molly. Everyone deserves kindness; everyone needs to be loved by someone. The least we can do for those around us is show kindness. Do you understand what I mean?" I responded.

She tucked her bottom lip in, a childish trait that had never left her. "So, we have to always be kind—even to the mean ones? Like that lady and girl?" she asked.

I looked down at my daughter, stopping both of us on the sidewalk. "Especially the mean ones," I said, smiling at her. Molly smiled back, and we continued on our way to our apartment duplex. "We will always be the good guys, right, Dad?" Molly asked, stopping again on the sidewalk.

"Sure thing, Molly. There's no reason to be anything else but the good guys," I responded, and Molly beamed. I gave more thoughts about my statement. "Sometimes, Molly, it's not always going to be easy to be the good guy. What makes a person good is this: actively making a conscious decision to do what is right in spite of the consequences. If you can stay true to the fire you keep in your heart, and be implacable in your values, you will never stop being a good person—that is at least, from your own view."

My daughter's smile turned into a frown. It would be many years before she would know what I meant by that, just like it had taken me many years since it was first told to me. Not wanting to confuse Molly more, I smiled at her. "Now come on, your mother is waiting for us. It's board game night!" I shouted, racing ahead as the two of us ran home.

Chapter 3

We sat on our living room couch. It was dull brown, appearing to look like midnight in the light from our television. My wife and I were finishing watching something—I wasn't sure what it was. The whole time my mind circled like a cyclone in a toilet around the events on the field today. *Had I done enough*? I wondered.

I had given my father's advice, which he had given to me as a small child: *keep the fire going,* he had informed me. That was how we stayed good people—by kindling the fire, stocking the flames high whenever we could. Only, had I done that now? My father's advice had always been more geared towards helping our family and ourselves. Helping others? Well that was advice better left to more caring men, I suppose.

My wife Diana was leaned towards me on the couch, her golden hair now brown from the television's purple light. She stopped talking, looking at me with both her eyes, worry stitched across her forehead." Are you alright, smart guy? You have that long look of yours again." She was referring to a thing I was known for doing. According to my wife, I would just disappear sometimes, recede like the curtains of a stage play before being privy to my world of thoughts.

"Huh? Oh yeah, you know, just thinking about today," I responded, looking at my wife, her angular cheeks riding high in the dull light.

She sighed heavily. "Yeah—I figured that's what it was. You know, James, you can trust you said the right thing to Molly. She's eight years old; she will have a traumatic event every couple of days in her life. That is just how childhood is supposed to be," she stated.

"I know that, Diana, but you know, sometimes I worry about her she's such a sweet—" I had started to respond before a thick pillow slapped me in the face. I grumbled out the last few words I had into the feathered silk sack. Then I moved the pillow from my face and felt a wet kiss tap lightly on my cheeks. I flushed red. *Love was when a kiss on the cheek still made you turn red after so many years,* I thought.

"James, baby, you take things way too seriously sometimes. Molly won't be sweet forever. She will grow up big and intelligent. She has the best nerdy and sensitive father she could ask for in her life. Don't forget that whenever you explain your long points, people have to figure out things for themselves; kids, especially, need to be exposed to the bad to overcome life. Molly will grow up soon enough. No need to rush everything with a lesson." She stretched, getting up from the couch, her low-riding pajama top edging slowly up, showing the pale skin on her back. "You can't fix everything, James, not even people. I'm sure you did the right thing," she added.

She was right, of course. Diana was very rarely wrong. I took the pillow Diana had hit me with and tossed it at her as she stood near the staircases leading to the upstairs of our home. "I'm not that sensitive," I joked back to her.

"Of course you aren't, big guy," she winked, turning slightly and motioning to head up the stairs to bed with her body. "You did well today, like you always do for both of us, James. Don't forget that. Now come to bed, dude, you have more good to do." Diana cocked out her hips and lowered her cotton-pajama bottoms. I arched my eyebrows. *Duty calls,* I thought, as I left the couch, following my wife upstairs.

Chapter 4

It was light; I didn't have to look at the glowing letters on my alarm to know that the time would just sadden me more than anything else. I was deep in my thoughts about what had occurred earlier today. Had I done the right thing for that girl? Her parents—if that is what you could call child abusers, and I'm not sure I would—were obviously not the kind of people who deserved children.

Yet I had let them take that girl without any kind of protest. What was I going to do, though? I had Molly with me; sometimes it was just best to stay out of things. I had no real evidence of child abuse other than a bruise on a young girl's head. I had to put my own family first, but it all felt rotten enough to wake me in the middle of the night before my alarm went off. The implications of what could be a huge mistake ate away at me. Even what Diana and I had talked about failed to put me at ease with the situation. *Fixing people is hard,* I thought. *Machines: it's just about connecting point to point. People: you had a better chance of conjuring fire in your hands than understanding why the average person did anything.*

I was bothered by my thoughts and the time. That was okay though, I had the rare gift of sharing my bed every night with my best friend. Even now, as she snored lightly beside me, I didn't feel any annoyance. In fact, it almost made me want to giggle. That was our thing, though; we completed each other in many ways. At my job during the day, I could never relax, but once home, the gloves were off, and my humor was in full swing. She married me for my corny jokes. "What do you call a fish with no eyes?" I would ask, waiting just long enough to tell her "A fshhhh," and still she'd laugh, every time.

Somehow this wonderful creature beside me would support my awkward jokes and still have enough seriousness for the both of us. My wife Diana, always being motivated by her job as a nurse, and me, I was more concerned with caring for my wife and child. We made a great team.

So, what were a little snoring, and the occasional passing of wind (I would always blame it on the dog, even though we both knew we had no dog). It's the little things like that make you feel good, and not like a fool, for falling in love. As I lay in our bed thinking of all the little times we had shared through years of marriage, a thought did occur to me.

Something made me wonder why I would wake up so suddenly. It wasn't such an oddity (after all, waking up worried about life—is life) and it had never bothered me enough to actually keep it on my mind. What father hasn't had a restless night, worried about his children? Then again, maybe the father of that girl might not. I hoped her father was out there somewhere, caring for her. My mind wouldn't let me accept anything else; I knew the truth, even if I didn't want to admit it. I had met monsters today; I had let them go with a little girl. I shivered at that thought.

I rolled to my right, overlooking my wife's slender form in the darkness. My alarm clock read 4:23—way too early to be even entertaining the idea of playing the sleep game now, with my shift starting in only a few hours. *It's nothing,* I thought, as my eyes naturally drifted across our room.

I always thought our room was too wide, too open, but like most of my home interior design battles, I had stepped back. Which was good, it gave me a reason to thank the angel next to me, because if I had my way, the posters and beanbags from my bachelor days would still be a thing. A wide room wasn't a problem for my wife; she always found a way to fill a space with "love" as she put it. Shapes in the darkness were just that—shapes in the darkness. Nothing to be concerned about.

I decided it was just me being weird and I should get some rest—Lord knows that 6 am would always come earlier and earlier. As my eyes closed and I drifted, I thought I saw a shadow entering the room. *Must be the dog,* I thought. *Only we didn't have a dog.* It took almost a full minute for my brain to make the connection of that thought. I opened my eyes to see a man standing there at the foot of the bed. His form was clear, even in the darkness of the night. An almost docile face, looking lost, which I'm sure must have matched my face upon seeing him. His broad shoulders, looming with a tussle of long, wavy midnight hair, adorned his shoulders like a thick cape made of the darkness itself.

I tore the covers from around me, lunging for the hammer I kept in our nightstand next to the bed. That was when the man's docile face, all round and guileless, snapped into vivid snarls of rage. His face transformed into a looming beast right before making the final kill. My heart pounded in my chest and I felt my body tense up, stopping my hand just over the hammer. The man came through the room with impossible speed, blowing away the covers concealing our naked forms. I panicked in the cold, feeling the chill of danger, like the slow warning you get when touching ice—you've ignored the clues around you too long, and now you're too numb and too stupid to do anything. The man took hold of my wife's leg, pulling with animalistic ferocity and speed. He moved her so fast it was as if his hand wasn't even on her leg.

That was able to pull me from my stupor and into action, my body taking flight like a jet engine. I dove for the man, but ended up passing right through him like a whisper from the wind. I landed hard on the ground, my tackle useless against all but myself.

Wait, that couldn't have been it. I had clearly hit him square in the chest. He was right there, I thought. I couldn't have missed. I smacked hard into the floor, the sudden noise finally waking my wife. Her face was one of concern, utter bewilderment at the look on my face and the seemingly animal-like man holding onto her leg.

"James, what is going—"

Diana was cut off as the man yanked her out of our bed; greedy and fast, like a young boy pulling rats from a wall by the tail. Diana screamed my name as she was torn away, and I dove again, reaching out with both my hands. I felt our fingers touch for the last time.

That was it; Diana was being pulled down our hallway faster than my mind would allow me to comprehend. The speed was unreal—mind splitting—and the insanity was going to have to be put aside for now. Until after I killed the son of a bitch for taking my wife.

I sprang forward, crashing into the door on the way out with my shoulder. *Strange,* I thought, *I had closed the door* (we didn't lock it on account of Molly) *but I didn't hear it open from that guy coming in.* I never once opened our bedroom door without it making a sound. The frame was slightly too big for such a narrow doorway, so the door always scraped when opened, period—this time included.

Our house wasn't a big one, it was a simple two floors. Yet in those moments as I chased him, it felt like the house was a living and growing thing, its hallways replaced by some never-ending mansion.

"James!" Diana screamed again as the man continued to pull her faster.

That was when every husband, father, and mother would hear the one scream that would shake anyone into pure animal instincts. Instincts that would drive a man clawing and biting at anything which harmed his children. It was my own child's scream—Molly. My sunshine and the greatest gift my wife had ever given me. Her scream almost took me off my feet; it was all happening too fast.

"Daddy!" her voice pitched, almost crippling me into panic. Her room was downstairs. At the same time, the man had my wife, heading in the direction of my office, almost out of sight in as he sank into the gloom. A man's worst fear: who to go for. Your small daughter, or the love of your life?

I didn't have to think. There are just some things every parent knows: it's kids first, no matter what. I took off down the stairs and ended up losing my footing in my haste, hitting the bottom wall hard. I recovered, calling out, "Molly!" I managed to navigate in the darkness using my daughter's screams. I reached her room at the end of the downstairs hallway, crashing into every object like a seasoned drunk coming home.

I could hear no more sounds coming from Molly's room as I approached her doorway. Without waiting, I kicked her closed door in, storming into her room. Unlike most eight-year-old girls, my daughter liked everything black and purple, which made the already dark room seem like a black hole with no light. Once the adrenaline of the situation eased, I was able to smell the room. It was the first things I noticed; it was a festering stink that dug its way into whole parts of your childhood nightmares—you knew it from the time you smelled your first pet. It was death, the smell everyone in their lives would learn at least once. Even if it was the chemical mask used to block the odor of your dead grandparents in the funeral home, you would know the smell, because death wasn't a smell that could ever be truly covered up.

"Molly!" I screamed into the shadows of her room, while fighting the urge not to cover my mouth.

"Daddy, I'm here, where are you?" she responded.

"Daddy's right here, pumpkin. Don't worry, nothing will hurt you." Only that was a lie—I had no idea if my Molly was safe, but come hell or high water, I was going to protect her.

As we talked, a metal taste entered my mouth, and my nose; I couldn't see Molly's silhouette clearly, my body was pumping so much blood from the adrenaline. I waited for her verbal confirmation, but I had to be quick. The reality that my wife was upstairs with a slippery and potentially brutal person made me swallow hard. "Molly, are you okay? I need you stay right here, honey. I have to go get your mother, okay? I will be back, I promise."

I said to her, turning to leave that room, my heart sinking deep into my body.

It was becoming hard to breathe, and the race was still miles from the finish.

"Daddy, please don't leave me, don't leave me alone," Molly said from behind her bed, reaching out for me.

"I'm not baby, just stay down here, and close the door. Don't let anyone in, I will be right back with Mommy."

"Daddy, no, please don't go!" I saw her small hand stretching towards my leg. Never before in my life had I wanted to scoop her up and carry her from that place more. But I had just made a decision. It was to go find my wife, now Molly was safe. I couldn't risk her being hurt. Molly had always been very dependent on Diana and me. I wasn't going to leave my daughter alone for long. I could see Molly's hand on my leg now; she must have been almost in shock, and I never known her skin to be so pale before. I took off out of my daughters' room, slamming the door shut behind me, before my fear overtook me.

My tears stung my eyes as I pounded up my staircase, taking three at a time, and all the while I kept praying my daughter would be safe. I thought again of the park. That decision was haunting me—I had woken myself up from sleep, worried about something I had said to my daughter. Now I would be thinking about how I just left her alone, I would likely never sleep again.

Focus on getting Diana, James, I thought to myself, as the images of my ordeal flashed like a computer screen in my head.

My thoughts were too fast. Thursday's spaghetti night hadn't seem like such a bad idea, until now when I was about to throw up. I kept it down, though, as I made my way down the hallway, my bare feet sticking to the ground from my sweat and the rising heat in my house. It was like standing in a furnace filled with lava, my whole body drenched from the heat.

Once at the end of the hallway, I came into my office out of breath.

I didn't know what I was going to do, but I knew I was going to save my wife from this man.

I had to. Somehow, I had to be that guy, who would do anything for his family.

It was dark, and I could only see the outline of my desk with my desktop on it, silently humming in the background. My hand found the light switch, in spite of the darkness. It didn't take long; it's amazing the muscle memory you develop after so many years. When the lights didn't turn on, I felt a chill. The darkness had such a way of turning simple shapes into your biggest fears. Shapes become different in the gloom when you're afraid.

My office rounded out to another hallway at the end, connecting to a small balcony overlooking the city. Fear kept me from entering the room—the idea of being alone in the dark is a feeling ingrained in us all. Still, I couldn't make out any shapes in the darkness that looked foreign, from my quick glance over. *If they weren't in my office, that just leaves the bathroom and balcony; if I can just sneak up on the son of a bitch, I can save my wife,* I thought. I stepped forward into the darkness of another hallway; I didn't want to use my hands to guide me, for fear of knocking a family photo down. I trusted my eyes as I walked, my sight allowing me to see light coming from outside, which gave me some relief, but also increased my panic.

My thoughts came to one conclusion as I moved slowly: *it means the man has deliberately shut down our lights to our duplex. This isn't random—it must have been planned.* I would worry about the why later, once I got my hands around his throat. I passed the bathroom and the door was open. I could see by the fierce light of the city coming through the windows that it was empty as well. Nice thing about all the light from the city; my house was never completely dark. *So, the bathroom is empty; where can they be?* I thought.

As I passed the bathroom, I stepped onto the balcony, and was greeted by the coldest of winds one comes to expect in a Carolina winter. I was reminded that I wasn't clothed. This wasn't exactly what I had planned for the night. I felt vulnerable, the fear of what might be happening to my family making me even colder in the wind.

I realized as I stood on the edge of my balcony that I was alone. Not a single sign of my wife, or the intruder. I was the only one out; the streets below were quiet, early morning traffic bustling along without any care in the world, no idea of the horror I was facing up here alone.

Oh God, where is she? They still have to be in the apartment. I didn't hear any door close; why didn't I call the police? What am I, some kind of badass? I'm just a computer guy who works a nine-to-five, five days a week. Even if I find them, what am I going to do? I began looking around in a panic. Everything around me sounded so loud in my ears. That was when I saw my wife.

She was on the ledge overlooking our neighbor's house next door. I blinked in surprise; the distance was easily over the width of an average-sized road. How in the world had she got up there? And what was she doing up there? My wife had nightmares coming out on the balcony some nights, let alone being on the roof that high up. She could get hurt, the wind wasn't blowing that hard down below, but up here at this height, it might as well be a hurricane some nights. If my heart could beat any faster, it would have exploded. I had to do something fast, anything at all.

"Diana, what are you doing up there?" I cupped my hands around my mouth to shout to her. "Just stay there, honey! I'm going to call for help!" I strained my voice, but it wasn't audible over the wind that had suddenly picked up.

The wind rustled her nightgown, exposing more of her tender legs, which even from a distance would still make my heart race under normal circumstances. At the sound of my voice, Diana turned her face to me. She had on a smile when her lips moved, and she spoke something right before she jumped. I would never know what the words were. The truth is a part of me never would want to know what they were, although it seemed that her words were: "Your fault, James."

I had killed my family.

Chapter 5

Her body plunged to the sidewalk below, head first, exploding out with the impact, smearing blood like a melon dropped in an experiment.

"Jesus Christ! Diana, no!" I caterwauled like a creature into the night sky, my tears unable to hide the image of her body down below. I could not fathom what I had just seen. It was like my brain was being torn to pieces by fingers, and my heart was being eaten by some terrible beast. This couldn't be real; I was supposed to be in bed with my wife. We had made love; we had gone to bed just like any other night.

Not this, please. No, not this.

That was when I heard the screams coming from below, where people were emptying into the streets in a wave of panic. An endless sea of terror unfolded—the disparate picture of a peaceful city just a moment ago now long gone.

Cars began to drift, moving at odd angles almost like they were being pushed by some kind of invisible current. The screams from the people below me caused me to back away from the edge; the nightmare below me played on, and I couldn't escape. Curiosity had always been something my mother said I was known for—I always had to look. When my parents were preparing to put out Christmas gifts for my sister and me, I would sneak into their rooms when they were gone, and find my presents for Christmas inside. Sometimes, I would get sad from seeing I was only going to get clothes, but mostly, I got exactly what I wanted (which always made it hard to act surprised, come Christmas morning). I knew that was wrong. When you're ten you just had to; curiosity got the better of you. The same thing applied now. I knew I should look away, I just couldn't help myself.

Peering over the balcony, I made my body flat with the ground. I must have lost my mind at some point; it was the only explanation for what I was seeing. People were being torn to pieces by some unknown invisible force. Their limbs and faces were peeling off like cheese being run through a cheese grater; once off, their flesh floated off into the sky. It was like watching a sea of pollen, only bleached red as the pollen drifted into the air.

My body was fighting desperately to get away from the horrible images in the dark below. I cast my eyes skyward, a trick I'd learned as a kid whenever I would watch horror movies, so that I could pretend that I wasn't scared—only above me wasn't much better than below. In the sky, there were people floating, almost flying somehow. They seemed twisted, lost in some kind of vortex. The wind picked up all around me and buildings in the area began to crumble.

I could hear a choir of screams for help. That was something a man was never supposed to hear in his entire life. That many cries made it sound like some kind of warzone. As I watched, a huge light appeared in the distance, filling the cold night enough that I could have thought the sun had risen. I covered my eyes in response. That was when I noticed the houses around me and the street below. The street was quickly being filled with the body parts of the living. A storm of the human pieces, in shapes that would make even a butcher gag.

I have to get out of here fast. Something bad is coming. That was all I could think.

I couldn't scream anymore. The terror was too fresh and bludgeoned my soul, hammering its way into my core. The screams, they were shaking my body—shaking, shaking, they just wouldn't stop. I felt myself moving in rhythm with the screams all around me.

Slowly, I found my way to my feet, when a body was torn to pieces right above me, showering blood all over me. I looked at the blood on myself, the blood around me was all my stomach needed to finally give up the fight with last night's dinner. I heaved everything I had onto my balcony and I didn't stop. My feet managed to keep driving me, carrying me back into the safety of my duplex as my stomach fought to contain itself. In a far back corner of my brain, the part that was trying to fight to stay alive, I knew that my apartment offered next to nothing in safety, if the world was breaking away.

That safety was nothing more than the blanket people wrap themselves in whenever they're faced with extreme horror. I could smell that metallic odor. It was blood, and my body just wanted to fight to get away from its clutches. I ran through my house heading downstairs, making my way down to my daughter's room. *I'm not sure what to do, I just have to get Molly, hunker down somewhere until this all blows over, just somewhere that isn't the house.*

I kicked in her door, hoping that she had hidden from the world outside and not looked out the windows. I prayed. worrying I wasn't going to be the same father, let alone the person I was after seeing that. *Please, just don't have let Molly see anything; she couldn't handle it,* my thoughts raced. Molly had a habit of always being curious at everything around her, a trait just like her old man. A trait that I normally loved in her, but right now I had to protect her young mind from the monstrous things that were taking place all around us.

For that matter, I would have to find a way to deal with everything I had seen. The worst image was my wife's face. For the first time, I was glad that I couldn't see well in the dark. I might have seen my face after losing my wife. That is a face I mustn't see yet, not if I wanted to save my daughter.

My mind sharpened back to the task at hand of finding my daughter. I reached her door, opening it without any hesitation.

I could tell the room was empty even in the low light, still I called out for her. "Molly! Molly, where are you honey? Daddy is here, don't hide!" I rummaged around her room, throwing open the closet and searching behind her clothes. It was pointless; I could barely see my hands in front of me. I had no other choice but to open the window. I gulped hard, hoping that Molly was just hiding under the bed and wouldn't see the outside. I opened the blinds and the room was greeted by the mayhem around. I turned quickly, not wanting to see anything that I would regret.

Chapter 6

The room had plenty of light now, enough to show me what I hadn't noticed before. On the floor was Molly, her head split open like a dropped melon, and her neck puffed up. My mind snapped back like a rubber band, my eyes were now fixed with her image. It would long lasting, over what was once my sanity.

My only real job, the only task I had to do, was now dead on the floor below me. *My daughter and my wife, both dead; what the hell is going on?*

"Molly, no…" I couldn't scream, I couldn't breathe; I collapsed onto the floor, reaching for my only daughter, my princess. Molly, gone. It was something that was just wrong, like the sun not meaning warmth, and ice cream not tasting great on a long summer day. It was something just unnatural and didn't make sense. It couldn't be true.

I was numb all over, Molly's image tattooed into my mind's eye. I stayed lying with her, weeping for her, alone with my daughter.

It was everything I could do not to notice the gathering group outside the window. We were on the sixth floor, and no one would be this high. As I set clutching the lifeless body of my daughter, noise gathered outside the glass window.

It was the glass shattering that finally snapped my attention away from Molly to turn around. Faces lost, like the man who had taken my wife, faces all covered in blood and gore. Upon seeing me, their forms came through the wall, like a person moving through a sheet of water. They reached out to me, with a hunger in their lifeless eyes.

I didn't tell my legs to act, so I wasn't graceful when my hands scooped up my daughter and I took off up the stairs. I wish I had let myself be taken by whoever or whatever the forms were that had entered my house. Instead, I was moving on autopilot.

My feet didn't fail me, but my heart was failing. I wanted to be back in my bed, or wishing this was all a dream and that I would soon roll over and kiss my wife. Wake up and start getting ready for work, not running with the dead body of my baby girl in my arms.

I ran up the staircase as the picture frames on the wall flew off, some hitting me, some shattering into the wall opposite me. The whole duplex was shaking with something like thunder, like a million people had now entered the room and were all jumping at once. More than once, my feet left the ground and almost came out from under me. I was more floating than running for my life.

I bolted down the hallway, thinking fast and moving faster. My office was a dead end, and the balcony was just suicide. That left my bathroom at the end of the hallway. Under normal circumstances, the idea of dying in the bathroom would really strike me as a kind of morbid humor, yet now the reality was staring me in the face. I didn't want to die on the shitter or anywhere in the vicinity of the bathroom. Out of options, I hit the bathroom door when I ran in, making sure to slam it shut behind me.

I had doubts about the lock holding back that mass of people. It would give me a few seconds, at most, to gather my thoughts before being taken by that swarm. I wondered at that point if it would hurt to have my flesh peeled away like the others outside. Or maybe the numb feeling inside my heart would block out all the pain. A dim part of my mind was already giving up, accepting my fate in this bathroom. The door buckled in like a painting shattering at the frame and showering splinters of wood upon me.

I placed one hand to cover my face, but it wasn't enough. Through the cracks of my fingers I could see their lost faces reflecting their various forms of separation from their bodies; separation in this case meaning their bodies were in pieces. I stumbled back in fear, my legs hitting the huge iron tub that my wife had insisted on buying. I landed in the tub, pulling Molly's body after me. No way was I going to let them have her.

The first person came forward reaching out with his hands, his face now a snarl, almost in pain from his desire to touch me. I closed my eyes, anticipating whatever agony was about to come. When I heard shrieks go up, I saw red sparks above me; a wild snake-like image flew around me. One second the man reaching for me was there, and the next he was not. That red snake came down upon me and I started to scream, as something played in my head...

It started with me sitting in the middle of a movie theater, all alone in an empty black room, with a massive projection screen showing me images. The images were slow, disorienting; I was seeing a black wall, with small objects in the distance. Somehow, I didn't feel alone.

Then a light shone, and gloved hands reached in and pulled something out. I knew that the hands belonged to a doctor once I could see the room I was in. It was filled with strange instruments of a medical nature which I had never seen before. As I tried to grasp at the implications of this, more images came: I saw a baby growing up, the love of his parents, the first days of school, the awkwardness of his first thoughts about women, all the way up to a strange light that tore his body into pieces. I had just learned everything there was to know about that man in his life, from his happiest and best moments down to a time he cut his fingernails. Every secret, every single thing that made that man who he was. I shivered, feeling my stomach toss. I gasped his name, he had been named Thomas. And now, something in the light had taken him.

Another person rushed to take the spot of the missing man, only to go up in sparks upon touching my tub in the same fashion. This time it was an older woman. Same as with the man, I had a vision which showed me everything in that woman's life. When it was finished, I started to gag, from the images playing over and over in my head.

It was hard for me to concentrate. Everything felt too close, too cluttered with the images flying through my head. Like I had spent years with these people, touching them, feeling them, loving them.

A trick I had learned from all my years of working in IT was to focus on one task at a time, to compartmentalize tasks. I focused on calming down my breathing, keeping the vomit inside and my mind where I was. *Think, Jim, look around you. What's around you, what do you see?* I could see the invaders standing inches away from the tub after the woman went up. That did the trick—the crowd pushing forward were halted, and pierced me with their gazes. They were stopped for now though, at least.

So many of them were in front of me that I couldn't see the end of their mass, and yet none dared to come closer. I screamed in a panic, expecting the worst, but they did not attack me. After a moment, I realized something was keeping them back. It had to have been the tub; something about it seemed to have turned the invaders into sparks. I hoped my thinking was right. Anything to keep my mind from all that was happening. I made sure to press Molly's body further behind me, shielding her away from them.

Even though the people weren't coming closer, I was still afraid, as there wasn't enough distance between me and them. *Maybe if I just close my eyes, will they all go away? That worked every time as a kid; if the boogie man was in your room, hide under your blankets. That would show the old boogie man a thing or two.* Only, when I tried this and opened my eyes again, those things were still staring back at me with the same cold expressions; their faces searching for a way to devour me.

I was thankful again that the lights were out; seeing any more of those monsters in the low light was turning my stomach into knots. From what I could tell, all were standing perfectly still, and I wondered how long it would take before one of them dared to reach into the tub and take me. It still hadn't come, and this made me feel even more uneasy. What were they waiting for?

I should ask them something instead of waiting for the inevitable, I thought. I mean, my job had me coming into contact with customers all the time. An army of angry users unable to connect to the Internet is worse than any group of zombies, or whatever the hell these things were. *Yeah, right,* I thought. *You're just a simple IT guy. You hide behind a computer screen because you are scared of talking to people.* Even so, I had never seen anything so horrific, absolutely heinous and without end. Their limbs severed, their hearts exposed, as still as a fish left on a shore too long.

I sat for a while longer, all the while never letting my gaze leave them. I couldn't tell if the closest one to me was moving. With my heartbeat finally calming down, fatigue was catching up to me. I kept an eye on the nearest person. From what I could tell, she wasn't breathing; and even in the darkness I could tell she was a heavier set woman. Her legs stretching up to a loaded body, long since past the point of being able to fit into the women's big and tall section. She looked familiar. I wasn't sure where I had seen her before, but something about her made me wonder. I kept searching all their faces, looking for basic signs of breathing. This was the only thing I could do to keep my mind off my wife and child. If I could just keep my mind moving, I would make it.

Both of their faces flashed into my mind periodically, threatening to tear their way into my thoughts, kicking and screaming. One way or another, I was going to remember what had happened. I dreaded the implications of that. Instead, with my own thoughts being dark, I thought about the images I had learned from the first man who had tried to touch me. It was like coloring in the lines of a character in a coloring book. Sure, I had a guideline, but the whole thing felt like I was simply following what someone else had done. I had stepped into the mind of someone else. That made it hard to focus on either the man or the woman's memories. Everything floated in my head, like bottles in the ocean.

Time passed, and I could see the sun shining in the distance, like land for a sailor lost at sea, I perked up. I didn't think I was going to live to see the sun again, nor did I think I would ever see a sunrise without my family. However, a part of me knew that was going to be how it was from now on. That made me start crying again, but nothing was coming out this time. How fucked was I when I couldn't even weep properly? I was just beyond the point of tears.

Something deep and primal began to rise up in my chest. Why was I being put in this situation? These fucking things came into my house and murdered my wife and child. Now I am being watched like some kind of animal at the zoo, like I was the monster.

No, that wasn't right. It wasn't like an animal at a zoo, or a monster. A monster would have caused them to fear me. I was more like a small mouse waiting for a cat to make a move. That was what I was to them—a mouse waiting to make a mistake. *Well,* I decided, *I am nobody's mouse, and I am certainly not going to go down in an iron tub inside my own home.*

"So, are we just going to keep playing the staring game, or is something going to happen?" I shouted, asking no one in particular; yet as I said it, the entire group snapped their heads towards me, tracking me with their lifeless eyes. Rows upon rows of eyes, greeting me with the same endless seas of an dark ocean. All waiting to dunk me into a world made of water that had drowned the land, sending countless to their deaths.

I shuddered in fear. *Maybe this wasn't such a good idea. Shouting at hordes of apparitions can't be healthy in the long run, but then again, I probably didn't have much longer.* The room started shaking like before when I was running to the bathroom, only this was much worse. The medicine cabinet flew open and everything in the bathroom jetted towards me. I must have been rammed a thousand times with my toothbrushes, and even a bar of soap. The sheer number of objects hitting me was uncountable in my state. Every time I would grasp onto something; other than pain and terror, my thoughts were beaten in, tenderized like a chunk of meat. I felt myself suffocating, reaching out to breathe under the weight of all the toiletries.

I covered my face and crotch, screaming out in pain, as a shampoo bottle took me in my stomach, knocking the wind out of me. The pain was incredible. I fought hard trying to breathe, and every moment felt like being drowned. I bit down hard on my tongue until I tasted blood, forcing me to let out a scream. That got my body taking in air again, remembering to breathe, despite the terror. I had never been a tough man, and as my body continued to be rocked and slammed, the whole bathroom was coming apart. *Protect Molly,* I screamed in my head, turning my back to the crowd as more objects tore into my skin. *I have to protect her.* A crack started forming in the ceiling, like watching thousands of spider webs being woven over a gaping hole, one I knew was going to pop up soon above me. Surviving bathroom products hurtling at high speed was one thing, but it was another to survive my roof caving in. A moving force that almost seemed to have a will of its own shook the tub, breaking the water pipe used to feed water into its iron hold. Water sprayed out onto me, and even amidst this nightmare, I was aware of how dry my mouth was. *How long had it been since I last drank anything, or, for that matter, eaten anything?* It was amazing the things your mind could grasp at when you were about to die.

The glass in the bathroom window shattered, raining shards down on me and causing deep cuts. I pushed my hands forward, trying to block as much damage as I could. I was too slow, though; one piece of glass shot into me, burying itself deep in my neck. I gagged, fighting the pain; I had to find a way out before I bled to death. The glass continued to pelt me with quick strikes, cutting through my skin like a hot knife through pie.

"I'm going to die!" I howled, like a wounded animal would, into the night hoping someone or anyone would hear me and save me from this nightmare.

I felt another deep cut on my back as I turned to shield my body; it was no use, though, every part of my body was littered with cuts.

I could feel hot blood running; a decent sized puddle was forming in the tub. Too much blood. In fact, if it was that much, I was pretty sure I would be dead. It was hard to think; I was screaming, trying to breathe, trying to make sense of it all.

That was when I noticed it was Molly's blood, my only daughter's blood. Blood, black and twisting beneath us in the darkness, like an eel. This was not going to happen, I was not going to let these things destroy what was left of my baby girl. She was mine. That pulled my mind back. *I am her father and it's a father's job to protect his daughter from anything. I am going to eat these things, these creatures. This is my house, my daughter, and I am not afraid.*

"Do you hear me, you sick fucks! I'm not afraid of any of you!" I shouted, raising my hands just far enough from my face to let my voice travel.

Their response was a thunder of voices, slamming into me like a tidal wave. I went back into the cold iron tub from the force. I had always wondered what it would be like to lose your hearing like in those war movies. To not be able to hear someone a foot away, and your whole head ringing in a dull silence, unsure if you're actually hearing anything. My curiosity was appeased. As the creatures opened their mouths, they unleashed a stream of words. I covered my ears in pain, thrashing in and out of the tub, fighting back against their screams. I couldn't make out anything they were saying; it was all babel, all pain.

That was when my ears popped, and I finally understood the movies. When you lose your hearing, it's not that you don't hear any sounds, but rather all sound becomes stuck inside your head. I fought the desire to press my temple in until it exploded; my every thought was crying out to me to get away from these monsters.

All around me, I could feel the bathroom shaking to pieces, including the floor. I had to plan my escape; the tub was my only chance, it was the only thing protecting me. But no way in hell was I going to be able to move this beast of a tub. When my wife got it delivered, it took a dolly and three sturdy grown men to get it in place. The thing was, though, the floor below the bathroom was my living-room, and there really wasn't a lot holding the tub up. With the water lines busted and the floor shaking, I could tip the tub over. It was a long shot, it probably wouldn't work, but I wasn't just going to die this way. *It beats just sitting here.*

I placed my hands as far up on the side of the tub as I dared to go. My fingers ached from the glass cuts. I wasn't sure if I actually had any skin left on my hands, or if it was all heated sand, and exposed muscle that would fall out soon. I bit down again, suppressing another scream. I started to shake the tub. At first, nothing was happening. It was too heavy to be moved from the inside and I was too weak. All I had left; melting like snow on a warm day.

"No, you don't get to give up. Don't you die, don't you quit…" I growled against the screams. I continued to push and shove with my shoulders and feet, but it gave no inch. So, I started to kick my feet down, and my hearing came back in the midst of the howling and I could tell that water was running from somewhere; the bathroom was flooding quickly. It was only a matter of time. I kept kicking and I felt the first shudder of the tub. The ground beneath was breaking; something was moving with enough force to cause the floor to crack. I kept shaking and cursing with every word I knew. I kept seeing Molly's face being killed by one of these things over and over. I slammed with all my might. I decided that when my body would feel weak from that vision, I would keep fighting.

I'm not sure how long the shaking and the screaming lasted, I only noticed when I finally felt the slide of the tub. In one sudden motion, the floor opened up, and then I and the giant ass tub were flying. I slammed with the last of my strength against the side, causing the tub to roll over. I tucked Molly into my side and fell face forward.

I had just enough time to feel my body plop onto the floor below, then the iron tub smashed on top of me with an ear shattering jolt, shaking my bones. I felt a popping and I thought the tub was going to break apart and squash me under it. Or worse, I would keep falling down. Instead, I was trapped in the darkness of this cauldron. Through the curves of the cistern, I could see feet all around me. Most importantly, it showed me the floor I was on was damaged and covered in water, but sturdy enough for now. I breathed in deep; I had Molly—that was all that mattered. I was surprisingly safe for the moment. Trapped inside a tank with enemies all around, but safe. The pain was worth it.

"You hear that, fuckers? I survived your little waterboarding trick! Better luck next time." I got no response from the crowd, only the beating of my heart.

Chapter 7

I felt pretty good about myself at this point, in spite of the coursing pain running its way through my body. It was okay, though. Sometimes in life, you want to be in pain, pain in order to snuff out the greater pain happening all around you. Because some day, all these pains would heal, but the hole from my daughter and wife would not be filled. It was safe for me to indulge myself. After all, how many fathers in the history of fathers have had to lie with their own daughters on top of them, dead, while surrounded by hundreds of strange beings? I started laughing, thinking about that. I covered my mouth from the sound. *I was going mad, that must be what all this is. Yes,* I told myself, *and if I count to three, it will all be over.* I tried, breathing in, trying hard to calm down.

I tried keeping it in; the pain in my chest was becoming too great until I couldn't contain it anymore. I pulled my hand off my mouth, and unleashed a roar of laughter, echoing inside my cave.

It was a strange sound for me to hear, even in a night full of strange things. I would say a part of my mind that was rational was hiding in fear. I laughed until I hiccuped over and over again. Then I continued to laugh, I think it would have continued, if not for me realizing Molly was still on my back. Her crumpled form would soon start to decompose, while I lay laughing under her weight. The power was out, obscuring our forms in the darkness, causing shapes to appear all around me. I closed my eyes, thankful I couldn't see what was left of Molly in the darkness.

She didn't need to be exposed to all of this; she deserved to be placed in a proper burial place. Not hiding with her "questionably" sane father under a behemoth iron tub. The thought of Molly got my laughter under control. I made a mental note to lose my sanity later. For now, I had the task before me of figuring out how to survive the horror.

I had spent the better part of my thirty-two years troubleshooting and building computers. In all that time, I had learned one very important lesson: how to troubleshoot any situation I faced. The first step was to identify what the problem was. That was simple: I was in a room full of monsters, and I was currently stuck under my wife's 300-pound tank and excuse for a bath. But that wasn't it—the problem was deeper. That was the thing, when looking for the root cause of a problem. Start from the simplest thing. I had plenty of oxygen, due to the design of the tub. So, running out of air wasn't an issue for the time being.

What I didn't have was any food or water. Though the exposure to Molly's body and my wounds could end up being something serious, pretty fast. The nub of the problem was even if I could manage to escape the tub, I was still hopelessly outnumbered, and for that matter, outgunned. Something unnatural had caused my bathroom to come apart. Something unnatural had taken my family.

That chilled me, causing me to shiver; thank God the heat in my apartment was still on, I thought. That meant the power was coming back on. That was something; a lot of options. Maybe I could find my phone, or try to call out for help. If the grid was still up, it meant someone from somewhere was still doing their job in this city. That was the best course of action; just ride it out until the military showed up. I had spent a great deal of time working for the military; it was my job to assist with communication work at the local National Guard. It was a big city, but not too big; a well-coordinated offensive could retake the city very easily—this is what they do, the military retakes things. *Just let them do their job; let someone else save the day. I'm not the hero.*

That made me uneasy though, I wasn't sure how much the government was actually going to be able to do. It made me shiver again. The iron walls were becoming colder, and the feet of my enemies just got closer. This was getting me nowhere; my voice was too weak to carry very far. Calling out wasn't the best option at all anymore. I felt like a turtle trapped inside his shell with a dog about to eat him. I pushed those thoughts away fast, trying to stay focused on the task at hand.

What I was left with was the Hail Mary approach. I could just try communication with them again; try less threatening words and tone. It was a better plan than waiting to die. Who knows, they might respond to that.

Out loud, I spoke, "Hi, I feel like we've gotten off on the wrong foot here. In spite of your rude break-in to my house, and for that matter, with its destruction, I am willing to forgive, if you leave and don't come back." My voice sounded harsh, even to me under the tub. I must have lost a good amount of blood during the whole thing. There was hope, though, that these people were still people. Not mindless freaks of nature. That everything that had transpired tonight was a bad dream.

Silence stretched out for what seemed like an endless storm, until at last, I finally heard something. It was not the voice I wanted to hear, though.

"James, James, come out from under the tub." I would never forget her voice, her name, and all the nights we'd shared together. This voice was my wife's. The voice belonged to Diana. Honeyed pitch and tone, always soothing away any pains my body felt. I'd never felt a stronger desire to see her. Just to see my wife again, just to get the image of her jumping out of bed to kiss me. I had to flip the tub and see her.

I braced my hands against the side, preparing to turn the tub over again. That was when I caught myself. This wasn't right; I had seen my wife jump. As painful as it was, I forced myself to replay the image of her death. She had jumped over a hundred feet down to her death. She had died upon impact—there was no doubt about that. So, who's was the voice I was speaking to?

As if my thoughts were being read, another voice sounded out. "Daddy, Daddy, it's me, Molly. I need your help, Daddy. I'm cold, and I'm stuck. I need you and Mommy." Molly squeezed out her voice thick, with what sounded like tears. That brought tears to my eyes.

"I'm here, baby girl. Daddy is here; don't cry." My voiced cracked and my eyes tried to shed tears once more. It was painful; all I wanted to do was take her into my arms. My hands found their way to the curve of the tub, reaching under. I placed my face close to the crack; I had to see her sweet face. This heap wasn't going to keep me away from my daughter.

Two unmistakable little fingers slid their way under the tub, very careful not to touch the cold iron sides. So slowly, the hands moved, when my real daughter's hand fell off my back and landed on my arm, casting a shadow over the small hand crawling towards me. *That's odd, that's Molly's hand on mine on the inside.* She had never left from being top of me. The end of the fingers reaching towards me came into focus. It was a man reaching in, his face peeled back, showing his teeth and the muscles stretched tight over his skull.

I jerked back Molly's and my hand as the man reached forward for us both. He let out a snarl of rage once my hand shot back, frustrated that I had moved. A low-pitched gurgle sang out.

"That was a nice try, you freak, you almost had me there," I snarled back at the man.

That was when I started hearing voices all around me, voices that I had heard my entire life. "James, what have I told you about playing in places like that? Come out, you bad boy." The voice belonged to my great-grandma Anne. It was hard to forget her always-judgmental tone. Even when she was being sweet, you could feel that you were in trouble with her.

I could hear the voices of my father, sister, wife, and daughter. Hell, I think even my seventh-grade math teacher Mr. Kice. His lips slurred every word, "Jim, whhyy donn'tt you coomme out." Their voices were all ringing from everywhere, all haunting me with their memories.

The voices continued, gaining in tone and pitch each time. Sometimes the voices would be low, sometimes they would scream so loud that my teeth would shake. I wasn't sure when I had finally dozed off, but when I came to, it was dark in the duplex; I couldn't see anything except the outline of Molly. A stench was starting to come off her. It didn't take a scientist to know she would start rotting soon—my dead daughter rotting on top of her still-living father.

I closed my eyes again, wishing for water, wishing for my wife to come back. I just wanted to wake up from all this to find that I was back in my cold office, sitting in front of the servers, sharing tasteless jokes from cheap websites, and bickering about useless stuff until I could head home to my wife and daughter. I kept my eyes closed—this nightmare wasn't going to end. And for the first time in my life, I thought about how much easier it would be if I just died. If I stuck my hand out under the tub, and let the freaks take me. *What was more pain? It would be over soon.* My thoughts darkened; I was a man in a jar of sand, and the pot just kept filling with dirt.

"We will always be the good guys. Right, Daddy?" I heard Molly's words from earlier whisper into my mind. *That's right darling,* I thought. *Good guys didn't kill themselves.* I felt myself pull from the darkness back to the situation at hand.

More time went by, light showed again under the tub; my skin was on fire from the cuts, and my whole body felt weak. I dared to glance out from under the tub; it had been about a night and a morning since I had heard the freaks. I wouldn't put it past them to be waiting for me to look out.

I couldn't see much. My living room looked abandoned, in spite of the hundreds having previously been all around me. None of the debris looked weighed down; it was like they simply had no mass to them, or my kitchen table was a hell of a lot sturdier than I imagined it to be. "Damn IKEA..." I mumbled, racking my brain for an explanation.

I rolled over to the other side of the tub, taking caution to move Molly's body gently. Again, no freaks in sight, but this time the tub faced towards the stair case. Littered throughout the house were the photo frames and various different kitchen utensils. But not a single person. It looked like they were gone, but I had to be sure.

"Hey, is anyone home?" I didn't wait for a reply. "Anyone want to hear a joke? I have a couple of funny ones. What has no face and scares the shit out of me? No response? Okay... the answer is a freaky person coming into my house, or freaky people, in this case."

I waited five minutes to hear anything. All I got was silence.

I decided to give it another twenty minutes or so, just to be on the safe side. As I waited, I pondered the best way to get the tub off of me. I had never been a gym rat, and I was still amazed I had even gotten the tub to fall through the floor. My strength was almost gone from the fatigue of it all; I might be able to flip the tub over if I had something to wedge the sides with, I thought. I looked around the tub. All I had was Molly and some broken pieces of glass, none of which would actually be able to help.

I looked at Molly. My baby girl was dead, and I had been powerless to save her. I tightened my fist in a rage. I couldn't save her, but I was going to find her murderers. I tucked the rage back inside, trying to keep my mind on getting out of the tub.

"Escape first, then..." I let the statement trail off as I closed my eyes, breathing deep. I knew what I had to do, it just sickened me. I was grateful I had not eaten or drunk anything for a while.

This next part was going to send me to hell; I hated myself for being so resourceful, I truly did. Moving my body and Molly's, I was able to twist her small form into itself. I turned her body onto its side, sliding it under the curve of the tub. Once her body became firmly wedged under the curve of tub, I moved back around, bracing both my feet on the opposite side of her.

Here goes nothing, I thought, as I gritted my teeth and pushed with everything I had. My eyes never left Molly, and I hated myself every second of the whole ordeal. I kept pushing and pushing, until I felt the tub start rocking on its side and tip just enough for gravity to send it over. The weight of the tub slammed down, smearing what was left of Molly's body into a thick goo.

Don't turn to see what you've done, I thought. It was too wrong for me to ever imagine. I leaned forward and threw up what was left of my stomach. That hurt, but not as bad as what I had just done. *I will get those who forced me to do this to you, honey. I swear, just you watch. I will get them all,* I thought. Still, my mind flooded with images of her small body being nothing more than a smear on my hardwood floor.

When I was growing up, my father was always into athletics. So go figure—his only son would rather have spent time slaying orcs rather than lifting weights. Still, my father had invested a great deal of time in "improving" his nerdy son. The biggest lesson my father had taught me was how to push through the pain. Isolate what was bothering you and move on. He used to have this saying that whenever misery became too agonizing to handle, you had to remember that pain wasn't going to last. That you had to seal off pain and compartmentalize all of it, or be brought down in it. Compartmentalize. So the pain of what I had just done to my daughter, I stuck it down somewhere with a lock and key. I had no idea such a thing existed inside of me. It would remain there until it was time.

There would be plenty of time to loathe myself when this was all said and done. First things first, to find out if the house was really clear, or if those things had set some kind of trap. When I thought of their faces, my knees became weak and unsteady like a newborn deer taking its first steps. I would have fallen if I hadn't caught myself on a piece of broken furniture.

I pulled in a long breath. *Compartmentalize the key out of this hell; one thing at a time,* I mumbled, searching for my breaths in the air, as if every inhale I took was going to be my last.

If the monsters were in the house, they should have swarmed me by now. This should have been when the monsters jumped out—once I started to feel safe, and that made perfect sense to me. Regular animals do it. Why should people be any different? I let that thought trail off as I made my way. I needed to be quiet. I could see light coming into the duplexes' interior, casting a dull glow over the destruction laying before me. It was like watching a living fire, only without the flames.

Closing the blinds wouldn't be a bad idea, I thought, in case someone was trying to get in. It would offer me some protection. As I crawled my way across the room, me behaving like this just felt odd. *Why was I trying to keep from being found? Shouldn't I be trying to signal for help?* A part of me seriously doubted, after what I witnessed last night, that there would be very many people left in the city, and another part of me didn't want anyone to see just how much I had failed. Or worst of all, that I was losing my mind. My mother had always joked to me as a kid that video games would rot my mind. Too many years I've spent working behind a screen—maybe this was what my mother had meant.

I kept moving, though, trying to stay low, I fought the urge to peer out the windows before closing the blinds, I decided I had seen enough gore for one day.

I pulled them close. In the darkness of my home, shapes became foreign, and more alive than I had ever seen them before. Everything looked like something found in the deepest of undiscovered caverns. I continued to stay low, my body instinctively taking me to the kitchen. I wasn't sure how much time had passed, and hunger was now driving me. The thought of water made me quicken my crawl, even daring to get up into a low hunch. As I passed the stairs, I peered up into the darkness above, hoping I wouldn't see anything.

I breathed a sigh of relief when I noticed nothing. It just didn't seem like a good time to go monster slaying. It just didn't seem like a good time for anything bad.

I got to my kitchen, and ripped open the fridge. The inside was scattered and looked like World War Three had been fought over my leftovers. Yet in the mess I found a bottle of water. I guzzled it down greedily, thinking to myself the whole time that I should conserve it. That was easier said than done—I was always bad at keeping to diets, or having willpower. First chance I got to do something bad again, I would jump all over it.

When the bottle grumbled dry, my heart sank. *Please don't let that be the last drop I ever get again*, I prayed silently. I looked around for more. Most of the food was splattered around, and it looked like decomposition was already setting in on most of the fruit.

I fished around in the cabinets, and was able to find another bottle of water. I looked at my sink, longing for more water to come out, but I knew it would be useless; the pipes upstairs had burst, and the fact that the whole place wasn't completely soaked through told me the pipes had already run dry, or the water had found somewhere else to go. I would have to leave the apartment if I was to eat or drink.

That wasn't an option, I decided. Picking my way through the dead was a bit too much right now. Even after the little water I'd had, my body felt weak and ready to collapse. I looked down at my hands, seeing how my skin was littered with scratches from the glass, and who knows what else. It was going to get cold soon, and my limbs were freezing just thinking about it. I needed to rest and clean my wounds up before I could even think about doing anything else. My fingers trembled. I didn't have time to waste. An obscure thing had festered its way into my house, and was now festering its way into my head, like some kind of deep root, slowly but surely rotting a house from beneath. Whatever, or whoever was responsible for what had happened to Molly and my wife might still be here. None of it made sense, and I wanted to just wake up.

I was going to find the monsters, though, and do all the horrible things that they had done upon me and my family. I promised myself that. My anger deflated when my stomach growled, though. I wasn't going to fight those monsters like this. "Be reasonable, James. Be a reasonable man," I muttered in the cold silence of my kitchen.

That left me with only one more thing to take care of, as I looked around my destroyed kitchen. I needed to find a way to defend myself. Violence wasn't a thing I considered myself attuned to, but those choices remained. *Come on, James. Use that head of yours. If you're going to be smart, you have to be creative as well.* That was something I would tell myself every time I was stumped on a server problem. Just being smart wasn't enough; you had to be more clever and creative.

I looked around my kitchen at all the items that had been thrown around. Everything was moved, or tossed to a different location, except my cast iron pan. Still set atop its rightful place—its throne—my stove. My wife and I always fought over washing it. I remember one of our biggest arguments came from her trying to wash it. I smiled at the memory of that argument. Needless to say, I had won it, and the pan never was washed. (*It's the only way to treat cast iron—preserves the flavors,* I argued.) It was twelve pounds of kickass right now. Twelve pounds that would stand between me and anything coming my way. Like a blanket for a small child when they're scared. It felt that way for me right now: my blanket.

I picked up the skillet, its weight feeling like a long sword, or so I imagined. Not exactly a sword, but it would do. I remembered how the tub had turned those things into spinning colors. And there was something else that came in the colors, something that didn't feel like my own. As I gripped the pan, my head started to pound, furious and red hot to the touch. I bent over and could hear music in my ears, taste an ocean breeze, feel hot sand under my toes, and smell something cooking. In my head, I could see children and adults swimming in a lake. I tried fighting the urge to throw up and all the sensations stopped abruptly. I was drenched in a thick sweat, hunched over my kitchen counter.

After a few minutes, I stood, facing the window as the sun was setting. My pan didn't feel so strong; whenever it was dark out, I didn't feel so strong anymore. A cold chill was drifting from somewhere in the house, causing me to remember that I was still, in fact, naked and covered in blood and grime, not to mention that damn iron tub still felt like it was wrapped and entwined round my soul now. I was going to need to get some clothes on, fast.

I kept close to the wall as I made my way out of the kitchen, my footsteps feeling heavy along with my breath. Fear was causing me to shake, the pan in my hand becoming heavier and heavier. I got to the bottom of my stairs, peering up into the darkness leading away. *The entrance into Hades,* I thought. *It's just my home,* I told myself, *only that isn't right anymore.* I was ascending stairs that seemed to stretch on for eons of darkness—a vast sky with no stars.

For so long, I'd had my wife to help keep me grounded, but now I was all alone. My legs started to shake from it all, so I stopped myself halfway up. I just had to compartmentalize again. There was that word once more. If I just took every step one at a time, I could do this, and nothing could keep me down. I found myself heading up into the darkness above, as my legs started the climb once more. My bare feet crushed the glass deep into places unknown to my body before. I gritted my teeth, not wanting to call out. When I reached the top, it was completely dark. My body acted like it was living in Hyperborea, surrounded by an angry winged god.

I kept going forward, and then I heard it. Laughter. It was coming from somewhere in front of me; somewhere off in the distance in my house, I could hear giggling. It stopped me in my place, my heart sinking with every laugh. "Move." I whispered. I kept moving, sucking in my breath as I made my way further down the hallway, the air becoming still and not appearing to move at all. A pressure was building inside my chest, a feeling that was trying to burst its way through.

I knew if I stopped, I wasn't going to move at all. As I neared the bedroom I'd shared with my wife, my feet stepped into deep puddles of water; I could see light coming from under my doorway. I could hear giggling again, sounding like multiple voices. *We're laughing though, all of us somewhere.* My hand was freezing as I approached the door. *Whatever was behind this gate,* I told myself, *I would have to face it alone.* This was something that was here and now. Not in front of my screen from some remote location, thousands of miles away. This was the terror that was invading my home. *What are you going to do, James?* I'm not sure what the answer was. *Were you going to let pain eat you, or were you going to seal it away, back to where it came?*

I opened the door screaming, expecting to find hundreds of those things. Instead, I saw only light.

Chapter 8

Light blasted me, causing me to shield it away with my hand. When the flare cleared, I was at the park. My wife was on the ground tickling my daughter; I remembered this day. We had all gone for a picnic. It had been a few weeks since my last real day off, and too many weeks since we had gone out somewhere.

One of the drawbacks of my childhood had been that my father was obsessed with his work, and never had a lot of time for my sister and me. I never wanted to be like that, so any chance that I got to be with my family, I took us somewhere, even if it was just the park. I wanted us to spend time together. I wanted to reach out to them, feel their hair, and smell that fresh cut grass. I wanted to sing with my daughter, and kiss my wife. I wanted it so bad, my fingers trembled reaching closer to them, and I could feel the breeze, the hot sun soothing away the aches in my body.

It was like a morning gospel at some church. Joy was filling my insides at the sight. Only, my insides were empty, I had spent two days in a tub not eating anything; hiding away from countless monsters. It was my stomach that clued me on this not being true. I blinked my eyes several times and their images went away, like cutting the power off on a television.

Instead of open fields of green, there was only my broken bedroom; and at the center was the thick woman from earlier. The illusion was gone, replaced by the bitter truth; it was all gone. I knew it, but more importantly, so did the woman. She darted forward with surprising grace, her round and once-gentle face replaced by a look of ferocity. It was so unreal that my mind was still trying to catch up, I was not in the park with my family now, I was about to be attacked by some woman in my bedroom. She was a foot away from me when every warning bell in my body fired on all engines. My hands shot up, swinging the skillet in an overarching uppercut.

On contact, sparks of coloration filled my vision, disorienting me, causing me to almost lose my balance. I had to blink several times. The woman was now gone; all traces faded into the unknown. My whole body was shaking, whether from fear or rage, I did not know. Visions of the woman played through my eyes—I was seeing her life. It was her younger, and in a much thinner time. She was getting married. Just like before, I could feel everything, see everything with all my senses. I shook my head hard as it pounded in fury. I stood there naked in my bedroom, clothed in fear—for how long, I wasn't sure, until I felt I was able to move again. All the images of her life played before me like a personal show. I pressed on, not daring to drop the skillet, despite the shaking in my hands. I tried to ignore the images of her life as they went through my head.

All I wanted to do was find some clothes and be done with it all. Water hadn't soaked everything in this room yet—that was going for me, at least. I found the warmest clothes I owned (which wasn't that hard, since North Carolina's winters would surprise you with their endless snows). I made sure to also take my pea-coat too. *Its thick warmth and pockets will see me through until this all ends,* I thought. I didn't follow that thought down the trail though—it was going to be a long time before this nightmare was over. Sometimes it was best to never follow the thoughts—they only led to pain, and dark places inside of your own mind that seal off all happiness. Before you know it, you are so far down, that pain will cripple you from moving forward. That would not be me; I was going to take this one step at a time.

As I slid on my work boots, (ignoring the pain in my feet) I decided I was forgetting the most important thing. I looked at the mountains of photo albums sitting atop my dresser drawer. My wife had made sure to actually preserve our many moments together. I used to say it was a guy thing to just not take photos, or that I sucked at taking them. Truth is, if it was not for her, I would have no pictures at all of my family. That was right—I had a family, and I could never forget that. I turned, walking away from my room with one of the albums.

I didn't want to take them all, mostly from fear of having too much stuff in my hands, but more importantly, I was afraid to ever enter that bedroom again. That fear ended up causing me to take almost all of the albums. It's so easy to lose a photo. As I walked down my empty hallway, the floors grumbled under the weight of my boots, the water sloshing at my feet. I listened very carefully for anything, but all I heard was the agony of an empty home. When I reached my living room, I found Molly's body and the tub, exactly where I had left them. I had one last task to do before the night was going to be over.

I had to take care of my daughter as any father should. With a little light remaining, I found a blanket from the downstairs closet. I placed as much as I could of my daughter in the blankets; the iron tub had splattered her almost into liquid. This was something I never thought I would have to go through in my life. It was something no father should ever have to endure, but I had to; I couldn't leave her like that. Not in that way.

I took her body to the fridge; the inside was still cold and would keep her for a few more days. I just hoped that was long enough for me to find her a proper place. I closed the fridge door; for now, I was going to have to keep that door closed. I made a silent promise to find her mother's body as well; keep them together at least. I would not rest until that was over, no matter how difficult it would be to find Diana. My hand rested on the handle, and an unknown amount of time passed. I didn't care; everything I ever cared about was at room temperature inside a fridge, slowly rotting away. And I was covered in the blood of my offspring. It's funny that on a normal day the fridge was my first stop after getting home—I would always go for a beer. Now it would be the last place I would ever go.

“Well, I am pretty sure it’s beer time somewhere. Might as well pound a few,” I mumbled. The silence was starting to get to me; I had this feeling, though, as I closed my cabinet, that making too much noise was a bad idea. In fact, just making noise in general seemed like the wrong play. The fridge door felt like it weighed a ton. My hand had no desire to open it once more.

From my cabinet, I went for a bottle of Jim Beam. I think someone had given it to me at a holiday party a few months back (it was the only liquid or food not broken in my home). I was never much of a whiskey man, but hey, what the hell. No point in not living a little. I took the bottle out to the tub; the tub felt exposed and should have felt foreign, being that it was in my living room.

“Right now, though, you look like the Titanic with your beauty, you old iron eye-sore.” I curled in tight into the tub, with my whiskey in one hand, my trusty skillet in another. My eyes circled the room—only dark forms, as far as I could see. Nothing that seemed to be threatening my immediate surroundings, I thought. It was going to be a long night, and I was not about to go to sleep after everything I had seen.

Chapter 9

It lasted about five minutes before my eyes betrayed me and I was out. I didn't dream—instead, I only thought of the man who had come into my room, and what my wife had said before jumping. A part of me kept telling myself I was imagining it, that she had not said anything. That didn't work when all you had was time. Time would keep spilling out, like water from the spring.

The thing that bothered me the most was my wife had a funny way of smiling. It had looked like it was her crooked smirk, right before she jumped. When you've lived with a person twelve plus years, you know every one of their mannerisms, down to the letter. So when I awoke, I expected to see my wife's smirk again. Instead, I got the empty duplex. Just the shell of a place that no longer felt like home. *What had she said before she jumped? Why was she up there in the first place?* My thoughts raced in the late hours. I suddenly felt the desire to leave my iron safety. Despite my stiff muscles, I couldn't convince myself to look out of the tub. *Don't take the chance again of finding another monster.*

My notion of time was completely skewed. My best guess about anything involving time was that it had been three days since my family was taken from me. I waited for a few minutes in the tub, the cold of the iron sinking into my skin. Even with my coat and clothes, I couldn't escape the cold. It was like falling into a frozen river, only my body wasn't in shock. *It sure wanted to be, though; or maybe I was, and this was all a part of the dream?* I ignored that thought. *Dreams don't last this long, usually.*

It was my stomach that won out, with me sulking in the tub, a deep rumble; rolling its way through me. I kept telling myself about an article I had read once, saying that most Americans mistook gas for hunger pangs, that most Americans wouldn't actually know what going without food was like. How factual the article was, but who knows now; I never really worried about not having something to eat. I am a computer guy, in job as well as looks. Tall, skinny, and more than likely out of shape, so junk food, or food in general, was something I never thought would be gone.

As my stomach continued to rumble, I reassured myself that it was probably the jitters and cramps from being in the tub. I just needed to stretch my legs, or stop drinking the whiskey. That seemed to help curb the pain in my stomach though, but it did nothing for my thirst. That was something that you couldn't lie to yourself about. Sooner or later, thirst would always win. My throat felt more edged than a blade, and my head was on fire. I thought it might have been the whiskey, but I had only taken one sip. No, my problem was something much more insidious and primal. I was dying of thirst and hunger.

That would be ultimately what would lead me out of my tub and into the real world. I gave one last hard look around my duplex; light was starting to form out from behind the blinds. I thought I saw a movement from outside, and that sent me sprawling back down into the iron tub. When I heard the chirp from the bird outside, I realized how ridiculous I must have looked. I waited another five minutes, pain in my stomach forcing me out finally.

My legs rolled out stiffly, almost causing me to fall. I was not a tall man, and I did have pair of long legs that hated every minute of the tub that I kept subjecting them to. I bear-crawled my way to the front door. My body was aching in pain, and somewhere I could still feel something bleeding. I made a mental note. First, I needed to take care of my body. I hoped I wasn't putting it off out of some misplaced self-loathing, my lack of taking time to heal myself. Only

I thought about it more, and it wasn't very misplaced. *Don't let the guilt and pain keep yourself frozen in fear,* I thought.

I kept crawling my body along the floor until I reached the door. On the key hook on the wall above me were the door-keys. Somehow, they were still there; things were looking up for a change. I stood up enough to get my keys, and then slid back down to the floor, feeling my heart kick up from just that tiny movement. *Maybe I was being a little over cautious,* I thought. I mean, there was only a flimsy door between me and the outside world. If something was out there I was in trouble no matter how big my skillet was.

Then again, if I had taken more steps to secure my home, I wouldn't have been in this situation. Thousands of people would not have tried to kill me in my own bathroom. On that thought, a chill ran through me: *where were all the footprints?* It had taken a long time to dawn on me—though there was water all over the duplex now, mud was still mud, so where were the footprints in the mud? People leave them like smoke from a fire. I didn't see any though, just lots of blood and water. That made me seriously doubt my plan to go outside. It was impossible, with everything that had happened in the last few days.

I had no choice though; it was either be a man now and do something, or—it was that simple once I thought about it—go outside or die. Dying didn't seem like so much of a bad thing, though. It was getting harder to keep that negative out of my thoughts.

That was hard to do, considering the things that had happened, none of which I understood. Instead, all I got were a bunch of crazed sociopaths, bursting into rainbow flames whenever I hit them with my iron skillet. *It's all explainable though, it always is,* I thought, shaking my head.

The rainbow flames aside, my logic was fine; science would be able to explain all of this in a few weeks. Until then, I had to get through this; I made a quick mental list of everything I would need on my outing. First things first: I had to move my wife's body, find some water, and get some medicine for my wounds. It was simple enough, I was pretty sure my neighbors in my complex would have most of what I needed.

That was easier said than done, though; my desire to go anywhere was broken. As I ambled around my apartment, my body broken, my soul rusting away with what little merit it had had to begin with, I had lost the value of trying. Now, I made it my mission to survive for my family. It was my duty to carry on. I was going to have to be a solider for them; I had to.

Through the wreckage that was my house, there were visions of a destroyed world, filled with gore and more blood than there was water in the ocean, an image that almost made me throw up. "What are you doing, man? You know they say to wait until rescue comes." I wasn't too sure if that was true or not—fear was keeping me there. I sucked in my breath, unlocking the latch on the door. The sound of the bolt sliding back must have been what prisoners felt whenever they were freed from jail. Did that sound actually mean freedom? And if they were free, did they find the world beyond the bars any better? "You're procrastinating, just get going, James." I said it out loud this time. I opened my door into the hallway. It was empty, and looked to be no more dirty than normal. That was weird. I figured with damage like what my duplex had gone through, there had been a battle beyond my sheet rock walls. I stepped out into the hallway, letting the door shut back on my home.

After everything that had happened, I was a little disappointed almost; the hallway felt foreign. With each door I passed, my unease became more and more gripping. I felt myself clutching my skillet closer to me, waiting for something—or someone to jump out. However, nothing came. When I reached the third floor, I decided it was time to stop and see if anyone else might have survived in my building. I picked the first random door. It was duplex 314, and the outside looked normal, which made me wonder if it was perhaps a good idea to knock or not. *Just be a man and do this. Who knows, maybe they will have some kind of answer.* I went with the subtle polite knock, waiting for any kind of sound coming from inside. I heard nothing, so I knocked again, this time louder, hoping for someone to come to the door. I was let down once more, no one came at all.

My heart was beating faster. This was getting ridiculous—where the hell was everyone? I swung back my hand holding the pan and slammed it against the door, over and over again, until the pan bounced out of my hand from effort. I was panting, my breath coming in waves. "What the fuck, why isn't someone answering..." I didn't want to know the answer to that. I kept seeing the bodies that had flown off into the sky. It made me shake. I knew this was beyond just being off—a part of me was still trying to rationalize it all. It must have been what the first person who discovered fire had felt like; it wasn't a feeling of discovery, it was a feeling of being very small in their world.

I shook my head, looking at the door-frame before me. The banging from the pan had left heavy indention's and splinters in the wood. It wouldn't take much more to kick it in. If anyone had been inside, they surely would think I was a looter by now.

Maybe I am. Maybe that is what I am, right now. It's hard to argue what you are once your stomach knows true hunger; once your body is eating itself faster than you can feed it. I reared back my foot, wishing now that I had not picked my pair of Converse to go kicking down doors and playing around in the apocalypse. Somewhere, someone was shaking their head because of that, but they are probably dead by now. I kicked forward with all my might, and my foot met solid wood. River beats of pain exploded at the base of my heel. *What the hell, is this door made of steel? I don't think even mine has material like this.* I made a mental note that if I found my landlord, I would give him a piece of my mind. I stepped forward again, planting as many kicks into the frame as I could. I tried to keep my blows in roughly the same place every time.

I felt the give of the door before I heard the crack. One more kick, and the door flew back, leaving an indention in the wall from the door frame. The duplex was empty. Its shelves and cabinets were lonely, and all of this was taken in as I came through the doorway. *Tell me I did not just break into the one empty apartment in this whole God damn building.*

I didn't want an answer to that, as I walked room to room. The duplex was well lit and echoed my every step as I entered the living room. Again, it was just another empty room. Another uneasy feeling seeped into me. I must have made a big mistake, and I was going to pay for it soon. Opening up another door would require a lot of effort. I looked at the skillet in my hands; maybe I could use it like a crowbar on the door frame. *That's not such a bad idea, only maybe I should try an open room first—might be some people left besides me.*

I turned around, avoiding looking out the window, I imagined thousands of birds picking through the dead. A sea of black feathers and beaks—*don't see that until you have to.* As I walked to the door, something caught my eye which I had not seen the first time I had walked in, or maybe it had not been there before. I walked to the kitchen, and in the middle of the room now sat a plain nightstand.

It wasn't the nightstand that made me shake; clearly it had not been there a moment ago. Or maybe it had been there—I was shaken up and more than likely overlooked this alien stand in the kitchen. It had a folded-over letter with the clear hand-written name of "James" across the front. I stared at the letter from halfway across the kitchen. My eyes danced uneasy—the letters of my name. Dumbfounded was a word that meant speechless. I didn't know enough words to describe how confused and afraid I felt upon seeing the letter.

I stepped across the room, picking up the letter, and my eyes took only a moment to scan its surface. I read it over three times before I could set it down.

"Dear James, by the time you have found this letter, you of course will have plenty of questions. Below is where you will need to go in order to have any and all of your questions answered. Don't worry about finding your wife; she is safe now, with me. If you're wondering who I am, I am a friend to you, James. Across from the Wells Fargo building on College Street, in building 303, you will find me.

P.S. I look forward to meeting you; you have such a lovely family."

I crumpled the letter in a rage. *Who was this son of a bitch, and what was he doing with my wife's body?* I took the nightstand and threw it at the window, shattering the glass out of the frame as the stand went to the street below. I was through with being treated as some kind of fool. It was like I was being labeled some kind of sucker of this world, a clown by destiny instead of design. I left the duplex in a hurry; I wasn't going to waste any more time being someone's lab rat. As I made it to the lobby, I noticed the main elevator was still working. I ran to it, and someone was coming down. *It has to be Mr. Slick who placed the nightstand behind me. Well I gotcha now. You think you were that quick? let's see how quick you are with a pan smacking you in the face.*

The bell from the elevator sounded off as soon as the red light above said One. "Here we go, don't be afraid now, James," I said to myself, gripping my pan tighter. I had never been a violent man in my life, but that was quickly changing now. I gripped the handle of the heavy skillet so tight my knuckles turned purple and red. The doors parted, and my feet came forward, along with the rest of my body, swinging the pan wildly every which way in a fury of blows. I didn't stop until I had banged the pan against the safety rail. The elevator was empty except for one confused me, facing an oblivion in the form of cheap steel and poor lighting inside a tiny box.

I stepped out, unsure as to why the elevator was working with no one in it. "Must be set to some kind of timer," I said, mumbling to myself, I needed to calm down and get my head straight. That could have been just another scared and confused person trying to find some answers just like me. I blushed red, thinking about how dumb I must have looked to someone else.

That made me feel guilty. I wasn't the only one who had probably survived from whatever this was. I should be looking for others and try offering help. Only, as I turned, walking through the lobby to the outside, I didn't want to find anyone. A part of me was longing for human company as much as someone would long for a juicy steak after a long diet, while another part of me wanted to be alone. Yet, I was alone, and that was what made me so conflicted. It's one thing to cry alone knowing there's someone that loves you; it's a whole another pain when it's just you.

At the doors to the lobby, I looked out expecting to see a sea of blood and metal from that night before. Unlike the room above, the outside was untouched, shining in the North Carolina light, otherwise unscathed and mundane. I expected my lungs to be filled with smoke from fires, not crisp morning air. *This can't be right,* I thought, pushing the doors open. I ran to the building across the street where I knew my wife had been standing before she had jumped.

Where I was standing below had to be where her body had fallen, I was sure of it. She had to have landed where I was standing. I was directly below that spot. I placed my face to the warm pavement. I only felt rocks, while my nose just took in the gas fumes and tire marks left behind from hundreds of vehicles. No blood and no sign of my wife, just hot tar. And no sign of anyone else I had seen on that night. *That's impossible—I saw the damage. It would have taken years for the city to completely clear away the destruction from that night. It took the city some time collecting the garbage from our building alone. Something is way off today; things should always be moving in the city,* I stated to myself, walking along the road, feeling a steady flow of uneasiness.

My wife and I had one car in the external garage beside our building. I never used it much—didn't see the point when the bus was cheaper. I would have added stealing a car to my list of growing crimes for the day, only as far as I could see, there wasn't a single car in sight. Only hollow buildings, that appeared more like tombs than actual homes of people. I picked up my pace into a slow jog; I had never heard the city before, but I'm sure it wasn't like this; it had always been so full of life and noise that it felt like a living thing. Now, all around me, it reminded me that buildings were in fact made of stone, places where people spent their lives, not truly lived their lives.

I decided it was best not think of all that was around me, I needed to compartmentalize, and take it all one task at a time. I came to the parking garage, and I looked at the elevator ,feeling like that was a bad idea, so I took the stairs again. It had been about two weeks since I had last driven the car again. *Why drive? Taking a bus is so much easier—good call,* I thought sourly. From what I remembered, it should be somewhere on the fifth or sixth floor.

Looking at the stairs only made me wish I had done stair climbing more often—or any form of exercise. Oh well, no one said it was going to be easy. Going up the stairs, I tried peering out at the various buildings, and saw no movement. No life, neither human nor animal. It was as if I was the last man on my block. When I got back from finding my wife and dealing with this sicko, I would have to make a search through all the buildings. The street below the garage was filled with lots of apartments. Someone else must have been around here somewhere.

Before I knew it, I was at the level of my car, with my feet almost causing me to trip in my nervousness. I came out from the staircase into darkness. Parking garages are naturally creepy places; every sound and shadow can set you on edge. Now what I faced was an almost endless expanse of cold steel and no lights. It was haunted machine house, a spooky garage where the ghosts were all cars.

My hands, though shaking, managed to find my keys jammed deep in my pockets. I clicked my sensor, setting the alarm off. My car was at the end of the garage. *Why am I not surprised?* I picked up my pace again, this time heading towards my car. My mind filled with images of the faces from my bathroom chasing me. It only served to make me run faster. I reached my car, my breath ragged and strained. It took me half a dozen tries to get the door open. I slammed myself shut in the safety of familiarity. I couldn't see anything in the garage. What little light came from the emergency exit signs casting red shadows in every direction.

I wasted no time peeling out of that haunted tomb, I would never park there again. Even after I left the concrete structure, I still felt as if I had somehow barely made it out of there alive. My heart was racing, and I was pushing my jeep to the limit. I looked at my gas gauge; I was at half a tank. *Plenty of room to breathe, plenty of gas to the Wells Fargo bank and back,* I thought as I drove across the empty streets. I got the feeling it wasn't a good idea to get out of my car. It was probably the safest place I could have been.

As the miles stretched by, so did my faith in finding help. Not one sign of anyone. It was as if some all-powerful force was allowing me to get there as soon as possible. I thought of the note addressed to me. "We have your wife, James." My hands tightened their hold on my steering wheel. I wasn't a man of violence, but I was going to be, once I found these people.

A few more minutes and I came upon the bank (the quickest time I had ever made). Its imposing features jetted out of the ground like a massive steel ant farm. It was amazing the amount of effort men could put into building a gigantic structure such as this building, but not find the time to actually place the people that need a home in such a location. I had a feeling that space would no longer be a problem in this city anymore, which was something that truly frightened me.

I stuffed my fear into a place deep inside. I was starting to store a lot down there. I wondered whether if too much tragedy was inside of a person, would they actually explode. I thought about that as I circled the building again.

I caught myself doing a third lap around the building and I kicked my foot on the brake, sending the tires into a quick stop. "This is ridiculous man, grow a pair and go in." I said. If only my voice had sounded surer. From what I could tell, the building was again empty like the others. I wasn't sure what I was looking for as my car idled on the side of the road. In the movies, this was when the action hero's trusty sidekick would come up with some ingenious plan that would make it through the enemy's defenses with no problem. Only this wasn't a movie, and my sidekick was in a garbage bag inside of my freezer.

The thought of Molly made my teeth shake, my whole body fighting the fever of anger that was taking over. Even when I was inside the tub, I hadn't felt this powerless. I mean, here I was, being led around like some kind of dog. I was the master of my own fate, and fate had picked me. If not that, then I was the luckiest husband in the world who happened to have a nagging wife who bought something that was sensible and apocalypse-friendly, which is the only reason I had pulled through the night. I took deep breaths, reminding myself that every door I'd opened today had ended up not being as bad as I thought it would be.

That was the thing about opening doors. You open some and you may find many great things. All it takes, though, is the one door with something really bad to overshadow any of the good you once had.

Chapter 10

I came through the lobby doors, the rotating glass still as interesting to me as it had been as a child. I remembered Molly had loved them as well; we would play on them every chance we got. Spinning in circles, never minding the stares. At the customer service desk inside the lobby, was another message. This time it was a dry white board with the words: "James, glad you could make it. Come on up. By the way, consider taking the elevator; it won't bite." I wasn't sure if that was supposed to give me any kind of relief, or just fueling my anxiety of the situation.

I came to the elevator, its steel doors opening before I could press the open key. My hand jerked back at the ding. I wished then that my skillet was longer. I was getting tired of being so close to things that were jumping out at me. I made sure my skillet was tucked for quick action. Once I got to where I was heading, I wasn't going down without a fight. I stepped into the elevator and the doors shut behind me. I was strapped in now, ready or not, and I wasn't remotely surprised when the elevator automatically headed to the top floor. As the elevator climbed, my heart rang in my ears. Each floor was a mile, one long endless mile.

I reached the top, another ding indicating that it was time to see what was in store for me. "Here goes nothing man, hold on to your lunch,." I said as the doors opened, and I was greeted by my work center.

"What the fuck..." I spoke, not even trying to control how baffled I was to find myself at my workplace. The same rows of cubicles and desks, and the same office jokes depicting various Internet technology humors. "This had to be how Alice felt," I muttered, making my way out of the elevator. As I passed the cubicles, people kept saying "James," or giving me a greeting; just like any other day.

A guy I work with asked me if I had caught the latest episode of some show. I didn't respond; my legs were already carrying me to my desk. On a normal day, I would have come in with a smile and talked to most everyone I passed on my way to my desk. Just like another day at the office.

I made it to my desk, which had a small plaque with the words "Lazy Administrator" scribbled in cheap plating above my name. I took a long look at my name, feeling the eyes from everyone I worked with around me. *Where was I, and what was going on?*

"James, are you alright? You've been staring at that plaque for the last two minutes and fifteen seconds. I know it, because I've been timing you. I know you computer guys are weird, but don't make this awkward for me."

I turned around to see my friend and colleague Lieutenant Colonel Douglas Wilson. Wilson is a black male of average height, nothing that would make you turn your head twice at him, except for his eyes and his voice. Wilson's voice was quiet, yet firm. the kind of voice that conveyed authority in every statement. Wilson was someone who didn't have to raise his voice in order to control any situation. But whenever you made eye contact with him, you weren't worried about him not making the right call.

He was someone I needed right now. Something wasn't right. Why was everyone so calm? Every alarm in my head was going off in unison. I wanted to answer him, "No, nothing was right. I have single-handedly crushed my daughter, and my wife killed herself. All of this in the same night, or did I only dream of smashing strangers in my home to pieces with an iron skillet?" I wasn't sure. I wasn't sure of anything.

Wilson must have sensed my uneasiness. We had known each other for five years, which was plenty of time to get to know someone and see all of their personality quirks. Wilson just smiled at me, noticing the pan in my right hand. "So, I am assuming the reason why you're late is because your wife made breakfast?" Wilson asked, crossing his arms, peering down his hawkish nose at me.

"What? No, she didn't. I am just working on eating out less. You know, diet is everything." My response seemed weak, even as it came from my mouth.

Wilson either bought it or didn't want to press the issue. He still smiled a deep sheepish grin. *Funny,* I thought, *I've never seen him smile like that.* "Whatever it may be, man, get yourself cleaned up; we've got a long day on the upgrade." he said, more than a little bit of annoyance in his tone. I couldn't tell if he doubted me.

"Right away, boss, I will get right to it." I hoped that my voice wasn't shaking as bad as I was on the inside. Wilson just arched an eyebrow and shook his head as he walked off. I turned around pulling out my desk chair; I didn't want to be disturbed so I slid my headphones on. It was a universal meaning amongst computer people. Headphones off meant it was free to bother me; headphones on meant war if you talked to me.

Once I was logged onto my work computer, I pulled up a quick search engine. I decided to search for everything from natural disasters to zombies, alien outbreaks even. Nothing came back that was of substance. This worried me—the most exciting thing I could find in the news was the local football scores, and the return of the tomato festival next month. Otherwise, my city didn't have one mention of what I had experienced the night before. Not even on a national level. It was as if nothing had happened at all.

This couldn't be right either. I know that I'd seen what happened, and the amount of blood and destruction was real. It had to be, after everything that had happened, what would it mean if it hadn't? *Oh God, I can't be a father if I had dreams of smashing my child's head open.*

A far worse thought burst into my brain with such a force I almost knocked my headphones off. *Maybe that was what Diana had said before jumping; I thought she had said this was my fault. Did I cause everything that had occurred? Like some long awaited mental disturbance that was crawling its way to the surface, like a maggot under the skin?*

I started to vomit once more, but only green stomach bile came out. After a second heave, I began to dry heave. It was real. No way of being unsure of that. I looked up, seeing a sea of faces peering over their cubicles. I was sick, and now I was losing my mind, to boot. I took off, running towards the bathroom, my whole body breaking out into a sweat. As I burst into the bathroom, I ran over to the faucet. I turned both knobs until they were about to tear free. At the sight of water, my tongue shot out like an old school cartoon character, greedily sucking down the nourishing liquid. Thirst was the one thing that would get to you most, before hunger, before any pain. Water truly was the life-sustaining force that kept you alive.

Beyond just keeping you alive, water provided one more key feature that was useful to humans; it cleaned surfaces pretty well. As my hands rested in the sink, the cold water washing away all of the damage done the night before, I felt myself drift off, if only for a moment.

I had heard stories from the military people in my office that it was possible to be so exhausted, so run down that images would blur, that they would fall asleep while in formation marching. To be honest, I never really believed them until that point. A lot of the guys I worked with were former military types, and I figured it all to be a joke on us "civilians." It was like being carried away by a huge gentle wave in that moment. The wave's power was so swift, I couldn't even feel it coming until it was too late. I was suddenly on a beach, with a tiny and pretty woman holding my hand, next to me. She had angular features, and a skin tone that I couldn't quite pinpoint where she was from. Yet she was lovely, the most ravenous creature I had ever seen. My heart swelled, and I took her hands into my dark ones, holding her tight. I blinked, my eyes opening back to the bathroom. I was breathing hard, the lights in the room feeling like millions of glass suns on a planet far away.

I felt myself falling, which was enough of a sensation to bring me back into reality. My momentary disassociation from everything around me was over, or so I thought. I had no idea who that woman was, or why I'd wanted to hold her hand so tight. My whole life, I had always only had eyes for a few women, and none had looked like her. I shook it off, my body wanting to collapse on itself. I opened and shut my eyes. When my eyes found their way to the mirror, I wondered again if I was asleep. I was wearing a long black tie, my simple double knot (the only one that my father ever taught me) hung past my belly to my belt. I was wearing a deep black sweater and my khakis; the average attire of the working-class man.

The blood and dirt that I was covered in only a few seconds ago was now gone, replaced faster than any waterfalls of a shower could do. "That's it, I must truly be insane—there's no other explanation for it," I grumbled, turning my back to the mirror. The image of myself looking fresh and new was too unbearable. It was one thing to have been covered in the blood of my daughter; it was another to try and be free of it.

I let my legs wander and carry me back to my cubical. Along the way, the office was a jungle of key typing and various different videos, conveying images of pop culture icons. On any other day, I wouldn't have thought this strange at all. It was normal to see things like this in my office. Only today wasn't normal, not by a second, not by a mile. I strolled to my desk, and as I looked past the desk of one of my colleagues, the image on his computer screen showed me the horror.

I couldn't mistake it; it was the image of me and my wife lying in bed. My quiet fan causing my wife's hair to seem like it was dancing to its own beat. On another desk, right across from my colleague, was another image of my wife and me. Only this time, it was from the perspective of the man who had taken my wife. I watched in horror again as my wife was dragged out like a farm animal being taken to the slaughter. It was sickening, seeing the images on screen, and my hands tightened at the sight. I never before wished that I could have jumped through the screen and destroyed someone. I turned my head, walking away, but I couldn't escape the videos. On every desk, from every radio, computer, and cell phone, I could see the long night that had forever changed my life; hear its taunting noises.

It was the overwhelming noise of it all. I felt as if I was reliving that gloom, sinking into a pit until my breath was all but a sad thought. My hands reached my hair first, pulling out my furry mess, that on a normal day would be held down by half a bottle of product. Only today, it had my fingers pulling the threads, my screams shaking the roots. My coworkers around me took notice of my behavior. I began to see their faces line up, peering at me from their cubicles. Instead of seeing a sea full of different people, I saw only me, over and over again. I was surrounded by almost a hundred of myself. All of me smiling, all carrying a coffee cup, all wearing a red tie. Those in the back, slowly started looking like me, their forms twisting and conforming into my shape.

"What the fuck is this!" I yelled at the nearest me, but he only responded by tilting his coffee cup to his lips. As I focused on the one in front of me, a slow murmur started to dance its way up to my ears. It started off weak, gradually growing stronger until words started to form. "Star-man," said all the mes. A chorus of my own voice, only on key, and less monotone than I had ever been at singing. I would never forget that song; it was one that Mother would often play while I watched her cook my dinner. I used to think it was the most soothing song on Earth, yet now I only thought it was the closest thing to hell that a man could ever find himself in. I had to get rid of it; I couldn't listen to it anymore. I cupped my hands against my ears, attempting to drown out the sounds. It was to no avail; I wasn't going to get away from it. My teeth were clenching so hard, I wondered how much they could actually take until I had shattered them with my own force of fear.

No matter how much I jammed my hands over my ears, I couldn't get away from the damn singing. My head was spinning, spinning so fast. I was losing control, my whole body floating away into the endless swirl of pain. I was a small ship, forever trapped inside a bottle. The more I screamed, the louder the singing got, and the voices continued to sing.

My legs fell first, and my head bounced off of the floor. Still, I could not escape. I looked up and saw the doorway to Wilson's office, his door being the only one not open as far as I could tell. *Wilson is my friend; he can help me get away from all of this singing.* As I crawled, the mes gathered closer around, pressing closer than a junior high school prom. I crawled my way onto the shoes of the nearest me in front. I looked up and his smile made me want to snarl and rip his throat away. The singing reached a pitch, almost taking my eardrums once the final note was hit. Then, just as soon as the singing had initiated, it stopped, leaving my ears unsure if they would ever actually be able to hear again. I looked up again, and seeing the nearest version of me, I was afraid. I was afraid of what was about to happen. I didn't know what was going to happen, but it didn't seem like it was going to be very good.

A roar of laughter broke out again, forcing my head to split in the loudness. As I thrashed my way on the floor, trying desperately to escape the laughter, I turned my eyes to the ceiling. Above, small black snakes were crawling out of the ceiling. Trilling and scaling along the surface, as the snakes passed over the heads of the mes, they extended their bodies down, growing long enough to reach to the men below. Once upon the men, the snakes wound their bodies around the heads of the mes—every single one of the mes that had been singing in the office.

In union, the snakes lifted up, taking the clones of me into the air. This neither affected nor deterred the mes. They still kept singing that song, smiling. Snakes were always a huge fear for me, and now that I was seeing this I made a silent prayer that if I got out of this, I swear I would kill and skin every snake I would ever see from this moment until the end of my days. My prayers were answered; the snakes became obscured by something far worse. As the bodies of the mes hung, they got ignited in a fierce flame. The heat became so great my body become soaked in sweat and the lick of heat.

Only the mes didn't burn, they kept right on singing as if they weren't actually being burned alive. "This is it man, you've gone crazy and gone to hell, you must go now." I pushed off the floor, my arms and legs feeling way too loose to actually be of some use to me.

That didn't deter me—I was going to get away from all of this or die trying. I started moving while covering my ears. It was too little shield against the onslaught, yet it was better than nothing. I made my way to Wilson's door, not pausing to knock; I just kicked at the door knob until I finally managed to get the wooden door to swing open, onto the set of elevator doors from the main lobby.

I couldn't fathom what had just happened; I was utterly confused and at a loss to understand it. I turned around, expecting to see the familiar desk of Wilson's, all covered in the vast array of awards that he had accumulated over a long career in the military. I shouldn't have been surprised when I turned around—fear had long since robbed me of that—but still I was. The room became white, as colorless as fresh snow piled on the walls, covering the floor. I wasn't in my friend's office now. The suddenness of the change shook me. I felt vertigo, my whole body wanting to lay down and crawl upon the ground.

Inside the room was a thick, overlapping mist that sprawled white in its form, coating everything in a silvery splendor, so that as I stepped deeper into the fog, I felt myself feeling more at ease. The mist calmed me; it was a lot less unnerving than watching myself burn while singing the childhood songs of my youth.

I gulped down the mist; it was almost marshmallow-like in form, chilling the inside of my throat. I was calming down, with every step the world felt dull. My cuts on my arms and chest became further, and further away, and the ground seemed as good as a place as any to rest.

Just sit down and let that cold blanket take over me. I had earned that, right? I had gained that freedom to relax, to simply rest, for a long while. I was beyond fatigued at this point; everything that had happened could be forgotten just for a while.

My feet stopped walking—*why had I entered this room in the first place? I was looking for my friend. Yes, this is his office, I am sure of it, and any moment I will find his oaken desk and my friend and I will catch up.* That felt clouded to me though, like an answer to a question that was far off and just at the edges of my teeth.

I looked at my hands; the tips were freezing, the hair on my arms standing like the bristles on a paintbrush. Bumps littered my arms—*was I afraid? Why should I be scared when I was just looking for my friend?* I thought.

Fear is such an odd thing—something that I always had following me around like the cold white mist in this room. Like a blanket with teeth that surrounds me, gnawing, hungry for a chance to continue feasting on its favorite meal: me.

A shiver ran up my spine and into my brain, taking me back to the task at hand. I had entered this room to get away from the chaos in the other room. Now I was in what was supposed to be my old friend's office. Instead, I had entered in a white frozen hell.

I cleared my throat, the saliva in my mouth turning into ice. I was shivering all over, and this room was endless. I turned back, and the wooden door bearing the letters of my friend's name was gone. Instead there was only the thick whiteness, encasing and enveloping me in a never-ending flash of a fury of cold.

My feet betrayed me first, jumping into the toothy grin of fear, thrashing out in the piles of snow that were now sticking to my clothes in white clumps as I trudged forward into the thinning air.

When you're cold—I mean in the meeting place of when your body can no longer remember what warmth feels like, when your blood aches for the heat of the veins—that is when you know cold. Your feet will be gone first, followed by the bite up your legs, ending in the tear of the cold reaching your balls and the rest of your body as it lashes out in a pitiful attempt for anything but the cold.

No escaping it, I thought. I slammed my mouth shut. I forced myself to not cry out for fear that my teeth would clack together, breaking under the pressure set upon me by the cold. The snow was getting deeper, and I was lost in it. Enfolded in my snowy tomb. After having survived all of this, I would go to my grave having not rescued my wife. I had lost both her and my child to the things of nightmares.

My face was stinging red in the frosty air; I was crying. *My nose is sniffling fast to hide the shame of a grown man weeping. I have to get ahold of myself; I need to get this under control,* I thought.

My walk continued to drift as I plowed through the ever-deepening snow. Burning in my legs, smoking everywhere, I thought things were supposed to be cold whenever ice was affecting you this much. *Great,* I thought, *I would die warm in an ironic situation: my face on fire as it melts from the frost.*

As I thought this, I fell to the ground, my tears still falling, no closer to escaping. *I was going to die. I mean, that is the logical outcome in this kind of situation,* I thought.

On my wrist was the watch my wife had gotten me for my birthday—a few back, if I could recall. Its metal edges gleamed a sunspot on the snow in front of me. I snapped out of my trance and followed the light from my watch. It led off into the distance, a small light shining through the haze.

I picked my legs up and started walking, breathing in the stale cold air as it burned my lungs from the heaviness of my breaths. I didn't care, though. That was light, and light equaled warmth. And I wanted so desperately to escape the lowest circle of this hell.

As I walked in the snow, my pace quickened. I was almost at a slow jog, and the storm let up as I continued to move through the thick currents of the snow, until the ice stopped just below my toes. I had found the source of light, the suddenness of it blinding me, forcing me to cover my eyes from the unusual flare. I blinked, squinting back more tears as I noticed the fixture above an all-white wall, protruding like a cyst on the side of a giant's white neck, leaking a long copper chain that ended at the edges of a curved iron tub.

"I guess the mind really can only take so much before it snaps," I grumbled, stepping to the tub. The snow had stopped falling, and the mist had receded to the edges of my vision. I was in a room, all white of course.

"That color is going to be the death of me," I stated.

"I don't think it will be a white, lover. I think it will most likely be a dull gray, kind of like a buzzing sensation you get when you've been in a silent room too long," spoke a smooth liquid voice from somewhere inside of the room.

My heart thundered into gear, snow falling inside of an endless room at the top of a building or not, I would never forget her voice. You always know your love's voice, you just can't remember it at other times, like stepping off a long flight. Sure, the first few moments are hasty and unsure, soon enough though, your heart's racing and you remember to walk; you remember their voice.

"Holy shit, Diana!" I exclaimed, running around the tub to see her curled against its iron safety, her long legs pale and glowing in the white of the room. I froze. It was my wife alright, I could never forget an inch of her, but her skin was different—bleached and almost marble in appearance. I traced up her body, naked and smooth. I stopped at her face, though; the lower half was all that there was.

The top half of her head was caved in, glowing green and empty, where her brain was supposed to be. I collapsed to the ground, tears already running down my face. *When was this nightmare ever going to end?* I thought. I covered my eyes; I didn't want to see her, not like this. I just wanted to see her sitting on our couch, waiting to watch some stupid movie. Not an off-white with her head caved in, during the worst couple of days of my life.

I kept weeping in the cold, expecting my tears to freeze up or just to go away for good. *Everything else was gone, can those leave as well?*

"You're a strange one," spoke Diana.

I flinched from her voice, uncovering my eyes, and looking at the body of my wife. Diana was close enough now that I could feel her cold breath on my own; I scooted back in fear. Her lips moved like plastic stretched to breaking point, though her voice was still the hum of energy I was used to. It frightened me.

"What? This isn't real," I stammered into the cold air around me, as Diana continued to speak, inching closer to my mouth.

"Oh, this is real, lover, this is all too real. Once, you and I had met on a bus a long time ago. It was rolling, rolling along the paved road. The driver drenched in sweat, stains seeping from his armpits down to his waist. I sat two seats behind, melting in the sun on a typical North Carolina day, dying of humidity in the rain-forest that is our state. You awkwardly sat across from me, wearing that weird Thundercats jacket—it's hideous and you really should throw it away, by the way," she stated, pulling me back to the moment we had met on accident while taking a bus into the city.

Love is an accident, I thought, *just like this moment in time with her in this room.* It was an accident; something had broken inside me that wasn't supposed ever to be broken inside of a person, like a glass bowl shattering on the ground. I wonder if I could ever recover from this mishap and be able to pull myself together. *Why was this all happening to me?* Diana moved forward again, taking my hands into hers. "Look at me, James, look at me," she said, her voice smooth with sensuality.

I looked up, and she snatched my face in her palms, her fingers digging into my cheeks. "Are you looking at me James, this is all so real, even for me," she whispered, and tilted her head towards me.

I had a good look now inside her head; it wasn't empty as I first had thought. I was shown the day that we had met on the bus. My wife right across from me, two seats back from the sweaty driver. She was wearing loose clothes and had the University of North Carolina shirt on, and the bus was mostly just the three of us, save for a Filipino man and an old woman sitting near the back.

I looked at the two; the old woman was staring out the window as if searching for something in the traffic as we moved past hundreds of people living out their lives inside of the city. The Filipino man was staring at me. I caught his look, and he shifted his glance to the ceiling. *Weird,* I thought, shaking it off and returning my thoughts to more important things, like the beautiful woman sitting across from me.

She was reading a book, its cover too worn down for me to get a clear view at the writer, but the title was all I needed. It said, "Memory Study." I chuckled. There was a beautiful girl, her hair as yellow as the paint markings on the road, reading a book on memories in one of the hottest summers I could ever recall. That very morning, I had spent most of my day sitting in class bored, learning about how computers adequately stored memory.

It was all very technical, and I was sure it meant a lot to someone, somewhere, but I was more into the creating aspects of computers, I had just come up with what I was sure would become the next big seller in the video game world. That was much more interesting to me. Not sitting around all day learning how they worked.

I shifted my gaze from her to my hands, trying not to be caught staring when I heard her yawn. *Nothing that beautiful creature could do would ever be considered ugly,* I thought, *she was the inspiration for any artist anywhere, her very yawp something that could send me into my wildest of fantasies.* I turned red at that thought; I wasn't very good at talking to women. In fact, I was getting to that age where it was weird for a young man not to have a girlfriend. I could see it now;

soon my parents would think I was either gay or weird.

I gulped. *She is just a girl, James,* I thought, clearing my throat in the process. Yeah—just a girl with legs that could walk on the sun, the moon shining down on her, glittering silver, and I was just a mortal dreaming of a goddess. I shook my head; *I've been watching too many bad movies lately. All they ever do is replace the words that you know you need to say, man,* I thought. Movies were terrible for that, replacing what I should say with their clever lines.

When all it ever took to talk to a woman, like Dad always said, was, "Stop worrying about the heat in your pants and cheeks. Just ask her out, you big dummy!" My father's booming voice rumbled inside my head. He was right, though; I just had to have the courage to ask her out—she was only human.

My hands were sweating, my collar too tight and I suddenly regretted wearing such a thick jacket on a hot day. I liked this jacket though, so comfort be damned. I fingered my collar, and when she spook to me, her voice was like honey over the loud "thud" of the bus moving on the hot pavement.

"You know, if you stare long enough, I might just burst into flames," she stated.

"What?" I stammered.

She sighed. "Guys are all the same. They look at you all day, and when you finally ask them why they're staring, they just respond with 'what?' with that stupid look on their faces. You would think by now, that the collective male species would have unilaterally come up with a better answer for when a girl catches them peeping," she stated again, with almost an air of indifference.

I shifted uncomfortably in my chair, pointing my eyes at the dirty bus floor. The floor was covered in what appeared to be an army of hair, and moving dust clumped together from the many people that had ridden the bus today. That's all we were, though, just many people riding the bus, never knowing anything about each other, never getting to form anything in each other's lives.

That's the key, I thought: *memories.* I responded before I thoroughly thought out my words, but I had no regrets—I didn't want to be just another memory floating on the ground of a dirty bus. "That may be true about the male population, but I think you forgot about one thing during your analysis," I responded, trying to sound cool.

"Oh? Do tell me what that is," she asked.

I moved my glasses, shifting the frames back on my face, "All those times girls catch guys staring and being creeps, and females have never formed any ideas about what to do when a guy stares," I stated.

She growled a low noise I would never have thought possible from someone so beautiful. I almost flinched from her anger at that moment. "And what, do you suppose, we should have learned?" she returned.

"That boys like staring at girls; some of us just want to make some good memories with each other. Right here—on a stinky old bus on the hottest day of the summer," I retorted, laying my arms across my legs.

She blinked and rubbed her head to my response, "I'm not sure if that made any sense. At least you had the courage to dig for something. Most usually get scared whenever I ask them that," she stated, holding her hand out towards mine. "Diana."

"What?" I asked again, confused at her.

She rolled her eyes. "My name is Diana, and yours is Clueless Staring Boy on a Dirty Bus, or something with more syllables?" she asked with a genuine expression.

I smirked at her; she was enjoying picking on me. "Well, when I'm not being an overworked and underutilized computer nerd, folks call me James. But for the sake of the rest of the bus ride, you can call me Clueless Staring Boy With a Great Smile, so let's form some memories together." I flashed my biggest grin, hoping it didn't look too weird on my face.

She blinked, this time laughing. We continued to talk for hours; it was one of the best days of my life.

"That's how it went. After a few more awkward returns, we sat next to each other on that bus for hours until it was the end of the line. I ended up having to call one of my girlfriends to come pick us up, as it was so late we couldn't take a train. I told them it was worth it though; I had met the smartest, but possibly the worst at flirting boy I could ever come across on a used lime green bus, which looked like an olive that had been sitting in a pickle jar far too long," whispered the Diana in this white room to me.

I tilted my head back and cried at the memory. That was the first day we had met. My head was swirling with the images she had shown me, and inside her head, the bus ride continued to play, bleeding over to the next time that the two of us had been together. I couldn't stop staring as my mind went back to that day.

It was Diana and I sitting in a park, two Star Wars coloring books set before us, and a half-finished bowl of macaroni. We had both agreed to bring something to the park that day as a picnic. I had produced the coloring books, and Diana, being the more sensible one of us, had brought the actual food. I didn't forget the coloring pencils though—after all, what good was a coloring book if you didn't have colors?

As we sat in the park that day, enjoying the sun in all its bliss, we were quiet. The comfortable silence of two people who valued each other's company, who relished the good times—as so many artists had put it in so many different ways.

By this point, I had my arms around Diana. She was reading, and I was the happiest I had ever felt in my life. "Think you can squeeze a little less there, big guy?" she joked as I turned red, releasing my hold on her. I was still trying to work the kinks out of being comfortable with someone so attractive next to me. Diana just caused me to go crazy whenever I was near. Not that I hadn't ever been with a woman—I had been with lots, but none had ever intrigued me like Diana. None had ever made me forget about the world as she does.

"Sorry," I mumbled, relaxing my grip and trying to smooth my sweaty palms on the checkered towel below us. "You say sorry way too much, you know that?" she stated, shifting so that her face was in front of mine.

"Well, I have to get your attention somehow; otherwise you will keep your nose in that book all day," I replied.

She smiled. "It's an excellent book. You would like it, you know," she insisted.

I cleared my throat, acting disgusted by the act of reading. "Unlike you, I don't read my textbooks for fun. I get enough forced upon me just by going to class," I countered.

"You're missing out. Books are normally written for a reason. Some may not be good; however, they still have a purpose," she said, suddenly growing serious.

I was feeling sheepish by this point, so I decided to humor her. "Okay, what did you get from your textbook, then? Your answer can't be something that prepares you for your test. Don't lie to me—I can tell." I quipped, sticking my tongue at her.

She laughed. "Well, the whole book is about memories. How memories are the controlling force in everything that is human."

I thought about her words for a moment; *I suppose, so memory is normally the first thing you relate to anything in any given situation.* "So, what, we remember things that happened to us? It's nothing more than a defense mechanism, like hitting your toes on a coffee table or touching an open flame with your bare hands," I said, taking off my glasses, pretending to clean them.

It was something I always did whenever Diana started to get deep into a conversation. I avoided such talks—after all, what was the point? Diana loves philosophical discussions. I didn't see why; numbers explained everything. If something seemed like a choice or unexplainable, you merely had to look at the numbers: everything added up. She didn't see it that way, of course. The way she saw the world had a level of uncertainty to it. Neither of us believed in God, but Diana always seemed to look on the more spiritual side of things, or the "feeling side," as I put it.

"I think it's true, I mean even now, I know from memory that whenever I say something that can't be rightly explained or something that you can't dismiss, you go into your head," she declared, moving out from under me. She placed her hands behind her back and looked me in the eyes. "Think about it, everything that we learn, everything that we value stems from a memory of something. It's how we are shaped. We are like clay, every single one of us," she said, pleading her point to me.

Why was this so serious to her? I mean she may have had a point, but what was the big deal? I thought. "Okay, memories are a learned experience, but I don't see where you're going with this. I'm not running away from the conversation like last time. No need to bring that up," I stated defensively.

She rolled her eyes before making her point. "You always run away," she smirked. "My point is that I learned something from this book. Just like I learned a lot about you from our conversations or lack of conversations on some points. I did it all with memories. Memories gained from actually doing my homework, memories gained from paying attention to you. We are creating memories together, James, so stop being uncomfortable and let the most powerful thing that makes us human be created," she informed me, taking my face into hers, and we finally had our first kiss.

She was right that years later, in an all-white room, my wife bleached and missing half her face would make me cry at that memory. It was something that had shaped me, something that had lead me to be the man that I was today. Only that man… that man had let both his daughter and wife die. Now I was in hell for it, seeing everything that I had done wrong.

"Forgive me," I muttered into the hands of the thing before me. It sounded like my wife, spoke as my wife did—it was a hallucination, though.

"Forgive you? No, no, no, why would I ever do such a thing, such a wild and unnatural thing that is forgiveness? Even now, you're deciding that I'm not real, James. That none of this is real—just the twisted guilt of your failure. You don't get off that easy; no one does. If you want forgiveness, start by forgiving yourself," she hissed with such a tone that my ears started to bleed as her rough hands gripped harder on my head.

My head was under pressure, breaking me like a bottle at the bottom of the deepest trench in the blackest of oceans. I was losing my mind; I had to find my way out of here. I tried shaking my head, shaking free of her grasp, but her strength was unreal and she kept pulling me closer. She suddenly stood, lifting me off the ground, holding me inches away from her face.

Her breath was icy, and she spoke again. "Fight, James, fight all you want. You never give up, except the only way for this story to end on a happy note is for you to stop fighting, start forgiving." She shook me, and I screamed out in pain.

I gasped, spitting into her face. Her head had caved in to the point that she had no eyes, just that strange floating chasm within her skull. She smirked, though, which allowed me enough time to unsling my pan and smack it into her elbow. She released me, and I fell to the ground hard on my face. I looked up, and she was still there, clutching her now missing arm, shrinking back away from me.

"I've lost my family, both my babies. I failed them, and I have even been led to this place... just to... just to see my wife again. Instead, I found you here, showing me memories of my wife—" I stopped myself and looked at the creature before me. The intrusions and deformities aside, she looked in every part my wife. She was my wife—or at least some part of her. She had to be her. She was exactly how I remembered her.

That's the key to this whole thing, I thought; *I had come to this office. I had come here not because I was led, but because I had memories of these places in my life. The people in my life filled the areas, making them real, making them tangible.* I looked at Diana, I looked at her shape. "I came here for my wife, for answers. I didn't find any of that. None of this is real," I whispered to Diana.

The ground around me shook, and Diana twisted and convulsed into herself. The walls became tarnished pieces of filth, peeling away the layers of an abandoned apartment building. I had the letter telling me to come to the bank in my hands; I had the pencil. A drop of blood rolled out of my nose and landed on the letter, and I fell to the ground. The whole event played through my head; I coughed, crying on the floor again. *This was getting old fast; be a man, James, and take control of your situation.* Diana's words about memories played through my head; I was going to have to hold on to something. Something that would keep me here. What was the most significant thing? that was the question. As I left my apartment complex, finding my way back to my car, it came to me when I opened my dashboard, searching for a map.

I saw their faces; first, I saw how all three of us were smiling. It was a family photo of Molly, Diana, and me at a park. What I had just imagined, it had felt real. Felt like something I had endured, twisted and visceral, taking me closer to the edge than anything in fiction—or in real life, for that matter. But my family, those memories were real. Love could not be made up. It was painful—one of the hardest things for me to admit was that I hadn't made the logical choices in my situation. That I had failed and failed hard. I had made up a story just because something rattled me. *A change was on its way,* I thought, *I was going to get ahold of myself.* It was the guilt for letting them down. It wasn't over yet; I was going to find my wife's body. I was going to see her.

I wasn't losing my mind, but I was just scared. I had failed my family, and that was beyond the ideas of pain, but the pain is a part of life—and if it is a part of life, then love must also be.

Chapter 11

Drinking was never my go-to whenever life was throwing me curves, but now, now as I sped along the abandon roads of my city, I would have killed for a drink. My wife, she was the partier out of the two of us; she knew how to have a good time. People loved her for it; people always commented on how she was the spark for us. God, I see it though, she was the spark for me.

I let that thought flutter around in my head. It was nice; something to keep me distracted from what had happened at the tower. As I was driving, I spotted a bar. *It was one in the afternoon, the world had ended, and I saw ghosts in my home. What the hell, why not have a drink?* I parked the beast on the curve outside of the bar, as close to the entrance-way as possible, (making a quick escape was starting to become a new staple in my life).

The lights were out on the inside, and the door was open. However, inside, the counters were littered with glasses and the remains of half-consumed food. A stench was floating in the bar, quickly engulfing me in its rotten odors. I covered my nose, and slid one of the stools from the bar into the doorway, propping the door open. *Completely worth it,* I thought, as I came around the bar.

I tried the first tap, leaning over the wooden edges of the counter. Liquid gold came spilling out, foaming a deepening stream of beer onto the ground behind the counter. *Good enough,* I thought, as I fished out a glass from the tray above me. I filled the glass to the top and started to drink. The beer was warm and bitter in the afternoon heat. That didn't matter; it was just lovely to have something to drink again finally. Just to do something that required no thinking.

As I sat, downing my first, second, and third beers, last night played through my head. I had imagined the entire journey to the bank. All the horror had felt so real; it was like trying to explain to a young child after bringing them to a haunted house that none of it was real. Sure, I could rationalize now that something had snapped within me and had caused me to go to that bank. Some part of me had gone to the bank in the vain hope of finding the truth about everything that had happened. I sighed—maybe I should have just stayed in the tub, I should have just looked for Diana's body, instead of hoping for something else.

Hope is a drug; hope is a limiter that people hold on to. Something that people crave instead of facing the reality of the situation. The truth was: that I was alone. I couldn't explain it; I didn't even have a grip on what was happening now. I'd just drunk in a bar, alone with no music on and shitty beer straight from the tap.

I started tapping my fingers on the counter. What should I do next? Should I continue looking for Diana? That seemed smart, but it appeared brighter to start looking for other survivors. I took a long pull on my drink; I wasn't in a rush to find other people just yet. In fact, only being around someone else sounded terrifying to me.

"Care to get me one?" asked a voice, that was drawled fast and had an almost rising intonation at the end of his sentence. I spat out my beer and fell off my bar stool. I came up quick, pulling my iron pan free, ready to go to war.

In the doorway was a small man, lean and brown. His hair was neatly trimmed, and his clothes were fitting surprisingly snugly. I looked at my now-soaked pants and jacket. Covered in a knock-off of a knock-off brand beer. I flushed in embarrassment momentarily, bringing back up my pan, hoping that whoever he was wouldn't come charging at me. Despite the beer, I was starting to get headaches from the lack of food. I knew that I couldn't go a lot longer without food—all the running around I was doing, that was burning what little I had to spare, the internal food clock inside me could only go so long.

The man pointed at one of the stools opposite me, and he came through the doorway with both of his hands held above his head. I debated tagging him with the iron pan—if he was another one of those things, he would let me know quick. And if I had to fight him off, he was about a head shorter than me.

"You have hands," I said, widening my stance. At any moment he was going to charge at me or turn into something from my worst nightmares—it was only a matter of time. He came down the bar stairs in an almost effortless way, like he was a man walking through a park entirely at ease with me. Despite the darkness, I could make out his features as he came through the doorway, making his way to the bar. He was someone that I wished I had never laid eyes upon, someone that would haunt my nightmares for many years. Despite my wish, he seemed familiar, as I gazed at the man.

I knew him, but I couldn't remember where I'd met him, He was a Pacific Islander—his round face and square nose told me that much. Along with his jet-black hair and tanned skin, I guessed him to be a Filipino, though it was difficult to say. Charlotte is a big city; a lot of surprising characters make their way here. I could have met him anywhere. He was cast in shadows that made his features all seem a lot darker than they were.

His looks weren't the thing that would stay with me; it was his eyes. They were the color of blood and shone brighter than the reddest of flames. His eyes were an unnerving bright red that glowed like the colors of fresh death. I swallowed, fearing I had just come across someone very dangerous, when the man pulled out one of the stools at the bar and promptly sat. He looked at me, shook his head, and reached into his jacket pocket.

I readied my pan to swing; this was it, he was going to attack me. I felt droplets of sweat fall down my face when—he pulled a cigarette box from his jacket pocket. He tilted it towards me. I looked at the box; inside were about twelve long and golden white cigarettes with a purple lighter tucked in with them. I paused, taking it all in; he wasn't trying to kill me, just instead offer me a cigarette. Not trying to kill me though—well at least not right away with those.

Looking at the man closer, it was hard to guess his age, I put him somewhere in his early thirties, his all-too-bright red eyes betrayed him. I worried what his true façade was beneath his calm smile and friendly demeanor.

He smirked, popping one of the cigarettes into his mouth, taking a long pull as he leaned back in his chair with what could only be described as absolute ease, absolute serenity in an otherwise awkward situation.

I thought about trying my pan again. If he were one of those things, he would be gone in an instant, but if he were normal—it would probably kill him. Eyeing my half-finished beer, I ignored my unwanted guest. I had come here first; this was my bar to brood in and he could find his own.

Beer has a funny way of going fast—down the hatch and out another faster than you realize would be possible, even for people like me. I grimaced at the remains of an empty glass, catching the red-eyed man cutting daggers at me as I set the glass on the smooth oaken countertop.

"Are we going to do this or what?" I grunted, pulling my pan into my lap; if he noticed the movement, I couldn't tell. His posture was as still as a statue, defiant in the stiffest of breezes.

"You know, no one wants to know the story of a badass. I mean, people love the tales of action heroes able to lift the sun, able to swing a heavy blade and take out an entire army of invaders. The truth is, those stories are hard to get into. Things are never that easy and identifiable as him or her being the bad guy. Everything stays in a gray state, in between them both. Anti-heroes are the best; it's the rawest and most honest description of everyday people. And has more depth than some guy lifting up a building just because he can," he informed me, still staring at me. I swear he hadn't blinked in the entire exchange.

My energy for dealing with any more surprises today was at an all-time low. I half-turned in my stool, "Anti-hero, hero, no one is coming to save us today, my friend." I informed him. I set my now empty glass down on the counter, keeping my weapon in my lap.

"Perhaps you have a point; I don't think there will be anyone coming to save anyone anymore. Or at least not for a while. The world has gone and moved on in a hurry. Do you have anything else to add to my point?" the man asked, entirely turning in his bar stool so now his face was positioned to my right.

"You didn't make any points; you just made a statement. A point means that you effectively convey all your ideas—from the look of it you're a talker. I normally don't mind being enlightened, but seeing how—and this is probably just me here—everyone has fucking died in this city! Not a trace, thousands of people torn apart to be replaced by images of beings, ones that a goddamn frying pan can turn them into nothing. I can't seem to make head nor tail of it, so if you have anything to add to that, I am all ears, otherwise shove it up your ass." I stammered, standing up from the barstool, causing it to fall over in my wake.

The man across from me roared with laughter, his eyes flashing in the light of the room. Like his eyes, his laugh caused me to want to bolt from the bar. I stayed where I was, though; my arms found them resting on the handle of my pan, ready to bolt at the first chance I got.

"I had no idea you would be so funny. It's good to know not everyone in your generation is so frozen by fear. Back in my youth, we most certainly wouldn't have hidden behind the slow caskets of social media. I blame that on the corruption of your generation; see, I've been studying you people, making all sorts of connections and viewpoints. You see, human beings by nature are nothing more than animals that developed abstract thought. A rocket to the sky, or an iPod playing a track on repeat—fundamentally, we are still all animals, and what has happened to you people is to become hidden, instead of growing and adapting in the wild. You're trapped like animals at the zoo, throwing piss and shit at each other. It's different from fighting it out in the wild; humans were meant for the slaughter, not meant to be a part of anything more. Just one collective strain of mixed thoughts that don't yield a thing," he informed.

Under my breath, I spoke. "Look, I'm not sure what you're trying to get at; I am just trying to find my wife, I'm not trying to be nobody's hero. Honestly, I just want to take a long shower, sleep this all off like a bad hangover, and bring my wife home; I don't care about any of that nonsense. I don't care about them, I don't care about you, just finding my wife," I declared.

His eyes regarded me—taking in what, I wasn't sure. He stared so long that my skin itched. Itched to be away from those cold red eyes.

"You have a daughter, correct?" he asked.

I stammered, "Yeah—I have one little girl."

"You also have a wife. Yes, you had both of those things. I look at you, and I can tell. I can tell you had more than just a wife. They were both taken, right? You don't have to answer me; your eyes say it all. You have that look of a man who's lost everything. Death is the extreme of life, the meaning of loneliness. That is why it is so important. The fear of death, however, is relational and polymorphic in its presentation. It's shocking; we convince ourselves we have an eternity to live this life—the primary immortal narcissism of man. We all have to die—just spend some good times with your loved ones while you can," the man said, suddenly sounding very far away from that isolated bar in my now empty city.

I was starting to feel like I was running around in an endless circle. *Why was I still in this bar talking to him?* Every time I began to leave, he would ask me a question. *Why was I getting so mad and staying here?* I thought. He was almost ignoring everything I was saying, as if he was reading a puzzle about my life.

"And did you love them?" he asked again.

That was one of the dumbest things anyone had ever asked me; my family was my love. My family was all I had. I had to find some way to get my wife back. He was trying to play a game. One I wasn't understanding. *I just have to keep playing his game,* I thought as my heart kept drumming faster. He was unnerving in the small quarters of the bar, and my thoughts were spinning. Maybe I had drunk too much.

"I knew my wife better than anyone else alive. I knew everything about her, from her smile to her awkward farts in the middle of the night. Everything about her—she knew everything about me in return," I sputtered.

His cheeks sucked in, and his eyes didn't move. That was the first reaction I had seen from him since I had entered this God-awful dreamscape.

"Yeah, only a married man would know bodily functions," he said.

"What are you getting at with all of this?" I asked.

The man tilted his head slightly, never breaking eye contact as one of his fists came under his chin.

"And what is your goal now? You don't have your family anymore, now your daughter is dead. Your loving wife is dead. Seems trivial, from where I am sitting, to do anything except lie down on some road somewhere and get hit by a car," he stated.

I leaned back, hitting the wall behind me, causing photos of bar patrons to come tumbling down to the ground; he had a point. What was I doing now both of my girls were gone? It was the truth; they were gone. "I just want my wife back… I can… I can take her home and put her with my daughter," I said, casting my eyes to the ground.

"That's a noble cause, one I could understand. What's the point? When the hero looses, what is the point in going on?" His tone was now dangerous. His eyes narrowed; he sounded suddenly fatigued. "Why carry on when the closest thing to relief you can possibly find is at the bottom of one of those bottles on the shelves," he said, gesturing towards the liquor stock on the bar shelf.

I sucked in a deep breath before answering, "Because my wife was the power to my cord; she was the display for my heart," I mumbled, tears rolling down my cheeks. "I could never leave them," I said, drying my face off with my sleeves.

"But you're here in this bar now, instead of being with them. If they were so important, why did you let them go?" he asked, boldly and without fear.

My anger boiled to the top, I was a steam engine long since past its red line. I was ready to blow. "I did not go," I growled.

"Excuse me, what do you mean you did not go?" asked the red-eyed man. It was the first time his smile had disappeared.

I continued, my voice becoming louder with every word. "I did not go! I went for both my wife and daughter; I went for them. I did not abandon them; I did not leave them. I took my daughter, my seed, and was washed in pools of her blood. No great funeral, no great sermon by a crack priest. No, instead I used a hefty bag while I searched for her mother's remains. I did not go! I was surrounded by monsters trying to claw into me, trying to take my family and me. But I did not go! I was unable to save my family; they left, and I was given the worst thing a man could ever be given. Not just any man, but all the people on this planet. I could cry and howl at the moon until my lungs burst in my chest, until my tongue fell from my mouth. My family is gone, and I did not go with them..." I snapped, seething with every word.

I caught his reflection in the mirror; his face hadn't changed, and he just regarded me curiously, like I was some kind sideshow exhibit.

He turned his gaze away from me, looking at the bar, and drew a long breath. We were both silent, the tension between us growing and swirling into an almost moving force that was striking from the wooden floors of the bars to the dusty and molded ceiling fans above us.

"Don't take this personally—I do feel for you. To be thrust into such a situation so abruptly, so raw that you haven't even had time to fully process the level of torment that is your existence now," the man said almost sorrowfully. He peered off, his eyes casting long into the past. I had no desire to find out what would make someone so strange, what would make their eyes so impossibly red.

"Why did you leave your family? You don't look old enough to have a family, but only family men are so concerned about a family," I hissed, hoping to scorn him like he had done me.

Silence stretched between us before he talked. It was like counting raindrops on windows—so many drops, so much time to wait until it was all over.

"I did go, I left my family," he said calmly.

Anger, once started to a point, is almost impossible to come down from—not without a release. Like a pot holding soup that is being cooked too long, sooner or later the soup will burst from the container, and someone could be hurt in the process. That was me at this moment, looking for a chance to break forth and to attack this man. Not just because of my general confusion and the ambiguous nature of this conversation, but because I wanted to hurt something. After everything that had happened, the trip to the bank, the strange encounter with Diana, and holding Molly. I let the thought die. I couldn't fathom even thinking about her death.

But I wanted to hurt someone.

Had I always been like this? I thought. As I looked at the man, my words stuck in my throat. No, I had never had so much as a violent bone in my body. I cried during most games as a child, or whenever I had the smallest of cuts. Here I was, thinking about hurting some man that I didn't even know the name of, instead of being happy I had found another survivor.

"So, who is James, then?" he asked, interrupting my thoughts.

I looked at the man, startled by his question. *I am me, of course, I've always been myself*. Though as I stared at the wooden bar before me, my mind drifted. *Who am I now? That was a simple enough question, wasn't it?* Before everything had started, my answer had been simple: *I am a family man, I am a computer systems administrator for a tech firm contracted by the government. I have a loving wife and an amazing daughter.*

I had everything I had ever wanted, and now they were all gone. Only that wasn't true in the slightest. I was happy with my wife, immeasurably so, only I hadn't been doing what I loved. What I loved was working on my video game. Spending hours programming a world into existence. It was a world I could control, one I had created wholly the way I wanted. It was easier, less complicated, than the stresses of life. The life I had, I would never trade it—yes, change a few things, but I wouldn't change it as a whole. *Or was I lying to myself*? I thought.

Most people on this planet stressed and worried about day-to-day struggles, finding security and providing for a family and their needs. Paying bills, getting out of debt, trying to find a foothold in life that was stable. And then possibly trying to achieve something of merit before life ran out. When someone has none of these "real-life" issues, and no worries about falling into poverty or not making ends meet, or losing their job, they still find problems. But those arguments, those fears of things that came along with choosing my family, they were worth it. I had my family, and my dreams became theirs.

Only they were gone now; I was all alone in a bar drinking a cheap drink, with a cheap man, having a cheap conversation at the end of the world.

"Let's start over. I feel like emotions are running high," he said, staring at the mirror on the shelf above the bar. For all my bravado, he wasn't fazed. Maybe it was easy to spot a killer, or perhaps he was just curious. Either way, my anger deflated, and I picked up my overturned bar-stool.

"What are you getting out of all these questions?" I asked, trying to avoid contact with his red eyes in the reflection.

He turned, casting me with a long look before answering, "I wanted to see the measure of your character. After all, these are crazy times." He paused, searching for the words, and my heartbeat increased. For the first time since I had met the man, my mind was working again. I glanced at the door. If I could find a way to distract him, maybe use my empty glass, I could make a break for the door.

"I needed to confirm a few truths," he said, finishing his statement.

"And what truth did you find out?" I returned, playing for time as my hand reached for the glass on the counter.

"Just what your part is in the coming storm," he answered, reaching into his pocket and pulling out a long purple knife, its hilt crested in such profoundly purple diamonds that they were almost black. I flinched, nearly falling off my barstool in reaction to him taking out the knife. He smirked at me, eyeing my wariness towards his knife. "Everyone thinks they're doing the right thing. Therefore, no one is truly evil. Depends on the perspective, though. All I do is try and make sure people are walking the path they are supposed to be walking, as opposed to their futility. I just do my job—my job is my morality. To do otherwise is useless," he whispered.

I barely heard him over the beating of my own heart, and I became scared in this moment. "If everything is so useless, why do you insist upon heroes having their own roles then?" I answered back, searching the bar out of the corner of my eyes. I saw the beer dispenser, its nozzle stretched out. I could use it to blind him with a quick spray; it was most likely powered by pressure just like the beer tap. Might not be much—it should give me some time to distance myself from this psycho, make it out to the car, and drive away fast. Get back to the search for Diana; that was the problem here—I kept getting off task and chasing down rabbit holes instead of looking for the body of my… of my wife, like I should be doing.

"Because we all have to play our part. It doesn't have to make sense; each of us does our duty, and we connect throughout everything.

Love is the universe's connection, the opposing force to total nihilism," he remarked.

"What are you, some cosmic hippie devil?" I slung back to his remark. My legs were shaking; I had to do this now.

He smiled, his teeth gleaming like a shark. I was his meal, judging by his smile. "That's a new one on me. When you find yourself in the darkest of hours, your loneliness of nights, ask yourself if you wouldn't sacrifice it all for love. Was it ever love to begin with? That to me is the difference between the good guy and the bad guy. The choice on what to do when love is lost. I am interested to hear your thoughts on it as well," he queried as if searching me with his words.

The sun was starting to get lower. The bar filled with shadows and the man became shrouded by them, merging almost. He was a man in shadows. Dread is the only way I could describe what I was feeling. My sanity cracked at the seams, and my mind flashed with the loss of Molly, her corpse on top of mine for days, her foul stench overriding me, smoking, and filling my lungs with her death.

I lurched forward, almost falling off the stool again, though my hand made it to the beer nozzle. A part of me remembered the plan. Good I wasn't completely losing my mind just yet. I hated being asked questions that made me feel, that Diana was right, that I did go into my head and shut down at them. When I didn't respond, the man in shadows turned, facing towards me. "What's your name?" he asked, as I readied myself for my assault, stepping onto the wooden floor. *Just keep buying time for the right moment,* I thought, clearing my mind of Molly.

"My name is James," I spoke, shaking my head. I could almost smell her as I looked at the man.

My heart sank—he moved in an instant and snatched the beer nozzle out of my hand with such ferocity that the tube connecting the nose to the bar was pulled completely out. I gasped. "James—we all have our weapons and tools, don't be the kind of man that can be summed up by only cheap tricks and one-liners," he said soberly, almost disheartened.

"Oh yeah—do you plan to use that knife of yours on me? A little unfair to say I used cheap tricks." I gestured and dropped my hands to my pan, ready to attack.

The man stepped away from the bar, taking his knife with him. I walked forward, ready to attack with my pan. He gestured towards his knife, its purple hews gleaming in the light, causing me to be enveloped in a blanket of stars from the ruby on the hilt. "And if I did use the knife, James, would you regret it? I could end it all for you right now, I could end it for you. No one would blame you—you've seen horrors and have only just begun to experience them. If you don't have me do it, you will wander alone, searching for companionship until the end of time. It really only leaves one option for you: kill yourself. I can end it for you; I can take away all the pain," he said smoothly, brandishing his blade inches from my chest. "Just say the word," he whispered.

I looked at the blade, and I looked at the man. He was offering to end it for me; a part of my mind jumped at this. This was the only way to end it, to escape grief and bereavement. I thought of Diana, I thought of Molly. I wanted to be with them so bad. My body became heavy and for a moment, I pressed into the blade. I felt the sharp edges pierce my skin, drawing a cold shiver throughout my body. *This was it, this is how I die,* I thought.

"We will always be the good guys, right, Dad?" Molly's question played through my head. I wanted my family; I wanted them so bad I was inches from death at the hands of a stranger in a bar. I steadied myself, not trusting myself to move away from the blade.

"No," I whispered back.

"What's that, James? I couldn't hear you."

"I said no, no thank you," I responded. Strangely, I couldn't trust myself to say I wanted to live. *I would go out on my own terms though,* I thought.

The man pulled his blade away from my body. "Try and get some rest, James, you're bleeding." He pointed at my chest. I looked down, seeing droplets of blood coming from my nose. I looked back, and the man was at the doorway. He had a black ten-gallon hat now, its shadow forming a farmhouse on the walls next to me in the setting of the sun.

"Wait!" I shouted. My head pounded, and I felt like I had in the room with Diana, just before everything shook back into place. "Is any of this real? Who are you?" I shouted at the man.

He turned around, speaking once more. "My name is Ghost." He smiled as I staggered forward, falling to the ground.

Chapter 12

I was in Molly's bed, reading her a story. Since she had been a baby, she always enjoyed the story of *The Three Billy Goats Gruff*. Molly demanded every night to have the story read aloud to her. That was okay with me—it had been one of my favorites as well, when I was growing up.

As I finished the part of the story that dealt with the biggest Billy goat, Molly's eyes were struggling to stay open. Her lips were doing her dance of trying to stay closed without drooling.

I took that as my cue to let her sleep. I tucked Molly in while kissing her on the forehead as my parents did to me as a child. She was a sweet kid, and I hoped she would stay that way for a little longer. Though she was only eight, I knew that some day soon she was going to start growing older. Soon she wouldn't like Barbie dolls and ponies, but rather boy bands and texting apps. "Oh boy, I should have had a son," I whispered, tucking her legs under the sheets.

As I turned to leave her room, Molly called out to me. "Daddy, wait; you forgot to check for monsters." Her voice was still halfway into dream land, carrying that trust that only children can convey in their tone.

"Sure honey, one sec," I said, leaning to the edge of the bed. One of our other daily activities was me checking under the bed for her; which of course never yielded anything.

Molly was smart, though, and she knew when I actually looked rather than just leaning over. "Dad, you aren't checking." She was still in that stage, I guess.

I laughed and dropped to the floor. I lifted her purple bed covers, revealing the underside of an eight-year-old girl's bed. Beneath her bed was littered with old toys that Molly had grown out of, and starting to accumulate a decent number of shoes, with heaping clumps of dust. No monsters.

When I was about to turn my head to report my findings of all clear, I spotted a tiny hand at the end of her bed. I squinted my eyes to catch sight of the hand, but it disappeared into the darkness. I blinked several times in confusion. *Had I really just seen what I saw? I just needed sleep; it's late and all the dust under here is getting to me. This whole house probably needs a good cleaning. Too many long hours at work to give it the proper once over.* I turned my head to move again, when I saw my daughter lying in the far-right corner. Molly's strawberry hair appeared jet black in the darkness. "Baby, is that you? Why are you hiding in the dark?" I asked, honestly confused as to what I was seeing.

"Daddy," spoke Molly in a terrified tone, different from her normal scared voice. Every child has one, and every parent recognizes it.

My heart exploded in nervousness. All it took was her to be in trouble, and I would be there. "Yeah, baby, what is it? Come out from under there before you get dirty, you squirt." I shook my words out, reaching my hand towards Molly.

"Daddy." Molly stated, her words causing my hand to stop a few inches short of her.

"Molly? It's too late to be playing games."

Molly remained silent, her eyes shining in the reflection from the small aquarium we had set up in Molly's room. I sighed deeply; she was still in play mode, and there was no way of pulling her out now. Well, if anything else, this might help her grow out of the "monster under my bed" phase. "Fine, I will play along, Molly," I grumbled, pulling myself out from under her bed. I looked up and there was Molly, lying on her pillow, perfectly at ease, exactly as I had left her moments before. Molly is a fast kid—she wasn't that quick though. I spoke, "Molly, weren't you just..." I couldn't finish the sentence. My mind was too far blown to respond fast enough.

"Daddy, there are monsters under the bed," Molly stated, sitting up in bed.

What did she just say? I didn't understand what was happening, and I felt cold. Something wasn't right, and this was too scary to be a good joke; besides, Molly never joked in such way. "Molly, I don't know what you're trying, but you need to stop, right now."

Molly looked at me for a long time; once again, the light from the fish tank played scenes of purple colors across her face. "What do you mean, Daddy?"

"Honey, how did you get out from under the bed so fast?" I asked, trying to convey my irritation over the brief scare I'd just received. The kid had managed to scare me pretty well. I wouldn't have called me exactly a coward, but man, it would be hard not to have your heart racing after something like that.

"Daddy, something is under the bed. Can't you hear it?" She tucked in her bottom lip; she only did that when she was scared. It felt like a cold hand traced its way all the way down my spine.

I bent over once more, this time more cautious as I looked under the bed.

Molly was under the bed again. This time, closer to me.

"Daddy," Molly whispered from under the bed. "What?" Was all I could mutter.

I looked up in time to see Molly from on top of the bed come flying at my head, her teeth bared like an animal.

I leaned back away from her, using my arm as a shield, as her mouth bit into my arm. My flesh tore away like the paper from an artist's notebook. I screamed, the surprise of the bite almost worse than the pain. I shook my arm as hard as I could to fling Molly away into the wall. I tucked my arm into my chest. The blood was coming out with no end in sight.

"Molly, what the hell is wrong with you?!" I shouted, standing to my feet. "I'm sorry, Daddy, but you taste so good," drooled Molly, rising to her feet. My blood was smeared around her lips, and she was not stunned in the slightest from the blow. Her nightgown was soaked red, and in that moment, I didn't see my daughter anymore. She wasn't the greatest gift of my life, she wasn't her anymore. *She's a monster.*

I stepped back, looking for room, when I felt another bite on my lower left leg. I shrieked both inside my mind and out of my mouth. Being eaten was the single most painful thing that I had ever felt in my life. As I screamed, the walls around me changed, and faces appeared from the purple walls. Eyes and little bodies peeled from the walls, until the room was littered with Molly's.

From somewhere, a Molly came from on top of the bed, swinging off and charging towards me, taking my other leg out from under me. Her strength blew my mind, as I felt another chunk of me taken out while I was confused by the sheer bite force. My confusion turned into disarray as the entire room full of Molly's lunged at me, biting and clawing me like a piece of meat in the lion's den. I fell under their weight, my vision a swirl of red.

I could hear tendons popping, and razor-sharp little teeth grinding on the bones of my leg. As I twisted my body to roll a Molly off my leg, another Molly smiled at me. I screamed once more as Molly bit down on my nose, easily breaking the bone in her bite.

The pain was endless, and when I finally blacked out, I came back. I was lying inside the bar, my whole body drenched in sweat. I brushed my arms across the battlefield of cuts on my body, but otherwise I was somewhat intact.

I felt cold; I couldn't get the image out of my mind, of being eaten by my daughter—or, well, daughters, in this case.

Chapter 13

I had been in a bar, right? That man, that man with the red eyes, he had said something to me, and I had fallen over. I shook, remembering what had happened with Molly. It was still daytime—how long had I been out? *Why was this happening to me? Why did I keep seeing all of this horrible stuff?* As I wrapped my arms around myself in the cold, abandoned building, I felt another letter in my pocket.

As before, it was addressed to me in a descriptive style, this time in an overly done lettering style. The message stated, "Just say the word, James," I assumed it was from the man—it had to be. Whatever he had done to me, he was rubbing it in by leaving a letter like this; taunting me.

I crumpled the paper into my fist, rage suddenly blasting away the cold that was plaguing my body. *Fuck that guy, who the hell is he anyway?* I wasn't sure if I wanted that answered, if I was honest with myself. His eyes haunted me more than being eaten alive—which was saying a lot, considering the state of my life; I looked around the bar, looking for something to help fix some of my issues. *I've got to get some of these cuts taken care of.* Working to take care of myself would distract me from the horror that had just happened.

I left the bar, taking note that the sun was now getting lower. I must have been out for a while. I was thirsty, famished to a new level I never knew existed. I used to go to the gym when I was in college; mostly it amounted to a few wasted cans of protein, and any results were blown away just as quickly from all the drinking. Until today, however, I never knew what real soreness felt like, what being in pain meant. Real soreness was like being run over by a bulldozer twice.

On the steps leading out the bar, my eyes became blurred and I started to see spots. I didn't know how much longer I was going to make it. I collapsed on the stairs, staring off into the distance. I wondered, as the sun lowered, what it would be like to just float off into the distance and just let it all go. *I mean, what was I even doing? I had lost everything that I held dear to me in a single night. To make matters worse, I was slowly losing my mind.* There was no other way around it, around the thought of Molly.

I bent over and proceeded to dump all the contents of the bar out of my body, along with most of my stomach acid. I wiped my mouth on my shirt, keeping my nose away from the smell.

My eyes just wanted to shut, only for a few minutes, just to let it all drift away. That was when I heard the small voice of a child. I opened one of my eyes half way, hoping that whoever it was would finish me off. Or God forbid, give me some water. A small Asian child stood before me, three feet tall and wearing a wrinkled Yoda shirt."

Hey mister, why are you lying on the ground?" The kid was bending over close to my face. Flashes of my dream, my daughter tearing me to ribbons, flowed into my mind. It made me more than a little uncomfortable, having another kid so close.

"Give me some room to breathe, kid. It's been a heck of a day, and I am all out of milk duds." The kid still stayed near my face; I looked up, opening both my eyes. The kid looked perfectly normal: no fangs, no strange nauseating marks. He appeared perfectly average, which should have been my indicator that something was wrong, I was either too tired to notice, or too tired to care. I sighed deeply—he wasn't going to go, and I wouldn't get a chance until he left. "What do you want, kid?" I asked, a lot gruffer than I intended.

"Can you help me, sir? My daddy is stuck in the coffee shop," said the kid, his whole body trembling in the light breeze of the day.

Upon hearing that he said his daddy was stuck, I shot up to my feet, my fatigue vanishing. It is amazing how much you miss human contact; I didn't realize how desperate I was for another human being until I saw the boy. "You're saying your dad is stuck? How is he stuck?" I asked, almost shaking the kid in the process as I stepped towards him. I wasn't the only one in this nightmare—he was real, and there were others as well. Thankfully, finally, someone normal and in need of my service. I was starting to doubt my mind being alone. Maybe this was a sign, just what I needed to stop seeing the nightmares.

"My Dad is inside the coffee shop. Come on, you have to help me!"

"Shush, kid, I will help; I need more information first, though. Things... have been crazy, to say the least."

The kid just looked at me, his face lacking all empathy. "Come on, my daddy is stuck, mister, please help me!" pleaded the kid, his body inching towards the coffee shop.

I looked up, scanning the shop. There didn't seem to be anyone in it; the lights were also off inside. The establishment was across the street, how had I missed people when I had come to the bar? That was probably where the red-eyed man had been hiding at—or is hiding now. I gulped. I didn't want to meet that guy again. He was just... disturbing. I thought of his letter; the words shook me. *He couldn't have caused me to have that dream, could he?* I shoved the thought behind; the day was starting to burn away like a firecracker, and I didn't want to be caught in the dark from whatever was going on. Ignoring every bell in my head, I went with the kid quickly around the shop.

Around back, there was the emergency door, shielded by a turned-over garbage cans. It looked like someone had tried to block the entrance. That made me feel uneasy; it also made me question how the kid might have gotten out.

"Kid, how did you get out of there?" I asked, turning to the boy. His hands were jammed deep into his pockets with his eyes cast to the floor.

When he heard my voice, he locked eyes with mine again. "Hey mister, can you help me find my dad? He's stuck in the coffee shop." repeated the boy, his eyes pleading for me to help him out. I couldn't place my finger on what it was, but something felt wrong; I was still trying hard to forget about what I had seen in my dream. Logic meant thinking, and thinking meant remembering. Neither of those felt right at the moment.

I looked at the boy, realizing that he must have been scared out of his mind. Hell, I didn't blame him. After all of this, he probably was about to piss his pants. I know I would have done, if I had some real water.

"That was it; I am simply hallucinating from dehydration," I stated.

The boy's eyes just regarded me worriedly. His face had that strange look, almost lost, as if I wasn't in front of him. I got the feeling that maybe the boy didn't see me in front of him, or instead was lost in his nightmare; it was something I wished on no-one, especially a child. That made me feel abhorrent and isolated. Here I was, motivated only to help for some human company, because I was feeling scared.

"Hey bud, what's your name?" I asked the boy, holding him with what I hoped was a gentler gaze.

The boy's face squeezed in, searching almost for the sounds that formed who he was. After a moment longer, I was just about to drop the question again, when the kid said, "My—name is Sam…" like he was tasting the words in his mouth for the first time.

I looked at the boy, and I had an idea. "Sam, huh? I used to have a dog named Sam; he was a lot of fun and such a brave dog. Do you know what, Sam? Do you think you can be brave like Sam, the dog?"

Sam just looked up at me, his gaze shifting from being lost to recognition. "Yes, I want to be brave. Can you help me find my daddy?" Sam asked again, his gaze quickly flowing back into his lost river.

"Sure, kid, I can do that," I sighed, moving to the garbage cans. I was able to move them to the side quickly enough. If his father was stuck inside, I didn't see how; the cans could easily have been moved by anyone larger than the kid.

"Sam, what's your father's name?" I asked, looking at the boy, as my frying pan became more burdensome as the sunset. I was going to have to find a way to tie the pan around me soon—something tighter, maybe a sling; it was starting to waver in my hands from holding it for so long.

Again, the boy was lost, like water in the desert.

"Sam, I know you're scared, but you have to help me here, pal. I only want to help you and your dad," I said, leaning towards the door.

"His name is Kim," Sam said softly. I almost didn't catch it.

"Alright, Kim it is. Sam, I am going to need you to wait outside." Sam just nodded in response to my statement.

I took a deep breath, my right hand shaking on the door handle, my left holding the pan firmly. "Here we go," I whispered to no one in particular. I opened the coffee shop door; I was surprised that it hadn't been locked. I slipped inside to the back storage area. The smell was like something out of a coffee heaven; I could smell fresh beans with various creams. "Oh man, it's been four days without my coffee—I must be dead," I mumbled, searching for any light in the storage room. As I made my way deeper into the room, I could see the light coming from under an exit door ahead.

Calling out for Sam's father seemed dangerous; something told me that I had already made a little too much noise for this adventure. I crept along, watching my feet from hitting any of the spilled items that were in this back area. It looked like someone had come running through the room in a hurry. I got to the door from the storage room. Outside the door was the central kitchen area. It looked to be more well kept than back here. I pulled my breath in, almost as a test to see if this was another nightmare or not.

Cooking utensils and heavy baking bowls were scattered all over the room. I picked my way through the clutter, with my feet making soft scrapes on the linoleum floor. I made it out to the main entrance from the kitchen; out to the serving counter. I looked out the serving window; the store was void of people. There were only chairs and tables. It looked like a perfectly reasonable coffee shop otherwise. Overly bright signs and comfortable back-lounging sofas. A pleasant place as any, even with matching colors of brown and light orange. *A sunrise and a drink for you. Good enough environment. Then again, so was my eight-year-old's room—she still ended up dead.* I kept my guard up. Now was not the time to relax.

The sun had finally gone down; I was now in the darkness of the shop, the light from outside gone. I went through the service doors, searching for a light. Maybe the power would still be on in here like it was in the bank. I found what I was looking for; the light switches on the wall. As I went to flick the switches, I peered off down the long hallway, leading outside the coffee work area to the back. I thought I could see something odd at the end of the hall. *It must have been a box of some kind or just a shelf.*

Absentmindedly, I flicked the lights on in the store; amazingly enough, they worked, and electricity shot through the shop. Casting the room in a dull glow from the fixers above, I squinted my eyes from the light. I couldn't see anybody or any places where anyone could have been hiding. I looked down the hallway; it was empty and led to an unknown area of the store. That was weird, though; *I could have sworn I had seen something standing in the hallway.* I shook my head, fighting off the sleep. It was taking everything that I had just to be standing here. My back hurt, and my skin felt like it had been stretched tight over a blanket of spikes.

"I need to get back to Sam; he is probably scared out of his mind." I went to flick the lights off again; no point in wasting energy if this was a place that had power. I could bring Sam in and see if I could make us something. I turned the lights off, and the outline of something obscured was again at the end of the hallway.

"What the..." I turned the lights back on, but once again the hallway was empty. I looked around the rest of the shop; I couldn't see anyone in the room. "Sam, is that you, pal?" I spoke into the emptiness of the room. Goosebumps were running down my body, and I was feeling entirely justified in the uneasiness weaving its way deep into me.

I took a deep breath, steadying one hand on the switch while wielding my pan with the other. I flicked the lights off once more and shapes appeared all over the restaurant. The shapes changed into bodies, and soon the entire shop was filled with people. I felt the light switch in the darkness, realizing the futility of the situation. They came back on—slowly, though. I was surrounded. I glanced back down the hallway; more people now filled the corridor. I couldn't go back the way I had come. As I stood there, nothing moved in the coffee shop. The people remained motionless.

I dared to move around the counter, never taking my eyes off of the people in the hallway. I made my way into the shop, bumping into a table, sending a chair to the ground. My hand was shaking until I saw the light glinting from my pan. The second I took my eyes off of the hallway, the lights stuttered and shut down. I was in total darkness, though not alone. The shapes were in front of me; I could feel them as well as see them. They wanted me, and I was now trapped alone in the dark. I gulped, raising my hands high, ready to defend myself.

When I turned back, other shapes emerged around me—two in front of me, and two more behind me; I was fenced off. I could feel a hissing, a slow, steady rhythm of sound screeching like the brakes from a car; yet I could still hear my beating heart. I waited. I didn't want to make a move. I didn't want to be there. That was when the lights came on again; I blinked in surprise. Before me was an Asian-looking man. I would use "Asian lightly"—his form was distorted and twisted, his skin all too pale. He opened his mouth, baring long needled fangs, and so did the other two with him. All three looked the same. *I was about to be attacked,* I thought.

"Not today, not again," I growled as I stepped forward, bringing the pan down on the nearest one to me. Everything changed, and the lights went gray. The walls turned to a dull storm cloud color. I blinked in surprise. The people before me had moved positions, and gone were the comfortable and inviting couches. Instead, in their place were bright red booths, with polished, circular, white tables. I stood up straight. Around me were people moving into the colorless void, some actively eating burgers and fries, while others took orders in checkered and plaid shirts. Even in the gray light, the coffee shop gleamed with the appearance of a much older and far more extrovert burger shop. I lowered my pan; no one was attacking me, and people moved around me, taking orders, playing songs from a neon jukebox.

A world of the past, come alive before me. I sniffed the air; my stomach growled fiercely and hunger set in—it was finally here. The smell of melted cheese, crisp lettuce, and salted fries threated to send me to the ground. No one noticed me; everyone had their places. The servers served the food; the patrons ate their food. All rolled on as intended, like the wheels on a bicycle.

"Dad would have liked this," I mumbled while watching two teenage kids share a milkshake and fries. My father had grown up in restaurants just like this when he was a boy; he always said the classics were the real burger joints, the classics knew how to do things right. I continued to watch the two teenagers for a moment longer; their lips closing softly, while the frozen treat at their table melted in the hot sunny day. I felt the sun on me, radiating on my skin and moving through the hours of the day as a calmness and a feeling of safety drifted over me.

I turned my head and looked out the windows of the restaurant. Gone were the high paneled glass buildings—instead were rectangular and open doorways of glass, showing not a city, but rather a vast and sprawling urban neighborhood. Outside, children played in the hot sun, and splashes of water from buckets filled to the brim with soap drizzled the children, and their laughter took me out of my serenity.

Sam, I had come in here for Sam. No—I had come in to find Sam's father.

"Sam," I spoke, and the music humming in the background of the restaurant stopped abruptly. A plug was pulled out of the world around me. The people distorted, twisted from their wholesome and pleasant feel. The windows shattered inward, convulsing until a wall of impermeable darkness covered every shine of the light.

I pulled my pan up to my shoulders, sweat drifting down my forehead. *Another dream,* I thought—*no, maybe this was happening.* I was encased in absolute darkness. The darkness that greets a person in the middle of the night—when all is foreign, and objects move at the edges of your vision. The wretched and foulness of claws; teeth, even! In the comfort of your home; in your place of safety. Because in some darkness, if it is a safe place, you remember you have no claws yourself, you remember your teeth have trouble with small chunks of lollipops. And as you make your way slowly to the light switch in the darkness, and you pray that nothing has teeth and claws, as something moves in the edges of the night.

My tongue caught in my throat as the darkness became deeper, as my vision became black and the hairs on my neck tried to run away. I turned in circles until a dull rhythmic melody cascaded across the sealed-off tomb I now found myself in.

As my heart raced, the melody heightened in its pitch, rattling my chest, causing my knees to shake, and I became lost in a maze of reality, under the surface; I was frightened by the marvelously terrifying bleakness of my minds conjuring's in the entanglements of my nightmares.

I had to run—I had to move, I told myself. I shouted as I inched my way forward. I couldn't see my hands in front of my face; I just ran from the music playing around me. My legs started walking, started running as I took off from the sounds of the music, and my body shot forward until lights bolted around me, fleeing the darkness.

I squinted in the sudden light. Figures appeared before me. It was the teenage couple who had been sharing the milkshake and fries. Their hands were locked, their bodies moved with grace; they began to dance to the haunting melody around us. As the tempo picked up, the couple pulled tighter into each other, and their movements became faster—more spins, more lowering of the hips and flaring of the arms.

I stepped back; they were only a few feet away. As I moved, they turned towards me. Their bodies close together; their fingers dug deep into each other's shoulders. Clawing and tearing at the exposed flesh covering their bodies. The couple's skin sagged and withered, turning old in the bright light of some unknown origin until they both were old. I gawked and felt myself eject any hope of ever making it out of the coffee shop alive. As the couple distanced themselves, they plunged their hands into their bodies, pulling the skin free as if it were a simple sheet on a bed. They were now only muscle, their tendons flowing, and organs jumbled together, despite their outside casing having been stripped away. They glowed the same cherry red as the tables had. The couple held their skin before them, taking their bodies into their hands, and started to dance.

I heaved over, almost dropping to the ground from the repulsiveness of the scene. "I am so sick of this… this snuff-film, torture, mind-fuck!" I shouted, charging at the old man with my pan. He looked at me, his features lost and unknown in his exposed muscled form. I smashed the man with my pan, and colors shot in every direction around me as I fell to my knees.

A bright light burst forth from the man, showering me with the images of his life. It was like being in the heart of a tornado; his entire life flashed before my eyes. I could see his adventures with his son, many nights of staying up late playing with his son, and some of his army men. I heard the love from his mother when he graduated from high school.

I smelled the scent of the first time he came to this coffee shop, the freshly ground beans attracting customers, the feel of his wife's hair when they first made love. I saw how the man had grown up watching old television shows, shows about burger restaurants. I learned how the man loved taking his wife dancing, how it had always felt like they were the center of the world, the only couple dancing in an endless sea of people. Everything about this man was shown to me in an instant. I was more intimate and aware of what had made him "him" than I had any right ever to be. The suddenness of it all caused me to collapse to the floor. It was like the woman from before in my bedroom. In a moment, I had stolen and looked into everything from this man's life. It—it felt wrong.

It became clear to me in that instant who the man was, and how his life had come to a violent end only a few feet from where I kneeled. The darkness cleared away, and I was back inside the coffee shop; around me were more people. I was on my knees; three attackers stepped forward, not wasting time on my stalled movements. Their dirty hands reached towards me, promising nothing but wicked desires.

I couldn't get what I had seen out of my head; I needed to live through it all, to find Diana. So I rolled, dodging the blows as they came down only inches away from where I'd been. I smacked my pan into the nearest attacker again, and once more I learned everything there was to know about the teenage girl attacking me.

She was sixteen and loved music—she felt that a perfect day was ZZ top, mixed in with some fresh double mocha. My eyes watered from seeing her life; she was too young to have ended up the way she had. I didn't want to stand anymore; I wanted to cry for the girl and the man. However, the desire to not be consumed by the attackers' advance was enough to dispel any feelings I had of quitting.

I swung for the nearest leg of an attacker, bursting her into billions of lights, it was the mother of the teenage daughter, and she was just having a day of fun with her girl. I didn't realize I had stopped until the other attacker was almost upon me. I let loose a scream and shielded myself with the pan; the movement saved me, the attacker burst into his memories.

I fell to my stomach after the assault was over. My whole body was convulsing under the weight of all the information. I once studied for a certification for my work for two months. In those two months, I put in a solid four hours of studying a night, but even with those nights, I'd never had my mind feeling this overloaded in my life. There was no comparison; it was like someone had placed every movie and book I'd ever heard of inside my head at the same time.

The final attacker lunged with his dark hands; I fought back, landing a blow into his chest. Again, his memories flashed into my mind, and this time it made me cry. It was some small boy; I had just killed him.

It was becoming so hard to breathe, with waves of emotions slamming me into the current. I was a lonely island in a sea full of pain—and yet love. That was the thing all of my attackers had in common besides the pain. Each person had loved others in some form. From the man whose memories told me of his love for his prize German Shepherd Max, to Sam's father bringing the young boy into his work with him every day. Everybody knew love in some way, but all knew only death now, and its extended hand.

I picked myself up, my cast iron skillet getting heavy again. I had a feeling that before long, it was going to weigh as much as Thor's hammer Mjolnir. It had to, to help me face what I was beginning to understand as my punishment for abandoning my wife and child.

My feet were moving again while I was digging a hole into the darkest reaches of my mind. As I strolled down the hallway, I walked like a man in the darkness of the shop, like a man who had been coming into the store every day for sixteen years. It was to be expected that I now knew everything there was to know about Mr. Myung-Kyu Kim and his young son, Sam. I made my way down the hallway into the storage room at the end. I knew what I would find once I opened the door; there was only pain behind those doors, but I knew that a first aid kit was hanging on the wall.

It was like reading a massive autobiography on them; every thought down to the least abstract. That's why I knew when I opened the door to the storage room, there I would behold the bodies. I wasn't surprised to see them, nor smell the decay as I picked my way through their torn limbs to the first aid kit.

I thought of Sam while I tied and applied the gauze to various parts of my body. I thought of all the memories that he wouldn't get to have. It made it easier to stomach my lost memories. I ignored what had happened in the coffee shop, I ignored the itching memories in my head, and I ignored the dead bodies around me. After I finished patching myself up and cleaning up with a bottle of rubbing alcohol, I made my way out of the shop.

I found Sam cowering in the alley, exactly where I had left him. He hadn't noticed me yet; he was just staring at the door I had entered earlier. Something wasn't right about the boy. I now knew he wasn't the real Sam; the real Sam had died being protected by his father, scared and alone in the dark of a coffee shop.

Looking at him, I couldn't bring myself to do it. Sam wasn't my responsibility. Besides, I was becoming a lot of things, and a child killer was something I couldn't become—not willingly, if I had a choice.

Chapter 14

I walked away briskly into the quiet of my city. It still seemed as dark and empty as it did during the day, only now the buildings swayed as if they were tree limbs in the darkness. I was on edge now, though; I wasn't going to be caught off guard again. Or at least, that is what I thought. Somewhere overhead, lightning had started.

I looked up into the darkness of my empty home, feeling like I was trapped inside of some steel tomb. *Nothingness, nothingness, as far as my eyes could see. At this point, the rain couldn't make things much worse,* I thought. I tucked my coat tighter and started my way back to my car.

It started to rain. I was wrong—the cold drip of water made my loneliness much worse, much worse indeed. As I made my way through the darkness, the sky continued to be lit up with a spray of gold and light from the battle of the gods above me raged on.

The lightning led to thunder that became so bad my heart started pounding. I wasn't afraid of the thunder before, but I also hadn't been the only man in my city before. I took shelter under the porch overhang of a nearby building. I was having trouble remembering where I had parked my car exactly; I was having trouble keeping my thoughts clear, my own memories slightly muddled by the ones I had just gained. The information wasn't as fresh now, it felt more like having an infinite source of reruns of television shows, causing my head to throb in pain. I decided to rest a few minutes; maybe the rain would clear some as it fell all around me like an unturned swimming pool. *Everything—just felt so puzzling; I had left the coffee shop to find my car. I think that was it. Maybe I should go back—I don't know where "back" is, though.*

I lowered my head, looking at my feet as I tried to center myself with my breaths (the old man's wife had apparently always asked him to do that when he was upset—sometimes it worked, sometimes it didn't). I took a few deep breaths, concentrating on my wet shoelaces. My heartbeat slowly returned to normal for the first time, in what felt like ages. The old man's wife was right, it did help, some. I was feeling better; I looked up and the thunder cracked, revealing a couple of things in an instant.

First: my van was parked down the road in the direction I had been before, I had walked a fair bit of distance from it. Second—this was the kicker—around me were hundreds of kids. I stared into their faces as the thunder above showed me more. Their eyes were as black as coal, their faces as withdrawn as the waves from a shore. Some were younger, some were older, about Molly's age at the most. In addition, most of them wore gas masks covering their features, though I could see their eyes.

They chilled me. It was like looking into the deepest pit's never-ending bottom, far away. I straightened up, and each of the children reached out with a little hand.

"Oh boy…" I mumbled. At the sound of my voice, they sprang into action, and torrents of screams came from their muffled mouths, eyes ablaze with an animal-like zeal. I turned, not waiting to see their tiny hands racing towards me.

As I ran, I looked back to see them following me; gaining on me quickly, despite the heavy downpour. I dug deep, racing towards my van, wishing again that I had taken a jog more often. If I got through this mess, I would become the biggest gym rat alive.

My feet tore forward, and I almost lost my balance in the rain numerous times. All the while, the children still kept coming. I reached in my pockets as I neared the van, fishing out my keys with my one free hand while I kept my pan from falling. I had made it to the door when I finally slipped in the rain, falling forward.

My weight and momentum carried me forward and I knocked on the door hard, dropping my keys somewhere in the rain. I spun back around quickly, as I fell. I could see scores of the children racing towards me, the rain passing through them like a giant drain. I swung the pan up and covered my eyes, bracing for the impact of their tiny bodies.

It never came, though, and I waited, breathing in deep rolls of fear as the rain poured down on me. I stayed that way until the rain passed. Only then I finally uncovered my face. Before me was nothing, just the emptiness of the city.

I wanted to cry so bad during that instant. I wanted to just have Molly and Diana back in my arms. I was ready to do anything, anything to be taken away from this nightmare that seemed to never end.

When I made it to my car again, I checked for my keys. They were jammed into my hands so tight they started to bleed. I looked in at the backseat first before getting in (I couldn't be cautious enough now). I drove home quickly; surprisingly, my thoughts stayed away from all the pain of the day. In the distance, child-sized shadows continued following, guided by my lights.

I shook in fear. Why had I been targeted by them? They had me dead to rights by all accounts. At some point, the human mind just couldn't register anything worse. I was at the point of total numbness, which was fine by me. I didn't want to have to feel anything anymore.

I opened my door to the darkness of my house, and I felt the rumble of my stomach once more. I was starving. It had been four, or wait, maybe five days since I last ate. Four sounded about right; yeah, four seemed more bearable than what the truth was. In addition to the first aid kit found at the coffee shop, I'd taken as many bottles of water as I could find, and I was sucking one down now greedily as I walked around my home. It would do until I found food.

I downed three of the bottles in a matter of seconds and was working on the forth when my body started to groan from water expansion. Then it was just me and the darkness of my house. I had never felt so alone in my entire life. I remember thinking of all the times that I complained to my wife about not having enough "James time," as I used to put it. How selfish I truly was to not spend every waking moment that I could with her.

I made my way to the tub, feeling my way through the darkness, using the now destroyed walls of my duplex to guide me. Once at the tub, I considered its iron depths, its shallow bowl seeming to stand out like a giant mouth waiting to eat me. My body didn't care what my mind felt—it needed rest. I stopped to listen before getting into the tub, and I wondered if I should perhaps check the house before settling into bed. It was no use though; I'd never felt so drained. I was not looking for another night in this thing, though a night in the tub seemed more appealing than being exposed to whatever might be leering around my house.

I closed my eyes, and then a monster reached into the tub, telling me that it wanted to devour what was left of my skinny ass. I snapped my eyes back open, peering into the darkness. My heart was beating like the heart of a rabbit chased by a clever hunter. Nothing was there. It didn't make me feel better, so I would just have to try sleeping again.

Once more, as my mind began to drift off down the river of sleep, images of the day flashed through my mind. *I wasn't going to be sleeping tonight, not by a long shot,* I thought. I pulled my pan up closer to my chest. It was my own iron teddy bear. Like most children though, I knew that Mr. Iron Pan could only do so much against what I was facing. I held it tighter, and my mind drifted off into sleep.

I was out. *How long had I slept for*? I thought, hearing something in the darkness. I heard his voice again. The icy Pacific dialect that inspired a chill to run up my spine: "James."

I snapped forward at the sound of his voice, swinging my pan overhead in wide arcs. I looked around in my house; it was still destroyed, and still spooky, but otherwise, I was alone. "I will kill that son of a bitch if it is the last thing I ever do."

I believed it as I settled back down, and my stomach roared in protest. "Yeah, yeah, I know. Please let one of us get some rest, how about it, stomach?" I asked my stomach as I lay back in the tub.

I looked at the ceiling, staring into the darkness. I remember reading as a kid that Michelangelo nearly went blind painting his masterpiece. I wondered if the same thing would happen to me, looking into the darkness for so long. That made me think of something bothering me the most, over the day's events (that being a lot of things). *What had happened to all the destruction from the night before?* A part of me was still in denial about meeting the man in the bar and being in my work office with all the 'mes.' It had to be the product of a lack of sleep, along with my nightmare about Molly and my wife. Maybe everything that had happened at the coffee shop along with those children—none of it could be real. It felt real though, it felt all too real.

The thing that drove my mind in circles over and over was my wife. I kept replaying the image of her standing on the neighbor's roof. Overlooking the dark below, that trace of a smile on her beautiful face and those words she spoke: "It's your fault, James," just before she leapt to her death, so very far down.

Wait, don't think that, man, that isn't what she said. You had nothing to do with her death; but a voice in my head knew that wasn't true in the least. When the time had come for me to make a choice, I had gone for my daughter, not my wife. That was something that I was never going to get away from. I reached up, pressing my fingers onto my temples. I wondered how much pressure it would take to actually split my skull—that was how much I was feeling now. The death of my wife would have been easier to swallow if I just could have found her body. *What had happened to her body when she jumped? Why had a letter telling me to go to a bank of all places shown up in my building?* The questions were piling up and no answers seemed in sight.

Perhaps it was something I would never know the answer to; it certainly wasn't something that I was going to solve tonight. It was nights like tonight, when, before all the unexplained shenanigans that had plagued my life in the last few days, I would sit at home and work on my video game project.

For the last two years, I had spent most of my free time juggling work and my family, while programming my very own video game. It was a sort of a side project of mine. I remembered that on the nights that I couldn't sleep, I would find myself wandering out of my bedroom down to my office. Programming always put things into perspective. Everything in programming has a variable, just like in life.

I would sit at my three-monitor set up, blasting only the best classics, keeping myself in the zone, one C++ line at a time. That had been my life for two years—typing out one logic code and leading to others. The funny thing that always made me laugh or chuckle was how much I truly believed that it would succeed.

It wasn't a thing now, of course, I thought. My thoughts drifted into the black cloud that seemed to have shrouded my life as a whole, but when it had been a part of my life, every long day of my life, I thought it would be the one thing that would make my existence more meaningful, something beyond the mundane. Maybe that was me being selfish.

The nice thing about working on the project was that I wasn't alone at all; my wife was on board from the very start, supporting me every step of the way. That made the long nights more bearable, seeming more like the world had a finite place in the grand scheme of things.

But, my mind had been all over the place. It's amazing the things you think of when you're alone in the middle of the night, typing away at the key bindings of your favorite desktop—a gift from my wife when we first met—just pecking away one key at a time, trying to make a better life for yourself. That was the thing; I wondered many times if I was truly doing it all just to overcome the situation I was in, or because I was greedily casting myself out like a small fish in the middle of a massive lake. A small fish wanting to be big.

As my eyes adjusted to the outside around me, I imagined the voices that were in the leaves, the faces in the branches, the whisper in the twigs, the tickle of the grass. *I was totally at peace with the world, which must have meant sleep, right? That was how it worked, right? If you made peace with the world around you, that must have meant peace, right?* Again, that would have made sense before; I had to be free from the obligations of the world around myself if I were willing to make peace with everything.

I tried closing my eyes, knowing that it was a fruitless endeavor that would only end in me wasting more energy than it was worth. I shook my head, pondering the thoughts that were keeping me awake, thankful my brain wasn't completely gone. Even though these ideas seemed like they weren't the ideas I should have been having, I was still happy they weren't the ideas of what all I had endured since the genesis of the horror that was now my life. I felt like I was in the middle of some swath of a desert, trudging along like a slave in ancient times. Nothing to look forward to, just following the past instead of the future.

Once more, I shook my head, trying to focus on what was around me, which was the best way to fall asleep of course; *if I didn't let my mind wander like it was, then I was surely good.* I rolled over in the tub, trying to find the best position for me in the cold darkness.

That was when I saw the glowing, a shining star in the darkness. A little dot of light guided me out of the tub. I followed it uncertainly, later more confident as it danced around me, sending swirls of bright light into my eyes. I reached for it, almost wanting to take it into my hands, wanting to feel it and keep the luminosity for myself. After all, who else was more deserving of the light than me? I had lost everything in the last couple of days; I was more than qualified for the task at hand.

A glowing light had to be only good, right? I told myself, as I shifted in the tub to get a closer look at its clear form; the light disappeared up the stairs, flowing into the stream. I followed it, reaching my way out of the bathtub. The bright sphere now guided me into the darkness of my house; I followed the light as it led me through the gloom. It was something I couldn't understand, and yet it was something I wanted to touch, no matter what. Even in the darkness as I followed the light, I was still confused as to my role. *I mean, here I was, nothing more than someone filling a role. What choice did I have, then, but to follow?*

That was when I knew I was fatigued beyond the understanding of myself or any man. There weren't many men alive today who knew what it was like to be this tired, and yet still having to fulfill one's role. My role was to follow this light, and nothing more.

Into the darkness of my home, I followed the light. I tripped over the various bits f debris and still, I kept my footing—I had to see where this magical light was going. That made all things at peace in the world around me. All my thoughts were gone—*just follow the light, James.*

A slow thought from deep within formed; it began to worm its way through the layers of my fog of sleep. *Why was I following this strange light? More importantly, where did this light come from? It doesn't matter though; I am just enchanted by its mysterious glow.* I followed the orb upstairs into the darkness, my feet sinking into the wet carpet.

Maybe I should try and touch it? I expected the rational part of my brain to speak up, but I was given no response. *Well, that must mean it's all good.* I extended my hand towards the orb of light, licking my lips almost like it was a juicy steak after a strict fast. When my hand came close to touching the orb, the light disappeared, leaving me shrouded in darkness. My heart became crestfallen, my own light from within vanishing with it.

My eyes still hadn't adjusted to the blanket of complete darkness over my house, still leaving enough for me to see the outlines of the wreckage of my place. "Well that's what I get for chasing after strange lights. I am pretty sure my mother would have made a comment about me doing too many drugs."

Wandering around in the dark at who-knows-what hour, I turned around, heading back down the stairs. As I made my way down the stairs, I met my wife coming up them. She was as elegant as I always remembered her being, and I could see her outline in the shadow. I could never forget her shape. My heart skipped fast in my chest, and I found myself bringing my pan up. I wasn't sure if I should swing or not.

It was another trick, or I was about to be attacked again? I need to swing now while I have the chance, do something before it's too late. I tightened the grip on my pan, rearing back to land a blow.

"Who's there?" spoke my wife, Diana, her voice flowing into me like smoke.

My only logical response was "What?" of course.

"Where am I? Why are the lights turned off?" she asked, her voice coming off more surprised than afraid.

My hand let go of the pan, causing a thick thud at the top of the stairs. "Diana, is that you?" I said, awestruck at the possibility of it all.

"Well I am, whoever that is. More importantly, I am confused about why everything is so dark," said Diana, the warm light of her voice lifting my body up. She always had that effect on me, that ability to uplift almost anyone with just a few words. "What's up with the pan, guy? Going to make some waffles?" she chuckled in the gloom.

My eyes watered up; it was her all right, and my world was back. This was all just one giant nightmare and my wife wasn't dead. I jumped forward to wrap her into my embrace; my gusto causing me to forget that I was in fact on the stairs still. My body went head first down the stairs and I rolled down into my war-torn living room. As I lay, my mind replayed what had just happened; I wasn't sure how I managed it. I pulled my body into the sitting position on my back, which was now feeling like it had taken most of the fall, and somewhere on my body I could tell that I was bleeding. "That really hurts," was all I could let out, without a scream.

Above me I heard giggling—Diana was laughing at me.

"Oh, hardy har har! Laugh it up. It really hurts, Diana!" I shouted back in response, feeling like my cheeks were a high shade of red.

"Ha, are you okay? Sorry for laughing, that was just kind of funny. I wish it wasn't so dark in here or that would have been too funny," Diana joked, as she moved down the stairs with grace, silent in her movements. I looked up to see her coming towards me. She was wearing the same clothes as she had on the night when everything went crazy. Just plain shorts and one of my long t-shirts—it was her all right. All long legs, and looking more beautiful than the night sky to me.

"Well, you have a point there; it definitely would have been a laugh to have seen. If you give me a minute, I can find our candles somewhere in the wreckage," I grunted, gesturing around me, not sure if she got my point in the twilight of my living room.

Even in the shadows, I could see the frown that was forming on her face, Diana only made that look at me a few times in our entire marriage, such as when I was explaining the rules of Dungeon and Dragons. And another time that Molly, as a child, had fallen off her bike. It was a look of confusion, bordering on irritation. Diana didn't get sad, she got mad and figured out her problems. It was something I loved about her—she handled her life; she wasn't emotional unless a situation called for it.

"You keep calling me Diana, plus you referred to the candles as our candles," stated Diana, walking up to me and extending her hand, "I honestly have no idea who you are or where I am," she wondered.

As Diana spoke, her hand reached mine and phased right through my own. The sensation sent an explosion of pain bursting into my body. It was like I had been plunged into a frozen river in the middle of winter. My entire hand shook from the touch, causing me to jerk from the motion, while my legs flared out from under me.

I was gasping for breath, lost in an ocean of pain. It was wild, it was fierce, and it flowed through my body as if it had a mind of its own. I closed my eyes, trying to block out the sensation the best I could; only managing to take the edge of it away. I looked at Diana; her face was just as confused as mine. Whatever had just occurred shocked me back to reality. Something wasn't right with this situation.

"Are you okay? You're shaking badly; you might have taken a harder fall than it first seemed. Let me help you," Diana whispered, reaching towards me again. I jerked away like a wounded animal in a cage. Diana stopped her motion halfway. "Oh, it was my fault." she said, turning away from me. That made me feel bad. She was only trying to help; maybe the fall had caused some latent internal effect in my hand, or maybe not.

I stood up, calling out to her as she headed back up the stairs. "Diana, wait! I'm sorry. It's okay, see? I am alright. Only thing broken is my corny jokes." I tried in vain to comfort her.

When Diana heard me call out her name, she froze halfway up the steps, like my words had trapped her in an invisible net. Her head snapped back around, and it made me take an involuntary step back, "Again, I don't know who you are," Diana whispered, gazing with a snarl of rage; I had never seen a trace of anger come out of her. Once she had stubbed her toe on a table, and she had cursed for a few minutes—that was about the worst of it. This, however, was something different, something primal and unnerving. I wasn't sure what to do.

My mouth did the work for me that my brain was unwilling to form. "What do you mean, who am I? I'm your husband, the hopeless loser you decided to have a daughter with. "I fumbled my words while taking a hesitant step closer towards her.

"Daughter?" Diana said like a question.

"Yeah, we had a daughter together—she has beautiful looks just like you. Going to be the smartest girl in the world some day," I stated, edging closer. If Diana had somehow lost her memory, I thought the best way to help was to be slow and steady with her.

It was hard, though; every fiber of my being only wanted to take Diana in my arms and close the door on the entire world. "I have a daughter and a husband…" Diana wondered, lowering her gaze into her palms.

"Yeah, we've been married for nine years," I affirmed, now only a foot of distance between us. "Wait—why did you say 'had'?" Diana whispered, her eyes leaving her palms and meeting my own.

I couldn't hold her gaze; I didn't know if I ever could hold her gaze again. After all, I had left our daughter alone, I alone had let whatever darkness that was around me take her away. Maybe it wasn't best to tell her that yet. She was, after all, suffering from her own problems in the last few days. Who knows—the fall could have caused her memory loss, she could have been looking for me for days as I had wandered all over the city like some lost puppy.

"Her name is Molly, and she is our daughter…" Diana puzzled again, almost like she tasted the words to see if they made sense to her, which they seemed not to. Her face was withdrawn into her thoughts.

I tried smiling; what else was I going to do? I had to help Diana; I had to just hold her one more time. "Diana, I am so sorry… for everything, I'm here now, though."

As I reached to hug Diana, her whole form begun to shake, from her core to her eyes. She was like a small child coming out of the cold during a wet storm.

"Diana, are you okay?" I asked, reaching out to steady her.

Her shaking stopped at the mention of her name. "You're James—my husband… my husband!" Diana screamed, launching herself at me. Her eyes were ablaze, like nothing I had ever seen before. Her skin had become stretched and a slow line of blood was trickling down her head.

"Holy shit, Diana, are you alright?" My desire to touch her was now replaced with an even greater desire to distance myself from her.

Diana sneered and leaped towards me. I saw it coming and stepped back, trying to put distance between the two of us. She hissed at me like a snake; her teeth, normally white as chalk, now shown only cracked and deformed. Her whole form was twisting up—she was looking like someone who had fallen from a building.

I was scared, scared of my own wife. That was a new feeling that I did not understand. Your significant other should in no way ever be someone that scares you; sure, someone you fear for when they are away from you. But not someone you worried was trying to hurt you. Because I had no doubt in my mind about the sinister intents of my wife as she took another swing at me. She wanted to only hurt me, twist me in ways I couldn't imagine.

I stumbled back, losing my footing on the debris in the dark. Diana didn't waste any time taking my imbalance as a chance to attack once more. The only thing that kept me from being touched by her was me falling over my cabinet door, now in the living room. I rolled quickly, trying to get away.

"James! What's the matter, I am your wife! Come here!" Diana hissed, blood coming in thick pools from her head now.

"Diana, something is wrong, you need a doctor," I gasped, regaining my feet as I made my way into our kitchen. I had to keep talking to her until I could figure out my next move. Had to keep talking to whoever it was who looked like my wife, no matter how much it hurt seeing her like that.

"What I need is you! Even now, I can feel the way your body beats with life. Your blood is flowing, and your veins are alive like electricity. Let me have you!" Diana hissed again, almost flying towards me. My reaction was to use the pan—I had left it on the stairs, though. *Why was I so stupid? I should have known something was up as soon as she appeared.*

With no other options, I threw up my hands trying to block her from getting me. Her eyes showed only hunger and that was something that truly frightened me. I felt wetness in my pants; I could smell the urine coming out as she bore towards me. I was afraid; I was about to be torn to bits by my wife. I let loose screams as Diana took hold of my hand, her twisted form coming into itself. I watched as her body rolled into a ball. All I could do was blink. *What in the hell just happened?* The ball floated inches away from my hand; it was similar in shape to the glowing orb I had seen earlier. Only this ball didn't give me any comfort or make me think I was safe. It was black in color, swimming with shapes in the inside.

The ball sprang towards my hand, and my senses thundered in a shower of cold pain. My hand felt like it was breaking apart. I imagined my skin tearing away, piece by piece, a puzzle being disassembled and never placed together again. Though my hand was freezing off, the rest of my body was reacting. To stop the pain—it was so bad—I smacked my hand on the counter. I did this repeatedly until I fell down.

Fire started to make its slow march up my hands, stretching past the tips down to my thumb. I had to get her out of me. I looked around in the darkness; not a single thing I could use. If the iron in my hand had killed the others, maybe I could use it to draw her out. I sprang to my feet, the pain causing me to become blinded. As I stumbled in the dark, I landed on my staircase, looking up to see the pan near me.

Go, was what a voice from deep within said; I made my way to the cold iron. Its weight crushed down as I held my other hand. "Here we go—please work." I held the pan towards my left hand, the iron causing my skin to boil and erupt. The reaction was like someone pouring acid on me; I could feel heat bubbles and blisters. Otherwise, my hand still felt cold. I could feel her anger at me for using the pan. More blots shot up my hand, now moving further along. I could feel her pain, cowering at her hunger. I didn't know how I knew these things; It was like I was listening to a soundtrack of her emotions on top of my tortured ones.

Inside, a message was becoming clearer to me; she felt this was entirely my fault. She was blaming me for the pain she was in. She was feeling the terror of being stolen in the middle of the night, mixed in with the pain of her jump. Her purposeful love abandoning her in her greatest time of need.

I picked myself up, somehow closing my mind to her thoughts and mine. If I was going to make it through this, my hand was going to have to come off. I made my way up the stairs to the hallway, until my legs collapsed beneath me. My marathon was only starting.

I couldn't see my surroundings and the pain was causing my brain to circle around anything but useful information. I needed something to cut my hand with; I was at a loss for anything sharp.

The gloom, combined with the pain, left me with no other choice. I had read somewhere once that the human jaw had around 120 pounds of bite pressure to it; to be honest, I wasn't sure exactly what that meant. I think in practical terms, it meant my bite would have around that amount of strength for biting. Considering the amount of pain and fear running through my body, I was sure that number would be doubled.

I didn't hesitate, just stuck my hand in my mouth and bit right at the wrist. My mouth filled with blood and flesh; it tasted of salt and metal. I started to gag as I spat out chunks of myself. I knew I had to take more bites as I spat parts of my body onto the ground. My biggest regret was being that my wrist was so big, it took three more painful bites to cover my whole wrist; the whole time spitting more blood, chunks of meat, and veins out. I felt myself starting to fade away, it wasn't enough. I think she was sensing my new tactic; she retaliated with a blizzard of pain in my hand, getting closer to my wrist.

After another big bite, and I came to my bone. There was no way I was going to be able to bite through that. I placed my butchered hand under my right knee, knowing my hand would be forever altered, never to be the same. I gulped in a fresh scream and slammed down with my iron pan on the bone. The hit caused my vision to go black, but I had to fight. I had to stay awake. "Come on, you pussy!" I screamed, slamming the pan again on the bone, feeling a crack. "Here we go! I'm sorry, Diana!" I screamed into the darkness as I hammered down with everything I had. I felt the bone shatter under that blow. It did the trick; I looked down to see my hand hanging on only by a few tattered pieces of skin. My hand was beyond painful; no words could describe the excruciating pain I felt.

Somehow, I was still awake though, feeling the blood rush out of my limb at disturbing speed. I knew I had only a few minutes to go before I passed out; if I passed out now, I was going to die.

I rolled over, crawling towards the stairs, ignoring the feel of my severed hand as I made my way. At the top of the stairs, I was now overlooking a mountain of wooden steps. It was daunting task at hand; I would bleed out before reaching the bottom.

I made the choice to roll down the stairs again. It was a quick method of travel and the only way that would get me down. Tilting my way to the edge in a blur was all it took. Like a rock on a ledge, gravity did the rest. I fell head first into a roll, slamming my back against uncountable aches and bruises. I tried my best to protect the exposed gore of my hand, but it's hard keeping your arms tucked when falling.

I reached the bottom in agony, everything on fire and my vision becoming even more strained. I had to keep moving, keep going forward. When Diana had gone into me, I didn't receive all her memories, (which I was grateful for, you just aren't supposed to know what someone was feeling in their last moments) I received enough though. A few years back, we had both agreed to quit smoking if for nothing else other than our daughter's future. As I gained from her memories, I now knew where her hidden stash was. Diana was keeping her smokes in one of her old coats inside the downstairs closet. "Thank God for our bad habits…" I mumbled, regretting wasting my strength as I made my way closer to the closet.

Luckily, the door was wide open from the trashing the house took the other night. I found her coat while pulling everything down in the closet on top of me. I found her lighter. I took the smokes with me as well; I was going to need one soon. I crawled my way into the kitchen, my legs too bruised to walk.

Pulling out my stove was a bigger task than I thought it would have been. *Was it this thing that heavy when I put it in a few years back?* Then again, I had both my hands back then. I undid the hose from the back, and immediately I could smell the gas.

I flicked the lighter on the first try, the small flame lighting up my kitchen in a swirl of orange. I had lived in this house for almost eight years now. I still remember the first night we moved in, the first night I spent it without my daughter and wife. Here I was, about to burn away everything I knew. I hesitated, knowing full well I could die any second, as I felt my blood start to turn cold in my body—or maybe it was just my body turning cold. Whatever the case, it was time to get things burning.

I flicked the lighter behind the stove and watched as a fire engulfed the stove and clothes that were thrown all over its top. The kitchen counter caught alight and went up just as quickly. The heat was tremendous, singeing my eyebrows from this close distance. I rolled forward towards the crumbling timber of a now-burnt cabinet door jotting out of the fire.

I looked towards the flame on the wood, wondering what it must feel like to be consumed by the fire. I didn't relish this one bit; I pressed the ruined stub of my left hand into the fire. I screamed into the night, trying to jerk my hand away, but somehow I held on. As my meat begun to burn, my bones charred to the color of the darkest night. I held my hand in place, the pain searing away any tears I had.

Finally, I couldn't take it anymore and got my arm out of the flames. I didn't want to look at my hand, I only wished I had just set myself on fire along with my extremity; let the flames finish the job. *Yes, that doesn't sound like a bad idea, just let the flames take you away.*

As the fumes of smoke and flesh danced their destructive waltz through my nose, I coughed, spilling something wet. I was going to die now; I was going to join my family. I crumpled into a ball, the pain searing away my thoughts—*just die, James. You can join them as soon as you let go.*

My eyes were heavy, and I couldn't move. I thought I saw someone though, moving at the edge of the flames. *I should tell them to go, just leave me here. I'm not worth the risk of this burning place.* I leaned up to protest and finally the pain caught up to me, causing me to fall onto my back.

If only, if only I could just burn away—if I only could just burn, burn. Oblivion sucks when you face it all alone.

As I drifted, I was being steered down this dark and befuddled road. Nothing more than a page in the oldest book of the oldest library, made for a purpose, but a purpose that lacked any bravery, lacked any semblance of hope. *I am that mouse, hearing my feet pad on the ground as the cheese guides the way.*

Chapter 15

Snowflakes were falling in the wreckage of my kitchen. A fire had seen fit to burn away a section of my roof, leaving me exposed to the elements for days now—as I sat covered in blankets, looking at the ruins of my hand.

Hours after I awoke, snow had started to fall, the first flakes of an early winter covering my house in a gray that seemed infinite in its mass, all the proof that my world was moving on. To what end, I did not know. I just stayed where I was as the cold fell around me.

As my body lost all the warmth, like the very idea of anything warm, I grew colder, as if anything made of light was not permitted here by some malevolent spirit. I was okay with this though; warmth seemed like a distant memory. A ship that was built yet never meant to sail, just to float and dream of the idea of waves.

I could only dream of heat, a dream of love. An illusion of life that was beyond this place of wrath and agony. Suffering was long gone and a new terror entered: isolation. It was that very isolation that was with me now—better than warmth.

Despite the cold, despite the hunger that nibbled at the edges of my mind, I stayed in my kitchen looking at the remains of my hand. My left side hurt—the bandages I had placed on the wound would need changing soon. I kept sniffing for infection for the first two days. Afterwards, I hoped, I begged for the disease. Death seemed like an escape to warmth—more tempting than to wait in the cold, watching my hand.

Every so often, I would brush the snow away from me, place more blankets on top of my brittle form. I made my way into other homes slowly, ignoring the food. Just taking the sheets, the clothes of the families that had once lived there. Taking anything else felt wrong—it felt like I was cheating my sentence.

My punishment for my crimes was to die in the cold, watching what remained of my wife. She had gone into my hands. I had chewed my flesh and killed her. For that, I had no more warmth to look forward to. I was back to watching my hand, looking for any sign of movement. Looking, hoping that something would move. Nothing happened, just snow and ice piling around my dead hand as my body slowly died.

Someone had pulled me from the fire, I was sure of it. I had been spared a peaceful death in my sleep. The kind-hearted asshole had even seen fit to wrap up my stub of an arm; my best guess is that whoever had done it knew what they were doing. Otherwise, it would have been infected, and I would have been smelling myself by now.

Instead, every time I changed the bandages, I just smelled pork. No other way to describe it, my flesh smelled like pork and every time I looked at my hand I felt myself cry. Tears were running down my cheeks, snot leaking with no end. In all my life I'd never cried as much. Not when both my parents passed away, the birth of my child, the day I was married to the love of my life. No—this was something primal, something that I could never have understood before. I had lost a part of me, burnt away like water on a computer chip. A fuss that would never work the same, a life that would be forever changed.

And that was why I wept for what seemed like days—no thoughts, just the pain of losing my hand, losing my family. I was a long way gone Why hadn't death come for me yet? Why had that person saved me? Why did I have to be alive?

Anger boiled from my tears first, not the desire to live. No, it was the fire—the fire to harm the person that had saved me. That was my driving force, the fuel to my inferno as I sat in the holed-out remains of my kitchen.

Soon enough, my fire from anger boiled away. Hunger had come. It was on a day that the snow came halfway up my legs that hunger stopped being at the edges and started to come full force to the very reaches of my soul.

My body became a thing, my skin hanging off my stomach, like collapsing dough sagging from how fast it shrank. Still, instead of finding food, I buried myself deeper into the cold, deeper into my solitude.

"What are you doing, James?" I asked myself as the snow continued to fall. It had been some time since I had left the kitchen last. At least a fortnight or more since I had stopped looking for food.

Tracking time was hard. Every moment my eyes stayed open was spent on drying my tears away and watching my hand. I wasn't sure what I was expecting, Maybe I was hoping my hand would come to life—just one sign of Diana. She had gone into my hand—perhaps, just perhaps there was a chance that she was still inside there. My hand never moved. Diana never came.

Another night passed, and I could hear the howling of dogs in my neighborhood. Hear the whisper of cats and the caw of birds. Animals had gotten the better deal, and humans the short end of the stick, at the end of the world.

For those that had managed to escape their homes, life was back to the natural pecking order, and since humans had an abundance of food at any time in most trash-cans, it was good eating. No fear of some asshole speeding down the road and running you over.

No waiting on some self-indulgent owner to walk you outside just so you could take a shit in the middle of the night. No more humans equaled a peaceful and natural return for animals to the world. As we fell apart and disappeared, they feasted and returned for now. Though something else existed in the world now. Sinister and without any explanation for their actions were the ghosts.

At night, I slept with my iron pan in my hands, ignoring the hunger. A few had come to my apartment. I hid in the tub, piling clothes on top of me. Peeking through the clothes, I could see them in my living room, almost searching for something as they moved through my destroyed home as if nothing was there. It was as if they were leaves in water, being pulled and walked along by some outside force.

They would float through any obstacles in their way, my hair would stand on end, and my breath would disappear as the snowflakes drifted through their bodies. Soon enough, they left me alone; they stopped coming into my home. Like shadows vanishing into the light.

I think they were looking for something. Maybe me, or perhaps just something living. I stopped hearing the animals whenever they came around; I ignored the hunger. More days passed and I finally started to get sick, and something was zapping my energy. The sun still wouldn't come out; the cold just kept on coming. Now my hand was frozen, and I ignored the hunger.

One day I got up and fell in the thickening slush of the snow below me. It took every ounce of my strength to drag myself through the ice. I was soaked, drenched in my many layers of clothes. I ignored the hunger.

The hunger was starting to win—all thoughts of my pain were numb compared to the craving. I searched my kitchen, through the snow, finding nothing, the food that I'd once had in my home hadn't been restocked. It was grocery time in another life of mine.

My legs gave out on me in the snow. How long had I been here, how long had it been since I'd eaten something? My inanition had become my tomb, but starvation was a hard thing to succumb to willingly.

I couldn't let myself starve to death. I made it out to my living room after what felt like hours of dragging my dying body through the wet snow. Over chunks of wood and splintered photo frames. I kept pulling myself until I made it to my door at last.

Looking at the thin piece of wood separating me from the outside world sickened me. One thick piece of wood was all that kept me from getting some food. I reached for the knob, my hands too numb to turn the door. The metal lock laughed at me, taunting me for being so stupid that I had allowed my body to become this weak in the cold.

I flicked the door off and placed my back on the frame, taking a rest as my breath became haggard and strained. What was I going to do? Everything felt dark at the edges. The snow looked deeper and broader than anything I had ever seen in my life. A vast ocean of white that I couldn't dream of climbing my way through again.

I closed my eyes, my thoughts were lost. My dreams, my dreams were no more, I was going to die. Then I snapped my eyes open sheepishly. Some part of my body was fighting back. I wanted to shout at myself to stop, to quit fighting. What was I planning to do anyway? There was no food in my home, nothing left except a dying man and a hunk of frozen—

I knew where there was food.

The idea of food spurred me to move, giving energy back to my limbs as I crawled my way through the frozen snow. The thought repulsed me, but hunger—true hunger—is a ravenous terror, for which only those who have tasted the madness caused by its onset can know its debts.

And madness was my driving force as I dragged and crawled my way through the snow. The snow cooled the pain from pressing my missing stub into the icy drifts, for which I was thankful. A pleasant feeling of warmth on my burned skin.

I knew what I was heading for; I had to have it, something so wrong. So far removed from the fundamental elements that were my life. Here I was, crawling in the wet snow towards my burned-down kitchen, to devour my hand.

I reached the kitchen. I dug in the snow—the very same spot that I had been watching for days now, the place that contained my hand.

I found the gnarled end first, causing me to dry heave from the gore. The bone was protruding, fractured from the blows with my pan. Pain flashed in my mind—the night that I had removed my limb. The tearing of my veins and the way my blood had dripped to the floor.

It was too much for me; I couldn't do it, I thought. But hunger causes you to do things in ways that you never thought possible. It didn't matter what, it didn't matter where—

Where. That was a good question. Where was I? I was in my home of course. In the remains of my house—my destroyed kitchen, to be exact. In the spot where my wife and I had made memories together.

The funny thing about memories, I thought, was that they never disappeared. If your mind can still recall the pages of your life, they stay. When you feel the texture of something that was a great memento of a loved one, or the rough edges of a scar, you remember. Standing in the kitchen now, I remembered. And I remembered the first night Diana and I had moved into this house.

The power had gone out. We had just put Molly to bed, and then we had shared a glass of wine with the heavy rain beating overhead. In this very same kitchen, where I was now picking out a pot from the snow, wiping away the sleet as I placed pieces of my house into my sink. All the wood and paper I could find.

I pulled the lighter from my pocket. The striker was challenging to start using my one hand. The flames burned awkwardly and dangerously on my fingers. I was numb to the pain though; hunger had robbed my mind of pain being anything to worry about anymore. If I didn't eat soon, I would die.

I fished out my separated left hand, gingerly taking the gored remains with me over to the sink. The fire I had managed to light was crackling, quickly taking hold of the wood inside the tub. I was surprised. I thought the snow would have prevented me from having a fire. It seems the elements were on my side, at least for the moment. Standing near the fire, my body became warm, and I felt the hunger subside just a bit—not enough. Starvation is a bull rampaging in a glass house. It was only a matter of time until it broke free.

I gulped, dropping my hand into the fire, watching my fingers slowly cook as my mind went back to the first night Diana and I spent in this kitchen.

We were laughing about something—I couldn't remember what it was; the wine was hitting us both hard by this point. "You did it, huh, you finally got a home," I teased Diana as I poured her another cup of wine.

"You mean 'we.' We finally got a home," she countered, the tone of her voice breaking into a giggle at the end. We both laughed, continuing to drink into the night, when Diana asked me a question after a moment of silence. "James, I have a question," she said, suddenly unsure of herself.

She very rarely frowned. Seeing her like that sobered me up fast as I sat my glass down and turned to her. "Yeah, baby, you can ask me anything that you want, you know that," I responded.

She looked at the candle near us, its flames licking the darkness away around us as its wax slowly melted down through the night. "What's a home to you, James? I mean really, what does all this mean to you?" She gestured to the kitchen. I knew this was one of those times that I should have said something, a message to my wife that was from the heart and was honest. I had come a long way since my old days of being so robotic that I could hardly handle being asked if I liked pizza or not.

I thought of Molly; she was in a crib next door to us. She was everything that I could have ever wanted to create in this world, tucked away safe behind wooden beams with the love of her parents. I thought of Diana, how she smiled and opened my heart up every day to greater distances of love than I ever could have imagined. I was a long way gone from the days of cigarette ash covering me like snow inside my parents' trailer home.

I thought to the rundown and recycled dorm rooms of my college days. How distant both those places had felt; how they'd felt like just a place to sleep. Not a place to call home; not a place to live in love.

"I think before I met you I would have said that a home is a structure or shelter that provides safety for one another. That's not true anymore." I sucked in a breath, turning away before speaking to Diana again. "A home is this—it is where I choose to carry your heart. Where we let each other live. Where we dance with each other, where I can grow, where I can love, and—most importantly—be loved. The one place on Earth that becomes separated from all things unexplainable and explainable, because it has you in it with me. I know it's a home because of that; because every time I come home, I see you and I know what living is. Living is home; living is you. And that to me can withstand any storm, as long as I have you in my heart and I have you in mine. I will never be without a home," I whispered, breathing hard at the end. It had been difficult for me to speak of feelings in the past, but it wasn't anymore—Diana was my ocean whenever I went to sea.

I looked at my wife; she was crying. I became crestfallen at that moment. Had I hurt her somehow? I started to talk when she stuck a finger in my mouth, saying, "Kiss me," and I did. I did for a very long time.

My heart ached for her lips now as the skin of my hand started to smell of pork. It was done. My hand was done. I looked at it, the flesh burnt black and red, the fingers cooked together. If I hadn't known better, I would have thought it was just a piece of meat and not my hand. I swore under my breath hunger was causing me this—hunger had trapped me.

I thought of that night with Diana, and of kissing her, while I pulled my hand from the flames. The meat was hot and blistered my fingertips as I held it towards my mouth. There was no going back now; I was a long way gone, I thought as I bit into the remains of my hand.

II

Part Two

"It is not death that a man should fear, but he should fear never beginning to live."
– Meditations by Emperor of Rome Marcus Aurelius

Chapter 16

I overlooked the endlessness of my city; it stretched before me, paved in tar and metal. On a morning like today, in a time much different from my own, I would have gone out and enjoyed the sun with my family. Family was something that I didn't understand anymore. It was a word that I never dared let back into my thoughts—not on the darkest of nights. But, sometimes, when I was weak, and all my nights were dancing away, I thought of my family.

I thought of Molly. She was such a shy kid, never talked much. She was the sweetest girl I had ever known. She always found a way to brighten my day. I would sometimes cry at night about the idea of the person that Molly could have grown up to become. I wanted to be there to walk her down the aisle when she hopefully married a nice tech nerd like her father, or to be there to provide corny father advice when she had problems.

Of course, I thought as I looked from the rubble of the decaying building, maybe it was for the best I'd never got to see that side of her. After all, it had been her father who had let her down—she shouldn't be with someone like me. I had grown old. My body had grown skinny; a defined skeleton replaced all traces of a comfortable adult male. This savage life had left little to the imagination. So I spent a lot of mornings tightening my belt, and a lot of nights experiencing real hunger.

I ignored that feeling of hunger; I had a can of something or other waiting for me later. Once you know starvation, you can never be full again. After twenty years of barely cooked meals, you lower your expectations, so I ate whatever I could find. I stroked my long beard and wondered what it would be like to try a steak again. Or Hell, I would settle for a trip to McDonald's if it would end up being cooked in something other than a can.

"Hey Jim, I know you're tired of getting beat. Can you at least pretend that you feel like playing? Brooding time on the ledge should really only be five minutes. Otherwise, you look just cheesy or constipated," snorted Holly, the impatience only so restrained in her voice.

I sighed deeply, cranky in my old age. A little silence for a man's thoughts every now and then wouldn't be too much to ask for, would it? Then again, I wonder how my sanity would have held out, had I not had Holly all these years. My thoughts were always quick now, always changing, keeping the worst of my feelings away. I turned around, back to our game. We had found a sturdy table and two rickety old chairs that were battered by the elements (Holly had insisted that we have two, though I didn't see the point), the paint peeling away in chunks. I think the original color was a light green, the kind you would find in almost every old woman's house in the world. Sturdy, practical above all, and a truly off-putting color.

It was our normal tradition to play a rousing and intense game of something or other we had borrowed (again, Holly insisted we call it that instead of stealing) from the local toy store. But I preferred to think of it as stealing two heavy green chairs and carrying them into a broken building.

Today, we were playing "Game of Life." It was ironic that I had sucked so much at life and yet I was winning at a game of it. In the game, I was working for NASA, I had made sure not to have any kids or wife, and I was a millionaire living the high life.

"You know, I find it a little annoying that you rush to get through our games so much," Holly said accusingly, her now-green hair blazing in the light.

I just looked at her with what I hoped wasn't a guilty look. "What do you mean, kiddo? I am just winning. Don't suggest the game if you can't take the beating," I retorted defensively.

"It's not about that, old man. I mean, look at the board. My piece has just got out of college and is married with three kids, while you're way ahead in late life and are approaching retirement. Don't you think it would have been better to have experienced a little more? Going on a vacation, going around and doing something else?" Holly said while floating above her chair. It was an act that I had become used to, but it still made a shiver run up my spine every time I saw her doing it.

"Holly, would you please?" I rasped, clearing my throat.

"Oh, sorry, boss. Sometimes I just do it," Holly lied. I didn't believe her tone one bit. It wasn't that she hadn't proven her usefulness with that ability. It was just too early to remind this old man that he was living in a world where ghosts were real and they floated.

This was our mundane routine; it was about as normal as our days got. From day to day, I had learned to live with the unexpected. Holly must have sensed that I was going down one of my thought paths again and interrupted me. "So, Jim, do you think today will be the day?" she asked anxiously.

I knew what she was asking. She was asking if today was the day we would find her body. "Hopefully, Holly. We just have to clear one block at a time," I guessed, swallowing the hard pill of an old lie. It was Holly's turn, and she claimed I cheated on her spins for her. I just moved the pieces—that was always my response as I moved her car to another spot on the board.

That was one lie I was never going to admit. I wasn't going to lay the fruits of that decision bare for Holly to see. I knew what it would mean if I did, I knew what would happen. I am an old man, a bitter and lonely old man. Yet once I was a father, and a father never wants to give up on his children.

Once we finished, I folded up the game board into a chest that we kept in the burnt-out building. I had won. Playing here was my idea; it provided much-needed vantage points of the city around me. When things could float and come through walls, you just never knew. Besides, the spot gave me some tanning locations during the summer. I had Holly keep a lookout as I placed the game in the heavy chest. The chest was made of iron and had I nearly broken my back bringing it up here. But from experience, I learned that anything that the ghosts could get into would be a thing they could use against you, so keeping a big iron chest around was as good a deterrent as I could think of.

We made our way down the broken building. I had meant to repair the stairs for a while. Now, at least, it wasn't high on my list. With only one hand, I had accomplished a lot of engineering feats that would make most inventors blush. I still had my limitations .

Outside the building, I went up to the "Beast," my Ford Explorer that was covered in more iron than most small buildings. Holly reached the door almost before me. I cut her off fast. "Did you forget this morning, kid?" I asked teasing her.

"Oh shit, well, you know I haven't had my coffee yet," Holly answered in response.

"You can't drink coffee, Holly…" I hinted, gesturing towards her and sighing.

"You know, Jimbo, bite me. Keep it up, and I will sing again." Holly implored, materializing sunglasses onto her face.

"Oh, anything but the singing!" I said dramatically, almost falling over and using the Explorer to steady me.

"Laugh it up, smart ass." Holly snorted, moving into the Explorer as I opened the door for her.

I looked at Holly, getting serious. "Holly, I am getting worried about you. First, it's the green hair, and now you're cussing. I think I heard you even use a word beyond two syllables. Are you okay?" I questioned her while closing my door.

"This is coming from the guy with a Jesus beard and a raggedy old coat, huh?" Holly scoffed, unable to hide the smirk growing across her face.

"Yeah well, back in the day, I used to dress pretty sharp, I'll have you know," I stated while watching the road.

"I have serious doubts about that—you carry around a frying-pan, for crying out loud. Wouldn't it be easier to use a—I don't know—a spear?" She gestured, pulling her arm out until it formed a spear.

I shuddered and looked at Holly. "First thing first, kid, spears are barely better. They would keep me from having to get so close, but you never know when you will need a snack in the middle of a rough day. The pan is all around good defense and good eating," I smiled. Holly returned her arm to normal and faced forward in the Beast.

"We've been together for all these years, and I've just now figured something about you, Jim," she stated.

I was confused by her tone, the sudden shift causing me to worry. I never stopped being on edge anymore, so I wouldn't be surprised if I had aged worse than my father had when he was my age. I remembered long lines and deep wrinkles my father had as his skin became taut and stretched over a lean form in his elder years. Wordily, I asked her, "Yeah, Holly, what have you learned?"

"That you freak out too easily," she admitted, sticking her tongue at me.

I rolled my eyes and started to pull out.

Holly could have easily kept up with the Beast by flying aside it. I had learned, though, that letting her fly outside was a bad idea. The other ghosts loved to come after her, just as much as they did after me. I think it had something to do with the fact that she radiated so much more emotion than the bad ones. The bad ones showed a lot of emotion, mostly just the emotions they'd felt in their final moments. Which often was painful, a sheer sealing of their whole lives, ending in an instant. I figured this out from a few encounters over the years; for whatever reason, they wanted us both.

I didn't blame them for wanting something else, in a way. I understand their role in the world; it was no different from the living they'd done before. Life for them now was finding meaning—dead or alive, humans don't change. As we drove, I occasionally saw glimpses of figures here and there in the buildings. I knew, though, that they weren't the good ones. It had been a long time since I'd seen a good ghost or a person. To be honest, I wasn't sure when that was anymore. As the years ticked off like the sheets of a calendar, so did the confines of my memory. Only that was partly correct—like some hubristic young prince of old, the memories I had gained from the many ghosts I had killed stayed with me, always rushing forward. Yet my own memories were starting to slip. I wonder if it was from old age.

I stopped the Beast on a bridge. Holly was busy playing with her hair, with a deep frown on her face. I knew what she was thinking. She was wondering if today was the day. If today would be the day that she would be set free. I was never very sure what to say to her when she made that face.

"Nah, it's not that. I'm thinking about why we haven't seen any birds today," Holly stated, twisting her hair in a nervous gesture. She was right. For weeks now, we had been noticing a decline in wildlife. The ghosts wanted to be alive; they wanted to be in something living. It didn't matter if it was a rat or a worm, the ghosts wanted them. Most of the time, creatures like birds and dogs were too quick for them. Most didn't realize, like Holly, that they could change their appearance to anything that would suit them. Generally, the ghosts stayed in the forms from their time of death, which was often gruesome and torn to shreds. I think that was easier for them to understand.

What was worrying Holly and I the most was how few animals we had seen. I was writing it off to the lack of food sources around the city. That wasn't true, though—the wild always found a way to provide food to those strong enough. It scared me to think of the alternative.

Something was wrong in this world, something new in a world

that was always showing me a surprise. I didn't want to follow my thoughts down that road if I didn't have to. I tried to change the subject. "You know, it is getting colder out. Birds are flying south," I remarked in a tactful manner.

"I know that, asshole. I read more on the subjects than you do, you know." Holly grumbled defensively.

"Language!" I fired back. It was true though, and we had emptied out all the libraries in the city with books on tape. I think it made her feel safer at night, while I slept, to hear other voices.

"It gets colder the further from the equator you go. Birds fly closer to the equator during the winter since it is warmer there and the weather is better. Where they go depends on the species and where they started off. Everyone knows this, old man," Holly informed me, twirling her fingers.

"Well, everyone being you and me, kiddo. We don't know that many people," I sneered, tapping my fingers on the wheel, hoping that Holly was right.

"You're hopeless, old man. What would you do without me?" she asked.

"Probably get some peace of mind for a change. Your antics in changing your look every day is going to give me a heart attack. "

"Yeah, right…" Holly says, beaming with a smile on her face.

I glanced out the window; it was still early in the morning. Time for "birds" would be later. No need to waste any effort on a few missing birds, though this had been the third time that one of us had made that observation. I ignored that chilling thought. For now, it was back to the usual grind.

"Ready to go, squirt?" I asked as I pulled the Beast into the driveway of a house on the new block we had started yesterday.

Holly, still smiling, with her avocado green hair, seemingly closed her eyes. I exited the Beast and went to the trunk, pulling out my bag, along with various other tools. Most importantly, I secured my iron pan in my sling. As I waited for Holly, I took in the wooden structure of the house we were about to enter.

Like most of the houses on the block, the wooden frames had long since caved in and sunken into the earth. Its original colors were a seeping yellow, now bleaching over the old white. Formed from the wooden support beams was what appeared to be jagged brown teeth; stretching high to the windowless eyes, narrowing as if to devour the prey about to enter. Once I was ready, I sat down on the tailgate of the Beast. I always hated this part—I knew that the condition of the house had probably blown away any batteries or canned goods. Most importantly, I knew that we would find nothing inside, nothing that would stop the search.

Holly came around the vehicle at that moment, appearing before me. I shied back, reaching for my pan in reaction. Holly just stuck her tongue at me in response. I groaned. Holly loved to mess with me always, "All clear kiddo," I asked.

"Yeah—good to go, Jim. Just walls and a roof," she responded. I acknowledged with a head tilt and closed the Beast's trunk. Just walls and a roof—our "all clear" sign. Still, I never could relax even as we entered the house.

True to my guess, we found nothing. Well—nothing that was too useful. I managed to snatch up a can of peaches, and Holly found a preserved poster of a man wheedling a chainsaw, somehow still maintained. She insisted we take it, and I agreed only because it wasn't some kind of boy band.

At about noon, we took a break. I sat on the porch, eating the peaches we found, grumbling at how long it took me to get through it with a knife. Can openers were impossible to use with one hand, I had gotten good at holding the can between my legs and cutting the top off with my knife in response. The process always frustrated me though, made me feel destitute of anything resembling an adult.

The peaches tasted fresh in the can, long since turned to mostly sugar. I licked my fingers when I was done and sat back on the stoop of the destroyed house, watching Holly look up into the sky.

I looked at the stub of my hand—as useless as I sometimes felt, not being able to use both my hands, Holly must have been on an entirely different playing field. She couldn't even change the CDs on her books. Sleep and rest no longer mattered to her, and her only company at nights was the words of some long-lost-to-time writer and, during the day, a long-lost-to-time father.

I signaled to Holly that break was over, and it was time for our next house on the block. Holly dipped her head and followed me back into the Beast. Both of our moods were a little gloomy after the first home.

We checked two more places before finishing out the block, as we both slid into the confines of the car.

"Didn't see any birds, Jim," Holly mused.

"Yeah kiddo, I didn't either," I answered solemnly, as we pulled up near a broken bridge.

Maneuvering in the city was tough. Nature had taken back its land with a fervor, and simple bridges like the one we'd traveled across now used to be an afterthought. Now they just made me nervous, as we crossed their damaged structures.

"It's nothing unnatural, I'm sure they will be back soon," I responded as we slowly moved across the destroyed overpass.

"And what if it is natural. Jim? What if this is a sign that there is nothing left in the city? Charlotte is huge, no question there, but it doesn't have a lot to offer in the ways of ghosts. I mean, after all, it's just one cranky old man driving a tank with a green-haired girl," Holly stated.

"That's not true kiddo, that's not true," I mumbled, desperately trying to change the conversation. Still, Holly did have a point, as little as I liked to admit it; *something was off about the birds; what could that mean? And if it did spell anything bad, how could I protect Holly and I from it? If the animals were afraid, should we also be worried?* I had seen and been the victim of terrors that no human being should ever be subjected to, but the idea of something natural causing change scared me worse. *What could I do against something that was a force of nature?* I thought, completely lost and no longer driving.

Holly always had a knack for interrupting me at the right moment, or letting awkward conversations die. "Hey Jim, daylight is burning. Feel like doing something else today?" She asked, causing me to come out of my daze. Whenever I went into my head, it was like a bear crawling out of hibernation, everything slow and unresponsive. "Jim?" she asked again.

I finally came to, back to us driving through the graying and decayed city. "Yeah—Holly, what did you say?" I responded glumly. I hated being in just my head; I was always called back, though, back to the darker thoughts that I kept below every day.

"I was saying let's go do something fun, old man, while we are both still able to," she advised, appearing much older than her child form. She stayed that way often, changing her hair color only, an act that continually served just to annoy me, I was sure. But she always remained as a child, the same as the day that I'd met her, and I hesitated to ask her why. We all have our secrets, things among us we never discussed. Like my wife and my hand and her never-ending style choices.

"Fun—I'm not sure if I can recall such a word in my old age," I spluttered, trying hard to fight the smile forming on my face.

Holly caught my smile. "Oh yeah, I forgot; a fun time for you is mostly cheap liquor and those old video game magazines. I mean, honestly, Jim, there are so many better books than that," she pointed out to me.

I scoffed. "Those magazines are good reading, a lot better than all your vampire books," I shot back.

Holly's hair and face turned blood-red, I could almost imagine the heat she would have had on her face if she could. "I don't like those vampire books. I mean I do, but I don't, there's just a million of those at the bookstore. That or superheroes, okay," Holly vacillated. I smiled, bemused by her embarrassment, "Hey old man, I don't make fun of your bad habits," she deflected, and I burst out laughing, fighting hard to stay on the road. I was glad we had left the bird conversation and we were able to laugh again.

"You got me there, Holly. Anyways, what is this "fun" you have in mind? It's a little early for us to go fishing," I queried.

Her hair turned back to a lime green, slowly matching the shade of baby grass growing at the start of spring, before answering, "To tell you the truth, I think we should do something we've always talked about doing for the longest time. It's time we did you-know-what," she hinted.

I turned, hesitantly. "Are you sure, Holly? We've been putting this off for a long, long time, and there's no coming back once we've done this," I cautioned.

"I think trying something new sometimes is the closest thing to being alive. Besides, our noon break went way too fast. What's an hour or two of watching you get beat?" she opined. I snorted in response, flipping the car around and heading in the direction of the movie store.

In a remote part of the city, Holly and I had found an old film store, the grimy and overly polarized shelves of a service that had long since died, even before the world started to end.

I took a basket, placing within it an assortment of different films. Holly would every so often push one off the shelf; I would grunt, more from the annoyance of her moving things, as she did. It always unnerved me seeing her do things like that. She wouldn't move, not in the slightest, yet something would fall.

Things have to be explainable; that was one thing I struggled to understand, no matter how many times she told me. Still, though, I didn't like it too much when she did it. However, when the others did it... I changed my thoughts before they could sour our moment. *This is break time, James, don't go down your hole.* I struggled to come back to reality when Holly spoke. "Jim?" she asked, concern in her voice.

"I'm good, Holly, I am just excited to win, like always." I grinned at her as she gave me the finger. I shook my head—that was something I needed to work on more than anything else; her profanity. I looked at my basket, seeing that at some point I had placed a few of the little airplane bottles of alcohol into my shopping basket. We both had our vices. And I left it at that as we started to leave the video store.

"Jim, don't forget," Holly reminded me as we passed the weathered kiosk. "Oh yeah—you're right," I remarked, setting the basket down on the counter and pulling out a separate pouch from my waistband. Inside was thousands of dollars' worth of money. I had been collecting it, mostly for starting fires, emergency toilet paper, and mainly for paying stores such as this for their services. It was another thing that Holly insisted we do—if nothing else, it gave me a reason to have so much on me. She said it was in the spirit of kindness; I said it was just so that she could annoy me.

Either way, I counted out a couple of hundred, figuring it to be about even for the cost of films, as I set the money on the counter and walked out of the store with Holly floating nearby. I popped the Beast's trunk, pulled out a foldable table, and placed it in the middle of the lot behind the movie store.

After that, I set out all the movies that Holly and I had both picked out. We had both figured out a long time ago that neither one of us would ever agree on a film, so the only way to settle it was for a "fire-fight." Back in the trunk, I pulled out a nerf gun and laid a stack of nerf bullets near my feet.

"You know kiddo, we've done this before, and you always lose," I stated, adjusting the sights on my nerf gun.

"Well yes, but we have never been to this—movie store," she said pointing out the old building around us. Its sign was long since faded to the ages, and soon the building and all the movies would be as well. I shook my head, turning my attention back to my gun. She was right, though; we hadn't been to this store.

Thankfully, this was a remote part of the city, far away from the highways, with never too many ghosts around. It provided some level of safety during the day. Generally, we spent our days looking through the houses in and around the surrounding city. Sometimes, when it had been a fruitless day like today, we would come out to the more remote parts of the city like here. Today's trip was the first time we had gone this far. It always made me uncomfortable being so far out of the town. Like it or not, it was my home, and I hated being away. "You know the rules, right, you old goat?" she sneered.

I fired back. "Just don't cry when I win again. May the best shot win!" I shouted, taking a stance and shooting at the movie covers laid out on the table; hoping that my shot would take out one of Holly's horror films.

She always picked the goriest and most unsettling films. Still, though, they beat romance films. I avoided all fiction entirely, choosing instead to go with safe nature documentaries. You couldn't go wrong with a story about ant farms and trees found in Africa.

"That's not fair at all, you, cheater!" she fired back, lifting the bolts of foam near my leg, sending a dart flying perfectly, taking out the video case of a documentary I had found on soup making in Italy.

"I really wanted to watch that one," I regretfully said as I fired a bullet, taking out the cover of one case with a man holding a chainsaw. I shuddered, looking at my left hand momentarily, thankful it hadn't come to that, as Holly lobbed another bolt, easily taking off another documentary. We both fired until there were no more bolts remaining and only one movie remained.

"Hah—I win, old man, the best hands in the east!" Holly snorted, firing her fingers towards the sky and blowing on the tips as if there was smoke coming out of them.

"Cheating—super aim," I grumbled, putting my nerf-gun back into the trunk. "Why is it always the guy with the pins coming out of his head?" I mumbled, pulling the projector from the Beast's trunk. I cleared the table of nerf bullets and video disks, placing the projector on the center portion of the table.

Next, I pulled out a battery pack; an assortment of wires and batteries was a must have for everybody's essential survival pack. I plugged the battery pack into the projector, snapping the power button on the old player. The bulb flickered, stuttering before firing up and displaying the movie from the disk tray that I had added to the projector, (using a straw and a lot of hot glue).

I was thankful the bulb worked; it was getting harder to find bulbs. I may have had most of my supplies inside the Beast, everything from screws, to batteries and nerf-guns. However, bulbs—any lights, in general—were hard to find. It was as if the coming of this new world meant the end of the light.

I walked back to the tailgate of the Beast and sat down. Holly appeared next to me, and I moved away slightly. Getting close to anyone, including Holly, made me uncomfortable; if Holly noticed she didn't say anything. "Next time, just let me win for a change, kid," I stated, as the movie started to play.

"Next time aim better. Honestly, you can't hit shit," she replied.

"Language," I grumbled as the movie started to get scary. I tightened my coat. I always seemed to lose.

Chapter 17

After the movie, Holly and I returned to the road, heading in the direction of the overpass from earlier. Holly was smiling and humming a song. I listened, enjoying her tune, and slowly maneuvered the Beast around a section of the bridge that had crumbled away. It was slow work, but it was relaxing, and gave my mind something to think about other than the disgusting film Holly had subjected me to watching. I was so deep into concentrating on the road that I didn't notice Benny until he was banging on the side of my car window.

My reaction was quick, the ridged metal fitting into my gloved hand with ease as I expertly found the gun under my steering wheel. My heart was pounding first, which then turned into anger upon seeing Benny. Benny had made his unsolicited boney ass a thorn in my side since meeting him some four, maybe five winters back.

Our first meeting hadn't been a good one; Benny had brought with him a hoard of malevolent monsters, all intent on taking chunks out of him. On a normal day wouldn't have been a problem for me—he would be the dead one after all. Only that day I was caught off guard and was almost taken by the apparitional fiends, if not for some quick foot work. I still shuddered at their memories; twelve was the most I had ever sent packing; the act was like running a double marathon back to back. When I had finally come to, Holly said I had been passed out for almost three days, while Benny had made off with all my gear.

So my anger towards Benny was something I felt was warranted.

"Hey… Yo, Jim, is that you?" asked Benny, rasping on the side of my car with his walking stick. He was covered in hanging iron trinkets, shining bronze light into my eyes.

I responded with my anger turned up to full ten on the old man. "Benny, what the fuck is wrong with you?! Who else would it be driving this thing? And if you don't stop sneaking up on me, I will make sure that I am the only 'last man' in this city!" I shouted. I'd met all manner of disturbing and disgusting things over the years, both human and the unknown. It had taught me to always keep my weapons on hand; I spoke little, swung more, now, as an alternative.

"Oh, so that must be you, Jim. Do you ever stop yelling at me?" Benny asked, looking as strung out and bleached of all abstract thought as a person could be. I believe he might have been a fairly handsome dark-haired man at one time, but now, like me, it had been years since he last saw a bath. Years since he'd had a decent shave, and too many years since he'd been sober.

His pupils long since changed to a hazy red, and his skin was more malleable than putty. He was a junkie, plain as day. I didn't know how he could do mind altering substances in a world designed to alter your mind as it was. The creatures that now made up this world could be anything. Any guess was as good as mine when it came to Benny.

Still, last I checked, he was flesh and blood, however dirty his might be. We were all that was left in the city. It had been three years since I last saw another human being, and ten years since I saw someone before Benny.

I decided to calm down' no point in ruining my morning so soon. I looked at Holly and nodded. She was quiet as, well, a ghost—which was unlike her at all. Normally I couldn't get her to shut up. "Holly, are you okay?" I asked.

"I'm fine; you know, we should just go. Nothing that cracked-out tweaker says is worth the trouble. Just drive, Jim. Don't do this to yourself," Holly whispered, still casting her thousand-eye stare into the distance. I knew what she was thinking. She didn't understand, though. Even though we had each other, I still longed for some kind of human contact. I don't know why, as being alone was more than a temporary bind. It was a suffering as long as an endless winter in a land once full of flowers.

Holly kept me from ending it all. She was, after all, someone that pained me beyond words every time I looked at her. Despite the pain, I wanted contact—a small part of me did. I sighed deeply. She was right.

"Piss off, Benny. I'm not in the mood today," I grumbled, facing forward, getting ready to take off.

"Is that Holly Too-Crazy-Hair? Hi, Holly. How you doing? Still with this crazy old man?" Benny snorted, pressing his face and hands on my window.

Smoothly, Holly answered, "I think I prefer my company a little less smelly. Thank you, though."

Benny's eyes wandered around the inside cavern of my car. I didn't like the way he was looking at my gear, or the way he was looking at Holly. Sensing the tension, I decided to defuse the situation. The sooner I was away from Benny, the better. "What do you want, Benny? If you don't mind, I am in a rush today."

"Rush?" Benny said, almost tasting the word. "How can anyone be in a rush anymore Jumim."

I always hated the way he said my name. I never could place his accent. I had heard a lot of Southern drawls, and Benny's sounded almost comical if you weren't used to him doing it. My impatience was starting to become uncontrollable. The longer my conversation was with Benny, I was about to just shoot him on the principle of wasting my time.

"I found a stack of them, Jim." Benny smiled, gesturing his hands out wide.

For once, Benny's term was something we both knew. A "stack," as Benny put it, was a collection of human bodies. "So, what, Benny?

Take care of them and send them on their way." I said matter-of-factly.

"Well normally, I would have, and I was about to burn them up and be on me merry way. That was when I saw one that looked pretty familiar. She was all long legs and looked a lot like green hair there," Benny hissed through the gaps in his teeth.

At the mention of that, Holly turned towards me, making eye contact. We were both thinking the same thing, only I was afraid by Benny's words.

"Wait, how do you know it looked like me? Did she have my hair, or my fucking eyes? Man, come on, stop busting my balls!" Holly screamed, almost jumping into my lap—she would have if she wasn't floating above my legs.

"Language!" I shouted back, my hand gripping the steering wheel tight. For countless winters, we had been looking for her own body. We weren't ever going to find it.

"Well, it's tough to say. It was dark in the place I found them, and I had to get out fast. So, I wasn't sure what I saw. She looked a lot like maybe a little older than you," spluttered Benny, sliding away from my door like he had just cured cancer and was about to get a Nobel prize for it.

Holly looked at me again, her stare almost sending blots of electricity out in her excitement. "Jim, this sounds promising, we have to go check it out!" she beamed.

"I don't know Holly; it could just be another wild goose chase. Besides, we still have two more blocks to clear out here first."

Holly sighed deeply. "Jim, you made a promise to me, remember?" she asked. I remembered just like it was yesterday, when I had first met Holly and we had agreed to work together. It was on the condition that she would help me find my wife's body, and I would help her find hers.

"Holly, what if we are wrong? It will be just another... failed attempt at something. Something... we should let go. I mean come on… after this long, anybody would be so far gone to decomposition that no one could be recognized."

Holly's gaze shifted to one of anger at that remark. She held Benny in a death stare. I was sure that she would have attacked him if she could have phased through the car door without hitting any iron.

"Well, old Benny here has a solution, ha-ha," Benny admitted, cackling while clicking his tongue in the back of his throat. The sound causing me to flinch with every pop he made. Benny went on. "See, these bodies don't have to worry about no worms—no worms indeed. See, these bodies are kept cold by the machines at the factory I found them in."

I blinked at that. *Surely the junkie wasn't that stupid? There was no way anything electric could be working anymore.* "Benny, get the fuck out of here with that now. This is no laughing matter; you know that electricity is long since gone. You have a better chance of aliens coming out of the sky than getting the lights back on in this city." I scoffed, raising my hand like I had seen someone do on one of those conspiracy television shows long ago.

Benny just smiled, his look more than a little belittling. "Not these machines, Juimm. These machines are being kept by someone much smarter than you and I," Benny informed me, still with his smile; talking down to me with more words than anything his junked-out mind should have been able to speak.

I narrowed my eyes at Benny. It was possible, I supposed. However, I wasn't going to trust Benny as far as I could throw him. I decided to humor him a little bit more. "Oh yeah? And how do you know this person who keeps the machines running isn't someone bad? I mean, after all, if they were smart enough to start those machines up again, why would he or she still have the bodies there?"

Benny looked slightly confused at that, while Holly floated above my eyes, fixed on Benny, not letting him escape her gaze. "What do you mean? I don't know why some sicko would leave the bodies there. What do you think I am, some kind of mind reader?" he asked, every bit as confused about the situation as his story was.

"That's what I thought, Benny; this is another one of your stupid games. That's it, step away from my car before I kill you. You have ten seconds."

"No, wait, I promise this isn't one of my tricks, Juimm, I swear. This time, I am telling the truth. I found the place because the lights were on and then I found the bodies. I wouldn't be telling you all this if I was lying. I know how it sounds!" he pleaded, placing his hands on the window.

He had a point, though; no one was stupid enough to actually fall for a story like that. But still, I didn't want to trust him at all. I looked to Holly to find answers; indecision had been one devil that never left me my entire life.

Holly was buzzing with energy. I could see the thoughts racing through her as she thought over that entirety of what Benny and I had said. "I think we should go check it out, Jim." Holly stated, and her eyes were set to stone. I knew that there wasn't anything I could say that would get over that wall. I wasn't going to win.

"Alright, Benny. If you get my car dirty, I will kill you," I sighed. Today was going to be a long, long day.

Chapter 18

Making our way through the city was surprisingly easy. We passed cars that had long since held any semblance of use, but were parked mostly out of the road. Only occasionally did we find the odd vehicle left in the middle of the street. They were so far gone that I couldn't even tell the make anymore.

It was a grim reminder that when the city had changed for good, the change had been sudden. No one had expected it, and not many had survived. Doors had been left open, for cars whose batteries had long since ran dry. It was if someone had snapped a picture of a still-breathing world and decided to edit everything out. The original painting still aged, but the original subjects were long gone. No evidence of the destruction I had seen that night. I shuddered, staying away from thoughts like that. They just served to remind me that I was in fact, going mad.

"Make a left at the end of the road, and go about a mile past the exit by that power plant." Benny pointed with his walking cane; it was amazing how far he must have walked to come to me. He had been walking with a limp since I had first met him. I wasn't sure how he had gotten hurt. I didn't ask; we all lived with our scars.

At that thought, my left hand started to hurt; I dared a glance down to see if it was really gone. The stub of my arm was fractured and scarred with heavy lines. The pain had been enormous; an endless ocean that still felt like it was happening today. I had once heard the term referred to as the phantom itch, or something like that. The itch was like a reminder that you still felt the pain, even though it wasn't there.

The itch didn't stop there. I heard voices, voices deep in my head, always calling out to me. I would see images of many people's lives, so many lives. Their most private moments, mistakes, and laughs. More and more, I worried that I would become the man who talked to both the living and the dead. *Rather that than talking to myself like a crazy person,* I thought. That I could deal with, it was everything else in this world that put me through the ringer.

Agreeing to come with Benny to this part of town was ludicrous in itself. All around us, I could see forms hiding in the shadows. They twisted, ran and scrambled. I could tell they were there. Always watching, always waiting for a chance to attack Holly and me. As I tightened my hand on the wheel, more voices flew in my head. Waves of emotion started passing through me and I felt myself getting dizzy and sick. A burning fire lit in my skull, the likes of which had only been seen in ancient cities like Pompeii.

I was buckling under the weight of their emotions. One moment happy, the next I knew a despair that would make even Poe afraid. *Here they go, driving their way deep into my mind like nails being chased by a hammer.*

I blinked, suddenly aware that I was still driving. Holly was looking at me, her face lit up in concern and her lower lip tucked under. I opened my mouth, breathing in the stale air inside the Beast. I heard people could lose their minds, go crazy. I wondered how long it would be before that happened to me.

It wasn't like that for me, I swear; I always felt the presence of Diana though, worming her way into my hand. I wasn't going crazy, it was just her—she never left. My hand hurt every night, in time to the beating of my heart. It would never be the same again. I shook my head, trying to refocus on the task at hand, when I looked up to see Diana crossing the road in her white wedding dress. She was as slender and beautiful as I remembered her. My heart stopped, and my lips moved. "Diana..."

"What? Jim, what are you looking at?" asked Holly, looking at me with concern. Diana suddenly morphed into a horror. She twisted into an image of pain, and her lips formed the words I knew better than any in my vocab. "It's your fault, James."

My one hand on the wheel lost hold as my feet continued to accelerate. I could hear Holly and Benny screaming from inside the car. We hit the pile of metal on the side of the road, causing my head to smack down on the wheel.

Chapter 19

I dreamed; a dream of ash and steel. All around me danced the memories, and the ghosts of the lives that they had once lived. I called out for help amongst them. I called out, ineffectual from fear that was holding sway over my voice.

None replied. It was a knock on a door stranded in time; lashed by a sea on a lonely gray wind. I was filled with the gift of all, the knowledge of everything and nothing at all.

I am the bottle inside the ship; the ship in the bottle hanging on the wall.

I am ghost; I am invisible. They cannot see me; but I can see them.

Chapter 20

My head was screaming, and I could feel blood trickling down on my forehead. "Holly, are you here?" I called out, trying to get my head to stop moving.

I looked down at my dash, My airbags had somehow deployed, after having had them for over twenty years. "Good Beast," I mumbled, unbuckling myself from the harness. Both Benny and Holly were missing from their seats, with the doors of the Beast wide open in their wake.

I fumbled my way out of the car, falling to the ground. Diana was nowhere in sight, and I wonder if she had actually been there. I didn't waste time though, pondering things that might or might not have happened. I got to my feet, trying to shake off the crash as I made my way around the explorer. I had long since reinforced the Beast with loads of iron. The car easily had about five hundred pounds of iron all over it, the only exposed sections being the windows, I popped the truck to pull out my bag.

I had always been a firm believer in carrying a tool bag, and cities full of ghosts required tools for every situation. My iron pan was always slung to my side, ready to go at any time. And like the Beast, I had iron stashed all over me, from keys to pieces of collapsed buildings. I pulled out my shotgun. It was the only gun I could find that was easily loaded with one hand.

I opened the chamber and checked there were two shells; I stashed a few more from inside the bag in my pockets. Finally, I pulled out an iron rod and shoved it into my boots. I locked the chamber back into place. I was going to find Holly, I had to.

I looked ahead of me, scanning the road as I made a quick dash to the end of the section. Everything was quiet as always, and I couldn't tell if Holly or Benny had made their way down this road. It was impossible to track a ghost, but it shouldn't be too hard to find a man with a cane. Blood was coming down my head, and I knew from a doctor (whose memories I had gained) that the wound was probably more superficial than damaging. I also knew, from another set of memories, how to tactfully move from position to position; pieces of cars are a great makeshift defense. The memories had caused me just as many problems as they seemed to help me with.

I started to panic. *What if Holly had gotten hurt in the crash? She could have accidentally flown into some of the iron in the beast. I had been careless; she could be gone for good and I would never know.* My mind was speeding out of control; it didn't take much to send it into the wasteland. See, a normal person could be overloaded just by their own thoughts.

My thoughts were like being inside a movie theater, with screens covering every inch of the room. Every screen blasting nonsense, showing the memories of people that I did not know, did not love, or hate. Just the memories, never ending, never leaving, showing everything about every ghost I ever came across. It was maddening, sometimes crippling. They weren't my memories, though; mine were locked far away by using a trick I had learned a long time ago. I was able to count binary over and over to keep my mind intact during situations like this. Sometimes, the weight of the memories would be too much. On those days, it was best to run, because my brain would take that one-way trip to crazy town, and there are no cookies in crazy town.

I ran through multiple equations in my head, trying to keep my mind under control. It was like pushing up against a huge wheel; my attempts nothing more than being able to hold back the destruction. As I rounded the end of the road and made the left Benny had spoken about, my mind started coming back into place, the sinking feeling floating away. *That's right, the feeling that I am lost in a maze is leaving, and I can find Holly*. Reassured and renewed with a gumption that was endless in feeling, I took down the road, running faster—while hoping I was going the right way.

I looked down the streets empty and barren with no sign of any electricity. I had known that more than likely, there wouldn't be any kind of electrical works, but my heart took a dive nonetheless. I couldn't see anything that looked like it would be where Holly and Benny would be. I looked down the street, my eyes searching with a fever, until I saw a massive warehouse at the end of the road.

Its doors were wide and surprisingly well maintained. It was not that the destruction to the city was so great, but more like the city was slowly falling apart. I was used to seeing things more run down. The metal moving on from its original form into heaps of scrap. Windows bleeding into the streets, sparking like razor snow from some of the more ruined buildings, wood now rotten to the point of dirt.

And yet, despite of everything in the city now being coated in brown rust, this shed was, for all purposes, just fine. Someone had been fixing it up, which meant one thing: either I was seeing the images from some clever ghost, or a person was fixing it up for what reason I did not know. "Nothing good," I muttered, running to the cover of the closest car. I was breathing hard and my body was shaking. Fear is something that will never leave you; no real mortal can be without fear. Neither the richest man nor the most powerful women was powerful enough not to be afraid.

I was no exception to fear, I just learned a long time ago how to deal with fear. About the time that I lost my hand, I made the decision that death wasn't the worst thing to happen to a person, that being tortured through life is much, much harsher; a life ruled by fear.

That made me always go into situations like these with nothing to lose, except for maybe Holly. She kept me from just barreling through with my gun blazing. I gulped in a fresh scoop of air, trying to dispel the fear growing inside me. I looked through the door, not seeing anything, only the darkness of the inside of the warehouse.

I waited half a breath for something to appear in the darkness. When nothing came, I came from behind my cover, moving towards the steel doors. Upon closer inspection, I could see the weight and girth of their frames. They were heavy, which meant they were used to keep things out, and the frames looked almost too heavy for me to move with only one hand.

I don't think Benny could have had the strength to move these doors. That made me even more afraid. What was going on? There wasn't anyone else in this city anymore, other than us. Hell, counting Holly, I hadn't met many intelligent ghosts that still had their minds not twisted by the darkness.

I moved through the doors with caution, straining from their weight as I tried to open them as quietly as possible, hoping to bring in more light. Inside the warehouse was barren and swept clean. I couldn't tell what had used to go on inside the warehouse, or what it was now used for. As I made my way farther into the dark, I saw lights glowing from inside. I stilled my breath as I came forward.

Benny was standing over a metal dog cage from what I could make out, with a long rebar in his grip. Inside the metal cage was Holly, her face tearing up in anguish. I erupted in a fury of steps, bolting in the direction of Holly. Steel didn't kill ghosts like iron did, but it was much worse. It was their version of a long suffering, forcing them to be burned away in slow peels of their paranormal bodies. I think it was the iron deposits inside steel that caused the reaction. Most of the time, the pain was minor, and wouldn't deter a ghost that wanted to get through bad enough. When there were a lot trying to get through a piece of steel, the metal would almost seem to age faster and break down.

Iron was the ultimate way to end a ghost. I still had no idea why, and I probably never would. Skip ahead to the future, once all books would be gone and the Internet would be no more, and human beings' attempts to understand the world would be broken. That is why discovery was a luxury that I did not have, or rather one that I didn't want to bother with. Why discover anything new when it was a struggle just keeping Holly and I safe? Still, how had Benny lured her into that thing? He must have tricked her. Holly could be a little... impulsive, just like me.

Seeing the iron in his hand made my legs move fast. I am going to kill you, Benny, if you hurt her. *If he did anything bad to her, he is a dead man,* I thought. I went to tackle Benny, leaping through the air, about to make contact with Benny, when I was hit hard from the side.

I smacked my head against the ground and my vision blurred, though not enough to keep me from seeing a towering form. I could smell a stench radiating from the person who hit me. It was rotten, noxious and putrid in nature. I almost gagged from the smell. After a second too long, I opened my eyes to see the towering form before me.

His shape was odd, and his height was bizarre, towering over me at least a few feet. It wasn't his height though, that was making me want to shield my eyes upon seeing him. His form was made up of pieces of animals and humans all stuck at different angles. I could see faces, so many twisted and deformed in place, somehow defying all logic by staying together.

When the monster had hit me, my shotgun had gone off flying in some direction. I wanted to turn my eyes to look for it; I had learned that lesson a long time ago not to take your eyes off the monsters, even for a moment. I would just have to make do without my gun.

My trusty pan was still attached to my harness at my side; I had serious doubts in its ability to hurt this thing. As I lay immobilized in fear, the monster charged forward, its massive legs moving at a surprising speed.

My body reacted before my mind; I was up and turning away from the monster and sprinting towards the nearest staircase. My old legs were strong, despite the exertion; I'd been running from monsters for a very long time. I had perfected the art of running for my damn life. I made it to the top of the stairs, feeling the added weight of the monster as it made its way towards me, stretching with limbs made of the bodies of the dead.

His stench fought towards me with a hunger and malice unlike anything I had ever felt before in my life. I ran faster, scanning down the walkway; I couldn't see the gun or anything I could use, and the end was quickly coming. "It's time to move fast, and think fast, James! Come on, you're a computer guy, figure it out!" I shouted to myself as an idea took form in my brain.

I reached into my coat pocket with my only hand, searching for my long coil of Cat 5 cables, which were, as I have found out time and time again through the years, surprisingly useful; I had managed to tighten a loop in the cables before coming out—having a lasso of some shape often paid off, I had learned. I looked at the railing, seeing the rust and degeneration in the metal. I could smell the monster as he neared; I was only going to get one chance at this.

I picked up my pace, putting everything I had into my run, my legs straining under the exertion. I reached the end of the catwalk; I didn't look to see where Benny or the monster were. Instead, I placed one foot on the railing and struck down hard with my hand until a bar broke free; I had a feeling that the metal was weak. I looked up to see the monster only a few feet away.

I slung the circle end of my cable and pulled tight as the monster approached. The monster flung a meaty hand towards me and I dove between his legs, hitting the twisted corpses attached to his body. I rolled again, tracing a pattern around the behemoth's legs.

The monster swatted at me again. I barely avoided it. I could hear the songs of the dead drifting from the beast. Wails of the former lives distracted me long enough to be taken hold of by the monster. I was pulled in the air, like a tiny toy in the creature's hands. My right hand was gripping the cable tight, cutting into my arm, but it was also wired tight around the monstrosity, while the rest of me fought the sensation of moving pieces under me.

I fought with the stub of my left hand, banging down on the fleshy grip holding me. It was to no avail; it was like watching an animal show where a tiny rat would wriggle helplessly in the clutches of a vicious cat.

The pressure from his grip matched his size. From somewhere deep inside, I could almost feel a pop, as my bones were broken by this horrible thing's will. I managed to untangle my arm, blood spraying my face as the cable came free. With my right hand, I made it to the rebar attached to my leg. I pulled out the bar and struck down hard into the nearest piece of fleshy meat. The creature loosened its hold enough for me to fall out, over the catwalk. I held tight to the cable as it pulled the metal handles above.

I fell hard to the concrete floor below; the fall hurt a lot worse than I had expected. "It always is…" I mumbled, rolling to my feet in time to see that the monster was entangled in the cable and metal bars of the walkway. A pipe was protruding from the center mass of the monster.

It hurt just standing; my legs were bruised and full of pain, nearly as bad as the pain coming from my ribs. It felt like I had cracked more than one rib; it was something I couldn't help now though. *Get going, old man, you have your gal to save.* I looked to see the monster clawing at the metal pole.

I turned around to meet the big barrel of my shotgun pointed into my face. I've watched plenty of movies where the action hero claims that the barrel of a gun is ridiculously huge when you face it. I believe those movies now. It was like staring into a cave, knowing a monster leered deep within.

"Can't you just, for once, stay down, Jim?" Benny sneered from a surprisingly firm voice. I wasn't the first person he had pulled a gun on, and judging from the hold of the gun, he was going to pull the trigger.

"Well, you know what they say about us old people—we are all too stubborn to stay down," I bluffed, placing my hand in the air.

"Now they will say you're dead," hissed Benny, his finger pressing into the trigger. I closed my eyes tight before I heard the scream; it was Holly's voice shrieking in a terror that set me off in a fear and trepidation.

I opened my eyes to see Holly melting through the steel bars, her movements strained, like the bars were holding her back with an invisible force. I could see the pain the movements were causing from here as she passed through the bars. But I could see something else; that fierce determination to save your loved ones no matter what. the drive that enabled mothers to lift cars off their children. She had someone to protect. *I'll be damned—she was going to save me.*

Benny must have seen the look on my face; he turned his head in time to meet the full-force attack of Holly. Holly opened her mouth and chaos is the only way to explain what happened next.

A force that seemed to shake even the air around me erupted, and then I felt the wave and I shot back like a bullet into the far wall. My back hit something solid, and the air left my chest. Benny was dumped on another section of wall, bent over in a heap. I was shocked; Holly had never done something like that. In fact, no ghosts I had seen were capable of such a feat.

The most I had ever seen was that first night in my house. It even seemed that all the ghosts could do was throw around debris and shake the house. Generally, what I have received from the ghosts is shocks and, well, scares. They were filled with the emotions of the violent ends that they'd suffered, while the worst ones, they were the things that would snap my mind.

But this, this was raw; like an emotional tide pouring forth from a whale. Some force of her emotions had crossed her world and entered mine and taken hold of it. Shaking it like this earth didn't belong here, and we were the ones that were a paranormal force.

Holly kept screaming, her voice causing my head to spin. I fell to my knees; everything on the inside feeling like it had shifted a foot. I had to save Holly, but like her, I was having my own feeling of protection that was overriding all my senses. I stepped forward, the force causing my legs to shake like twigs in a stiff breeze.

One step forward, now take another one; keep going, you have a job, old man, don't you quit now. It was a game of inches as I edged into the sound of this poor girl screaming for her life. The agony in her face broke my heart as well as encouraging me to keep going. *She wasn't some poor girl, I thought to myself with a very quiet voice.*

I reached her finally and tried to wrap my arms around her. I felt the cold sensation of our imitate touch; my attempts to hold her phasing like she was wind through my fingertips. It was painful; I didn't care though—she was mine. Holly's screaming stopped, and all I could do was try and put my arms around a little girl. It was like standing in the coldest of rivers during a snow storm, my fingers freezing to the point of numbness.

"Holly, it's okay, I got you. It's okay." I fumbled my words, trying my hardest to hold and comfort her.

If you ever been a place in your life when someone was in pain, pain that you couldn't possibly imagine—even worse, when it was someone you cared about, then all you're left with is to try and show love and affection. Show that human nature isn't all dark; that we were capable of more. Yet, in those times, no words, no comforts can help that person. Some pains the comforter just wouldn't understand. It's like seeing a man fall onto a subway train track, and you are in a wheelchair; you're powerless to really help the person. I couldn't help but hurt on the inside. If I could have died in that instant, I would have, rather than face this alone.

"James, I know this is hurting you—you can let go now," Holly voiced.

At the sound of recognition, my heart started again like a car. I had been worried... worried that she was gone. "Holly, are you alright?"

I tried putting it into words without my voice breaking. I had no idea just how much this girl meant to me until now.

"Yeah, I am alright; let's get out of here, please," Holly said, stepping away from me. I nodded, standing to my full height. I looked down at Holly, and her face was miles away. I wish I knew what she was thinking. We were going to have to do some deep talking when this was finished.

But first, before I left, I had to deal with Benny once and for all. A cold resolve slid over me; it was time to kill Benny. I turned around, to see the meat monster right behind me. He was tangled in metal bars and Cat 5 cable. The monster roared and hit me again, sending me flying in the direction of the generator. It was still chugging along, spitting coughs of grey smoke into the air as it burnt what had to be some of the last gas left in the city. The monster stepped towards Holly, I couldn't tell if it could see her or not, its many faces snarling in hate. Holly did the unexpected again and charged forward into the thing—she flew towards the monster. I knew what she was trying; once we had tested what would happen if Holly tried going into the form of a dead animal. The results had been bad.

Once she was inside, the animal would come back, not the same, though. It was all fangs and teeth with no control; I still had marks on my arms from when I tried to kill her when she was inside a dog.

I shuddered at the memory. I had to help her see that she was in way over her head. "Holly, stop! You can't do what you're trying to do, you know this!" I shouted, still stunned from the blow.

"Shut up, Jim, and do something, smart guy!" retorted Holly as she glided towards the monster.

I watched as Holly flew towards the monster and phased inside. The monster stopped moving, its form seeming to freeze in place. I leapt into action. I looked for the gun. Somehow it had been tossed only a few feet from the generator. I fumbled to my feet; my body was not going to be able to take another hit from that thing. I made my way to my gun and popped the chamber. One shell still inside.

I had serious doubts that it would be able to keep this thing down, though.

I snapped the chambers closed, in time to see it making its fiendish steps towards me. Holly lay down on the ground behind it, not moving. I aimed the shotgun and fired. The first round hit its center mass, sending out chunks of gore, but the monster still lurched towards me. "Well shit, this isn't good at all." I took another step back from the monster, not daring to take my eyes from the thing.

The generator kept sending up puffs of smoke. It was a wonder that it still held up with as much shaking it was doing. I reloaded the gun, a few shells in my pocket—not enough. As the monster stepped up beside the generator, my hand put together the thought before my mind did and fired at the generator. I missed the first shot. I swore, taking another quick shot, and this time I was lucky. The shot sent heat and force towards me. More importantly, it ignited the monster like a dry leaf in a fire, as the shot found its target in the generator. The smell of its rotting flesh managed to make me throw up, and finally I could hear its screams. It was like hearing a chorus of wails. I was unable to shield it out, and I just had to listen to the horrible toll of it all.

Once I felt steady, I walked towards Holly. I made a wide berth away from the flaming monster on the ground—just in case. Its shrieks still echoed in the warehouse.

"Are you okay, kiddo?" I asked, kneeling over her. "Yeah. Jim, it was horrible, all those poor people and creatures. They were stuck in that thing; it wasn't right at all." Holly looked towards the burning heap.

"Yeah, I know. Listen, stay here for a second and get some rest," I said soothingly as I started to reload my gun. I had someone I had to kill.

Benny was still crumpled into the stairs. He had a pool of blood coming from his head, and his eyes were wide with anger. "You son of a bitch! That was my brother!" Benny screamed, struggling to his feet, but not fast enough. I had no problem with smacking a wounded man with the butt-end of my gun.

The meaty give of his jaw made euphoric chills race up my spin. It felt good putting scum like him in his place. I wanted to hurt him, put him through the most painful experiences my mind could fathom. He had nearly killed Holly. That was all there was to it. I eyed my gun. I had never killed a man, but it didn't feel that hard. I balanced the shotgun over the ruined stump of my left hand.

Benny's mouth was bleeding and I could see pieces of a tooth lying on his shoulder. "Bye, Benny."

My fingers were about to pull the trigger, when I felt Holly's cold hands bleed into my back. "Stop, boss. He's not worth it. Plus, he was telling the truth; that was his brother."

I kept my gun pointed at Benny. His face was one of pure hatred. He would get up and try to kill me in an instant if I took the gun away. Holly continued, "I read the thing's mind—it was sick and full of so many painful souls. When I looked into the memories of his steel cage, I found that Benny was just trying to save his brother. He has been alone for as long as you have, James."

"That still doesn't explain why he lured us here. Nor should we let him off the hook for trying to kill us, Holly!" I growled, my face flushing from the heat coming from the charred meat of the monster.

"No, it doesn't, Jim. However, there aren't a lot like us left; killing him will only put another ghost in this place," Holly whispered, taking her icy hand out of my back.

I turned my head towards Holly; *she never ever referred to the ghosts as 'ghosts'.* "Holly, you aren't like the rest of them—" I replied, some of the anger still coming through as I fought to urge not to run to her. Being isolated is deadly—feeling like you can't relate to those around you can lead to roads paved in stones of furlough and anguish. *Those roads are one way.*

"It's okay, Jim. I'm dead and there isn't anything I can do about that. I won't know anymore what it's like to be alive again. And

I don't want to have him in my heart, as well as my mind." Holly sniffled, staring at Benny. Holly and I had figured out a long time ago that the ghosts read people's memories too, like when I read theirs after killing one. The difference was that the ghosts could pull the memories from an object that meant something to the person. They wouldn't learn all of the memories of a person, just all the memories associated with that object. So, there was no telling what Holly had learned while she was trapped inside that cage. As she had once put it, *Everything has a story to tell.* It often made me wonder if the chairs I sat on told something I wasn't aware of.

"Holly—I know you have a caring heart, but letting this guy live is a mistake we can't afford to make. He threatens every chance of survival we have." I couldn't take it anymore; my vision was red, and this scum was still alive. Just lying there, glaring at me; it would be so easy just to pull the trigger and be done with it.

"James, you don't even know how bad it is with him. He is being tortured," she whispered, her eyes cast to the ground.

I dared a glance at her over my shoulders. "What do you mean?"

"Inside his head, it's like he is being kept in one giant continuous loop. It's—sick, Jim. You have no idea; he is crawling away in the darkness from a flame at his feet. Above that, his feet are bound by wire to his head. As he crawls, his feet pull his head back and the flames continue to burn. On his back, I think it's some kind of... fridge that is pumping cold blood into him, I can tell from the steam. Benny is in a great deal of pain, Jim, Benny is in agony," she murmured, meeting my gaze.

I absorbed that, my anger deflating only a little. "Even more reason to put him out of his misery," I replied. Every instinct in my head was screaming for me to pull the trigger.

"If surviving means killing someone, then I don't want to be existing in this world; you once told me the secret to life was fighting for those that are precious to us. Well, Benny was fighting for his brother, however fucked up it may have been; he was only trying to be with the people that are precious to him. That is something I can understand," Holly avowed, placing her hand above mine; I looked down to see her hand causing the hair on mine to stand tall from her gesture. She was right; in our roughest moments, I always told Holly we were the good guys fighting for what was precious to us.

"Let's go, Jim, please," she urged, her voice tiny in the large area. I wanted nothing more than to paint the room red with the blood of this… this wasted life, as I looked at Benny. I drilled holes into him with my stare, but no matter how much I yearned to end his life, I couldn't bring myself to do it. I wanted to end Benny, but I just couldn't do it. Not with Holly so close. That was why I knew I was going to walk away.

With my back to Holly, I spoke. "Holly, I left the doors open. Get to the car and rest."

"Jim—" Holly whispered.

I waved my hand behind me. "Holly, go. I won't kill him, I promise."

Holly waited a couple more seconds; I could tell she was debating if I was telling the truth. She must have seen something cold in my eyes. "Fine. You're not a killer. Just remember that, Jim," Holly consoled, fading through the side of the factory.

I turned my head back to Benny, watching him twist under my gaze. His hand still covered his mouth and I could see thick globs of blood. My fingers were sweating; my fingers were aching to kill. I debated if Holly would hear the fire of my gunshot. I didn't trust myself to move as I spoke. "Benny, I don't know why you did what you did, or if I am making the right choice leaving you alive. So, I will make this really easy for the both of us. If I see you again, doesn't matter if you're a ghost or you have the cure for this fucked world we have to share. I will kill you, slowly and painfully. Do you understand me? I want to kill you more than anything right now. Don't take my lack of action as a weakness. I'll have both my eyes on you from now on."

"You said you would make it stop! You promised!" Benny shouted, spitting out blood, whimpering into the air. Benny's eyes were staring past me—far away as if speaking to someone else. *That was odd. Who was he talking to? This world could break any man,* I thought. So if what Holly said was true, Benny was losing his mind. My choice here wasn't about doing anything to make me feel better, but Holly was mine, and that was a promise I would keep this time around.

And Benny had come close to taking her away, to sending her to a place I could not go. My skin burned, heating to the point that my very blood had to be lava, trapped by a thin layer of flesh. *I had to hurt Benny, I had to hurt him very bad.* I let my rage take over. *Hell, why not indulge yourself in the sins?*

I aimed the gun first at Benny's face, until I felt it lowering. At his knee, I finally pulled the trigger. Chunks of red and knee showered my chest, but I didn't feel the resolution I expected, as I listened to Benny's wails and cries.

Instead, I felt very tired as I turned, walking away with my head held low.

Chapter 21

Outside, the sun was still fairly high in the sky. It had been years since I last bothered keeping a watch. There was no point anymore when it was day to day, and ghosts didn't give a shit about the time of day. Day or night, your ass was the target for whatever was around you. As far as I could tell, the world was back to survival of the fittest. In this case, though, I wondered if it had ever been different. And like time, the city was devolved back to its core elements. *A rotting tree made of metal and glass, a sea of rust, and the memories of all that had once lived here. Just gray* I thought, *just gray*.

I looked to my car parked in the distance; Holly was shimmering in the passenger seat. She was always surprising me with just how alive she seemed to be. She needed rest from time to time, and seemed to feel pain. That was evident from her power display back at the factory. I tightened my hand on my iron pan, making sure it was there. I had never seen one of the "good ghosts" move anything like that, without becoming twisted and wanting to kill me.

As I got closer to my van, I could almost picture my wife sitting where Holly was, her long blonde hair sweeping down in waves that reflected the afternoon sun. Only that was the best I could remember about my wife, without picturing the night that she was gone for good from me. I still saw her, just not in the ways I wanted. I had thought I seen her walking around earlier, and that was something happening more and more lately. She was always there, existing in the background like a living and breathing malevolent force. I didn't know why I was always seeing her; I didn't want it to stop though.

Her memories, however brief, were all I had left.

I reached the door of the Beast and climbed in, shutting the heavy door behind me. I looked around—no signs of Benny or any kind of ghost. I turned back to Holly, and she was staring at the floorboards.

"What's up kiddo?"

Holly kept looking at the floor of the Beast, her eyes miles away. Even from this angle she showed pure lethargy. My voice seemed to bring some of her energy back. "Oh, are you talking to me Jim? I'm okay, just really ready to be on our way..."

When she spoke, I flinched, I couldn't help it. I had learned that when you let your guard down, the ghosts seemed to attack that moment more than anything else. I didn't feel bad about flinching away from her as she spoke again. I could see an uncertainty in her features, a lack of the normal guileless glee she would bring to every situation. That made me feel bad—she was a sensitive ghost.

She caught my movement and to my relief, smiled. "Don't worry, old man. I am still me, driving you crazy, while you can go on being grumpy and complaining about not having enough toilet paper to wipe your ass." She smirked.

I smiled back, hoping to get her attention. Holly's focus stayed on the floorboards while a long silence stretched its way between us. I was never very good at handling awkward silences; words just felt petty when you didn't feel sorry for your actions. I decided to just cough and make a small suggestion. "Well, ready to start our day," I asked, as Holly remained quiet.

And that is how it went. Holly didn't mention what I did to Benny. She was smart. It felt wrong to ask what was on her mind or anything else she might have learned from Benny. There are some things you just don't ask.

We ended up finishing clearing the block we had started out on that morning. Holly and I would search house by house for any sort of supplies, food, or Holly's body. When we were finished, I would hammer in an iron nail at every corner piece in the house. This, I found, kept ghosts from wanting to even attempt to come into those dwellings—well, most of the time. Figured it was the best to keep the places safe that we had already visited. Once all the hammering was completed, I would scatter any steel in the house all over the floors for good measure. Then pack up the Beast, and it was on to the next one.

Most of the time, this task was easy in the sense that I did need supplies, even if it was just for one person. It was the other reason we searched that caused me dread. That never got any easier; a lie never should, for that matter. I knew full well where Holly's body was at. It was buried deep within a steel framed fridge, under the rotting wood of bad memories.

I thought of that every time Holly and I would go looking through one of these abandoned homes, of the families that once lived there. Whole entire lives snuffed out like sand flung over fire. In an instant, everything gone. Everywhere I looked was the reminder of the skeleton land I now called my home.

Sometimes while Holly and I were looking through a home, I would pull out the only photograph I had left of Molly and Diana. It was all I could manage to hold on to, the only thing I knew was certain to be real after all this time. I kept it under the visor on the driver side in the Beast. I never wanted to keep it on me or inside the shelter, in case Holly ever found it. There was no telling what she would say or do if she found the photo. That's why I would take "breaks" out in the Beast, to stop and look at the photo. It would give me peace while we searched, make my lie a little easier.

But lies are never supposed to be easy things to stomach. Despite the hiccup with Benny, by any sane logic I probably should have called what transpired insanity. Only, the fact it involved another living human (no matter what state that human may have been in), made more sense to me than anything in this world. Beyond that, though, I wanted to avoid thinking about all that had happened, to get lost in the search.

If you see a box with a turtle in it, you can deduce only a few outcomes: that the turtle was placed inside, and that this had to be done for a reason. This was something I could understand or at least acknowledge as something possible. That is why Benny wasn't frightening me. Even the creature, made up of all those parts, was something I could understand. After all, I had seen Holly go into something dead as well, and drive it around as if it was alive, when in terms of all known neurology, it was dead. Some force had powered the creature, but now the creature was dead; leave it at that, just like the turtle in a box. No need to explain the situation, just fix the situation.

What bothered me about the ghosts was after twenty years, I could still not explain the reason why they were here or all their behaviors. Holly was as far from the ghosts as turtles are to birds. She was something else; something I couldn't understand. I feared the day would come when I would find that box with a turtle, somehow alive in the middle of a great fire. There would be no way either should be unharmed, but they would be. That day, I wouldn't be able to explain, I would just have to let it happen. I shuddered at the fear of that. I was trying to rationalize the irrational and every day, it just made my head hurt.

I looked at my wristwatch—I had long since replaced the one my wife got me. I had plundered the many abandoned timepieces that seemed to be littered throughout my city. It was a common thing for people to present them to loved ones. So common that nearly every house I went into had a watch. I tried to leave any that had a description on them though; it just felt wrong in some way.

It was getting later in the day; the sun was still high, and the air felt very dry as I tried to suck in breath. I got out of the Beast; it was time to get back to living my life. *Living the life of a lie*, I thought. I shoved the photo back down into my coat pocket just in time too. I glanced out the side mirror and could see Holly floating nearby. Her eyes had deep bags forming under them and she looked... well, tired. Which was a new one for her.

"How are you feeling, kiddo?" I asked her as I turned around.

She regarded me coolly for a second, as if she was unsure I had spoken to her. "I'm good, Jim. Say, do you want to cut out early? I was thinking... well, it's been kind of a rough day and you found a whole lot of cans..." she muttered, her usual jubilation all but gone. Facing terror was normal for us, but today had been particularly rough.

I looked at her... I mean, I considered her. *We had both had a long day,* I thought. "Yeah, want to go ahead and call it a day, kiddo?"

She smirked at that. It got her spirits up. "Well, I was thinking we could go fishing," she said.

The sun was getting lower, our timer for the world becoming heavier. My eyes hurt, my everything hurt. Holly's eyes were stretched wide—it was our favorite thing, fishing. In the distance, Diana stood, bleeding in the road. She smiled, waving me towards her with her hands. *She was there, gesturing me, all I had to do was cross the street. Cross the street and I could hold her again,* I thought.

I started to move, and my leg ached, leading up to my back. Instinctively, I rubbed my lower back. "Is your back hurting you, Jim?" Holly asked, concerned.

I looked at her, turning away from Diana. "Yeah, something like that, squirt."

When I looked back, Diana was gone. "Jim?" Holly asked again.

"I'm fine, Holly. I say we go tomorrow. Let's get some rest," I stated, heading towards the Beast. My walk was out of step and my back had a knot forming somewhere under the surface. I was feeling light-headed. That monster had done a number on me, when I opened the door to the Beast, Holly flew in, I closed the door sluggishly, moments later, and fell back.

"Jim, are you okay?" Holly asked solicitously.

I looked down the road again. Diana wasn't there. *She is gone James,* I thought before responding to Holly. "Yeah, it's just been a long day, you know?"

Holly paused, biting her lower lip before responding. "I know what you mean. Can you get us back to the house?" she asked.

The house was a thirty-minute drive, and the sun would be down in a few hours. But everything felt dull, slowed to the point that I was shaking as I felt sweat trickle down my forehead.

I shook my head. "Just get some rest, Jim, we can go tomorrow," Holly voiced as I flipped the chair back. My eyes were closed before the chair was tilted back. The world rushed to close around me and Diana whispered in my ear, "Sleep well, lover."

Chapter 22

When I awoke, Holly was floating near me, her face lines of worry. I grunted, "I'm fine, kiddo, don't worry." I looked at the road, the light causing me to cover my face with my hand. "How long was I out for?"

"Long enough. I was getting worried there that you had died in your sleep, old man," she smirked, but her eyes showed her concern.

I grunted again, pulling the driver's seat back into position. "Let's get a move on, kiddo. We have some fish to catch."

If you drive deep enough into most towns, you can find shopping centers, and my town was no exception. There was a standard-sized mall, connected to a parking garage about twenty minutes from where we were scavenging today. For the most part, our mall was made up of generic food stands and overpriced clothes stores. However, our mall was special. It wasn't how this mall looked on the outside that made it special; it was the vast fountain on the inside that had made it one of a kind.

Somehow, against all odds, fish had made a life there inside the fountain. The circular base around it was no wider than two of my cars side by side, and with a massive obelisk in the middle, the fountain was surprisingly well lived in, its murky waters teeming with fish.

Before everything had gone to the waste side of Ghostville, I had hated fishing. I mean, come on, all you did was sit there and wait. You were more likely to catch a cold than an actual meal. It just didn't feel very effective when there were thousands of cheaper fish, which probably could be consumed at almost any restaurant.

Holly and I had been driving by, one day, and she insisted that we find a new book store for better tapes. I grumbled and lamented the prospects of a boring day after she had complained enough. When we had cleared the mall, and decided it was safe, we noticed the water was moving.

At first, I had thought it was ghosts coming out of the water (nothing made me scream more than when they did that—it was like watching the reflection of a window suddenly shift when you weren't expecting it).

We had both gasped when we had seen the fish inside. To my knowledge, there wasn't a pump that could possibly be running. From what I could gather, it was probably a bird that had accidentally taken some fish eggs from the local creek nearby and it had landed in here.

Either way, Holly was less considered about the 'how' than I was; rather, she liked to see them. I think it made her feel more secure, maybe more grounded in this crazy world. For me, I liked seeing her happy. It was a refresher from the abnormality of fearing for my life at every turn.

I sat at the edge of the fountain, watching Holly dive in and out of the water, the water remaining still as she entered and exited. It was as if nothing was coming from it, nothing at all. The only indication that she was even in the water was that the fish inside would become panicked by her presence and would shoot off in all directions. Occasionally, one would flop out of the fountain from her chasing them. I would reach down and throw the thing back in.

In this way we would 'fish.' It was relaxing for us both. We had been there for about three or four hours, sitting in the hollowed-out remains of the mall. It had long since been picked clean by us and who only knows who else. I figured it had to be after the ghosts came. Besides Benny, it had been years since I had seen another living human being. People survive, people go, and Holly and I are just another chapter in this abandoned building's life—indifferent to everyone, just trying to hold it together.

That was fine with me now, though; I couldn't imagine the kind of people that could keep their minds intact after all of this. Benny was probably considered sane compared to all that had happened. My mind, tired and haggard as it was, was probably the best thing that someone could have hoped for in this world. Even so, I was glad to be alone—people would scare me. I mean, what would I even talk to a normal person about these days? *Are you missing any limbs and hunted by your dead wife?* I thought, looking down at the water, where the setting sun was casting a dark green pool across its surface.

Holly came out of the water where I was looking. I jerked in surprise and she smiled. "It's way too easy to make you flinch, you know that, right?" she joked mischievously.

"And you're way too forgetful of how much I hate when you do that, don't you?" I asked back, pretending to have a heart attack from the scare. We both laughed—it was nice. I looked at the sun. It was getting close to night. I would rather get out of all this before the darkness came.

Holly turned her head to me. "Jim, do you mind if I ask you something?"

"Sure, fire away, it's never stopped you before," I snickered.

I could feel Holly's grin as I turned to her, she rolled her eyes and went on. "I was thinking about the fish. How there is the very real possibility that they aren't real. That none of this is real—have you ever thought that? I mean, deeper than in some book or movie, have you genuinely considered that everything around us is just in the imagination? I mean, at that point it wouldn't even be real, would it? Just something we made up to validate our existence."

I blinked, unable to think of a response that would actually make sense. "I… don't know Holly, I'm not very good at deep thoughts. You know this," I remarked.

"Just humor me please, Jim. I mean hell, for all we know the fish we are seeing in that fountain aren't actually there. Just something our minds placed there to deal with how fucked up everything is. Every night, it's a wonder that I am even still here, as far as I know. I am some made-up thought inside of someone's head. Like anyone you've known in your life, from your wife—"

I slapped my hand down on the hard granite fountain.

Holly stopped, covering her mouth. "Jim I'm sorry, I didn't mean to bring her—"

"It's okay," I muttered through clench teeth. After twenty years of being together, we both had agreed that we didn't need to know anything about each other's pasts. Holly could never remember anything before the moment we met in the smoking ruins of my old home. And to protect her—to protect her, I never talked about my family. It would be too much, and she would eat me, just like Diana had. It was easier, leaving that all unsaid.

Anger is the best way to keep people from asking too much, I'd found. Getting angry prevented her from questioning too far. I took a deep breath, gathering myself back up before speaking. "I don't know, Holly, about any of that. I get pretty hungry, and that seems real to me." I growled, still trying to soften my voice.

Holly made a level gaze with me before speaking again. "Can you try to be deeper this one time, Jim? I could really use outside thoughts on this one," she pleaded, on the verge of tears.

I looked away, sighing deeply. "All of this—all of this is real."

"How do you know that?" she asked.

"I just do," I replied.

"But honestly, from day to day, things change. From the water to the air, Jim. How can all the loneliness—all the signs of happiness that once lived here—not make you wonder if our memories are made up?" she asked again.

"No," I stated.

"Why not?" she asked once more.

"Because you can't replicate the heart; you can't fake love," I stated, standing up from the fountain. Everything suddenly felt very hot inside the mall. "That's the shitty thing about love—when it's real, it's real. And no amount of time and change can ever make that up. Love is a home for the memories worth keeping. So yeah, I don't think any of this is fake. If it were, it wouldn't hurt as much," I muttered, walking away.

Chapter 23

Holly remained quiet for a while, both of us not looking at each other. Just watching the fish in the pond, watching their world swirl around them in what had to be the biggest thing they would ever know. Their world—the only thing that mattered in the end to them.

We stayed, watching the fish, neither one of us talking as the silence lapsed into the hours of the day.

I looked at Holly, and she seemed a lot more relaxed than earlier. *That was good,* I thought. *At least the day wasn't a complete loss. Who knows, soon all this would be behind us like everything else.*

I have my doubts about that though; things always got worse when you needed them not to. I thought of the picture, and I ached to see my babies. I needed to see their faces one more time before the evening was up. I looked at Holly. "Why don't you go ahead to the Beast, I'm going to get a quick smoke in," I mumbled, while gesturing towards my lips.

"You don't smoke, old man; I bet you couldn't light a lighter even if you had two hands. If you want time to postulate on the stars, just ask next time." She laughed, gesturing with a twirling motion to the cracked ceiling above.

I smirked at her, "Get out of here, will you."

"Yeah, yeah I will be in the Beast—oh, Jim?" She paused.

"Yeah, what is it?" I asked.

"Never mind—thanks for taking me out here today."

"Sure, Holly, not a problem."

She smiled, vanishing into the air, and I knew that she had gone to the Beast. I waited in the cold vastness of the empty mall for five minutes, making sure that Holly was gone. That photo was my addiction; it hurt every time when I saw it. It hurt every time when I didn't, but I had to look. It is the only way that I could be sure that I once had a family, which meant more to me than anything else I knew. It was the only concrete proof that I once had an old life outside of this endless abyss.

I looked around once more, just to be on the safe side, like a person who was ashamed of a habit. One that I should have let move on, like everything else in this world. I reached into my pocket, and my hand came out blank—no photo. Just pocket lint from years of wearing the same clothes repeatedly. I panicked, and my heart started beating faster than when that monster had cornered us earlier.

Frantically, I dug into every pocket and pouch on me, and I turned up with no photo. I looked around the fountain. Maybe it had fallen out when I wasn't paying attention. My heart was pounding louder than my footsteps inside the mall. The only noise I could hear was the steady rhythm. I retraced our path all the way to the main door. Nothing, just dust and the memories of a past that was long gone.

Where could it be, where the hell did I put it? Had I left it in the Beast? I froze—*if I had accidentally left it in the Beast, Holly could have found it.* I ran, slamming the ancient glass doors open, and raced towards the Beast. I calmed as I approached; I could see Holly floating in the passenger seat, her head down. I breathed a sigh of relief. No need to get stressed. I was good; she still didn't know and that meant everything was going to be okay.

I opened the driver side door. "Man—I need to quit smoking, I am breathing so hard." I fake-coughed, trying to clear the anxiety that I might be displaying. I looked at Holly, and she was staring down at the ground. I stopped talking; she had a down-cast look. I spoke again. "Holly, what are you looking at, kid—"

I didn't get a chance to finish my question; I saw what Holly was looking at on the ground. It was the photo of the day that my wife,

Molly, and I had spent at the park. All three of us together, very much looking like Holly was Molly; sitting between Diana and I in the photo. A question that I had feared for twenty years was coming to the surface; I could feel it.

"Who is this in the photo?" Holly whispered. My tongue froze in my mouth; I started to answer when I glanced in the dash mirror. A young girl with jet black hair and a barbed face littered with cuts was in the back. She smiled when I saw her. Her fingers raised, and I screamed too late, but then she was gone in a flash. So was Holly.

I was alone again in the Beast, watching as Holly was running outside the van with that girl. They were both holding hands, skipping into the darkness as the sun came down. I blinked, confused by what just happened, as the two girls got further and further away. They were going to be gone soon, my Holly was going to be gone and all I was doing was sitting there slack-jawed and scared, just like before with Molly.

I wasn't going to let that happen again; I wasn't going to let her go.

I got out of the Beast, giving chase after the two, unaware that the world around me was changing slowly. The mall was soon behind me, and I was flying past the city, my feet making the only noise as I struck hard dirt. The sky was turning into the darkest of nights, the buildings washing away like sandcastles by the sea. Soon, as I was running, all I could see was the glow of the girls off in the distance, and the rest was the pitch-black. The girls seeming almost crepuscular, off in the distance. I had to catch them before they got away.

The dark veil began to pull away ahead of the girls, gently and quick like a lover's hand in the darkness of your bed. There was a small house, its features non-descriptive even without the darkness. The girls made it to the door, giggling. I was getting closer and my heart was pounding. I had done a lot of running today, and I was starting to wonder just how much more I was willing to throw out before my body quit on me. I was spurred on, though, the flash of

Holly lighting my way through the darkness, all fatigue forgotten. What had I done? I had been careless, and because of that, I was going to lose her.

The darkness swarmed around me, as if it was alive. The whole city had become a void so endless that the steady drum of my heart was the only evidence of life in the hushed world.

The dark-haired girl opened the door, and Holly turned back at the sound of my voice as I shouted at her. I wasn't sure what I saw in her face; it didn't look like anything good.

Holly went in after the girl and the door to the house slammed shut. All around me, the world was slowly turning back into darkness. I had to go through the front door without looking, The twilight around me felt alive, itching to get me. I made it to the door, and I could see it used to be painted a deep shade of red on the outside, only now time had chipped away and rotted the wood, leaving a musky brown in its place.

I tried the knob and the door came open easily. I stepped through, slamming the door before the darkness could get to me. The inside was as murky as outside. I couldn't make out anything in front of me, so I opened my ears to the sounds of the house. Spooky shrouds or not, this house was made from things of the earth. Things of the earth made sound; you only had to listen and stop your own chatter to hear something. The problem with that is I was tracking two girls who were, by all definitions, ghosts. Ghosts didn't make a noise unless they wanted you to hear them, which made it almost impossible to track them—only I had found a way by using batteries.

I stowed away my gun into its slot in my jacket (I had taken it out just in case of trouble while running), and removed the laptop battery in my other pocket. I was thankful for my overly complicated plans for a change—I always messed up, but for the most part I planned for most scenarios. *Just relax, James. Think.*

For some reason, I found that batteries would give off a small shock at the presence of a ghost. I used laptop batteries because their design made them easy to hold, plus while the small shocks were mildly discomforting, a laptop battery could be used for a variety of special needs. From powering a computer, to finding your lost ghost daughter.

One of those needs I was hoping wouldn't have to be used, but you never know. I swiveled with the battery going all around me until I felt a small shock from the direction to my right. I waved the battery forward and felt the shocking sensation once more.

One of the worst feelings from not having two hands was in the darkness of that hallway. If anything attacked me, I was going to have some trouble. This ghost seemed to be up to something I hadn't seen before. She was smarter than most, not trying to attack me head on. I thought of her appearance inside my car—who was she? She had a look to her—maybe Molly's age at the time of her death—but she was too big and had a tussle of black hair.

She looked familiar, I just couldn't place where I had seen her before. I had to have at some point—why else would Holly have gone off with her? *Because she found out you lied, you old fool,* I thought as my shoulders suddenly became very heavy. *There was always smoke where there was fire. My day couldn't get any worse.*

Stay focused, James—think and find Holly. I inched my way down the hallway, all the while feeling the slow shock steadily. I remembered seeing the outside of the house before coming in; it shouldn't take long to reach the end of the hallway, but that was the thing that was starting to bother me. I had been walking enough steps to have reached the end. I tried keeping a mental count: one... two... three...

A dull purple glow shot out and blinded me as I walked. I covered my eyes to see light coming from the wall next to me. I jumped in reaction, nearly dropping the battery; the shock was sparking like a small bolt of lightning in my hand when the wall became alive with color.

I looked down the hallway; I had only fifteen feet to go before reaching the end. That didn't seem right, though; I had seen from the outside that the hallway wasn't this long, and I was sure I had been walking for a long time. I stopped, thinking to myself that I remembered having this thought already. I shook my head, ignoring the light, and started counting again.

I turned back to the direction of the door, expecting to see it far behind me. Instead, I was still right next to it, having traveled no more than a foot from its threshold. That didn't feel right at all; there was something wrong. I started again down the hallway, pulling my pan into my right hand. No point in keeping my battery out, so I stowed it away into my jacket.

I took a deep breath. *Steady, James, steady.* Reorganized, I walked forward at a faster pace than before. The dull purple from the wall provided a decent amount of light. I knew it was a trap, I just had to figure a way out to make it get snapped at the right moment. I kept walking and the end seemed no closer.

That made me stop again. I looked back from where I had started, and I was further along. Yet my progress didn't result in anything like reaching the end of the hallway. To top it off, I wasn't sure how long I had been going down this length. As I started walking again, the end came closer, then it stretched out once more.

This is getting ridiculous; I feel like I've been walking for hours. Or wait, did I just get started... I turned back towards the door; again, I was only a few paces away from where I had entered.

I turned back and quickened my pace almost to a slow jog; I needed to quit being slow and get to the end of the hallway already.

"Hey mister, can you help me find my dad?"

I froze in place; it had been a long time since I had heard that question. But it still came back fresh in my memory. I turned around to see little Sam, his face in the wall. His eyes were just as wide as they had been many years ago when I had first met him, only this time, his eyes were coated in the white paint of the hallway.

"Hey Jim," said another face coming out of the wall next to Sam.

So many voices, belonging to people—people I had said goodbye too. Slowly, like watching dirt turn to mud in the rain, faces showed in the wall. I didn't know most of their faces—I knew enough about some of them, though. A very cold chill ran down my spine and I took off, running down the hallway as the faces appeared, all speaking my name.

It was haunting hearing them again, and I couldn't move my feet fast enough to get away from their voices. I pounded forward, my feet echoing in the empty hallway that seemed to stretch forever. Even moving as fast as I could, I still wasn't getting any closer to the end of the hallway, as their voices called out to me repeatedly.

I couldn't take it anymore. Switching to my pan, I swung it into the wall of faces, shattering the face of young Sam. Instantly, the purple veil lifted, and the faces melted back into the wall. A black shade slid down the wall, enclosing me in total darkness again, like a hand over a flashlight.

I was breathing as I made my way along the wall, using my hand for sight.

The hallway finally ended, and I found myself in the open. I wanted to take out the battery again, but I didn't want to risk being without iron in my one good hand. I was afraid and alone in the dark; my mind beginning to construct horrible images of something attacking me, of tearing me to shreds, and there wasn't a thing I could do to stop it. My whole body started shaking. I would have dropped my pan had it not been tied to my side.

"Is this how you fight for those who are precious to you, James?" whispered Diana. She was gone in more ways than one; all the ghosts stayed with me in a way; otherwise, though, they were gone. Except for Diana—she never left. It was more than just memories. Diana would never leave; never stop reminding me of how I'd failed. She continued like a serpent in a garden looking for a weakness (she had already found so many ways to haunt me). You live with the ghosts you create in your life. I had created a memory of my wife that had forever twisted and replaced the very image of her being inside me.

"Why don't you just lay down already, James? That's the kind of man you are. The kind who doesn't act, or provide for his family; you've now lost your daughter twice in one day. You aren't grateful enough to have had her in your life to begin with," she sneered, coming up to me in the darkness. I felt her hot breath brush against my ear. I was in total darkness, my breath cold, hers warm.

She was right; I didn't appreciate Holly for what she did for me. She was my lighthouse while I was lost on a raging sea. *I think... I will just lie down and let it all go, go off into the sea. My lighthouse is gone, I'm lost.*

I fell to my knees, and all the while, Diana kept speaking. "That's right, James. Just give up like you always do. It's easy, just let it happen."

I failed you, Holly. I had failed her so many times, it was neverending, this pain. My life a circus of terror and the punchline of what was shaping up to be a cruel joke was how I kept fighting it. I kept swimming upstream in a river which had no direction, had no flow but down, down, down into the darkness.

I failed you, Molly. That was when her name triggered something inside of me, something I had forgotten. *Holly is Molly; she is my everything, my will to step out into the awful world every day.* It was that love which started a fire again inside my heart. I thought of all the times she and I had played board games on the roof. All the times we had spent glowing and growing in each other's lives. *Love didn't need a hallmark card, or shiny song; love only needed to bring people together and enrich their lives with happiness. Love was all there is; all I had and all I would ever need.*

Fear wasn't beating me today, I thought as my hand snaked its way to my small pocket knife inside my coat. I flicked the blade out, cutting a small patch out of my arm. *This is real, this blood of mine is real,* I thought as the cut slowly trickled hot liquid in the dark, down my arm. *Everything else, that's up for debate, but I am real. I had the love of Holly, and she is real.*

That thought was building me back up, bringing me back to my knees. Like that, I started forming a wall inside of my mind, blocking out Diana until my head was my thoughts only.

I took a deep breath*; my fear is great, but my love is stronger.* I walked through the darkness with a purpose, no longer afraid. I had a daughter to find and by God, I was going to find her.

"You can't ignore me forever," she hissed.

"Stay awhile, baby, and find out just what I am capable of," I responded.

Chapter 24

Finding my way along walls was easy enough, and soon I had managed to go up a flight of stairs as well, without any problems.

Which started to worry me, I didn't gain memories when I had hit the thing on the wall. So, something was still in this house with my daughter and me.

Now I was inside another hallway, still just as lost, with no clue where I should go. The whole house seemed larger on the inside than on the outside, an effect that made me nauseous. Rationalizing what I had seen in my life worried me. *I might be making false memories in order to work through the pain,* I thought. *Even if this is not real, you must find her, you know you must. It was just hard; the realities of life are simple, and just because I said I would do something didn't mean I could do it.*

I shook my head. *What was I doing? I just needed to find a clear direction.* My direction was made for me when I looked at the end of the hallway to see the girl with the dark hair.

She was glowing with a light that wasn't natural, a beacon in the darkness, causing me dread rather than hope. I readied my pan to take her head-on if need be. The girl looked me in the face and I saw eyes that were too intense to be on someone that age's face. I had long since made peace with destroying the ghosts, including those that were young kids, but it still felt hollow and horrible when I did it. *Don't let her age fool you—her eyes say it all,* I thought.

She vanished and teleported down the hallway. Her speed was alarming, and I threw up my pan, ready to fight. The ground gave way below me and I was thrown to the floor below. Something had ahold of my leg, and I couldn't see what it was; I only reacted with muscle memory and hit the thing with my pan. I felt the hold give, and I rolled out in time to see the girl standing before me.

I swung my pan arm upward and missed her as she teleported again. The room had become filled with light as she vanished. That's when I saw the shadows playing on the walls, twisting at her will.

She assaulted me with various shots of shadow, and repeatedly they shot out of the wall, like the tentacles of an octopus. My pan would send the tentacles of shadows back into the darkness, only for more to come. The exchange was going on longer than I wanted it to. I honestly don't know how many dodges I had left as I sprawled and rolled, praying my body wouldn't give out.

Her shadows whipped around like the merry-go-rounds I took Molly to as a child. I nearly had my head taken off twice by them. I took one hit on the side for moving too slow. Old age and the strain of it all were starting to catch up with me. My mind was still moving, doing as much mental gymnastics as possible on how to defeat her, as my body was tossed aside like a rag-doll.

I had nothing I could throw on her—her shadows were being used liked shields, so anything I could use would be blocked. Shooting her with my gun was useless and would probably just piss her off more than anything. I did, however, have a big battery deep inside my coat pocket. I dropped my pan into its sling at my side, dodging a shadow swipe from above. She was being cautious now, trying to keep me at a distance, probably just waiting for me to get tired and go in for the kill.

I found the battery as I rolled, and slung it nearest the wooden stairs. Now the statistical chance of a lithium ion battery exploding is slim at best on a good day. Only I had what it needed: a little age, and a big goddamn fire-breathing shotgun.

I tossed the battery close to the ghost, sending small electric sparks everywhere. I aimed, taking a deep breath. Most shooters had trouble being accurate, let alone when they were missing one hand. My hand shook from the weight of the gun. I didn't want to miss this—no, I had to hit it.

I fired, and the first shot missed. She hissed, sending one of her arms to take me. I breathed deep; *for Holly,* I thought. I missed a second time, swearing as a shadowed limb struck through the floor beside me, missing by a hair. I swore under my breath, rolling closer this time. *I can't miss from this close,* I thought, sucking in a breath before firing. Somehow my aim was true, and my shot found the battery. What happened next shouldn't have happened; I had time to register the force of the explosion and the flames licking up all the shadows.

I was rocketed somewhere with my feet flung out below me. I hit something hard and my eyes went black, the last image being the house burning before my eyes. I could see Holly off in the distance, standing at the rails, overlooking the fight that had occurred between that girl and me.

Chapter 25

I woke up to a bright light shining from a high moon above. The explosion must have ripped the house partway out of whatever world I was in. That was a plus; at least now I knew I could get out if need be—assuming I wasn't just trapped in the world I had been before. Or, for that matter, if this was all real. Rationalizing the irrational is impossible, so instead I focused on the small bits of every situation, the underlining fabric to the thick comforter that had become my existence. *Figure out what you can, smart guy, focus on that.* I curled in my toes and wiggled my five fingers. I was still whole—shook up, but whole. I had no real way of knowing exactly how long I had been knocked out. That's when I remembered the ghost; she was still alive somewhere nearby. Fire wasn't enough to stop them. That made me afraid; I reached for my pan beside me like a man does in the night when he is afraid his wife has left, like a man does whenever he realizes this situation could be endgame at any wrong choice.

It was still there, still attached somehow to my sling. I rolled over to see a massive hole spanning the entire room. Somehow, I was lying on a ledge just wide enough for my body. In the light of the moon, I could tell the hole went down about three, maybe four floors. The house was bigger than it looked from the outside—*that confirmed it, making zero sense,* I thought, as I stared at the light from the moon. *One thing at a time old man, one thing at a time.*

I tucked myself into the wall, hopefully out of sight. Things looked a hell of a lot higher, the longer you kept your eyes wandering.

Instead, I focused my eyes on the wall nearest to me. The wall looked consumed from the fire; it did have enough of an edge I could walk over. Its old wood was popping from the embers still burning dully. Looking at the burnt edges of the wood, I should have been engulfed in the flames—it had to be Holly. *There was still hope; hang on baby-girl, I'm coming.*

I shifted to my feet, feeling the boards blackened by the flames somehow still supporting my body weight. "What the hell? That isn't the first time I had caused a battery to explode, no way. It should have been a distraction and nothing more. But this, this is like a bomb went off when I fired my gu—" I mumbled as I peered over the edge into the darkness below.

Enough light showed at the edges to reveal to me the young girl with black hair; she was pissed, and I could see the hate in her eyes. I stopped talking. If she got ahold of me I was a goner. I had the high ground, though. Even if she could fly, I was safe up here. I could hit her long before she even tried using those black arms of hers.

I never stopped jinxing myself, I soon learned. The black-haired girl took a step back and started gagging. She was coughing ectoplasmic goo, drizzling from her mouth. "Oh, this is going to suck!" I shouted, looking for a way out of the situation. The stairs across the room were largely still intact; I would just have to make my way across the ledge.

She gave one more cough and suddenly a head appeared in her mouth. That made me stop for a second, feeling the scream in my throat replaced with terror. The head soon pushed out of her mouth and arms, and a long white torso followed.

Another head appeared at the end of that body, and each had long flowing black hair. I couldn't make out the faces very well from a distance, but I knew it was the girl. She had a scar on her head—a discolored patch that stood out from the moment I'd first looked at her.

I placed my back against the edge and started making my way to the stairs, one sidestep at a time. It was good timing; she shot her heads out until the torso of arms and heads could reach the ledge I'd been on just seconds before. She crashed into the wood, sending splatters of chips everywhere. The arms reached out to me like thousands of worms wriggling from the ground. I did my best to keep moving along the edge.

I was moving fast as the long body of the girl took another swing. She missed only because I had made it to the staircase. I fell, landing hard on the wood, and pulled myself up the stairs as fast as I could.

I only missed the third swing by inches when the wood was cracked and sent flying everywhere. I kept moving forward, not turning around until I made it to the top, doubling over, out of breath.

I heard her roar and my mind filled with the image of her many arms tearing me apart. The hands of the lead head connected to the staircase and the long trail of bodies collapsed into her, until she was pulled to the top. Her body language was easy enough to read; she was pissed and would be killing me very soon. I gulped; she wasn't going to go down easy at all.

She pulled herself up and the fire was still in her eyes. I took off down the hallway, pounding my feet along the wooden floor. I turned back, and she was gone. I readied my pan in front of me, expecting the typical ghost behavior. Instead, I only saw the emptiness of the hallway and the rooms beyond.

She was playing a trick; I just had to be smarter.

Ghosts loved to have the element of surprise; anything to gain the edge. They would stalk me as if I was prey, trying to break my grip on reality itself. After years of scares and thrills, I had learned how to steady my fear in my heart. The trick was to keep something solid and real in my mind.

Right now, my 'rock' was Holly, wherever she might be inside this maze of a house. *Holly is here, I just have to find her.* I sniffed the air, searching for that distinctive flavor of fear.

I've learned fear is something that can be smelled; its odor is one animals produce when trapped in a cage or in dire situations. Same for fresh recruits' experience when they arrive at their training destinations. No matter the catalyst, fear can be smelled.

The key is to not have the typical reactions to fear that normal people have. Such as sweating or gasping. I learned how to control the beating of my heart, to remain calm even in the most terrifying moments.

I slowed my breathing and my steps. As far as I knew, the line of sight for ghosts was the same as humans; they only appeared all-knowing because they were quick. The black-haired ghost was looking for fear, and I had none.

I stepped into the shadows. *It is time the prey becomes the hunter, for a change.*

I waited and kept waiting inside the cover of a dark room. What little light from the moon above cast odd shadows, so I had to blink to make sure the shadows were real. I wasn't sure if they were, or if the fatigue was finally landing its nasty little hands on me.

I kept moving my joints slowly as the time trickled by, my mind closed off to keep my eyes from seeing anything more than what it needed to. I had seen too many heartaches, too many hardships to be able to maintain focus, if I ever allowed my thoughts to drift.

It was a game she was playing; somewhere in the house, she was looking for me and I had the feeling we were both waiting for the other to make a move. *In a waiting game, I am going to lose to a ghost, no other way around it. They don't need to worry about the simple aspects of a good night sleep, or food and water.*

I readied my pan as my body became tense, my missing hand feeling electric for some reason. I was about to step out, when I heard her voice behind me. It was Holly's—that is, her crisp voice sounding oddly mature. I turned around, fully expecting another trap, only to find my wife sitting there on a chair facing me.

She was naked, her sex on full display, causing the old gears of arousal to spin once more in my head. I couldn't help myself but to gasp, and a sudden image of the sex we used to have came steamrolling its way from my brain down to my loins. *God, it had just been too long since I had last been with a woman, too long since I had seen anyone naked beside the twisted scars of my body.*

I looked closer at my wife's face and realized it wasn't her. She had the same heart-shaped face, but her eyes were the same blue oceans, just like mine. Her nose was also flatter than my wife's ever was. It was Holly, no doubt; she was all grown and filled out.

Any attraction I had been feeling had now left me. I felt vomit coming up to my throat. I cursed it back down as I made eye contact with Holly. "Um—Holly." My cheeks were burning from carnal feelings inside me, returning to the chest from which they came.

"Hi, Jim—or I think you go by a different name, one we both wouldn't know any more, would we?" Holly smiled; it was about as friendly as a copperhead lying in your bed.

"Don't say it, Holly… let's just get out of here, please." I couldn't even meet her eyes as I said that. I couldn't hear the word we both knew; she was right, it didn't make it hurt less, though.

"Oh? You don't want me to say a simple word, huh, Jim? What damage can one lousy word inflict? Can it bring down a mountain, with unholy scripts of lettering; painfully removing the shrouds around us, stained by our own selfishness? In this case, the selfishness would be you, huh, Dad?"

Before the word could hit home, Holly stood from the chair and pulled my body forward somehow. I flew until I slammed into the chair. I tried fighting, but it was useless. She had power over me that was somehow keeping me down, as if I was strapped in.

"It is time for an introduction into the lesson called 'Pain,' Father." Holly came forward and stuck her fingers into my head. My head felt like it had been invaded by eels, and all I could do in response was have my screams run out into the room. I could feel her, feel her inside of me, chasing for answers to things I didn't want to admit. Things I didn't want to know any longer.

Chapter 26

At a certain point in your life, you start to ask yourself questions. One of those I never asked myself when I was younger was: "Am I good person? Are the choices I've made worthy to damn me?' That was something I never had to question myself about—after all, I had a beautiful wife and daughter. For the most part, I was well-to-do, and I never went out of my way to harm anyone.

But, as time goes on and in the body of lies or whatever form your sins may take, you slowly realize one thing. *I am just a shitty human being, maybe not for the reasons some people are—I didn't kill anyone. But I might as well have with the actions I've taken in my life.*

It was my very own actions which had led me to the path I now found myself on. A slow aching pain, trudging my way through the roads of life. I deserved the immense pain I was in now, I deserved the horror.

At some point, I stopped screaming. I opened my eyes to the darkness all around me. I was still in that chair; still in that room. I closed my eyes, the pain fading into the back of my mind like a bullet train speeding past. I was untied now, free; my mind wasn't working that fast yet; not enough time had passed since Holly had invaded my skull. With shaky legs I stood from the chair, looking around the dark room. I felt warm, very warm. I could feel a heavy liquid weighing me down as I stepped. Everything smelled of copper—*yes, almost blood-like. It smells of blood,* I realized as I made my way through the pools that stretched before me.

The way the blood moved as I walked, was revolting, abhorrent, a sickening thing that nobody should never have to go through in their life. I fought back the questions of whose blood I was walking through, as the blood continued, endless in its amount.

As I trudged through the blood, I only heard the slow lifting of my feet out of the vital fluid all around me. I heard a beating, my heart matching the rhythmic tempo of my footsteps.

I wasn't sure where Holly or that girl was, and it didn't seem like the smartest of plans to start calling out into the darkness. I felt for my pan—it was gone, as were my clothes. I blushed at the embarrassment; I wasn't used to being so exposed.

I breathed in, steadying myself, and tried to make for shapes in the darkness. Ahead of me, I could see what looked like trailing arms from the ceiling. Fear almost took me in that moment—I imagined the arms were attached to a horrific beast found only at the bottom of the deepest pits, or worse, the blood was from its victims.

My skin felt alive at that thought, burning, and aching to run away from the area I was in. It took every ounce of my mental will-power just to not bolt into the darkness. I fought that down, steadying myself and again feeling my way through the darkness with as many senses as I could use.

I was thankful I felt nothing besides the cold wetness of the blood on my feet. I would have screamed if it had been something else. I made my way to the dangling arms, and I quickly realized how wrong I was. It wasn't some horrific monster. It was paper chains peeling from the ceiling, thousands of them all looped together by their tiny paper loops. It was at the end of them that scared me the most, though. I could see clearly—as if to remind me that I was not in some world where I would be spared a tragedy, that dull purple light from the hallway shone out.

"What is this shit?" My hands shook as the words came out. At the bottom of every one of the arms were photo frames, containing pictures of my whole life. Things from my times with Diana and Molly, to more recent stuff with Holly and me. Everything presented to me as if I was on trial for murder. *Maybe—maybe,* said a far-off voice at the back of my head.

I looked at the nearest photo. It held an image of Molly and me sharing ice cream—some twenty years ago, today. It was our last day together, it was our last time as father and daughter.

"Exactly," whispered Holly's voice, as all went black.

Chapter 27

I was sitting in a movie theater. It was empty, save for myself and Holly right behind me. "Let's see the truth," she hissed, digging her fingers into my head. The feeling started out as if I was fishing seaweed from a thick current, only to be replaced by waves of cold. An image started to display on the wide theater screen before us; my head had become the view projector for Holly. Images of my life flew before my eyes. I struggled, fighting the pain through tears. She sifted through my thoughts like it was all stacks of paper. That is probably all it was at this point.

Just a collection of an old man's ruin that didn't need to be kept in any real filing system; this was how she was gaining the truth from me.

Behind every deception, she was there, pulling at them like weeds in a field, trying to hunt down her answers. She came first to an old memory, one where I was still young, and Holly and I were finding survivors almost every day.

It was me and a young couple—I couldn't recall their names anymore—setting up long lines of fiber cable with scraps of iron at various angles. We had managed to zigzag hundreds of feet between two buildings, and that had effectively kept the ghosts from our area.

It was a smart plan, one of my better plans. Only I didn't foresee that the couple would try and steal my equipment in the middle of the night. They claimed it was for survival, that we had enough as it was. Whatever their reasons were, they put Holly and me in jeopardy. When I figured out that they were in the process of stealing from us, I put a bullet into the man and chased off the woman. He didn't die—he ran off as far as he could with his wife. I just cleaned the blood up before Holly could find it. Not saying a word about what had transpired.

Several weeks later, however, I found the woman's body being eaten by cats. I told Holly that I never found her. Holly was devastated for weeks, believing she had somehow caused the couple to run off. Most people are uncomfortable with having ghosts around. They had a point—most were trying to consume you. After that, Holly was quiet for weeks. I worried she might turn. Turn just like Diana. I told her I would go look for them, told her that they hadn't run away because of her. Instead, I went looking for the ghost of the wife., I found her hiding in the spot where her lover had fallen by my hand. I never solved how she became a ghost or how her husband had become one too. I just handled my business.

I dispatched her with my iron pan. After that incident, I never trusted another survivor again. It didn't matter anyway, as it turned out survivors after that either avoided me altogether, or humans started dying off faster.

I felt Holly's rage at that reveal, her fingers like spider legs scurrying over my brain, forcing another wave of screams out of my mouth.

She went probing deeper, peeling the years back like an onion. Learning the constructs of my mind and any defense I might have been able to throw up, she hammered them down.

My eyes kept flowing, as Holly reached a painful memory too far back to give her what she wanted. It was the day in the park that we had spent playing in the sun. Everything was so perfect that day between my wife and my kid, I remembered thinking I didn't want it to ever end.

We had been approached that day by a rather large lady with curly black hair and a doughy face, but still with an attractive appeal to it. That woman would soon become my boss, and she would also become someone I for whom I would murder her own ghastly image in my own house. She was a colleague from work—I never made the connect until just now that she had been my boss. Maybe I had blocked it out. Whatever the case, I remembered her now. It had been my boss Debbie, who ultimately decided that I stop being a freelance programmer of a video game that wasn't ever going to be finished, let alone do any good. She introduced me to the exciting lifestyle of governmental work. Who would have known that I would someday destroy her in tattered clothes with a cast iron pan?

Holly became agitated at the string of seemingly useless memories that she was finding. She trashed my head back and forth, with her fingers still inside of my head. I knew what she was looking for, and she had every right to know.

Only I couldn't let her. I remembered in that instant what happened when Diana had regained her memories of our relationship. When she regained the knowledge of who she used to be, the loss of that twisted her into the monster.

It ended with me losing my hand; it had begun the first days of my long struggle. And the last attempt I ever made trying to help a ghost regain its memories. It was too dangerous, helping them remember who they were, turning them into demons. The things that I had been fighting for twenty years. I had lied to Holly—kept the fact hidden from her that she was my daughter in order to protect her. I gave her a name, a different name, when we first met. Weaving a story that burned like paper in a fire once exposed. It was too dangerous otherwise. That was the curse of man; if we ever figured out our existence, truly, the existential self-actualization would probably drive us into a murderous rampage, like it had Diana.

While Holly was processing that information, that old fighting spirit of mine kicked in to protect what was precious to me.

I began sealing off parts of my mind; just the parts that had to deal with the final resting place of Molly's remains, and the relationship of the women in the photo to Holly. I felt the knowledge of her mother secured first. Holly shrieked in almost a painful rage in response.

She suddenly pulled her fingers from my mind, and the cold pulled back like a frozen curtain from my bare skin. Holly was breathing hard in front of me, her chest rising and falling. I wondered for a second whether if Molly had grown up, she would have looked like Holly did now. Like the adult version of my daughter before me. My eyes, and all the beautiful looks of her mother; I would never truly know. I used the pain from that thought to reinforce the locked box containing the worst memories.

There are some things a man should never admit, no matter how much pain it caused. No matter how much pain the lie was causing, we all have our secrets; we all have the things that are kept in the box.

She looked at me with utter hate. I was the victor, but it tore my heart out, seeing that look from her. I had sworn that I would never let Holly end up like her mother. I hadn't failed at that yet, I would die keeping her from losing who she was now. Holly would not become one of those things. I could tell she wasn't completely lost, or else she would have just had gone inside me and taken my body.

Holly's face became one of stone, and then it became one of understanding. She walked towards me, placing a hand upon the seam of my pants. "I can't physically touch you, Jim. However, we both know that there are other ways to gain knowledge," she stated while closing her eyes. I knew what she was doing.

She was trying to pull the memories from the blue jeans that I was wearing. My experience told me that she was seeing everything I had ever done in these pants. Which had been a lot over the years. The pants had become little more than patched-together rags, but everyone has a pair of pants that they've done everything in. If our minds can gain memories, a recording of everything perceived around us through our senses, there was a strong chance that the grimy, deodorant-stained, rock-and-roll t-shirt you wear every summer had to have memories of you in it. After all, it was made from something living, once; life remembers, if nothing else. We live all day amongst the dead and the living without even realizing it; everything is captured, recording the world, without us ever being aware.

She quickly lost interest in whatever memories my pants held. After all, I had to change my pants often, due to my sewing abilities with only one hand being subpar at best.

She traced her hands along my boots and found again a similar story as to my pants. I was thankful for the first time ever that I only had one hand. I'd always liked saving things in the old days. If I had both hands, I would have probably kept my original clothes all these years. Her eyes rolled up in the back of her head as she finished with the memories of my shirt.

She twisted, smiling at me; I could see the gears working their way through her head. She was forming something insidious inside her mind. Or maybe it was something far worse than an evil plot. Maybe she was forming something that would cause me to do what I feared the most: tell the truth.

Holly disappeared, and I was all alone in the room that was now illuminated with the glow of the moon. It was like the moon was passing into the exact place needed, like a spotlight shining on pirates lost at sea, exposing those wicked scoundrels out in the open; in the middle of the act.

She reappeared after a minute, in the light. My hand was still bound tight and I didn't think that I was going to be getting out any time soon. I still fought, just sitting there, not doing anything was torture enough already. I tried moving, tried reinforcing my walls.

Next came the black-haired girl, her hair as dark as coal in the moonlight. She had a lost and distant look, as opposed to Holly's sinister and never-changing sneer. I had no idea what she had planned, but felt certain this was going to be bad. I started to reach for my iron pan with my fingers. The sling was only inches away. If I could reach it, then I could defend myself.

My fingers crawled the slow dance of a desperate man towards the strap, when the sling was snapped, and the pan flew into the back wall. Puffs of smoke went up from the decaying wall.

"Jim, I've been with you for what, twenty years? You really think I don't know your every move by now?" Holly walked around me as she asked her egocentric, but justified question, oozing with every word flowing out like blood from the veins.

"Today, every heart that beats, and those that do not, will love for the first time. Be set free by the fire of integrity and honesty. Today, our hearts have won first prize." Holly slid on top of me, her nakedness too close for comfort, though her cold body froze any desire within me.

She continued, "See the young girl behind me, Jim? You've been battling with her all morning... she has a major hard-on for you. Not because you're some kind of stud." Holly sneered, turning towards the girl. She turned her gaze back to me, and that's when I felt the flames in her lonesome stare. I was done for, and there wasn't a whole lot I could do about it. I would take my secret to the grave, though; I would do this last thing for my daughter or die trying in the process.

Holly continued. "Like me, this young lady experienced something that no princess should ever have to from her father. After all, any girl born to a man deserves to be treated as a princess by her father. Only, both our fathers failed us. This princess's name is Anna, and she suffered. Oh, Jim, she suffered a fate far worse than you and I could ever truly understand. When Anna was a girl, her daddy would sometimes call her his little princess." Holly sniffed, gesturing towards Anna. She started back. "His precious little princess, his little something above all..."

I was scared, listening to Holly's speech; my wall was weakening. I didn't like the direction that the story was heading.

"Despite Anna being Daddy's little princess, he sometimes would take her in the middle of the night. Carry her deep down into the basement below this very house. He would find the longest and coldest metal chain, attaching her to the hot water boiler, which you blew up only recently, by accident—good job on that. That's not important, though. What is important is what happened in that dark basement between Daddy and his little princess. See, Daddy would sometimes touch his daughter, not in the ways that a man would touch a young child, but as a man would touch much older women. Anna would scream and scream during the whole ordeal. All her father would whisper was for her to shut up. He would trick her with adult mind games and trust, asking if she wanted to make her daddy happy or not." Holly spat with the fire raging in her voice.

I looked at Anna; she had been about Holly's age when she had died. It burned my heart seeing her. I couldn't hold my gaze any more, but Holly wasn't through with me yet. A small force coming from Holly pulled my chin up.

"It's not over yet, Jim, not by a long shot," Holly whispered into my ear only inches away from my face. "Little Anna would be bruised and bleeding on the worst nights, especially if Daddy had a bit too much to drink. Anna tried to tell her mother. Her mother, though, was worse than her daddy. You see, her mother knew all about her daddy's late-night antics, and she dealt with it behind a veil of drugs, and would even help Daddy carry Anna downstairs sometimes, if that meant she could have five more minutes of her own high."

Holly pressed on, like stabbing a cold dagger into my heart. I had witnessed many horrible things since the world had changed. Still, no man who had a daughter could sit through this and just not feel utter terror.

"See, Daddy, Anna's daddy, betrayed her just like you did to me. You lied to me about knowing who I was. It makes me wonder, though, what else you might be lying to me about. What other evil things you might have, twisted up in that smart brain of yours."

Holly jeered, coming up behind me. I could feel her fingers wiggling their way into my brain again, and the pain came right back. As I screamed, I looked at Anna. She was such a skinny thing; she looked like she didn't eat much. Probably liked to read and never imagined her life would be cut so short; that someone who was supposed to protect her no matter what would do such evil things to her. Looking at her though, I could have been completely wrong, just like I had been so much with my own kid.

And still I wondered why my heart felt so bad, why my soul was bleeding at the sight of her. *Is it because I knew that I was no better than Anna's father? Was I using my own daughter for my own selfish reasons? In that sense, her father and I were twins.*

"Anna… Anna, my name is James." I spoke slowly, trying to talk through the pain, the tearing of twenty years of lies bursting through like water from a dam. I was crying, and I didn't remember doing it. I pressed on my conviction, using its steel in what was probably going to be my last moments. *I was going to do right for Holly, I promised that, if it is the last thing I did.*

"When my daughter was a little girl, she used to love *The Lord of the Rings*. She would sit in my lap and tell me she wanted to be just like Aragorn when she was an adult. I teased her about why she didn't want to be like Legolas, since he is a beautiful elf. Molly was always very smart, and put way too much faith into her old man. She said 'Because Aragorn reminds me of you. He would always be there to save the day, plus you have a beard like his', she always believed in me and trusted me."

I couldn't help but laugh at that memory. It was one of the better ones I ever had with her. *Then again,* I thought, *there never were any bad ones with her.* She was always my sunshine, and no matter what happened, I would always cherish every moment I got with her.

I felt Holly's fingers loosen enough to stop the fierceness coming out of my voice anymore. I coughed first, clearing my throat. "I let my daughter down once. When she needed me most, my wife was pulled from our bed like an animal in the middle of the night. I gave chase the best I could in the darkest of nights. And that's when I heard her scream from below. See, without making excuses, I couldn't leave my daughter, I could go save her or save my wife. I picked Molly instead of my wife. I didn't know that she was dead when I found her, until later—by then both her and my wife were just gone. And when I did find her, I died right there along with her. She is my little something, something that I bore from the smallest parts of me. Life without her wasn't the life that I wanted. So, when I was given a second chance at being with her; to be her dad again, I knew I had to have her back. To keep her, though, I did something that made me as bad as your father."

I paused, the pain choking in my throat. Anna kept looking at the ground, her body motionless.

"I chose to lie and tell my daughter that I was not her father, and that I didn't know who she was, to prevent her from ending up like her mother had. Now, I know that isn't right, that I am scum, but by God, I would do it a thousand times over if it was the only way to save my daughter. Anna, what your father did to you was not protecting what was precious to him. He did it for his own desires; he did it for himself. And I know that must have created a deep, deep, deep hole inside you. Let me tell you, though, you're not broken; you're not evil. I may not be your father, but I love you and will care for you for the rest of my days, like I did for my own daughter. We are all family in this world now. Now come… come on back to us. Anna, I am so sorry for what your father did to you. I am so sorry for what I did to you."

Anna looked at me, into my eyes for the first time. Inside, I could see the pain that happened to her when she was a child, but I could also see something more. There was hope beginning to sparkle from deep within. She was listening. I knew I wasn't going to make it, seeing this girl… this girl made me want to protect her no matter what.

"Beyond all of this, Anna, is a place that I don't know about. I think no man is ever supposed to. Sometimes life becomes a prison of fire and all we want to do is curl up into a ball and let go. I'm telling you now that there are worse things than your parents. And one is being alone, being unloved. Come back, Anna; come back from the rage within, Be the beautiful person that I see within you. You're a splendid flower in a field of darkness, so shine on with your little petals and nothing can break you again."

I pleaded while facing Anna's gaze. *Please, just please, Anna, believe me. I need to be able to save one. I couldn't save Diana, and Holly would forever hate me. That is something I could not change. Anna, though, she didn't deserve to be locked away in a prison of hate. I deserved that—not her, not Holly, and not even Benny. No one deserved to face hate alone.*

"Jim." Holly spoke, coming around to the front of me. "Would you say the same things to me?" Holly spoke with such uncertainty that I thought she was Molly again. *That's because she is Molly—let the truth have its day,* I thought. *Fuck it, why not? What better way to go than doing the right thing for your own?* My heartbeat was settling down, my thoughts finally meeting a resolution point that was manageable.

Inside my head, I opened the chest and my heart readied itself for the pain to come. Only no pain came. I looked at Holly before me; pain did not break her face. She was crying and pulling in her bottom lip, like she always had done when she was a child.

"You did all of that for me, Dad? For twenty years?" Holly asked, shrinking back down to her normal child size, her elder form all but gone.

"Yeah Holly, I would do more for you. You're what's precious to me. And I did what I did because my life would not be the same without you. Without you, I would never have found the strength to get through normal life, let alone this hell. Let alone a world as fucked as the one we have now. Whether you're my eight-year-old princess making me play with Aragorn meeting a Barbie, or my crazy friend singing random songs wrong as a ghost floating above my dinner table, you will always be my daughter. You will always be where my heart goes to, and I could never say I am sorry for loving you. I will just say that I am sorry for not trusting that my daughter would not be lost to me if I told her the truth. I love you, Holly. You're my daughter, and you're the best part of everything that makes this world turn."

I ached to hold Holly in that instant, to comfort her one last time. She disappeared, turning invisible, and so did Anna. I felt the hold on my arms go away.

I left my iron tool on the floor as I rubbed my left arm where the hold had been. I could see bruises already starting to form, even in the low light. It didn't matter; I made my way out of the room in a trance-like a state. I had to find Holly; I had to find Anna as well.

I needed them probably more than they needed me. They were both my girls, as far as I was concerned, and they needed me to love them and care for them.

I walked over to the railing, peering down below, and I could make out two forms at the bottom in the pale light of the moon. It was the girls from what I could tell, standing over something.

I pulled out the longest of my fiber cables. I had never attempted holding this much weight with a cable before, except for the monster in the warehouse, but that was probably luck more than anything else. I shuddered at the thought of that creature. Whatever twisted evil had made such a thing, I was lucky I'd had my cable. I hoped it worked now. *If it held the meat monster, then it will certainly be able to hold my light weight,* I thought, mustering my courage.

I tied a quick knot the best I could over the railing, and hoisted myself over slowly. I had become very good at tying one-handed knots—the trick was the loop. *Just like all the mistakes we make tend to loop back around, it's up to us to tie them off.*

The tug went taut around my arm and I descended below the best I could, as the cable became harder and harder to handle. Seven or eight feet from the bottom, the cord ended, and I let myself drop the rest of the way.

I landed hard on ancient plywood and nails. I kicked out my feet as

I made my way over to Holly and Anna. Both girls were overlooking a small skeleton with remnants of hair and the same soiled white dress that Anna was wearing.

I knew right away that was Anna lying there. I could see the long metal chain attached to her body. I followed it back to the hot water heater that had blown up when my shot had hit it. She had died a long time ago, alone and attached to that heater, her remains now partially burned from the explosion. How her bones hadn't eroded by now was beyond me—*probably due to her being in the basement,* I thought. *If a ghost's bones dissolved before being burned, I wonder what would happen? No clue to that one, I spent more time killing them rather than burning the bones.*

I felt fury and pity for the girl—that was just a rotten way to go. I knelt down to eye level with Anna. "Anna, I know that is you. Are you asking me what I think you are?" I spoke as gently as I could.

Holly spoke. "For some reason, she can't talk as you and I can. I think it has to do with the amount of energy she has... boy, does she have a lot, Jim... She could have torn you to shreds at any time if I hadn't been holding her back."

"Well, thanks for that Holly-biz," I responded.

"I didn't do it for you, Jim—believe me, I was happy with letting her eat you alive for a moment there. It's just that when I was listening to you telling your story, I could see inside of her. Someone is controlling her. Someone that can power us up... I don't know how anyone would do that—she is just in so much pain. Like someone has that chain wrapped around even her soul, Jim." Holly spoke softly.

"Does she want to be released? I mean, how do you know if she is being controlled by someone else?" I asked just as softly.

"Because somehow, you were able to make her feel loved again, you big asshole. There is no other way to describe it. By love being real, like an actual curing thing. Who would have known it could break the hold on her? It was enough for me to consider not killing you. I'm not saying that I forgive you yet... Just that I don't want to kill you any more, Jim, if that makes any sense at all—I don't know." Holly looked up towards the moon. "Might as well give the whole love thing a chance. What is the worst that could happen?" she mumbled.

I chewed over Holly's words, letting them sink in. "Love is a mysterious thing; it causes us to be fueled like the best of drugs. All right, Anna, are you ready?" I asked the girl. "Now like I said earlier, I don't know what happens after I do this. For all I know, I could be sending you some place worse… Are you sure you want to do this? Holly and I, we can be good for you. We can protect you and love you," I told her.

Anna placed her hand upon my arm. She transferred memories into me. I saw all the pain her parents had caused her, all the abuse the poor girl had suffered in her very short life. However, I also saw when she was a little kid, she enjoyed playing with bugs.

Anna had liked to make bug circuses and dream of faraway magical lands where bugs ruled with humans and all was peaceful. It gave my heart some joy in knowing that Anna had some good memories buried under all that tar inside of her. She had died very young and alone—her parents had left her attached to the heater when the world had changed. I was thankful she had memories of better worlds before the end. I let the memories flow until they came to her ghost life. It was all blank; it was as if for one second she did not exist, the next she was staring at the Beast as we drove by.

That was definitely something; before I could investigate that thought anymore, Holly interrupted me. "Jim, she deserves to be free. Do it, Jim—and you gain some ground with me, which is trust, and you need that very much right now," she demanded from behind me.

"Holly, relax, I am going to help the girl. But the best way to help her is to figure out who put her in this position in the first place." I mumbled back, letting her memories fly through my head once more.

"What do you mean, who put her here? I was sure she has just been here like you and me," Holly said, confused with the anger finally coming out of her voice.

"That's the thing; the ghosts normally have new memories of their ghost's life as well. They're normally random as shit, and often very redundant, it's as if she was born today. I can see up to the point when she died along with everyone else. There is this gap—everything is just blank up to when she sees us today."

"Well, how do you know it was us today, and not us from another day?" Holly asked.

"Good question. Today was the first time you've had green hair. She has been following us since the bridge," I responded, feeling a dread in the pit of my stomach.

"What does that mean, Jim?" Holly whispered. I could hear the fear in her voice and I hoped mine didn't match hers.

"I don't know, Holly. I think we need to keep a closer eye on everything..." What I didn't say aloud was my suspicion about everything that had happened these last few days. First, it was us noticing the animals, then the whole thing with Benny, and now this girl. It was like some strange force was moving everything around us.

I wasn't going to be able to figure it all out now. Maybe it would be a little bit too late when I finally did. I stuffed it away for later; for now, I had something much harder to do. I looked at Holly and nodded to her. She sighed, and closed her eyes, gathering herself. We had only burned two ghosts before, and each time something a little different happened. Though in the end, it was like a nail being removed from a coffin filled with them; like one less torment for the world, one more free soul to move on from this place. We truly lived in a world of wrath and tears, agonizing in its touches and unforgiving in its mercy.

I looked at Anna, and I almost envied her. She was finally moving on from this twisted place; she would be free. People used to tell me all the time that life was about holding on to it, that every moment was precious. I stopped believing that a while ago. *Life is hell, and the afterlife, if it exists, probably isn't much better. It is freedom from this place, though. Holly—was the only thing that made this life worth living.*

"All right Anna, if this is for sure what you want to do, let's get you going, kiddo." I beamed my best smile at Anna. She gave me a half-effort smile back that did give me some peace.

I went over to her remains; they weren't completely bones and ashes yet. I could still see some scraps of flesh here and there. I did notice as I approached her body that there was an extra set of footprints right next to hers. They were too perfectly intact, which meant they might have been fresh. I made a note of this and covered the tracks up before Holly could notice; I didn't want her worrying about anything more than she needed too.

Just like that, I had made another choice, a decision without her. I am an old man trapped in his awful ways. I pulled the lighter from my back pockets For some reason, remains that belonged to ghosts lit up as if they had been covered in gasoline, it was amazing how quick it was. I looked at Anna one last time and my heart died a bit, knowing that some day I might have to do the same thing to Holly.

There was no way around it now; she had caught me. I smiled at Anna, trying to send some warmth her way. Dying just isn't easy for anyone, no matter what kind of pain it sets you free of. I flicked the button of the lighter, causing the flame to ignite and engulf Anna's remains on the ground below. The bones charred within seconds, and the last thing connecting Anna to this forsaken world went up in smoke.

I took a deep breath as a blue light cast over Anna; inside the light were all the memories of her life, the bad and the good. A look of relief swam over her face. I didn't know what she was seeing; I hoped it was only happiness as she slowly disappeared from our sight.

Understanding something clearly at last was the closest thing I could describe to peace on Earth. The feeling was beautiful, and it was as if my own memories seemed less harsh, a long time ago and not such recent pain.

I closed my eyes, and when I opened them, the light was gone, and so was Anna along with it. The room was silent, and I looked at Holly who was now crying. I had never seen her cry before. That cut deep, deeper than any crevice at the bottom of any ocean.

I couldn't physically comfort her at all, and I wasn't much for conversation comfort. I did the one thing that let her know I was there for her. "Let's go, Holly. Let's go home, kiddo."

Chapter 28

Our drive home was uneventful, and I couldn't have been more thankful for that than anything else. Holly kept looking out the window the whole way. Any attempt at communication on my part was met with a cold shoulder. The roads were dark, and we occasionally passed wonders and ghosts of the night; some followed us, others even dared to touch the Beast before bursting to pieces on its iron coating.

I sometimes wondered if the ghosts got scared of the dark like we did. I noticed that they did seem more active at night. *Was that a predator mindset, or was it simply that the sun caused some sort of discomfort?* I had never asked Holly which it was; now wasn't the best time to start that kind of conversation, though.

By the time we crossed the bridge where we'd met Benny, Holly finally spoke up. "A part of me is always going to hate you, James..."

"Yes, I know," I responded, keeping my eyes scanning ahead; I'd had enough surprises for one night.

"But, I guess it is normal for most daughters to hate their parents, right?" Holly asked.

"Huh, well, there was a time when I hated my parents. I grew out of it at some point. It's just puberty." I realized how dumb my response sounded as soon as I said it.

"Well, that's one prize you never have to worry about father. No red bomber, and a trip to the tampon isle, huh, old man?" Holly jabbed at me.

"Holly, I'm—"

"Relax, Jim. If I don't ruffle your feathers every now and then, you get bored and depressed. Besides the dictionary describes puberty as changes in the body. I think that is wrong," Holly stated.

"Oh yeah? What do you think it is, then?"

"It's just a bullshit excuse for everyone to put their foot in their mouth at kids, and for parents to come to terms with the fact that their children are going to grow older," Holly informed me plainly.

"That's a good observation kiddo. A little dark, don't you think?" I asked, making the turn onto our block. I started to relax as we were home. Of course, as I had learned over the years you're never safe until you're behind the actual doors. *And even then, safe is another bullshit word from the dictionary. No matter how many doors you have, no matter how much planning and money you've spent, none of us will ever be safe from everything.*

"Yes, well like father like daughter, ah pop?" Holly said, looking in my direction for the first time the whole ride. I didn't know how to respond to her; instead, I pulled the collection of garage clickers from inside the glove box as I slowed down. With one flick as we passed a marked section of a particular building, the garage doors for all the houses around us started opening.

Long lines of fiber cables became stretched out in the air. Attached to the cables were hundreds of iron keys that I had looted from an old civil war reenactment shop. It had been neat picking through all the gear—most importantly, though, were the loads of iron keys I had found. It took me a while, but I managed to wire the garage doors to all open at exact moments, with the help of some people we had met; not to mention more generators than most music concerts.

And back when I had help, I had arranged all the keys to crisscross at multiple angles, effectively making a huge net for any ghosts chasing after us. I was always great at fixing and building things; part of every Saturday I spent fixing and maintaining the garage doors.

That's why whenever Holly and I would go looking for her body, we would spend a great deal of time searching through houses for everything useful. The average household held something that was of some use to us. From duct tape to nails, people didn't realize what they had.

We came upon our home that had no apparent entrances and looked close to collapsing under its own weight of metal. I had picked the house because of its one floor and stone structures. It was the only home on the block that had pillars made of rock, which I used to absorb heat during the winter, and more importantly, it could hold all the metal that I had placed all over the building. On the outside was steel, enough to scare the weaker ghosts off. On the inside, I had tacked onto every inch of the house hundreds of pieces of iron, from the ceiling down to the floor.

The only place not coated in iron was Holly's room and a pathway that led into and out of the house for her. Since she could change her shape, she was the only one that knew exactly how big she would need to squeeze through. In all effect, the house had never been breached, but it still didn't make me feel as safe as I would like. The last time I had felt safe, a man had stolen my wife in the middle of the night. No, this house provided comforts from the outside horrors, not from the evils that dealt within the tomb.

And right now, Holly wanted nothing to do with the kind of comforts my home could offer as a sanctuary. She now viewed me as a stranger, not as her friend and partner. Holly had to view me as a hedonistic old man, more concerned with his own thrills. That or some manic liar, which didn't seem to be false in my own mind. It was my home though, and for that I couldn't complain; people need a home.

It's true I'd begun to enjoy somewhat this lifestyle, or at least become used to it. That is why man is disturbed truly; we can be locked in a cage long enough and find a niche within the confines.

"If I go in there with you, Jim, what will actually change? Will it mean anything to you, now that I know the truth." Holly didn't really ask that last question—it was more of a statement. In truth, I could feel where she was coming from. Under normal circumstances, I wouldn't trust me. Where did she have to go, though; neither of us had anywhere to go other than each other.

"It means everything to me, Holly, that you've come back. I promise I will start being honest with you from here on out."

"Do you mean that, Jim, or are you just saying that in some vain attempt to maintain whatever lie you're forming?" Holly asked. She wasn't playing around. If I didn't tell her the truth from now on, I had a feeling I was going to lose her again.

I nodded my head towards her and said, "Yes, I promise."

Holly sighed deeply. "Promise me that you will take me to my body tomorrow."

When she mentioned her body, the nails went into my coffin. Any last shred of hope I had left slipped away. It took me a long time to answer, to get my thoughts in order. Finally, I spoke to her, watching her with her arms crossed standing next to the Beast after we had parked. A deep frown in her eyebrows; she looked a lot like her mother in that incident. "When you read some of the memories, you saw that I liked to visit a certain location, huh?" I asked.

"Yes, it wasn't so clear what you were doing there, but I noticed that you had a lot of memories of you going to that place. It didn't take much to work my way through the rest."

I smiled at her observations. She truly is my daughter, just as clever and hard headed. I gulped in some air, feeling the cold night all around me. "You know, when you were a little girl, you used to make your mom and I take you outside all the time. It was the strangest thing, on nights like tonight, you especially liked—"

"Jim, answer me now. You will take me to my body tomorrow, or else I will leave now, and I will never return." I could hear the conviction in her voice. That was her mother in her and she didn't even know that.

I couldn't make eye contact with her. How could anyone, when you're about to fess up to a lie that you've been carrying around like an atom bomb in your luggage for over twenty years? "Yes Holly, I will take you tomorrow… I—I promise."

"Thank you, Jim. Let's go inside already; come on, old man," Holly said, floating past me and heading to her entrance on top of the house. She was gone from sight in an instant.

I sighed again, thinking about the long tomorrow I faced. "It's good to be home."

Chapter 29

I lit all the candles inside my house when I entered. I had electricity, I just didn't use it. I saved it for the event of an actual emergency. I waited for a noise as I scanned my home by candlelight. The walls were covered in thick smoke stains from all the smoke over the years from the lack of windows. The iron keys stuck to the walls caused shadows to dance across the rooms, in shapes of my every fear. Like skeletons unlocking my final resting place.

Holly ignored me, shooting off into the darkness of our home as I continued to light other candles. I heard the pop of the stereo and the familiar sound of a book on tape. It always amazed me that Holly could touch things as small as buttons, to reach from whatever plain of existence she lived in now, and interact with my world. It also put my mind at ease as I heard the familiar words of *The Outsiders* playing. It was her favorite story, which she listened to only on the hardest of nights, I'd noticed. I debated making my way to her room and trying to talk to her again.

I stood outside her doorway for a second and changed my mind. Sometimes not talking was a more effective argument than anything I could say. *Holly and her mother were always the good ones with words; I am a computer guy, not a poet. Or rather, I'm not used to some roles changing—me still being a father will never change. As much as Holly will never stop being my daughter.*

I walked around the house, checking the iron and steel for any holes. After today's surprises, I didn't want anything more to happen. I made my way to my room, which was little more than a closet. It was easier to sleep when I didn't feel like there was an entire room where something could jump out.

I set my candle down, reattaching my hammock to the hooks from the ceiling. Beds unnerved me with their comfort. It felt too large for a single person to ever need that much space. It also made it easier to not be sleeping with my wife anymore. Pulling someone out of a hammock was as likely to get you stuck before you could get someone out of one.

I doused the candle and slept with my gear and clothes on. I peered through my doorway, searching the darkness for something. Once I was satisfied that nothing was coming to eat or scare me during the middle of the night, I felt myself drop off into a deep sleep. I think I dreamed of my wife for the first time in years. She kept smiling and repeating "It's your fault," over and over.

I awoke feeling like the closest thing to a zombie that a man could be. My back ached in places I didn't know existed and my body shook like I was standing in the middle of a blizzard. My mother used to have an expression that said when people got cold it was because someone was walking over their grave. I hoped not; a grave had never seemed like a good resting place for me.

I had a few nightmares about what would happen if I ever turned into a ghost; *would I be cursed to wander around as a memory-less husk for eternity, since no one else would be left to burn the bones?* That thought did make me shiver like someone had walked over my grave. I shook it away and started my morning routine.

I started checking my body for bruises. I did this every morning. I found after a few times of sleeping out in the open, that the ghosts liked to hit me during the night. Sometimes, I would be so beaten and scared when I awoke, I would find bruises that matched the size of my own hand. How they found their way in was anyone's guess. If they had come in, I'd assume they would have finally taken me. Maybe I was imagining it all as I searched myself. Holly never said anything either—*I was just getting old,* I thought.

This morning, I was in luck. No bruises that I couldn't write off to yesterday's misadventures. "Oh, joy…" I mumbled. All I had on my mind was to have a pack of American Spirits and some coffee.

Thankfully, one of those needs could be answered. I went to the makeshift kitchen area, which was little more than a heavy iron chest laden with cans of food that I had been collecting over the years. I cracked open a can of beans using a wedge that I had fastened to the side of the chest.

While I ate my beans, I flicked the switch on my battery backup cluster. I had enough energy for up to eight years if I used them all in succession. I had found a nice hardware store loaded with computer parts a couple of years ago, that would have given me a nerd orgasm in another life. I reached into the trunk and fished out powdered packets of coffee, which I had taken from packs of MRE's from a military store in town.

Powdered coffee is an abominable disappointment, but beggars can't be choosers. Rats seemed to enjoy coffee, and I was lucky to have the powder. I poured the contents into the burning pot and set it on the hot plate connected to the battery backup. I tilted the last of the beans down my mouth and spilled some on my already ruined shirt. I thought about changing it—however, changing shirts, especially buttons, was more trouble than it was worth with one hand. While the kettle boiled, I stretched out my body. I was never into going to the gym and getting into shape like my wife was.

I did quickly learn, as the years progressed, the error in my ways, which had become clearer, so I started doing my morning yoga. It was the only exercise done quickly, and with zero harm to my already-battered body.

I yawned and completed my stretches just as my coffee was finishing. I poured the contents into my Darth Vader cup—Holly didn't have to insist for this one. She insisted on a lot as I snorted at the memory. The black coffee quickly hit the spot, starting my motors on the inside. Before everything went down the shitter, I couldn't start my mornings without a cup of coffee of some kind. If the ghosts ever wanted to get me, they only had to find a way to poison my coffee supply; that would do the trick.

I finished my drink and started lighting candles. It was impossible to tell the time of day from inside the house, as every section of window was covered in a metal of some kind. My last mundane activity on most mornings was getting Holly up, as she didn't sleep anymore, but sometimes I would wake and she would be just gone. I don't know how else to describe it; her eyes would be rolled into the back of her head and sometimes objects would be floating around. I would later ask her if she remembered any of this; she would tell me no. I believed her; I think it was her way of dreaming as a ghost.

I was apprehensive to find her this morning. I slung my iron pan in my hand, readying for what I feared the most. I had never talked a ghost back from losing them. Then again, I had only done it once—with Diana. I still had nightmares of that day. I walked into Holly's room slowly, like a cat burglar.

I came to her doorway and pushed the door open gently. Holly's room was covered in movie posters that we had taken from a local store. She also had a bed and two cabinets. She said it made her feel normal if there was something in the room other than just empty space.

I didn't see her when I came into the room; hers was the only place in the bunker that had any light shining in it, from the strips of Christmas lights lining the ceiling. *Twenty years later and she is still afraid of the dark, only I don't blame her for that fear.* I felt my heart rate increase and my hold on the pan tighten.

"Boo," sneered Holly from behind me, I snapped into a roll and swung my pan, almost taking Holly's head off with it. She was expecting it and faded back with only inches to spare. "Fuck, Jim, you almost took my head off there, you jumpy old goat!" she shouted at me.

"Holly! What the hell is wrong with you! And for the last time, language!" I shouted back while breathing hard. Holly was laughing at my expense, and gesturing with both her hands in the air.

She stopped laughing and her eyes grew very serious. "You can relax... I'm still me. Very much pissed off at you still. Just think of me as the ghost version of premenstrual syndrome right now," she informed, with her twisted smile at the end.

"Wait, that's a thing?" I asked, genuinely perplexed by this. She had never mentioned it in all these years.

"No, Jim, it's called being coy or a smart ass, if that's easier for you. Relax, old man; you don't have to have the birds and the bees with your ghost daughter," she stated matter-of-factly.

"So, do you need to have the 'talk', Holly-biz?" I asked.

"Jim, you're a moron. Did I hit you too hard last night?"

We both laughed at that, it felt good to feel a laugh from me and to see her happy. I didn't think I would ever smile like that again. I didn't think she would ever smile like that again.

She turned and started to float away, Holly cocked her head back to me. "Jim, can you look nice—nice for today, please?"

"Sure, Holly, I will put on my nice flannel," I said, turning and going back to my room. As I rummaged through my gear, I realized I had nothing in the way of nice clothing that wasn't torn or patched to shreds.

I settled on a mostly clean shirt—it smelled that way at least. *Holly wants you to look nice, old man; do something about it. Then again, she wants me nice because this means goodbye.* I considered the only mirror I had in my house. I kept it for hard-to-see stitches, otherwise I made it a point not to keep mirrors around. Mirrors have a way of playing tricks on you. I rarely used it.

It's amazing just how much your body can change without you realizing it; I had become an old man. It seemed like it must have been overnight. Long gone was any extra fat on my body. Now I was a hollow version of that much younger man so long ago.

I reached into the dresser drawer. I placed the mirror on the dresser and fished for my cutting scissors. I began trimming my beard; twenty years of growth with no maintenance had left a curly mess. I quickly finished and managed to leave a decent dent in the jungle on my face. I could finally see more than just my eyes.

I took a moment to breathe in deep… once and then twice more. *Listen, man, sometimes doing what is right isn't supposed to feel good. Yeah, right,* I thought, turning around and walking out of my room. *Doing what is right is never easy.*

"Holly, I am going to be out in the Beast!" I yelled as I opened a small peephole on my house door. I scanned the surrounding area and tried to stretch out my senses the best I could in all directions. Human beings are naturally born with our own survival instincts, no matter how pampered and civilized we think that we have become. We can never truly shake that animal inclination of checking for predators. I didn't sense anything after another minute of looking. I popped the peep-hole cover back on and opened the door. The sun was rising on the horizon and I could see the wetness on the earth around me.

North Carolina is a cold place during the winters, and the bitterness of the surrounding landscape made the coldness that much harsher. It made me glad that I only cared for myself. It was hard enough keeping just one of us warm, let alone two of us.

I walked down the path leading to the Beast. I inspected every inch of the car while I waited for Holly. The time alone allowed my brain to wonder, I wondered how that girl Anna must have gotten into the Beast. I looked at the doors and realized it was probably when I had left them open. I would have to remember to check the back seat the next time we took the Beast out. *Though what had she been doing in the first place? Her memories showed her following us for some reason.* It wasn't uncommon for ghosts to follow us, but it felt like she'd been following us for a purpose. That concerned me—losing Holly concerned me more, and I shook the idea away.

After a few more minutes, I became satisfied with the safety of the

Beast. I checked it again, just to be sure. The sun continued to rise, and I scanned the houses surrounding my home. I had long since set up dummy traps for the ghosts that happened to make it past all the iron lines.

I found out playing music or having human interactions would attract ghosts like a honey pot. I had set up an old record player, rigged to go off at a certain time. I think it was the idea of something from their old life that attracted them to the sounds. Keep everything sniffing around, but completely lost. That's how I had stayed safe for all these years. Though having a pan had helped with that as well.

It was one of the reasons why I worried about Holly's books on tapes, though. I thought a couple of days of my long silences would probably drive her crazy. I didn't blame her for wanting to escape that.

I started tapping my fingers impatiently on the hood of the Beast; I never understood why she took so long. It had to be just to annoy me; I turned around, looking back, to see Holly appear from her hole at the top of the house. She had made herself grown up again; I couldn't help but stare at her with incredulity. In a way, it made me proud to see just how much she looked like her mother. *Diana, if you could have only been around to see how our daughter looks...* I cut the thought off as the feeling of regret began to flood my mind. Regret is a weakness worse than fear; it served nothing in the way of survival. Holly had made her hair match her mom's; however, it was red in color like my own, minus all the gray. Both of us shining red-headed beings in the light of the morning.

I looked at her. "Ready for this?"

"Yes Jimmy, let's hit the road. How... do... I... look to you?" She asked as I opened her door for her.

"Just like your mother."

Chapter 30

We sped along the old parts of the city, heading back to where our previous home was in another life. I tended to avoid this part of the city and Holly could tell. I had to backtrack several times around the decaying rusted jungle that had overtaken the land.

It was hard to tell anymore where the wilderness began and the city ended. It was a color palate of gray, deep browns, and lush greens that left me often breathless, unable to fathom what I was seeing. Nature had won in the end, despite all our attempts. Humans were dying off faster than everything else. That made me scared; *loneliness is hell, I don't want to be alone.* Being alone meant I would end up like one of these buildings, just broken-down rubble standing in the middle of growing trees.

It scared me knowing that there was a very distinctive possibility that I was one of the last men on Earth, and how much I did not want that responsibility, that privilege of upholding what it meant to be human. As of right now, I had not done a banged-up job in the human category. Maybe I could settle for being a good father as I looked at Holly. She was admiring the outside world, aloft from my very existence, right next to me. She and I could never exist in the same world, not in the sense as the old days—yet she was there now.

I existed for her sake now; I realized that as I continued my drive through the overgrowth. *If today is going to be my last day with Holly—I am going to make it the best I can for her.*

As we made our way deeper into the city, the path came back like the words to a long-lost song, the pieces falling into place and instinct taking over; I no longer felt lost.

The buildings in this area of town were mostly crumbling brick and mortar at this point. Several times we had to stop and take a different path, due to trees bending into the roads, or collapsed buildings. I imagined now the shocks that must have traveled through the earth whenever one of the buildings came down. Like Atlas dropping the world, enough weight that it would send dry thunder through the dirt without the storm.

We ended up stopping for a break about an hour into our journey; I started to have a hard time planning the way around the forest which had taken over the road. I had Holly stay in the Beast as a lookout (also to keep her safe); I didn't see any ghosts. *They're phantoms, though; when you think you are alone, expect to find them right behind you. No more risks, James,* I thought.

The city started to make me uncomfortable in the high humidity. It isn't uncommon for North Carolina to be cold in the mornings and then hot enough by noon to drink the air.

I wiped my brow, looking for the ghosts, looking for anything other than Holly and me. The feeling of being watched was weighing heavy in my mind. I knew someone was following us, I just couldn't see where. Or rather, I had the feeling; normally that feeling was right. It was probably just ghosts—only they never followed more than a few miles, and then they would normally lose interest.

"Jim, is everything okay?" Holly asked with concern in her voice.

I looked around once more at the buildings around us and then responded to Holly. "I'm fine… it's just I feel like… it's nothing. Let's get going."

I got back in the Beast, keeping an eye on the gauges; we had used up a lot of fuel on this adventure. I still had a full gas jug in the back; I would have to go scavenging for more soon. I did the math; unless I started scavenging more than a few hours out of the city, I was going to run out of fuel in about four years at my current consumption.

I had never gone more than three hours out of my city in any direction since everything changed. This city was a tomb of so much pain for me, but it was still my home. *Home is always a place that will stay with you. Calling back to you silently in the back of your mind. Maybe after Holly left, I would leave the city. Yes, I think—after her, it's time to leave this rotten place,* I thought.

We started again, and I took my time navigating around the trees. "Still no animals even out here…" Holly mumbled from her post at the window.

"Yep," was all I could say. It bothered me even more than before. *How far was this reaching?*

As I started to follow that thought path, Holly shouted, "Jim, look out!"

I looked up and crossing the road was a huge black bear with one small cub. Holly and I watched as the bear looked at us, sniffing the air for a treat. Satisfied, the bear went back into its forest. Despite bears being found only in the woods of the Appalachian to my knowledge, one was out here in the outskirts of our city. I had never seen one before. Holly and I both smiled at each other after seeing the bear. It was a first for us both. Finally, my mind relaxed on the animal fear. No more worried by us than it would be a deer in the woods.

We had found our first animal in who knows how long—we weren't alone. Something else was out here making it, I traced the outline of the bear for as far as I could before the dense overgrowth obscured the view of the momma and its young cub.

"She was beautiful, don't you think, Holly?" I asked, and turned to see her crying into her hands.

"Yes—yes she was. She is making it out here with her little one, despite all of it. God, I hope they will be okay." Holly's voice cracked, and she continued to cry into her hands. I knew that I couldn't wipe my daughter's tears; I couldn't hold her. So, I just struggled for the right words like always.

"She is a parent; no real parent would ever let something happen to their kids." I stated, putting the car back in drive and going down a road that I didn't want to go down anymore. I did not want to lose my own cub; I could not lose my own cub.

Holly's face stayed in her hands for a little while until she looked up, sniffling into the air. No signs of tears on my seat, no indication other than sight that a young girl was suffering next to her fool of an old man.

I swallowed that pill; *it's too late for regrets now. You made a promise, old man; do right by her.* I avoided my own gaze as I checked my mirrors; I wished that I had sunglasses. Our path along the road ended up back-tracking us onto the highway until finally, we passed the old Wells Fargo bank, which felt eerily familiar. It was like I had been there before, like some old memory of a moment reaching across time and space to tell me something. Most of my early days meeting the ghosts now seemed hazy, like trying to peer through a dirty mirror. An image was being shown, but the dirt was too thick, too dusty to show me what was worrying me. I ignored that feeling; more important things were happening.

We were getting closer, I thought, keeping my mind back on task. A long silence stretched between Holly and me again. After a time, any attempt at conversation seemed pointless. Instead, I focused on my driving, when Holly spoke up again. "Do you ever think about things that you miss from before all of this?" She asked as I turned, avoiding a ruined section of a road from what looked like a fast food restaurant pole.

"I miss people more than I actually miss things..."

"Hah—no, Jim, I knew that you would say something along those lines. Let's take a step back and smell the roses for a second—everyone misses something." She leaned back in her chair for the first time since we had started the trip. I turned and looked at her, amazed once more at how she could remain in the actual vehicle while we were driving. That was something I had always wanted to ask her. *This may be the only chance you get, old man,* I thought.

Aloud, I said, "What if I tell you something I miss, if you tell me something I've always wondered about? Deal?"

Holly seemed to chew it over. Her face went curt, then back to normal. "You got yourself a deal, old man. Tell me your thing."

I sighed and scanned the surrounding roads. *It's nice to have a simplistic conversation; she isn't gone completely yet.* I dared to think, I dared to dream. "I would have to say, out of everything I miss from before, and believe me on this, I've had a lot of time to think about it: A Wendy's Frosty," I stated, scanning skyward the best I could out of the Beast.

"Wait, out of everything you could have picked, you picked a Frosty?" Holly laughed, the skepticism evident in her voice.

"Oh yes. It's something I actually had a lot of, back in the day. Back when I had a lot of time on my hands and more meat to spare," I said jokingly.

"I thought you said you were a computer guy before all of this..."

"Yes, I was. Still am, in a way."

"But I figured you would mention that game of yours. You know, about that man going around trying to spread world peace or some shit by slaying magical dragons."

I frowned. "Since you look like an adult today, I'm going to give you a one-time pass on your language. On that note though, no, my game was about trying to solve a mystery with dragons; one of the byproducts of that game was finding peace in the world. Or that was how it was supposed to end, I think. I never got to finish it; work got too busy, I had to provide for my fam..."

I stopped myself before "family," not wanting to cause any uneasy feelings to come to the surface, now that I had her talking again. If my word had caused her any problems, I couldn't tell. Holly could win a poker tournament with her expressions.

"Anyways though, no, the game was always more of a hobby that I ended up quitting—kind of like your snoring," I teased.

"Oh, I don't want to hear it, how many times have you woken yourself up on that piss -smelling hammock from your own breathing at night?" Holly snorted and did her best impression of me.

"That reminds me. Since I answered your question, care to answer one of mine?"

"I suppose that—that would be the correct nomenclature in this conversation." Holly sighed, being dramatic, "Ask away if you must, curious George," she said, flicking her flame red hair.

"This actually is going to be two questions. Before you freak out on me about how that's cheating, I will explain more about the Frosty."

"Okay." Holly agreed to my request, so I went on. "What did you do at nights while I slept? Surely you couldn't listen to books on tapes all those hours."

Holly sucked in a big gulp of breath, or rather, imitated the motion of breathing in. "A lot of time. I was actually watching you, Jim," Holly admitted, staring out the window. I wasn't expecting that one, and I felt a little bit of a shiver run up my spine. She may have been the ghost of my daughter, but she was still a ghost. A lot about her I would just never understand.

"So—why were you watching me?" I asked after a moment.

"Well, some nights you would scream, or rather, most nights you did scream. I guess... I don't know, I was always worried that whatever nightmares you have would get to you. The first couple of times it happened, I thought it was one of the bad ones attacking you. I found myself going out a lot to check around the house to see if anything came in."

Holly's words caused me to blush, I never knew that she did that. I had always assumed that my anguish was kept in check while I slept. I suppose it made sense, considering how I was during the day.

"Thank you for telling me that. I may never be able to sleep again," I gulped, making my eyes go wide.

"Shut up," Holly said, touching my arm, causing a shock of cold on the section of my skin. I gritted my teeth, not wanting to ruin the moment.

I quickly changed the subject. "So, here is a question I am surprised that it took me twenty years to ask. How are you able to stay in the Beast right now?"

Holly looked at me and laughed. "You know, I am surprised as well. I figured you pieced that together a while ago. It is easy. I attach myself to a memory that is in the car. All around us, everything has a memory of some kind imprinted on it. Whether it is alive or not, everything has a story. What I have to do, is just hold on to whatever that memory is and make it a part of me. For example, while we are sitting here, I can sense from the memories of the car all the times that you've sat in the passenger seat. I always assumed it was your wife's car since the memories were always you in this spot. So, I think of you sitting here. It's like I become grounded. I don't know how else to explain it."

I blinked. That information astounded and utterly flabbergasted me without any kind of response. "Wow, I had no idea that much went into it. That is very impressive, dear." I meant it; Holly's gifts always amazed me, and I had never seen another ghost riding in a car like that. Well, that Anna girl had managed the same feat, so she must have done something similar. *I wonder if there is a way to prevent memories then? I could keep the ghosts away forever if they couldn't connect.* I let that thought trail off, I was with Holly, not a good time to be planning for war. I continued my previous thoughts—Holly is truly amazing, I thought, as we pulled down the street that leads to our home so many years ago.

My stomach dropped. I knew it was going to happen. I just had hoped that the road would take just a little bit longer. I instinctively slowed the car as we passed huge mounds of building and forest. It was hard to tell buildings anymore. I knew which building was my home—home is home. I could never forget. My mind reconstructed what the area looked like twenty years ago. It had once been so full of life.

I saw all the neighboring buildings and amenities that had lined the streets. Once, this neighborhood was on the high-end of society to live, and now it was gone and replaced by the new world order: Mother Earth. Or maybe it was always just going back to the way it is now, back to the living. The dead can't rule over the Earth. Only the living, only the wild.

Twenty years had done nothing to deter the memory of where our building had been located. In fact, it was still standing mostly intact. I parked the Beast in front of our high-rise duplex.

It had been twenty years since I had last seen this building. Twenty years since I had last witnessed anything that resembled this much of my old life. Holly was mistaken earlier when she said I visited here often. I hadn't; I'd just dreamed of doing so. Each time, I would pull up outside my old home and just stop. Now I was living my nightmare, having to go into that old building. It's amazing the false memories we can twist with fear; something intangible can become a nightmare that never leaves us if given enough fuel.

It took too much effort to turn my head to Holly. she had been talking and I had ignored her. "Huh, sorry Holly…" I responded as Holly looked at me, her brow turned down in the signature look of her father.

"This is the place, isn't it?" Holly spoke, her voice becoming strained.

"Yes, Holly. Here is where I left you."

Chapter 31

We made our way up to the duplex; I stepped through the thick brush obscuring the way. I did not bring any of my primary weapons with me. I had serious doubts that any ghosts would be in the area (they tended not to be in areas without people). Then again, I avoided areas with people and still ran into the ghosts all the time. Yet another mystery I couldn't solve.

We moved slowly, and all the while, neither of us spoke. Each step made my heart pound in my chest. Every step became a mountain that I wouldn't and couldn't climb. It was the most nerve-racking moment of my life. I now understood what it was like to be a prison inmate on death row. You're going to your doom with every step, there's nothing that can be done except to go forward. Despite all my regrets, despite my pleas, I had to go forward. I had no choice, and I had made a promise—and I would keep this one. I kept repeating "For Holly," over and over as I made slow and deliberate steps into the apartment doorway.

The glass doors had long since shattered. The main lobby was grown thick with grass and small bushes. All around were the remains of the hallway walls, mixed in with the evidence of animals that had used the main building area.

I thought about how the animals weren't much different from the animal that had once lived there as well. Living in its walls, but ultimately never to be a part of it.

"Jim... I honestly don't remember this place." Holly had stopped following me and was looking at the molded remains of a building structure piece. I looked at the beam and wondered how much more the supports could take before it all came crashing down one day.

I answered Holly, though, trying to put myself more at ease than her. "Well, to be fair, a lot has changed in this building since I—I mean since we lived here."

Holly turned to me, her face asking "How so?"

"When you were a little girl, you used to love coming down here and annoying the floor security guard. His name was Chris, I think, and every day your mother and I would find you down here talking to Chris about different animals."

Holly laughed and brightened up at that statement, "That sounds good enough to be true," she stated, floating to where Chris the security guard used to sit. His table was only there in lumber and raw materials, an ashy brown that had seen too many years, before becoming dirt.

I smiled and said, "That one was true. Come on Holly. We have a couple of flights of stairs to take."

I turned and walked towards the stairwell to the left of us, pushing open the doors. The staircases appeared to be sturdy enough for me to make my way up them. Inside, the building was dark, and looking above made me feel like I was looking into the mouth of an ancient monster from Greek mythology. The darkness was absolute in its concealment, my imagination the only thing allowing me to see.

I fished out the flashlight from inside my jacket pocket and flicked the 'on' button. A small stream of light came up as I made my way up the familiar staircase.

Our journey was quicker than I thought it would be. Once or twice, I had to test a step before I was willing to put weight on it. That was the worst of it. No ghost had shown itself the whole time.

I did get the feeling of being watched again. That caused me to look down to check my progress on a couple of occasions. Each time, Holly would give me a questioning look. We had cleared out plenty of buildings before, so we knew each other's tells for danger.

I shook my shoulders as if to say nothing. I couldn't figure out what it was anyways. *Just a feeling, no need to get Holly alarmed.*

She must have sensed my uneasiness from something; she began to fade out to go invisible. Holly only did that if something might be in the area, so I spoke to calm her down, "Relax, Holly. I don't think it's anything. Stay with me; no need to split up on this one."

"Are you sure, Jim?" she whispered from somewhere nearby me.

I fought my body's natural reaction to freak at the disembodied voice. "Yes, it's nothing... just my nerves. Might have drunk too much coffee is all."

"Hmm, okay," Holly said, skeptically reappearing.

I took a few steps, and my legs began to shake. I was afraid, I realized. I felt that whatever was following us was getting near. Holly still hadn't taken notice of it, or else she didn't want to let me know.

I had to try and get a better read on our would-be follower; I suggested that we take a break. *It could be nothing,* I thought, shivering in the darkness. I just had a feeling, as I glanced below us, that something was in the darkness with us. I sat down, Holly agreed, and there on the stairwell, I took the time to start eating.

Food was always hard to come by, and it made me thankful that only one of us needed to eat as I took a can from out of my pack. The label had long since worn off the can, and it prevented me from telling exactly what food I would be consuming. I cracked open the can, using the rail on the staircase, and I tilted back the contents. It was a comforting and soothing taste of old pears. I wiped the excess juice running down the side of my face.

I looked at Holly as she floated, wondering if she had any inkling of the situation beyond just finding her body. I sighed. *Holly is a smart girl; after all, she takes after me. She is quick-witted enough to figure it all out. Holly is just ready to go, I understand that, but every step I take is one closer to saying goodbye to my child, and no parent should ever have to say goodbye to their children, especially twice.*

I left the pear can on the stairwell. No use in carrying it anymore. As we made our way up the stairs, I thought about my plan after Holly. I suppose I could finally finish off that bottle of whiskey I kept in the house. I drank a lot these days, but I'd managed to save the good stuff.

Maybe if I got lucky, something would take me in my sleep. It was a sobering thought that I could face easier than the loneliness already creeping into me. *Yes, I could face that quite quickly.*

My eyes stayed fixed on the ground as we walked. All the while, I remarked on how these stairs used to signal the end of a day of work and my return to my family. *Now, what do they mean? What does it mean anymore when so much has changed? I am now truly removed from anything that I could ever understand.* I felt my face blushing and wondered if I might be crying. If I was, I hoped she didn't see it. I had done this to myself; *I must be a real father,* I repeated.

"Jim, so you never did answer from earlier why you think a Frosty is the greatest achievement of mankind," Holly said, appearing before me, as I almost ran into her in the suddenness.

"Oh, well for various reasons, kiddo," I mumbled in response, wiping my eyes and hoping that Holly discounted it as sweat.

Holly smiled and shrugged her shoulders as if to say "Go on." So I told her my absorbed, yet what I still felt were logically sound, opinions. It helped pass the time, and I was able to get quite a few laughs out of her as we navigated the corridors of the apartment building.

Before I knew it, I looked up, and we were at our old home. It had been so many years since I had been to this place. And as I looked towards the door, the cold hand of the devil consumed me. Reality had set in, and the repercussions of my life were coming to fruition.

Holly stopped laughing long enough to notice that I had stopped. Her smile gave way to confusion, and then confusion gave way to understanding. We were here; we had come to the final resting place of Molly.

Chapter 32

I stood before the door, awkwardly staring at the wooden frame, now nearly rotted away, leading to my old life. I wasn't sure how long I stood there; I was lost in all the times I had spent in my life coming and going out of this passage. I think a part of me was more worried about not returning out of that door, rather than what I was going to fine on the inside. As I looked, carving daggers into the wood with my eyes, Holly coughed.

I turned and smiled at her, seeing a look of nonchalance on her face. Holly was calm as a rock, unlike her old man as of late. I took a deep breath and opened the door, knowing that I would not fear what was behind any door.

The door was unlocked, like I had left it many years before. I remembered when I had finally gained consciousness; it had been like waking into a dream. Every shape of my home had become mountains of wood, simple debris, and photographs that littered the floor appeared like Egyptian hieroglyphs. I was neither able to translate them, nor pull any meaning to connect why I was seeing them.

My stub of a hand was raw and festering with charred black skin. I risked smelling my missing hand; it smelled like burnt pork. It had never got infected from what I could tell (I had never gotten its smell out of my mind). And sometimes, like now, when I looked at my stub, I still saw the charred skin. Though now it was simply scar tissue, you never forget some images. I felt myself gag, and my stomach emptied onto the floor.

I wiped the saliva from my mouth, standing straight at the same time. I was able to see more clearly now, if not a little shaken from the amount of liquid leaving my body faster than I was putting it back. I ran my fingers through my hair, a gesture I always did whenever my nerves were getting the best of me.

I didn't know how to take my apartment in; the flames had somehow been put out, though the kitchen was now a pile of ash and steel. The light was shining into my duplex; I had no idea what time it was or how long I had lain on the floor. All I knew was my hand hurt, and I had thirst and a deep hunger, quickly overriding any other sensation. If I were going to keep on going, I would have to leave the duplex. There was no way of knowing what chemicals might be festering, now that I had set half of my home on fire.

Still, as I surveyed my kitchen, I couldn't believe how the fire had gone out. It was like it had suddenly stopped where I had been lying only moments before. I brushed down my body with my good hand, checking for any burns. I was covered in a black tar from the smoke.

I was burn free, meaning not even a loss of any hairs from the heat of the fire; I couldn't fathom how that was even possible. I should have vanished into the flames of my apartment, which had somewhat been the plan when I had started the fire.

I tried thinking back to that night, my mind filled with the images of my wife racked in pain, chasing after me, and the horror I felt taking my hand. All I could feel was a numbing awareness that was unable to free me from my reality—that everything had burned away, yet here I was alive.

I turned away and walked from my kitchen, finding my pan at the bottom of the stairs, its iron edges covered in the gore from my limb. I sniffled back, another vomit wave spilled, and I tucked the skillet under my left arm. I looked around my apartment, the closest thing I would ever get to seeing a war zone.

When I had been a younger man and video games had been an everyday hobby for me, a scene like this would have come off meritable, almost. It would have painted the perfect picture of pain and war. The irony to me was not lost; a few years ago, I would have enjoyed the state of my duplex.

I wiped my face once more, knowing that I could not stay in my apartment anymore. I had no idea what was beyond those doors. I shook as if I was standing in a cold breeze. However, in a way I was—I was standing in the most biting wind of fear, and there was no way to go but forward.

I didn't take anything with me as I let my body go forward, searching for nourishment, reacting from total muscle memory as I tried to block out the pain. As I stepped on glass, shattering the heated rock beneath me, I saw a photo of the day Diana, me, and Molly had gone to the park.

Our were faces lit up in bliss from a beautiful day that my wife said we would always remember. It was always a treasure and allowed us a euphoretic escape whenever things got too dark. With tears, I bent over and snatched the photo, folding it into the pocket of my pants. I knew if I stopped to examine it more, that apartment would have become a tomb for me. Instead, I had left my home that day, leaving my memories in a dungeon buried in drywall and flame. I had eaten my hand, I had suffered the loss of my family, and I left my home that day and never returned.

Those memories faded, and I was back to standing in the doorway of my old home with Holly floating nearby.

Thinking back to that didn't make me weak like I had expected it would. I was only numb and for the first time in a long time, more concerned with the here and now of the moment. I had finally opened the tomb of memories of my life. I cleared my throat and turned to Holly. "Well, Holly bear, this is our home. What do you think?"

Holly floated past me, avoiding the rotten and degraded wood, and the mounds of mold and flora that had taken over our previous home; completely bypassing the whole section of our living room that had collapsed through to the floor below from the water damage.

I closed the door and skidded my way around the hole and tested my foot on what I hoped was sure wood. The structure creaked and groaned under the weight of my steps. The construction proved genuine and held me—and my beating heart—surprisingly.

Holly floated to the staircase and stopped. She paused with an eerily stillness that only a ghost could perform. It was complete motionlessness that no human could ever replicate, because we had to breathe. She stayed that way for a while as I watched her; I wondered if she was reconstructing how the house used to look. I wondered if she was rebuilding the textures and the years of happy memories that had once lived in the frames on the walls, now lying rotten on the ground.

After a short amount of time, I cleared my throat loudly to catch her attention. "Holly—"

"I'm fine, Jim, I'm... fine. This house is just... all a little bit too surreal, and believe me, I feel like that's an understatement, considering we fought against a monster made of petrified meat."

I smirked at her comment, thankful that at least one of us was having some sense of humor. That was the trick—to survive any horror in this life was to smile, let that be your weapon in the darkness.

I made my way to her at the bottom of the staircase and sat upon the bottom step. I felt myself sink into the wood—I was pretty sure it could hold the skeleton amount of weight that I had left in my body.

"Well, Holly, strange things are always abundant, truth be told. I am surprised that you honestly are surprised by any of this. This has been our life for the last twenty years."

"It's not that I am surprised by this Jim, just trying to take it all in. So, this—this was our home..."

I looked around the apartment and watched how the light seemed to make the wet wooden floors look like comforting mud on a dense and wet jungle floor. “Yeah, Holly, this was our home a really long time ago.” I stood up and stretched my arms out and letting loose a long yawn. “It belonged to the three of us, it…” I let my sentence trail away, before my voice cracked.

I changed the subject. “Well, come on lazy bones, let’s go see your room.” I walked away, overstepping the piles of my former life. Holly followed behind me; when I turned around, a small smile crept into her lips. I couldn’t help seeing her mother in that instant. That was loud enough for me to keep moving through it all, to galvanize me into action. We made it to her bedroom, where I opened the door and was amazed at how well the room had managed to stay somewhat the same.

The shattered glass had let in plenty of animals over the years, judging from the torn sheets that were on her bed, and the ceiling was starting to cave in over her dresser.

Her fish bowl had cracked from something, and as we stepped into Molly’s old room, I made sure to plant my feet over the blood that had stained her floor. Holly floated past me and moved towards her closet first. I saw her eyes tracing the chips of purple that had long since held color on her closet doors. She was taking it all in, seeing her life before she was forever transformed into an eight-year-old girl.

“Did I really like purple this much?” Holly asked, looking towards me as I drifted into the room more.

I smiled and responded, “Actually no, you were starting to grow out of it about that time, but it sure beats a lot of the hair colors I’ve seen you pick since then.”

Holly turned to me, smiling. “You do pay attention to my hair, huh?” she said.

“Only when it’s appalling, which is every day.”

I caught her sticking her tongue out at me as she continued her search through Molly’s old room.

I couldn’t quite finish my statement without feeling a sickness deep inside me. I looked at Holly, seeing the wonder and fear in her eyes. I didn't want to see fear in her eyes if I could have ever helped it. I sighed and continued. "About that time the ghosts first came, you started getting into darker colors and wanting to be a professional football player. Honestly, your mother hated it. For the record, I still think you could have made a hell of a running back, kiddo," I admitted, turning my back to Holly and walking out of the room. I called back, "Take your time and look around for a bit, Holly. I am going to check upstairs."

I left Holly alone in her room, hoping that her experience back in her old room would just be a positive reminiscence about her old self. It wasn't my place to be there with her during her experience. When I got to the staircase, I pulled out a battery from my pocket. I felt a small shock when I waved the cell in the direction of Holly. Otherwise, the house wasn't giving off any shocks in any direction as I moved the battery around me. From what I could tell, the house was safe, but it still didn't help me breathe any easier. It did give me the courage and steadiness to move towards the upstairs. I approached the rotten stairs, taking one step at a time, out of fear and out of caution; the steps had seen better days.

At the top, my memories took over. The ones buried deep within, the ones that I had kept locked away like the riches of treasures at the center of the Earth. Only I had never planned to ever open this treasure chest. My head became filled with the sights and sounds of Holly and me playing on the railings; the many times that I took Diana in my arms when I came home early.

I walked to my bedroom, taking the doorway slowly, as I remembered the fat lady that had come crashing in so many years ago. She had once been a boss, and now she was a cautionary reminder. The room was empty, save for the remains of a filthy bed. The sheets were surprisingly preserved, in place after the last night that Diana had slept in them. Still turned down from our frantic explosion.

I felt a rage burn its way into me at the sight of the sheets.

Something about seeing them again, knowing that I could not do anything to change that day, despite how much I had learned was burning its way into me. I tore the soaked and molded sheets to the ground.

My anger did not let me stop there; no, I was just getting started as I flipped the bed, using my right arm to prop the bed up as I got low. I took my pan and begun smashing the dressers and closet pieces into chunks of offensive boards. My breath came in waves as I tore into the wall, repeatedly breaking with everything that I had.

I was making so much noise that Holly snuck up on me. She came to the doorway, calling out my name. I was only feeling a numbness that was fueling the rage from within. Never-ending, never ceasing fury. I swung once more, smashing the pan into the old nightstand next to our bed. It gave a satisfying squash as the iron skillet buried itself flat on the side of the old wood.

I was breathing hard; my hand covered in blood from my knuckles. My crusade against my former bed was complete. I immediately felt remorse for what I'd done, while scanning the broken timber beneath my feet. *Try as you might in life, you just can't beat the things you did wrong with force. It took something else to overcome some sins.*

Holly was behind me, I knew she was, but I just couldn't turn around and face her yet. I couldn't look her in the eyes just yet. Everything had become too twisted and a fabricated piece of personal hell. I stomached what was left of my pride, if that was the word for it. I had no more words for a broken man. I was as far from anything that could be right as a tree is to flying in the sky.

I tilted my head towards Holly and walked past her, not meeting her gaze. Once I was nearing the end of my long hallway, I turned back towards Holly and spoke. "Your body is downstairs…" My voice choked in my throat as I continued. "If it matters to you at this point, Holly, I did it because I love you." Holly stared at me, unblinking and seeming a lot further than a foot away.

I left the room, headed down. At the bottom of the stairs, I combed my way through our kitchen towards the old freezer.

In twenty years, I had meticulously organized and utilized every aspect of my environment. I had left nothing that could be used, with the rare exception of the times I had been chased. I scavenged everything, from keys to dog food. In my old home though, I hadn't taken anything except a pan—and some ragged clothes.

I had left behind more than one body that day. I came upon the freezer, observing the layers of dust that had gathered. Placing my hand on the freezer handle, I lifted the lid, freeing the contents within. I hadn't anticipated the twenty years of trapped, decomposing tissue imprisoned inside a metal tomb.

The smell was atrocious, very nearly bringing me to my knees. I placed my hand over my mouth and nose to keep from sneezing as I searched the freezer for Molly. My little girl's skull floated, fragmented in the murky ice water below.

Even though I had placed her in the freezer, it still felt wrong disturbing her final resting place, I thought, as I stepped away to let Holly float up to the freezer. *Maybe I should have visited; I should have left more flowers.*

I couldn't see Holly's face as she looked over the fridge. She could have quickly moved through the metal. Now that I realized just how powerful she was, she scared me.

Holly gave her former body the respect that she deserved, not disturbing the remains of a poor little girl killed in a violent way; a girl destroyed by her father's failings. Then Holly did something that surprised me; she has always been devoted to doing the unexpected. She stepped from the freezer and went to the balcony's massive burned-away hole that was inside our former kitchen.

She was gazing out at the city, the light flickering on her long red locks. "Jim—James, I mean. Now do you know why I picked this color for my hair today?"

The question found me clueless and taken off balance. "No Holly, I have no idea why you picked red." I wasn't sure where she was going with her color; all my mind could comprehend was the impending doom awaiting me.

She blew out a breath and clicked her tongue before answering; it was a trait that her mother did a lot, now that I thought about it. Holly spoke, "I picked red because red is the hair color of my father, the hair color of a man who fathered a girl named Molly. That girl is not me, James; I don't know if you always wanted me to replace her or whatever. I just can't be her anymore, James, and I can't be some anchor that exists just so you can torment yourself about the past any more. I just can't..." Holly sobbed, placing her hands over her eyes.

My mouth was full of pain, and my feet remained glued in place. I opened my mouth again after shutting it many times to speak. I couldn't, though; it was true I had been using Holly for many years, so that I wouldn't have to be alone to bear the harshness of this life by myself. It was more than that—I had kept her around, inflicting wounds. I had treated Holly as an open sore, to remind me of a past life rather than a new future.

I was ashamed to speak. anything I came up with in my mind sounded pathetic and wrong. Holly did not wait for me to find the strength in my voice. She spoke through tears. "Did you ever really care about me, James? Did you even try to help me when I was alive? This is hell—never growing old, never sleeping. Having all the memories of food, being forced to imagine what it would be like to have a pizza, or the memories of some long-lost parents feeding me sweet ice cream on a hot day. To wonder every day if what I see in my head is even real; if I am even real in the larger sense of the word. All around us is a world which is, at the very least, explainable in some terms. But I can't be explained; I can't be understood, when I don't even know what is real and what is not! Is this really what you wanted? To turn me into a husk?" Holly shouted, turning towards me. Her cheeks were red, her nose sniffling, yet I could not see tears. I could not see all the pain of my daughter. I knew it was there, and that softened me. I noticed that my hand had made its way to the handle of my pan.

Holly followed my eyes to the pan and looked at me. She shattered any idea of getting through this. I breathed in deep and noticed again how much Holly reminded me of her mother. She was all that remained of my previous life; a memory in living image, always by my side. Despite all the pain, I was the cause. She was still floating in front of me, giving me a chance, in spite of it all. Holly was a better person than I could ever have dreamed of becoming.

She was alive; I was the one that was a ghost.

Holly stuck around, needing me as much as I needed her. She was on edge, and I could tell she was close to breaking. Now, more than ever, Holly needed her father to be a man and do what was right. She wasn't turning into what her mother was at the end; she wasn't what her father is now. She was something magnificent, a perfect portrait of peace after a raging storm.

I looked at the floor while rubbing my hand on my pants. Drenched in sweat, I blew out my lips and started on words which I hoped would convey to Holly that I was truly sorry. "You probably don't want to hear this, but whenever you were a baby, I would hold you above my head. You would smile, even as a newborn—you always smiled at me. You wouldn't do it for anyone else; only me, from the moment that you held on to my finger, to today when I—I would have to say goodbye to you. I knew that you would always love me. And I knew that I would fight any monsters for you; you're my partner. You're my best friend, Holly. I am your father and I always will love you."

I had never spoken the words out loud, and they hung in the silence between us. I continued, "I never wanted to send you to this… place. If I could trade every second of my life back, I would, to just kiss and hold my girl against me. I can't, though; I can do what's right though, at the end of things."

I stepped towards Holly, placing my hand on her shoulders, as close as I could to touching her, aching to hold her. I settled for making eye contact with her. "You're not a husk. You are my daughter, and I will do whatever it takes to protect my little girl from everything. That includes a stupid old man."

That's when I uttered the words that I had forgotten. When love can only associate itself with pain, the mind forgets—but the heart cannot, no matter the pain. "I love you, Holly, I am so sorry I failed you as a father." I was crying in front of Holly, all shame gone. I was here at the end of things and did not want to waste another moment on my mistakes. I was doing this right; I was going to do what I needed for my daughter.

Holly whispered, "Dad, I forgive you. I went through your memories last night. You did everything you could; you did what a real father is supposed to do."

I dropped my eyes and cried, and Holly floated as close as she could to me without causing my skin to fester under the cold of our touch. We must have stayed that way for hours. I told Holly everything that had happened with her mom, everything that had led me to fighting for her body from the hordes of the ghosts. How my protecting her body was to prevent something from taking her over at first, but later became my selfish desires. I explained why I never told her that she was Molly—I was just so afraid of losing her.

In return, Holly told me of all the times that she had let me win in our board games. All the times she had protected me from ghosts without me being aware of it. It turns out I probably wouldn't have survived this long without her. *There was no way,* I thought, *without her I would be dead.* Talking to her then was one of the happiest moments that I had experienced in over twenty years.

That moment together, that brief moment, made me human again. I was a person; not a ghost, but a man. We stayed that way for some time, absorbing each other's memories. I let Holly see all the pain I had locked away. In return, she let me see she had been suffering the whole time as well.

When it was finished, I had shed my last tears, my knees ached, and my back felt like it had lifted a ton. I managed to stand with understanding though, resolution and peace. I imagine it is that moment every man feels, right before meeting their end, an acceptance of one's faith. It is a feeling that all is right and in place in the world, despite what may be about to happen.

Holly's face seemed untouched and unchanged, save for a small smile at the corner of her eyes. To ease the tension and to obscure her from seeing any more of my tears, I turned away.

"Well Holly, I know you are ready to get to this, I imagine."

Then Holly surprised me again. She floated next to me and placed her hand on the stub of my left hand. "Does this ever hurt?" she asked as the cold between our touches erupted, sending a shiver up my body.

I shook my head at her after a moment of thought. "No, the worst of it passed a few years back. There are some nights when it keeps me up; just nights where I could have sworn that I just felt it, before I remember it's gone."

Holly seemed to take that in; she tucked in her lower lips, and her eyes wandered to the fridge where her body was. "You know, I think you have enough on your hands—I mean hand—to have to worry about being by yourself. Honestly, Jim-Jim, I don't know if you could even find your way out of the house in the mornings without me. I—think that I will stay with you for a while longer yet." She stood, clasping her knees. "There, that settles it then." Holly snorted, slamming her fist into her other opened palm.

I stared, dumbfounded, trying to make sure I'd heard her right. *She must have not said that right. Not in my wildest dreams would I think that Holly would want to stay.* "Holly..." I started, before Holly interrupted me.

"No, James, shut up. It's time you let that big brain have some relaxation time and let me take care of it. I can't leave you here on your own. Mom... Mom would not approve of it, and you would end up doing something stupid. And I am afraid it would be something that you couldn't return from. You're already almost a ghost walking; I can't allow things to get worse, and you dying would probably haunt the whole world." Holly turned to me, her expression serious, leaving little room for doubt. She continued, "You've made sacrifices in the name of doing what you thought was right. However, you also made choices that were wholly selfish. All I am suggesting now, Jim, is let me make a choice that is a little selfish. Let me make a mistake that may come back and bite me, or which might well end up being what both of us need. I just can't leave you, old man, so if that means I have to put up with your smelly old ass for a little while longer, that will be just fine with me."

I looked at Holly and saw the same steel resolve in her eyes as her old man has. *She is truly my kid,* I thought, *therefore, it's a waste of breath to argue with her.* "Alright, we can stay together Molly."

Holly looked momentarily pained at the mention of her previous name. She winced. "Actually, Jim, I was thinking that I would like to keep going by Holly if that is alright with you. Molly was and is no longer me; she died, Jim. I'm not a clone of your daughter; I am your new girl. Just like how you're my new father and friend. If it's alright with you, I would like to continue to be called Holly instead of Molly. Names don't give or show love; love shows love, Jim. We've both have walked a long road to where we are now, and I'm afraid there is no going back. This isn't so bad, though, what you and I have now. Our life is the father and daughter relationship that matters now. And like the animals that seem to have taken up in this place, we have to do the same; make a home for ourselves," she said, speaking the words gently to me.

She was right, though, my old life was gone. *Let the James of that world stay at peace with his family. It was time for the James of here and now to embrace my life with my daughter.*

I walked to the other side of the kitchen and begun rummaging through the debris. Holly hovered over me. "Jim, what are you doing?" I continued to dig until I found the remainder of an old bloody tarp that had been used to cover my hand after I had burned it. The tarp was almost white in color from being exposed to the elements and had a decent amount of my blood still coating it, which flaked off to the touch as I moved the tarp.

I stood up and faced Holly with the tarp tucked under my armpit. "Holly, it's time we put Molly to rest in a proper place, don't you agree?" I waited for Holly's response.

Her eyes glazed over for a fraction of a second before she answered me. "Yeah Jim, let's have a funeral for me, you, and mom.

Chapter 33

After gathering Molly's remains the best I could (it was mostly bone fragments and ash), I placed her inside of an old gym bag that belonged to her mother. Holly waited outside as I cleared the rest of Molly out of the fridge. I sat down when I was finished, my hand soiled from handling my twenty-years-past-dead daughter. *Here I was, one-handed, burying the body of my only child, while the ghost of my only child was outside. Life sure could be fucked up.*

I let out a long breath and sighed, hoping for a cigarette. Hell, I would settle for aspirin. It's amazing there used to be many ways to fuck people up. Make people forget.

Maybe it isn't such a bad thing that I can't forget, and maybe it isn't such a bad deal either. Memories are the only way that I can keep Diana and Molly alive; keep them with me, even as I go through an endless amount of hard times.

I had my daughter back; she wasn't going to be leaving me. I wasn't going to be alone. Molly wasn't dead; she had been with me for twenty years, and that was a measure of comfort that blew any painkiller out of the water like a tactical nuke dropping on a city.

I reached the bottom of my apartment building and looked to the sky, seeing it was about mid-day. Getting caught in the dark wasn't the end of the world, I just didn't want to risk this day turning sour. I saw Holly floating above a small patch of yellow flowers, her long red hair flowing down in ruffles like her mothers had.

I walked next to Holly and set the bag down. "This is the place, kiddo?"

"Yeah, I always liked these flowers." Holly gestured to the yellow sunflowers which had remained the same after all this time. I remembered once how I took Molly to play in the flowers as a child; I had never seen a happier kid than her that day. *It made sense,* I thought, *somewhere that she could be at peace.*

I scooped down and started digging out dirt the best I could with my iron pan. I shoveled and scooped with the pan for an hour, having to take more breaks than I would have liked (digging with one hand is just hard), before the makeshift hole was deep and wide enough. I turned back to find Holly staring at me; no ice was in her eyes, just the same sweet Holly that has been my friend for such a long time. I stepped back from the hole and poured the dirt over the gym bag while wiping my hand on my pants.

None of this was how I'd ever wanted my life to end up; maybe we died and are just living out our gray memories of what life really is, or maybe I was just lying to myself. A part of me wished that was true, more than anything. Wishing was something that took away from what I had. And what I had was that girl floating next to me.

I stood as close to Holly as I could physically get, and I felt Holly's cold touch press into my hand. We stayed that way quite for some time, enjoying each other's silence. The cold from Holly's hand started to hurt so I stepped away "Ready to go, Molly?" I asked.

"Sure am, Jimbo," the young girl whispered turning towards the car. I followed suit until she stopped and turned back to me. "One last thing though Jim, keep calling me Holly." She pointed at the grave site and continued, "Molly is dead and gone, she is in the ground—I am pretty sure with the rest of our family. I don't have many memories from her, so I feel like based on that, I shouldn't be called the same as her. I have about as much in common with her as someone does as looking in at their reflection in the mirror. We look the same, but we will never be more. Like I said in your old home, that was her life; this is mine now."

I chewed on her words and lowered my head. She was right, of course. "Alright. Holly—that works for me. One last caveat, though, our family isn't dead and gone, kiddo. There's you and there's me." I pointed at Holly, then back to myself.

Holly smiled and called me a dork; we walked back to the car, feeling at peace with the world. Nothing was able to stop the feeling that we were sharing. As we reached the Beast, I heard footsteps. Silent and moving with a purpose. Someone was trying to not be heard. Years of listening for creatures that made almost no noise had made me an expert at hearing. If I had anything that was keeping me alive, it was my ears.

I whirled around and shouted at Holly to get behind me. Holly wasted no time and made herself invisible in the bright sun. I pulled my pan from its holster and wished that I'd had the foresight to bring my gun. My heart raced and geared up, once I realized that it had to be Benny. I wasn't sure how he could have made it to us, especially after what I had done to his leg. He was the only other living thing in this city.

Out from the side of the apartment complex stepped a man I hadn't seen in years—it had to be a ghost. He wore the tattered remains of black clothes and an all-black jacket. His face was hidden by an ancient-looking dark gas mask, now discolored to a seaweed green. On his belt was an assortment of blades. He stopped and regarded me for a long moment; I couldn't see his eyes behind his mask, and my fear doubled as I thought of ways to escape him if I needed to. I'd never been a fighter, and this guy looked tough. Some men you could just tell, from his shoulders being back, to his chest being out. His body radiated a confidence that mine just couldn't.

We faced each other; neither of us changing our stances; suggesting violence. I was sweating, I realized, as it dripped into my eyes. I ignored the sting, keeping my focus on the imposing man. Even from this distance, I could tell that he easily stood a head taller than me. Compared to this guy, Benny and me looked like starving cattle next to him.

I didn't think I could take him in a fight; maybe I could last long enough for Holly to get away. I was going to die trying before I let anything occur to my girl.

"Holly, get out of here..." I started, keeping my eyes on the man, my pan feeling way too weak, even with its heavy weight. I'd been swinging this pan at spooks for twenty years. Impressive, but then again, those ghosts didn't have any resistance when I landed a can of iron justice on their backsides. That naturally made me doubt the power of my swing, and I hoped that Holly wasn't sensing my fear.

"Nah, Jim, I think I will blast him if he takes another step. How about you get in the car and rest your old ass?" Holly snapped, causing the air to crackle around her. Somehow her hair was moving, and even the leaves in the bushes around us danced under the sway of her power output. As she slowly reappeared out of the corner of my eye, I took a step to the side slowly, remembering the way she had flicked me across the warehouse floor like a child would do to a kite.

The man in front of me either wasn't fazed or he had a pair of brass balls. Neither inspired any form of confidence in me. My throat suddenly felt very turgid, my mind was thinking worst case, and I wasn't seeing any way out of the situation anytime soon.

First, he spoke, breaking the tension by raising his hand in the air in the universal "We come in peace" gesture. However, I noticed his right hand stayed strapped to his belt. "Why don't we calm down for a second, everyone. I mean, James, is this how you greet old friends after so many years?" said the man in the gas mask. His voice came out muffled and louder than I think he intended it to be, but there was no mistake in his words—he had spoken my name.

"Who are you?" I sputtered out, while trying to find my voice from behind my tongue. I had no idea why I was so rattled by this man. I had seen a lot of scary stuff in the last twenty years; hell, the last forty-eight hours alone would be enough to break most people.

Then he did the unexpected and moved both his hands to his mask.

I flinched and felt my hand rising to protect myself. Holly seemed to be a little bit more in control, which was good thing. That girl had a cannon on her that I am sure she could flip a small car with.

"Geez Jim, tense much?" said a familiar voice as the man removed his mask to reveal an older version of my friend Wilson. His dark complexion was now highlighted by a thick ruffle of grey. His eyes still shined as bright and black as ever, with a fierce determination that I couldn't help but admire, even after all these years; I was dumbfounded, and my mouth had to be open. Seeing my old friend was a new one. *Figures,* I thought, *I was seeing every ghost from my past these last few days. What was another one? Though this one was pretty convincing, if nothing else.* I looked to Holly, and her face was strained as she looked Wilson up and down.

"Jim, he's not a ghost—" Holly whispered over my shoulders, putting off more of that energy that seemed to suck at every part of my body.

"That's not possible. It's been, what, twenty years?" I pondered out loud.

"Not possible that I am still this good looking? Thanks, Jim. Now are you going to keep standing there with your mouth wide open? Or come say hello to your old friend?" Wilson spoke smoothly, taking his mask down to his belt. A huge smile lit his face, just like it had always done so many years ago.

I was confused and too tired for any tricks. "Forgive me for this—on second thought, don't!" I shouted while dropping my pan into its sling, the heavy cast iron coming back and smacking me in the leg as it had so often done over the years. I reached into my pocket and searched for my piece of iron rebar.

I turned to Holly and nodded; she nodded back, never taking her eyes from the man. I turned back, and the Wilson look-a-like was still smiling and seemed completely at ease, despite the tension that I was feeling. I flicked the rebar at the man, and it landed a foot to his right. "Pick that up and touch yourself with it—now," I spat towards the rebar.

Wilson arched his eyebrows, but still he kneeled to pick up the rebar. His fingers grasped over the metal, and he didn't go up in sparks. He traced the rebar all over his body and made sure to over-exaggerate the movements, to show both Holly and I that he was not a ghost.

Feeling somewhat satisfied, I spoke to Wilson. "Alright, so you're real; why the fuck are you here now in front of us?" I growled at him.

Wilson placed both of his hands in the air, dropping the rebar. "Easy, Jim—no need to get tense. It's me. You have nothing to worry about. I know it's a little sudden, I suppose." Wilson puzzled as if we were two people running into each other at a grocery store.

"Just a little tense? Yeah, that's funny if you've been alive in this mess for five seconds. Tense is not the word that comes to mind," I shot back.

The Wilson look-a-like regarded me as if he was looking at a flock of birds in the park, more observant of Holly and me than actually afraid. That felt wrong. I know I wasn't the most imposing man, but Holly should have been at least enough to make him feel a little vexatious at least, and not that peaceful. He would only be that calm, I thought, if he had been aware of what we could do. That meant that he had to have been sure that we weren't going to blast him on sight.

It dawned on me that he must have been following us for who knows how long. If this man had been following us, there wasn't much of a chance he was a threat. Threats tended to come from behind when we were least expecting it. I kept my pan ready to go, tucked near me in my sling as my eyes stayed on him. *It was a trap; he must be the diversion.*

"Jim, are you crazy? Why are you putting your weapon down?" Holly whispered so quietly, I could almost hear it in my head.

"Just keep your eyes on him," I murmured back.

Wilson walked towards me, very slowly crossing the few feet between us. When his impressive form got within striking distance, I raised my weapon, ready to go to hell and back.

He either didn't take the show of force part seriously or he meant us no harm, because his walk did not stop until he was barely a foot away. I involuntarily took a step back from him. "That's it; I think I've had enough games for a few days. How about you step back before I start swinging?" I threatened and readied myself to attack him with everything that I had.

He froze at my movement, and I finally saw something human come out of the man: fear from my potential attack. "Alright, James, look. I know this is pretty fucking weird to be seeing me." Wilson sighed, giving me an ample girth.

"Yeah, pretty fucking funny indeed; if you don't mind, we are going to leave now," I snarled, and without turning, I spoke to Holly. "Holly."

"Right boss, get in the Beast." Holly vanished inside the car and was waiting for me to pull us out.

"I'm not sure if you're real or a very smart new trick. Honestly, I don't have the time for this shit." I growled while backpedaling to the Beast, my eyes never leaving the man. His dark eyes tracked mine the entire way.

"What if I was able to prove it's me, James?" Wilson urged.

"Even if you prove that it is you, I have other people to worry about." My back reached the Beast, and my heart took a jolt.

"Jim, I promise you, if you and your daughter get in that car and drive off now, you're both going to die. That is guaranteed; you two will not live to see the next five minutes if you don't come with me now," he stated, his face as grave as the darkness before a thunderstorm.

"Are you threatening me, you piece of—"

"I'm not," Wilson said, cutting off my defense. When he spoke next, his foreboding was evident, and my heart knew that something was wrong, even if my brain wasn't picking it up yet.

"What you don't realize is when a train comes, you not only hear it, you feel it. Something so unnatural and powerful, bulldozing its way across every piece of effort that your body possibly summons. It's that realization as you hear the train, as you feel the train, that you come to an understanding for the first time in your life—that all your efforts are a small thing compared to a giant hunk of metal, able to shake the very earth around you."

Wilson spoke quickly yet deliberately; I was still processing his words when he suddenly yelled. "James, get in your car now! We are in danger!" He started running towards me. As he ran, his steps muffled by the overgrowth, I heard a fierce howl in the air. Then I felt it like Wilson had said. The very ground shook and I heard barking in the air. I looked into the distance, my vision limited by the forest grown over the city.

I saw the dogs first, silhouetted in the sunshine, followed by every animal that had disappeared. "Well, that explains that mystery..." I mumbled as Wilson ran past me into the Beast, slamming the passenger door shut behind him.

"Get in the fucking car, James!" Holly screamed, snapping me out of a trance. When I ran to the Beast, almost falling, behind me were the empty gates of the jungle. The monsters had come to play, and we were smack in the middle.

I had the Beast started and reversing before the door closed. The first dog came running through the apartment complex, howling as if he was about to gain on hopeless prey. As I drove, I hoped that we weren't the prey.

I spun the Beast around, facing forward, as the tires screeched in protest. In my rear-view mirror, I watched my former home collapse under the sheer number of ghosts. I had never figured out how ghosts were able to have an effect on the physical environment, and I vowed if we made it out of this, I was going to devote time to figuring the answer to that.

The apartment shot dust in all directions, and the beasts followed with cries like a thunderstorm on Jupiter. I could feel it, their desire to hurt us as I drove, the Beast's steering wheel rattling in my hands, and somehow, I felt that the already large amounts of iron on my car weren't enough. After all, I couldn't put that much iron on the windows, plus Holly always needed a ride. That left me at least somewhat exposed. I had doubts about the weakness of my car and whether it could hold off that many.

I tore away, the road behind me clouded by the horrific sight of animals in various states of decay. I slammed the gas pedal very nearly through the floor of the explorer, the weight of the iron causing her to lurch forward far too slowly. Chunks of the apartment building came collapsing down all around us; on top of the car, I could hear thick pieces of ancient concrete dent into my frame. The hood almost bowed in above me as we made our escape. I risked looking in the rear-view to see all the animals of the land bring down a building and even the trees around them.

Other than Holly, I had never seen such a display from the ghosts; all I had witnessed was noticing doors slamming or random movements of my clothes. At the most, flying objects. For that matter, I had never seen ghost animals. Or creatures made of different parts, I thought. What was behind me was like a bomb going off in the middle of a war zone. Just another day of the unexplainable.

I faced forward, focusing on the road, amazed at the sheer numbers of beasts that were hunting us. We were in the middle of a wild hunt; we were just the sick deer for the slaughter.

"James, those things are going to catch up to us; we need to find a way out," directed Wilson from the passenger seat, his face controlled and calm despite the panic that was on the faces of both Holly and me.

"No shit, gas man, what do you want me to do about them?" I shouted, while veering the Beast over a curb. The first ghost animal hit our car and showered into sparks of colors. *Our vehicle shook slightly from just that one—if more hit, we were doomed.* I went faster, trying to navigate around the remainder of the city and the overgrowth now taking its rightful place over the jungles of man.

I rounded another curb and the Beast almost flipped from the sheer number of the animals that slammed into it from behind; blinding colors of the rainbow flew around us, showing several lives of the monsters. It took everything I had to keep all four wheels on the ground. That was when I saw the black bear from earlier; she was pinned down, pawing feebly at the ghosts as her fur shook, melting from her body. A last howl of pain into the sunny day as both her and her cub passed away. *Don't think about it James.*

I scanned the roads ahead and saw more turns, more endless fields of rusting machines. *We weren't going to make it,* I thought. I didn't get enough time to follow that rabbit down its dark hole. I looked over, and Wilson had his window rolled down, a medieval looking axe brandished in his hands.

"What the fuck, are you crazy? Roll the damn window up!" I shouted over the festival of noises.

"Focus on the damn road—I got this!" yelled Wilson, slashing at what appeared to be the ghost of a tiger pawing at the rear of the car. I turned my head back around; I was just going to have to pray he wouldn't use that axe on the two of us.

Pressing forward, I felt the engine of the Beast going into overdrive as I began to red-line my reliable car. As the creatures got closer to us, their snarls ripped into me; the force enough to make the frame vibrate and my teeth to chatter. The animal's volume continued to grow, and my vision began to go dark from the level of noise. I was worried that my head might explode from their force. I dared to close my eyes for a second, and we almost flipped again when I opened my eyes.

Wilson sneered with a look. I shot him back with what I hoped was a "Shut the fuck up." We continued forward until Wilson slumped into his front passenger seat. His face and body were drenched in sweat. His breaths came in heavy waves as he gathered himself before his next bout with the monsters.

"James, I can't keep that up for much longer, and judging by the way this thing is heaving, she doesn't have much longer either." Wilson pointed at the dash of my car.

I growled under my breath; I knew he was right. "She's got it where it counts; don't you worry," I responded. "Darn it; we did not go through all that just to end up as puppy chow to pet seminary's wet dream," I fumed, while gripping the steering wheel until my knuckles turned white.

"I have an idea, Jim," Holly interjected, sticking her face between Wilson and me. The movement made both of us flinch. *Good,* I thought, *he is at least human; that little maneuver would scare any person. It just isn't a natural feeling for the human body.*

Looking in the rear-view mirror, I made eye contact with her; she had a calmness to her eyes, and I knew she had a crazy stupid plan. After all, she was my daughter, and it was only something that I would do. "If you're thinking of splitting up, don't try it."

"Jim, I—" she stammered while I shook my head no. Holly turned around and looked; the sky sounding like a large moving ocean as we drove across the wasteland. I glanced in the mirror again—those things were running on the sides of buildings; we were doomed.

"You won't make it ten feet with all of that going on out there," I pointed behind us with the stub of my hand.

"Well, what are we going to do? We are at least an hour from our home under normal circumstances. We—are trapped in this thing like a tin can in a lake, Jim."

"I know, Holly..."

"Do you, Jim? Because things look pretty fucking bad from back here," Holly said skeptically, pointing at a beast that hit the side of our "tin can."

"Language, Holly!" I shouted over the roar of the animals.

"Listen to you two, arguing like children in the middle of a crisis," interjected Wilson, as he lay hunched in his seat.

"Shut up!" Both Holly and I shouted at him from our spots.

The beasts continued to bunch over the roads and hummed as I tore through anything I could to get away from them. "I have an idea, James. If you can make it to the founder's bridge, I can get us out of here."

I thought about Wilson's words for a moment. The bridge was outside of the city, but it did offer the potential safety of the river. Though water did nothing to stop the buggy creatures; *unless the bridge was completely made of iron, we were fucked.* "That won't help us in the slightest; we are too far away," I stammered back to Wilson, catching a violent shake from a ghost that looked like a brown bear.

"Well, we could always go to the old Catawba dam. The walls are thick and full of more iron than a railroad car," suggested Wilson; I ignored his statement, focusing on the road.

I looked out my window at the ghastly monsters aching to devour us if they could penetrate the holes of the Beast. "How do you even know that?" I asked Wilson, my attention between him and the road.

"The Fort Mill Dam is where I stay," Wilson admitted, rolling his window back up. The creatures were getting too close for comfort. There for a second, I thought I saw one of their furry paws come through the window.

"I don't think that's a good idea. We got Holly, and I can dig in deep in our place. You will… just have to hoof it."

Holly turned to me after I said that. "Jim, we don't have a choice right now. I don't think we can make it this time. I mean I want to make it, we just can't."

I ignored Holly as well; this was all turning into a shitstorm. Here I was, with a ghost from my past randomly showing up during an already chaotic couple of days. Especially on the day when I was burying the ghosts of my past. The dead just didn't want to stay dead in my life. Things were moving fast, things never slowed down, and it seemed no matter how hard I tried, I was just paddling myself deeper down an evil river.

I wasn't about to bring 'Wilson' back to our home; I had long since learned the hard lesson of bringing strangers into your place. I thought about the safety of all the traps I had set up in the neighborhood; they would work on ghosts, but if people attacked the house, it wasn't a good defense.

I couldn't put Holly and me at risk; I couldn't place her in any danger. It was just safer at our home. *There was the chance, though, that we couldn't make it back,* a small voice whispered as I drove frantically down the barren roads. And down my descent into the waves I went, as my thoughts distracted me from the creatures. I felt one of the wheels of the Beast start to wobble, and I turned the wheel as hard as I could in the opposite direction, the problem being that a man with one hand can only put so much strength into driving. *We were going to flip.* I closed my eyes.

Wilson's hands overtook mine on the wheel, and together the Beast remained steady, and we bounded forward, smashing the monsters outside. I looked at Wilson who had fear in his eyes, which I knew had to be in mine as well. I saw something else for a moment when I looked into Wilson's eyes; it felt strange, almost like it was the first time that I'd had a good look at the man. I understood that after the way the world has been that no one would probably have the same look in their eyes as before. It was as if this was the first time I had ever met the guy, like a casual encounter on a walk home when you accidentally bump into someone. You don't have a clue who they are, nor do you care. After all, they're strangers, and you're busy with your life. Not at all like the recognition that you feel when it's someone that you've known for years.

Before I could think about it any more, Holly screamed. "Dad!" she belted from behind us. "Do something before we die, please!"

That caught my attention, and I looked at Wilson. He was as good as a stranger, even if we had known each other.

"Alright, lead the way, Wilson. But if you fuck with us in any way,

I will not stop until I have killed you. And if you turn into a ghost afterward, I will kill you again," I stated, hoping my voice could do what my eyes would have said if I could spare a glance.

"Thank you; was that so hard? Turn toward South Carolina, James old boy. We have a road trip and monsters to lose," Wilson reiterated with far more humor in his voice than I was comfortable with—just too coolly.

I looked in my rear-view mirror; Holly was biting her lower lip. "Why can't something just be easy for a change..." I mumbled, and steered the Beast.

Chapter 34

We had managed to drive through the city, the beasts getting closer the entire time. I drove like a mad man weaving and dodging around traffic. Wilson would provide directions based off of ancient landmarks that surrounded and littered the city. Places that used to be people's offices and homes, now just forgotten stones in a new world. *Funny—twenty years old was now considered ancient,* I thought.

As we crossed the South Carolina border, the ghost animals slacked off; I could still hear their cries over the hum of the engine. At least it wasn't inside my head any more. I looked at my fuel gauge. The speeding and the long journey had left us almost on empty.

It had been twenty years since I had left Charlotte and now we were going to be stuck in the south with no gas; I think there was a movie or two about that very same thing. I wasn't sure what made me feel worse: the monsters chasing us, or the monsters that we might be heading towards.

As we traveled the roads, the forest had reclaimed more of the world than even in the city. The woods were thick, and the way was made harder. Roads were vanishing, while the world grew back.

Other than directions from Wilson, the three of us remained quiet. I looked at Holly in the rear-view. She met my eyes, and I could tell she was as nervous as I was. Our home in Charlotte was filled with pain and horror; it was still our home, though. We weren't prepared to leave it, and we both felt uneasy about Wilson.

"I would say a few more miles, James; you will love the hideout. Not much in the ways of comfiness, though, but security can be the most comforting blanket there is," Wilson said casually.

I turned around a tipped-over semi truck and continued to drive the Beast as the ghosts followed. "Before we get to your supposed safe house, I want to know how and what were you doing in my city," I queried.

Wilson waited to reply; I hope it wasn't to come up with a response. I should have just taken Holly and ran as soon as we had seen him.

"Well, to put it simply, we are running out of supplies at the dam. Like most people who survived the first night, I left for the military base down south. They set up a camp based at the dam. From there, we made it by raiding surrounding towns and local areas—just like you or anyone else unfortunate enough to survive in this world."

"Charlotte is a long way to come scavenging; there is almost no way you made it all the way to us on just your feet alone. In fact, I find it even harder to believe that you had managed to get to us—all on your own."

Silence after my statement weighed heavy in the air between the three of us.

"Well, to put it this way, it is creep central all over any of the big cities. Frankly, I've been to Charlotte plenty of times in the years that have followed since all this shit began. I reached the city the same way that you're entering my home—I drove my happy ass over into the city and avoided all the crowded places. I don't know about you, but today is the first time I've seen any animals in weeks. In fact, I haven't seen a lot of ghosts—I think, I believe, that something is wrong. This is why I went north looking for answers; no idea I would run into you, a computer nerd and his daughter trapped in a tomb of ghouls." Wilson spoke smoothly, in spite of the threat.

"Yeah,we—" I looked at Holly in the rear-view, she nodded her head, and I continued. "We had noticed the same thing—I wonder what it all means," I responded as a clearing in the forest came up. The road was mostly intact, and it looked even as though someone had taken the time to keep the jungle at bay. I could hear the river before I could see it and in the distance was a large fence that stretched across the remains of a concrete dam. Its sand stones were chipped away by time, exposing in sections gleaming rows of iron that appeared like the teeth inside of a giant's mouth waiting to devour us.

"Well fuck me, you weren't lying."

"I will say, sure beats that shitty bunker we have, huh, Jim?" Holly gasped, leaning between Wilson and me.

I blinked and mumbled, "Yeah, I wasn't expecting this."

Chapter 35

A gate connected to the road, its heavy iron parts standing menacing even from a distance, as the Beast shot forward. I dared glancing behind us to see the legion of animals stop at the fence and howl in a frenzy. We had escaped their wild hunt and somehow made it to the unknown.

Even with the gates wide open, the creatures remained outside. Perplexed, I gestured to Wilson. "We keep iron on the ground. We've noticed that ghosts can sense it and turn away."

I grunted in reply, "Well, where should I park—anywhere in this heap?" I asked.

"Anywhere is fine. When you're done, help me close the gate—it makes me a little scared with that many out there."

I couldn't disagree with him; I could see an almost endless amount of the ghosts staring back at us. I wondered what it was they wanted. *Why were they chasing us so relentlessly?*

I had been chased by the creatures before; they typically only gave chase for a line of sight. Once you were away, they seemed almost to grow bored or move on to do something else. Often the ghosts stayed only in the areas where they died. Getting away from ghosts was surprisingly easy if you knew your way around enough. That's why I liked my city; I knew every street, every tree, and crumbling piece mortar. It was my home. With everything that was going on, I was getting nervous being away from it. First, it had been that super-powered girl and now an army of dogs. Something dangerous was going on here.

I looked at Holly as I held open the door for her. Her hair had turned a bright blue, and she regarded me with worry. I smiled the best reassuring father smile I could. "Everything is going to be alright, kiddo. I promise."

"That's the thing, Jim, I think we are a long way off from anything ever being alright again. Something doesn't feel right about this place—or him." Holly gestured towards the dam.

"Yeah, I know what you mean. Just play along; just as everything clears up, we will run for the hills, I promise," I pronounced, turning and watching Wilson exit the other side of the Beast.

Stepping out of the Beast felt like jumping into an ocean filled with sharks. If keeping Holly alive—at least not any less than she was now—was all I had left in this life as a mission, that was what I was going to do. Besides, the best I figured was that Wilson would lead me inside and eat me, or the ghosts outside would eat me. At least I would die in the country. *Dying in the city feels like one giant stomach,* I thought.

We followed Wilson as he made his way to another section of the dam. I could see the water trapped by the dam and as the sun started to set, I felt a moment of relaxation and peace. *It is moments like this when things seem like you're about to die; the moments when life appears to be throwing you problems that you began to push forward. For me, whenever I started pushing forward, I found solace at that point, and was able to be whole at least for a moment.*

Outside, monsters of all nature and reality were trying to consume us; I was heading inside, into a decayed brick dam with a strange man from long ago. I was still at peace while I walked in the intense sunlight. I had never forgotten how much the Carolinas made me sweat. A breeze topped it off, and I was able to walk with it all around me, despite the tremble my legs made with every step. *Just enjoy your last few moments,* I thought as I readied my mind for anything.

As we reached another fence, I could tell that someone had switched out the regular steel poles with iron. Dirt was piled at the bottom of each pole, and an extensive amount of work had been done to the security of the dam. *They must be intelligent enough—that might be worse than crazy people. Assuming there are people in there,* I thought darkly, trying to keep my mind calm. Once inside the wall, I could see at least three sets of footprints. Two of them looked small. Most likely a woman or a small child; the other set might have belonged to Wilson. There was no way of knowing with the amount of rain that a place like this got. The ground was still muddied from recent rain, in fact; I was surprised to see any prints.

We reached a rusted-in double set of doors with a light at the top, indicating the entrance. Wilson caught me eyeing the light. "Best we were able to configure was electricity to run the lights for years. What we weren't able to figure out is how to keep the original bulbs working." I arched my eyebrow at this.

He was right, of course, keeping lights on, even in a place as complex as a dam, would be hard enough, while finding the parts for the dam must have almost been impossible for them to maintain the upkeep, year after year. At the door, Wilson pulled it open without unlocking anything.

Why wouldn't they lock it? The remoteness of the dam aside, other things can get through those gates beside ghosts. I pondered that as we stepped through the threshold. Holly floated quickly enough through the second fence, dodging the iron.

It bothered me how calm Wilson was around Holly; he should have been on edge more about the whole thing. Instead, he was acting like he was used to being around ghosts like Holly. Holly was, well, the only ghost I had met like her. That was setting my teeth on edge: Wilson was just too calm. We stepped through the doors, leading into a hallway framed in deep shadows and trails of cold stone all around us.

Once through, we entered a poorly lit room. A table was laid bare before another door that was closed. This one looked like it was sturdy enough to take an assault, the steel thick, the frame broad.

Wilson walked to the second door and spoke. "James, before you two come in and meet everyone; I must lay down a few ground rules." I puffed at Wilson as if to indicate that it hadn't been our plan to come back here in the first place, so there was nothing to be worried about from us. Wilson went on. "Here, we try to get along with both the living… and the not so much," Wilson said, gesturing towards Holly.

Holly blinked her eyes but otherwise stayed floating next to me, her hair suddenly changed to a darker blue. I swear, any chance she got to make a scene or change her damn hair, she would. I shook my head at this and smiled as Wilson continued.

"So, if you don't mind, James, put your weapons on this table. This is—well, for lack of a better word, we don't trust outsiders," Wilson said bluntly.

I dreaded the idea of being unarmed behind whatever was back there. Holly and I exchanged looks. She had a power that they didn't know about, and I was pretty good at throwing right punches. Still, being without any defense was against our creed, our very way of life by this point.

I took off my frying pan and slid the rebar from my belt on the table. Wilson just smiled back, completely at ease with the whole thing. When Wilson was satisfied that I wasn't hiding anything, he turned to unlock the door.

I felt strangely naked, and a wave of fear hit me as the door was opened to another long hallway. This time I could make out rows of offices that led to a green door at the end of the hall. The whole building was well lit and contained many signs of having been lived in; it was someone's home. Down the hallway, as we made our way, I could see a lot of bedding and changes of clothes everywhere.

"You know, Jim; that's one thing I don't regret about being dead and all. I can't smell anymore…" Holly piped up, holding her nose and waving in front of her face. I agreed with her and moved on, trying not to gag from the smell; human beings are animals, after all.

I'm sure my home wasn't much better.

We reached a lime green door, and Wilson paused. "Promise me that you two will be good. Also, don't mind the uncleanliness; you guys should know how it is here."

He opened the door, and we came to the generator room. Huge turbines stretched in a permanent decayed state, and would never be used again in any form. At the center of the chamber were many worn couches wedged together to provide comfort, a sense of shelter in an otherwise colossal room. A sturdy table was holding many lamps that provided much-needed light in the darkness, and three strong hands belonging to three very different people awaited us. They were in the middle of a card came; when we all came in, their eyes locked with mine and I would have felt fear if I had not seen what I had in my life. Four random survivors and a horde of undying ghost animals; what a great day.

One was a man about my age or older. His hair was long since gone and replaced by a crescent moon balding formation. His body was littered with tattoos, and most importantly, his legs were gone from the knees down. As he observed me from behind his hand of cards, He scoffed, pushing wire glasses up his nose.

Next was a woman of my age. She had long black hair and a beautiful but very run-down face, the kind that appeared older than her. Still, a sense of beauty in her twilight years. Her eyelids were like pools of black that offset her willowy figure.

Next to her was a younger woman with broad shoulders, a bulldog face, broken from many fights. She had broad shoulders yet still looked slightly feminine, and a tattered mess of green hair lit the room with a neon jade.

Oh great, another one, I thought. When I tried sizing her up, she stared daggers into me. I took note of this and tried not to let anything show on my face. If they saw that I was weak now, Holly and I would be goners.

"James, Holly, welcome to the ghost family." Wilson beamed,

clapping me on the back and walking around to where a cooler sat near the table. "We don't have much to offer in the way of drinks, but we do have some food." Wilson reached into the cooler and threw me a can.

I caught it with my hand and turned it around. It was beans, from what I could tell by the sticker. It had long since worn away, leaving only the outline of a smiling green figure. "Thanks." I grimaced, tucking the can into my jacket pocket.

"So, is anyone going to say anything, or are we just going to keep staring at each other?" asked the man in the wheelchair.

"Oh, sorry about that. James—Holly, this is everyone." Wilson gestured. "This strapping young lady with green hair is Christina; her old man used to run this place," Wilson indicated, pointing to the woman in the middle, she smiled, and I flinched. It had just been too many years since someone hadn't been trying to kill me.

"Still does," she shot back keeping her eyes on her cards.

"I am just messing with you, honey," he winked.

"Wink at me again and I will pull your eyes out. You too, pretty boy." I could see the fire in her eyes as she arched her eyebrows in my direction. The golden loop in her eyebrows gleamed in the low lights of the flame. Wilson just smiled like a father does to a child.

"Hey, I think you look great with green hair," Holly admitted, complimenting the woman. "Thanks, kiddo. Blue is just the right amount of kick for you, by the way." Christina grinned while winking at Holly.

"Moving along, now the wheel-chaired man to my left is Robert, or Fast Rob, as he likes to be called." Wilson smirked, gesturing towards Rob. Rob took a look at me and smiled, going back to playing his game, either uninterested or unthreatened by me—I couldn't tell.

"He will talk when he is ready. Don't mind him. You will want him to shut up afterwards, trust me—this is Kim, sitting over to my right." At the mention of her name, Kim looked at me. She had large eyes; her features were weathered by harsh years, no doubt, of trying to survive in this world; she still had an attractiveness about her that was strangely alluring. Or maybe it had been that long since I had been with a woman. I kept looking at her longer than the friendly two-second stare. I adverted my eyes, smartly, before it became to awkward.

"How do you do?" Kim hesitated, stretching out her hand. It had been almost twenty years since I had touched a woman. I felt a strange stirring in my stomach, and I chased that down. I had more important things to worry about than a potential lay. I tilted my head and grunted without taking her hand.

"Who's the ghost kid?" said Rob from behind a curtain of smoke—he had quickly pulled out a fresh roll from somewhere. I had missed that—a mistake that I wasn't going to make the rest of the time that I was here.

"An old colleague that I used to work with back in the day. That's his daughter," Wilson answered, coming around the table and standing next to me. "Isn't that right, Jim? Say hello to everyone."

"Hi." I said, feeling very awkward and out of place. I couldn't remember the last time that I was around this many people like this.

Wilson must have sensed the weirdness and uneasiness in our interactions, and offered to show us the rest of the dam. "Come on, James," he gestured, pointing to another set of doors. I hesitated for a moment. The group looked harmless enough, but look what all I had accomplished with just one hand.

The dam was impressive; the turbines looked long since out of use, but helped support the safety of the compound. Apparently, as Wilson put it, they had been covered in iron, which was quickly stripped and put to good use. Despite its age, the structure of the dam remained intact and imposing as ever; a fortress of stone gleaming in the darkness. It had been a polished white that now drooled a dull gray. Wilson even took us outside to show us an area behind the dam they had been using for fishing. My mouth watered at the sight of fresh meat for a change, and not something that had come from a can.

When we were outside, I saw that the animal ghosts still lingered beyond the fence line, across the river, even leading back to the entrance. The dam effectively had only one direction; everything else was fences and a lake. "How long do you think they will be out there?" Holly asked.

"I don't know, Holly; I'm not sure what it is that they even want—"

"Probably the same as the rest—they want to be alive, just like us," Wilson interjected, interrupting my train of thought.

I grunted in agreement; he was right, though it seemed that everything in this world was, one way or another, wanting to be alive if nothing else. That was something all of us could understand now.

"How soon can we get on the road?" I turned and asked Wilson.

Wilson turned towards me and spoke. "I imagine not long. Ghost or not, they're animals, and animals will move on after a while. Once they leave, I can take you into town and get gas for your car if you want."

"Sure, that works for me," I stated. "Wilson, can you give Holly and I a few minutes to ourselves? We will be back inside soon."

"Sure thing, James, whatever you need." Wilson nodded, looking between the two of us as he turned and left back downstairs.

Once I thought he was out of hearing range, I spoke to Holly as low as she could hear. "What do you think of this place?"

"To tell you the truth, Jim, I am still trying to piece it all together. I mean, what a big place this is, and way out here in the open," she whispered.

"I agree. Makes it even worse that they have our weapons and we are all out of gas," I responded.

"That's the thing, Jim. One of the books that we took from the library talked about this dam. It's called the Fort Mill Dam in South Carolina, and the route we took down here was the long one."

"Are you sure?" I asked.

Holly nodded and kept her eyes fixed on the door leading back down towards the turbine room. Holly might have been on to something. She never got her facts wrong from those damn books. A trip to the market could take hours since the destruction of the cities now, and that was most likely Wilson's reason. "Well, a point could also be made that he was taking us around any obstacles in the road."

"True…" Holly muttered. "Still feels pretty fishy to me. What was that you used to tell me as a kid? 'If something smells fishy than it most likely is fish, and unless you're eating it, it's not a good thing.'"

I looked at Holly very plainly, "You might have a point, but maybe Wilson has a reason for all of this. Besides, we aren't going anywhere for a while," I puzzled.

Holly dropped her hands to her side. "I agree, Dad. He has plans, but he has something that we aren't seeing planned—call me crazy, I can just tell." She cautioned me skeptically, her eyes big and her voice full of concern. It was the youngest she had looked in years.

"Normally I would agree with you, Holly, without question. And I mostly do. But this place is better than anything that you and I have back in Charlotte, and to top it off, I used to know the guy." I hesitated, leaning over the railing to get a better look at the horde below us. The river flowed right between us and the ghosts, nearly canceling out their cries over the sound of gushing water. We were high above the river and the fence line. *I'd never liked heights, and what awaited me below was far worse than any roller-coaster,* I thought.

"That's the thing, Jim; you would usually not give a shit about whether it was Mom, or the devil himself. It is just you and me. And just because you know him doesn't mean that we can trust him," she said defensively.

"Well, you got me there. What has you so to the races with him, Holly?" I asked, folding my arms in the sudden cold.

"The thing is, I remember when I was a kid, you introduced me to all of your office friends. I don't remember him from your office, and

I can't picture his face out of all the others. A lot of memories have been coming back; some aren't so clear, but I just don't remember his face in any of them."

That stunned me; Holly didn't forget anything, not anything in almost twenty years. Even if she had learned about her past life recently, she still had remembered a lot, from what I could tell, in the last few days. Holly was almost made of memories. The way she could recall any information, it astounded me. Any story, any scrape, that's why even though she'd just found out about herself; she knew almost everything about her life as Molly.

I couldn't wrap my mind around how that was true; I had seen him plenty of times at work. I even had memories of us spending time with each other's families. Our families were close, I was sure of that. It was possible that Holly's memories had been suppressed from all the years and trauma. *Or she could be right,* a small voice said at the back of my skull. *Being too eager as ever for human company, James. Remember what happened with Benny...* I shook my head before speaking up, ignoring the voice of someone in my head.

"Either way, we are stuck here until we can get some fuel. We can't solve the mystery tonight. I'm not saying you're wrong Holly, I just think we must work with what we have at the moment. Try to act normal for a bit," I cautioned, walking past Holly to the door. "Coming with me?" I asked.

"Just—just keep your eyes open," she stated, walking through the door leading down to the turbine room.

"I never get a break; I never get a break," I mumbled, following behind her.

Chapter 36

When I walked downstairs, there sat a little boy about Molly's age before she'd died, floating above Kim's lap, along with Rob and Christina dancing to a tune Wilson was playing on a broken guitar. The boy floated over Kim's lap. *That explains why they're at ease,* I thought. The juxtaposition of the two was everything if not beautiful. It had been so long since I had seen actual people interacting. For a moment, I lost myself in it all. Listening to Wilson play his songs softly, watching the disabled man and Christina dance, while the mother played with her boy. From an outsider's perspective, they were having fun, they were a family here in this dam. It was utterly foreign to me.

I saw the kid float off towards Holly and the two began to play games in the background. They both changed their shapes and morphed into creatures and chased each other around for many hours, seeming to hit it off quickly. Everyone was relaxed—*too relaxed,* I thought. It was a struggle to fight off, the feeling of it all being dangerous or fake. I lamented my distrust once the attention of everyone was on Joey and Holly; it's hard not to laugh when a ghost transforms into a dragon and is slayed by another using a lightsaber. I let loose a torrent of laughter and let my mind leave the never-ending record player that it had been for more years than I could count.

Wilson soon brought out alcohol. It had been many years since I hadn't drunk myself to sleep every night; before the apocalypse, I hadn't been much of a drinker. That was always more Diana; she used to tease me and say I was too afraid to live with the little amount of anything bad I would do. The first few drinks of smooth whisky hit me hard, much better than the cheap airplane bottles I kept on me—though I ached for some of those right now; they were the perfect shot amount.

As I tilted back a smooth shot, Christina came up to me. "How are you doing tonight, darling?" she coaxed, sitting across from me. She was layered in grease and had on a thick leather jacket, the inside lined with fur. Still, in a certain light, I could see her being someone you wouldn't want to meet in a back alley. *Then again,* I thought as our conversation went on, *she has a great personality, full of a lot of life.* It turned out she wasn't as tough as I'd first thought. I even felt myself laugh. That felt odd to be coming so naturally out of me that I stopped twice mid-sentence to make sure Holly was still nearby, and someone wasn't trying to attack us.

"James, relax. This night is all for you. You're around friends. Trust me, nothing is getting in this place." Wilson gestured from behind his guitar strings. I smiled back and went on talking to Christina.

"So, that is your daughter over there, correct?" Christina gestured to Holly.

"Correct, that's her," I responded.

"She's beautiful. Has some pretty blue eyes," Christina said

"She got that from her mother—almost everything from her. Her temper and language, now that's from me."

"Oh, yeah, it's weird the things our parents give us, right? Tell me about her mother. What was she like?" Christina asked casually.

"Bit too early for that kind of talk," I grumbled.

"Easy, big guy. I'm not trying to cause any heartache on a good night like this. They're few and far between us, as I'm sure you have noticed. I am just curious. I see the way you look at your girl. You care about her, that's who you are, so never be afraid of who you are and keep doing what makes you… you. After all, that's all we'll have when death finally comes knocking."

She stood up and touched the gnarled remains of my left hand. It had been the first time in twenty years an actual person had touched my arm and I had not killed that person. "Just checking to see if I should be worried about you or not." She winked and turned walking away and sat next to Wilson. She and Wilson shared a silent laugh, obscured by the sound of his guitar.

I stayed where I was at and continued to drink as the night's hours rolled on. Christina soon passed out right where she lay, and Wilson headed to bed in another room. "You're welcome to any of the rooms back in the corridor that you came through. I will wake us early to start hunting for some gas. Good night, and get some rest," Wilson informed me, waving goodnight.

I stared at my left wrist, looking hard at its form, and thought of the night that Diana had turned forcing me to cut off my own limb. Tooth marks still dotted the outer edges, where the flames hadn't been able to sear it shut.

"You know, whenever I have that look on my face, it means I am thinking about my legs. Is that the same thing you're doing right now?" asked Rob, rolling his chair up next to mine.

I smiled. "What gave it away?"

"Tell you the truth, nothing did. Just that is what I think of every time when I drink. I think of how I lost my legs. It seems like a mountain of ash and bullshit ago. That's anything in this fucking life, a mountain of ass and bullshit, I tell you," Rob muttered.

True to form, Rob had a cigarette lit and a thick haze of smoke enveloped him in a matter of seconds. His hands were quick and deliberate, I noted. He had to be a mechanic of some kind, or maybe he had been a construction worker in another life.

"Oh yes, how did you lose your legs, mister fast?" I asked, making conversation the best I could through a drunken buzz.

"Easy enough question. One I can't give a very good answer for you, I'm afraid. It's real easy to tell a story, that doesn't mean it's of worth. It's so much harder to get a story of value to any peckerwood these days. Stories have to mock something, not have substance—maybe they never did. If you aren't mocking something or showing a big booty wedge between a meathead, no one want's to hear it," Rob stated, looking around the room, as if to decide the atmosphere was right, then he started talking again.

"If a man knows anything, if he knows anything in this life, it's that there are only a few constants. One of those is don't tell a story quick or without a lesson, those are constants to storytelling like in life. You will need to shit, to cum, to eat, to love, and you will make memories during all of these over the course of your life. Only, in my case, my memories are almost like tangible things. That, I suppose, is true for everyone. You can take the memory of two people witnessing the same event and check on them twenty years later and I promise you, the memory will be completely different. The size of a car, the curve of a lady's hips, the horror, or the good that comes from an incident. They're nothing more than a catalog with an index written in pencil that can be changed anytime; ultimately irrelevant, since those memories don't actually keep you alive like a lot on my list." Rob took a long drag on his cigarette.

"So, basically you don't remember, I take it?" I guessed.

Rob laughed and turned, facing me while looking me in the eyes. "Fuck it, kid, it's another mark on the black road of my life, knowing my memory of a life event. If you want to know, to time travel back to that place and time, the facts are simple: I lost my legs; I tattooed many people in my life. I got to be a part of mankind's extinction at the very end. Good, bad, no matter the memory, it is what it is. Nothing more exciting than that, I am afraid."

I thought about what Rob said, letting it sink deep into me before I answered him, wondering why I was allowing strangers to be so personal. "When I was a different man, my wife died and tried to take over my body. In response, I took off my own hand with an iron frying pan. The more I think about those memories, the more I want to forget them. Not just because of how painful they were, but because that was the last time my life made any sense. The last time I could recall the shape of a room and know that it is accurate; do you know what I mean? To trust that what I was seeing might be real,"

"I haven't got the foggiest of an idea. Then again, I've had a lot to drink tonight," Rob snorted, as we both laughed at his comment. I shared a drink with him and he even insisted that I share one of his cigarettes with him. He explained that before the world turned into "Ghost," as he put it, he had been a tattoo artist who also dabbled in chemistry from time to time.

He said he used a screen door combined with scraps of paper; anything from photographs to scratch paper. When pressed with water and a sponge (and a little bit of pressure, as he put it), he was able to create paper. I was impressed, he said I hadn't seen anything yet. I laughed at that; noting that the hour was starting to get late, even as I was getting to know everyone at the compound, I still didn't trust them enough to go to sleep.

I am a byproduct of the apocalypse and realized I would never feel safe anywhere ever again; that was okay with me, I thought as I sipped more of the harsh whisky. Against my better judgment, I still kept sipping away; Holly looked at me as she played with the young ghost boy, her face clearly one of concern. I smiled and waved to ease her.

After a while, I heard snores from Rob; he was slouched deep into his wheelchair and showed no signs of waking up any time in the future. I started to doze when Kim came up to me this time at the table.

"Rob always did like to party. Sorry about that." Kim spoke softly, her voice honeyed in the smoke trapped inside the dam, a rare treat in the middle of the night. "Don't worry; I am only a drink or so from being in the same boat."

She smiled and spoke again. "You don't seem like the partying type, if you don't mind me saying."

"That is correct. In the past, my wife was the one who liked to smoke and drink. I was just always around for the laughs and the good times. I just never could stand the taste of tobacco and one beer was usually enough to do me in. 'Clean health,' I always said."

"Except for now—I've seen you downing every bit of liquor we have in this room. What caused the change? You don't live long in this world by trusting strangers," Kim stated.

I thought for a second before answering. "To tell you the truth, I'm not sure; to say if I think it is smart, I do not know. I will say this, that I can still handle myself in this situation, in spite of whatever you may be thinking—"

"Easy. I'm not planning anything insidious. It is just nice to make conversation for a change with a normal-seeming person."

I laughed again. "I'm normal to you?"

"Oh, by a mile. Look who is around me: a mechanic who is more man-like than most men, an alcoholic in a wheelchair and an enigmatic leader who spends his days hunting for ways to stay alive. And me, just a mother. You, on the other hand, are older and yet you have still been carrying your daughter with you for who knows how many years. Most guys couldn't handle a real girl for eighteen years. That is impressive enough to me."

"Thank you." I said.

A silence stretched before us. I thought of something to say, but nothing ever felt right, as I took a big drink from the whisky. "So, the boy is your son?" I asked pointing at Joey.

Kim smiled deep, the corners unable to hide the frown, "Yes—he is my son. I know that may seem crazy—"

"It's not crazy at all, I feel the same way with Holly," I said, interrupting her before she could finish her statement. We both flushed and turned away. *At least I wasn't the only one bad at flirting,* I thought.

I decided to dig deeper on Wilson, as she'd mentioned him. "You stated that Wilson focuses on staying alive. How does he do that?" I asked, trying to seem disinterested.

"Let's see, he mostly scavenges and forages for any goods he can get ahold of. My son and I owe a lot to him; without him we would have died a long time ago. "

"How long have you known Wilson?" I asked.

"Well, not long. We've only been with him for over a—" Kim was saying, before her son appeared next to her.

"Mother, how much longer do you think Holly will be staying here with us?" He asked. The boy had piercing blue eyes that shone like bomb propellers from a great war plane, and they were slightly unnerving with a blue tint that just seemed unnatural. I wondered then if he was changing his eye color like Holly did sometimes. I wondered if ghosts appeared as they were, or if they all changed liked Holly did from time to time. I suppose it was no different from tattoos or plastic surgery. *People liked to change—that is the nature of humanity,* I thought.

"I'm not sure, honey. Why don't you just go play some more and let Mommy do some talking with Mister..." She smiled and looked at me.

"Mister Smith," I said slyly.

Kim nodded her head at me, not believing me, but not going to question it either.

The boy regarded me with a dull look that I wouldn't think any living eight-year-old would have been able to give me. "He seems—" I started, but was cut short.

"I know what you're thinking; Joey is all I have, though, Mister Smith. We are all each other has. When he came back, it was a sign from God. Like I was getting a chance to have my boy, my little boy back forever. Even if I could no longer hold him, he remained with me. You must know how I feel," she said almost pleadingly.

The truth is, I did know how she felt. Having Holly back was a blessing I didn't deserve. Only parents could understand that. "Can I ask: is he okay? He's a little tense." I asked.

"What do you mean? He is relaxed right now," she replied, confusion evident on her face.

"I mean, is he alright, after everything?"

"Oh yes; yes, he is charming, perfectly reasonable. I think the best answer would be that he is trapped as an eight-year-old form in his mind," she said pitifully, staring at the table. We were both silent for a spell as we listened to the two play. I was thankful that Holly maintained her intelligence. She was my rock, and I couldn't imagine her being anything than what she was now. I realized that in spite of my daughter dying, I was lucky I still got the chance to have her the way I did. She could have easily ended up as Joey, void of a personality.

I took another sip from the whiskey and enjoyed the silence between the two of us. It had been a long time since I had talked to another person; I thought I would have more to say. Even before the ghosts came, I wasn't a big talker. After twenty years, an introvert is still an introvert. I spoke after the silence became uncomfortable, and I wasn't sure if it was the whiskey or the incredible fatigue that was setting in.

"It is a sad, sad thing, when love turns out to be true. In the end, we all must lose, for it's very rare for both lovers go at the same time—one will always remain. To live one's life without a partner is to live one's life in total darkness. To live in total darkness is to be without any meaning." said I softly.

"Where did that come from?" Kim whispered.

"I think too much while drinking, but also from an old project of mine that I used to work on, just something for fun."

"Don't shrug it off, tell me what it's about. I might learn something," queried Kim.

"It is—well something silly from a different time. You know how it is." I coughed, looking at the table.

"Yeah, I do, I get that. What was the project, if you don't mind me asking? And answer, please; it's just nice to hear a different story from someone for a change." Kim asked, sliding closer to me.

"What the hell, why not? When I was younger and a lot less—well, let's just say younger—I worked as a server administrator," I said smoothly, setting my drink down and turning to peer at Holly and the young boy. The boy was now transformed into a miniature T-Rex, with Holly pretending to be in danger.

In a great way, it made me smile, and I think it made it worth it to talk to someone about my life for a change—to really talk about it, not being afraid of my life. Out loud, I spoke, "Anyways, I had this idealistic vision for a video game." I waited for laughter from Kim. Whenever I told people about me making a game, they used to laugh, especially when I mentioned the overall goal of said game. Instead, Kim kept her eyes focused and level—as well as someone could at the hour of our conversation.

I was a little taken off-balance by how non-committal she was. "I am surprised you aren't laughing. My wife laughed the first time I told her," I smiled, chuckling at the fact that I could still be embarrassed in spite of it being almost twenty years since I'd worked on the project.

"Oh—I've heard worse dreams from men. Men have the great fortune to be the biggest dreamers of them all. That being said, they will follow their dreams first—only their dreams," Kim jeered, wriggling her hands into themselves. Her teeth were grinding.

I decided to pick my words wisely through my drunken haze. "When it came to my dreams for my video game—that was it, just a fool's dream about a game, that was all. I was happy my wife supported me, and it gave me something to do after getting off of work. That was a very long time ago," I guessed, looking at the ceiling. "It was my story, though—I think I wanted to make something fun that had a deeper meaning, you know? Not a greetings card, just something that would make you think. And not end in you throwing up from how cheesy it is," I sighed, sipping at my drink. *I was done with this conversation,* I thought.

"I have to ask—were you the sort of man who put his family first, or did you go after your precious 'dreams?'" Kim asked, the fire in her voice. The woman was scaring me. One moment she came off as gentle as a bird; the next, as fiery as a hell hound—that or my paranoia was finally kicking in. *Why was I sitting here? I don't know these people...*

"When it came time to be there for my family, I was there. And that is all I will say about that," I growled, meeting her fire with some of my own.

"I'm checking, is all. My husband... well, let's just leave it as he made his choices. He picked certain things over his family." Kim sniffed, looking at her son as he played with my daughter.

That made sense to me, or rather it didn't need explaining. There are a lot of things in this world that didn't need to be overly explained. When the world became less filled with the living, the world became easier to understand. It was survival and nothing else. She had a past, I had a past. We also both had assholes—no need to explain beyond that.

We sat in silence again for another long, awkward pause. I stood up, stretching my sore joints. "I guess it is about that time—it was real nice talking and all, Kim."

"Wait; sit down for a little longer. I'm sorry things got a little on edge there. I understand it's none of my business in any of your life, just like it's none of your business in my life. I just really would like to get to know you better," she said, somberly.

Kim sidestepped towards me; I instinctively went for my weapon on my leg. Of course it wasn't there, and I swore under my breath for agreeing to such ludicrous measures. Kim sensed my uneasiness from her reach and pulled her hands back. I looked at her and saw a searching and need in her eyes. In that, a moment a hunger sprung into me, not hunger in the sense of a man loving a woman, but the desire of a man truly needing another person around him. If you can't give a man someone to love, at least give him someone to talk to.

As defensive and queer as I felt, I desired to keep some conversation going.

"Alright, let's drink a bit more," I replied as we drank. The conversation remained small as Kim asked for more details on my video game. And I asked for more information on how they had been surviving at the dam this whole time.

It turned out Christina's father had been the actual manager in charge of the dam. Her father was overseeing the entire conservation of the whole lake and all the various dams that were a part of the river system for protection. I had no idea it was that big of a problem—*just another little thing everyone had taken for granted in the world before, I thought.*

When the crisis began, Christina headed to the natural place she knew best. The Fort Mill Dam; she had visited the dam almost every summer. Christina had stayed at the dam for an unknown amount of time all by herself. I wondered, then, if that would explain some of the personality I had seen. One day, when Christina was on a supply run, she found a torn-to-pieces Rob on the side of a flipped truck. Rob was almost bleeding out and dying on the pavement.

By the time Christina met Kim and her son, Rob was nearly dead, after a few days of Christina frantically trying to save his life. Kim, being a former nurse, was able to stitch up the poor, disabled man and save him from death. They spent months together, hiding in the dam, hiding from the strangers in the wind, as they called the ghosts. The three apparently almost starved from lack of supplies; then, as if out of thin air, as Kim put it, Wilson showed up.

Wilson was able to get everything the four needed and more. I tried probing exactly how Wilson was able to obtain all the supplies they needed, but I couldn't get anything more out of Kim. The very mention of Wilson's name turned Kim almost into a dream-crazed teen. She was a little girl looking at a pony for the first time; the man could do nothing wrong in her eyes.

Finally, Kim asked me a question, as I was sleep-talking for a lot of my responses by this point. "What was your wife like?"

I opened my eyes slowly. In the two hours we had been talking, we had moved very close to each other, a lot closer than I would have liked to get to a woman. A lot closer than I wanted to get to anyone. *A truly alluring thing, women,* I thought. And that was the attraction I had felt for Diana years and years ago; no matter how old my body became, no matter how racked with guilt and misery. Diana's elegant, yet unusual way of always making my knees weak, was something I couldn't forget. The way my stomach seemed to rumble, the way my heart beat fast and my pants would suddenly become entirely too tight.

I would normally avoid the thought of Diana, like a huge snake in the middle of a trail. I couldn't help it now, though; maybe it would do me some good to speak of her for a change.

"My wife… she was a picture out of a frame; a bird that could not be caged, a river that is too wild to be fished. I kept her heart; she carried mine. I don't know how else to say it. She was my everything, and she gave me the greatest gift anyone could ever ask for. But, she also gave me…" I let my words trail in the air. I remembered the night she changed, the night it all went wrong, and she came for me. I had bitten and torn through my flesh in an attempt to get her away from me. And since that night, she wasn't my wild bird that I had been lucky to capture—now she served as a reminder of my mistakes over and over again.

I looked up, and across the room, Diana's mutilated form was smiling at me. I was never going to lose my bird. She would always be smiling at me from across the room, above me in the middle of the night, with me in every mirror I checked. She would whisper those words and they would play in my mind like a contagion drowning me in the poison I had created in this hollow world. Before falling down the pits of Diana's traps, I gulped the last of the whiskey and downed the hot liquor, until the bottle ran dry.

"Damn—I wish someone would talk about me like that." Kim

flushed, with her cheeks turning a bright shade of red. My hand was shaking, and I dropped the now-empty bottle of whiskey to the ground. As it shattered, Diana or whatever part of my mind that allowed her to show up, disappeared. "Are you okay?" Kim asked, with concern evident in her voice. It was refreshing to hear a woman's voice concerned for me. I looked up and found myself staring at Kim's bosom. I felt my face turn red as well and I looked away, mumbling between words as my tongue fought to stay in its place. *Twenty years since I'd had sex, and my wife is gone. Keep it together, you old fool.*

"I'm fine—how was your husband? I mean, what was your husband like?" I asked, quickly changing the topic from something other than Kim's breasts. It had been too long, and I was in need of a very long shower.

"My husband, well, he was something else." Kim spat, staring darkly at the ground. I didn't notice the difference in her tone until she said "else."

"When it came time for him to step up and be a man, as you said, to do right by his own, he tucked tail and ran off with a little slut who he had stashed away," Kim hissed. Venom was leaking out of her every word, finally catching my attention before it was too late.

"I'm sorry to hear that—"

"It's completely fine, James. Men like you, you're hard to find. People like my husband were, well, let's just say when I finally found his ghost, I didn't lose any sleep when I stuck a piece of steel down through his balls. I hoped it was painful and every bit as excoriating as that prick deserved," she growled while standing up, to her full five-foot-nothing height. I was impressed by her anger—*she was justified,* I thought.

She suddenly changed again and spoke. "You must think that I am crazy, don't you, Jim?" she asked.

"Not at all. Actually, I get it. The feeling that this world creates, crazy for us all, somehow," I said as I recalled what I had done to

Benny inside my mind. I had left that man to die. By now, some ghost had come along and more than likely torn him to pieces. I felt something at that thought. I didn't want to lament Benny, or for that matter, regret what I'd done. *Benny had tortured my only daughter, my seed. He deserved what he got, didn't he?* His face, though, pained and crying out for mercy, struck inside my mind like the strings of a jump rope, turning over and over again.

I felt suddenly sick and asked Kim wearily, "Do you have anything more to drink and also, could you show me where Holly and my quarters are?"

"That was the last of it, I'm afraid. You can find your rooms down the same hallway you came through. Just pick one of the empty ones."

"Well, it can't be helped—it was nice talking to you, Kim," I started as I began looking for Holly. She had been off with Kim's son the last time I'd checked. Panic began to sink in quickly as I looked around the suddenly clustered room. Rob was snoring lightly in his wheelchair, and the turbines looked as formidable as ever in their desolate, forever-off state.

"Holly, Holly, where are you?" I called out, trying to keep my panic out of my voice.

"Calm down, James, I am pretty sure she went to Joey's room," Kim responded coolly.

Joey? Who the hell is Joey? I guessed it must be her son; still, that information did nothing to change my uneasiness about the situation. She had told me that already: *Why was everything in this dam so weird?* I felt myself clam up when I normally wouldn't be, and things like names seemed to slip by like words in a stream.

"I need to go find her; she and I need to be in the same room," I declared.

"Oh—I understand now, I get it, pal, don't worry. She's okay, I promise," Kim said, getting to her feet as well.

I cut her off with a look. I didn't pay her attention as she lit a cigarette produced from somewhere on her person. I glanced her way again. "Those will kill you," I stated.

"Everything we did tonight will kill us," she stated as well.

I let her words go on to silence. I was about to shout again, but that was when Holly suddenly appeared from the ceiling above. She came down cross-legged and looked bewildered. "What's wrong, Jim-bo?" she asked, perplexed.

A flood of relief washed over me as I saw her. "Oh, thank God—I thought something had happened to you..." My voice was feeble and full of fear.

Holly understood instantly where I was coming from; she was like her mother in her ability to pick up on people's feelings. Holly smiled at me and shook her shoulders floating to my side.

Kim looked slightly bemused. "You two must be inseparable." Kim joked.

"You can't blame me. It was nice talking to you, Kim. Good night," I urged, rushing my way out of the open room, back down the long corridor. I found our "room." Candles had been placed on holders in the walls, and the hallway was surprisingly well lit.

I stopped before I opened the door, turning to Holly. "The room is all clear; just a sleeping bag and an overturned desk." Holly spoke with her eyes closed. I blinked at Holly, staring back at her. "Since when can you do that without having to go in?" I asked.

"I don't know. Ever since we met Anna, I feel, well, stronger. I can't... explain it," she admitted, flexing out her fingers in a gesture, almost as if she was working some invisible force.

"Met who?" asked Wilson's voice from behind us.

I froze in place, turning back around to find Wilson standing against his door-frame. He was eating an apple carelessly, seeming almost bored. "Oh, sorry, Wilson. Did we wake you? Sorry about that. Holly and I were just talking about some of our adventures out in the city." I laughed, trying to conceal my hand gesture behind my back to Holly. I twirled my fingers hoping Holly knew that meant to leave.

"I would love to trade some war stories with you, James." Wilson smiled and again, I felt uneasiness about him. I couldn't shake the feeling that it was not the first time I'd met Wilson before. It was like seeing a movie that turned out way different from what you'd expected from the trailers. Wilson was just foreign in every aspect, like a test from junior high school that you suddenly have to recall many years later. I vaguely knew him, I just couldn't understand the person I was meeting now.

"Well, have a good night, Wilson. Thanks again for letting us stay. We will have to talk some other time." I motioned, turning back to the room.

"Not a problem James. You and Holly are family. Enjoy the chamber," Wilson called out as I was already opening the door, letting it close behind me. Once inside the darkness of the room, I pressed my ear against the door—listening for what, I wasn't sure.

I held my breath, extending my senses out beyond the door, and I came back with nothing. When I was satisfied, I turned around to Holly glowing in the darkness. I flinched from the sight; I should have been used to it by now, but it was just unnatural to see someone shining in the darkness of a room.

"Douse the light a little, honey." I mumbled, squinting my eyes in the darkness.

"Sorry, I forget sometimes." Holly whispered.

I gave her my most disapproving frown. I had the feeling that it was lost on my daughter when we were both trapped inside of a closet.

"So, Jim, what's the issue? What's with all the weird hiding in the broom closet stuff?" Holly asked.

"For one, I think this is an office. Two…" I looked around the office, making sure that the room was empty. I lowered my voice before speaking. "Holly, I think it's best that we remain quiet. I do not like this place, and I think it's time we get out of here at the possible first chance we get," I whispered.

"Okay," Holly replied in a normal voice.

I cringed at her voice and spoke low. "Keep your voice down, kid."

"I don't understand the need for hush-hush. Also, I don't understand old people. I mean, just because the light's out doesn't mean that someone can't hear us; darkness doesn't affect sound."

I sighed heavily, wondering where exactly I had gone wrong in getting the biggest smartass in the world for a daughter. "That's not the point. If I taught you anything in the last twenty years, it was that perception is reality... I am having an uneasy feeling about this place, and I am trying to seem as normal and as hospitable as possible. If you don't believe me Holly, try to appear grateful to them at least. Or else we could be dog meat. I'm not saying we should run for the hills just yet, but let's keep our guard up and play it cool. I don't want to cause them any alarm; the whole thing just feels too easy..."

"Absolutely," Holly said shortly.

I wasn't sure if she wasn't sensing the urgency in my voice. "Holly, I am serious. We need to figure a way out of here. I do not like this place one bit—something is wrong."

"I get it, Jim—you're scared of being around other people after only being around me for so long. I—get it. You know, that Kim woman, she's pretty attractive. Who knows, maybe shave that beard of yours and a bath—you should be smooth sailing, if you understand me."

I flushed at Holly, my cheeks turning red. "Holly, you can't smell. You know that, right, kiddo?" I stated matter-of-factly.

"I know, I just want you to know that maybe for once, we don't have to be so paranoid about all of this. I mean, I spoke to Joey for a while. He is a weird kid, I can't blame him. Being the only ghost stuck as a little boy for twenty years with nobody—or the taste of ice cream—would kill most people. Besides, Rob is kind of funny and Christina is real sweet," Holly murmured. Holly looked down at the floor, as if searching for the words on the dusty floorboards.

"How about for once, we both just put our fears aside and take it all in. We've been searching for others for years. Maybe surviving and living are the exact same thing. Maybe we should try to have someone else around us for a change and roll the dice, to see if we can win."

I was taken aback. "I don't know, Holly. There are too many variables that aren't adding up."

"You're a smart guy, Dad; if you want to leave, then I won't hesitate to leave in an instant. Just make sure it is for the right reasons. We can't go anywhere; we might as well relax for a change and make the most of it. Like we talked about outside, we can't go anywhere, I think I was wrong in my first guess—hopefully you will be too," assured Holly, floating over to the desk and lying down. She hovered over its wooden surface, and I took that as the time to say what I had noticed.

"One last thing, Holly. I never told him you were my daughter. He had met you a few times before, sure, but I find it weird he knew exactly who you were. And you mentioned that you never remembered meeting him. None of this is adding up," I stated, In the darkness, I could see Holly turn her head to me.

"What does that mean, Jim?" Holly pondered.

"I don't know Holly, I don't know." Holly was quite for a while before speaking. "I think you should get some rest, Jim."

I murmured in agreement; she had me dead to rights. We couldn't leave even if we wanted to. I rolled into a sleeping bag on the floor and turned over, staring at the wall in the darkness, thinking I might as well not even close my eyes with how dark it was. Something still didn't feel right with the situation, though, and I just couldn't shake it. It all felt too staged.

As the night drifted, my thoughts became less frantic. *We were safe at least,* I thought, *if nothing else, we were with a friend of mine from long ago*. Though what worried me about that thought was how much people could change in just a day. Not a single person is ever the same from moment to moment. I know for sure I was nowhere near the man I used to be twenty years ago—a man who'd been weak, too afraid to do what was right by his family.

I turned, looking at Holly as she floated above the wooden desk with her eyes closed. *There is my family,* I thought. *There is the one person I will never be too weak for ever again, even if it kills me.*

Chapter 37

"James, James, why don't you wake up? Wake up James!" hissed a voice, My eyes were heavy, and my back was hurting. Years of sleeping on the floor had done nothing to deter the stiffness caused by cold, isolated hardwood floors. Beds were the worst in this new world. Those which still existed at this point were an ecosystem for germs and if that wasn't enough, try lying down on a fluffy, entombing, and rotten foam that wraps your body up like a sandwich in a world full of ghosts. One experience of that had been enough for me.

I sat up. Holly was nearby, a slight glow still radiating from her body. I considered calling out to her, as her eyes were open, and she was staring up at the ceiling. To be on the safe side, I followed her gaze up to the ceiling, but nothing was above us, only darkness. I breathed out, starting to rub the lower part of my back.

Muscles were starting to hurt that I wouldn't have believed existed until recently. I sighed, breathing out cold air. I started to cough. The dam offered very little in the way of warmth and the sleeping bag that had been in the room felt tattered. *Its days of doing its job had long since passed,* I thought.

"Just like you, lover, tattered and falling apart, bruised and flimsy on the best of days. I'm sure a stiff breeze would blow you over," spoke Diana, leaning against the desk, not too far off from Holly. I flushed with rage. The thing that was in the room now with Holly and I didn't deserve to be around my daughter.

"Don't you mean *our* daughter, lover? I'm everywhere; you might as well just speak what's on your mind," she sneered, idly rubbing her fingers together as if bored.

"Keep your voice down—and stay away from her," I hissed, pulling myself out of the sleeping bag. Diana moved across the room with speed, standing before me. She was naked, her flesh exposed, but any eroticism I once felt for my wife was long gone. It was hard to be turned on when she always appeared before me naked.

"What's wrong, lover, I don't turn you on anymore?" she asked, cupping my chin in her hands. Gesturing towards Holly, Diana spoke. "I get it, you're more into that shell over there. More into the image of a little girl."

I smacked her hands off my face. "No, I just like my company a little less like you," I grunted, moving away from her. I needed air. I needed to be out of this stuffy room. Holly was gone in one of her trances, and I couldn't pull her out of it if I wanted to. *She would be safe,* I thought, turning away from Diana. I started to move towards the door. *Diana will say anything to get to you—ignore her, James.*

"I notice you didn't correct me about our daughter being a shell," Diana smiled, pleased with herself.

Without turning to regard her, I stated, "She's my daughter, not yours."

"But she is just a shell," she cackled, and I turned ready to reply, to find an empty room. Holly was floating above the desk still. Otherwise, the room was darkness. I grunted, turning the door handle. I needed air, and it was too early for my normal ritual of arguing with Diana.

I wanted coffee, I wanted air. I was going to get whichever one came first. There was no way of telling what time it was in the dam as I moved through the long hallway. Gas lamps had been placed every couple of feet by long chains, providing what little light could be allowed within this small narrow cave.

I kept my hand on the wall. Having something solid in my hand always helped me feel like I was grounded, that everything was fine, because I was touching something real. I kept my hand on the wall until I came to the living room. Rob was snoring lightly in his chair, oblivious to anything else in the world.

I was the only one up, I thought—*that's good.* Last night was way too out of the ordinary for me—I was never that social with anyone. I crossed the open room to the doorway Wilson had taken us through the other day.

Outside, I could hear the barking and snarling of beasts as I approached the threshold of the door. The handle was cold, and I pushed it open. Snow was falling in heavy mounds all around me. Covering the ground in thick puffs of frozen tears. *I hated wet snow,* I thought, *it was no good for snowball fights, no good for anything that was useful.*

At the railing, I could see the ghost animals outside the fence line, searching desperately for an entrance. I gulped, thankful I was beyond those fences; if the situation had been reversed and we had made it home, I wasn't sure if my home would have been able to fend off this many.

I brushed the snow from the railing and leaned into the cold metal, resting my arm on the ledge. Beyond me, a soft pink sun was rising over the mountains, signaling the end of fall and the beginning of winter. I shivered, pulling my coat around me tighter, as I watched the ghosts fight desperately to find a way into the compound.

"Complain all you want, you bastards, you won't be finding a way in today," I mumbled as I looked down at the riverbank. Below me was the garden. Christina had a shovel and was digging something from the ground.

She hadn't noticed me. If I turned around now, I could sneak back inside and avoid an awkward talk. As if on cue, snow fell from the railing and landed near Christina. She jerked, looked at the snow, and finally turned her eyes up, seeing me above her. She beamed, waving her hand. "James—good morning to you, you scared the shit out of me. Want to come down here and give me a hand?" she shouted up to me.

If I went back in now, it would be rude. I grumbled, calling back down, "Sure," as I turned, heading down the frozen stairs slowly. Just like last night—my normal actions weren't happening. Holly was even acting different as well. *Maybe I was just comfortable around these people,* I thought.

I reached the bottom of the steps. The ground was frozen and hard beneath my feet as I made my way over to Christina, and before I could speak she handed me a shovel.

"Start digging that row. I will take care of this side. Make sure you go over the blade and that should be deep enough," she grunted, turning away from me, and started digging out a long trench along her side.

Perplexed, I hesitated and soon followed suit. I was hard work—the ground was thick, strenuous to break open, and I couldn't apply as much pressure as I would have liked to. Christina soon noticed I wasn't keeping up with her. She eyed my hand, a neutral look on her face, so I couldn't tell what she was thinking as I struggled to break the dirt.

"How about you just hand me the seeds instead, otherwise we will be out here all day," she spat, taking the shovel from my hand and threw me a heavy sack.

"Hurry up, we don't have all day," Christina shouted over the river nearby, as I juggled the sack of seeds, following after her.

"Place a handful of seeds about every six inches or so," she trailed off as she dragged her shovel across the ground, creating a wide ditch as she headed towards the river. Doing the best I could with one hand, I put the sack in my arm and sprinkled seeds every six inches like she'd instructed me to do.

We worked until the sun was over the mountain, and the birds finally started to call out as the compound became a shrine of gold reflecting off the melting snow, bleeding into the running river below us.

I sat the sack down and wiped the sweat from my head. It was hard work, but during the whole thing I thought of nothing else except for placing my seeds every six inches as I was told to do. It was nice, just focusing on doing my job—I would always be a working man. Christina went to the riverbank and dipped a bucket into the running water. She pulled it up and took a long drink from the bucket.

Under her jacket, I could see thick shoulder muscles moving along her back. *She had been a hard worker most her life,* I thought. I looked at my hands. A blister had formed from where the sack had rubbed on my skin while I planted the seeds. Otherwise, they were soft compared to hers. *Don't get in a fight with her,* I noted, wiping the last bit of dirt away from my fingers.

Christina eyed me, watching me as she drank from the water. Feeling nervous, I spoke out. "So, those were potato seeds I'm assuming, correct? I never had much of a green thumb. I heard you could plant potatoes all year round."

"Onions and garlic, to be exact," she said matter-of-factly at my statement.

"I see," I mumbled, turning away slightly, I was ready to get back to bed. I was drained from being in the field. And despite the hard floor, I had slept fairly well for the few hours I got.

"Well, I am going to get back to Holly—she will be missing me." I waved, turning away from Christina.

"My father lost his hand as well, during a wood-cutting incident. Lost it to a widowmaker," she said to me.

I stopped, turning back towards Christina. "I'm not sure what that is," I puzzled, trying to figure out what Christina was saying to me. She placed her bucket down, taking the shovel in her hands, and stopped a few feet away from me. I instinctively stepped back. I wasn't comfortable with anyone getting close to me, especially someone who knew she was probably stronger than me.

Christina leaned on the shovel, and explained. "A widowmaker is a branch that looks like it is free, and hanging from a limb, when it's actually still attached. My father was sawing down some logs one summer, while we were home from the dam. He accidentally got the chainsaw caught in the limbs, the branches jerked ahold of the saw and well—let's just say my father's days of sawing down trees were over." She sniffled at the memory.

"After that, my father would just stay working here at the dam as a conservation manager. I would work with him every summer," she went on.

I hesitated before answering. I hated having to confront any kind of emotion. Why was she opening up to me anyways? I was just a stranger. "Why are you telling me all of this?" I queried.

Christina straightened up, "Because seeing you and your daughter reminded me of my father and I, is all. Thought I could get to know you better, is all, if we were all going to be living together a bit longer," she announced.

I coughed. "I guess so. I wouldn't exactly call us 'living together,'" I mumbled.

"What would you call it?"

I looked around at the ghosts, snarling at the fence lines. "I would say begrudgingly shelter occupants," I scoffed under my breath.

"Well you could be outside of those fences. I'm not sure how long you would last then," Christina stated. Her words provoked me momentarily until I looked at the ghosts outside. Their numbers were endless. We couldn't have made it back to our home if we tried.

I sighed. "You have a point—thank you for taking us in," I grumbled, turning away from her again.

"My father said he could always feel his hand—you know, his missing one. Swore it felt like it was attached. He said it was like an itch that could never go away," she spoke over my shoulders.

I shrugged. "It's more like—more like remembering something was there that you see every day. Like a photograph of a perfect moment in your life. Sure, it gives you happiness, may even provide some level of comfort, but the thing is, that photograph can easily end up gone. Gone in a fire, gone from the ages, and what then? It's just another scared thing to remind you of what you lost. Everyone will stare at it, everyone will wonder whose photo that is or what happened to all the photos, but just like with missing limbs, once they're gone, they're gone. You can't remember what happened to them anyways, so why stare at picture of something when all that's left is bones and ashes?" I trailed off, wanting to head up the stairs already.

Christina was quiet, so I spoke first. "Is that why you called me down here, to trade war stories about how you think your father and myself are similar? Both crippled men with their daughters?" I snarled at her.

"My daughter has been my heart forever, she always will be, even when she died. On that day, I forever sold my heart. On that day, I said goodbye to anything bad. She was my light on this Earth. Living or dead, she is my heart. If you think I will let any of you hurt her, think again. I will eat you, I will kill you. There will be no chance—you will not survive," I fumed.

Christina raised her shoulders, squaring them as if for an attack. Neither of us moved for a moment, as I breathed hard into the freezing air. "No—my father was a good man. A good man, just like you. He wanted me to go beyond this dam. Worked his ass off to put me through college so I didn't end up working here. Turns out I did anyways, even after I left for school," Christina laughed.

She went on, "I just admire men who take care of their families, is all. Crippled or not, you seem to be doing a good job to me."

Christina continued, walking past me. "This was my father's home away from home. He spent most of his life here. He raised me here; it is my home. Staying here makes me feel closer—makes me feel safe. I called you down here to help me fix some seeds, nothing more. Not everyone is out to harm you, James. You reminded me of my father because of the way you just spoke about your girl. If we wanted to harm you, why let you though the fence in the first place? Why bring you back here? Try being less of an asshole. Oh and thanks for the help," Christina lamented as she walked past me, heading up the stairs.

I mumbled, my anger deflated in the cold. I was off to a good start with making friends. I headed back to the room, Holly started to talk to me as I threw the sleeping bag over my head and blocked out the world. I needed a few more hours before putting up with anyone.

Chapter 38

Later that day, I awoke to find the room as still as darkness covering a lake, as still and enclosing as a tomb. I rolled out of the bag, unsure of the time without any light. I looked for Holly and couldn't see her shape. My heart started racing at that. I had to calm myself down multiple times—Holly could take care of herself.

Under the door to the office, I could see a light shining and hear low whispers. "Everyone must be up," I said to myself, regretting having drunk that much. My head was on fire. In the darkness, I decided to freshen up as much as a hung-over man with one hand at the end of the world could do, which wasn't much. I left the room and entered the open area of the dam. The turbines looked like relics of an old sci-fi movie, gathering dust, still ready to blow a world up if necessary.

Gathered at the same table as the night before were Holly, Joey, Rob, Christina, Kim, and Wilson, slowly stirring a pot of something. That something made my mouth water as I could smell the coffee inside.

"Any of that for me?" I asked, walking towards the table hesitantly.

"Sure is, you probably need it, after this morning," Christina laughed, blowing into the cup of her own sweet nectar of the gods. If any of our conversation from this morning had upset her, I couldn't tell. She simply smiled and blew into her coffee. *I must have been really drunk,* I thought, replaying what we both had talked about. No need to bring it up if she doesn't.

"Morning James, how did you sleep?" asked Wilson as I accepted a cup of coffee from Christina, taking a seat at the table near Holly.

"Well enough," I grunted. I was never much of a morning person.

"I have some bad news for you, James," Wilson said somberly. I eyed him out of the corner of my eye, ready to swing if needed to be. "The animals are still outside the fences, so I don't think we will be able to head out today. I am sorry."

I made eye contact with Holly, hoping my message of *remain calm* was transferred between the two of us silently. "It is what it is. Guess we will just have to remain here," I responded matter-of-factly.

"Yes, it appears that way," Wilson agreed with a smile hanging deep on his face. I noticed he had his gas mask on his waist still. Was it some kind of memento? Had to be, surely it was, since no one else felt the need for one. As I looked at his belt, I could peer inside his jacket pocket and make out the outline of a purple object, glistening. Before I could ponder further, Wilson caught my gaze, shifting his body at an angle that obscured my vision. He carried a lot of knives and a gas mask—I needed more information.

"So, any idea what we can do today, people? Can't really scavenge; must be chores time," Wilson said like a concerned mother.

"Has anyone ever told you guys you're sort of weird?" voiced Rob, sipping at his coffee, making a face at the taste. That got a moment of laughter from the group and eased some of the tension, some.

Throughout the rest of the day, the group broke off into smaller groups. Kim and Joey spent time sewing a stack of clothes. Mostly Joey just watched everyone with deep ocean blue eyes. Rob, mostly cussed, and in general made an ass of himself as he helped Christina work on some old truck in the garage in conjunction with the dam. I noted they had made similar designs as the Beast. Both were surprisingly good mechanics, from what I could tell, as they expertly worked on the machine. Holly and I tried staying out of everyone's way, keeping watch, all the while offering what little help when we could. Wilson, for his part, inventoried a stock of canned goods. I made sure to keep an eye on him from time to time, most of all.

As he was tallying up the goods, I spoke, choosing my words deliberately. "Ever miss the old days back at the office?"

Wilson straightened up his posture at the sound of my voice and turned to me. "Are you kidding? Probably every day. All of you guys were a bunch of knuckleheads. Good workers, though, when you weren't busy shooting Nerf guns at each other and debating some of the dumbest things I've ever heard in my life." Wilson beamed, smiling at a memory. I pressed on, searching my mind for something that could be used to gain more info. I was still having trouble remembering. It wasn't the exact moments of my life I was having trouble recalling, it was Wilson. Every memory of him felt like I was looking through a screen door. I could see him, but nothing felt clear.

Wilson must have sensed something on my face, "It's all the ghosts you've taken, right? I have trouble sleeping, trouble remembering the happiest memories of my life. Sometimes I must draw something on paper each day to make sure it is, in fact, my memory and not some other ghost's." Wilson stared at his hands, pointed to the ground.

That shut me up. He was right, it wasn't old age that caused me to forget things, it was like trying to recall a million books you were forced to read every day for years. Sometimes, I would think I was a doctor, teacher, or even a plumber in a previous life. A teenager into punk rock, or an old man laughing with his old war buddies. Mostly, I was able to shake off those moments, easier than when Diana would visit me. If it wasn't for Holly being there every day, I was sure the madness would have consumed all my memories of my previous life by now, sunk like a paper boat in the ocean.

My voiced cracked in my throat, and I just nodded at Wilson. He understood what it was like, remembering—how hard it was. I understood why he liked the task of counting, or that he would draw his memories on paper. He didn't want to forget—it gave me more respect for Wilson instantly.

I turned to excuse myself to think. "She sure looked beautiful that night," Wilson said as I turned away.

"Who did?"

"Diana at the last office Christmas party. She looked great in that green dress," Wilson said calmly.

"Yeah—she sure did," I said coolly, walking away.

Chapter 39

As night settled in, we all gathered once again at the table. Conversation had been easier after my talk with Wilson. I was more at ease with the situation than before. There might have been validity to his story so far. It still felt too good to be true, but I was relaxing some. Holly was as well, from what I could tell. She had spent most the day with Joey again. It was nice seeing her with a friend. I wondered then what sort of friends Molly would have grown up to have. Holly was so different from her, so much braver, much more alive. I shook my head. It was wrong of me to compare the two and the whole thing still felt taboo.

Still, I was proud in that moment of both my daughters, they had both been good people. "Good ghosts…" I muttered, thinking about Holly.

"What's that, James?" Wilson asked, pausing from a story he was telling the group. "Oh—nothing, just saying 'good ghosts,'" I said, embarrassed.

"Ha, that's a riot, but I think you're on to something Jim. Everybody has a good ghost story. What the hell, anyone want to share theirs?" Rob interjected, asking the group. Everyone paused at that, trying to figure out what Rob was getting at.

When no one responded, Rob put up his hands almost defensively, "Come on people, everyone has a good ghost story—I mean, hell, when you're surrounded by a horde of ghost animals no more than forty feet away, might as well share some stories."

"That sounds pretty cool. Can I go first?" Holly asked, raising her hand. We all turned our heads to Holly, waiting to hear her story.

Chapter 40

"So, there I was in a classroom." Holly continued her story. "Jim—or my father—always helped me get books on tape. A lot of them talked about school. I honestly just wanted to feel what it was like. You know, to sit there and just learn like kids my age are supposed to. Anyways, I snuck out one night and headed to a nearby school we had passed once."

Holly glanced my way. I shot her a look, and she paused. I wasn't mad she had been sneaking out per se, just more confused at how she had been doing that. I guess that was the faith of parents to be fooled by their children.

"It was pretty boring, just sitting there—I had found this one classroom that wasn't completely molded over. It was cliché as fuck, but hey, why let a little thing like a skeleton hanging on a hook and boring 'be-strong' posters get in the way of a little hooky?" Holly paused, looking at all of us.

"At some point, I was sitting in the class. It had grown really dark outside. I mean really dark—all the lights in the sky were out. I'm not saying I got scared, just a little uneasy. I mean, an abandoned school like that would scare anyone. I was about to leave when it started thundering. The classroom lit up with light, this huge crack. I closed my eyes, you know—I was a little scared at that point and was about to leave. Then, every seat in the class became occupied with these kids... I'm not sure if that was exactly right, they all were quiet, all were completely still. None of them moved and as the thunder outside smashed around me, my heart beat faster. Jim had always taught me to run in situations like this. I didn't waste a second and booked it from that class. As I started to leave, all those kids flew after me," Holly said, showing herself with her arms out-stretched. All of us were hanging on to her every word, waiting for her to continue.

Holly continued, "I flew as fast as I could, those creepy things kept coming after me. I had no idea why though. I remember screaming my head off through the city. My voice covered by the thunder... I had never felt more alone in all my life—I mean, I guess in my time as a ghost. Either way, I kept flying scared and became lost." Holly stopped.

"Holly—why didn't you just come home? Our home could easily have warned them off," I pondered, my fatherly instincts taking over. I hadn't heard about any of this from her before.

"I was lost completely. The city at night—it's one thing during the day, but at night, it's a moving nightmare. I had flown so fast and so far away, I wasn't even sure if I was even in Charlotte at some point. I was still being followed by those things, and I was feeling weak for some reason. To this day, I had never felt as tired and scared as that night. They kept coming, those kids, and nothing I did seem to lose them. And I had no idea what they wanted. I flew into a building and I just stopped. I couldn't go anymore. I tried, but it felt like something was pulling me back. I had only a couple of seconds to think, so I flew into the nearest thing. Turned out it was a casket in some tiny ass church. I wasn't alone for long—those kids showed up, I could feel them all around me as I waited inside that coffin." Holly stopped again, gathering her thoughts.

"How did you know it was a casket?" asked Rob, sitting up straight for the first time since I'd met him.

"Oh, well I wasn't alone in that coffin. Someone was inside it. Or rather, someone's remains were. Not sure why a casket had remains in it, considering everything changed in one night per Jim. Regardless, I floated inches away from a skull for hours. And when the sun started to shine, I felt the kids leave. I left that casket and church as soon as they were gone, speeding the whole way home. It took me a while, but somehow I remembered my way back." Holly finished with a faraway look in her eyes.

Father or not, anyone could tell the ordeal had hurt her. I wanted to hold her, I wanted to comfort her. "Holly, I... why didn't you ever tell me this?" I asked her, everyone at the table quiet.

She just shrugged. "Crying inside the casket of some dead dude for a few hours doesn't seem like a fun story to tell your pops," she whispered.

I was stunned, and couldn't think of what to say. Thankfully, Rob was always on beat. "Well, I sure thought it was fun, had me hanging by the edge of my seat. Good story, Holly!" Rob roared, slapping the table.

"Yes, it was pretty scary. Going to be tough to top it," Christina added. Everyone else just nodded their heads in approval. I just sat there with my mouth closed, feeling very old.

From there, the rest of us shared our ghost stories. Mine was about a time Holly had picked up a sheet and screamed boo at me. Rob's, about him being caught by a ghost in a bathroom. Christina shared her encounter with ghosts inside the dam and Kim didn't want to share, saying she had enough nightmares. Wilson just smirked when we asked him to share, saying, "I think there are enough things every day that are far worse than any story."

After that, we all went to bed. Holly wouldn't talk to me as I closed the office door. I stopped trying after a while and decided to go to bed. Stories were great to help with getting through something; they could inspire people to do great things, or do great evils, but sometimes, just sometimes, stories told too much truth. The truth being that we were all strangers to each other, despite how much we loved and cared for one another.

No matter what happened, we all had our own ghost stories haunting us in the middle of the night. That night, Diana came to me smiling, saying once again, “It’s your fault, James.”

Chapter 41

After a while, cities all started to look the same to me, I thought, *covered in runic grays, with crumbling bricks littering every inch of the ground, as shoots of green fought to overtake the city. It was always the same, a moving photograph that reminded us we were all that was left of an old world. We were the ghosts now; this is their home,* I thought, as Kim, Wilson, Joey, and I moved through the city.

Wilson had told me the name of the city at some point, and I hadn't bothered to remember it in the slightest, just nodded and focused on the road as we pulled into the parking lot of a run-down mall. Factoids like that seemed miles away; belonging to a different me. My hand was sweaty as Holly left the car and flew off into the mall. Wilson said he had been avoiding the mall for a long time—now that he had us for help, he figured we could try.

Using the dam itself, we had managed to float down to a portion that had been eroded away by time. We crossed, free from the animals, about a mile downstream from the other section of the outer wall. It turns out Christina's Dad used to take her canoeing on the river every summer during their off days. She was an expert compared to the rest of us.

The idea to search the dam's waterways was suggested by Rob on the fifth day we had been at the dam. I think my constant pacing during the day was adding to the cabin fever at the barrier. *You have to keep busy to keep the mind from snapping. I'm not doing a good job of staying busy inside the confines of the dam. I need this,* I thought.

We left in the early morning, Wilson paddling ahead with Kim and Joey. Holly and I with Christina, since we had to go slower. The water was rough in the morning—higher, as Christina put it, because of the snow that was melting adding to the river level.

Sure enough, as Rob theorized, towards the end of the river, a section of the dam had in fact eroded away which is why the water banks had risen in the last few weeks so dramatically. We had our weapons again, which made me feel a lot safer, but the water had scared me. The entire trip I had gripped the sides of the canoe so hard, my hand was almost bleeding. I never liked large bodies of water in general. With the addition of ghosts in the world, things coming out of the water was always a possibility.

Once we crossed the dam and headed to the calmer parts of the river, Wilson signaled for us to lead to the riverbank. We disembarked, and Christina stayed with the canoes, tying them to the bank. Wilson had a map out, examining some portion as I came up behind him.

He turned towards me, looking up at his map, "Okay, there should be a city about ten miles upstream from here. Help us get into the mall inside the town. Afterward, I promise you can take one of our cars out of here," he stated.

I grunted in response, begrudgingly. The plan was simple enough: help them, help us. I wished we could have left the dam in the Beast, but beggars couldn't be choosers, and the animals still hadn't left yet.

"Holly, Joey, you two go on and scout ahead." Wilson pointed off into the distance along the road. Holly gave him a long look. Wilson didn't seem to pay attention or to care as he studied the map. I motioned with my hand: "Go." Holly did, and the rest of us minus Christina headed along the road. After an hour of walking, we came across a Honda that had rusted brown to the point that its original color was anyone's guess.

"I know what you're thinking—trust me, it runs. I've left cars all over this state in my searches. She works just fine," Wilson smiled as he slapped the hood. I looked around at the surrounding woods, feeling uneasy at all of this, as Holly and Joey flew overhead. Everything was feeling too easy again; this was about the time something terrible would happen.

I shook my head as we sped along in the car. *Keep a positive outlook man. I mean, after all, somehow this rust bucket of a car was running despite twenty years of sitting in the middle of the road.* Wilson explained on the way through town that he had picked up and used multiple cars over the years. With the help of Christina and Rob, many of them were kept running, but gas, gas was the hard thing to come by in this new world. *Don't I know it,* I thought as we approached the mall.

I hadn't told Wilson about the supply depot Holly and I knew about. It was one thing losing my car. Our best hope was making it to the warehouse and hitting the road, holding our chips from them, putting as much distance between the dam and us as possible; I had decided that maybe the people at the dam weren't all bad, though everything still felt out of the ordinary. Five days wasn't soon enough to stop being guarded.

And that's how we had made it to the mall—uneventful for the most part, no ghosts, no hiccups, just a quiet ride in a rusted car on a lonely road. We stayed in the car, keeping the vehicle running as it sputtered with the engine running low. "I think we should have just enough gas to make it back to Christina; hopefully, we can find something useful to get rid of those animals," Wilson mumbled. Wilson mentioned they had enough supplies of food and water to stay at the dam for years. What they lacked was everything else. The winters were hard in North Carolina, and gas needed to be found. Wilson hoped at the very least a generator of some kind or more blankets would be in the mall.

Keep to the deal, I thought, *help them find supplies then let them drop you off at the riverbank. You don't owe anything else to these people,* I thought. Holly and Joey soon came flying out of the mall, Joey's face as stoic as ever, Holly looking bored. That was good news for a change; this should be quick.

I opened the door walking out towards Holly. "How did it look in there?"

Holly hesitated, looking behind her at the mall. My heart dropped with worry as to what that meant.

"I'm worried we won't have enough room. There was a book-store—I mean hundreds of disks, Jim. Good shit, honestly; I don't think we will have enough room in the car." Holly trailed off as I pinched the bridge of my nose.

"No, Holly, I meant are we good to go in?"

"Oh, yeah—not a thing in the world in there, just the same broken and molded down building we normally find. Just walls and a roof," she informed me. I nodded my head and turned back to Wilson and Kim, then exited the vehicle.

Wilson rolled up his map and shoved it inside his coat before speaking, "I couldn't find any maps of this place—we will have to use the guide on the inside of the mall," he stated. I shrugged; he was right, I just wanted to be in and out of this place as soon as possible. I looked at my pan. Kim had a long piece of iron-rebar hanging from a cord on her arm, and Wilson had nothing in his hands. That didn't make me feel comfortable at all as the three of us went through the cracked in glass entranceway of the mall.

Get in and get out, I thought wearily. Once through the doors, we were met by a map guide framed behind the plastic-like material of a stand, long since overdue a good wipe-down.

Wilson rubbed the plastic covering the map and pointed out a few points of interest within minutes. "Okay, let's see, there's a hardware store on the north side of the mall, that's most likely where we will find anything of use—I will go there. James, you and Kim go to the food court area, see if you can't find any goods. There are three exits to this mall, one behind us and one in the West Wing and one on the North wing. As for Joey and Holly, you guys search around some more and find what you can. All of us, meet back here at this entrance way in thirty minutes. If anything happens, shout and run for the exit. No one be a hero. Any questions?" Wilson asked the group. Everyone was somber and quiet. I hated it.

Jumping into a building this size, especially without any arms, was making me nervous. Holly usually never missed a beat, and that put me at some ease. But I didn't know these people; I had no idea what they could or could not do.

The only thing I had seen on Wilson was his gas mask and that weird-colored blade in his jacket. Kim had an exotic and feisty look to her in a way. I noticed she walked with a limp in her foot. It dawned on me then as the group split up, Holly and Joey vanishing into the darkness of the mall, that Wilson had put the two cripples together. I grumbled. Being underestimated was a given considering the circumstances. And while I held no illusions I could carry more than one canister of gas, it was just a bitter pill to swallow. I was less of a man than Wilson is.

That thought haunted me as Kim and I delved deeper inside the mall. We both had flashlights shining into the darkness, the stale air moving particles of dust as if we were opening the chambers of a spaceship for the first time in thousands of years. That's the thing—when you smell old air, a sense is awakened; you know the feeling. It's the one that dismantles you in the mirror, the one that haunts you in the quiet moments of your mind. A ringing in your ear, a prickle on your neck and suddenly you need the light on—you need to turn the lights on because you can smell something wrong is afoot. A betrayal of your favorite aromas that you weren't expecting. Something haunting, grueling, and vicious awaiting you. Buried beneath all your rationale, all your lights and words of fighting the darkness, you know the truth: fear is coming, and you've just opened the doorway.

I shook as Kim and I slowly made our way through the mall, the two floors above us looking like the bones of a giant, clasped above us as we continued to the west side of the mall. Kim was silent. If she was as unnerved as I was by being in this old building, I couldn't tell. I had to give it to her though, after years of going into buildings with Holly, I still felt racked with fear whenever I entered them. Humans are just meant to be afraid of the dark; things eat us in the dark.

"You know, I'm embarrassed by you. I am about to completely shit my pants walking in the dark right now—you're taking this as a walk in the park," I called over to Kim.

She stopped, turning halfway towards me. "Actually, I'm scared out of my mind. The only thing keeping me going forward was the thought of maybe finding something to mix the fish with for a change. Let me tell you—not a single person in that dam can cook worth a damn," she stated.

I laughed, easing up the tension as the two of us walked through the mall together, this time closer. With Kim's walk, the way was slow, our time to search ticking fast by as our beams of light came across the first food signs. We had entered the food court. Around us were the remains of frozen treat stands and hot-dog venues. I let my mind fill in the smells that should have been inside the typical American mall.

"No cookies though," I mumbled.

"What's that, James?" asked Kim, as she shined the light into my face. I covered my eyes in response.

"Nothing. I just don't think we are going to find anything here. These kinds of stores don't keep canned goods," I stated.

Kim moved the light and went behind the counter of the nearest stand. She began to rummage through the cooking selves on the other side of the bar. I left her to it, as I shined my light in the open food court area. I made sure to sweep slowly so I wouldn't miss anything. Being in a room this vast and open screamed "attack." My flashlight gleamed over objects in the darkness, turned over chairs, half-eaten meals, purses and even the remains of a shoe stretched before me. The last moments of people's lives—over in an instant.

It was as if looking at a painting of people at a museum.

I could see a picture of how the world used to look, see a world that was familiar enough at least in shape, but I couldn't relate. I couldn't jump into a painting, or have a conversation with the people depicted. *After all, they're a picture, just a casual glance out of the corner of my eye. And I don't want to look at someone else's life, not even for a moment; I didn't want to have to imagine what people had to have been thinking before everything changed. It had to happen like dust being swept away in an instant. Like a painting in a museum, James, not an actual thing. Treat it like that,* I shuddered as I saw the piles of baby clothes tossed under one table. *Like a painting.*

"Hey James!" shouted Kim from behind the stand. I turned and she was brandishing several bags in her hands. "Jackpot!" she joked, coming over the counter. slowly. I noticed her lousy leg needed an extra moment worth of movement to see her over.

I doused my thoughts and started to walk towards Kim. "What did you find?"

"Well, I had a hunch the ice cream stand would have these, but powdered peanut-butter and some flavor mixes. This stuff will last forever, if we can find some honey, then so long, flatbread from Christina's garden, hello fattening snacks. Just have imagination sometime."

We both laughed at that. Christina had a green thumb for sure, but there was only so much you could do with fish and potatoes. Apparently all the garlic and peppers from last year's harvest didn't make it.

Noise from the other side of the food court stopped both our laughter instantly. I shot my flashlight in the direction of the sound and a pale leg dipped into the shadows behind a pillar.

"James," Kim whispered.

I kept my light fixated on the spot that the leg had been. "Kim, get back to the main entrance. Go find Holly," I whispered back.

"Are you fucking crazy? Leave it alone, let's both get out of here!"

"If it was a ghost, they would bring more; I need to take care of it before it's too late. If it was something else, they're probably scared out of their minds."

"You have one hand, what can you do? Let's go!" she raised her voice.

I didn't answer back. Instead, I charged off into the shadows as Kim shouted "James." I dodged around the overturned tables and chairs and made my way deeper into the food court. Pillars were all around me, and I swept my flashlight in the gloom, searching for the leg that I had seen.

There, near the end of the food stands, James, I thought as I saw a flash of pale skin again. I ran deeper into the mall; Holly had said the building was "clear." If this person were a ghost, it wouldn't be clear for long. Spirits traveled alone, and when there were this many of us, one was enough to cause problems. I kept chasing until I rounded the food stands, when my legs glanced the side of a table, and I fell hard. My flashlight shattered when it hit the ground, rolling away from my hand, its last few moments of light flickering before finally blinking off into the unknown.

I tasted blood in my mouth as I felt around with my tongue, making sure I hadn't lost any teeth in the fall. "Nope, everything is all in place," I croaked, spitting out blood.

"Go that way, James," pointed Diana, glowing a soft white tint in the darkness.

I grunted, "You're always bossing me around, Diana."

"Someone has to James; you can't even stay on your feet."

"Why don't you—" I started before Diana disappeared, leaving me in total darkness. Panic snaked its way inside me; I turned back around, searching for Kim. There was no light in the dark; there was only the midnight.

I knew what this meant right away; I had gone too far into the mall. I thought about shouting out, but if the ghost I was chasing came after me, I was finished. I couldn't see the end of my nose. If it turned out to be a person, I could be walking blindly into a trap. I outstretched my hand, my pan banging softly on my hip, letting me know it was still there.

You have that going for you old man, keep your head up, follow the path Diana showed you. Diana was always there, always a flicker at the edge of every corner, but so far, she had only tried to kill me once. I gulped, remembering her last words. *Don't think them, James, don't think them, just walk. By now Kim has found the others. You haven't gone that far into the mall, just stay where you are.*

Of course, that's assuming she made it. She was probably already dead—that's why her light is gone. Or the inescapable truth: she left you to die. Why would they want a crusted and handicapped old fool like you? Wandering around in the darkness like an old man trying to find the bathroom when he needs to pee?

Holly would never leave me; she would come back even if the others wanted to get away. Keep telling yourself that, James. How long has it been? Long enough for a clubbed-foot wreck of a mother to scream her little head off and find the others. Long enough for a swarm of those things to feast upon them. Might even be your dear little Holly, even.

"No!" I shouted back at my mind. Instantly the thoughts building inside me shook in defiance.

"No, he says," hissed a voice from behind me.

I spun. Wilson was frozen before me, a flashlight shaking violently in his hands as a ghost was latched onto his back. Pale, long limbs coated in powder white, all leading up to the mud-colored brown top of a woman ghost.

She winked when I turned towards them, the light from Wilson's flashlight casting shadows, illuminating her as if she were an enormous spider come to eat us flies below her. I recoiled in fear; I had never seen this before, Wilson was flung into the air, his body unmoving as he screamed out.

I kept backpedaling until I hit one of the pillars in the mall. Wilson continued to scream, and all I did was try and put distance between the two of us. A steel voice rasped in my ears, and I turned, seeing Diana. "Go on, James, go save him," she urged.

I involuntarily jerked away from her, my gut reaction to run, when I felt cold hands in vice-like grips pull my arms behind me. It was enough that my fear was being exacerbated by being in the dark—more so now I had Diana holding me.

"Diana, let me go!" I screamed at my wife, matching the maddening wails of Wilson above me. *If Holly was here, she could easily take care of that thing,* I thought.

"But she's not here; it's just you and me, James;. You need to stay away. I am protecting you." Diana slithered her words out as her tongue traced my cheek.

I was tired of her, tired of the same old song and dance. Every time I needed to be strong, she was here. *What gave you strength last time, James? Think—it was Holly, of course.* "Not today," I whispered to Diana, snapping free of her hold. I ran forward, looking at Wilson. He was dangling in midair, about twelve feet off the ground. *The fall would hurt,* I thought just before I unclipped my pan, launching it at the ghost above him. Throwing a heavy cast-iron pan wasn't something I had ever trained for, when it soared past Wilson. My heart went with my pan as well. Diana cackled from behind me.

Wilson cried out once more when Holly appeared behind the ghost. Kim shone her light, illuminating the darkness. With ease, Holly blasted the spirit off Wilson and he fell, breaking the tables below. I bolted forward; hopefully, he hadn't hurt himself in the fall. But I saw blood—Wilson had his forehead clutched in his hands.

"Are you alright?" I asked.

Wilson eyed me. "What do you think, James?"

"Dad!" Holly screamed, floating down to me, "Are you okay? Kim told us what happened." I could hear the concern in her voice.

Flushing with embarrassment, I shook my head. "No time; lead the way out of here. Is Joey with you?"

Holly nodded and pointed up. Joey circled over his mother's head, his face still long and blank. *Still as creepy as ever*, I thought with a shudder.

"Did you find anything?" Wilson mumbled, trying to get to his feet as Kim helped him stand.

"No time—well a few things, but fuck it, we have to go. More will come." I shot my hand out to Wilson, who took it and stood. I quickly went to my pan, bending over to pick it up."

Please turn out the light," spoke a voice in the darkness. I couldn't see anything, and only a fool would think it wasn't sinister.

I grabbed my pan, reattaching it to my sling, and slowly moved from the voice. "We've got to go now," I shouted to the group as the others had already started to run. They turned and fled the mall, but I hesitated. Something had called out to me in the darkness. It hadn't been Diana—she always left after being a pain in my ass.

As their lights slowly pulled from the darkness, I made out a woman standing in the shadows. At the edge of the light she spoke. "Please turn out the light." A grin pulled back her lips, as the light faded.

I stumbled back; more faces showed in the darkness, and they were hungry. "Please turn out the light," they whispered. Fear had come, and my legs shook. The nasty harbinger of fear, a twirl of the pen for the end of my story. I shot my right hand to a cut I had made on my forearm, just a few days earlier. I jabbed my finger into the wound until I felt hot liquid slide to the floor. Then, like before, my legs started to work. I gulped, turning away just in time as the hands in the darkness reached for me.

We fled the mall, all the while something lurking in the shadows. I never knew what. with the creatures in this world, and I didn't want to find out. I had to drive once we were in the car. Kim tended to Wilson in the back, we had gotten no supplies and only managed in nearly getting Wilson killed.

When we met Christina at the shoreline, it was getting dark, nowhere near enough time to scavenge for gas for Holly and me.

"I'm sorry, James. Maybe the animals will be gone soon," Kim mumbled as we launched the canoe into the lake.

I glanced behind in the direction of the mall. It was never going to be safe anywhere we went. Holly and I would have to go somewhere far away from everyone else. "Maybe," I mumbled back.

Chapter 42

"You mean to tell me a woman once got a flaming red dolphin tattooed on her ass?" Holly blurted at the table as breakfast was being served.

"Language," I snickered over my oatmeal.

"No lie, it was as red as the devil's pecker and looked like one as well. I will admit it was the strangest tattoo I've ever seen on someone," said Rob, leaning towards Holly with a heavy smirk on his face. They both burst out laughing as Kim began clearing away the dishes.

I insisted on helping and was met with fierce eyes telling me to sit back down.

"I have to say, I like all your tattoos, man. I think if I concentrated enough, I could get a tattoo on my body," Holly admitted with a high air of confidence that was too damn jolly for me first thing in the morning.

"Don't even think about it, kid, blue hair—or well, I mean orange today—I can't even keep track anymore..." I mumbled, playing with my bowl of oatmeal. I hated to be picky, and it felt like ages since I had eaten. I just couldn't bring myself to eat enough. Oatmeal just sucked.

"Aren't you just the sour one," Rob snickered.

"Don't mind him, Rob; my father just doesn't appreciate art."

I decided to suck it up and pound down the oatmeal. Lousy or five-star meals, I was going to need the nutrients. "It's not that I don't appreciate art, Holly and Rob, it's just that I appreciate the finer things. Like double barrels and a certain amount of comfort provided to me by protection. That, to me, is art, ladies and gentlemen," I responded. Rob snorted while Holly rolled her eyes.

As the four of us continued to bicker about various definitions of art, Wilson came in. He was again dressed from head to toe in black. And on his belt was a gas mask, coupled by an array of blades, this time displayed.

"Good morning, everyone," Wilson declared, entering the room and making his way to a coffee pot I had managed to rewire in the weeks we had been spending at the Fort Mill Dam. During that time, with the help of Rob, we had successfully gotten a generator working again. We had power at the dam. Overnight, it had boosted the morale of the entire group.

The animals at the dam had been persistent and determined to get at us. Some even managed to get inside the fences. It didn't end well, and I saw the sparks from the creatures fly everywhere.

For two months of staying in Fort Mill, the dam had turned into a second home for Holly and me. During the time, Holly explored every avenue of the dam, and I mean everything (she was able to find a whole compound that the others did not know about). Meanwhile, I assisted Wilson in maintaining the fences along with Christina, whom it turned out was a very good landscaper and constructionist, and a hell of a welder to boot.

Wilson and I had gone over a map of the surrounding area and towns. We had determined that the best and closest town that would have any fuel was about a thirty-minute drive towards Charlotte, as Wilson had put it.

While we waited inside of the dam, I made myself useful repairing electronics that could still be run by batteries.

When we weren't busy maintaining the dam, we were relatively safe. That was something I could never get used to. The others at Fort Mill stated the dam hadn't had its walls breached in almost twenty years. Coupled with the fresh water running into the dam and a thick vegetable garden running out back, the dam was a fortress that could last for decades longer.

Still, that didn't stop me from wanting to leave the place. Safe is only a made-up word used to help people who are in denial. Fools who think the world is a lot cuddlier than it actually is can never ever be truly safe. No one is truly safe, no matter how high the walls are, no matter how thick the iron that surrounds them is. And as the start of our third month began, it had been several days since any of us had seen the animals. Safe wasn't the word I would use just yet—I no longer knew what safe meant. Something had drawn them away one morning. Wherever the creatures had gone, their presence still hung in my dreams. Millions of teeth and eyes, all watching. Waiting for one of us to leave our hole. I shook just thinking about their eyes, and about being devoured by such things.

Christina entered the room while we were all sat about, huddling together in each other's company.

"I was thinking today that we make a trip out to the gas station," I stated, looking in the direction of Wilson as he stood drinking his coffee. His posture was calm and relaxed as always—something that made me jealous and uneasy. I considered myself to be tough. The years had proven that one to me over and over again. Yet here was Wilson, calm with two relative strangers, regardless of past relationships, like a man walking in the park since day one. He was in no shape or form intimidated by my presence. This worried me to no end. I just couldn't see how anyone could be so trusting anymore.

When I spoke to Holly about it again, she dismissed the idea as me being paranoid and felt I was being unreasonable. Maybe I was, to a degree; I just couldn't wait to be on the road again. And it also bothered me that Holly wasn't seeing my point in all this. I knew we had been through a lot, and I thought after the funeral she would always be on my side. Still, as the weeks went on, I was becoming more trusting of our group. That was what worried me.

"Sure, let's load up my truck; it's not too far off a ride to the last petrol station. Which reminds me, how were you getting gas for your ride all of these years?" Wilson finally asked.

I sipped the cold coffee in front of me, deciding there was no point in hiding that piece of truth.

"It was a little hard at first, for the most part. Everything I found seemed pretty stale and when added to anything with an engine, they would cough up a lung full every time. Fortunately, we lived in one of the most paranoid places in the U.S., if not the world. After the 2005 hurricane that blew away most of the state, many people began building bunkers. All Holly and I had to do was find a city planner, and there were loads of those in Charlotte—it was building up fast, as you know.

Next, we tracked down some old contractor's whereabouts; obviously, we found some of their contracts to construction sites. What that led us to was a few underground shelters scattered throughout the area. We happened across one of these bunkers filled to the brim with gasoline. The gasoline was clean, inside a stainless-steel container with little oxygen, and was periodically stirred using an automotive machine that was running on the gas it was storing. Some son-of-a-bitch foresaw a gas apocalypse and had saved enough to make an oil driller blush," I stated, sipping my coffee and eyeing Wilson's reactions.

Wilson arched his eyebrow and let out a long whistle. "Damn, Jim, I didn't know you were so MacGyver."

We all laughed at Wilson's joke as the early morning light began to shine in through the windows of the dam.

"Everyone pack up; let's roll out in ten minutes." Wilson directed, setting down his coffee mug and leaving the room. Christina smiled and wiped her brow, leaving the room.

"Well, I sure wish I could hit the road with you guys as well," Rob said over his morning cigarette—or rather, his standard cigarette that seemed never to end in one long, ashy chain.

"Don't worry, Hot Wheels; you will be with us in spirit," Holly replied as she began fading from the room. I placed my hand in front of her before she vanished.

"Holly, wait a second—"

"Not this again—I will be fine, I promise, Dad." She said defensively before I could even speak.

"Actually, I'm not worried about that for a change, just the opposite. I want you to help look after Miss Kim. Your old man can handle himself, and we both know you're quicker than I will ever be. Just take care of her."

Holly tilted her head before turning into a silhouette and vanishing into the light of the day. I looked up to see Kim smiling and blushing. I smiled back, turning red, missing the smirk that played over Rob's face. He enjoyed watching us all make a fool of ourselves.

"Well, I best be getting ready myself now," Kim blurted, hurrying out of the room. Kim and I had grown close in the last two months, having shared a lot about each other's lives. It's an effect that only a woman can have on a man; the effect that makes every man forget his damn brain. Or maybe that was the excuse we told ourselves instead of just saying we liked each other. Funny how you never really grow up.

It was one of the reasons while I was eager to be on the road from this place as soon as possible. It wasn't that getting close was a liability at best to mine and Holly's health, but having Diana visit me often in my dreams was causing me to constantly struggle with feelings of guilt, and on top of sexual urges I was starting to feel like I was back in high school. It wasn't as bad as before; now I wasn't hiding anything from Holly. But there are some wounds that just don't want to heal; some you just don't want to recover from.

I finished my coffee and left the kitchen and made my way back to our room. I quickly rolled up my pack (which hadn't been unpacked until last night when Holly demanded her book player to overcome my constant snoring).

Holly showed up behind me as I repacked my pack. "So, do you mind telling me what was with all the dramatic heroics back there?" Holly asked, floating around me to the front desk. Her hair was a blazing yellow which was anything but discreet, like I'd asked her to be for the next few days.

"I meant every word of it; she is a sweet lady and has a son," I said, while folding the length of a pair of pants. *The best thing about packing mostly for just one was how quick a simple backpack could be loaded full,* I thought.

"Yeah—but come on, was that like a pass or something her way?" Holly stated.

I sighed deeply, looking towards Holly as she shrugged her arms and let them fall. "Honestly, for once, this isn't something I have a hidden motive on, I promise. For once, I just want to try and do something good for someone else for a change, is all. Kim seems like the kind of person who needs it."

I let the statement fall, and I turned to see Holly perplexed, then smiling. "Have to say, I am proud of you old man; you aren't such a stubborn jackass after all."

"Watch it, Holly." I smiled, walking past her and turning back to see her appear with a similar backpack to mine. "I always loved adventures. Let's kick this concrete can." Holly stated, gesturing to the walls of the dam.

We made it outside to see a rusted red van pull into the front. Christina got out, talking to Wilson as he loaded his gear into the front door. Kim walked past through the door with young Joey, following not too far behind his mother.

I walked up quickly and noticed the lack of defenses in the van. I looked at Wilson who seemed as emphatic as always, chatting with Christina.

I cleared my throat. "Maybe we shouldn't head out in this heap."

Wilson turned and spoke. "Sure, we can trade this fueled-up vehicle for that giant eyesore. Oh wait, it won't make it ten miles down the road."

I bit back my return comment—beggars couldn't be choosers, it just became hard not to punch someone's mouth when they insulted a man's vehicle.

I grunted before speaking up, keeping my voice cold, remembering it was a very long walk back to Charlotte. "My point is, this thing doesn't seem to have anything in the way of defense, and if I might say we've been trapped inside by an army of hungry ghost animals for two months."

"I can make you feel better with this one," gestured Christina, taking her hands out of her jumpsuit. I noticed then that the suit had the old stitching with the name Christopher, must have been her father's. I looked at Christina and gestured with my hand pointing up, as if to say "Be my guest."

"The insides of the doors are laced with iron rebar and the entire engine cab is made of iron. In fact, this baby has more iron than most small buildings. Sacrifice was fuel efficiencies. It's a van, though, so that was already a given," she stated matter-of-factly.

I stood dumbfounded and rethought my ideas of Christina. She was an amazing woman and a damn fine mechanic, apparently.

"That must have taken you a long time to pull off; you're a genius," I muttered, searching for the right words.

"Sure did, but you can take a ride for, say... on the house, sugar." She offered, walking away as the morning sun shone above us, cutting bright light through the overhanging gray curtain.

I hummed and held open the door for Holly to slip into the back of the van with Kim and Joey. I made my way around the red van, getting into the passenger seat as Wilson started the car and we began to leave the compound. Christina got to the gate of the compound and waved goodbye, quickly shutting the gates and sealing off any chance of us coming back.

I waved, as soon as the gates were locked, I turned my survival sense back on high. Using Kim's help, I'd managed to fasten a better sling for my iron pan; one which was easier to unsling at a moment's notice. What happened at the mall wouldn't be repeated. I had my shotgun cocked, within easy reach of my hand. My senses were back to heightened alert, and I was feeling somehow safer on the road than I did back in the dam. *It's the little things,* I figured.

Chapter 43

"Where are we heading, Jim?" Wilson asked as we came to our first major section of highway.

"Just follow the road for about ten miles. We will be heading to one of the bunkers about halfway there—no sense in going all the way back to Charlotte," I stated.

"Agreed," Wilson replied, we had both decided not to dip into Wilson's stash; though I decided grudgingly. Wilson may have had me beat in security, I had him beat in resources. He was willing to trade me the time I'd spent at the Fort Mill Dam, plus a few recommendations, in exchange for a top-off of three jugs of fuel.

After a fierce eye battle with Holly in the back seat, I lamented and allowed the trade. In total, Wilson and I had calculated the trip was forty minutes away from Charlotte; however, due to the state of the roads, it was more like half a day. Holly and I would be lucky to be able to hit the road before dark; I was going to make that happen one way or another. I missed my city; its dreary walls made more sense than the stone gray of the dam.

Wilson drove smoothly and calmly, taking his time around the overgrowth. I peered through my passenger windows and saw the ghosts of the animals following not too far off in the distance. My heart thumped inside my chest, and I turned to Wilson and pointed at the monsters on the outside.

"I see them. Looks like they're turning back." Wilson pointed out quietly. We were both whispering, which made me feel awkward in the situation, two grown men so afraid they were whispering. It comforted me though. After all we had gone through, the man had shown something that was human: fear.

"Why do you think they're turning back?" Holly asked from between us.

"I don't know—honestly, I think the sooner we get off the road and back to the compound, the better," said Kim, hugging herself in the back seat. She had insisted on coming along, the morning before we left. Kim felt it was only repayment to Wilson for all the years of work he had done for her and her son, plus she argued that she needed more medicine supplies. It was sound enough, but I felt uneasy with her and Joey tagging along—this was a dangerous place to be out on the roads. I was completely against the idea, though I didn't give any objections. It was her choice at the end of the day. She seemed like more than a capable survivor. *Capabilities aside,* I thought, *when you involved your children, things became complicated.*

"I believe it might be because of them..." Wilson spoke up, his voice barely able to be heard over the roar of the road. I turned and looked at Wilson.

"Haven't you been noticing how all the animals have been disappearing? How the ghosts... are getting stronger these past months?" Wilson spoke to me with a reticent voice I did not think he was capable of.

"We have noticed... things are the same back up north," I responded, matching the level of his voice.

"It's not just north; everywhere I've been, it's been occurring more and more often. Animals are disappearing, and the ghosts are acting stranger," Wilson whispered.

I nodded my head in agreement. "Something is causing this. We just have to figure out what."

"Someone, you mean," Wilson stated.

"Someone?" I responded, confused by Wilson's point. "Don't rule out that this could be *someone,* James. To do so would be foolish," he remarked.

Wilson was right, though. Someone could be doing this. I felt a chill run up me like a snake in a river, slow and stealthily. The more I thought about it, the more I realized no human could be behind this. Things were just too chaotic; it was often too hard to tell what was real as it was. To think that someone living could have something to do this was like trying to tell someone from a hundred years ago that men could make a bomb which could level a single city in one blast. My mind just couldn't make the leap. There was no way any human could be behind this.

I shuddered and pulled my jacket a little closer; human beings had to be on each other's side, and this was too big to be the standard "evil person." I had to believe that.

As we continued on the way to the bunker, my thoughts kept going back to Benny. I had shot him. I had pulled the trigger on a man who was only trying to be with his family a little longer.

Benny had tried to take Holly from me, and he almost succeeded. That still didn't make it any easier for me. I kept recalling the image of his face flushed out in a burning pain as my shot tore chunks away from his knee. It was the same thing Wilson was doing for his new family, the same thing Kim was doing. Everyone was trying to survive, to be with their families. If the roles were reversed, I had little doubt in my mind that Benny wouldn't have done the same thing; he probably would have done a lot worse, then left me bleeding out on the ground.

I still felt wretched about the consequences of my actions, and I still wondered strongly if it had been the right thing to do. Leaving a man to suffer and die in the cold of a factory. After all, my reasons were the same as his. Benny could easily be sitting in the vehicle with Wilson, speculating on what was happening to the ghastly monsters that had ruled the world for the better part of twenty years now.

My reflection in the passenger mirror caught my gaze, and for a second, I thought I saw a ghost. I flinched and realized it was only me. I turned my head to find my friend Wilson staring back at me.

His gaze was all-knowing and piercing deep. "Jim—if you're scared and feeling like this is all too much, you aren't the only one. I am losing my damn mind more and more every day. I have to know, before I get out of this car, that you will have my back and that I can trust you. Because right now, I am shaking, and I won't lie, the best way for us to get through whatever is happening is working together."

I blinked at Wilson, which was unexpected—he was right, though. Pulling resources was the only way to win in this kind of situation. I extended my hand towards him. After all, it's not like I hadn't done this sort of work a thousand times in the last few years. My time in the dam had made me softer, more comfortable. My father always told me handshakes were a sign of respect, a sign of trust. Extending my one good hand to a man who felt like a stranger, it felt wrong. It felt lost.

My hand trembled as we both exited the vehicle, followed by Kim, Joey, and Holly.

We had arrived at the location of the "gas vault," as I called it, or the "fat vault" as Holly called it. Many tourists had begun moving into the Appalachian Mountains, especially paranoid, proud gun owners; people that had a bit of doomsday pre-madness. That plus a dash of money and what you had was the perfect combo for everyday survival you would ever need.

From inside my backpack, I reached for my laptop battery while Holly vanished. I felt no shock expect in the direction of Joey. Wilson pulled out his long axe. I looked at him quizzically; he just shrugged his shoulders.

I focused back on the battery in my hands. Who was I to judge? I was using a frying pan as a Ghostbusters weapon, and sometimes as an omelet cooker, if I was feeling magnificent that day.

Holly came back a moment later, appearing in front of Wilson and me. "Coast is clear, boss. Even looks like the garage hasn't caved in any more since last time."

"That's a relief. Alright, everyone, relax a little. Watch your step, though. The last time we were here—well, the place almost came down," I told the group, tucking the laptop battery back in my pocket and walking towards the shattered remains of a log home, perched high on the top of a mountain.

It had taken Holly and me three months of continued cleaning and moving of cars from the roads to reach the place. Though it turned out it was all worth it. The log house was a virtual gold mine of supplies. Apparently, the former owner had been a retired gunnery sergeant in the Army or something to that effect. Worth the trip out into the mountains.

We were able to confirm once we found the vault. His spirit wasn't happy to see us, and the smell of his corpse being trapped in an airtight vault for years wasn't much better.

I went in first into the log cabin and popped open the door. It swung wide to an empty house. The walls were stripped bare and the floors, despite the age, remained relatively intact.

I bent over, searching for a cord I had long ago stretched out across the floor. The cord was still intact; no one had been in the cabin since Holly and I had last entered. I let go of the breath I was sucking in, as Wilson came up behind me, hunched over in a protective stance.

"All clear, still?" Wilson Whispered.

I nodded my head yes, and Wilson touched my shoulder, sweeping past me into the log cabin, going upstairs.

Wilson had been military and I had not been trained like him; it was interesting, though, to see how we both had learned aggressive behaviors from different causes. *It must have been from the video games I used to play,* I thought. Or any of the ghosts that had been solders. It felt good having my friend back, though it felt even better to have an extra set of eyes for a change. If we got a chance, I decided that later I would catch up with Wilson on games. Meaningless conversation was a life saver, Holly would always tell me. I believed her—to hear someone's voice was a lifeboat.

Wilson went up the flight of broken stairs leading into the dark unknown above. I waited a beat and Wilson appeared from top of the stairs with thumbs up. I stood to my full height.

"You know, the thumbs up in Roman times would actually mean Caesar was about to have a gladiator kill someone." Holly spoke from behind me, and I jumped instinctively.

"Holly, stop sneaking up on me like a—" I looked at her and closed my mouth.

Holly stood near me, then walked through a wall with Joey in towards a hidden room. I shook my head and continued into the room avoiding the gigantic hole that had been torn into the roof by Holly and me when we first entered. Somewhere under the stacks of wood from the ceiling was a gray couch, if I remembered correctly, it was a home after all, not just some dugout.

"Does she do that a lot? Throwing out random pieces of information. Never mind, on second thoughts, I think that is a thing you both do very well," Wilson reasoned, while coming down the stairs and joining me as I looked at the huge couch under the debris. Mold had long since set in, and the house was falling apart. At least the part that counted. All I cared about was the wood flooring that covered the basement door.

"She likes Julius, is all," I stated, turning away from Wilson and going deeper into the house. Kim soon came in through the door, frantically looking around the room, becoming more at ease as Wilson and I relaxed our postures.

"Julius?" Wilson asked.

"You know, Caesar. Come on, history major, you should be aware of this."

"Oh right, sorry. Yes, I know all about him…" Wilson mumbled. I turned towards Wilson, seeing something odd in his look. The Wilson I remembered had been a history fanatic and a damn good one at that. He was once a military historian volunteer in most reenactment parades. He'd always been spouting out pieces of history any chance he got. He'd been so good that if I had ever been on a game show, he would have been my first choice for a lifeline.

I guess the effect of the end of the world made people forget certain things, I thought. I gave a silent prayer to myself, thankful I had retained my Internet technology skills, the ones that counted at least. I was the best there was at troubleshooting, and it had gotten me through twenty years of hell.

We came to the basement door; I opened the latch slowly and began the descent. The upstairs of the cabin looked mostly like a regular cabin (with the exception of the gaping hole). Its secret was in the abyss.

Kim followed behind and produced a bright light, shining it deep into the gloom. I found my footing in the dimness of the light and reached the bottom, searching for the simple stand. Kim shone the light in the basement to the plain room, which led to a long cascading catwalk.

My hands followed the grip of the railing until I stopped midway on the catwalk. "No sense in us all going down here. Kim, keep the light shining over my shoulder."

"Are you sure, James?" Kim asked.

"Positive. Just keep the light on me," I said, going further down the catwalk.

My hand found the vault door first; I smiled at the cold and mechanical feel of the door beneath my touch. Machines always made me feel comfortable, they didn't need to be talked to, or reasoned with. They'd just do what they were told.

As long as you knew what you were doing, machines did their job, and they did it well. I inputted the combination of the vault (when we had destroyed the original owner of the cabin, Holly and I had learned the combo from his ghost).

I heard the click and the door swung in; I turned around to see Kim and Wilson had come right behind me. I was annoyed to see them down the catwalk; I let it slide. No point in getting mad—they couldn't have seen the combo in the dark from that far away anyways. "Alright guys, welcome to paradise. Step in through and load up."

The others followed me into the vault rooms. An entire room was filled to the brim with various supplies. From water purification tablets to arsenals of guns; the man was a genius when it came to survival. He was even a clean doomsday prepper, organizing everything on coherent shelves.

After a few minutes, Wilson and I managed to get the generator working properly, and the vault came alive with sparks of light. I showed Wilson the entrance to another tunnel. This tunnel led down to another storage area. This time, though, at the end was a small door made of thick steel with a small handle attached to the front.

I showed Wilson the handle and I had him pull the door away. A nozzle was firmly secured inside the steel wall. Wilson produced two big jugs from behind him and handed them forward. Placing one of the jugs under the nozzle, I turned the knob until a thick stream of precious gas came flooding out. We both cheered and laughed at the sight of it.

Once the jugs were full, Wilson and I went back to the main area of the storage room and met Kim in the makeshift kitchen. She had stacked her pack to the brim with goodies and had taken one of the .22 rifles from the wall.

"This place is—wow, James, why the hell did you and Holly just not stay here?" Kim asked.

"We wanted to; certain things prevented us from doing that. Basically, on our last trip here, Holly and I ran into some unneeded company, and I accidentally set fire to the house. I became smoked out and would have died, had Holly not lead me through the ash..."

"Wait, so you drove us up here without even knowing this place was still standing?" Wilson said accusingly.

"Honestly? Yeah. It paid off, though," I responded.

Wilson laughed at me in response. "You have some balls man; you have some balls."

"When you ladies are done talking about your balls, we should probably start loading up the van with what we can. No sense in all of this staying here and wasting." Kim quipped, taking her pack and heading back out towards the catwalk.

When she was gone from eyesight, I turned to Wilson. "Well, you heard her, let's be quick. In my experience, ghosts don't pick your best moments to show up," I stated, turning to start packing my pack.

Wilson and I were quick like Kim asked us to be; we both loaded our bags and started down the catwalk. We made it to the top of the stairs into the living room to find Holly, Joey, and Kim all staring at the front door leading into the cabin.

"What?" I asked.

"There are children at the door," Kim quavered flatly. Her back was towards us, and she had a long piece of what appeared to be a chair leg made of iron. I made a mental note to ask her where she found that, as I made my way to the door, hunching down slowly.

"Holly, the curtains."

"Right." She whispered waving her hands, as all the curtains closed shut silently. "Jim, they probably can still see us," Holly implored.

I responded, "I know Holly, but any advantage is an advantage." We were in total darkness; I made my way to the door, hunched over and with my frying pan pulled out from my sling.

Once at the door, I held my breath, turning to everyone behind me. Holly had her game face on; it was fierce and showed wisdom beyond her appearance as a young girl. Behind her, Kim was ready with her iron chair leg. There was no hesitation in her face; she was ready for whatever came. She did this while also shielding her young son behind her and even though the boy was dead, she still cared for him. I admired that in her.

And behind all of them, crouched down, was Wilson. He had pulled the nastiest looking rifle from the vault downstairs. I couldn't shoot a rifle with one hand, I had figured out it was even harder to reload for me, (most of the supplies, namely the weapons, stayed on the shelves). It was comforting knowing that someone on my side could use one of the guns. Wilson leveled his head, and I turned back to the door and peered through the peephole.

Sure enough, by my count, there were four… maybe five ghost children standing in front of the door. Their eyes were solid black, and if I had seen them twenty years ago, I would have thought nothing was wrong from a distance.

It wasn't just their eyes that caught my attention and made me jump at every shadow in the room. It was their body language. All five of them stood tall, with their chests back and shouldered squared. A stance that is just unnatural to see in children at that age, with faces just too calm for kids, and the stance of warriors going to battle.

I shivered, stepping back from the door quietly, and turned toward the rest of the group. Everyone looked jittery, like they were expecting me to tell them there was a monster on the other side of a rotting thin wooden door.

I gulped and held up a hand, indicating five of them, not wanting to risk using my voice. Wilson lowered his head in understanding and took a step closer to the couch. With one hand, he slowly charged the back end of his rifle, and I envied him for being able to use an actual gun again. Though when it came to ghosts, guns were useless.

Holly looked concerned, it was apprehensive even from where she floated, staring back and forth from the door to me. A knock came from the door brought my attention back to the demonic children that were likely to become a common thing over and over again in my life. *There was always something knocking, always something coming,* I thought.

I wondered for a moment if these kids were just like the Anna girl. The poor girl was truly wronged, but wronged or not; if it were another attempt to get Holly, I would do whatever it took to fight them off.

If they were like Anna, that door was like a sheet of paper in the rain to them. That made me grip my pan a little tighter. I wished for a change in having more reach with my weapon. I was tired of getting so close to big and nasty.

Another series of knocks came, this time a little louder. I sensed the kids weren't getting happy rapping the door. I took a gamble and spoke. "Who is it?"

I heard silence on the other side, then the unmistakable tone of a small child. "Will you let us in?" pleaded an unknown voice. Now that was something I did not need to doubt my feelings on. Every instinct in my body told me to run to the hills as fast I could. Cold and shattering, their voice rang like diamonds frozen in the deepest of lakes.

"Sorry kid, I'm naked in here, and children should never have to be around naked adults. Come back another time." My response was met with more silence, and I prayed if it had done the trick; stranger things have happened to me.

The wind blew outside, and the seconds slowed down as an explosion of noise sprang from every direction. First, the wooden door blew in like a leaf in a storm, as feared. It crashed into me like I weighed nothing (which was close to true—a lack of nourishment had long since left me a frail ghoul), and slammed me into a back wall. Luckily, the door was rotten to the core. Otherwise, the impact might have blacked me out.

Second, I heard Holly scream above as children flew from the hole in the ceiling, raining down like Great War bombers. I heard Wilson shout "Get down" to someone as the room filled with smoke and gunpowder from him blasting his rifle. Guns were nothing more than a human comfort against ghosts; the intangible phantoms absorbed bullets like sponges and it likely scared them, more than anything else.

I think it was due to a distant memory of their former lives telling them that ducking out of the way of a screaming bullet was probably a good idea. Pieces of the decaying log cabin showered all around me as a black child with matching black eyes came silently through the doorway.

The kid moved quick through the wreckage that was becoming the cabin. Kim had managed to take down one of the kids, judging by the rainbow of sparks flying around the room. I looked in awe at the red mixing with the black from the gunpowder, forming some kind of sinister dragon in the ash, flashing its teeth at us. I imagined it was the closest an average person would ever get to see the horrors of war. Only this was a war—this war of mine was my life, and I had people to protect.

My body felt like lead and somewhere I could feel something cold on me. I shifted my knees up and hoisted what was left of the wooden door off of me, in time to see a child crawling down from the ceiling, reaching towards its helpless prey below. A large black tongue unfurled and reached out like a small hand; instinctively, I swung my frying pan, and the monster dodged out of the way, disappearing into the wall.

They're clever—shit. I spun around. Wilson had forced a group of children back out the front of the door, using a combo of his rifle and a rather nasty hooked iron blade. Joey and Holly were nowhere in sight; Kim was being forced towards a window by a group of the ghost kids; Kim's weapon was doing little to scare them away. The groups of dark-eyed children were swelling in numbers, coming through the walls like water.

Things were getting out of control fast; I continued to swing my pan, missing more often than actually landing a direct hit on any of the monsters. A small girl appeared in front of me after I managed to hit a little boy, turning the boy into a shower of sparks.

I stopped mid-swing; she was small-figured and had golden blonde hair, and my hand trembled with the weight of the pan over my head. The ghost child didn't hesitate; she shot forward, hammering into me with a force that sent me sprawling towards the kitchen. I lay on my back and looked up to see her inches above my face, my reflection showing in her black pupils.

She floated above me, a slow smile forming on her face, and I knew I was a goner. A room full of this many powerful ghosts was something I could do nothing against; for that matter, I didn't think any of us stood a chance in our present state.

I had never witnessed what it was like to be taken over by a ghost, except in a movie. In movies, the person would project vomit and suddenly learn an advanced vocabulary in Latin. Or maybe that was demons—it was hard to tell the difference when their eyes were so dark. The few times I had touched Holly, it had felt like a dip in the coldest pond in the middle of a blizzard, butt naked. And the one time Diana had gotten inside my hand—that had been an explosion. One moment I had a hand perfectly capable and the next the hand was on fire, feeling as though that frozen pond I had jumped into had sharks biting my fingers off slowly.

I closed my eyes, expecting the sensation to come back. Nothing happened as I lay on the cold floor. I opened my eyes, and the girl was gone. I could hear shouting from outside and a hole was missing on the side of the cabin. Wilson's gun lay shattered into pieces not far from where I was.

I rolled over, my back popping, and I had a hunch as I got to my feet. It was only a matter of time; I wouldn't be surprised if my back had finally given out—constant abuse from being thrown by other world demons could not be good for your health.

I walked—well more like dragged—my body to the front door. Colors of a moving thin shape swirled outside Wilson, all around him, disorienting his image in a bath of bright reds and deep greens, forming a crystallized image around the man. The ghost child Joey lay on the ground, motionless and as natural as the grass that littered the woods. The wind carried the swirling maze of yellows, greens, reds, and blues as I approached, and it created a mural out of the carnage around us. *So much chaos, so much beauty. A dichotomy I never wished to see in my life.* I looked on to see Holly ripping a black-eyed kid to pieces, and a volley of screams followed Holly glowing with anger I recognized only in myself. I knew she couldn't keep it up. She wasn't like me; killing wasn't in her, and I knew that later she would hate herself for all the ghost children she had to cut down.

That was when my breath stopped; Kim was being pulled away by a ghost child. I reached out in vain; she was beyond my grasp and I wasn't sure what I could do, even if I had been up close. Those kids were beyond anything I could do with what I had on me.

"Holly!" I shouted over the screams coming from Kim as she was being pulled away. Holly turned back towards me, her eyes a fire of hatred and anger harking back to that night she had been taken by Anna. I flinched from the sight.

"Go! Follow them! Don't attack on your own, though!"

"I have to get her back, Jim!" Holly screamed back, taking off into the air.

"Holly, don't! You can't—win!" I shouted back, but it was too late. Holly had vanished from sight, like the children and Kim.

Wilson walked towards me stepping over the comatose Joey. "Have you ever seen any of them carry someone off like that? I mean, slamming a door is one thing, but carrying her off like that without any effort…" Wilson muttered. He had his air about him again, calm in spite of the violence that had just occurred.

I felt flush with anger. He had just lost a member of his group and instead was more concerned about the semantics of classifying ghost behavior rather than being concerned about the fate of his friend. "Hey now, you son of a bitch! What is wrong with you!" I asked, coming up to him.

Wilson cocked an eyebrow, and his stance didn't change as he continued walking towards the house. "James, grow up will you, please. There isn't anything we can do right now. Neither one of us has wings. No sense in getting so upset."

I growled in my lower throat. "Still doesn't mean we just sit here.

Let's get gas in the car and give chase."

Wilson turned towards me and shook his head no. "Not a good plan. Those little shits have us outgunned. Your girl is the only one that stands a chance against them. Besides, why do you care? Kim isn't even one of you."

I fought back a response; he was right, my anger wasn't doing any good. I was virtually helpless, a worm trapped under the weight of a giant rock. I sat down where I was, staring at Joey as his unmoving form remained like a statue in the bright sunshine of an otherwise healthy day. I was unable to help him; I wasn't even sure what had happened to the boy.

Twenty years ago, I would often gloat sometimes about my ability to fix anything, which was mostly right. I was an expert on the power of Google by default, and that made me a jack of all trades. However, take away that electronic crutch and I was nothing more than a broken old man, incapable of helping the kid on the ground—helping anyone, it seemed.

So I watched Joey, waiting for my daughter to return with something—anything— that could help with the latest shitstorm which had found its way into my life.

"Give me a hand with the gas," Wilson stated from somewhere behind me.

I stood up, brushing the dirt from my pants. A lot of good I could do to anyone. I was like a doctor being forced to operate with no tools or any knowledge of what the wounded had suffered.

Chapter 44

After filling Wilson's truck to the brim with gas and loading as many gas jugs (numbering about four) as we could spare, I sat with my back facing towards the van. Holly had been gone a little over an hour, and I was starting to fear something might have happened to her. It didn't help that Joey was still in a catatonic state.

I looked at Wilson; he sat on the porch at ease, cleaning another rifle he had taken from downstairs. I had spent many nights sitting around trapped; it is a feeling that couldn't be shaken and only served to shake one's faith in themselves. Sitting next to that van, I wished I could fly like Holly. I wished I could be there with her now.

I held on to the fact that Holly had gone after Kim; she must have been helping Kim coming back, if anything. I'd never seen how fast Holly could go, nor any of the ghosts. There was no telling how far and how quick the little phantom bastards could move. I knew Holly could do it.

In the instant I looked down, Holly appeared in front of me again, causing me to jerk back in surprise, walloping my head on the truck. "Damn it, Holly, warning first, please?" I mumbled, rubbing the back of my head.

I looked at my daughter, and I could tell before she even spoke that something wasn't right. "Holly, where is Kim?" I asked.

She shook her head. "Well, I have good news and bad news, Jim—you won't like either."

Wilson came up walking towards the van slowly, as I stood to my feet. "Give us the veggies," Wilson said.

"Okay. Well, I followed those dark-eyed losers as far as I could. Let me tell you, they were booking it in a hurry. I kept my distance; it looked like they had knocked out Kim somehow and even weirder, were able to carry her. I've never—never—seen something like that," she said.

"Neither have I," I said.

Holly cast her eyes into my own, and any fear that had been inside of her voice was blown away and replaced by her father's steel. I was proud of that look; it was one I knew I could trust her with.

"They moved quickly and kept up a relentless pace until they came to this stadium. From what I could tell, the stadium was some football team's stadium. It had a bunch of strange panthers and such. Anyways, here is the real kicker; the thing was packed to the gills full of ghosts and animals. I mean, Dad, if you could have heard the moans... my ears shook. The place—just felt wrong... It felt awful, and I wanted to leave as quickly as I could. I stayed, though; I wanted to try and save Kim."

Holly had wrapped her arms around herself and shivered as if a cold breeze had brushed past her. I wasn't sure if ghosts could feel coldness. It is just plain tough, watching your child suffer, watching your child be afraid when there is nothing you can do about it.

Holly had trailed off from talking. I dug, knowing that the story was only going to get worse. "Holl—" I started.

"It's okay, I'm good. What I saw was even weirder. At the center was one of you, flesh-and-all warm bodies," Holly stated.

"Warm bodies?" I asked.

"Oh sorry—that was something Joey and I talked about when referring to the—well, living. You guys are a lot hotter than we are," Holly said.

"Makes sense," I commented.

"Right—we even call ourselves the cold ones. Anyways, they—the dark-eyed children—flew Kim to the center of the stadium. And at the center was a man—a warm body, Jim. The craziest thing is, it looked like that person was able to control all of the ghosts inside the stadium." Holly shivered while her voice grew quiet. I sucked in a deep breath and laughed nervously.

"Yeah right, Holly—there is no way anyone could control ghosts, let alone an entire army like you say," I stated skeptically.

"Are you doubting me?" Holly shouted, fury in her eyes.

"Easy Holly, I don't doubt you, it just doesn't seem real. Out of the thousands of ghosts you and I have come across, how many are like you and Joey over there? And to top it off, how many have you told me yourself would try and hurt each other if they could? Ghosts just can't interact in that large of a number, let alone be controlled by one of us. Everything we've seen suggests they would sooner try and destroy our minds before doing our bidding."

"I don't know, Jim. There was so many of them and they—weren't attacking either of the two. What else could it be?" she asked.

"I think I agree with your daughter on this one, Jim." Wilson stated.

I turned my head towards Wilson as he made his way up to us. I blinked at his shaved head in the bright sunlight, "How do you figure that, Wilson?" I asked.

Wilson sucked in his lower lip while wiping his eyebrow; it truly was another hot North Carolina day, and it was only getting warmer as the day dragged on. *Even the weather made no sense—everything is against us,* I thought. The situation was turning the heat worse by the moment as well. "Because let's assume this man—"

"Or woman," Holly interjected.

"Thank you, or woman—was capable of convincing a whole army of ghosts like Holly and Joey. What the hell would possibly be their end game? There is simply no way anyone could have any control over them." I shook my head. *I was right; I had to be*, I thought.

"I think this will be a lot easier if I just show you." Wilson said, gesturing for Holly and me to follow him. I looked at Holly, and the three of us made our way over to where the young ghost child Joey lay.

I had seen statues with more life, I thought as we came across the boy in his unmoving state. Wilson knelt over him, first muttering a few words I couldn't make out; it sounded like a prayer from what I could tell.

Wilson kept his eyes closed, until he opened them quickly, snapping his hands over the heart of the boy, and plunged his fingers into him. I blinked in utter surprise. Wilson had managed to go inside one of the ghosts, and he had physically disregarded any fundamental rules of our world and made his own. I was astonished once more by this sight of seeing Wilson do this. My reaction was very different from Holly's though. When she saw it; a different look came into her face. She looked wildly hurt and afraid, like an animal that had just been trapped. One thing was for sure; we were both seeing something unnatural.

As Wilson dipped his fingers into the form of Joey, his eyes snapped open and a pulsing light shone first from Wilson and ending in Joey. The light shot out in every direction, forcing me to cover my eyes. Once the light had cleared, I saw to my amazement that Joey was sitting up.

Wilson looked perfectly healthy, and his hands were now at his side. "Joey, transform like you sometimes do into a dinosaur," Wilson stated as Joey turned into a horned beast that I had never seen before. It was without a doubt, though, a dinosaur, with horns, and thick skin, dotted with feathers at every mark. The boy (now what appeared to be a triceratops of some kind) simply floated above the grass frozen, without any indication he was aware of his surroundings.

"What did you just do…?" I stuttered, searching for the words. One moment I thought Joey had died again, the next he was up and listening to Wilson's commands like a new trainee in the military.

"Joey, Joey, are you okay, pal?" Holly stammered, talking over to him, concern evident even in her body language. Joey neither heard nor cared as Holly approached; he remained still, like a tree in a lonely forest. And when he didn't respond, I could see the hurt forming in Holly's features. I knew what was next, the classic anger that was becoming worse and worse as the days went on between Holly and I. Holly snapped at Wilson, charging up on him and floating to his height until both were at eye level.

"What did you do to him? Release him now! Release my friend!" She screamed into Wilson's face with no fear and her hair twisting like some warrior goddess of old myth.

I motioned to step in when Wilson jumped back, pulling up his iron ax. No one moved out of the three of us. My heart was spinning like the propellers on an airplane. *This person is about to kill my daughter* was all I could think, and it took everything I had not to try and react. I watched as Wilson slid his ax near Holly, and Holly floated back slowly in response.

"That's what I thought. Do not touch me," snarled Wilson in a persona that didn't match his normal tempo. "Now, I was merely trying to show you two that controlling one of you is a lot easier than you would think—if you would please mind calming down."

Holly and Wilson continued to stare each other down like it was a high noon face-off as my hand made its way to the shotgun at my side. Wilson wasn't getting off a shot against my girl.

No one spoke as Wilson remained stout, with his ax ready to take a fatal blow at Holly at a moment's notice. Holly was almost on fire with her aura. It was something else, like she was sucking the very sun out of the sky and into her.

I was sweating and fighting to catch my breath, racking my brain to figure out how I could get out of this mess, when Wilson suddenly dropped his guard, causing Holly to flinch. "Why don't we relax, and I will explain a little," Wilson suggested.

"Release my friend, and I won't kill you," growled Holly. Her eyes had turned solid white, and she didn't appear to be my daughter anymore. She looked more like Anna had, that night she had taken Holly; more demonic than human.

I felt myself shivering, even though it was not cold. My hand stayed on the side of my leg, though; I wasn't taking my hand off my gun until the confrontation was over.

"Why don't you just kill him, Jim. You're always going on about fighting for those that are precious to you—especially that colored hair whore you care so much for," whispered Diana from somewhere deep in my mind. She sounded so close, I could have sworn that she was standing right next to me.

"I can't do that… he is my friend. I don't—I don't want to hurt anyone," I pleaded.

"That is your problem, Jim. You never react to anything, and you always let things happen until the choice is made for you. There is a word for that, and it's called a coward," she bit back with harsh venom.

Is she right? I thought. *Is Diana, right? Am I about to let my daughter be put at risk again because I feared protecting my daughter over my friend's life?* I didn't want to answer that question; I wanted to put as much distance between myself and that as possible. This wasn't supposed to be happening today—none of this was.

I didn't trust my hand to stop moving towards my gun, and I didn't trust my hand not to keep moving. "Yeah, maybe killing him won't be such a bad idea," I mumbled, answering Diana wherever she existed.

Wilson took his eyes from Holly and half turned towards me, "Are you thinking about killing me, Jim?" He asked, not in a mocking tone; it almost seemed like a plea. It rang a bell to my better judgment to gain control of my hand. I stopped shaking; *I am no monster. I wasn't going to kill this man; it could all be solved through reasoning.*

Humanity had been almost wiped out by ghosts, and there seemed to be no way of ever rebuilding, but we weren't beyond reason and logic. Monsters wouldn't turn us into monsters that we were not. Only that was hard for me to believe, wasn't it? In another story of my life, I used to think the evil that existed within men was something that could be cured.

Evil was nothing more than men failing to use their natural tools in the environment around them. After all, there was nothing that could not be fixed; people were the same way. *People are the same way.* I thought, in an icy voice. I had to believe that—if not for me, then for Holly, that we could fix things.

I looked up at Wilson; steel had replaced any doubt he may have had. I cleared my throat before going on. "Explain what's going on, man. No need for this to get out of control." I extended a peace offering.

Wilson finally took one hand from his ax and reattached it to his belt. "You know, Jim, we live in a world full of ghosts. It's just you and me. Think about that the next time you make a half-empty threat. The world can always hold more ghosts."

His words stunned me and the threat was clear. I sighed, "Let's not make any more today, shall we, old friend?"

Wilson tilted his head towards me and walked over to where Joey stayed transformed. "Ever figure what the most powerful thing in the universe is, Jim?" Wilson stopped and asked me.

"Come again—what do you mean?" I asked.

"What is the most powerful thing in the human universe? The most powerful thing that is always overlooked and is often forgotten entirely; because, man, I tell you: it's not a nuke or some black hole we can't see. No, it's something that is inside each and every single man."

Wilson stopped talking and looked at me with a long stare, awaiting my answer as I fumbled for words like a person trying to find the right key on a ring with over a thousand different keys for two thousand different locks.

Finally, I spoke up. "I'm not sure, Wilson. Is there a point to all of this?" I declared.

"There always is a point to everything, Jim. This isn't something you can find in any reasonable research. You only have to accept it for yourself. Memories are the most powerful thing that mankind has—and ever had," he stated.

More than a little perplexed, I replied, "I don't see your point. Logically, a bomb that can physically go boom is more powerful, pure, and straightforward."

"Ah—I knew you would say that." Wilson snickered, reaching back towards Joey and that same bright light showed again, this time though, it disappeared quicker. Joey fell to the ground, like a sack of potatoes, and Holly rushed over to the boy and cradled him in her arms. He remained like a statue, and I wondered if Holly could see something different about his form than us humans could. Maybe she was able to see something similar to whatever Wilson was getting at with his talk of memories. I could see easily how memories could destroy a man and I could see how memories could carry a man forward. Hell, it was the memories of Holly and me together in a much better way that had forced me to come back to the world.

"Memories can be the rock that sinks the strongest ship deeper into the ocean, or the adrenaline shot that pumps you a few more feet when your body and soul are broken. My point being, everything that has ever motivated any person in this world was based on something from his or her life. Whether that was a positive thing or a negative thing, it is the memories that lead to someone doing something in this world. And I don't have to be an artist for you to know that men are not bad at destroying each other. For that is something man is just so good at—hell, even the after-image of man, and spirits and ghosts, are causing havoc on this planet," Wilson stated, bending down to the grass, his long coat obscuring the green with dark shadows as I thought about his words.

"If you sacrifice a memory to a ghost, you can control them. After all, I think that's what all the ghosts want. Those that aren't calm like Holly and Joey there; they want to remember anything, something that isn't what was happening to them right now," Wilson whispered. "They are the lost, James, just like you and me. Everyone is lost," Wilson informed us.

Holly eyed Wilson with daggers as she held Joey. He remained unmoved and unchanged. "Control them, control them how? And what do you mean 'sacrifice a memory?'" As I asked my questions, I thought of Diana and our first encounter when she came back in the kitchen.

She'd had no recollection of who she was or who I was; and when I tried to force her memories back, she changed. It still made me shiver at her image, seeing her as a walking corpse. When I had met Holly, she had no idea she was the ghost of Molly. I trembled in that moment. *Could Wilson have been right about all of this? Were the ghosts that attached to memories*? I reflected.

"When I gave Joey there a memory, he kept it forever. I will never get it back; that's why I gave him something simple and small," Wilson said.

"So, in theory, whoever the person is could build an entire army of ghosts on his side?" I pondered.

"Correct, that is an accurate statement, unfortunately," Wilson sighed, making a grand gesture and stretching out, while standing back up. "

"Yeah, well, it's sick what you did to Joey. And whoever it is doing that is a monster as well. Controlling people like their slaves! It is just sick and wrong, and they need to be stopped." Holly snapped in defiance.

"One problem with that, honey—you aren't 'people' anymore," Wilson stated.

Holly jolted to her feet. "What did you just say? Say it to my face, big guy! You and I can go right now!" she shouted, and I worried another fight was going to break out between the two.

"Drop it, Holly; we don't have time for this," I said, getting in between the two of them.

Jim, you can't have this sicko's back, look at what he did to Joey!" she snarled, floating above my head to lock eyes again at Wilson.

"Yeah, but he also released Joey. Your friend will be okay, I promise.

Getting mad at a situation doesn't fix it, like I always tell you, kiddo. We can work our way through any problem." I spoke, trying to coax my daughter.

"For fuck's sake, Dad, people aren't machines. Dusting off something wrong is the same as letting a problem happen and then not fixing it," Holly shouted from above me.

Wilson considered the ghosts to be subhuman, and he was saying my Holly wasn't good enough, and for that matter, none of them were good enough. I wasn't sure how I felt about the ghosts being controlled. *It was sick, it was wrong, and it needed to be fixed. That wasn't just it, though; Holly is my daughter, and she was more alive than me at this point,* I thought. "Holly is my daughter. Sometimes when I am alone, I used to wonder if she was here; if she ever actually existed. This world has been cruel, and darkness is all around us at every turn. It took me some time, time to realize that Holly was indeed my little girl who had been with me all these years, not some figment of my imagination. Real love, you can't fake. Real love can't only be in the mind. It is in the heart. And I would go to the end of the world for my daughter."

"Jim..." Holly said in a small voice near me, the fire in her eyes all but gone.

"That is a beautiful thing you said and all—but monsters are monsters. Polish a turd with gold, Jim, still doesn't make it gold. Now let's get in the truck and go. The sooner you guys are on the road, the faster I think things will be a little better," Wilson said calmly.

"That's it? That is all you're going to say? What about your friend? We have to go after her!" Holly shouted towards Wilson as he turned back around eyeing her.

"Kid—you said it yourself; they have an army of ghosts. What could we possibly do? We are just an army of a loudmouth dead girl, two old men, a crippled drunk, and a mechanic. I like being alive," stated Wilson as he opened the van's passenger door.

"Fucking coward! Come on, Jim. Let's go get our friend since this guy is content with just getting some gas and going home like he is taking a trip to the damn grocery store." Holly flared, and for a moment I felt the wind move all around me from her anger.

I stepped forward, placing my hand on the truck door, and Wilson turned towards me.

"Kim was the first person in twenty years to touch me in a kind way, the first person not trying to kill me, or to take over my body. You know, I imagine that is probably the same for you. We are both becoming cold—becoming ghosts ourselves. The thing is, Wilson, I think we both need to do something about it. This is the world we live in. It is filled with ghosts and both of us will probably never live to see the world like it used to be. Let's not become ghosts—let's do something crazy, let's do some good for a change before our time is up. You said it yourself; we are a bunch of old men. Let's go get our friend back and start trying to make life a little more like life, for a change," I said, leaning in towards Wilson.

"It's an army, man—are you serious?" Wilson replied.

"I don't fucking know, but it sure as hell feels right to me. Doing the right thing helps—it really does," I responded, looking at Holly and remembering finally taking her to her body. I hadn't told her, but that might have been the scariest moment of my life. It had been worth it in the end. Ever since that day, I had felt a lot more at peace than I had in a long, long time. I smiled at Holly and turned towards Wilson, answering him with the most honest answer I had. "Let's go get one of our own."

Wilson looked forward like he was staring off at some unknown object, before turning back towards me. "Doing the right thing fucking sucks. I hope you have a plan, Mr. Hero. Get in the truck, you two."

I smiled turning back to Holly, "Get Joey, Holly."

Holly already had Joey scooped up in her arms, holding him like he was a baby. "Way ahead of you, Jim. He is so heavy right now."

"That's weird. I thought you guys would weigh nothing," I stated, opening the door for Holly and Joey.

"It's the same idea as when I am concentrating on staying inside of the car by focusing on something real around me. I—I guess we can touch each other if we can form a connection that makes us grounded. I don't know how else to describe it; it's like a string becomes attached between the two of us."

"Interesting. How does that work for ghosts, considering that, you know, you never get tired, kiddo? Running your mouth all day has to be exhausting."

"Oh, you're so funny, Jim. For real, though, the rope I was describing seems to be thinner with Joey for some reason. I think I will have to hold on to him the entire way to make sure he stays with us." She sniffled.

"Good idea, squirt. You stated that you have a connection to touch something—so how were those kids able to hurt you two?" I asked.

"Easy one. They scared us and wanted to harm us, While Joey and I both wanted to be safe, and for you all to be safe as well. So, we were thinking about protecting you, and we became more grounded and easier to relate to," Holly said as Wilson started the truck and we put the cabin in our rear-view quickly.

"Great—an endless army, one that never gets tired either," Wilson mumbled from the front seat.

I glanced out the window as the world flew past us in a whirl of green. "Yeah, we have our hands full on this one."

"That is an understatement," said Wilson.

Chapter 45

On the ride back, everyone was silent as we pulled into the dam's compound. The light reflecting on the river painted a false peace with its shards of orange on the backdrop of the Carolina's murky waters. Wilson was out of the truck almost before the car was parked, saying he was going to prepare the others.

I gestured my head. Any words to be said were lost to us both knowing what was about to come. I didn't turn to Holly, but I knew she was still in the truck with me. It felt oddly comforting to be just the two of us again alone (well, the unwilling Joey being the exception).

I watched the sun get lower over the river when Holly spoke finally. "How do you feel about this, Jim? Do—you really think we can actually beat an army?" she asked with her voice barely above the quietness of the river humming its continuous flow.

"To tell you the truth, I'm not sure Holly. You and I have always been much better on our own. Teaming up with anyone feels like a bad superhero comic, you know?"

"Yeah, I see what you mean," she said.

"It's not too late, Holly. I don't want to do this unless we both are on board before we attempt a suicide play," I admitted.

Holly breathed deep, phasing through the passenger seat nearest to me. I looked back, and Joey remained in the cab, despite her movement. "Invisible rope," Holly informed with a sad smile.

I tried my hardest to smile back, but the gesture felt too forced, so I quit while rubbing my eyebrows instead. "Always saving the best tricks for a surprise, huh kiddo?" I asked.

This time, Holly's smile felt more genuine before she responded. "Learned from the best—old man," she teased.

"You know you're right; I'm not getting any younger. I won't—always be around forever," I mumbled.

"That can't be true. My Daddy told me once he would always be there for me. You always said that," she stated

"You're right. Answer my question. Please," I added, turning towards her.

"I think it's something that goes against the grain; I believe it is something that is needed. If anyone in this whole world can bring Kim home, it would be you—Dad," Holly said.

I looked at the river and turned back to Holly. "I think when this is all done; it is time we leave this city. What do you say about that, Holly?" I asked.

"I would say that is probably the bravest thing you've said in a while. Can we go out west for a bit? Somewhere warm would be great!" Holly laughed while forming sunglasses over her eyes and stretching out with her arms behind her head.

"The west, huh? That sounds good to me." And it really did. *Do something a little crazy, maybe win big,* I thought. It would certainly be a change of pace. I turned back to Holly and spoke. "Alright then, it's settled. Let's go get our friend," I said, finally opening the door to the truck. Both of us got out, and we headed towards the dam entrance, looking less eerie than it had the first time we had arrived there many weeks ago.

"Hey, Jim, one more thing. I know Wilson is your friend, but I think we should stay away from him," she stated, holding Joey in her hands still.

"Holly, he is a bit rough around the edges, sure—"

"No Jim, it's not that. I get that this world changes people, and it's not just the way he looks at us ghosts. It's the way he looks at you. He looks like a predator who's about to chow down. I don't see anything resembling friendship—I only see hunger. Just—let's just not do this with him, okay? Something doesn't feel right. When he is around, everything feels heavier," Holly explained.

I looked at my daughter who very rarely made statements like that. In fact, I wasn't sure if she ever had said something like that before. "Holly—we can trust him. I know we can. He is just as confused as the rest of us. We already showed him one of our stashes and how we found it. What could he possibly get from us at this point?"

"I don't know, Jim—just, you're a good person Dad, I know this. I think this time, though, we need to be out for just ourselves," Holly pleaded, shrinking into herself slightly.

I walked towards her and got eye-level with her, bending over on my knees. "If you think we should watch out for Wilson, then I will keep two eyes on him at all times, I promise."

Holly looked at the ground before nodding her head in agreement. She floated past me, heading into the dam. I waited standing there, in the dark, with the safety of iron bars around me.

I shivered, thinking the iron didn't feel so safe anymore. *Maybe my mistrust of Wilson from the start was valid. Or maybe, I was just getting old,* I thought. I turned, walking through the second set of gates before going into the dam.

Chapter 46

Once we had recounted the events of the day, everyone was silent. It is truly a dangerous thing to lose someone without the ability to fight back, to feel utterly helpless. Like we were all sitting inside a building during a tornado. Only that wasn't true—I had never been one for quitting, and I wasn't going to do that today. We had the power to take back our friend. We would do that.

None of us could think of a reason why the ghosts would steal her away like they had. It just was so out of character for most ghosts to even do that. From the encounters I'd always had, they would launch out and attack, try to get in your body like Diana had previously. What motivation would they have to come after us?

It was Rob who voiced it during our meeting around the table; he said what we were all thinking. "It's for us, they're baiting us for a bigger score. I mean, fuck, we are probably the last humans on Earth, for all we know."

No one had disagreed with him, and everyone hoped it wasn't true. There were just too many ghosts in this world and not enough people.

We all agreed the risks were worth bringing back Kim though; she was one of us. So we gathered at the table like our first night, when Holly and I came to the dam. Once we were all gathered, we began to spit ideas.

"It's just really a fucked situation, man," Rob stated, fumbling with a bottle lid.

"I agree, things are fucked, but it's not proactive complaining about it. Does anyone have any ideas for what to do?" I answered Rob, trying to keep some semblance of unity together. Leading was never my thing, and Wilson seemed to be sitting back and reserved for a change.

"Mine would be to stick our collective head in the sand and get fucked, but that is just me—what do I know, after all?" Rob muttered.

I ignored Rob. What destroys a planning process the most is negativity towards the plan, as I had learned over the years. "I can see everyone's concerns; it can be done, though. I have a plan that... should work," I stated.

"Well, should be better than nothing. Let's hear it, guys," countered Rob, his dissent seeming to have an effect on the group as a whole. Even Wilson hung his head a little lower.

I searched my mind for the right words to start my explanation, when Wilson spoke. "Regardless of the way we take—this will be a rough one. No one here is a soldier. Everyone here is capable of coming with me to get Kim back. I will go with or without you. Look inside yourself, if you don't have any desire to work with us, get out of this room, you aren't helping." Wilson had skewered the acrimonious arguments that everyone had about not going in one giant sweep.

Everyone was quiet. I spoke, breaking the ice. "Thank you, Wilson... Now, let's get started. Based on what Holly reported, the plan is this..." I briefed the group, turning around and drawing on a board Christina had found for me. It took me a little over three hours to explain the entire plan and drill out any holes we might have had. In all, it was probably the best chance we had at getting Kim back and keeping our collective asses safe—no pressure.

"I think this is totally nuts; it might just work, though, right?" Christina asked the group.

"My dad is very rarely wrong; it would be the best way to extract Kim and get us out of trouble fast in a pinch," Holly said, winking my way.

"I mean, I find more substance in the flat Earth theory, but hey, what do I know about such things?" Rob rumbled, before taking a deep breath.

"Well, I might be able to cook you up some party favors to help us out with the whole thing. If there's as many as you say, we will need more than one bar of iron. I thought about putting iron into a bullet, once; the problem is, using wrought iron as a shot will jack up a barrel something fast after a few shots. The bolts just need to be smooth and able to slide through the barrel. I could load up a shotgun with a few rounds inside the casing, and just replace the already metal pellets. But that will leave you almost entirely on your own for any long-range issues you might have," Rob stated, taking a long drag from his cigarette.

"We have the rifles from your bunker. Hopefully Rob can make shells for them. That should cover you on the move from a distance, and I will do what I can. Besides, Christina's cannon idea should do a damn good job of messing things up. Provided we can get close enough to use it," Wilson stated.

I nodded my head in agreement. All of this was speculation. Joey and Holly had returned an hour earlier with intel that Kim was still in the stadium. So far it looked like I would be going in the stadium alone to retrieve Kim, while Holly, Joey, and Christina would be running distractions from the Beast nearby; Wilson would be following from the rooftops with his rifle, giving me something of long range support, and Rob would be covering the Beast from a close location, using the other rifle and, as he put it, "Something fun."

"Alright, Christina, you and Wilson, go to the welding shop and get whatever you need from that hardware store you said was in town. Make as much as you can with what you find. Be able to fill the van with iron, except for the passenger and driver seat. Rob, you get started on putting together the bombs. Any questions?" I asked.

"I have one. Honey, no offense, but you won't last long in there just with your frying pan. There are just too many of them to take a swing at everything that walks. If you give us a little more time, I can make something useful for you," Christina remarked.

"Okay, anything will help, but know that we can't delay much longer. Every hour lost waiting could let something bad happen to Kim. We don't know what we will find once we are inside. So, on that note, we will have to assume everything bad can and will happen. I would say the best plans are those thought out from start to finish. It's just frustrating..." I sighed, tired from the day and knowing we still had a long way to go to prepare.

"Alright, everyone, you know what to do. Let's get started. Time is wasting, and I'm not getting any younger," Wilson declared, standing from the table and leaving the room.

"It's a good plan, chief. Don't worry, this is going to work. And believe me, I hate saying such nonsense," agreed Rob, rolling out of the room towards his workshop. Christina left after Wilson. Their task was going to take the most time and I hoped they could come back with enough supplies. Apparently, there was an old iron hardware store in town. According to Christina, the guy who had owned it had all kinds of scrap metal.

"What can we do to prepare, Jim?" asked Holly, gesturing towards Joey and herself.

"I'm not sure, Holly. Neither one of you are good at holding things. I am going to help Rob. You and Joey go, scout one more time, okay? And be careful; let me know if anything changes. Keep an eye on Joey—make sure he is okay."

"Right Jim. Come on, Joey," Holly said to the boy.

He was still quiet as the grave, and he hadn't spoken one word since we told him his mother was gone. I was worried, but I figured a busy mind was a sound mind, if nothing else. I didn't blame him; I would be a little shut down too. I turned from the board and taking my gear, I headed towards Rob's workshop at the end of the dam. Every little bit would help, and three hands were better than two.

All of us worked throughout the night, helping each other in various ways. Christina and Rob were the most useful; they both were able to put their skills to the test. When the night was over, I ordered everyone to try and get some sleep. To my surprise, everyone was listening, and even Wilson nodded his head at me in approval at the end of our day. I'd never liked leading, but it felt right to be in this position for the first time. Like I was actually doing some good.

I went back to my room only to find little rest. The floor was cold, and I couldn't help but feel uneasy. "Holly?" I asked the darkness, and a moment later, I heard my daughter's voice.

"Yeah, Jim, I'm worried too," she responded from somewhere nearby.

I started to say something, but nothing good came out, so I rolled over and muttered: "Just—see you in the morning, kiddo."

"See you, Jim," she whispered, and the room became dark again.

Chapter 47

A light came through the window, and I could see my breath. I sucked in a cold gush of air and started to dress. This time, I took my entire pack. The plan was that after we got Kim back, Holly and I were going to stop by the cabin one last time and then hit the road west. I smiled when I thought about it; it'd be good to feel the dry air on me for a change; nice to see Holly smile from zero worries about our life here.

Once I was geared up and ready, I went out to the meeting room. Everyone was assembled, for the most part. I looked at Christina as she chewed on a plastic straw. Her eyes appeared black as midnight, and she smelled like metal. She looked like hell. "Did you get any rest last night, Christina?" I asked.

"None. Come with me out to the loading dock," Christina grunted, getting up from her chair. I followed after her, not sure what I should have been expecting. We made our way past the offices where we slept to the loading dock. The dock had two massive metal doors leading out with various scattered work tables, throughout indicating a high level of use. Their wooden legs were held up by various pieces of scrap, while their dull gray surface areas were beaten in, like the wooden tops had seen a battle.

All of us, except for Joey and Holly, had spent most of the last night loading Wilson's van and Rob's bombs up with tiny pieces of iron sheet metal we had looted from the hardware store. Small chunks of metal littered the floor as I stepped behind Christina towards one of her workstations.

"Before all this went down, I used to weld a lot, and it was my passion—my art. So try and take care of the suit, please. I've been working on it for a long, long time. We had a lot of scrap metal lying around. Hopefully, it fits," she gestured shyly, while pulling down on a chain that revealed a strung-together armor piece.

I was astounded by the assorted pieces of iron Christina had managed to weld. There even was a helmet crudely made and fastened with a chin strap.

"My measurements weren't made as well as I would have liked them to be, but you should be able to move around without being completely weighed down, at least. Just don't make any dramatic movements, or this baby is going to start falling apart fast—so take care of it, hero." She beamed, looking at the metal suit with pride in her voice. I couldn't blame her; the craftsmanship was insane.

"This is awesome, Christina. Great work." I marveled at her work, it was truly a thing of beauty.

"Yeah, well, you just remember what you're fighting for, fighting for all of us. You know what happens when one of the ghosts is killed. Try and do your best; because this armor won't keep all of them out. You'll gain all of their memories," she stated, sitting down on a work stool next to the bench.

She was talking about the memories gained when ghosts were killed. Everything that a ghost ever dreamt, ever cared for, every sin, every embarrassment that person had before they died would become known to you. Over time, I had forgotten most the details of my life; I had yet to forget a single thing learned from any of the ghost's lives that I had taken. Every aspect of their lives—it scared me just thinking about it. It had become such an ordeal, the differences between when I knew my memories and when I knew theirs. It felt like I had been alive for a thousand years, that I had been alive for countless lives.

I nodded my head to her and looked at the armor, wondering if it would be enough once I got into the thick of it. I was getting nervous, thinking about rescuing Kim; I felt my legs sagging, before I realized I was heading towards the floor. Christina had swooped in at the last moment, catching me before I fell. I breathed deep.

"Are you okay, Jim? You're pale right now," she said, guiding me to her chair.

"It's just the light in here; I'll be all right," I responded.

"Well, just take a deep breath. I assume you aren't used to things like this, huh? It's funny: by the way you coordinated this whole thing, I would have thought you did this for a living," she said concernedly.

"Nope, just a regular old computer guy; closest I ever got to war before things changed was playing a video game." I said.

"How many ghosts have you killed at once? I guess that is a weird question, since we can't kill what is already dead," she pondered.

I breathed in a shaky breath, not sure if I would throw up before I spoke. "Trust me, Christina, it is murder... you just aren't supposed to know all that about another person's life. Hell, I don't even think people know that much about their own lives. Every time I killed one, every time, it was like someone was shattering the mirror that made me into me. Like I had pieces of glass being taken away. And every day I was being told: *reflect yourself, show yourself*. But you can't show yourself when so much is missing. To answer your question, I'm not sure how many I have killed; I would say I have killed about twelve at the most at one time," I said, tasting a lot of spit in my mouth. It was starting to feel like I was going to throw up.

"Yeah, I figured as much. For me, it was two. And like you said, it felt like murder to me. I still have trouble forgetting their memories. Wilson gave me a tip once: he says if you keep your mind focused on just one thing, and one thing only, then their memories can't get in. I'm not sure how it works, but hey, it's better than nothing. So, just focus on something important to you."

"Good advice," I said, looking at the armor again. "Help me get this thing on," I stated, standing up and walking towards the armor. I unfastened a leather band first, before Christina jumped in and helped me get into the metal. The metal felt cold and heavier than I thought it would be, my skin feeling replaced by a permanent shell.

I felt like a turtle; I just hoped I didn't fall over. Still, the arms were able to move surprisingly well as I practiced swinging my pan. When we finished, I felt Christina attach my frying pan to a leather thong. "You know, I might be able to tie up a piece of sheet metal and give you some more range if you want," she suggested.

"No thank you. If I start changing things now, something dumb will happen. I'm superstitious like that," I joked.

Christina looked bemused as she finished the touches on the frying pan sling. "Anything else you need from me?" she asked. I told her about my shotgun, and she quickly attached it to my right leg after some adjustments to the straps.

I looked down imagining what it would feel like to have to go for either of my weapons. It is a sober thought, knowing you're about to go to battle. I liked Christina and Rob, plus little Joey. The three had become good friends of mine. *That was what I was going to do,* I'd decided. *Since I had to go to war, I was going to protect my friends.*

As I practiced pulling free my gun (it was pretty hard, the metal glove that was made for me was surprisingly thick and well strung together. It allowed movement, just not enough), Holly appeared in front of me.

"Ironman." Holly said with amusement.

"I know, it only took the ghost apocalypse to come true finally," I jested.

As the three of us talked, Wilson and Rob came into the room. Rob was still in his wheelchair, looking no worse for wear than normal. Only this time, he had a pump action pellet rifle in his lap, in addition to what appeared to be a big radio controller.

I cocked my eyebrow at him, and Rob smiled. "Party favors, man, it would only be rude if I didn't bring something to the clash," he stated, while reaching behind him for a bag. "Here, for when you need something out of your way. Just light what is inside the bag and throw it quick," Rob said, tossing me the bag.

"What the hell is it, Rob?" I asked, having difficulty lifting the bag over my shoulders until Christina stepped in and helped.

"Ah, nothing too fancy, just a mixture of low-octane gasoline with benzene and polystyrene, all tucked into a few small mason jars." Rob flushed with a smile for his cunning.

I was more than a little befuddled; chemistry was never my strong point in school.

Rob must have noticed my expression and explained. "It's napalm, brother. Type-B, if you want to get down to the semantics. Just all you need to know is light the bag, give it a toss, and run like hell, man." He gestured with an air of confidence that reminded me of an old mad scientist show.

I nodded my head just in time for Wilson to start speaking, ignoring the fact I had a bomb on my back and I was dressed in a suit of iron.

What a day this was turning out to be.

"I hope everyone is ready. We don't know what to expect out there, and we don't even know for sure who is behind this. What we do know is these assholes have our friend. Let's go kill some things," Wilson said, sliding his massive ax back into his belt, where he had another long purple dagger. He was dressed in black from head to toe and had an old and ragged-looking knife on his chest. Around his neck, though, was his gas mask. The protective seals looked like they had been replaced multiple times; in fact, I was no expert, but the gas mask looked foreign and just odd. Like something from an old war.

"Where did you get that ax?" I asked Wilson.

"Same place as I got my mask. There is a military history museum to the east of Charlotte. I'm surprised you never raided it yourself, Jim. Now, we should hurry and get on the road. We leave in two minutes, people." Wilson stated to the group, turning and moving.

I racked my mind for a moment, trying to picture where the

military museum he was talking about was located, and nothing came to mind. As I thought, Rob and Christina begun to load up their respective vehicles. I looked at Holly and spoke. "How are you feeling there, kiddo? Are you tired? I see you have you war paint colors on today." She did indeed—her hair was a bright red and gold.

She yawned and stretched her hands over head. "Just a little bit. Joey and I just got back. I am telling you, Jim, it's scary as hell just watching how all of them are standing there. It's like they're awaiting orders or something. And the screams coming from Kim... We just need to get her as soon as possible." She shuddered, and I felt that intense desire again to be able to comfort my daughter.

I smiled at her. "We will get her soon, squirt, and get to the bottom of this. After that, it's just you and me on the road for a while. I'm thinking the Grand Canyon," I said, chuckling, trying my best to cheer her up.

Holly cocked a half-smile and rose to my height, kissing my cheek. I felt the cold sensation. It was one of comfort for a change, as she floated away from me. "So, explain to me again why he couldn't wear the armor, Jim?" Holly asked from beside me.

"Honestly, I can't shoot worth a shit, and Christina is probably the most useful person here if something happens to Wilson. Wilson is our best shot, so having him cover me does make me feel a bit safer," I said, slapping my hands on the hard iron.

"Just promise that you will be careful, Dad," she stated.

I looked at her and turned, grabbing my helmet. "As long as I am breathing, Holly, I will protect us both," I said.

"It's not that I am worried about that, Dad. Besides, I'm the one who protects you now. I don't think you would make it out of your room in the morning," she teased. Holly suddenly turned towards me straight-faced and spoke again. "You know, Dad, we proved to be the good guys, after all," she declared.

I looked at her, puzzled by her words. Holly must have sensed my confusion and continued, "I've been getting some memories back lately… you know, from the ones before. Don't worry; I know I am still in control, no crazy boogie man coming out of me today. I was at a soccer game once, and I remembered tripping over this girl after she pushed me. Anyways, you took me out for ice cream after the game, and you told me to practice forgiveness as a way to make us brave. You said forgiveness was the only way to live with people and to be happy. Molly—I mean, I—didn't believe you, as you could probably guess. So I asked you if we would always be the good guys. And the answer was one that made me have faith in you forever; you said we would always be the good guys. And guess what we are, Jim! I just want you to know how proud I am, Dad; you rescued me from being lost and gave me a reason to keep on living."

I stood silent and more than a little red in the cheeks. *It had been a long time since I had a mentality like that,* I thought. As I stood contemplating this, Holly floated off near Joey and before the two disappeared, she waved. I waved back, smiling, knowing that everything was going to be alright. When I turned back to Christina, she had the van pulled towards me as I rushed to the passenger side. *It was going to be a rough day,* I thought, as I pulled the doors behind me and our two-car convoy line started out.

Wilson and Rob pulled ahead of our van and waved us on as we started the long trip to Charlotte. Holly and Joey had also spent time on their scouting mission, showing us the clearest and fastest route to Charlotte, so the ride was relatively smooth for a change. In the seat next to me, Christina tapped the steering wheel with a nervous rhythm. I didn't need to ask to know what was on her mind. Hell, it was hard enough for me to remain in my seat as we made our way closer.

As we entered the Charlotte area, a click almost inside my head went off. *I was home,* I thought. It never hits you how much you miss your home until you finally return. *Holly is my home, though, no matter where I am and what I am doing. As long as I have my daughter, I will always have a home.* I let that warm me as we got closer to the stadium over the long drive. Our voyage so far hadn't attracted the attention of anything on the roads. The heat was causing me to sweat inside my iron armor.

Whoever had decided in their mind to take Kim, I couldn't comprehend why. The thing that frightened me the most, though, was how easy they were letting us move this whole trip. Less than three months ago, Holly and I had nearly been eaten by a horde of ghost animals. Now we hadn't seen one sign of a stray phantom for miles and miles in any direction. Once more, according to what Holly and Joey were saying, none of them were moving, just frozen in their forms like statues on a beach, awaiting the return of a ship, or the massive swells of a hurricane pulling back for the main surprise.

I shook my head and looked at Holly quickly, keeping up with the van, flying a safe distance away so as not to be hit by the iron. I wanted at that moment to just tell her *never mind,* and for us to just leave. I knew I could never live with myself if I did leave Kim behind, though. I sucked in a breath, hating myself for giving a shit.

I tried thinking about the plan over again, and that was distracting enough. Inside the van with Christina and I were over two hundred bottle rockets filled to the brim with iron metal shavings Christina had spent hours making the night before.

All were designed to fire off out of their holders using a contraption Rob and I had made together last night as well. It was pretty simple for the most part. An ignition switch would prime a wire that sent a signal down the line to fire each rocket about a second after the previous one. We even added a pullout table to the back of the Beast. All Christina had to do was park the Beast as close to the stadium as she could get, and fire off several rockets, one after another.

The missiles would make it just over the front of the stadium and would hopefully take out enough ghosts before the largest portion of the astral army showed up. During that time, it was up to me to break into the stadium and find our missing companion Kim, while I was hopefully being covered by Wilson and Rob. No problems, right?

Right, and pigs could fly, I thought as we entered the last highway leading up to the stadium. Wilson and Rob pulled aside us and called through the walkie-talkie headsets that we kept inside the van. I hesitated to answer as I heard the squeak of an incoming call. Nervous, I reached out, taking the plastic machine into my trembling hand.

Wilson's voice came in harsh and ragged. "Listen up people, we are getting closer to the stadium. Rob and I are going to peel off now and be waiting near the parking garage. Jim, try not to get bogged down. Just get Kim and get on out of there fast. We will all be covering your back so don't be afraid. Good luck, everyone. Wilson out."

The radio went dead with silence as Wilson in his van peeled off in front of us. I set the receiver back on the dashboard and stared out the window as I could see the large facades of the stadium. Its arching was still intact after twenty years, though the paint had long since turned from blue into red rust, and the signs that once indicated the stadium was a place of fun were now long gone. Its arches resembled the ancient gladiatorial stadium of Rome, only the blood spilled here today would be only that of ghosts. Hopefully.

From our vantage point inside the van, I couldn't see anything. All I could see was the towering stadium surrounded by open lots, highways, and a huge shopping mall. *Relatively exposed,* I thought. Then again, from what I saw, it was probably the most intact section of the entire city.

We rolled on towards the stadium, stopping at the intersection ramp. Cars were blocking our exit down, and both vehicles had to come to a complete stop. I reached for the radio as Wilson called in. "What is this? I thought Holly and Joey reported that the road was all clear to the stadium."

"Someone would have moved it recently; Holly is never really wrong by what she sees," I said letting go of the talk button on the radio.

The radio sparked back a moment later. "Regardless, we have to get around this shit—can you and Christina handle this? We can go around to the longer path, by taking the other ramp," chimed Wilson through the radio.

I bit my lip before speaking as I looked at Christina and she nodded her head in approval. "Yeah, you guys know what to do—James out." I clicked, hanging up the radio.

Wilson and Rob reversed and backtracked the way we came, going to a separate ramp that would take them around the stadium. However, it would take longer, based off the maps we had looked at from the surrounding area.

I opened the van door making sure to fasten the heavy helmet on tighter. The temperature went up fast, and I started sweating before I even got out of my seat, my ears feeling like I was being dragged under water. "Keep it running; I'll pop the cars into neutral and roll them," I shouted to Christina.

"Be quick about it, James. This doesn't feel right..." Christina said, letting her words hang between us.

I didn't want to waste time agreeing with her. As my feet hit the pavement, Joey and Holly showed up out of thin air. "Jim, we are completely exposed right now—we need to get moving," Holly whispered, looking off in the direction of the stadium with a pained and anxious expression on her face. I walked towards the first car, positioned at an angle with the other car forming an efficient "v" shape.

I busted the first window with my pan and was amazed the vehicle was in such good condition. The amounts of rust on the inside, I noted, should be nowhere near this much and the outside should be far worse. Someone had been maintaining them. I ignored that detail, and kept pushing on, hoping these cars weren't from some place other than Charlotte. My eyes ignored my fear though. The plates had been stripped. *Great.*

I pulled the car into neutral and spun the wheel all the way to the right. The movement inside the armor was making everything strained, and I felt my breath coming in short gulps. I turned back and looked at Christina; her eyes were peeled, watching the stadium, and she had the van idling.

"Holly, do you think you and Joey could push this car for me? I only need a little bit; don't strain yourselves," I said grunting, and came out of the driver's seat. Keeping the door opened, I started to push as Joey came up behind the car.

"I don't know how to move things like Holly does; I'm sorry," the boy mumbled, casting his eyes towards the ground.

I grunted, "That's fine. Holly?"

Holly answered by appearing behind the car, and she flared her eyes, and I felt the wind pick up all around me, pulling towards her. It was like we were standing inside the eye of a small storm as debris in the road started circling over her fiery hair. A moment of pride struck me while watching my daughter. It was interrupted just as quickly when Christina began to honk the horn of the van furiously. I snapped back to see hundreds of human ghosts flying from the direction of the stadium.

I spiraled, heading back to the van as fast as I could, my progress hindered by the weight of the suit. Without looking back, I shouted at Holly and Joey to move. "Get out of the way, guys, now!"

"Jim, get down!" screamed Holly as she flung her stored-up energy at the cars. A heavy grind of metal on concrete ripped through my ears with a force that almost dropped me, as I looked up to see the cars flying towards the road below, along with huge chunks of the turning ramp.

I stood up on shaky legs and felt uneasy as the ghosts came flying towards us, their migration one far too frightening for my mind to handle, as my legs flew towards the van. Christina was luckily moving faster than me and met me halfway down the turning ramp. I stepped up to the passenger door and held on, with my feet on the stepping ramp attached to the side, and part of my upper body in the window.

Christina had the van moving at top speed as we rounded the curve. I closed my eyes as the van momentarily came off the ground from the maneuver. I opened my eyes, and we were still on the road. I looked at Christina, her eyes locked on the stadium in the distance.

The ghosts soon shifted their direction and bee-lined towards the Beast like we were a wounded animal in an ocean filled with sharks. I felt the first ghost hit near the driver's side of the van, and rainbow sparks flew off the vehicle, showering us both with visual images of the ghost's life. I closed my eyes, not wanting to see any of the spirit's life or the breakneck speed we were going. Instead, I focused on catching my breath and slowing down my heart. I felt the rhythm was too similar to a hammer beating a nail into a roof. One strike and down the beats went inside my chest.

More ghosts hit the side of the van as the armada caught up to us. The swarm began to form a horde, while sparks flew from the embedded iron frame. A few made it over to me and were greeted by my armor, sending waves of pain into me as their memories came flooding in.

I looked towards the stadium as we sped to it, keeping the image in my mind and my thoughts only on that image. *Holly, give me strength.* The ghost's memories swarmed my brain, and I felt my hands falling off the van when a stronger image took hold. I remembered Holly, and the ghosts' assault on my mind ceased as we sailed on the road. It was the image of us playing board games. Hours we had spent, just the two of us, lost in moments, but together on that roof. On that roof overlooking a dead city, the last two alive. The lost in our love, together on that roof. Turning my head back towards Christina, I could see the strain of all the memories take their toll on her as well.

She was bleeding from the eyes and ears. "Christina, are you okay?" I shouted over the roar of moaning ghosts as her passenger side window shattered in. The glass found ways to sink in, even through the iron armor. I clenched my whole body and looped my one good arm tighter on the inside of the door as we increased speed. Even with two arms, I wasn't sure what good I was going to be able to do at these speeds.

Looking up, we were a hundred yards out from the main entrance when a cluster of ghosts swirling around, imitating a cyclone, came at the front of the van. Christina saw them coming and started slowing down the van as fast as possible. Iron frame or not, glass was still glass and would break with that many ghosts heading towards us.

Without looking, Christina snapped her seat belt on and spoke, "Go get our girl, Jim."

I panicked, realizing what she had planned. "Christina—wait!" I said too late, before she hit her brakes, sending me flying from the van onto the road. The momentum caused my tumble to be a lot worse, as I felt pieces of metal shred loose along with my skin.

My breath was gone, but the fall wasn't nearly as bad as my mind had pictured. I looked up and realized why my skid wasn't as bad—Christina had shot me into the grassy bank full of shrubs and bushes.

She had slowed down just enough for me not to slide into anything too damaging. I got to my feet, tasting blood in my mouth and feeling cold, damp spots all over me. I felt like sandpaper rubbing a wooden chair raw. My skin was warm everywhere—burning, even.

I shook it off, running towards Christina. The van was swarming with ghosts, the front windshield now blown in, and glass was sprayed over the street. I reached for my frying pan as the helmet atop my head started to slide. The metal was tearing my skin now in sections, every time I moved. It was still holding, thanks to her craftsmanship though. Without it, that fall would have killed me.

I charged forward, heading for the van, when I started hearing Christina's screams. Doubling my pace into a full sprint, I reached the van, and slammed the first ghost with my frying pan. Blue and green sparks highlighting the creatures flew around me like being trapped inside of an amusement park ride, surrounded by neon, a glowing death that threatened to send me to a junkie hell. I kept focus on the task of saving Christina; nothing came into me, except for more rage at trying to save her. I went to take another swing at the ghosts, when Christina's screams stopped. She was no more, and that left the entire group of ghosts with a new target as they circled overhead. I looked in awe as the eidolons formed a cyclone, like fish do in the ocean. I was their prey at the bottom; I tightened the grip on the frying pan, readying myself for the attack.

A roar snapped my attention to behind the van, as a giant tyrannosaurus came smashing into the fray of ghosts. Using its powerful jaws, many ghosts were broken as the creature tore through the ranks of monsters. "Well—holy shit..." I gasped at the sight, losing the hold on my pan. I wasn't going to be able to beat that anytime soon.

Holly soon appeared from on top of the prehistoric beast and glided down above the van. Vengeance was the name, as her red hair sprayed shots of sunlight like fire and her fists glowed with a bright intensity.

"James, get going! Joey and I can handle this!" she screamed, tearing ghosts into shreds feet away from her. I couldn't see what or how she was doing it. Right now, though, that wasn't my daughter. She was a pure demon enraged at the loss of her friend.

I doubled back and pulled my bag from the passenger seat as the ghosts were too busy being occupied by Joey the dinosaur to pay any attention to me at the moment. I quickly slung the bag back over my shoulders, not wanting to look at the body of Christina. Out of the corner of my eye, I saw the blood—she was mostly muscle. Thankfully, the bag hadn't busted after the Beast had wrecked.

I made my way along the road at my quickest pace, and all the while the iron armor dug into my body and I could feel my blood flowing from somewhere. Running up the main entrance way, I could see how great the stadium had once been. It must have been a good place for a lot of people. A modern-day ruin, changed to look like ancient aliens must have built it, a whole generation of knowledge and skills gone. It would be hard for anyone to think men could build such things. "Barbarians must have felt this when they came to Rome…" I mumbled, trying to catch my breath.

The glamour of the stadium was under only a moderate degradation. Despite the time that had passed, only the paint had disappeared. The stadium stood tall, and flanked at the main entrance were the two imposing, giant panthers, which made me fear they might be animal ghosts.

My fears were put at ease as the monsters never moved from their cold spots. Like giant metal guardians, forever perched at their dutiful locations until the end of time.

I risked turning back to see Joey being swarmed by ghosts and Holly blasting off huge waves of their foes in all directions. I turned back to the main doors to see them locked and barricaded. I kicked at the glass doors, yet the glass held. It felt more like safety glass, and wasn't going to be kicked down by an old man.

Great, I muttered, *of all the times for something useful to still be working. Shooting the glass was only going to draw a massive amount of attention from the ghosts nearby,* I thought. *Think, Jim. Compartmentalize. Why? Because brother, you don't have much time at all.* I reached for my gun with the intentions of blasting my way in when I heard Holly shout from behind me.

"Need a hand, Jim?" Holly shouted while she channeled that massive swell of energy. Realizing what her plan was, I jogged and dove out of the way of the doors as a huge invisible force shattered through the glass as if it was a stretched-taut poster with a ball being thrown through its center.

I tasted blood in my mouth again; I bit my tongue when I landed, and mocking my stupidity, I stood up and gave the thumbs up to Holly as she and Joey continued to battle.

"Come on, Jim, be lazy another day—it's all just a little blood," I shouted, encouraging myself to move through the doors. So far, I had been lucky and faced almost no ghosts upon entering the stadium. When I got in, I could make out the remains of a caisson-stand and the once-populated booths of places where people would have fun on an average Sunday. I regretted now for some reason that I'd never taken Molly to one of these games—she would have liked it. *Reminisce later, old man.*

I stopped and searched through my bag. My hands fumbled on the flashlight, and I pulled it free from the bag, snapping it on. The light went through the first hundred or so ghosts, all leading up to the exit ramp onto the field I was searching for. Of course, that had to be the direction they were in. I cursed my luck wishing I could have found a way to coat the flashlight in iron.

The handle from the flashlight was sending large amounts of shocks up my arm as the battery was reacting to the huge number of aberrations. I dropped the thing, and the light shattered, and I was in total darkness. I fumbled in the bag again for another source of light, trying to move aside the jars made by Rob filled with what had to be the man's reenactment of Vietnam with as much as the pack was holding.

As I looked, thousands of lights clicked on at once, casting me in a red light; I squinted at the glare. My fingers no longer worked as a hundred sets of unblinking eyes faced me down, glowing red in the darkness. *Don't need a light anymore. The armor I'm wearing is the only reason why I haven't been attacked yet,* I thought. I searched frantically for the lighter. My hands found the lighter wedged between one of the jars. Blood came down my fingers in streams as I trembled for the lighter and pulled it free from the bag.

Using my one hand and a combination of shrugs, I was able to get the bag open. Dropping the bag to the floor, I blurted out in some form of mental disturbance, "I'm not sure how you assholes feel about fire, but me, I love it." I shouted to the group, before snapping the tab on the cool metal of the lighter. First try, and a small flame licked from the top, showering my hand in the darkness of the underbelly.

One of the jars was leaking something, judging from the smell; I knew this was going to suck and I had only one chance. I burned the bottom of the bag and took aim at the closest wooden stand. Molly had played soccer as a kid, and I only ever played sports on computer games. So when my kick landed on the bag, it went veering off to the far left instead of straight on.

"Shit!" I snarled as the bag suddenly became engulfed in orange flames, exploding in all directions, showering the whole underside of the stadium in light. The fire managed to make its way to one of the stands, catching the old countertops aflame in a matter of seconds—despite my aim.

Not wasting time, I dropped the lighter and pulled my pan free as I charged the first ghost. *Keep a good thought in mind*; I heard Christina's words whisper into my head. The first ghost met my iron pan and exploded into memories, and I continued forward.

The ghosts all reacted all at one time, a hive mind moving like a wave forcing me down under their weight like a tall tree falling on a weak bush below. I swung my pan left and right, not aiming anymore. Not thinking, not doing anything, just going forward. My thoughts were only on my daughter and on nothing else; my mind was clear and my legs kept moving.

At times, I felt my body being lifted almost from the ground, or being pulled down. As I moved, pieces began to fall from my armor. My walk was too slow, and the weight of their force was too strong to go any faster. Every time I became aware of their pushes against me, my image of Holly wavered.

I hesitated as more pieces of the iron suit came free, exposing me to an endless number of images. I felt my nose bleeding as I walked, continuing to swing my weapon. My pan made my arm too fatigued; I was spent, I couldn't hold the pan anymore. Several times, I dropped the pan from the weight, and it slammed back down on my leg. I pressed my left arm up, I was going forward, through blood and steel.

The armor on me snapped free when the ghosts sent a thick gush of air, knocking me to the ground, including my helmet. I sucked in a deep breath as the air felt on fire from the heat of the bomb.

Ghosts were all around me and everywhere I looked, I saw faces in flames. It was the closest to hell as any place a man could make on Earth. Faces crying, moaning in the darkness; reaching out to me. Tears drying in the rain, limbs unmoving in the flames.

I wanted to cry; I wanted to curl up into a ball and lie there, and let the monsters take me. My tears were drying from the heat faster than they fell. I breathed the word "Holly," and my legs came back up, along with the rest of my body as I slowly made my way to my feet. Ghosts continued their onslaught on me, taking pieces of flesh and clothing from my body. My shirt became a tattered cloth along with my pants; my voice worked fine, though, spurring me on. "Holly," I repeated over and over to my demons as I came to the exit of the ramp on the field.

The light blinded me, and I looked down to find my stomach and legs were smeared with blood. My hand trembled and was colored blue like Neptune; all life in my body had been taken away to a different planet. How I had survived my ordeal I wouldn't have the time to figure out.

The inside of the stadium was chaos. The Beast lay in several pieces and had crashed into the lower section seats, causing an impact crater that had done more damage than most bombs from an airplane.

It stunned me to see the devastation and even worse, that I hadn't heard any of it. When I tried to hear anything, both my ears felt painful. Pressure was built up in my head and I felt like I was miles under water. Everything rang.

I wasn't sure how the Beast had ended up in the stadium; my best guess was Holly had thrown the heavy machine over the massive walls. "Never piss her off, old man…" I mumbled as I looked at the top arch, now demolished from the flight of the Beast.

In the distance, I could see ghosts gathering in the background. They looked at me as the fire quickly grew. I could see thousands of red eyes staring at me, calling my name to come back into the darkness. Faces in the flames, voices in the smoke coming for me.

The only thing protecting me from them was the scattered remains of iron shavings that had been loaded into the Beast. On closer examination, I could see the pieces of metal were blanketing the area with a fresh bronze-colored snow. I gave a silent prayer to Christina for her ingenuity, and I stripped off the remains of my armor (the metal was pressing into my already-mutilated skin, but it was now used up). Thanks to her, this plan might actually work. Making sure I kept over the safety of the iron pieces, I made my way down from the lower section out onto to the field.

At the end zone, I could see figures; one of them was being held down by her hair and was screaming in pain while other more menacing ghosts floated nearby. I walked the line leading up to the group, all the while my anger growing. Ghosts followed my steps deliberately and slowly, nipping at my heels like dogs.

When I was about ten yards off, I stopped and pulled my gun free, pointing the barrel towards the ghosts holding Kim. She was crying, her eyes long since bleeding red from the number of tears she'd shed. Her skin looked almost yellow from her exposure to the elements.

"Let her go," I snarled to the group of ghosts. None moved, just continued to gaze unblinking in the flames. I pointed my gun towards the one looking at Kim, as I did this, hundreds of ghosts came to land behind the ringleader.

It's a show of power, I thought as the numbers soon swelled, and the odds were one human to a thousand ghosts. I was soon encircled, and the song of the ghosts started playing its anonymous tune all around me. Something I could neither understand and something I wouldn't want to know. The definition of sadness, beings lost without a way out, only knew the song of grief.

I spoke once more to the ghost holding Kim. "Let her go. Now."

The ghost finally turned its head from her to me and snarled, eyes gleaming black. All of the ghosts' eyes were black, as deep as coal. "Why don't you destroy us all?" implored the ghost, as the thousands of spirits around me repeated the sentence in union.

I thought about the words of the ghost. Was it challenging me to destroy them, or did it actually want me to kill them? I couldn't possibly take on this many and hope to walk away. Not even with Wilson's or Rob's help, who were still missing. At least Wilson should have entered in the stadium by now or provided some kind of covering fire—where were they? I was assuming they'd managed to make it in position and hadn't been caught off guard as the rest of us were. I was on my own, and I was going to have to save Kim or die trying.

A shot rang off in the distance, and I looked off to see Wilson coming from the other side of the field, his shotgun tucked deep into his shoulder as he blasted away a ghost that got too close. His gas mask was on, and I couldn't see his features, but I knew he was looking right at me. The mass of ghosts left him alone as well, and above us, circling overhead, were Holly and Joey; we were all here in the stadium. Still alive, still ticking. *Why, though?* That didn't make any sense to me. *Why were we all still being allowed to sit here without being torn to pieces?* They could easily overwhelm Wilson and me.

Why let us get this close? What were their motives? Surely, someone out of the collective ghosts had seen a crappy hero-against-villain movie? You never let the hero just come into your trap. Did they even have one? I thought while I turned looking at the faces of ghosts all around me. None looked lost; none had the traditional eternal sadness I had grown used to seeing. Instead, their faces looked at ease. Determined, like they were on a mission.

Like they were being controlled—that is the answer, I thought. They were being controlled. I was wrong, it was not grief driving them—it was dedication. I kept my gun pointed as I spoke, and let my voice ring as loud as it could. "Who is controlling all of you?"

I was met with silence. No one moved in the entire stadium, until the ghosts all answered at once. "WE ARE ALL LINKED TO THE ONE," the horde shouted.

"Linked? Linked to whom, who is controlling you?" I shouted back my response.

"WE ARE ALL LINKED TO THE ONE," called back the army in response to my questions.

I was getting mad as my heart started pounding from the fear and the anger. I wasn't going to get a straight answer out of these guys. I looked up at Holly and saw the concern in her face far above. I looked at Wilson; he had pulled his gas mask from his face now and watched me with sharp eyes. He nodded his head and mouthed the words "attack." Wilson wanted me to attack the group, to hurt them and rescue Kim from their clutches.

I shook with anger; I wanted to shoot them all for what they were doing to Kim. For what they had done to brave Christina and anyone else who had been hurt by them. So many people had died since these things had risen. *And why, what was their point? To simply die and hunt the living, to turn the city into a tomb crested in sorrow at every turn?*

Venomously, I spoke. "Take me to The One now before I kill each and every last one of you!" None of the ghosts moved; none stirred from my ideal threats.

"Jim, we are going to have to kill all of them; you can't talk to these monsters," shouted Wilson, eyeing the army of ghosts, his stance indicating he was ready to start shelling the crowd of ghosts around him with zero prejudice.

I looked at the ghost holding Kim; it appeared to be a teenage boy. His shirt had a gaming symbol on it. Another ghost nearby wore scrubs, and one more wore a cop's uniform. *An entire arena is full of ghosts from all walks of life. Everyone had lived a life; they had all been alive just like Holly. Just ordinary men, women, children, small, tall, black, white, and everything in between. People—that's what they were.*

Diana, she had been everything in my life—for the briefest of times I had her. The same with Molly—I had them both a lot longer than I deserved. Somehow, though, I was given Holly instead, and she had been my light in this never-ending night. All the times we had spent together, growing together. Becoming a family of our own, the old us was dead. James and Molly were gone, but Jim and Holly were here now though, and we had a life. And that life is what everyone here had; they weren't ghosts, they were people who had been twisted by something. Something that could never be explained, but they were robbed of their moments in life. Now they were being deprived of their second moments, these poor souls. That's what they still were, just people trying to figure out life and what happened to them. I was killing people; I wasn't making the world a better place. Just sending it into darkness, pretending to be the good guy for the sake of my family. All of them would do anything to be with their families, just like I would.

Suddenly, my gun started feeling a lot heavier than it did before. The wooden stock of my rifle dug into my hand; a weight that was going to have to drop soon.

I felt eyes on me from all around me, like I had in that hallway when I went for Holly. The eyes of every single ghost I had ever met, every single person I had met in my life. I pictured what it would be like to be heading west with Holly, the desert sands kissing my neck as we rode off into the sunset. To be free of the never-ending nightmare unfolding around us.

I wanted to be anywhere in the world; anywhere that was far away from everyone around me. I felt listless, my eyes drooping in the hot day. My back ached, my skin burned at the touch of the smooth red liquid racing to fall from my limbs. I was here though; I was in this situation. I had to face it, I had to make a choice. "The woman, the woman you're holding… she had—has a son. He is right above you now, actually," I said, feeling the words in my mouth.

I continued, "Let her go, let her be with her son. All—all of you had your lives. That doesn't mean all your lives are over. My daughter died. I cradled her body in my arms; I was trapped under an iron bathtub for two days with the shell of my daughter. And when my ordeal ended, and light settled back in my life, my daughter came back; I have since spent the last twenty years with my best friend. I have spent the past twenty years with the wind in my sails. I would die for her; she would die for me. I don't see a monster when I look at her. I see my daughter, with whom I am going to spend as many years as I can, making memories. I never controlled her; we control the world around us instead. I am so sorry someone is controlling you. I am so sorry you died, I am even more remorseful you lost who you were when you lost your memories. I don't care what you've done. Killing you will just create more ghosts." I fumbled my words, searching for what I knew was right. *Press on James, do the right thing.*

"If you can't believe me, if you have nothing to hold on to, remember this: we didn't need love; we weren't given love. Not by some higher power, not by some evolved intelligence. We—*we*—chose to have love, we opted to be there for each other, if anything, to face any terror in the darkest of tunnels. Hold on to love because that is the greatest thing we've created.

"I look at my girl above us, and I think of the memories we have created together in the last twenty years. I was a man before this world changed, I became a ghost after the world changed. I am becoming alive again every day; I am becoming a man again; a father, a friend, and I am making my way in this crazy world. We must create a heaven in our hell. So let that woman go, please. Let her be with her son. Let her continue her life with her loved one." I pleaded, dropping my gun to the ground. I undid my frying pan from my side, and I let the metal clunk to the overgrown turf—now a jungle of living grass.

"Jim, what the fuck are you doing! Pick your weapons up!"

screamed Wilson. Without turning to my friend, I walked to the ghost holding Kim, my feet crunching on the iron below me. "Make your memories. If you're lost, rediscover who you are," I spoke gently to the ghost.

The black eyes of the ghost never moved. All were silent in the stadium, waiting for the next moment. I was scared out of my mind; maybe it was because of all the ghosts that had tried to claw their way into my brain, or just the blood loss. This felt right; this seemed like the best chance we all had. Saving Kim wasn't the only thing I could accomplish today. "What is lost can always be found," I said, turning in a circle addressing all the ghosts.

One ghost finally moved, floating towards me. "I do not remember who I am. Will you help me?" pleaded an old male ghost. His features were distorted, showing signs of his death, having been crushed under some great weight. His head was nearly flattened into his shoulders, causing his words to drawl out in low rasps.

I looked at the man; this wasn't my specialty, saving a group of people. I thought of Holly. I thought of how close to a monster I had been becoming for so long, and I realized this was my chance to come back from the edge finally. "I can't tell you who you are, but I can help you find your way. Commit our meeting to memory. Once you have that down, find yourself. You're real, just by knowing this is happening. You're you; be the person you want to be and make the memories that you say." I spoke, touching the ghost hastily on the shoulder, my fingers easily gliding through.

The ghost looked at my hand. The cold sensation frosted under my fingers as I moved away, his force becoming more solidified. I looked once more at the man, and he began to change, his features coming back to normal. He no longer looked sinister; he no longer looked like someone who had been murdered. Instead, he was replaced by a man filled with light. The old façade of his existence dissolved away like sugar in water. His eyes were returning to normal; he looked like Holly. He looked alive. The other ghosts around him eyed the old man as he smiled, casting his eyes up to the sky.

Another ghost stepped forward. This time it was a teenage boy. "I want to remember this. I want to be alive again." The boy lumbered as his features began to glow, just as the old man had.

More and more ghosts around me began to speak, their forms changing to ones closer to human nature. Power surged from the group; I left my tools on the ground, my hand better off empty. The weapon's protection was unneeded and unwanted, clunky in its feeling; a sense I wasn't used to. It felt right discarding my tools.

Holly swooped down with Joey as he met his mother. I watched as Kim cried and did her best to touch Joey. Both mother and son reunited. I looked at Holly, and we both smiled.

For the first time in twenty years, I saw something on my daughter's face, probably something I had never seen before on her face: she was proud of me. I had finally done something good; I looked at the sky and was thankful I could leave this city finally on a good note.

Ghosts hovered near the ground, talking, shouting their questions about whom they were, as if tasting words for the first time. I walked towards Holly through the crowd of ghosts all trying to discover their lives, all trying to rekindle something they didn't have before. Life was a precious thing, and to be alive in any form was something that should never be taken for granted. I knew that now. I felt an old ache in my chest start to fade away as I looked to leave with my daughter.

The crowd of ghosts cleared, their songs of the lost replaced by the joyous sounds of the lost, only this time, they knew they had been lost, and that, I thought, is how you become found.

When the crowd cleared, I saw Benny walk from under the same exit ramp that Wilson was standing in front of.

What is Benny doing here? I thought as I was speechless at the sight of him. He walked with a slow, but noticeable limp in his steps, as he crept his way behind Holly.

I registered the hate in his eyes first as Holly smiled at me, waving. Her eyes caught the fear in my face first, as Benny's iron rod struck through her. Holly split in a bright ray of colors, flying into countless streams before me.

"Your fault, James," whispered Diana, and I finally understood what she had said, all those years ago on the roof. She had said, "Your fault, James."

I screamed, howling like an animal, and charged forward. *If I could just outrun her memories as they floated away, I could somehow put her back together. This couldn't be real. I had to put her back as she was; this wasn't real. Holly couldn't be gone.*

It was Benny; Benny did this. Benny had killed my daughter! He was going to pay. I focused on Benny; a cold smile played across his face as I ran through the mass of ghosts. Their bodies were freezing my own, causing me to lose speed and strength by the time I reached Benny.

My anger was enough to let me sail through as I hit Benny, taking us both to the ground. I went to swing, when two strong hands took hold of mine and flipped me to the ground.

I looked up, and Wilson snarled at me, his kind and cool features replaced by disgust. He looked at me as if I was some vile prisoner and he was the guard forced to watch me.

Wilson spat on me and twisted my arm, bending it behind my back. I cried out in pain and rage, "Wilson! What are you doing?! Stop him now! He killed Holly—get him!" The madness was growing within me as I wanted nothing more than to claw the eyes of Benny out, to kill him like he had killed my Holly.

"Jim, grow up!" snapped Wilson, letting go of my arm. I rolled to my feet, taking one look at Wilson, then one back at Benny. I ran forward again to destroy everything that was Benny, when Wilson swiped my legs, and I came crumpling down to the ground.

I tasted grass and dirt as I raised my head, only to have it kicked back down to the ground. "You had one job, one fucking job. Twenty years, I've had this planned. All you had to do was kill some fucking ghosts. That is all you had to do! Instead, you start some Sunday school special, save-me-fucking-Jesus prayer-fest!" Wilson yelled, pressing my head deeper into the ground.

A kick in my stomach knocked the wind from my lungs. I coughed, reaching towards Benny. He laughed while bending down over me. He said, "Told you you should have killed me, Jim." Benny smiled and then his face contorted to a snarl, and he spat on me as well.

As Benny stood, I struck out at his leg. He stepped back, and I could see the massive cast on his right foot. I felt another sharp kick into my back, and I rolled in pain as many kicks rocked me. I did my best to fight the blows off. I was never much of a fighter; I was never much of a father, either. I had failed.

My fury built inside with every kick. Every breath I took drove madness deeper into me, anguish boiling my veins into rage. Over and over, Diana kept taunting me, telling me this was entirely my fault until the blows suddenly stopped. "What's wrong, boss? Do you not think he is going to show?" Benny asked Wilson.

Wilson responded, "No—if he were coming, he would have shown himself by now. Clever little fuck will only show his shadowed ass when everything is exactly perfect. Twenty years of planning, down the drain."

I reached one broken and tired hand to Wilson, my left eye swollen shut from the kicks. He was my friend; I reached out to someone good. Wilson shook his head and walked away. I dropped my hand, succumbing to the weight of love, the weight that made me Atlas no more. I had been holding on to the love of my daughter for so long. Now she was gone, and I was just a bleeding old man on the ground. *Nothing hurts worse than when love is taken away; nothing at all, no damnation like the loss of love.*

"Kill him, Benny—we have no use for him," stated Wilson, as Benny stumbled his way over to me.

"For what it's worth, Jim, this scenario always ended with you dying," Benny said, pulling a revolver from his belt. I stared at the barrel. Its dark hole showed me oblivion as the sparks from the hammer flew back, and a bullet came screaming towards my head.

III

Part Three

Out of the night that covers me,
Black as the pit from pole to pole,
I thank whatever gods may be
For my unconquerable soul.

In the fell clutch of circumstance
I have not winced nor cried aloud.
Under the bludgeonings of chance
My head is bloody, but unbowed.

Beyond this place of wrath and tears
Looms but the Horror of the shade,
And yet the menace of the years
Finds and shall find me unafraid.

It matters not how strait the gate,
How charged with punishments the scroll,
I am the master of my fate,
I am the captain of my soul.

—William Ernest Henley, Invictus

Chapter 48

"For mourning: coffin too big for a small girl" played through my head as I came home from the funeral of my daughter. My darling Molly was now dead and gone. I tried to distract my mind from the funeral; it was to no avail. To march off to your child's funeral is no terror any parent should have to endure.

When you lose someone you truly love, one of the worst parts is the slow walk down the aisle towards the deceased in the middle of some crowded church. To be utterly alone in the breaking of your heart, but to not be able to grieve in solitude. A tradition only in place to serve as a support system; one where long-lost relatives and friends pat you on the back saying, "There, there, she looks so beautiful," and "Time heals all wounds."

I just wanted to tell them all to go to hell. I wanted to pull my hair, scream, and break every chair in that room; showing the world my rage from losing my only child. Instead, I had to share my final thoughts of my daughter's passing in a more intimate way than sex, more intrusive than a knife to the back. I couldn't be alone to view my girl; I had to share in her death with people who might as well have been walls—how could they understand? She was dead, and they wouldn't leave.

I loosened my tie and plopped down on the couch in my now-too-quiet house. It was late, and my wife had already gone to bed, or at least I think. We hadn't spoken much the entire night. Outside, I could hear the silent drops of rain playing along with the windowsills, making trails like fingers on the glass.

In my mind, I walked along the aisle again, everyone all around, as alone as the last planet in the eye of a massive black hole. I thought about how big her coffin looked; how small my Molly looked. How utterly far away she was, despite the proximity of her body and my own; she was now in a place where her Daddy could never follow.

I wiped away the wetness in my eyes, tears racing down my fingertips, damping the collar of my shirt. I stayed that way for a while longer, the night carried on, leaving me in numbness.

It was late when I finally moved from the couch, the lights out in my home, the silence louder than any engine. My steps rang out as I walked from my living room couch to my upstairs bedroom. The family photos on the stairwell appeared only as pictures in another father's life. Another different, happy family, not the broken one that now existed; I avoided them turning to focus on my bedroom.

Sleep of any kind was a morphine that had no price too steep. Upon entering my room, I was undressed and gliding to my bed in a trance before my clothes hit the floor.

I lay in the loneliness of my slumber, reaching for my wife but finding only the cold sheets of her empty spot. My thoughts plagued me; I didn't want to be alone. She was gone. I called out, "Diana, Diana, where are you, honey?"

I waited for her voice, met with only silence. I prepared to call out again when she answered, "I am here, James, in our daughter's room."

A pang of guilt collided into me; here I was lounging in a bed of sorrow while completely abandoning my wife to grieve alone. I pulled the sheets away from me and tiptoed out of bed. In the darkness of my house, I left our bedroom, closing in on the location of where her voice had been.

At the bottom of the stairs, I came to my daughter's room, the quiet bringing me to a stop. Shapes in the dark were stealing away any courage I had; going through that door meant the truth: I was going to go into her room and find it bare of joy. I found myself longing for my wife, longing for the sweet embrace of companionship. My solitary nature was giving way to the raw emotion of loneliness; fighting it, I walked into the offspring of my life's room.

The blinds were open and the storm that had sprung outside matched the storm that was beating in my chest. My wife stood motionless. Her back turned to me; she cradled my daughter, limp in her arms, nursing in the way that only a mother can convey.

My heart felt the tug of a lover—slender hands in the darkness. Only that slender hand felt wrong. It wasn't caressing my heart, only opening me up, exposing my heart to a world of senselessness and languish. I spoke, and my voice was frozen from the sublime. "Diana—what are you doing?"

The floors creaked, the ceiling wept, and my wife remained ambivalent to my very voice. My voice caught in my throat before my words could come, then Diana's head rolled backward, twisted and unnatural, her face now pointed to the ground, but her eyes eaten out as if by some beast—no, scratched out if by her hand.

I recoiled, stepping back as her laughter burst from her, calling me, mocking me, repeating words that flowed from a different time, blood gurgling in her mouth, dripping onto the floor around her like she was a lonely island in a sea of scarlet. "Your fault, James, your fault!"

I cried out, backing up until my feet hit the wall, when all the room turned into total darkness. Before me, my mutilated wife stalked towards her frightened husband; glowing green like the brightest blades of grass, smeared flat like seaweed rubbed raw across the ocean blue.

My daughter joined my wife in the chastising, edging the knife deeper into my heart, calling out, "Daddy, why didn't you help me? Why didn't you save me? Why? Didn't I matter to you?"

I answered back, tears in my eyes, their undead shuffle forcing the urine from my body in an explosion of shame, my words weak compared to the glow from their bodies. "I'm sorry… I'm sorry…

I'm sorry." Pressed for space at their slow advance, my legs scuffed the walls, and in a burst of fear I bolted forward, only to be seized from behind by thousands of arms.

The arms were glowing like the bodies of my family. I was thrashed, flocked, scratched raw, twisted in agony. The physical pain only matched by the quarrel of my accusers against me. I looked at the ceiling, fighting for air, as my lungs clasped on their last moments. A man in a gas mask peered at me, and behind him two red eyes beamed. I was being judged at my final point, my end, as the world shredded me to pieces.

Drip, drip, drip. The tendons in my hand snapped, the marrow in my legs slurped dry, my soul burning in the regret, the anguish cracking my heart, smeared by the fever of sorrow. I was too slow to acknowledge the knots in my heart, the dark spots in my face.

Chapter 49

I smelled his tobacco first before my mind came completely back. My sight was heavy; my breaths felt heavier; I couldn't get enough air. Smoke danced across my nose again, entering my lungs, and I coughed.

The cigarette was quickly dashed, and the squeaking of a wheelchair approached me at speeds I couldn't measure. A distant thought of escape from danger overrode all sources of numbness in my body. I jerked with all my strength, all the fiber of my being, and my eyes fluttered open to reveal a balding man with a thick black beard and layers of tattoos, legs lopped off at the knees; keen eyes staring into my soul as he came.

He spoke to me; I am pretty sure of that. I was muttering back something, but deaf to the words that came from my mouth. The weight of my non-responsive body loaded my frame down, almost like the stiffness of my makeshift bed.

Again I fought against my body, against the wheel-chaired man; I had to run away, I had to get away. His hands reached for my chest; I jerked like electricity ran in my veins. My anger was growing, something deep from within coming back, something that I had forgotten. Perhaps hidden away by some great kind of pain; I silently cursed my body for being weak. *No,* I yelled at my body for being weak, *come on, fight! Push through this, old man!*

An old man? Yes. I am an old man and my name... my name is... My name is James. That's right, my name is James. Why am I here in this bed? Why is he attacking me?

These questions forced my blood to rise, starting in my chest as I tried to evade my captor. Head ringing, ringing, I could hear a whistle from somewhere far off inside and outside my head. An elephant walking on egg shells stumbled through my skull, and I felt cracks of red hot searing pain at the memory.

I had been shot; I had been shot in the head by a man named Benny. Benny, the man that I had let go, Benny, the man that had killed my daughter; my little girl named Holly. Holly! Roaring and screeching everything that was hiding inside of me, it felt like I was giving birth to the devil himself, my voice scratching its way out of a throat far too parched.

Fatigue set in, my voice inside getting lower; the image of my daughter bursting in sparks of fire in the North Carolina summer, playing through my head. *She was lost*; the bullet, the blood, the dream, everything coming back at once.

I was growing silent, I was growing weak. My rage, however, was not. I reached deep within the monster growing in me, felt the fiery heat of its hate and called out. "Holly!" I screamed, causing Rob to pull away in fear. I screamed until my voice clogged and I began to choke on my tongue.

"Easy, Jim, it's okay. Settle down, stop screaming," Rob said, bringing a bottle towards my face with one hand and another hand lifting my head towards the bottle.

When the dampness of the bottle hit my lips, I greedily sucked the liquid down like a toddler.

"That's better, Jim. Take it easy; not so much." Rob cooed like a parent. I ignored his warnings and continued to drink until I felt dizzy, my head swimming in an ocean.

When the bottle popped dry, I settled back, my head feeling like a rock and my throat crying out from the lack of water. Sitting back, I closed my eyes and was assaulted by the visual of the stadium. *Yes, it had been at a stadium, where we had gone to rescue Kim. My daughter and I joined by friends...*

"You can get some more in a little while; I don't want you to throw up on yourself," Rob grumbled, taking the bottle away and pulling out a wet washcloth, pressing it against my aching head.

I looked past Rob, trying to see beyond him, and saw only a little glow of a lantern. Meeting Rob's voice instead of his gaze, I spoke. "Thanks."

My voice sounding foreign to me. Gone now was the father. I was no longer a father, and I had failed twice; I had failed both my wife and daughter. I had failed myself; I had let my loved ones around me die. A dream of terrible agony played through my head, and weeping, I called out before falling into a deep sleep. "Yes, yes, it is my fault."

And that is how the first couple of days after my awakening went. I stayed in a constant state of disturbed and restless sleep. Rob would always be nearby, with bandages or water of some kind.

Hours would pass, and I would develop a fever, I would look around the room often during those times. Doing anything and everything to keep my mind away from the horror, to be given some measure of peace in all the hell. My room was molded and degraded to yellowish walls, caked by the years of the apocalypse gray that matched the dullness of life. No windows were in the room, only a small nightstand, littered with many bottles and used bandages. A pang of anger shot through me when I saw the bandages; *why did Rob have to save me? At least I could have died. I could have stayed there and kept some level of dignity in death.*

I could have been with Holly; I could have been with my girl. "That will never happen, Jim; guys like you shouldn't be around children," slithered Diana, standing at the foot of my bed. She looked like the day I'd married her.

All bright blonde hair and long legs, centered by two beautiful blue eyes; she had decided to stay with me every waking moment since I had regained consciousness. Always taunting me and smiling, always saying how it was my fault. I hadn't been able to sleep; she was always there. A shadow that danced without movement; a night that never left the day. She was always there.

I ignored her, even though all my thoughts told me she was right. A few more days passed, or maybe it was only hours. It could have only been minutes; I wasn't sure when one nightmare ended, and another began. If I did sleep, I would be back at that stadium, Benny laughing at me as he killed Holly. I gave chase, only to fall every single time. Every so often, Rob would come back in the room and try and feed me, disturbing my dreams.

I fought him with everything I had, tooth and nail. I even managed to get a few fingers one time. After that, Rob started throwing water bottles at me. Said something about feeding myself; Diana would whisper that the bottles were for people that deserved them. Always wanting to be a good husband, I would consume the beverages in spite of her.

One day, I heard Rob cursing from the other room. I was sitting up in bed. Throughout my days, I tried pulling myself up further and further until I was able to see out into the other room. Rob was working on what could only be described as an extensive collection of batteries and a large metal box, the box being formed in the shape of a mad scientist's wet dream.

The cells were connected to the box, while Rob was inserting wires with one hand; the other cranking some hand device next to the station. "See what he's doing there, Jim? He is doing something. You can't trust him, though; you can't trust anyone in this world, Jim." Diana spoke into my ear, cupping her mouth and whispering to me.

"Will you be quiet already?" I spoke to her, not turning my attention from Rob.

Rob placed his hands down and turned, looking at me. "Are you trying to talk like a normal human being, or are you just wanting to kill me again?"

I looked at Rob. Someone had given him a fat upper lip, and he looked like he had taken a few shots to both his eyes. His glasses were being held together by hope or prayers and he had a twitch to him that wasn't normal.

I ignored his question and continued watching, keeping my distance. Rob realized that any form of communication with me wasn't happening; I only longed to snap his neck. All I wanted was to be away from him and Diana, then just die somewhere in a dark hole. I just wanted to be alone.

Every so often, Diana would cut into Rob and my pissing contest. She would pester me until I finally answered. It was always some comment about my failures in life. I gritted through them, determined to find a way out of the bed and be free of humanity once and for all. I maintained my watch, waiting for Rob to slip up, waiting for Diana to go away and that was when I would make my move.

"Are we just going to keep staring at each other? It's getting late; food probably wouldn't be a bad idea..." Rob asked from the other room.

At the mention of food, my stomach started growling, and I couldn't remember the last time I had eaten.

Rob, looking at me, spoke again, this time softer, "Tell you what, how about you try talking a little bit, and I will see if I can't get you something else other than just blended food?"

"You don't need it; tell him he can keep his nasty food," hissed Diana, next to my ear.

Without moving my head to speak to her, I acknowledged Rob finally. "Food, please."

Rob sighed heavily and turned from his station, rolling his chair to a side of the room I couldn't see. "That's a start, I suppose." I heard the popping and sizzling of something that smelled possibly like bacon, as Rob disappeared. I looked at Diana standing there impatiently, stabbing her feet; her face only showing hate and disgust for Rob.

"He is just going to kill you the first chance he gets. He is just going to kill you, Jim. And you're going to fail again," Diana snarled, her voice soothing despite the message, but no love was between us. Not a love that I could recognize, not one that I wanted. Nothing that I felt I could trust so quickly, though, she was starting to make a point, I think.

"What will you do, keep lying there in bed like a bum for the rest of your days, or are you going to be a man and kill someone?" Diana snorted, while still tapping her foot, the hardwood floor echoing her impatient mood.

I looked at her and my desire was to only get out from this bed and bring down every ounce of my hatred upon her. Instead, I just talked. "I think I will lie here until the time is right. Rest assured, when the time comes, you will be the first on my list of those who will go."

"You were always the patient one," she snapped.

Rob rolled into the room, a plate full of bacon and a bottle of water. His face looked long and full of worry as he looked about the chamber. "Jim, who are you talking to?"

I looked at him, ignoring his question as Diana smiled. I snatched the plate of food greedily and Diana spoke. "Good, Jim. Eat up. You will need your strength."

Chapter 50

I was back in the house, my old house, standing at my door, its frame simple and inviting in its textures, down to its milky white coat. I was standing at the door because of a knock. A tapping was taking place, slowly, every so methodically. *Tap, tap.* My heart kept beating, and the taps kept coming. And the door continued to stay closed. I couldn't move; the door stayed closed, my heart beat, the *Tap, tap* played. I finally threw open the door, and a man with red eyes and shadows dancing all around him smiled at me. I heard the *Tap, tap.*

That was the dream I had most nights when I could sleep. When I awoke; I would be covered in sweat, and Diana would be floating at the end of my bed. Rob would be in the next room, working on his batteries. After ten days of this cycle, I started talking to Rob. I had found out that I had been drifting in and out of consciousness for close to three months. During that time, the city had become a warzone of ghosts, an endless horde. Millions, was Rob's estimate. I didn't believe him at first, until I took my first shaky and unrefined steps into the cold North Carolina air; the city was alive with the dead in countless droves. I wasn't sure how far outside the city we were, but I could see their lights far off in the distance, as we set perched atop our lofty thrones.

I asked how we were remaining safe; Rob described his metal battery contraption was hooked to a power fixture throughout the house.

"You mentioned to me once that you found that electronics shocked you when they were nearby, so I thought about that and how the ghosts can move so quickly from place to place. Human beings are the animal equivalent of a lightning rod of energy, if you didn't know. Not a lot, but just enough. All that power wouldn't go away just because we became a different state, or being. I figured that the electricity wasn't tracking down ghosts, it was scaring them, somehow interrupting their internal making; I took some batteries and supercharged this place," Rob told me.

After that, I began working out while Rob slept. Rob finally needed to sleep, and I resisted the urge to kill him. The city below us soon emptied of all ghosts, and it was just the three of us for a time. Diana would visit any chance she got, mocking me, pestering me in the solace of my prison.

In the long nights, I couldn't sleep. I searched the room, finding a cracked mirror. Looking at my face and body made me drop the mirror, screaming out. It wasn't the weight that I had lost, not the sunken depths of my eyes, nor the length of my wild and untamed hair. My terror was from the stranger that looked back at me. I was dead and gone. Gone were Jim and James, replaced was this new person.

I kicked the mirror off into the distance, shattering the glass all over the floor, just as Rob wheeled into the room. "Well, something is wrong, huh?" Rob scoffed.

I looked at the wheelchair man, a strong desire to hurt him. "Are you ready to do something about it, Jim?" He asked me as I walked from the room. After the incident with the mirror, I spent many moments exploring the confines of my self-imposed isolation.

To drive out Diana and Rob, I began to do stretches and sit-ups on my bed every hour, on the hour. My strength was aching to come back, aching to be unleashed. I itched for a chance for more. A voice, somewhere deep in me, kept repeating, "Wait."

Two more weeks passed in the routine of me working out, me dodging Rob, and Diana continuing to harness my madness. *Madness gives way, breathing hate once, and hate flowed so much in me. I am filled with hate, the hate for myself, the hate for others, just hate.* My veins were heavy with hate, my heart pumping more venom and malice as the days went on. Using my pain, I became focused by that. I sent my condolences to the part of my life that ever had anything beyond anger, and I embraced it.

That gave me a way to fight the madness; I thought of that as I moved from the bed in which I had spent so much time living for the last few weeks, and I approached Rob. He looked up at me as he continued to work on the "ghost repellent," as he was calling it now. "Think you're ready to start doing something now?" he asked, sleep evident in his eyes.

I looked at Rob, his face edged into taut lines, his frame now loose and flabby. He had also lost a considerable amount of weight over the last few weeks. Only, I think his was worse than mine; he was suffering and looked sick. I nodded my head, and he set his tools down and motioned for me to follow him.

He stopped at the door and turned back around, stretching in his chair. "We are at the home of my parents, where I grew up." I looked at Rob, perplexed. He seemed to be around my age, the lines and graying in his hair made me think older. Guess I was potentially way off by decades.

He continued as we went down the conjoining hallway and outside a door to a small garden. The garden was spouting clumps of dirt and overgrown vegetation. "What am I supposed to see here, Rob?"

"Nothing. This was my mother's shitty garden back in the day. Follow me," Rob said, gliding his wheelchair quickly over the thickness of the grass. I was impressed by the strength of his arms, in spite of how weak he appeared.

I remained quiet as we came to a graveled road, where Rob struggled over the rocks. I offered to help; my hand came back red and sore. When we had traveled down the road for a short distance, a woman came walking up the street carrying a basket.

She had dark hair, starting to be replaced by the traces of old age, but that was still a refined attractiveness, which only women managed to pull off. When I searched her eyes, I knew exactly who she was. It was Kim, her hair in a ponytail, her clothes washed and clean, a long look on her face with a trace of remorse, which turned into delight when she saw me.

"Kill her, James." Diana spoke from behind Kim. It started slow, the fever that ran through my body, driving the loathing from my depths.

I sprang forward like a lion, pouncing on Kim, my hand extended, cupping her neck, and my weight carrying her to the ground on the chunks of rock below. Admittedly, my weight had considerably lessened in the last few months. I was energized though; I was reinforced by my rage.

I felt her hands slap at my right arm, and I pressed my left forearm on her throat, leaning forward and bringing all my weight down upon her. Her eyes began to turn red, and she screamed for her life as I applied more pressure to her windpipe. While my attention lay with Kim, I didn't hear the crack of Rob's stick until I felt it break across my back under the blow of his powerful upper arms. My grip was instantaneously loosened, and Kim rolled out from under me, gasping for breath as I struggled forward crawling my way towards her.

Through thick breaths of air, Rob spoke. "God damn it, Jim, don't make me hit you again. Just stop, she is the one that saved you."

I looked at Kim; she held her neck while still on the ground, her brown eyes tearing up. Rob's blow had brought me to my knees; I stood on shaky legs and marched towards Kim. My force of will carried me rather than any machine. She had helped the people who had killed my daughter. In my mind, she was the very image of death, the death that needed to be dealt.

"Kill her, Jim, kill her now," Diana hissed into my ears. I ignored her pleas, my focus entirely on killing Kim. Kim continued to hold her neck and attempted neither to run nor to fight back.

This time, I heard Rob roll his wheelchair across the gravel road, I turned in time to see the smack of Rob's piece of wood busting into my legs. My left leg gave out, and I fell hard onto the gravel.

I felt a fresh bruise forming already from where I had been hit; my determination not deterred in the slightest as I crawled my way towards Kim. "Jim, stop!" shouted Rob over my head as he brought down the full weight of his wood down on the base of my upper back. I smacked hard on the ground, busting my chin on the rocks. I reached out with my right hand and pulled my body as Rob hit me once more with his weapon—this time, on my shoulder.

Kim finally recovered enough. "Jesus, stop hitting him already before you break his arm!" Kim shouted at Rob.

"'Oh, thank you, Rob, for saving my life!' You act like I am the asshole," Rob spat, pointing the wood at me beneath him.

Kim coughed before speaking as I still slowly crawled towards her feet. "He is justified in his actions..." she gasped, stepping back from me.

I heard Rob sigh again before hitting me over the back with his whipping block. Then the sky went black, my ears rang, and I drifted into a darkness. I was only hearing that *Tap, tap* again.

Everything felt like fire when I awoke; I opened my eyes, and I was back in the bed, only this time, I was strapped down with old leather belts. I tried moving my arms and legs. The restraints were too great, and the blows from Rob were bruised already. I could feel a massive knot on the back of my head as I shifted my weight from side to side in an attempt to break free from my bonds.

"Hi, Jim," Kim drawled out, her accent clearly a Florida one (it was unbelievable the things you notice after being hit in the head). I hadn't noticed that at the dam. Then again, I hadn't noticed that Wilson would kill my daughter either. She reached towards my head, a light in her right hand. I snapped at her fingers with my mouth as she attempted to touch my forehead.

Kim recoiled her hand in fear as I snarled at her like a beast. I could smell Rob's cigarette before he spoke. "He is fine, girly, no need to check him for anything other than maybe a bad case of rabies."

Kim rolled her eyes and pressed her fingers above my eyelids, shining the light on them. "All this effort in saving him would have been for nothing if he had a damn concussion, you moron," Kim said.

Rob choked on his smoke. "Your choice; good luck." He snorted.

When Kim finished, I took another failed attempt at trying to nip her arm. She looked down at me; I avoided her eye contact. "That is your problem, Jim; you never had a killer instinct," Diana pointed out from behind Kim. She looked almost bored standing there.

"Wasn't that why you married me, you bitch?" I shouted.

"What?" asked Kim, looking towards Rob.

Rob shook his head as if to say it beat him. "He's been raving for months, spouting off random words and sentences," Rob said, keeping his hands on the stick in his lap.

Kim turned back to me, concern on her face. I exploded in anger; I was not going to have her pity. She was a killer, and that was that. "Why don't you untie me, and I will show you both a real time with my piece of wood up the back sides of your heads!" I snarled.

Rob coughed and spoke to Kim, "See what I've been dealing with? He won't let me touch him to change his bandages, plus there is that thing he keeps doing..."

I caught Kim shooting a glance at Rob. He stopped before he could elaborate further on the subject. Kim moved up to my head. "Settle down, killer; I need to change your bandages before you get infected and die."

"Maybe I want to die," I said. My words left my mouth, and Kim looked at me and swung the backside of her right hand into my jaw. My head snapped back, and she slapped me again, in a flurry of blows, my head was hit so many times until my face stung, raw from the abuse.

Kim bent down so that we were both at eye level before talking to me, "Don't you ever say that, don't you ever say something like that. If you want to die, die then, but it won't be because of me." She stepped away, turning her back to me. In the corner of the room, Diana smiled, a sharp edge pointing out with a blood lust.

"Jesus, and there you were harping on me. You just beat the fire out of the guy…" Rob said while puffing hard on what was left of his smoke.

Without facing me, Kim spoke. "My husband, he was always an asshole—but he was funny, you know? The kind of guy that a young and impressionable woman would eat up, all nice abs and few brain cells. The only thing he ever did right was knocking me up with Joey when I was twenty at the time, just starting nursing school." She paused, turning back to me, I expected to see tears, but instead I saw only resolve. "When all of this broke out, Joey was still just a toddler, but we made it somehow, managed to stay alive. Between my husband and the ghosts, I could never tell which one was worse."

Kim paused again to pull down her shirt; on her right shoulder was a massive and jagged scar. "My husband was a real asshole, the worst of them all. The kind that beats his kids, his wife, and still drinks. One day, my husband went out scavenging for food. Joey went with him—I don't know the exact details of what happened—my husband came back, reeking like a damn brewer. I asked him where our son was.

In response, he beat me—he beat me until I lay on the ground, spitting blood from in between my broken teeth. At some point, I blacked out, and when I finally came to, he was passed out on our bed, snoring the drunken snore of a pleased man."

Kim paused and walked closer to the foot of the bed. "I set him on fire in his bed. I would do it a hundred times over if it would give me a chance again to my son. I would do anything if it brought my son back. That's why when Wilson came along, he was my best chance at being able to hold my son again in the flesh. I think that is a sentiment that you can understand, Jim."

I wiggled my head and shoulders to the limit that my restraints would allow. I needed to be eye level with her. Gathering my thoughts, I spoke. "This is a sentiment I am sure you can understand. You played a part in the killing of my daughter, and I will assume it was you who healed my wounds. Regardless of actions taken afterward, when I have had my revenge on Wilson, I will kill you next."

Kim met my gaze and didn't flinch*; she is a strong woman, a lot stronger than most men, even.* "Wilson is just like any other man; he has control of my boy. What he did to you was wrong; you deserve your vengeance for what happened," Kim stated while stepping to the bed and untying the restraints.

I quickly got up from the bed, stretching my bruised and battered body. Everything intact for the most part, intact in the physical sense, at least.

"Oh, geez. Are you going to try and kill us again?" Rob asked grabbing the block of wood across his lap. The top part was dented in, like it had been smacked heavily across something or someone (that someone being my body).

I turned back to Kim. "It's not me that he did anything to, it was to my daughter that all of this is happening. For that, he will have to pay," I snarled.

Kim nodded. "Where do we start?

Chapter 51

Over the next several days, I was able to learn what had transpired from the moment I was shot. Rob had been ambushed and thrown from the van. Afterward, he had crawled, rolled and dragged his way to my body, which apparently was bleeding out, and I was presumed dead until I started talking. Rob, realizing the only way to get my body out of the stadium, strapped my bleeding form onto his lap. He said it took him about an hour to wheel his way out with me on top.

Then Rob told me the rest of his story…

Chapter 52

"Yeah, you guys know what to do—James out," spoke James' voice through the radio; gripping the tiny piece of metal, I wanted nothing more than to toss it out the window and run for the hills in the exact opposite direction of that.

I sighed, knowing that would be more of a chore than what we were doing, now being legless and all. I had an itch for a cigarette; this being on the front-line shit was stressing me out. Once more, General Wilson had been doing nothing but barking orders and repeating every last detail of the plan. I knew we all wanted to get Kim back bad, but he was driving me nuts with the level of meticulous detail. "When we get around to the back, remember to keep the van ready to go."

I looked at him and gestured to my legs and cocked an eyebrow as if to say "How?"

He eyed me and gave his traditional "I am Wilson" answer: "Hiding behind the excuse of your legs is something you never fail to throw out there, isn't it?"

"You're right, Wilson. In fact, I feel my lower extremities coming back. Wait, wait, they're moving! Lord, it's a miracle. Wilson, you must be the son of God reborn in the body of a black man." I said, clasping my hands together and praying at the roof of the van.

Wilson scowled at me. "Don't let me down, Robert." He turned back to the road as we pulled behind the stadium at the southern exit. I rolled my eyes as he put the van into park. He was out of the car and digging in the trunk for something before the engine completely stopped. *Impatient as always,* I thought.

Once he found a pair of bolt cutters, he went to the fence and began working on the old chain separating the doorways with a chain link fence. Wilson snapped the blots and stepped inside.

"Oh, thank God," I said, pulling a cigarette from my shirt pocket. I flicked open my golden lighter, letting the flash from its painted metallic surface soothe me. It was a terrible thing not to be able to help the gang. The most I could do now was stay in the car and keep it running like I was some joke.

Here I was, finally, for one of the first times in my life, trying to help someone else, and I couldn't. I had spent most of my days blaming my problems on other people. My old man had been right, I never did anything hard. I dropped out of high school just to make drugs with my friends. Yet, here I was sitting in a van with a pellet gun loaded with iron pellets. "Yup."

I looked down at the place my legs used to be, remembering the fire that had consumed them when our little experiment had gone upside down. I was so clever, so stupid back then, too high to get out of the way of flames.

Always too high to care about anyone other than myself; even when the ghosts came, I was stuck in my father's basement smoking with my friends, doing tattoos and drinking wine like I was the next great Salvador Dali.

My father had teased me with how lazy and insignificant I was, always lecturing me like Wilson does now. Always saying I couldn't be relied upon for anything. That is where everyone was wrong; I had a secret none of them understood. I finished my cigarette and flicked it out of the window of the van as I looked at the sky. The clouds were getting darker. I hoped that wasn't a sign for what was about to become.

I was a clever little half-man; I spent a great deal of time reading. And to top it off, I could do a lot more for myself than any of them realized. I fumbled for my shotgun in the seat next to me. Feeling its smooth metal barrel comforted me. I hated being out in the open like this, but I wasn't going to let down my friends either. The whole thing made me tense, as I thought about the rampart being blocked. Those cars, I swear they were ones Christina and I had fixed a few years back. I didn't make it a habit to remember every detail, but with so few cars on the road anymore… I shook my head. *It was a coincidence and nothing more. I needed to be there for the group.*

I was going to be the best, by God, the best lookout there ever was. I pointed the shotgun out of the driver's window and I waited for Wilson to come back through the fence with the rest of the Scooby gang.

Waiting there, my itch for another cigarette started again. It was a horrible addiction and I couldn't even remember when I'd picked it up. It was better to be in a tar graveyard than any other drug graveyard. I still remembered the withdrawals… thinking about them caused my skin to flake, moving almost like I was a snake trying to get off a nasty last layer of skin. I missed them though; I missed the release, the places my mind would go.

An explosion somewhere off in the distance interrupted my train of thought. "Things are really heating up from the sound of it, hope those guys are all right…" I mumbled, looking around the back of the stadium. I was thankful Jim had let us use the protection of the van. It may have looked hideous and like a clusterfuck, but that guy knew how to put something together.

He had to be a doctor or a former military type, with the way he thought things through, you would imagine. Surprisingly good guy, from what I could tell. It was nice he had his daughter. I envied him for that in a way. I looked at my watch; it was a quarter after twelve, and according to the plan, the whole rescue was only going to take twenty minutes. It all felt weird to me, the delay with the cars having been moved there in the last few hours. Joey and Holly hadn't reported any such thing. I was sweating and running through my thoughts like a squirrel outrunning a bird in the trees. Zigzagging and bouncing to every limb I could get.

What's worse was that someone had to have moved them there, knowing the front assault group was going that way. It wasn't that I was worried someone had put up a blockade for us. It was that someone was trying only to make it seem like they were blocking us out. Anyone with a brain should have known that was an easy fix, and once more, they should have had someone watching the back of the stadium. I felt a cold chill suddenly, like I wasn't so safe inside this iron tomb.

I repositioned the shotgun, becoming stiff with waiting, sweat trickling down my head. God, how I wanted another cigarette. Just one more, one more to take that itch away. I only had a few left, and I would have to make more paper soon.

At the rate the day was going, though, I was going to need a carton. I blinked away sweat from my eyes, wishing I had left the south. The constant humidity, even on a cloudy day, was unreal.

A shot rang out and interrupted my thoughts. It was a single shot from something a lot louder and bigger than the shotguns everyone had gone in with, powerful and full of viciousness. That was weird to me; I had been around weapons my whole life, so I knew what they sounded like—it wasn't a shotgun. I tried shaking the feeling that something was wrong as I waited for my friends to return. Last I checked, ghosts didn't use guns either. That sound belonged to something much nastier.

Wiping away my sweat again, I saw a ghost appear out of the darkness of the stadium. I flinched from his sight, almost dropping the gun out of the window of van.

I sucked in a breath and prepared to fire at the ghost as it came forward towards the car. I squinted, looking through the iron sights on the shotgun, when two more ghosts followed behind the first. More and more started filing out until Wilson came strolling calmly through the darkness.

His gun was pointed up, and an expression of pure malice was on his face. Next to him was a man I had never seen before. He walked with a limp and looked every bit how I would imagine a mountain man to look. All long-legged and bearded, and to top it off, even from this distance, I could see the red in his eyes. He looked like someone who had experience of addiction. His teeth gnarled, and his skin sucked in, leaking out puss from scars on his cheekbones.

Behind him were Kim and her boy Joey, hustling along to keep up with the stranger and Wilson; I couldn't see James or Holly. That seemed odd to me, and very wrong. Nor was Christina in sight. The plan had been for her to peel off once she fired her load. Hopefully, she had left. "Hope in one hand, dick in the other, see which one comes first," I mumbled in the stale air of the van.

Wilson spotted me and headed over to the rusting van, flanked by the ghost and the stranger.

I had seen enough horror movies in my life to know how this one turned out. Searching around the car with one hand, I reached for whatever I could find; my hands tightened over an iron bar lying on the seat. I quickly stuffed the iron down my pants, trying to hide the movement.

Wilson and the stranger approached the door. "What took you so long Wilson? Did you get lost—" I started to say, as the driver door was ripped open and I fell before finishing my sentence. I walloped my chin on the hard ground, tasting blood from somewhere in my mouth. "Wilson, what the fuck was that for?" I said, spitting the blood out of my lips.

"Should I kill him too, boss?" asked the stranger to Wilson, as they took the shotgun out of my hands and started emptying the vehicle.

I pulled myself to the sitting position and felt helpless as the stranger looted the vehicle of my friend. I was panicking and starting to freak out. *Why the hell is this happening?* I had never been one for shutting my mouth, as my father put it, especially when I was scared. I said, "Wilson, besides the big 'fuck you' for throwing me out, where is Jim?"

Wilson eyed me and handed the shotgun to the newcomer as he laughed at the mentioned of Jim.

I looked at Kim, and she avoided my gaze, looking to the sky. "Oh God, what did you do?" I screamed at the group. Wilson stepped in front of me, kneeling down. "Rob, I am going to need you to stop yelling now. I never much liked you; you had a sound mind though when you were sober." Wilson said, looking at the sky. "He never showed, you know. Twenty damn years of planning to be thrown away in a single afternoon."

I was perplexed, utterly dumbfounded and when I spoke, my voice shook. "Who—who didn't show?"

Wilson turned his attention back to me and appeared crestfallen and a lot older than his normal calm and collected state. "Just the person who was going to make this all better."

I had no idea what the hell he was talking about; I never cared too much for Wilson as a whole, but I always thought he was a decent enough man as they could come in this senseless place, now I wasn't sure who or what I was talking to.

Wilson stood up. "I won't kill you Rob, and I've done enough of that for one lifetime. You did a good job at being an idiotic and reasonable person all these years. It takes a great and controlled mind to resist the blade like you did, but I needed your help to stay alive. I have no more use for you now, Rob. Good luck."

Wilson then walked away. He entered the van with the stranger and Kim. Kim avoided my gaze, still getting into the car. Before Wilson could peel off, I shouted, "Hey, at least give me my chair! I won't make it long either way. At least in a chair, I can die with some dignity."

Wilson and the new guy talked it over. I couldn't hear the conversation, but I saw Wilson's nod. The passenger door opened, and the new guy came around to the back. He popped the trunk and pulled out my robust and faithful wheelchair. He looked at me and laughed, throwing my chair to the ground. "You should have just let me kill him. What's one more corpse in this stadium?"

He had a thick country accent. He was a local, that was for sure. Most likely from the western side of the state, I thought. Once he was back in the van, Wilson let the brake off and pulled away.

I flipped them the finger in a vain attempt at some kind of retribution. I dragged myself to my chair, pulling myself into it. The work had caused me to lose my breath. As I waited to gather my air and my thoughts, I looked off towards the stadium. *Need to quit smoking; that was way too much effort.*

I could see crows overhead. I thought of Wilson and that other guy's words. One thing about when I was growing up—I was a stubborn jackass, as my father put it. But I never listened to anyone my entire life. Now wasn't the time to change that, I thought.

I let the brake loose off my chair and started rolling myself to the fence line. I pulled the metal wire, twisting the frame until I could move through. When I crossed the threshold under the stadium, I felt it: I felt death. I looked back at the road and thought of them rolling away. Nothing awaited me beyond this point.

I had to see, though; I had to see what had happened to my friends. My old man had called me a coward; I had called myself a coward. In the short time I'd known Holly and Jim, I had gained friends. James was not a coward. That's what I kept saying to myself as I rolled through the darkness. It was the only way I could keep going forward. If I just kept thinking about my friends then I would do something about it.

I came to the clearing that leads to the exit off to the football field. I hesitated when I came to the opening; off on the far side of the stadium were remains of the Beast and most of the concrete overhangs blown to rubble.

My eyes searched until I saw a body lying towards the end zone. "Christ," I said. *Well, that's that; whoever that was is probably dead. Time to go, Rob; just roll your ass that way—see if you can't get a ride and haul up somewhere; just turn around. But I'm not going to, though, I have to know, and something just doesn't feel right.* I went forward in my wheelchair, and the overgrown grass immediately rooted me in place.

Straining with effort and a lot of heavy breathing, I was able to get over the clumps and make it to the body. When I got within ten feet, I could tell it was Jim. Every fiber of my being wanted to leave. Still, I pressed on. I had to believe Jim and Holly would have done the same thing for me.

I thought of young Holly without her father; she was going to be a wreck; maybe I could find some kind of clue on Jim to indicate where she might have gone. I gritted my teeth and kept rolling towards my friend.

When I finally got to Jim, the constant strain of pulling and pushing the wheels on my chair had left me drenched in sweat. I looked back at the exit and felt sick to my stomach with the effort it would take to get back out. *Going back would take most of the day,* I thought.

I did my best to wipe the sweat from my eyes as I looked at Jim. His body looked like road kill with numerous cuts and some whole sections of missing flesh. As my eyes traced the way to the top, I could see the blood drenched all over him; resembling an animal at a butcher shop, not a father.

And the big kicker: a huge gash and circular bullet hole at the front of his skull. "Oh fuck me, Jim—someone shot you…" I mumbled, feeling sick to my stomach. I looked at Jim's head and couldn't see an exit wound as he lay on his side. Judging by the size of the entry wound, it confirmed it was a revolver that had shot Jim. As to what kind, I didn't know. "Explains that sound." I continued to look over Jim, and I saw no obvious signs of Holly having come to the area.

What was I expecting to find, a handwritten note? She is a ghost, and while she is pretty impressive, she had her own law of the land now. I continued to chastise myself as I searched for anything, something I could help find her with, help save her if need be.

When it became apparent I wasn't going to find anything that would help, I stopped. I turned my wheelchair around and pointed towards the exit from which I first came.

I took one last look at Jim; I was sorry for what had happened to my friend. I truly was—he was a good man and didn't deserve just to lie dead in the middle of a field.

"Goodbye, Jim. Don't worry, I will find Holly—I promise." I meant it, which didn't feel hollow in the slightest. I raked my fingers through my hair, wondering if I should say more. I decided that was enough and started my labor back to the street.

"Holly," croaked Jim.

I froze. *It's impossible to survive a head shot, right?* I turned back around, and blood had spilled from Jim's mouth. But I could see the movement from his jaw line. *The son of a bitch was trying to speak!*

A memory I had from when I was a child came to mind, back when my father and I would go hunting. He told me how once when he was hunting, he knew a guy that had been shot in the head. He said that sometimes the bullet doesn't break the skull, and sometimes the shot breaks. Was this the same thing? The same as the person in my father's story?

I looked at Jim, lifeless, yet holding on somehow. It was unbelievable that he had survived. It frightened me. *I am a coward, what could I possibly do for him? I couldn't take him anywhere.* I had serious doubts I could make it back to the dam even if I had a car. The longer I stayed staring at the man, the harder it became.

Jim had taken a gunshot to the head, most likely by that guy who was with Wilson. After thinking further, I realized the worst part of seeing Jim there. *Holly wouldn't have ever left her father lying there; she wouldn't have left him to die alone.*

I looked at the pathetic man on the ground and knew I was never going to be able to leave him. "Why did I have to pick today of all days, to start growing a conscience..."

Looking at my belongings and Jim, I had no ropes of any kind. Besides, I might only end up making his head injury worse. I looked at his weight and my position on the wheelchair. This wasn't going to be easy; I would probably kill us both along the way.

"Thanks Jim, for making my life shitty at the end."

Chapter 53

I sat quiet, hearing Rob's story, once outside the stadium, Rob moved me to the closest safe place he could find. The remains of a hot dog shop, where he tried to dig the remainder of the broken bullet out from my skull. The bullet had broken on my bone—one in a million, as Rob had put it.

Not knowing much about stitching beyond that of an average person, Rob assumed ghosts were either going to get us or I was going to die of fever. The two of us stayed in the hot dog store for a day, until Joey appeared at the stadium. The boy was mute as ever, floating, looking at the stadium, according to Rob; not long after that, Kim showed up, looking for the kid.

Only Joey had already moved on by that point. Rob had managed to roll his way behind Kim stealthily enough and had ambushed her, though I didn't believe for a second he had attacked her when he told me. I had caught him more than once checking her out.

Either way, Kim had spilled the beans after little to no questions from Rob. Apparently, Wilson had, from the very beginning, taken control of Joey; Kim never had a choice as long as she wanted to be with her son. After that, Kim and Rob loaded me into a car (Kim had managed to steal back the van when she left Wilson).

It was Kim who had saved my life, cutting chunks of dead flesh from the wound. She did this as Rob drove, using the barrel of the rifle for gas and breaks. A feat he was actually proud of, from what I could tell.

Not knowing where to take me, and the city swarming with ghosts,

Rob drove us to the western half of the state in the mountains. A place near the Pisgah National Forest.

It was here we had spent the last three months helping me recover. Kim and Rob were somehow able to find me antibiotics, though Kim assured me by all accounts I should have died. They both described the amount of screaming I had done, the sleep they lost from the terror I was creating in them. I said nothing, and just watched Diana dance in the background.

When their story was finished, I went back inside, the sun setting low on the mountainside where Rob had grown up. Fall was giving away to winter, and the reds, yellows, and greens glowed in the sun, looking oily like one giant mural from the marvelous play of some god. I thought about how Holly would have liked looking out at this, and a pain shot in my chest like someone had taken a knife, all edgy and dull, sticking the blade six inches all the way through my soul. It was just too hard to breathe; too hard to think of her.

I went inside, and faced the mirror in the bathroom. Up here in the mountains, we were isolated alone from the rest of the world. *This must have been how the gods of Mount Olympus had felt,* I thought. A bunch of assholes hiding out from the evil world they had created below.

I took my bandage off and moved my increasingly long locks of hair aside. The wound was mostly superficial; still, the skin had been sewed shut and didn't smell or look too festered. My flesh was dug in around the shot, and as I pulled back my hair, I could see a trail of stitches leading up my head. The shot had gone through the top part of my face; it did not come out, though. All the blood must have fooled Benny, I speculated.

Tension grew in my chest at the mention of his name, my anger harboring in my heart like a deadly shark waiting for prey. Diana appeared in the mirror as I readjusted it, causing me to jump. "Looking good there, husband," she said, cackling behind me.

I turned walking past her, heading outside to be with the others. I wasn't in the mood to be haunted right now; she never went away, Diana. "Looking better than you, sweetheart," I said while closing the door behind me. Whatever game Diana was trying to play (presumably to ensnare my body somehow and ride it like a bad rental car), she was going to have to wait a while longer.

Kim and Rob sat near each other at the edge of the home of Rob's parents. Neither turned to look at me; that was okay. I stuffed my hand into the hoodie pocket. A thick gust was blowing, and I knew the cold was only going to get colder from here on out.

The next day, I dressed in an old pair of pants; holes in one of the knees, and a faded red flannel. The clothes felt comfortable enough; Rob's father had been a heavier set man, plus my weight loss had caused them to be a little baggy, which I was sure Holly would have found funny. It gave me plenty of room to breathe.

I stopped staring at the bed where I had been sleeping the last three months. Looking at the heap of dirty blankets, I could see the spider webs of my life, none of it making any sense, and I suddenly felt more human than I had in a while. None of my life in the last twenty years had made sense. I was like a fly caught in a web trying to understand what horrors awaited me, while every effort to escape made things worse. *If Kim is a long-legged spider, Wilson a grudging beast, then I will be the avenging devil. I will be the one who burned the webs to the ground,* I thought.

I left the bedroom, intending to never return to its confines. I found Kim and Rob rubbing the sleep from their eyes, gathered around a map of the local area. "Good morning. Did you sleep for a change, Jim?" Rob asked, lighting his standard issue daily smoke.

I looked at him carefully and didn't answer. Rob smirked, "Well, that is a better response than what I thought I would get." He coughed, covering his mouth until he was finished. His skin looked sickly blue, and his eyes were dark black. Kim looked at Rob, concern written in her body language and features.

"Don't worry about it, just got a little cold last night," Rob said, taking a long drag from his cigarette before ashing it directly on the table.

"I would usually say that is disgusting. It's your house, though. Fuck it," Kim responded, while pulling a water bottle from her backpack.

Rob caught me eyeing her water. "Don't worry about drinking too much up here, the main reason I brought us here was running water from the mountain. Nothing beats mountain water, especially from a well. Any who, if you're ready, we need to make a plan today. It pains me to say this, but we might have to give up our plan on attacking Wilson," Rob sighed, looking down at his map.

"I will kill him," I stated.

"I get where you're coming from, but let's face it, man. We are up a shit creek made of lava. I mean, he has an army, we are made up of three cripples and a—still attractive though, no offense—husband burning woman," Rob said, gesturing with his fingers.

"None taken, ex." Kim chimed in from her side of the table. Though she and I were on shaky footing, she still kept her distance. *I would have too, if she only knew the amount of effort that it was taking me to not kill her.*

At Rob's protests against attacking, I slammed my arms on the table, causing the frame to shake violently. "What was the point in waking me up? What was the point in saving me if we are not going to get back at this asshole? All of us have more than enough reason to kill him where he stands; including the people who helped him," I sneered, staring daggers into Kim.

She showed no fear, staying brave in the face of my threats, which only served to make me madder.

"I understand that, Jim, but he has an army. What exactly is your plan? Our best bet is to retreat for a while, maybe find a group of others and plan an attack from there. Or we can just accept that this one is just too big a mission for us," Rob said.

A part of my brain that was something else other than rage knew he was right. However painful it was, I knew there were some elements of truth in what he was saying. I just couldn't do it—I couldn't just give up on Holly. Life without her wasn't worth it for me. Walking away now meant only one choice for me.

I looked at Rob and Kim, composing the storm within me to coherent words. "You throw around words like mission and retreat. I am sickened by them, the double standard and the context you use them in. My daughter isn't even one foot in the grave, and we are giving up on her. Words like mission and retreat... They're military words. And what are we? What we did in the past didn't stop us from going after you!" I pointed at Kim.

I took a breath, steadying myself. "We came for you in spite of our better judgment or any skill we possessed, despite the odds. So, if you say Wilson has an army, well then we go get an army of our own." I walked around the table and slammed my fist upon the city of Charlotte.

"Build an army—that's not likely, Jim. He is sending out an army to devour what is left of us," Rob protested in defense.

I snapped my head in his direction and spoke, "Then why retreat? If we can't fight today, then a fight another day won't make the difference. No—I have a better idea for this. I won't be using humans, if we are all that is left, and we will fight fire with fire."

"Fight fire with fire..." Rob said the words like they were a bad taste in his mouth. "We don't even know how Wilson can control everyone; this is a man who can control people as well as ghosts. Something is unnatural and unreal," Rob stated.

"You got me there, but I don't see any other option. That is what I am going to do," I announced.

Rob lowered his eyes and shook his head. "Fine, fight today. Who needs to grow old? Not me, I am ready to die today."

"How do you plan on building this army? You don't know how Wilson even managed to do it." Kim spoke up finally. I looked at her, realizing Wilson hadn't told her all that had transpired when she was taken. In fact, not even Rob knew how Wilson had taken control of the ghosts. If it had not been for the confrontation between Holly and him, I wouldn't have even known exactly how Wilson had managed it. Kim had mentioned that he seemed to be able to make people calmer around him, make people do things. He seemed to be unstoppable.

I thought of what Wilson had said. He'd said that ghosts had to be given memories. When I thought about it, I realized how much it made sense. Holly had told me dozens of times that she had to make connections to stay in the Beast, for example. All I needed was to find a ghost. Which had never been an issue when living in a spirit world—there were plenty of them.

Not wanting to share any details with Kim unless I had to, I tried to divert her attention away from anything that would give away my plan. "We have to try! Worst case, we are torn to pieces by ghosts. Best case, we are all going to bring the thunder down on Wilson," I shouted, slamming my knob of a wrist into my other hand.

"Rob, do you have any idea how to attract ghosts? This area can't be empty," I said.

"Well—that's the thing. I picked this place because it had a low population back when the living was here. I am pretty sure there might be one or two around here somewhere… I suppose we have plenty of time actually to experiment and find a way to control a ghost—have to say, though, it just doesn't feel right doing this. Assuming it's even possible to do it, it's wrong to control someone, right?" he asked.

"That doesn't matter," I said, walking from the table. "Find a way to attract ghosts, Rob. We are going to need a whole lot," I said, walking from the room back outside. Diana followed and snickered every step of the way.

"Wow, it's interesting to see just how easy it is for you to have given up your principles just like that, Jimmy-boy," Diana chastised. I ignored her. Looking at my breath in the morning country air, time passed for what seemed like hours as I looked out over the mountainside.

I heard Rob as he came up beside me, looking at the valley floor below, possibly beyond. The man was always staring off into the distance. "Jim, you have got to be the hardest person to read I have ever met. I hope you know that too... Your daughter was my friend; she was a very kind and sweet girl. And believe me—that's something I never really say." Rob spoke remorsefully, taking a long pull from a bottle of what smelled to be ancient whiskey.

"Well alright then, let's not waste any more time," I said turning, heading for the van, its shining black paint and irons blazing like a black storm in the cold air. *Maybe that is what is going to happen; I am going to bring a storm to those who have wronged me.*

I opened the driver's side door as Kim came running out of the house. "Do you have any idea where you're going?" she asked.

"Not a clue. Hopefully, off of this mountain first," I said, as Kim jumped in the back seat before realizing Rob would need help getting into the van. She got out, helping the man into the back. I watched her lift the wheelchair into the back of the trunk. *Her strength was impressive for her age; she clearly did a lot more working out than I would have thought—might be harder to kill her.*

When she finished, she ran around to the front passenger seat; Diana appeared in the seat, exclaiming, "Shotgun!"

Kim jumped in, and Diana took shape around Kim; something must have shown on my face when she looked. "What?" she asked, looking around nervously.

Diana's silhouette smiled at me, and I turned my attention to the road, ready to start my revenge. *One way or another, it was all going to be over soon,* I thought.

"Jim—we can't just leave here and pull a plan out of our asses," Rob said, scooting closer to me from the back.

"I'm tired of plans, Rob, and I am sick of waiting."

Being so close to Diana and the others was getting to me. Doing anything was better than sitting around.

Chapter 54

By the time we pulled into the town of Canton, located about a mile off the mountain, we made our slow pace through the towers of huge pine trees. The air was thick with shapes; snow was falling creating a blanket of hidden forms in its vast folds. I placed the time to be about midday. You would never have been able to tell, though by the darkness of the obscuring white.

I pulled the emergency brake on the van in the middle of the street. The others looked perplexed. "Why are we stopping here, Jim?" asked Rob from the back seat. I waited before answering, watching the snow come down all above us. "Jim?" asked Rob, so low, I barely caught him over the hum of the engine.

"I'm just thinking, this is the town, correct?" I asked.

Rob answered, "Yes, this is the town—or was a town. It was never a big city, a mill town where everyone knew everyone and nothing exciting ever really happened."

I tapped my fingers on the wheel, keeping my eyes to the sky. "Perfect," I muttered, getting out of the car. I had always considered myself a bit of a modern-day Ghostbuster in a way. I mean, that was what I did; I caught and killed ghosts (mostly just killed).

I had been doing a lot of thinking lately about the ghosts, especially today. Rob had discovered that electricity attracted ghosts because of its heat, and he theorized and correctly guessed that if you reversed the pull of power (mostly using the combination of magnets and batteries), he was able to make a makeshift ghost repellant.

Rob had figured out the shock I used to receive from batteries as I was tracking them was the ghosts becoming grounded in the real world and electronic devices reacting to their presence.

In theory, all I had to do was make an enormous shock, and ghosts would show. If it continued, then they should at least be attracted to the output. I had witnessed it for myself, with ghosts wandering around Rob's house. Something kept making them come, something made them come closer. As they neared the batteries, though, they would just freeze. I had never seen anything like it before. It was like they were trying to become grounded. Once that happened, Rob would take the ghosts out from the safety of the house, using range to his advantage.

The only problem with my plan was that we lived in a world that had lost almost anything resembling electricity decades ago. But there still were a few things which would carry electricity. In this case, I would have to utilize an old and well-used cathode ray tube or some power supplies. I had collected a great deal of them over the years (the storage time of the electricity being beyond what the typical person would imagine). Thankfully, power supplies and monitors were easy to find. Most modern homes had at least one computer, and I only needed fifteen or so.

I went to the back of the van, popping the trunk, removing a huge monitor. Rob and Kim peered at me from the cab, wondering what I was doing as I pulled and lifted a rather large bag, hoisting it into my arms and carrying it over to what I believed was the center of the road.

I had long since had this planned in the past, as well a sort of shock-and-awe campaign, in case things ever got hairy. A part of me rejoiced at this prospect, while the rest of me was indifferent; it was just one more stepping stone on the way to having my vengeance. Sticking to the task at hand, I unloaded the van, digging for a long metal pole plus jumper cables. We were lucky no one thought to unload all the supplies in the vehicle. Otherwise, I wasn't sure if this small town would have had enough computer parts just lying around for what I was attempting. *Thankfully, Holly and I hadn't kept everything in the Beast,* I thought.

I cleared away the snow until I reached worn-away pieces of pavement. The winter had killed the grass that had taken root, but chunks of concrete remained. I looked up and saw I was still standing directly under the remains of a power pole. The only one that was still in place on the street- its metal form would be essential in my plan.

I unzipped the heavy bag and pulled out an aluminum tray fixed with over eighty tied-together power supplies. Their wires were routed and configured towards a fully charged car battery at the end. *This was overkill,* I thought—*it should do.* Once I had the tray in place, I flicked the switch on the battery and watched the power supplies all spring to life in a great hum. I thought to myself, *how the sound of working machines used to oddly put me at ease, twenty years ago. The feeling that everything made sense and was explainable, always comforted me. They still did, in a way,* I thought as I looked at the metal pole I had brought along. Only it was more of a comfort in being closer to ending everything.

Taking the pole in my hand, I wedged one end of the rod into the power supply contraption and the other into the power pole. When that was finished, I connected a pair of cables to the car battery and ran to the engine. I motioned for Rob to pop the hood as I came around the front of the car.

Rob opened the door of the van. "Are you sure about this, Jim? I mean, I think you just made a bomb…" he muttered, gesturing towards the pile of power supplies.

Without losing focus, I attached the red cable. "Honestly, no. It should be enough to attract someone's attention, though," I responded.

The instant the black negative cable touched home, a surge of electricity shot from the car faster than I could track, followed by a loud percussion of sparks and an explosion of white lighting shot everywhere. The front end of the van became a sea of static, shooting white dragons in all directions.

I dove into the snow, praying I wasn't fried on the way down. Just as soon as the storm of electronics had begun, it was over. I opened my eyes and smelt the damage first; the acid in the batteries smelling strangely like burnt hair. I pulled myself from the snow and looked at the jacket I was wearing; one of the sleeves was cooked all the way through. On my arm below, all the hair was smoked off. "Still alive…" I muttered, whipping the snow from my body, looking at the wreckage from my bomb.

The power supplies were on fire, lacing flames on the snow, while the pole was blackened at the point of conduct with the light pole. "Nice light show, Jimmy!" Diana clapped both her hands behind me.

The van door opened, and Rob fell out hard onto the ice below. He was coughing, coughing up a lot as I turned to look at the man. "Yeah, great job, James, plan on giving us a warning next time? That fucking electricity made me almost shit myself." Rob paused, looking down. "Oh wait, I did shit myself."

I turned back to my bomb. I hadn't expected a ghost to show right away. However, I did figure one would have come along already. Electronics attract them; I had just put on the biggest electronic display since the video game conventions back in the day, which I would spend hours watching on the Internet. *James, the Power-Man,* I thought.

"Well, don't just stand there like a kid in Disneyland, come pick me up, asshole." Rob beckoned from where he lay. Kim exited the van, a sour expression written all over her face. I walked back over to my car and reached into the trunk, getting Rob's wheelchair as he let loose another volley of coughs.

"So, what's the plan now, chief?" asked Kim.

She was standing on the other side of the hood, obscured more than I would have liked her to be. "We wait," I said as I unsnapped Rob's wheelchair. I offered to help roll the chair out for the man, and he pushed his way into the chair, moving aside my hand.

When he was settled, Rob spoke. "Wait for a cold is the only thing I think will happen around here..."

I ignored Rob, tucking my arms into my coat, keeping my eyes open.

The snow came down harder as we waited. Soon, Kim went back inside the smoldering remains of the van. Rob and I braved the cold, neither of us talking. "What exactly is your plan by the way? You don't have any iron," Rob pointed out.

"I figure it's the same as with us humans or any other creatures on Earth. Why would you show up to an all-you-can-eat buffet if you think there might be a danger at the buffet?" I stated.

"Must have taken you a whole five minutes to come up with that, huh? Smart ass..." Rob grumbled. We waited, watching the snow, my anger keeping me warm as the pellets of the forgotten landed upon my shoulders.

Kim opened the door and finally spoke after we had been there waiting in the silent frozen rain for hours. "I think it is fair to say that no ghost is com—" Kim started to say, just as one appeared behind her.

I turned, seeing the ghost. It was an older woman, her skin gray and the dress she was in was tattered, the color long since bleached out.

Rob followed my gaze and saw the ghost standing behind Kim. I shot my fingers to my mouth, letting Rob know to keep quiet. So far, the ghost wasn't moving. Kim's face shrank in terror. I could tell she was feeling the presence of the ghost right behind her.

I slowly stalked my way around the van, making deliberate steps to not crush the snow under my feet. Kim was breathing heavily, her angst and dismay reeking like a bad smell as I rounded the corner of the car. The woman was fixed on Kim, barely moving, and she moved her hands slowly over Kim, rubbing her as if her head was a crystal ball.

Kim rolled her eyes up from the touch; I could tell the sensation was burning her like she was on fire. That cold sting racing along her body, an incredible and perverse feeling that was anything but what a human being was supposed to be used to; like a trip into the endless cold of a dark lake.

Keeping my eyes on the woman, I stepped forward, sucking in my breath. I wasn't sure if the ghost could see the frost from my breathing, or the sweat that trickled down my face landing on the ground; she remained focused on Kim. I reached the woman and recounted Wilson's words. 'Think of a memory and once you have it, touch the heart. You have to keep your mind on that memory at all times, no matter what."

But what memories do I choose? The stronger the memory, the more powerful the ghost; only those memories that I give are gone forever. I recalled one of my earliest memories; I gave up the memories of a young boy named Sam. A poor boy looking for his father; we should have never met.

I had fought that day to save his father; I had failed. Even back then, I had always failed. *What was one less memory of a failure?* I kept Sam's round and guileless face in my mind. My hand touched the woman over what I believed was her heart.

The reaction was instantaneous, and my arm pulled into her like being sucked into a hurricane of ice. My hand splintered and the hairs on my arm exploded, like icicles falling from a house. I kept going until I felt something warm. The pain was causing me to shout out, but I pushed. I kept pushing, just a little bit more, inch by inch in what felt like miles. When I reached the warm center, it was like someone had made a fire in the middle of raw wood, heating at the center, barricaded by hateful cold on the outside.

I sprang forward with everything I had on Sam, the meeting of him in that dark alley. The shape of his hat, his favorite toy, his mother, and father; everything that made him Sam. I felt the drain of the memory pull from me; slowly, I lost the memories of Sam.

Like water drying from wood, the water had been soaked in, but water can't stay—just like memories. A relief of a burden I didn't know I carried, a weight I hadn't known I was holding slipped away.

And whatever memory I had just given away was gone. I tried to recall as I pulled my hand free of the woman, and it was like searching for a boat in the darkest sea without any light. I knew something was missing, something internal; I just couldn't put my finger on it.

When I was completely out, the woman glowed, and a blue rope shot from her to me. I flinched back in fear of the line; only I felt no pain from the touch. *Most peculiar,* I thought, as I felt the rope again. It was attached to the exact spot in my heart.

I looked at the woman. She stood still, without motion or any indication she was aware of what had just transpired. I walked around her, taking a look at her face. She still retained that motionless daze ghosts always carried—the look of the lost.

Her eyes had changed; gone was the confusion, now replaced by the eyes of darkness. The same black eyes I witnessed when the children had taken Kim; I shivered when I looked at her. *I wish she would close those.*

And she did. The woman closed her eyes. I stood stunned at what had just occurred. "Well I'll be damned, that is kind of cool," I spoke. I thought about her opening her eyes again, and she snapped her eyes, showing orbs of darkness once more.

Rob rolled up next to me, holding a long piece of iron in her direction. "Psst, Jim, what did you do to her?" he asked.

I looked at Rob, taking my eyes off of her for the first time. Cupping his hand, I lowered his weapon to his lap. "I don't think we will need that; she's not attacking," I said.

"How can you be sure; how can you know that?" asked Rob once more.

I regarded Rob before turning my head away. "It's a feeling. I can feel her head, and I can just feel her; I am pretty sure she is exactly under my control," I answered.

"You think! Well if it is all the same to you, oh great thinker, I am going to keep my weapon close. I think that is a smart idea," Rob shouted.

I rolled my eyes and turned back to the woman. If she was doing exactly what I wanted her to do with my thoughts, perhaps it would be possible to see into her mind.

I looked at the woman, and continued to search for her in the confines of my mind. I tried to hone in on her, to feel her presence. I searched until I felt a small tug, and it felt like an itch on my brain. A tiny, little itch that was showing me what it was like to be seeing from her point of view. I saw myself, my long beard speckled with gray, and the blond and red hair I once had was long gone. Only specks of color now existed on an otherwise white slope.

It was alarming, the weight difference between how I looked now and how I had been before. Before I was starving, close to becoming the walking dead; now I looked like the victim of a death march. My cheek bones high, my bones all too apparent. Next to me sat Rob, looking perplexed and nervous. The man was holding the iron, his hand shaking violently.

I am looking through her eyes, like a doorway into another realm, I thought. A painting at a museum, a window into another life. Somehow, I couldn't see into her thoughts, just my own painted on the inside of her eyes. *I wonder how that is possible. Holly was capable of many complex problem-solving skills. Hell, I was pretty sure she was more intelligent than I was. But, why was this woman not processing anything else?*

If memories determined strength, had I not given her enough memories? I thought as I searched inside her head and came upon a small ball, the image of a young Asian boy's life playing out inside of that ball. I wondered who the kid might have been, as I continued to search the woman's mind.

When my search yielded nothing, the answer came to me. It wasn't that I didn't give her enough memories. Those memories of the boy had been repressed by me for over twenty years.

What I had given up must have been weak, because it had no relationship to me. No meaning to me in the space forming inside my mind. Since it was not an actual part of me, my mind had suppressed it, like the body would do any infection; significant measures were taken to keep it from flowing into my head.

I thought of the space that used to be taken up in my mind, and it was like someone had finally turned off one of the televisions.

"So, do you think old lady is safe or should we run for the hills?" Rob asked.

I, talking through the lady's mouth, with her voice, said, "I think I will be fine, Rob. You're screwed! Boo!"

Rob jumped in his chair whipping the long iron pole out from his pocket. "Glad to see you're so funny, asshole!" Rob shouted at me with the iron in his hands. I tilted the lady's head back and let loose a laugh. I looked back at my body; it was motionless, not moving. *Strange,* I thought, *if I were a betting man, I'd assume staying in this body would be harmful over time.*

But I wasn't a betting man. I had never been, and surprises are not something I handle well. I started to climb back down the rope to my body, slowly edging my way from the tomb that was the ghost.

I didn't hear the click of the shotgun; I did listen to the boom of its cannons. I was still in the eyes of the old lady when I saw Rob rock back in his chair, the bullets taking him in the stomach.

Rob cried out in pain, and his chair fell over to the ground. I looked up, and Kim had the barrel pointed at the old lady.

I had a second to react as I pulled from the old lady just in time for the loaded iron shells to shred their way through the ghost. I was in my body as the ghost turned into a different color. This time as the ghost died, she flashed in a wave of black; no memories shot into me. The memories swirled; twisted like a monster in the depths.

They soon dissipated, and I made my move. I drove to my feet and ran hard. My boots were worn and quickly became wet as I ran towards the buildings nearby. Another shot rang out and hit somewhere overhead. I ran into the back alley of the cluster of old remaining town buildings. The foundations crumbled and caused me to trip in the already blinding snowfall.

I realized the only thing saving my life was the amount of snow coming down and the sky getting darker overhead. Kim was a decent shot; she wasn't taking her time at all, though; she was too busy trying to kill me fast instead of just killing me.

I rested on the side of a building, catching my breath in the icy cold all around me, my hands on the crumbling brick. *Thinking time, Jim, recall everything you have on that gun*. And I did. I remembered seeing Rob cleaning both shotguns the night before. His longer barreled, pump shotgun was still in the van. Loaded in the gun were a total of five buck shots. The pellets were all made of iron, from the assault at the prison.

Kim was a little bit more particular with her gun. Less range and a just a little less power—still capable of blowing my head off though. Most importantly, it was only loaded with six shots. I looked around me then, my position still in the clear with no sign of Kim knowing where I was.

I listened, doing my best to hear of the beating of my own heart, the rhythm of a speed bag in my chest. Off in the distance, I could hear the soft falling of snow on the ground. The fresh powder was breaking under the light weight of a small woman; *there,* I thought.

To my right would be the best exit, cutting through the buildings beyond the main street. Only, if Kim hadn't killed me by then, the cold more likely would. I looked down at my boots; the snow crusted already on the side; it would serve only to help her track me. I reached down and started untying the plain knot on my boots.

It was simple tying my shoes with one hand, once you understood the song—as Holly had put it when she found a book on the subject. I quickly sang the tying song as my fingers fumbled on the frozen laces.

The thought of Holly cooled my beating heart. *This was all for her. The woman who helped kill your daughter is trying to kill you. You better kill her first, old man. You better shoot that one.*

I was out of my boots, my socks soaking in the wetness of the snow. I wiggled my toes, trying to keep what little warmth I was quickly losing. The thing about North Carolina snow is how wet it is. *The powder is never tough and durable, just plain wet, probably from all of the humidity,* I thought. Which made it easy to move through, if nothing else.

I listened again; Kim was coming from the end of the alley I was in now. I chucked my boots at the opposing wall and hurried down the ally in the opposite direction of her approach. I cursed myself for not having some way to wipe away my footprints.

I ran hard, trudging my way through the snow, my feet scraping and burning in the cold. I rounded the crumbling structures of an old hotel building and circled back around the original building I had come from.

I could see Kim near my boots, bent over with her back to me. She was too busy trying to figure out why I had taken my boots off and was casting her gaze skyward to a hanging ledge above her. *I wasn't that strong,* I thought.

I slithered my way to Kim through the cover of the snow, as my steps sounded like a bull jumping a rope. I was a foot behind Kim when I stood up behind her; I tapped her shoulder, and she stiffened, swinging the shotgun around as my fist swung down with everything I had. My hit drove home and smacked her head back hard into the wall.

Size and power were on my side, plus I had the element of surprise to boot. My velocity was pure, my rage without fear as I attacked Kim until she finally dropped the gun. I felt her kick and swipe at my legs as I fell forward with all the limited amount of weight I had left.

Taking her head in my hand, I slammed her face into the wall. She fell to the ground, blood smearing her face. I was hot, I was on fire, and I was unhinged. I had never attacked a woman—for that matter, I had never done something like this to anyone before.

I didn't like it, standing over Kim, wounded and bleeding. She was going to receive no mercy, though, not for her crimes. Kim rolled over, her face looking at mine, crimson red; snowflakes melting from the heat of her blood.

The image of Rob lying in the snow flashed through my mind. I let go, let myself dive into the fury of what she did, and I landed upon her, my hand around her throat, while my legs were straddling her.

She gagged, her face turning purple, looking up at me as I drained the life from her. Holly flashed again in my face. This time it was when we had once been searching for a body. A long day it had been, the two of us searching through house after house. We had decided to take a break in a field of flowers. There were daisies—her favorite.

Earlier that day, Holly and I had come across a particularly nasty ghost. I had managed to slay the man-turned-ghost. In his memories, I had seen that he had been a loving brother and son. He hadn't done anything harmful to anyone, yet he had died, torn to pieces by ravenous beasts. No way to fight back, no way to run with ghosts all around him hunting his body until he fell to the ground. Dying in the dirt, turning the grass a stained red, to remain until the next rain fall. After that, the grass returned green, as if the man had never been there.

When Holly asked how I felt about killing his ghost, I told her it was merciful, me putting him down. She got mad at me for weeks after I said that, refusing to talk to me. When I finally got her to talk, Holly had told me not to kill, no matter how justified I felt I was, no matter how merciful I was. *A life is a life no matter what form that may be. No matter where they're from, their color, shape, or how evil.* Her final point was: *what is the purpose in trying to live if we are going to be killers without remorse?*

Her words stayed with me for a time. Like most things in life; words have the power to change you, the power to lift you from your darkest places. However, it is the person, not the words, that have to have the courage to be changed by words. It is always their own choice.

Only three months ago, I had made the decision to give ghosts, which had been trying to kill me for twenty years, the benefit of the doubt instead of destroying them. I had sought to save them. And the end result, had been my daughter dying right before my waking eyes! A split second decision had resulted in me losing everything to this person beneath me. It still felt wrong, draining the life from her body, as I felt Kim sliding away under my power.

I loosened my grip on Kim's neck, and she spoke. "Please, Jim! I'm sorry. I had to do this—he has my son! Please, it's the only way I can get him back." Kim begged weakly, her eyes pleading with tears. I felt my grip getting weaker; Holly would have understood. Holly would have told me to let her up.

My hand almost came completely off her throat; when Diana whispered in my ear, "Jimmy, she killed our little girl. She helped a madman, are you going to let her go? Remember what happened when you let the last guy go?"

A surge of rage raced into my hand as I choked harder on Kim's throat, her eyes going wide. She had killed Rob, and she had helped kill Holly. Kim screamed as my hand tightened around her throat.

"Yes, Jim! Do it, do it!" hissed Diana.

"Shut up!" I shouted back, my head turned towards Diana. Kim looked towards Diana, digging her hands into the snow. I pressed with all my might until I heard a pop, Kim's eyes rolled in the back of her head and she stopped moving.

"Don't let up, Jim, they always make it seem like they're dead, but to choke someone; you have to hold for a while longer," Diana said, circling Kim.

When the cold finally dug its claws into my bones, I let go. My fingers were stiff and raw from the attack. I pulled my way off Kim, her body still warm to the touch. I looked at her, the way she lay there—no breath, no life. "Oh God…" I said, vomiting next to her body.

"Wow, Jim, I didn't think you had it in you… It's a damn shame you didn't do that sooner for your daughter. Oh well." Diana snorted, dancing around me as I continued to vomit and sob. When I was finished, I looked at Kim, the snow covering her body. I closed her eyes. She had only tried to save her son, which I could understand. She just had to know my vengeance. Her eyes popped open and stayed open from the cold freezing her to the depth of the void, forever casting a mirror into a lifeless husk until some bird plucked them away. *A killer shouldn't be allowed to not see their eyes,* I thought.

I walked to my boots, the cold causing me to shiver. I was going to have to get somewhere out of this snow soon or I would die.

I found my boots, shaking the snow from them, putting them on quickly. I tied my knot fast, and my fingers never stopped shaking the whole time, I wasn't sure if it was from the cold, or from Kim. When I finished, I made sure not to turn around and look at Kim. If I turned back around now, I wasn't going to be able to look away. I walked back out to the main road.

Rob lay by the side of the van, his hands covering his stomach wound, while a puddle of blood rushed from his body; he was very blue and didn't look up at me until I was before him. He grunted, clearly strained. "Did you kill Kim?" he asked.

I remained silent, not wanting to answer.

Rob blew out a breath. "I figured you would. She played us both and shot me with my gun. What a woman." Rob laughed. I smiled at the man as he lay dying in the cold. He was with me, but he might as well be alone—death is a lonely ride meant for only one. A part of me felt like I had died back in that alley. The truth was, I had been dead since Holly passed.

It must have shown on my face. Rob rolled his eyes and grabbed hold of my left shoulder with a surprising amount of strength.

"Don't blame yourself. You observed your life and lived it the way you saw fit. We all make choices; Kim made hers, and she paid for it." Rob stopped coughing up blood. "I think you and I are the unlucky ones, Jim. We got to live to be old men while the entire world around us died off. But hey, you had your daughter, longer than most do in this nasty world. That's something that makes it worth it. Don't lose track of that. Hold on to her and settle this, one way or another." Rob wheezed, letting go of my shoulder and placing both of his hands over his stomach.

I looked at the man and suddenly realized Rob was the last remaining living friend I had on Earth, probably the only friend I had. "Is there anything I can do to help? It's just a stomach wound; infection is what we need to worry about most. Maybe Kim left some antibiotics back at your folk's house," I started.

Rob seemed to think it over and stopped me as I started to pick his body up. "Stop it, jackass, before you hurt me worse!" He snapped. I dropped him, feeling embarrassed, and crouched down next to him. "You wouldn't have happened to have a smoke, would you Jimmy?" Rob asked.

I smiled, looking off into the distance as snow piled onto the remains of a roof. "Fresh out, I'm afraid," I said. Rob sighed. "Figures. Well, if it is all the same to you, hurry up and kill me already. I don't have time to keep distracting you. You have a madman to find. You heard Kim. Wilson is trying to kill all the humans like a bad 80's movie," Rob snorted.

I looked down before answering, "I think—I think it's pointless. I think it's time to admit I can't beat this man. Might be better just to die against this car with you, man." I spoke, letting my words trail off into the cold. I mean, it made sense considering the fact that it was now just me—me, and a dying husk of a human being, much more content with self-loathing rather than self-respect.

Rob spat more blood before talking again. "Your real moniker is

James, right?" Rob asked.

I looked at the man, perplexed. "Yeah it is. Why?" I responded.

"Then shut the fuck up and listen to me, James. Doesn't matter the odds, even if you have to slap the devil himself, do right by the ones that loved you, or just sit here and die with me. It's that simple, you jackass," he said.

"Now if you wouldn't mind, kill me. You might as well. We both know you can't care for me. Hell, I don't even know if you can care for yourself. But I do know this. I never saw in my life a more loving father. I think the least I can do is help you finish your quest as a loving father. Besides, I think I will make a great ghost, don't you think?" Rob asked me, staring into my eyes the whole time, his complexion matching the frost of the snow.

"You don't even know if you will come back as a ghost—" I started to say, before Rob spoke again.

"Jim, please." I looked at the man and nodded my head towards his. We both understood. I stood up, picking up his iron bar which had landed on the roof of the van. "You know, all that work for one measly ghost, and we didn't even get a chance to share a smoke," Rob joked.

"Yeah, you're right—we will have to share one after we find Wilson," I said.

"I don't—" Rob started to say, as I came down hard with all my strength, using the iron bar. Rob's skull crunched under my fingers, and I felt his blood spray onto me. I looked down, seeing Rob's eyes roll into the back of his head as his body jerked in the last moments of his life.

I let go of the bar, realizing I was covered in so much blood. There was no telling whose it was; it was either Kim's or Rob's. I didn't know, and I didn't want to think. I sat down in the snow, feeling hot, despite the ice around me, and waited.

My body gave out before my stupidity, and I went into the van. Turning the engine on, I prayed thank you to the electricity gods. It was just too cold to sit there and wait. My feet and hands shook from the cold as the warm air blasted my limbs. After being in the cold so long, my body was stiff and numb to everything, except that the ends of my fingers burned. I knew it was the blood reentering them causing the sensation; it still felt foreign. To feel anything besides the cold felt alien.

I started to doze off when Diana appeared at the driver's window, a wicked smile on her face. "What do you want now?" I grunted, more than actually speaking.

Diana looked stunned at my question. "Look at all the death around us, Jim; I am so proud of you. You're finally becoming the monster I always knew you could be." She gleamed.

Even though she looked like a grown-up Holly, if I had a gun, I would have taken her head off. I imagined shooting her in the face with my rifle. It was comforting to think about, as sleep took me, and I drifted away.

I awoke sometime later, my throat dry and itching from being in the heat for too long. I clicked my tongue to the roof of my mouth, clearing the dry taste from my lips as I rubbed the sleep off from my eyes. It was night time and according to the clock on the dashboard (I had long since stopped adjusting the time), it was sometime after 2 AM. *Which was accurate enough,* I thought as I looked around the darkness, wishing I had a flashlight.

I yawned, letting a much-needed soreness from my body. My fingers found the headlight switch for the van.

"I wouldn't do that if I were you."

At the sound of the voice, I jumped and hit my head against the flat roof of the car. My hand instinctively went for my frying pan to find my side empty instead. I swore and reached for the door handle, when the locks slammed closed.

"Jimmy, calm down already, man. You're acting like such a pussy right now," said a mocking voice.

Growing scared, also a little angry for being woken up from one of the most peaceful sleeps I'd had in a while, I asked, "Who are you?"

"Who am I? I am—" The voice trailed until a red horned man appeared in the darkness across from me. "I am—boo!" screamed the man.

I jumped back, hitting my head on the window. The face disappeared, and Rob came back, floating in the seat. He was laughing, mocking me as I clutched my chest from the scare. "Rob, is that you? What the fuck is the matter with you?" I demanded.

"What's the matter with me? Man, you're one to talk! You shoved a pole through my head and choked a woman to death!" Rob answered, garrulous and as long-winded as ever.

I blinked at Rob in the darkness, his form exactly as he had looked when he had died (only a little more complete from what I could tell). "That must be you, Rob; you never shut up."

Rob laughed at me from nearby. "You got me there, partner," he responded.

It dawned on me then, to ask the obvious question. "Wait, how in the hell are you back as a ghost?" I asked, genuinely confused.

Rob looked at me, confusion evident on his face. "What do you mean?" he asked. I looked at the van as if to check and see if anyone might have been listening. "Oh, you mean you don't know? Damn—Jim, I always thought you were a smart guy," Rob stated.

I blushed red; I never liked seeming like the dumb person in the room. "Enlighten me, smart one." I said, twirling my fingers.

"Well, it is pretty simple. Everyone on the planet turns into a ghost when they die," he said matter-of-factly.

My jaw dropped. I had no idea that was how it worked. Besides that one couple when I was younger—I had assumed everyone else would die like normal. I figured that couple only changed because of it being close to the time all the ghosts had emerged. Another question shot into my head, as soon as understanding from his statement sprang into understanding. "So, wait, how are you able to remember who I am?" I asked sheepishly.

Rob sighed. It was becoming his new trademark with me, I noticed. "Well, that is a good question. To tell you the truth, I'm not sure why I remember who I am, or who you are for that matter—I guess it just is. All I know is, I came back and found you sleeping. I remember not knowing who you are, but when I touched you, it was if I had stepped into a moving stream. All this knowledge of who I am and who I was came back. I'm not sure how that happened, how I didn't end up with someone else's personality. I do know this, that even when you die, you will become just like me," Rob informed me, sending the hard pill down my throat.

I thought about his words; they struck home like a torpedo at the bottom of the ocean. For years, one of my biggest fears I had with Holly had been that I would die, and she would be all alone. Cursed to roam the earth forever, forever alone and searching in vain for her body—a quest she was doomed to fail from the very beginning as I had hidden her body from her for years.

If I had just died or had left, I could have been with my daughter, at least in some way, for the rest of my life. The anger inside me snapped back, driving out all the rest from my body and I felt myself physically expand from the pressure building on the inside.

Rob continued talking. "To be honest, I think the only ones who get to keep our memories are the ghosts that had a firm connection to their memories. I mean, really, how many people in life just go through life? One step at a time, on and on until their lives are over. So many people just *live,* never making any real memories. I may have been a fuck-up in my life, but I managed to make my life one big adventure. I loathed a lot, but I cherished every memory."

Rob quit talking when he noticed my face; I was deep in thought, thinking of Holly. "Hey now, you had no way of knowing Wilson set you up. Hell, he set us all up, Jim. I hope you know this, right? None of this is your fault," he assured me.

Rob's words pulled me back to the surface long enough to respond. "Yeah, it's not my fault, but it sure feels a lot different than that."

"None of us knew about Wilson, about Kim; the question is: now how do you intend to go on from here?" Rob asked.

I relaxed, letting my guard down; I couldn't stop Rob anyways at this point if he attacked. "I'm not sure. I'm a little empty on gas, and I am a little empty on an army as well… I suppose I could challenge Wilson to a one-on-one. Though he kicked my ass last time, which will likely be the same result," I stated.

"I think you forgot the most important thing about the world, Jim: there is madness in us all. Turn on the lights." Rob gestured to the headlight switch near the steering wheel.

"What the hell are you talking about?" I asked.

Rob, ignoring my stupidity, waved again. "Just do it."

I decided to humor him; I turned the light switch on, and the van's headlights shone bright over hundreds of ghosts. All standing near us, close enough to scare me, far enough to stay away from the van's defenses. Astonished, I asked, "Where did they all come from?"

Rob laughed before answering with the same cheery tone in his voice. "They were waiting for you to put down that iron the whole time. Your little bomb attracted a whole nest. The best part is while you took your little nap, you snored—loud, I might add. I got to talk to some of them while we waited," Rob mused.

"Why aren't they attacking me, Rob?" I asked.

"I think they're just curious. Most have no idea who or what they are," he responded.

Bewildered, I looked at Rob. Rob waited a moment before speaking, giving me the chance to piece it all together. "Means that you should get out of this death trap and build an army already." Rob said floating through the driver's side window. He floated outside, with his hands gesturing as if for me to come out and challenge him. He was no longer in a wheelchair (he'd even decided to grow back a pair of legs).

Diana spoke from behind me, *my very own ghost while I am surrounded by other shades—my real haunting. A devil to whisper in my ears, an encouragement of fear in her every word.* "You don't really trust this guy, do you, Jim? He can't help you save Holly, not like I can," she said. Fear would have pulled me into the dirt, to turn towards my wife and stay with her. Holly though, she was my flame, and she had died with no fear. I wasn't going to let her die alone again. *Daddy is coming baby.*

Without turning, I opened the door of the van. "I will build an army of warriors and take down the one man who killed our daughter; afterwards, I will kill myself for helping that madman. I had, in a way, let him kill everyone on this planet. I should have just let Holly take him out as soon as I saw him. I'm not sure why he is doing this, but like Rob said, there is a madness in us all—I have that madness now. I will say this, though, Diana. When it comes to deciding which memories need to be forgotten; I will trade every one of yours first. My wife was the love of my life; she was an amazing mother and wife. You're just a shadow of what she was." I exited the van, slamming the door on Diana, as the first ghost approached me.

It was a man dressed in a firefighter's outfit. His size was imposing, though I feared him less than I did the thing inside my vehicle. I thought of some of the memories I had with Diana the night she died. I reached forward and expertly knifed my hand into the chest of the bigger ghost. This time, entering the centermost section of his heart quickly; I let go of the memories of the night my wife had first returned as a monster, the night that I started my path to becoming a monster.

When it was over, I could see the rope between the fireman and me. I looked towards Rob. "We are going to need a lot more; I have a lot to lose."

Chapter 55

To live in the exact moment of my life without a past, present, or future was a discipline that I had never learned. In my normal life, I had never learned how to be exactly in whatever I was doing. I was always worried about what could happen and what I could have done differently. My wife would tell me, when we first started dating, that I was afraid to live. Now I was dead, I was finally relaxing.

As the numbers of my ghost army swelled, that became easier for me. My focus was on killing Wilson and Benny; nothing else mattering but that, and I used every drop of the memories of the ghosts I had killed, everything about their lives they gave me; I realized now it was a good thing I had taken so many. I had traded every memory of my life. From the simple ones like my first shave and one time I cut my fingernails, to more complex ones, like the first time I had sex, and my father's funeral. Everything that had made me who I was, I traded for my revenge.

I kept all my memories of Holly, all the ones of Rob, Wilson, Benny, Christina, and Kim. Everything else was gone. When I thought of my memories with Holly, I couldn't remember anything else beyond just the picture of her. Not the words I spoke, or the many profound moments we'd shared while we searched for her body. I couldn't remember who she was before she was Holly. *That was okay,* I thought; *I didn't need to know who I was before. That person I was before was a monster.*

For now, I was much better off only remembering the people I had to kill. When it was done, I had only the white of my empty mind and the reasons that were driving me. A man only needed love in his life, and since I didn't have that, I only needed someone to kill. What I needed to do was to be a monster; easy to do if you had no memories. Morality streams from the lessons we learn during our lives. If you don't remember those lessons, you have no worries.

As the last ghost approached me, she looked familiar; she looked like Kim. I looked at her, knowing it had been me who killed her, I didn't feel any hate towards her. I felt nothingness, only the absolute of my mission. "I'm sorry Jim, all I ever wanted was to protect my kid," she spoke in the cold air.

My breath cast a dull blue over her in the early hours. I nodded. What I was doing was all I knew, and it seemed right making her a part of me. I gave her my strongest last memory to give: my name. I no longer knew who I was as I turned from her and stood before an endless swarm of ghosts, all tethered to me by blue ropes all leading back to me. One hairy and tattooed man beside me spoke: "Have to say, Jimmy; this must have been how Darth Vader felt standing before his Storm Troopers. I'm surprised you got all of them so willingly—and so powerful now." Rob stuttered in fear.

Without looking at Rob, I spoke to him. "I have no idea who any of those people are. It's time to go, let's finish this." I said.

"Wish things could have gone differently for us both, I really wish they had," Rob called over my shoulder as I started walking in the direction of Charlotte. I could have taken the van as I walked past the hulking iron machine. Only I had no idea how to drive anymore; I gave away that memory, along with many others. Logic had prevailed and kept me from trading all my language skills, though only barely.

I walked through the fresh snow for about an hour, the cold seeping into my bones, my feet laden with ice, when I finally quit. I was over a hundred miles away from Charlotte, and walking there was only possible if I didn't mind losing a few toes in the process.

It was taking me a long time to catch my breath, and a cough had started to sink in. I looked ahead, staring off into the mountains before me and the mountains behind me. Maybe finding something that ran for a while wouldn't be such a bad idea.

Rob floating beside me, sensed my thoughts, and spoke, "You know, we could always just fly you there."

I looked at my friend floating next to me. My memories of him sharp, my time with him only limited. All I knew was that I was on my way to find a man named Wilson, to kill him for what he had done to my daughter. "Give me a minute, Rob; I need some time to rest," I said. Rob frowned at me and nodded as the two of us looked on at the mountains before us. I shivered while I rested, tucking my body into small enough of a ball to avoid the cold.

"The beautiful thing about being dead is I no longer get cold, really; I don't even get hot. It's surprisingly comfortable right now." Rob coughed casually. I looked at him, hoping my stare would convey much more than words would. They did not, however, as Rob continued. "Come on, Jim, let's just continue you on already."

"I am no longer that person, Rob; I am simply a man trying to destroy another man any way I can. I would appreciate it if you didn't remind me of all I have lost. Especially with names—they only serve to confuse me more," I said.

Rob sized me up with his eyes before speaking. "Fair enough."

I tried to focus on killing Wilson, but the hate I had for the man, while intense and burning, lacked context. I knew I should hate the man; I knew I had given up memories of my life. It all felt like I was trying to recall a very long textbook. Turning to Rob, I spoke. "Can you tell me about different ways of fighting ghosts, please? I need to know something about them," I asked.

Rob flaunted his chest out and began telling me details about ghosts. About how to kill them, how to trap them, how I was able to control them; I looked down at the iron bar in my hand, and even though I knew the weapon killed ghosts, it felt fragile with the numbers around me. It was impossible for me to believe in the abilities of the weapon, since I'd never actually tried using it.

While we sat, the other ghosts around us slowly returned to their normal personalities, though their ropes to me remained. The mountains became alive with conversations as all the ghosts spoke to each other. I had trouble thinking under the weight of their words; it was maddening. I stood up and shouted at my army behind me. "Everyone, shut the fuck up!"

And they did, they all obeyed. Standing tall, I paced forward turning my head back to Rob. "Okay Rob, you claim you guys can fly me to Charlotte. Let's see it."

Ghosts moved in around me; I was lifted into the air with an invisible force that ruffled my clothes and spurred me higher. We flew over the Appalachian Mountains, our speed intense in the harsh winter air. For miles across the forgotten lands below me, I drifted. I was an angel floating above a world without God.

Soon we were approaching Charlotte, the few remaining buildings appearing below, like we were giants from above. *It's the first time I have seen the city,* I thought, *but it isn't. I have lived there my entire life.*

I couldn't fathom or understand what it was like to have lived in a place like that. *What must it have been like?* My mind craved to indulge itself in the experience of learning about the city. As my thoughts trailed, I chastised myself. I was like a small child. *Keep focus, keep your mind on the task*; I had the memory of me deciding to give up my memories. It was just like swimming upstream, trying to keep going on the path I had set before.

People must make up memories of their lives, I thought. This was all made up—that was the only way to describe it. My body felt tired, and I was covered in scars. But for all I knew, being a one-armed person was normal.

I listened to the chatter of the ghosts around me as we flew; *they must think of me as some banshee, a ghost among ghosts.* I had no idea how I should fight this Wilson. Rob didn't strike me as the planning type from what I could remember; it was truly the blind leading the blind as I looked down, seeing a ruined stadium below us. I wasn't sure what the best way would be to attack this man. Maybe that was best—if I couldn't remember who I was, I was free to be whomever I needed to be.

I had the most dream-like memory of the events at the stadium; it was there I had lost my daughter. I suddenly wanted to be on the field, and it was like seeing pictures of faraway cities—my mind knew Holly existed, and the only way to know of her existence was to be at the place of her death. The only way to believe it. Same as with those cities, how could you know they were real if you did not go there?

I sent a command to all the ghosts to land in the stadium. On cue, my entire army glided to the stadium below. My feet touched gently on the overgrown grass; I could see the damage from footprints stepping onto the turf, covered in a fresh powder of ice. There were no other visual signs of anyone else having been there. My heart dropped into an empty world. I was surrounded by ghost people with all my memories, yet I was a man on the moon, missing what I could not have.

I looked up into the sky. Traces of the morning sun started to peel back the black of the heaven with a glow of orange on the horizon. I looked around the field, playing the memory of the stadium assault in perfect detail (when my mind only held the memories of the last three or so months, it was all too easy to recall), I saw in my mind how the Beast had destroyed the top archway of the stadium, tearing into the seats below, how the ghosts circled me like I was a small fish in a shallow lake, how Benny had clumsily and without being provoked killed my child. I gripped my heart at that thought, not from despair, but from the raging bull dying to get out of me.

Rob teleported next to me, looking at the part of the field where I stood. He remained silent as I looked upon the graveyard without bodies around me. "You know, a place just—it just feels wrong. It just feels wrong when you can barely remember why you were there in the first place. It's like looking through a glass; you just can't get close enough to the memory around you that way," I whispered, letting my words hang in the air.

"The world around us sucks more often than not, friend. At least we get a chance to be a part of it, still," Rob said soberly.

I turned toward my friend. "Some of us get to be a part of it, Rob, only some of us." I looked up at the sky; more light was shining down. "Well, it's getting to be that time," I said to no one in particular. I was lost as I looked around at the sea of faces around me.

So we stood, awaiting some of the ghosts we had sent ahead. After a time, Rob spoke. "Before we get started, though, the scouts report that the numbers Wilson has collected are a great deal larger than we originally anticipated. To be honest, and blunt, it's a metric fuck-ton more than we could have seen coming. Not only is it animals and every beast of the sea, but it's also almost the entire world's population—maybe some living ones as well." Rob swallowed.

I thought about the things Rob said. I tried to piece together what it was like to see so many numbers. I wasn't a general; I wasn't anything, from what I could tell. A man who was a vessel for memories, a conduit for those around him, yet how was I going to be able to beat a man who vastly overwhelmed me?

I shifted through the memories, the ones of Holly; especially the ones when she had powered up and performed incredible feats. Wilson had told me that the stronger the memories, the more powerful the ghost. I had given personal memories to a lot of ghosts; I had even given my name to one ghost. *That couldn't be the only way to power up ghosts,* I thought.

I looked around at the ghosts around me, their many faces showing husbands, fathers, mothers, sisters, sons, daughters, old, healthy, doctors, janitors. All had former lives; all were regaining who they were through the powers of my memories.

Rob and Holly had managed to do incredible things when they became ghosts; however, ghosts like Joey, and the old lady I had first taken over, were weak compared to them—the question was: why? Why some stronger, while others were weaker? Was it like humans, humans who could grow and train to be stronger, or was it like the human spirit that made ghosts stronger. If it was that, did the ghosts have the equivalent of a soul?

I looked at Rob; he sat as calm as a cloud floating in the new sky. "Rob—what makes a stronger ghost to you?" I asked the man.

Rob smiled at me, smiled at me like he was a proud teacher viewing a student's first solved math problem. "I think it is the same as when we were alive, Jim. What makes a person stronger? I believe you have the answer." Rob smiled.

Same as when we were alive, huh? I looked down at the blue lines connecting all of us together. I was a far cry from anyone I had known in the world before as being alive. People wanted freedom; people wanted reasons to live. Wilson had a vast and massive army, an army which would fill every grain of sand in a sandbox, but he had no real people in his army.

I cupped my mouth and shouted to all of my ghosts around me, my men, my troops that would be following me into the breach, "Everyone, quickly—tell me your names!"

Chapter 56

It took longer than I would have liked. In the end, though, I had learned the names of every single ghost in my army. I had heard about who they were, who their families were, what their dreams had been, what made them them. I rolled over their stories in my mind like a tumbleweed guided gently by the wind. To my surprise, every walk of life had a tale; some bigger than others, some much smaller, but all full of power from their stories. A life of any kind, no matter how long, has a story to tell. The stadium was alive with chatter as I spoke to Rob.

"Surprise is on our side; Wilson doesn't suspect anyone would come to the front," I stated.

"Just because we don't think he would expect that doesn't mean he won't be expecting it," Rob countered.

"True, you make a good point, but I don't think even Wilson could have foreseen this," I said, turning around and gesturing at the thousands of... people. It was hard thinking of them as ghosts now. I had few memories of the ghosts as anything else, so far. The only memories I had of people were those trying very hard to kill me, or trying to kill my friends. To me, the ghosts now seemed like the safe ones.

All around me, my people were coming together. I could feel a hum almost, a feeling of power in the air. Rob exhaled a long breath before speaking. "Just remember your promise. If you forget, you are liable to end up exactly like the rest of us pretend-breathers," Rob reminded me, gesturing towards the other ghosts.

He was right in reminding me; I didn't think he should have worried, though. I was going to free the ghosts like I had promised when this was over. During the process of learning everything, it was agreed I wouldn't keep them past this one task. Some broke down and cried; I think most were just happy to have a life in some way. Talking to Kim, I had learned that Wilson wouldn't let her have Joey back. So, she had left in anger, and after that, she had found Rob and me. Kim stuck around to hear our plan. When it had run its course, she thought Wilson would be proud if she stopped our project. If she hadn't left Wilson, I would have died. That was that.

I made another promise to her: when this was over, she could find Joey; what was done was done. I needed every single ghost's help if I had any chance of beating Wilson, whether it was a victory, or my death at the end. I was going to let them all go. When I had promised this to the army, cheers had gone up. It was strange, knowing we were all probably about to die—or, for all of us, again. We were about to die a second time. Maybe that was how life was, a black blanket quilted with the stars above, and throughout our days we were always becoming different people; always dying. That left us with the stars; there millions of them, just like we all had millions of lives despite the black quilt that enclosed us.

The world had goose-stepped us into a slow march to doom. I, for one, was willing to face it, so long as I could see the whites of the eyes of the men who had killed my girl. "I'm coming, baby…" I mumbled, turning to find a short and stocky man. His hair was cut close, his clothes tight over the massive muscle for his build. Next to him was a gentle giant, affectionately named "Tiny," his chest at my head level; I looked up at his face, strangely at peace.

"We are ready, boss," Tiny stated.

I nodded at the shorter ghost named Kyle. "Let's get the ball rolling, boys," I said as I walked next to Rob. "You might want to hold on tight for this, Jim," Rob suggested.

I looked at my friend, puzzled. "There's nothing to hold on to,

Rob." I said ignoring his comment about my name. It wasn't my name; it hung like the paint on a faded wall. Something that once meant a great deal to someone now meant nothing at all to me.

"Geez, man, you could lighten up before the end of things." Rob fidgeted nervously as the other ghosts surrounded me, lifting me up into the air with ease. I kept my iron pan tight to my side and my shotgun strapped to my other leg (somehow both my weapons had remained exactly where Rob had left them in the hot dog stand across from the stadium). Maybe it was luck, maybe it was just meant to be. Either way, when I felt the cold steel in my hand, I felt ready.

Then the sound of steel and cement rippled across the stadium. Even in the air, I felt the shudder of the massive structure starting to come lose, as the old dust hit me, forcing me to cover my eyes. With a massive grumble of stone and steel, the stadium came free. I looked behind me, seeing everything except the turf in the stadium floating behind me, scores of ghosts holding the circle structure with their power.

All around me, ghosts had trees and cars suspended in the air by their power. *There's something you don't see every day*, I thought, as we made our slow crawl towards the center of town. We flew for twenty minutes, a creeping wave of materials and debris floating above the city like bombers on a final desperate mission.

I saw Wilson's massive army before I noticed the building. It was an endless ocean of shades, banshees, ghosts, and men. The number was almost beyond anything I could comprehend; at first, I thought they were all small buildings, moaning. The very air around me shook with them, and I suddenly felt afraid, high above the earth.

I was about to try and attack that, and I must be off my meds, I thought. That was a solid wall; it could not be defeated. Rob floated near me, mumbling; I wasn't sure if it was in fear or something else. "Sail rocks into the sea, sail skipping rocks into the sea; sail boulders into the ocean, for that is the only way to make a splash, you shall see," he muttered in the fierce wind.

I looked at Rob, and my mouth would have hung open if it was not for the blast of cold North Carolina air engulfing my face. I pushed through the wind anyways, shouting, "What the hell does that mean?"

Rob turned looking at my face; his features tense and on edge. "Just remember the boulders that caused a splash in your ocean, Jim; the men who killed your daughter are below you. Let's go kill them," Rob shouted.

I nodded, turning my attention back to the tower, wondering if Wilson was staring back. *Are you watching, asshole? I hope you are, because when I find you, you will be sorry, and you will know the horror.*

I motioned for the army to start landing a hundred yards out from the opposing force. Flyers stayed in the air with their payloads as Rob called them ready to be slung for distraction and shock, more than anything else. All was calm, and the only one making any noise was the heavy breath from me, the scared meat bag.

I pulled my frying pan from my sling. I looked at the rusted metal; it had served for over twenty years. I thought of the memories that had passed into the iron throughout the many hours of my life. *I was here now; I was here now. I was grounded and a part of the world that was here.* I took a deep breath, flashing Holly through my mind, veins in my neck ripping their way out of my too-thin frame.

I looked at the faces of the lost across from me, so enslaved they couldn't even show fear. I was going to plow my way through a million ghosts if I had to; I was going to get into that tower.

All was calm, all was silent, and all was in place. I took the fear that had built its ugly fire before my heart and shoved it deep down. I had no name, past, present, or future; I was the avenging father!

"Now!" I bolted forward as cars, trees, buses, an entire stadium, and everything we could get our hands on slammed into the group of ghosts in front of us.

Swells of colors flew everywhere; a legion of memories looked for a mind to play their stories, like a movie reel in an old theater, long forgotten to time. Shock was written on the ghosts' faces as I came forward with my army behind me. We had filled the vehicles with every scrap of iron in the city. Which wasn't much, since I was the only one who could touch the metal. *It would just have to do,* I thought, over the noise and confusion lighting up the early morning sky like the last concert for the god of rock.

I had the strongest ghosts work together to accomplish this. The results were total panic in the enemy's lines as my pan struck the first ghost. Its memories charging into me. I quickly diverted them along the power lines connected to me, feeding my army with every swing of my pan as I kept my eyes on the entrance to the towers.

Dust blew in from every direction; I became lost in my charge. Ghosts attacked me, pure malevolence in their expressions as their hollow forms chased me, spilling energy and memories into the air. I dodged, running for anything that would provide me something of a breather. The cold air was slowing me down; my breaths felt too heavy, too sluggish to be of any use. I knew my body was old, but I just didn't feel old in my mind. *I should be faster—I needed to be faster. Making it to that tower is all there is, nothing else. I had my mind;* I kept repeating this to myself as even my bones became tired. The memories I had felt like textbooks, nothing more tangible. Everything felt like I was grinding a stone against the ground and trying to place it back together.

In the distance, I could see an overturned bus; its windows shattered onto the field below. I risked turning my head; five mindless beasts were chasing me. Their forms twisted, and a wicked zeal written across their brows. I took off as fast as I could for the bus, pumping my legs hard as the ghosts cut me off. They soon encircled me; I raised my hands in defense, readying myself for their attack.

Even though I could feel everyone in my army around me, I felt alone with the force presented before me. But I didn't feel fear. *Fear is a learned trait; learned habits are the lessons you carry in your memories. Good thing I had none, I had no fear.* I stiffened my back and charged forward towards my attackers. Before I reached them, Tiny and Kyle the ghosts came charging forward, stomping all five into sparks of black.

I gasped. Tiny had transformed himself into a giant, while Kyle had enlarged his upper body to the point that it was almost comical, his muscles on the verge of exploding. "Okay, thanks for the help, guys," I called, leaving the bus and continuing my charge towards the building.

All around me, ghosts exploded; the few humans amongst them screamed in sheer terror. I blocked it all out, keeping my focus on the building as the battle raged. Ghosts of whales swam by, slamming me down at one point, only for Rob to blow them away; my path remained clear and I was thankful the power they possessed was on my side.

I dodged groups of animals, ghosts so twisted that their forms were borderline demonic. A monster made of body parts swooped its disfigured torso limbs, nearly taking my head off as I ran forward. I couldn't recall the creature—the smell though, I almost gagged. My teeth clenched together so hard, I felt something crack, blood spilling into my mouth.

Occasionally, blasts of something would propel me forward and I would trip, falling onto the ground. If it wasn't for the few ghosts I had around me on my side, I knew I would never have made it to the entrance of the tower. On the stairs of the building, I stopped, catching my breath.

Let's go, old man, let's go—no time to rest, I repeated to myself. It was to no avail; *I am just too old, too broken down.* I turned around seeing the carnage of war, my mind slipping from the madness. Shots of black and red memories flying in every direction, screams from the dying, screams from the undead, their songs forcing my brain to close; I gripped the handrail before I fell over.

Kim came, half running, half flying up the staircase towards me. "Run!" she yelled, phasing through me as a large rhino came stampeding my way. "You have got to be—" I shouted as the monster almost took a swipe at me. I was already moving towards the doors, age having shattered the glass a long time ago. I dropped through as the monster missed me with its horns—not with the force of its will, though. I was shot across the lobby, landing hard on the broken tiles below. The bottom lobby shook from the rampage of the beast.

I curled my body tight, expecting to be impaled, when Kim challenged the beast. Little Kim, who I had killed with my bare hands, beautiful Kim, mother of young Joey; her hands glowed with a bright light, and I knew she wasn't going to lose.

Without taking her eyes from the rhino, Kim spoke. "Are we square now?"

I hesitantly got to my feet, my back bruised, feeling the abuse of the beast. "Yeah, we are square. Give him hell," I said, giving my thumbs up as I made my way to the stairwell entrance.

"Count on it," Kim screamed, charging the animal.

I was aching as I walked, my movements slow as I made it to the first steps. I looked up, and it took everything I had not to sit down. I wanted to just lay down and die, but I couldn't. Rows upon rows were above me. I started climbing up the steps as the sounds from the lobby wafted in; they were mixed in with the voices of other ghosts.

Too many to differentiate between who was who. I kept my focus on the steps. I had no idea where I was going, just the idea that *if I was one of those assholes, where would I hole up in a building like this?*

"Right on the top floor—fuck," I said, ignoring the flattened feeling I had on my back and taking the stairs two at a time as I charged them. *I'm coming for you, asshole. I am coming for you, Wilson. I have no more memories of fear; I hope you can say the same thing. Because when I find you, you will know what I mean.*

Chapter 57

I found Benny in a bathroom, shooting him this time. I waited until his ghost appeared, then I killed his ghost, this time allowing his memories in. I needed to know why...

"Get down there now! Fix this shit, Benny!" squeaked Wilson's voice from my radio. I set the radio back on my belt clip as I looked out the windows at the mayhem below. It was madness, pure insanity, and I was trapped in a God damn tower with only one exit.

It was too chaotic outside to leave now; I had no choice but to try and hide. Wilson though I was dumb enough to run out there. I don't know what he honestly expected me to do anyways; he was the one controlling the army.

What made it worse was we had no idea who the hell was attacking; it was like some rogue faction of ghosts had started to attack our much larger force. Which made no sense at all. I mean, what the hell was a damn bus cruising around in the air for?

I turned away from the window, shuffling my left leg across the battered floor. I wandered down one of the better lit hallways, already sweating from the couple of flights of stairs I had gone down . He never did anything besides yell and stare out the window. Playing around with that blade of his. Shivers raced across my body. *That blade scared me—I knew what it meant whenever it came out. Always making me do everything,* I thought.

I would like to see Wilson have gone down all those stairs. My leg twitched like a son of a bitch. "Thanks to that damn Jim..." I growled. Wilson was always telling me what to do, but I fought down the resentment; I remembered the twisted pain I had been in. The painful torture—Wilson would send me back, he said he would. That promise, I knew he would keep.

Just thinking about that prick caused my leg to tremble. I floundered my way to the nearest candle fixture, taking the dwindling wax into my hand, and I started walking. No matter the size and ferocity of this army, Wilson wielded a force made up of every living thing that had lived on this planet.

He had reserves constantly in the air at all times, and not only that, he had an army of regular humans all under his control. It had something to do with that purple dagger he was always playing with; he never let it out of his sight. Wilson said its power was running out, and that was why he needed me so bad.

He sure had a funny way of showing his gratitude, though; he spent half his time getting mad at me. He shouldn't have relied on that girl and that wretched no-good killer Jim. My leg hurt at the thought of his name, crying out in an electrical sensation that had never fully healed.

He'd sat there and blamed my brother and me for making things harder—how were we supposed to know he gave that much of a shit about his kid? We could never have guessed she was going to be that powerful. I only freaked and grabbed her when we wrecked. That crazy coot was mumbling and fussing about seeing some woman on the roads. Yeah, it was that asshole's fault—had he just let us take his daughter and done away with her, none of this would be happening.

Matthew would have had a new body by now, and Wilson would be off our case. Now, I was being smacked around like I was some damn hunting dog or something. *Well, I'm not a damn dog, I am nobody's fucking mutt. I am Benny Cogburn, and my brother Matthew and I were born to raise hell and piss fire, by God.*

I smiled when I said our names, thinking of my brother. It was hard not having him around. I never realized how much I missed his stupidity. It had just been him, me and his fat wife and that little brat.

She was always screaming and being a bad little girl. What I wouldn't give to just skin her hide one more time. That was something which had always made us all happy.

That girl was spoiled and a total whore in training. She had it easy; she complained her daddy was touching her every night. Well, Matthew and my father beat us every night, hit us really good. The nights he came home really drunk...

Vomit started coming up my throat, and I pushed back the acid in my mouth, trying to forget about our daddy. *He was a fag for what he did to us—not us,* I thought as I came towards the end of the hallway.

I paused, hearing running. It was a man's footfalls for sure, secure and confident as they glided up the metal steps. Ghosts started to appear at the end of the hallway, flying towards the next floor as their pressure blew the doors on my floor wide open. I gulped, and my hand shook. I didn't want to be anywhere near that as I took the first door. It was a bathroom, the stench causing me to cover my mouth. Wilson would completely brainwash his followers with that dagger; they would piss and shit themselves if Wilson didn't always remind them they could go. But without power, it was tough for anyone to get the toilet right.

I went to the nearest stall and plumped down on it. The sounds from the battle below sought their way into the uppermost part of the building. I wasn't about to die for Wilson today, or any other day. My brother was now gone and any chance I had at reclaiming my family was gone. *Wilson was losing his power with his knife; I was free. He couldn't hurt me anymore,* I thought. I was scared, though, he would know even in this shit bathroom I was speaking ill of him. I shook my head; *he couldn't do that, could he? I had to get away from Wilson; that was that.*

I am quitting right now. So much time, psycho, best of luck with whatever you're trying to do. I would just have to wait out this battle, or whatever the hell was going on. A few intruders had made it in the building. It wasn't impossible, I suppose, but Wilson would repel them soon enough. Once that was over, I would casually sneak out of here.

I was good at hiding, at not being seen. Coming and going as exactly as I please. My whole life, people had written my brother and me off as being stupid from our accents. Mocked us for our lifestyles; yet here I was, though, alive and well. Most of them had died on this sticking shitstain of a planet, but not me. I was smart; I have always hidden away from the danger, avoided unnecessary conflicts whenever I could. Some people might think it made me a coward; I was anything but that. I was simply a survivor; today was no different from any other time.

I let out a giggle, unable to contain myself in the dim light from my candle as I set on the stall. My giggles masked the sound of the bathroom door opening. I heard it despite my voice, then covering my mouth and dousing the light from the candle. I sucked in my breath along with half of my bottom lip, my heart beating fast.

I listened to the footsteps. Whoever it was, they were moving calmly, sure of themselves, not taking care in any of their steps. Not stalking, instead moving with confidence—it had to be Wilson. I tried peering around the edge of the stall door, hoping to get a better look at who had entered the bathroom. The darkness kept my visibility only to nose length.

The footsteps moved in front of the stall, and a small light came on, placed at floor level. I covered my eyes from the light as the door was pushed open; and there stood James. He looked like hell; he looked like the devil himself, his eyes full of hate and his face strangely calm.

I started to piss myself. I had always been a coward; I had always been afraid my whole life. I didn't want to die inside of a bathroom. "Jim—"

"Goodbye, Benny, take it easy," were the last words I had heard before the click came…

Those were the last memories of Benny. I let that thought sober me as I sent his memories to the rest of my army. “Goodbye, Benny,” I whispered again.

Chapter 58

The air had become electric; a sensation was kissing the back of my neck along with sweat. Outside, and through the building, there was a raging conflict between my men and Wilson's.

Glass shattered; explosions rang out through the day, as a thick rain began to fall in the city. I could hear the soft pounding on the windows over my breathing.

Rob and I had split up; he took a group of six ghosts around the building and was heading to flank Wilson. I went on my own. Rob had found Benny for me; said he was in a bathroom. I had taken care of him, this time without any hesitation. *If only I had done so before,* I thought dryly.

The last door was before me, and I glanced down the long and winding path I had taken all the way to the top. *Don't think about how many stairs it will take to reach the top.* I shook my head and focused on what was in front of me; beyond that door was the man who had killed my family. By his plans, he had ended Rob's life and numerous other friends. *It is time for him to pay.*

I popped the breech on my shotgun. I had used one shot to kill Benny, and it would only take one shot to bring down Wilson. I flicked the breech closed again as I walked through the door. I would like to see that son of a bitch try and take more than one shot.

The hallway light was on; I could hear the chugging of a generator somewhere in the distance. Closed doors were on both sides of the hall; I kept my arm up as I tiptoed, keeping my eyes opened for Wilson.

A door to my right pulled in and I turned, seeing Wilson reaching for my shotgun, his gas mask concealing his face. I had a split second to register it was him as he pulled the gun from my hand and smacked me with the butt of the rifle in my chest.

I lurched backward from the blow, losing my balance as I felt Wilson's leg kicking at my heels. The ceiling above me came into view, its fine white textures now stained in green high above me as I winced in pain. I coughed out my breath to draw more air into my lungs. Wilson loomed over my head, his gas mask darkened since the last time I had seen it.

"Your lungs have had the air knocked out of them; it will take you a moment to catch your breath," Wilson sneered clearly through his mask, with only a hint of his words being muffled. He was used to speaking inside of it.

Through clenched teeth, my voice carried up. "Why the hell do you wear that mask all the time? Should I even ask you that? I barely know you, after all."

Wilson laughed, leaning down towards my face. "I have followed you longer than I should ever have; you weren't worth the twenty years I spent, all wasted on you," he taunted.

"That's cute, you do care about me," I mumbled back in defiance. Wilson remained silent; then his hands shot forward, hoping to land a blow on me. I lifted in the air, both my feet towards his stomach and pushed up, flipping him over.

Wilson was as surprised as I was that it had worked, regaining his footing almost as fast as it took me to stand up. I saw my shotgun thrown a few feet away. I dove for the gun, but I was tackled to the ground as I went for it. I landed hard, my chest feeling like it was about to cave in when Wilson fell on top of me.

My hand reached for the gun, and Wilson punched down on my elbow joint, I cursed him, feeling the bone bruising from the hit. The shotgun slid away, and I rolled with his weight, trying to wriggle my way out from under him. Wilson, in response, brought down both of his fists on my head. I saw stars and my mouth watered from the lack of air in my chest. "Give up, Jim, just stay down," Wilson growled from behind his mask.

I was not a strong man, and it was becoming clearer Wilson could kick my ass in a fair fight. I had to start fighting dirty if I had any chance of winning this. Wilson lacked his weight though, shifting up to get a better angle for another punch.

As he moved, I pushed up with my right arm, spinning my elbow to his face. Wilson blocked it with his shoulder, lowering him closer. I kicked my knees and legs up with all my might and swung my head forth. I felt the soft spot of his nose break in a grinding crunch.

Wilson let go, and I stumbled forward, picking the shotgun up and turning. He clutched his nose, and I could feel the hate radiating from the man without having to look at him. I brought the gun up and attempted to aim; my head was still spinning from all the blows it had taken. I fired the gun, and one of two things happened.

First: my shot ended up being about chest height, due to my arm not swinging up fast enough. I didn't have time to aim properly. Second: When the pellets hit Wilson's chest, a purple light shone out, eclipsing all the light in the hallway as I shielded my eyes from the flare. The light lasted for a moment and was gone just as quickly as it had appeared.

With the light gone, my eyes were out of focus and black dots filled my vision. Wilson recovered first and charged; I dropped the shotgun and pulled my iron pan from my side, as his steel ax struck down on the metal of my pan.

His strength was more than mine, and I fell to my knees bearing his weight. I gritted my teeth and pushed up with all my body; it was no match—I couldn't win with only one hand. Wilson surged forward with his ax, and I dropped my pan to the ground with my right hand still on the handle, uselessly. Wilson's ax gleamed like a golden and blazing sun inside Apollo's hands. The blow would have lopped my head off easily, had I not lost my footing on the broken glass below.

I closed my eyes, and a weird sound flowed around me. It was weird because of what my thought was—it was the sound of water, but we were high above the earth in a tower. I opened my eyes and saw the remaining tatters of the walls around us peel away. The walls themselves began to swell, protruding outwards. The flow increased, and the drywall shook, cracking rocks and plaster onto the molded carpet below.

We both turned to see a tide of blood spilling down the lobby. The blood stained the ceiling and left no room to run. Wilson stopped his onslaught, and we were slammed with the force of the blood as the whole tower shook. I was lifted from my feet, and I was tumbled around the hallway.

I couldn't see anything in front of me except for red; I clenched my eyes shut as the force tried to rip me apart. I felt someone while I bounced around, and I swung with all my might, kicking and punching out. Hands wrapped around my throat, and I lashed out and landed a blow somewhere mid body and the hands let go—presumably Wilson.

Then the lack of oxygen hit as I was slammed into a wall, forcing the blood to spill into me. I was gagging and fighting for air when suddenly, the blood stopped and disappeared. I looked around the hallway; Wilson was bent over as I was, both us trying to catch our breath. His mask had been almost pulled off, and his nose oozed blood from where I had hit it.

"Do you realize what your shot did? Do you have any idea?!" Wilson heaved, throwing himself in a frenzy towards me. We both locked eyes and ran towards each other. The hallway was dry, with no sign of the blood that had almost drowned us. I disregarded that, my focus was on killing the man who had murdered my daughter. Right before my pan struck against his ax, as we swung our weapons, that purple light surged in the hallway again. This time brighter, like a living purple tentacle stretching for blood.

It didn't blind us. Instead, this time it transformed us, made us different. Everything became gray around us, and my body became a million different memories, my hand replaced with the images of a thousand different lives.

Wilson was the same when I looked at him, only the outline of his body showing, and the rest of him memories. I kept swinging my pan and dodging his swings. When our weapons connected, the light would blaze up, and we would both be blinded in a flurry of images.

Wilson managed to land the back end of his ax handle into the side of my cheek. A lump immediately started to form, and I fell back into one of the doors behind me. I braced myself to have my head lopped off, when Wilson tripped forward, and I brought my pan up in time, the clash of metal bringing the pan into my chest. I folded over and rolled to the floor.

Wilson was breathing hard. Though he was stronger and faster than me, I had endurance on my side—hate gave you all the energy you would ever need. We both had returned to normal, the light having gone away.

"You son of a bitch, you destroyed the dagger!" Wilson growled at me.

I spat blood when I opened my mouth to talk. "You helped kill my daughter. I think a broken dagger is the least you can do to make up for it." I spat on the ground again, standing taller. "You were my friend, Wilson! We had known each other for years; you betrayed Holly and I, fed us to the wolves, and for what? To build an army on a planet that has no one left!" I boomed, my chest blowing up in testament to my resolve.

Wilson just stood and cackled loudly until he started coughing. He ripped off his mask, spitting in my direction. "You want to know the truth? The truth is, Jim, I never knew you before; using that dagger, I implanted what I wanted you to know. You knew exactly what I wanted you to know. All I had to do was override my face over a friend you'd had your whole life. You know what else? None of that even matters now! I needed that dagger to fight someone much stronger than you. Feed you to the wolves? I would feed you to every beast of the Earth, if it meant I could be reunited with my family. Get over yourself with your thinking you're the only one who has suffered." Wilson coughed before bolting in my direction; his weapon held high in his hands.

Holly was right; I didn't know this guy. I shouldn't have trusted him. A part of me had known it. I should have believed her; his memories confirmed this much. Wilson swung his ax, and I ducked, stepping forward and tackling him to the ground. On the way down, he beat his elbows into my back. I held on tight until we were both on the floor; I tangled with his arms. I couldn't overpower him, though I could manage to disarm him. I applied enough force, and his ax hit the adjacent wall beside us.

I had spent too much time tracking the ax with my eyes to notice his fist until it hit my eye. My eye almost swelled shut from the impact; it was effective in causing me to roll over. Wilson started kicking me, his blows landing over and over my body. I cried out in pain; I wasn't a hard man—I could endure this, though.

"This has gone on long enough. Just die, already!" Wilson shouted, stomping on my ribs. I reached up with my hand, the strength fading from my body. I couldn't give up now, though; I had to do this for Holly. I rolled onto my stomach when I felt Wilson had stopped kicking me. I crawled with one limb in front of the other, trying to gain distance.

"Go to hell!"

Wilson stepped towards me, leaning in ready to pounce, "Yeah James—we can't go to hell if we are already there!" he snarled.

I heard the swish of Wilson's ax, then the sickening sound of my left arm being cut. Pure agony came from my mouth as I pulled my severed arm away from the sharp blade. The cut had been done at an angle, the bone bristling white under the fountain of blood that spewed from my arm. Wilson lifted his ax up; I was able to roll away over the soggy carpet of the hallway before the next blow, as the ax gleamed inches away from my head.

I curled against the glass windows of the hall; my screaming only matched by my beating heart. *I am going to die,* I realized as I looked up at Wilson towering over me. He wasn't smiling like he enjoyed what he was doing. Rather, he just looked tired, and he seemed like a man who just wanted all this to be over. "I don't want to kill you, Jim—you only wanted to save your daughter… I can—I can understand that. Call off your ghosts below; only I have the power to return our families back to us," Wilson offered, extending his right hand towards me.

I looked at his hand; his hand was clean, but I knew it had a history of blood. I knew those hands had plunged into the deepest pits of waters I could only imagine. Now, he was telling me he understood what it was to have lost everyone you could ever love. I had no idea who this man was. I was through with taking the hands of killers.

That is something I couldn't fathom. I wanted Holly back with all my heart and soul, and as I looked at Wilson, I realized the difference between the two of us at that moment. He was truly a man who would do anything to be with the ones he loved. Wilson had turned himself into a monster; he was no longer a man. I was becoming exactly like him—we both were shades of what men should be.

I was tempted to take his hand. I longed to be healed, to stop hurting. I wasn't about to sell my daughter down the river—not so quickly. I smacked his hand away instead of taking it. I looked down at the ground; I looked down at the ground, and I remembered.

"Let me tell you a story you think you know. When I was a young man, I had a wife and a beautiful daughter. My wife—she was my bird in the sky, she was everything I would ever need, and I only wanted to fly with her forever. Together we had a home, just the three of us. Then suddenly, both my babies were taken. My daughter, she was pulchritudinous in every sense of the word, and still wonderful in her spirit. Like a beacon, she shone. As light, she shined, until her fire was dossed, never to glow again." My voice broke, and I started to cry in the one eye I could open.

"And when she died, all the warmth went with her. I thought the light was gone forever from my life. I had to live with that eating away my every step, my every fiber of my heart. I watched my wife, fall to her death. My home, my love, plummet to the ground like a fallen star. You know what that is like, watching something so amazing—just end, taken away from your life!" blood poured out of my lips, my eye locked on Wilson, he would pay

"No, no words can describe her—she was my home, my reason to walk in the sun. Both of them, gone! I went on, though—life continues, it goes on even if you don't want anything remotely resembling this disgusting thing called existence. This virus—a curse given to me. A curse you will soon know the horror of, I will tattoo it into your corpse! You stole the light from my life, Wilson. You stole the light, took it, and murdered it! To lose both the loves of your life as if they were candles in a sandstorm! For that, I will kill you! I will slay you; I will end you. Even if it's the last thing I can ever do! Their names will be engraved into your soul and I will eat you before this is over, take away everything you've ever loved!" I shouted.

Wilson sighed. "You put up a surprisingly good fight, Jim. But for someone like you, who isn't willing to sacrifice everything they have for their loved ones, you can never win. My pain is much greater; yours isn't enough."

Wilson readied his ax, tilting it back, I looked at the blade—it was huge and would most likely kill me quick. I looked down, seeing the rope, its threads connecting me to every single ghost in my army.

I reacted with a blaze, sending every ounce of my will into the nearest ghosts that could come to me. And they did—six came teleporting through the window.

Wilson jumped back, and my ghosts attacked, their fury guided by my thoughts. I started to stand up again, still clutching my arm to my chest. I was bleeding out; I wouldn't have much more time before I would collapse. In fact, my eyes were already closing as I looked up, seeing Wilson fighting the ghosts. He was winning. I gave a mental shout out to Rob, and I called his name as I started to fade.

Rob appeared in front of me. Even as a ghost, he looked drained—worse than I probably did. "Shit, Jim—you're about to bleed out, buddy. Don't worry; I will find you some help." Rob panicked, turning his head towards Wilson.

Speaking low, with my voice already one foot in the grave, I reached for Rob. I fumbled my words, trying to touch him.

"What, Jim? What are you trying to say—"

Rob never got to finish his words. He never had an opportunity to help his friend. Wilson had stated I didn't have enough pain to save my loved ones, that I did not have what it took to do whatever was needed. He was wrong; I lifted myself up with my wounded arm and stuck my hand into Rob's chest.

Rob reacted instantly, going quiet for the first time. I had ever seen him like that. I gave him my memories of earlier that day, just to get him under my control. A blue line connected me to Rob; I absorbed his memories, and I wasn't done even by a long shot. My vision was getting black; I was going to pass out soon, and it would all be over then. I thought of Holly—my daughter was my strength. She was my strongest memory. *To correct what had happened to Holly, I would have to sacrifice everything I knew about Holly; this is my damnation,* I thought, *I love you Holly—I am so sorry I couldn't save you.*

I opened my mind and poured everything I had into Rob. Every smile, every laugh, and every bit I had about Holly. The good, the bad, and everything in between; I gave up all the memories in my head, except the ones of that day, the day she died.

When it was finished, I felt nothing; I knew nothing except I was bleeding and needed to heal my arm. I had no idea of a life beyond where I was. No concept of anything more—I was a caveman, only concerned with my next meal; nothing more.

I could feel the power from Rob; I could feel the surge of energy running through him, burning like a sun. I gave him one command; I told him to save me. Rob disappeared, like smoke from a fire; my injured arm started to tingle. Then, the blood stopped pouring out. I looked down; it was like seeing a see-through cloth was holding back all the fluid on the inside of my skin. Some force that I couldn't see was keeping me alive. I still felt drained; all my body wanted to do was to rest for a thousand years. But I wasn't going to bleed out just yet.

Hesitantly, and without confidence, I made it up on my elbows. In the distance, I could see Wilson slaying the last ghost, its form bursting into black shades of memory. Wilson turned back explicitly towards me, his posture tense; he was without fear.

I extended my hand in his direction, silently cursing him. Wilson was almost unstoppable; I reached out to all the ghosts that I had left. My army was gaining traction in the battle. They were pushing back Wilson's larger force. Extending my senses, I could feel an enormous energy stored in my hand, more than what was needed to keep my blood in. I pumped all that energy down the blue rope jolting out of my chest, letting it flow from my body like a faucet. I gave one simple command: *Stop this monster; bring down this tower.*

Moments later, the whole building shook, shattered, convulsed, until a crack came from below. The vibrations from the building tearing reached the top of the tower, and I was trying to stand on floating ice-lake, my legs shaking.

Wilson turned to me, this time with fear in his eyes and a knowing of what I had just done. One more titanic shatter ripped through the building, Wilson and I fell forward towards the glass, shattering it easily as the building started its plummet to the earth.

With my arms spread wide, I was floating out in the middle of the sky. Wind rushed into my face, and it was hard to keep my eyes open. I was gliding over a massive battle below, every kind of beast fighting tooth and claw, every kind of man doing the same. I sent another command to any ghosts listening and suddenly I was lifted, my fall guided to the bordering building. I smacked hard through glass, onto crumbling floors.

I cast my gaze up to see the slow fall of a building toppling before me. It was like watching the collapse of a steel giant; somehow graceful, like a titan being kicked off of Mount Olympus.

My ears popped from the noise when all that metal hit the ground below, completely dwarfing the carnage in the streets; I closed my eyes as a curtain of dust and debris ascended beyond the building I was in.

I waited to open my eyes until I could hear something again. I blinked, thinking there was something around me, only to realize it was just air coming back into my head. The very air a living entity of dust and debris choking out life. A volcano made by man, a building no more.

I was covered in dust, my clothes and skin copper brown. I started coughing, coughing a lot. Blood came out, and pieces of broken teeth along with the blood. That building collapsing had cost me. The energy I had felt before I ordered the building to come down was now gone. I looked around the empty floor I was on—ruins at this point. The floor was completely bare, save for the construction poles exposed and unfinished, in a building that was nowhere near complete. I was shocked the framework hadn't come down when the other tower gave way.

I kept scanning the room; I spotted Wilson on a wall nearby. A jagged piece of metal punctured his shoulder, and he had multiple small lacerations crossing over his forehead. The man was still standing; he was somehow still alive. I had dropped a building on him, and he was standing against a wall.

"I bet you think you were the only one who figured out how to get your ghosts to be able to touch objects? That was... the dumbest shit

I've ever seen, bringing down a building on the both of us," Wilson swore.

Beyond just today, I had no memories of who he was. I just knew his name was Wilson because his name had been spoken. I knew he had killed someone crucial to me. It was everything else that was torn and gone from me; I had no recollection of anything. For all I knew, today was the first day of my life; I had been born into a world of cruelty and violence. *Suits me just fine,* I thought. *I had been born into a world of fire and ash. I was incarnation of fire.* I dragged my legs, slouching my body up, facing my adversary. We both were bleeding, we both hated each other, and we both were on the verge of dying.

"What, you think this changes anything? You think you have won! I will not lose to you! You, who have lost nowhere as much as I have for your loved ones; I will kill you!" Wilson screamed, walking in small steps towards me. He was wounded, he was bleeding.

I was walking with pain. Somewhere, glass was sticking into my legs. I tasted only blood in my mouth as I met Wilson. Wilson's right arm hung uselessly at his side, and with his left, he threw a wide punch. I couldn't move my legs fast enough to dodge. Instead, I took the hit directly into my already smashed eye. My head jerked to the left; the blow, though, was without enough power to bring me to the ground.

I swung my left arm towards Wilson's face; stumped, bloody, and degraded beyond repair. I fought with my broken arm. I had nothing to lose; I had nothing to hold me back. My only memories of the wounded man before me were of hatred. Pure, unbiased hatred, born unto me from someone I didn't know. Wilson cocked back another fist when I got in close. I feigned a fake punch with my left, and Wilson tracked my clumsy punch, easily dodging. He didn't see my ruined arm though, its bone sharp edges gleaming the blood of a madman. Using all my hate and anger, my severed arm tore into the bubble of his eyeball, the bone from my arm going deep into his eye socket.

Wilson let out a shriek of pain. He was dying now, like a top apex predator who had managed to get wounded by the much weaker prey. Confused as to what had happened, the top player dying to someone so beneath them, so pitiful and groveling in its last moments. Still enough to take down the noble and superior creature, despite the imbalance.

His blood sprayed onto my face, painting the dust on my hand crimson, leaving me caked in earth and blood. I yanked out my bone stub and took Wilson's eye with me. Wilson screamed, his voice trembling; he was already dying. Part of his brain was still wanting to fight, still believing in that victory which had died first. Wilson slid to the ground, falling into the wall behind him, back first.

Wilson was breathing heavy, his voice weakening. "Barbara...Rachel...Jackson... we all go to the grave in the end." Wilson sighed, looking at something very far away. I had no idea who he was talking about, but he continued.

"I witnessed the monsters of the stars, worlds on fire—all gone like sand in a storm. I loved them; I loved them, Jim. You... I see now that you loved yours, I'm—" Wilson said, then going quiet in that building, slumped before me, his one eye still looking at me as his breathing became still.

I knew at that moment he was dead. The only other person I knew in this entire world. The only person I knew, disappeared in the ashes of our war. Like snow in summer. Like the trails of fire bleeding into the night sky.

Chapter 59

I coughed, falling forward onto Wilson's lifeless husk, my hand above his head. A strange energy played before me, and I learned the story of Wilson...

"Staff Sergeant Douglas E. Wilson," buzzed a voice over the intercom as I awaited the multitude of uncomfortable and desperate people inside the lonely hallway of an even more alienated building. That's what it felt like, waiting on the aid of someone else. Knowing full well, that even with the help of a stranger over an intercom there was an excellent chance that you would still die in the end anyway.

In a lot of ways, lines were the best example of human life. You spent lots of time every day waiting for something. A chance to deposit hard-earned money into a greedy bank or become entangled in lines of traffic, all the while rushing to get to your destination, only to be stuck behind someone slow at the office microwave. All these events were happening throughout your day, taking up the time you had left and extracting it from your body, leaving you gasping like a fish soon to be flayed, wondering what happened to the seventy to eighty years of your life which passed by in the end. *And what do you do to change it? Nothing, nothing at all. Why would you? The teller says "Next in line," the traffic light says green. If you wait long enough, you will get your turn. And that's what hallways are, a chance promise that at the end of a long wait something must be waiting for you for your good behavior.*

What people got wrong about lines, though, is that you chose to be in them in the first place. You decided to murder your own life, one long awkward moment after another, frivolously ticking away the minutes until you become the raw materials for a carpet rope at a rundown movie theater, hundreds of years later.

I hated lines, and I especially hated this one. When my name was called, my hate was forgotten. I had waited long enough; it was my time to be served. As I made my way through the sea of people packed into the long confines of the hallway, I kept my eyes on the pair of military police at the end of the hall.

I glanced at the people around me, their eyes envious behind masks of sorrow and fear. *We are cattle; we are the desperate many tucked up in a hallway awaiting the arrival of a savior in the form plastic and rubber respirators.* I was one of them, but I was one of the lucky few who would survive the coming storm.

I did all of this for my family. *We were going to make it through this now. Ignore the envious faces, just keep going forward.* I told myself that—something I'd learned from my time in the military. *No matter how desperate the situation, just keep going forward.*

I approached the guards, straightening up my uniform. A lot of good it did me. Sleeping in the same clothes for going on three days now was making them the nightmare of any dry-cleaning agency. *The guards are young, very young,* I thought, *that was a common thing to see on base. A nineteen or twenty-something, covered in sweat from the tension of their bosses and the anxiety seeping off those people fighting desperately to remain calm before their sanities broke.*

"Douglas E. Wilson?" asked the closest guard to me, his eyesight barely coming over the edge of his clipboard.

I cleared my throat, trying to keep my relief from showing quite as much. "That's me." My voice trembled with fear, trying to keep the hopelessness from carrying through. *Just get through this, get what you need for your family and go.*

The guard gestured to the opposing guard, and the door obscuring another hallway opened up.

"Aren't you going to check my ID?" I asked, glancing between the two. The guard holding open the door shrugged his shoulders, and the other went back to glancing at his clipboard, pretending that I wasn't still in front of the two of them.

I coughed, moving past the two into the next hallway. *Just get what you need for your family and move forward, man,* I thought, worrying about my ease of access. Things just weren't that easy when it came to going anywhere on base. Normally, you always had to show an ID. Always going through another fence or past two guards hating their lives, still doing their duty if for no other reason than just being there.

I was worried. Worried I wouldn't get what I needed before it was too late. The news I had heard this morning while my wife and I furiously packed our lives away into two tiny suitcases was the yellow storm still had days before getting to our area. We had time; I kept reminding myself. Someone had to be working on the situation; humanity wouldn't die off, choking and burning alive to yellow particles floating around in the air.

I rounded a corner of the hallway and came to an open loading dock area, the noise level causing my heart to panic at the realization that this was the true waiting area. In the dampness of the warehouse, the room was thundering with angry voices and wafts of gasoline, as vehicles fired up with the clear indication of getting as far away from that place as possible.

Not wasting any more time, I took off into the crowd of people, pushing aside disgruntled humans on the verge of becoming an angry mob. I made it to the front of the loading dock; five soldiers stacked boxes full of supplies into the back of a tailgate on a massive truck, whose driver I could see thumbing the wheel nervously. They were about to leave.

Glancing around at the crowd around me, I picked up a couple of things. Despite that a few of the angry individuals in the warehouse wore the same uniform as me, they didn't have guns. We were a mixture of civilians and military types. At this point though, we had all become civilians. No other name for us at this stage, not when we were at the mercy of people with guns.

Fear is an emotion I never dealt with growing up; not that I hadn't ever been afraid, but rather that I had never been deterred by fear. I never let fear sink its claws into me. I wasn't going to today. I approached the nearest guard by the loading dock, making sure to position my body a safe distance, to come off as non-threatening as possible. Things were about to get worse—I sensed it in the air.

"Excuse me, ma'am—" I started.

"Wait in line like everyone else, sir," barked the solider as she turned away, talking feverishly into her headset. After a brief exchange of dialogue with whoever was on the receiving end, she twirled two of her fingers in the air at the loading dock crew. They all started hustling the boxes full of supplies.

Supplies that I knew had my family's gas masks in them. I had been promised four for my family. I would be damned if I didn't get my hands on them. The woman speaking into her headset turned back and addressed the crowd of now dismayed and horrified group. They knew too late that they had been lied to as well. Just like I had been—we weren't getting the supplies we'd been promised.

"Listen up, all of you. Return to your homes. There will be no more rations given out today," yelled the woman guard into her speakerphone. Glancing at her rank, she was the same as me. Just another devil dog forced to do as she was told.

The crowd surged forward, in a panic of bodies and voices reaching out for the woman. "This is a bunch of bullshit!" screamed someone from inside of the group. The loaders on the dock stopped what they were doing, reaching for their rifles as the crowd got closer to the truck full of supplies.

At any moment, someone was going to do something stupid, someone was going to do something that would strike the whole place off like matches to firecrackers. I just had to be the one that started it; it was the only way to ensure that my family would be safe.

Years of service, just to be fucked in the end, I thought, as I skidded around the crowd, moving towards the tail-bed of the truck. In a green container sat the familiar shape of the gas mask carriers. I couldn't forget. It had been my people who had helped assemble them and put them together. A lot of us were in this room now, putting in all that work to not even receive our own masks in the end.

When I was within five feet of the box, I spotted the nearest soldier amongst the growing crowd. He was young, younger than the guards at the front. *Forgive me for what I am about to do,* I thought as I shoved hard into the man nearest the guard and me.

The force was enough to propel the man into the guard, causing both to fall in a heap of bodies and confusion. It provided me what I needed most, though, a chance to go for the box. I shoved the remaining people out of my way, rushing towards the container.

The other guards didn't stay still, though. As soon as their comrade fell, they all reacted. The whole crowd froze just for a moment before the perfect catalyst for a perfect storm was triggered.

"Get back now!" shouted the female guard, all pretense of restraint gone and her gun raised along with three other guards coming around the truck, rifles in hand. One was heading in the direction of the pileup; my distraction was running out. I had to get the place more chaotic, and I was going to lose sleep over this for a long time. *But rest versus, losing my family—I would rather become an insomniac.*

I cupped my mouth and shouted, "He's got a gun!"

The guard heading in our direction turned, and sure enough as I expected, he fired at the first person standing in the crowd. Fear was something I did not let control me, not ever, not in the slightest. I know how it worked its way into people, a worm that spread until it stretched to the deepest and foulest parts of the human soul.

The crowd gasped, and then the tide came in, and the people rushed the people with guns. I closed my eyes and ignored the screams over the shouts as I slid to the box, I couldn't see what I had done, but I had to save my family. This was all for them as I took hold of the green box and jumped off the dock. My feet landed hard on the road below, and I dared a glance back.

A rifle hung loosely in the passenger seat of the truck. Someone had forgotten it in the commotion. I went for it, sparing precious seconds. I would need the defense—this world was about to descend into madness. I snatched the rifle, setting down the box that was hopefully full of gas masks, and threw the rifle over my shoulder, just in time for one of the soldiers to grab hold of my arm.

"What the fuck—" he screamed, and I snapped my head back, crushing his nose, spraying blood on the back of my head as I turned. The young man held his hands to his nose, and I kicked forward with all my strength into his face. I heard a crunch again; I had probably just killed that poor young man. *For your family.*

I swept around, tucking the box into my side, and started to run as fast as I could. Not fast enough though. The guards had retreated from the wave of the mob. "Hey!" they shouted over the noise of the warehouse as I pumped my legs fast, trying my best to round the corner of the warehouse and hopefully take the mad dash back to my car. Shots rang overhead, and I ducked. Sweat stung my eyes as my mouth fought for air.

More shots scattered around me; I hoped their ammo was running low. I had yards to go still, and my luck was going to run out. And it did—I came to the corner of the warehouse to find that the entire parking lot in front of the building was becoming a battleground. Small arms fire erupted at every angle; bodies splayed out on the ground bleeding red into the black pavement, creating a rising tide of brown, in the hot summer day. I gulped, searching for my car as I took cover behind the nearest vehicle.

Where did you park man? Where did you park? I thought. I scanned for my blue Honda; it was somewhere in this parking lot, I was sure of it. In the distance I could see more soldiers piling into the parking lot, and some of the civilians had guns. Things were about to get ugly as more firing started from somewhere.

I tucked the box under one arm, secure in the weight as I pulled my clicker from my pocket. It was the best plan I had, as I kept my head low and began my journey through the smoke and blood towards my car. I dodged broken rubble and debris, stepped over the corpses of the fallen, and still was getting no closer to locating my car. When you're in a firefight, time doesn't slow down. It's not something that suddenly causes a river to flow backward. No, it is rather that when you find yourself in a firefight, the world collides, splashes like mud dumped into the water.

Thoughts become reactive, and the world dissolves all around you, forcing what kept you together to become a question of death or survival. Survival—that was something I understood all too well, as I rolled out from under a car I had been using for protection. Just like my other times in war, the only thing going to get me through was what I was fighting for; I knew this as I ran into the dissolving day.

I was fighting for my family; enough said, I told myself as I dashed until my lungs filled with the black smoke all around me. I coughed, feeling trapped in the endless sea of cars all around me.

"M4s make a surprisingly smooth hole. Sure is a good fucking rifle," gagged an old man, soaking in his uniform. Through the mess of his white hair, I could see the build of a hard man, the kind where someone had spent much of their life fighting. I glanced down at the old man. His hands were to his chest, and he had only moments to live. His body was propped up by a red Lexus.

"I'm sorry, old man," I muttered, risking to stand at my full height to find my car. I was starting to panic, my natural shell breaking. I had witnessed a lot in my life, things that most men would only hear about from old veterans sitting in front of a grocery store on Memorial Day. But this—this was total war. A complete breakdown of the world.

The old man spoke again, this time taking hold of my pants leg that had become tattered to pieces during my flight from the warehouse. I could see blood on my leg; it could have been mine, though I didn't have the luxury of seeing if it was. "Young man, listen to me. The holes are round," he muttered as the light in his eyes twinkled out, slowly rolling back into the depths of nothingness. I almost kicked him in reaction when I noticed car keys in his hand. I dared a chance glance at the keys; they looked like the electronic type.

I pulled them from the old man's hands gently; *he didn't deserve to go in such a way,* I thought. As I clicked the auto-lock open on the Lexus, I moved to get into the car quickly. I prayed that no one had heard the chime of the doors being unlocked in the mayhem around me.

In the distance, as I crawled into the driver's seat, I could see a tank shelling into a cluster of parked vehicles with a small group of people firing back. *Fools—rifles couldn't do anything to the armor of tanks. You were better off shooting your friend and hoping that they slowed down the enemy fast enough for you to get away in that kind of situation.*

I set the box containing the gas masks on the passenger seat, buckling in the robust container. I breathed in deep as I started to pull out; I was getting closer to saving my family. Just a little bit more to go. I gunned it out of the parking lot, speeding past the wreckage around. Cars twisted and folded, looking like crushed coke cans as I flew out of the base gates.

Outside, people fled in terror and as the night sky became lit up with the flames of the dead. I prayed. Prayer seemed like a waste of my time; usually, I was by no means a religious man. I didn't plan to become one. But honestly, no matter what you believe, when people are being blown away by the very government that swore to protect them, riddled with bullets and adding to the flow of an almost endless sea of blood, what do you do? You pray—nothing scientific about it, it's the logical response to fucked-up situations, like peeing your pants during horror movies. I prayed to no one in particular—I mean my thoughts were just a comfort thing, not a callout for a conversation with a deity. I wasn't losing my mind, after all. No one answers prayers.

This horror was real, this was visceral, and if I was unlucky, my entire family could die without these precious masks. I punched down harder on the accelerator at that thought; *I am coming, babies.* With the Lexus red-lining most of the way, I reached my home. *My neighborhood was a nice one, square houses and a sea of green preserved grass. Trees, all in perfect harmony, same species, the same flare of different colors during the start of fall. A modest suburban neighborhood,* I thought as I sped along, passing the last few blocks before my home.

The area was empty. Even as a yellow snow blanketed the world around me in layers, I could see no footprints, no signs that anyone had been through there in a while, save for the tire marks. Marks that were crushed deep into the yellow snow. I panicked again, my heart praying once more that the marks were probably from another family that had been led into staying longer by their boss, too stupid to ignore all the signs that they should have been on the road sooner. Not waiting around for aid that would never have come. I was a fool for talking my wife into staying here. I'd honestly believed that if I did my duty for work, my family would be helped.

Who was I kidding? The guards protecting the masks had probably been about to run off with the masks themselves, had I had not pushed that man. At the thought of his death because of my intervention, my heart sank. I had killed a man, a man who was probably there in that warehouse trying to get some gas masks for his own family.

I shook that thought away as I continued to follow the marks edged into the road. The trail was leading closer to my house, and my gut started to twist into knots. *Don't lose your mind just yet, man, that could easily be tire tracks leaving the neighborhood as easily as tracks leading into them,* I thought.

I made the last left leading to my home, hoping that my wife had our kids ready to go. *The sooner we hit the road, the better it would be,* I thought. The drive from the base had taken hours of rerouting and backtracking with the traffic caused by the fighting. The sun had come out, turning the already yellowed ground into a glowing sheet of gold.

I yanked the brake on the car when I neared my driveway. Outside was one of the trucks from the warehouse, coated in yellow now, but I still could see the green and brown army-coated paint.

It was the guards from earlier; they had somehow found my house. How, though? How had they found it? I started to feel my uniform pockets down, until I noticed the holes on me. My clothes were in ruin. More specifically, my pants were almost entirely shredded through in some parts, especially around my back pockets. My wallet was gone, most likely fallen out when I had slid off the loading dock.

My hands gripped the steering wheel—a useless gesture. I could no more tear the metal free than I could undo my mistake in being so careless. *It was worth a try, though*; I thought as I tightened my hold and gunned my car down the remaining distance until I spotted someone coming out of the truck. It was the woman with the headset; she panicked when she saw me coming.

She turned, reaching for something in the truck's cab. That was a mistake, as I mounted the curb and leaned back in the seat just as soon as the Lexus made an impact with the thick metal door of the truck. Blood sprayed the now-broken glass of the windshield, and I was rocked hard into the back of the seat and then shot forward as my head slammed into the airbag.

I was dazed momentarily, before shaking my head and reaching for the rifle in the seat next to me. The box had landed in the foot area of the passenger seat, but otherwise looked okay. I breathed in, trying to pool my nerves back in after the crash.

No time, I thought, *no time to waste. There could be dozens of them inside my home at this very moment. And I had no idea what was happening to my family.* I spat the blood out of my mouth and wiped my nose with the back of my hand as my legs came shaking, one step out of a time, out of the vehicle.

The woman with the headset was in half, part of her body twisted onto the front of the car and the rest of her more than likely gone under the truck. I paused, catching my breath so I wouldn't vomit. *Don't think about what you did to her. There is nothing good about them being at your house right now.*

I slung my rifle and crouched, moving forward fast to the entrance of my house. Outside, tarps and boards were scattered haphazardly around my yard. Before I was called back into work, I had meant to finish sealing off the house in case of looters while we were gone. *It's just stuff anyways,* I thought, and after what I had just done to that woman and that man today, I imagined that I would never be able to come back into this house ever again. *So be it.*

With the rifle firm to the inside of my shoulder, I went to the door. The doorknob wasn't broken, and I heard nothing. *That is odd; the guards must have tricked my wife into letting them into the house, they're waiting for me behind the door,* my gut instinct told me.

Unsure about whether the door was locked or not, I drew back my leg. I've kicked open doors before on my deployments; it's not an easy thing to do. It's not about strength; it's about placement and the confidence of your strike. Slack just a little on your kick, and you could give away your entire team's entrance or have too short a force behind your blow—and congratulations, you've just shattered something in your knee in the middle of combat.

I breathed deep, aiming my kick at the knob, and pushed forward with all my might. I had weight and strength on my side as the red door to my house flew open and I ran through before the door could hit the inside wall.

In the living room behind the couch was one guard, raising his rifle above his head. I charged my gun and shot the man, pulling the trigger three times, taking him square in the chest. He fell, and I moved on as his body slumped to the ground. I swept my rifle from side to side scanning as I entered deeper into my house. Heading down the hallway leading to our dining room, with my gun tucked in my shoulder.

I came through the threshold of our eating area, when a black-gloved hand shot down, knocking my gun out of my hands. I turned as a fist came barreling into the side of my face, knocking me into the wall.

A young dark-skinned male breathed heavy as he charged forward to finish his onslaught. Seeing his fire reminded me of myself at that age. Always willing to get into scraps, always thinking that I could beat anyone once I had them on the ground. That was the way fighting worked in the dangerous neighborhoods I grew up in as a kid. Being a black kid where I was from had been rough—it did teach me a lot though; namely that when you're about to get your ass kicked, be prepared for anything.

The young guard reached forward, thinking that he could overpower me. I pulled his arm into me, tucking my legs over his shoulders and let gravity do the rest as my weight came down upon him. *I learned that from the military,* I thought. My right hand came free and took hold of the knocked-over flowerpot that was sitting in our living room. I lifted the clay pot up and smashed the vase against the head of my attacker.

I'd learned that from all the fights I had as a kid. The guard stopped moving, and I stood up, taking the back of my boot, slamming my heel into his neck repeatedly until I was sure that he was dead. *That was a horrible thing to do anyone—just another person to think about later,* I figured.

I found my rifle on the other side of the room, as I tried to listen to the sounds of my breath. Nothing was making a sound; *another trap was trying to be set,* I thought. I just had to out-think the invaders inside my home. Think how they would take out someone like me. *The answer was simple—stay near my family,* I thought. Most likely they were in my kitchen. It had a back door and could provide a quick getaway.

I coughed, spitting more blood out as small droplets of crimson mixed with the yellow dust on the ground formed orange clumps of blood in the sand. I coughed again, wishing I had on my mask. That dust was going to start killing me. What little amount I had gotten on me was already burning my skin. According to the news, the dust was acidic, able to burn through anything given enough time. Through the kicked-in front door of my house, dust was coming through, slowly burning the wooden floors and plastered walls.

I had to act quick, and get my family their masks before something bad happened to them. Slowly I inched my way out of the dining room, one foot in front of the other, until I came back to the living room. I just had to check the kitchen and then head upstairs; hopefully, there weren't too many more of the guards.

Back in the living room was one of the guards, weapon held up ready to fire, but he wasn't aiming. "What the fuck—" the young man yelled from across the room to me.

I shot six times, taking him in the chest until he crumpled to the ground. *First mistake, kid, you should have just shot me when you had the chance.* I let go of my breath and entered the living room again; holes were in the wall behind the dead guard. Holes that were round and looked like they had been made by my gun. I recalled then that when I had shot the first guard behind the couch, some shots had gone wide. I popped my clip; it was empty. In my panic, I had fired more than I thought.

Oh no, no, hopefully they're upstairs. I ran into the archway leading from my living room into the kitchen, opposite the way from the hallway, and came to the horror. My family had been tied against the kitchen cabinet walls.

The words of that old man with the Lexus played in my head: "M4s leave smooth holes," he had told me. I could see that now as I looked at the bodies of my children, my wife included. I dropped the rifle to the ground. One of the rounds had blown out the window to the kitchen, and my skin burned from the dust.

I collapsed into the dust as their blood pooled towards me, a creeping hand only inches away from pulling me into oblivion, a nothingness without my family. *This is how I lost my family,* I thought, *I have killed them.*

At some point I went back out to the car and took the gas masks out of the box, ignoring the charred and twisted form of the woman I had killed. I came back in and stood looking at my family, forever frozen in their state. My eyes did not leave their bodies, even though the breath had left their lifeless forms and death had become their new niche; entombed forever in decaying flesh. My heart thumped in my chest, beating faster and faster. So quick, in fact, that my lungs were struggling to keep up; like my heart was always winning this unseen race against my breath.

I pulled my family deeper into my embrace, trying to will the life back into them—it was fruitless. My mask prevented me from laying a last kiss, that a man deserves, on his family. No poem or amount of wishing upon any light would grant me my desire.

As the death clouds above me glistened, a shadow against the backdrop of the now yellowing sky above, the very air was instant death that would cause me to drown in my blood as my body would fight for oxygen. Because of that, my mask had to remain on. I just didn't know it would be so hard to see them dead. My family had died without any breaths and their bodies were shamefully covered in their blood and shit.

My mask was sealed tight, and the pressure remained, even as my tears clouded my lenses. I released my wife and children from my arms; I had to leave the place of death that my family had been lost in, gone forever. *If I had only gotten here sooner, they would still be alive.*

I was still alive; and it would only remain that way if I got to shelter fast. I looked around me at the barren wasteland that was now my only friend. For as far as I could see, the world was poisoned and even the soil was starting to crumble from the bereavement in the sky. I remembered weeks before the incident, I had convinced my wife that we had to leave the shelter of our home to survive the overuse of fossil fuels. Whatever the case, a sickness that was either man-made or sprung from the bosom of Mother Earth had managed to wipe us all out.

I was alive to witness the end of days, something that should only exist in the realms of a sick man's imagination. I looked back down at my wife and two kids, seeing the flesh of their crumpled forms slowly being eaten, soon to be nothing more than a puddle of forgotten dirt on this dying earth.

My exposed skin was starting to burn as I stood there.

I quickly bent over and stripped my family naked, taking their clothes into my hands. I allowed myself one last look, one last look that was almost enough to make me stay with them there. To just remove my mask and let death take me.

For them, I told myself as I wrapped their clothes around every piece of my skin. Their clothing slightly burned as it touched my skin, but I ignored my pain. It was nothing compared to what they had gone through. Out in a shed behind our home, I pulled a gallon of gasoline out. I poured the full contents over me as the fumes slowly caused me to gag. The news said gas was great at keeping off the dust. Also great at lighting me up as a dry tree in a heat storm.

When I was ready, and my skin no longer burned, I picked the direction that I thought was north. Not that the north had anything else, according to the T.V.—this yellow devil was everywhere, and you could not escape its terror. I figured the north would be the last place bandits would think to look. You would think that a horrific apocalypse of mustard-colored clouds would stave off the worst of mankind.

My walk was long and would last for many hours, and all the while, the landscape never changed. The ground was still void of life and I passed thousands of dead families, animals; even the bugs were not spared from the wrath, as I trudged onwards.

Now and then, I would stop to replace the clothes on me that were starting to melt through, pouring more gas whenever I could. I would keep my mask as protected as I could, feeling the rubber heating against my face. After a day of walking, my legs finally collapsed. My throat was burning, and the stalled air brought on by the filter of my mask wasn't enough anymore. I dropped in the dirt.

I considered taking the mask off again, to join my family and let this yellow hell above me consume me. Flashes of their demise circled inside my head like some predator. Everything was covered in what looked like yellow snow, and off in the distance, I could see the outlines of a fierce lightning storm. I felt as the mud shake beneath me as if to cry out in pain. The whole world was baking in an endless sun with no night, as far back as I could remember. It was too hot for rain, too painful for tears. I put my head to the ground. First came my shoulders and my back. I was slowly falling into the ground, trying to find an ounce of comfort in the dirt.

When I awoke, my body was covered in yellow, the clothes that I was wearing almost burned through in many spots. My skin felt blistered and burned beyond repair. Squinting my eyes in the golden haze, I saw something moving in the distance; at first, my mind created forms of an angelical being coming down from its lofty throne to save us sinners from our doom.

But as the weakness cleared from my mind, my senses were able to make out the form of a lone man. A tall figure was walking, his shoulders held high, a chest stuck out as only a person of confidence could radiate.

I called out in vain, my voice muffled by my mask, unable to reach the man. I could see that he was not walking, as I was, without a purpose, but he was going somewhere. Staying alive was the only thing that my body could muster the energy for. Grudgingly, I picked myself up from the ground and followed the strange man in the yellow haze. *If he knew where he was going, I should support him*—my brain held onto that thought.

The man never stopped as he fled across the wasteland, I did not stop as I followed my footfalls, sending puffs of yellow poison in my wake. The distance that the man traveled felt almost like another day. Some force of nature greater ensured the man was carrying this lone outlander through the thickening haze that was growing like flames in the wind.

Past the point of no return, I pushed my body, the image of my family replaying like the melody of a tortured song. I felt my bladder empty, and I was thankful for the coolness it provided on my aching body. Anyway, the smell was better than the sweat inside the mask.

And on I followed the man, the whole time, watching as his strength remained high somehow. I was amazed; I was walking with a giant in hell, and that gave me some solace in the heat. About the same time as my mind was rejoicing in a stranger's abilities, my body began to fatigue past its breaking point, unable to overcome the stress that I was placing on my frame. My steps became smaller and my breaths became larger as I followed the man. I was falling far behind.

We had made it to an area of the world that wasn't completely void of man, however. Across the wasteland was ruined road and hunks of twisted metal already starting to break down in the heat, and at the end of it was an empty building double-layered and somehow intact. I could see the paint on the outside was obscured by the yellow poison and any attachments had long since melted away.

The stranger quickened his pace; he began to run towards the building. He entered the building through a front door, escaping the world.

I watched as the man entered the building, leaving me alone, dying in the yellow heat of the devil breathing his fowl mustard musk upon me. I felt a punch of jealousy in my gut. This so-called champion I had been foolishly following the last day had abandoned his relentless march through the wasteland, only to hide away in a building.

It wasn't fair, I thought, and I only wanted to punish him for leaving me out in the open all alone. My body found the strength it needed to continue; I was injected by rage that would serve me through any force of nature. So, I followed him as a cat would stalk his movements, taking in his scent, even in the howling wind that was threatening to plow me over, if I did not take a firmer stance.

I made it to the roasted hot door. The heat was scorching, and I was afraid to put my ear close to its frame. I took a gamble and opened the door, fleeing the yellow death just in time.

My skin instantly broke out into a cold sweat, relieved at some semblance of coolness. The coolness soon vanished; the yellow particles had wormed their way through the many layers of clothes I had been wearing. I stripped down to the tattered remains of my clothing—just my boxer shorts and my shirt. I felt exposed and vulnerable, the pieces of my soul showing that I had never allowed anyone but my wife to see. I tightened my mask around my head, the heat causing me to sway; still, I would not risk being taken by the yellow cloud, so close to being saved. The champion had done the same: I could see a ruined yellow mask like my own, piled on top of seared clothing.

My breathing was coming in fast. The lights all around me seemed to flicker and anxiety begun to sink in. It took every ounce of willpower I had to slow my heart, to slow the beating that was hammering its way out of my chest. Over the pounding, in my ears, I could make out a small voice.

Like a branch falling from a large tree, my mind snapped back to why I had entered the building. I had been following someone; I was getting closer; I could make out a voice. I looked around at my surroundings; the walls loomed high, coated in the yellow from the outside, yet the lights remained, bitterly glowing and still holding power.

I crept along in the light, noticing long-since-abandoned work-stations, monitors showing the lives of taxed worker bees as they lived their last breaths in this terrible world. My eyes traced images of smiling families and now-probably-dead house pets. The people here had died, and most likely the families who had loved them too. I pulled my eyes away, focusing on the voice of the stranger; I had seen too many bodies, and I did not want to see the faces that loved the lives in the photo frames on the desks.

I could hear a voice; I followed, and it guided me through the dim-lighted building. The closer I came to the sound, the more I could make out another voice. I stopped at the bottom of a metal staircase, waiting for enough noise to conceal my steps as I tiptoed up one step.

Another few steps and the voices became clearer; I could make out two. One belonged to a woman; I could hear her accent slowly drawing out, and all her "r"s. I couldn't place the accent—*maybe Boston,* I thought.

The other accent was unplaceable, though I thought it might have sounded a little Asian. It was rather hard to describe. It sounded like an American accent with a tinge of Spanish. There was a melodic quality to the speech.

I reached the top of the stairs and made my way across a metal catwalk until I came to the corner. I felt something heavy in the air, the closer I got to them. It was as if some unnatural force was pressing against me.

I felt like a single drop of water in the blistering sun, so inconsequential that my place here in the building was a mistake. I was better off staying outside. That was when I made out a few words through the muffled rubber covering my face.

"I could reverse this; none of this damage has to last. I can," pleaded the frantic voice of the woman. I stopped in my tracks, the fear building in my legs and chest. I had to hear more, though. *Could she be serious?* I thought. I stepped to the corner edge, peeping around until my eyes locked on the owners of the voices.

The woman was beautiful in every sense of the word. Though covered in as many rags as me, and despite a windswept look in her face, she still radiated beauty. Her black hair was cut short in an exotic way that perfectly matched her well-endowed bosom. Standing still, across from the woman was a man. I couldn't see his face and his stature was small. His black hair looked barely tousled on his brown skin. His presence was enough to make my knees cave. His clothes were a smooth black suit, held in place by a long golden tie. He was crisp, he was sharp, and most importantly he was yellow-dust-free. That set my heart racing.

I could see fear in the woman's eyes. I could also see a courage there that only burned in people every so often. The kind of courage that allowed an old woman to stay sitting on a bus, or the courage my mother showed even as her body became racked with cancer. It was the look of an unbreakable woman, an indestructible soul.

I dared to lean closer to the edge, feeling my way to a safe distance from the man. Something about him made me feel like he was pure evil. I did not want to see if my instincts were correct.

I listened to the voices. "It does not matter if you can save this planet or not. In fact, that is the very reason I am here. It is the way things work—I am sorry for this, truly." The man said this while taking a belt of blades from around his waist, setting them down on the table next to him. He was preparing for something, though I could tell what. I wasn't sure if I should stick around for whatever it was.

The woman spoke. "But I can stop all of this. You don't have to do this. Just let me disperse the agent; this planet can be saved."

Making out their words from my vantage point was difficult. I could hear every other sentence the two were saying—the heat was making it harder. My head dripped with sweat as I strained to listen.

I could see the frown on the man's face from hearing these words. "This can no more be escaped than a fish can escape being out of the water. I didn't want it to be this way though. I prefer ending these things much cleaner, if that is any consolation. You seem like a good person. But alas, we both have our roles to play."

I felt a chill run up my spine. This was the most surreal thing I had ever seen in my life, and my mind was being tossed like a ball at it all.

The woman spoke again, this time her voice a little louder, more pronounced. "I had lost you—I had lost you in that fire. How?" she asked.

"I use the blades, like this little blue one." The man gestured, placing one blade next to the others. "That blade allows me to go wherever the shadows are, when and wherever that I choose to go."

The woman looked as lost and as perplexed as I felt, and that was when I saw the fear take hold of her eyes. She was breaking and was going to crack; this man had broken the unbreakable woman with words alone.

Without looking, the short-statured man reached behind him, seizing a curved white blade. I noticed three holes in the hilt of the blade as the man pressed it towards his mouth, as if it was a flute. "Goodbye, hero, this is the way things have to be," he said almost sadly. The man pushed the knife towards his lips, and a haunting melody came forth. Shadows begun to dance near the man, moving as if his song was causing them to come alive. I was frightened, but not nearly as much as the woman. The shadows twisted, taking the shape of animals, horned and fanged in the low light.

The woman turned to run; it was too late, the shadows shot out like snakes, devouring her in strikes. She sprawled to the ground, bloodied and bound by the shadow serpents. The darkness held her as a bigger one formed from the center of the man. Out came a black hand, draped in the color of death, and it launched its way towards the woman, clasping around her throat.

I was stunned, watching her fight for air, as the man kept playing his blade, while stepping closer towards her. The woman's fingers fought the shadows to no avail, as her eyes turned red. I knew it was only a matter of time.

She was a goner—I didn't need to be any doctor to see that. My body reacted despite my desire to close my eyes and put my knees to my chest. I crept down the scaffolding, using the adjacent staircase at the end of the stairwell, until I was behind the strange pair. The woman was about to die; that wasn't going to be me. I went to the man's desk and snatched the blue blade and some purple dagger, counting my blessings by not making any noise. There were other blades, but the closer I came to the shadows, the more my legs couldn't stop shaking. *Don't be stupid, hurry up.* I made sure to tuck the blue blade deep in my pocket; he had mentioned that it could send him anywhere. *Thank God for classic villains being overconfident and talking too much. This chance would never have happened.*

I left the room as she lay dying. Her eyes flashed at the sight of me, and I knew that if she could, she would have screamed "Help me!"

I whispered back "No," as I raced down the hallway leading out of the room.

If this blade did what that lunatic claimed, then it would transfer me anywhere I wanted to go. And the anywhere I longed for was me willing to sacrifice my whole life to get back with my family. I found the underlying cause of the stairs and ran back to where I had been at the beginning.

I looked the blade over. It was small and shaped like a butterfly knife, only it had three small holes on the top hilt and one on the bottom. The blade was as blue as the day sky; it didn't look all that sharp, though. I thought of the grizzly image that had just happened. *That man hadn't used this blade for the stabbing—he'd used his blades for much, much worse. The power,* I thought, as I gazed at the blade through my gas mask; *that kind of authority must be used for something awful.*

I pictured the moment that yellow fever had consumed my world. I went back even more, before the violence, to cryptic messages from my government. The vision was strong in my head, the moment when everything was best with my family and me. I waited for a feeling, rush, or displacement that would land me far away from my current place. But nothing came, no sudden sensation of weightlessness, not even a spark from the blade. *It should have worked, magic is easy, right? Just picture something and it will happen.*

I opened my eyes at the blade and concentrated harder and harder, feeling my heart beat in my ears. Nothing happened. I was still standing in the middle of the abandoned factory, now listening to the last dying breaths of a brave woman.

From the choking sounds the woman was making, I could tell that she didn't have much longer. I focused harder, until I was gripping the blade so tight that it bit through my skin as if it was alive. The screams became quieter and finally I heard a loud snap. The woman was dead, and I had stolen the killer's weapons.

I panicked, the blade suddenly weighing a lot more in my hands. I felt like a child who had just broken his mother's favorite lamp; it was only a matter of time until mother found out, and when she found out, I was going to pay.

I began twisting and playing with the holes in the blade, anything to get it working. My franticness soon turned into cold fear, as I imagined the man looking for his blades and realizing that someone else was here. *It must not work for me; maybe it only works for him.* As dread filled my belly, I turned around to see the man standing at the top of the stairs. His eyes were as the darkest pit of blood, like I was looking into a dragon's stare. I couldn't help but feel terror, and I felt my body take steps back.

His face was blank as his eyes sized me up; they stopped at the blue blade in my hand and time froze. We both knew in that instant what I had done. We both knew what was going to happen next.

The man pulled back out his white dagger and pressed it once more to his lips. *The sound was beautiful,* I thought, as the shadows near me began to chatter and shriek.

Sound, sound... Wait, that must be it! I jumped back from the shadows and opened the door to the outside world, thinking that the sunlight would blast away the shadows. The light had no effect and the shadows continued to move towards me, picking up speed as I moved away from the yellow heat and animals of darkness all aching to consume me. I looked at the blade once more, knowing that I was either going to die by this man's shadows or I was going to die by the yellow cloud.

As I pulled up my mask, I thought of how dignified the yellow clouds were at least. That was something that I could relate to others in the afterlife. Death at his hands felt unnatural and wrong in every sense of the word. I pressed the three holes up to my mouth and stuck my fourth finger under the hole on the bottom, remembering the way I used to play a flute as a child. *Only I was never good at playing,* I thought.

All the while, I never took my eyes from the man as the shadows came closer and closer. I breathed as hard as I could into the blade, until a heavy tone came out from somewhere on the blade. I felt my body dissolve, almost turn into a black substance, and disappear, just as the snakes came towards me.

I broke apart into countless pieces, my scream lost into fragments that were beyond the sight of any microscope. I floated above the red-eyed man, his eyes still locked on the place I had been.

Suddenly, I felt a draw to an area behind the man; I started to reform, a piece at a time, like glass being placed back together, only when I came back, I didn't feel as whole and my body threatened to fall and shatter like a sheet of glass, into shards of memories.

I dry heaved and threw up over the edge of the stairs onto the hot metal below. I reached up instinctively for my gas mask, verifying that I hadn't somehow lost it while broke apart. Structurally, I felt fine but in my mind, my thoughts were having a hard time coming together.

While I fought to get my bearings, the man took notice of me, turning around. His features lit ablaze like his red eyes and fury that made me feel more than dread was plunging into me.

I took a step back, searching for room away from the man, room that I knew wasn't there. I blinked, and the man zoomed to meet me, throwing a lightning-fast fist that would have taken my head off, had my body not stumbled back from the speed of his movement.

I was on the ground, the man above me moving with pure malice, I rolled over the guard rail at the last moment by sheer luck; his speed and strength were unreal. My body dropped like a dead weight to the floor several feet below. I looked up to see the man easily clear the railing down towards me. I screamed and reached into my pocket, searching for anything that could be used in defense against the animal coming at me.

My hands found the hilt of the purple blade and I brought it up screaming, as the man landed on top of my body, the blade the only defense between us. The blade found home inside him, the impact so great from his momentum that my arms shook and collapsed.

Suddenly I wasn't under a stranger's weight, or inside a factory being bombarded by a yellow death. I was alone on an island, overlooking a sea caught aflame. All around me, carnage rained, and the golden sand ran crimson as voices cried out overhead. *I was in the middle of hell,* was my first thought. I stood up, digging my feet into the sand, my boots becoming wet in something that I did not want to see.

I ran forward, dashing through shouts and the whizzing of bullets overhead. I couldn't tell if any of the shots I was hearing were aimed at me or someone else. My feet found footing, despite the perilous beach. A shattering of earth and metal caused my teeth to chatter.

I came to dense foliage of a jungle and I kept my feet moving. I quickly became lost and all around me, unnatural jungle noises met the terror of my heart as I realized I had no idea where I was heading. I placed my hands on my head and began screaming into the air, trying to grasp the horrible reality unfolding around me. All around me, colors of green were exploding in bursts of orange and red, sending pieces of the jungle over me.

This is maddening; this is all a nightmare. I was in the middle of war; I was going to die. I looked around and a family of four ran past me at top speed. If they noticed me, I couldn't tell, they sped past as if I was a statue, forever motionless.

Looking to see what they were fleeing from; it was a wave of men bearing old guns, flashing in the bright sun. Bullets came close to clipping me, and I heard a language I did not understand, mixed in with screams from all around me. I gave chase after the family, bolting in their direction, running towards what I hoped was safety. My feet burned, and I felt myself drenched in a new wave of fresh sweat; the humidity so great that I could drink the toxic air, which was quickly becoming more smoke than oxygen. I was thankful for my mask—without it, the intensity of the jungle would have been too much for me.

I kept on running, seeing the family ahead of me. I soon overtook them, sidestepping around the youngest kids, and kept moving. I considered slowing down; I considered turning back and helping them. I'd considered a lot of things lately—but not them. I turned my head, glancing at the man that was taking his family to safety; he was filthier and much thinner than when I'd last seen him, but it was *him.* His round and guileless face seemed almost harmless without those flaming red eyes.

This all had to be in my head, I thought, as my mind fled away faster than my feet were moving. I came to a clearing and ran along the beach until I met another forest.

I sprinted into the jungle, not looking back as more bullets came for me. I heard the scream of the children with the man. *Don't think of your own children and how they met death in such a way—don't think of dead children,* I thought. *Something unknown and strange had cut them down like blades of grass;* I remembered seeing their bodies sprawled out on my wooden floors, splintered and holed as their blood soaked into the floor.

I ran for what seemed like hours over thick bundles of limbs, dodging trees that stood so tall, the sun was blocked out in some sections, before my chest finally heaved and I felt myself throwing up. I was arched over and my breath stinking of vomit, when I looked up. The jungle was silent, and I couldn't hear anything all around me. Suddenly it was more terrifying and more alive—like a beast that had without warning stopped stalking its prey. I listened for movement, anything that could be dangerous, any sound in the moment of silence.

I stood frozen, listening to the silence, until I was satisfied that I wasn't hearing anything coming, before picking up and moving on. My body was shaking, and I had never been so frightened in my life. I walked in the direction of where I had come, trying hard to retrace my way in the endless maze of foliage and limbs. Luckily, all the destruction from bullets flying into trees was all around me, so I had to be going the right way. *If I could get back to the beach, maybe I could find my way back to the factory... but what is going on here? Was any of this real?* I thought, looking over my shoulders. Fear shot up my spine, going deeper into the woods was death. Following a trail of death somehow felt safer. I shuddered at the thought of the forest, its green legs and tendrils belonging to an entity of another world, more dangerous than the men chasing me. Something propelled me towards the beach. I started walking; I picked my way carefully, every step bringing me to the sounds of gunfire.

I panicked with every burst of screams that floated to me like a banshee woman, cursed to roam the woods at night, forever alone. I walked more in the direction of the gunshots; something was overriding all instincts of mine to stay alive and pulled me in the direction of the massacre.

Eventually I found my way back to the beach clearing, where the man I'd seen earlier was in front of me. He was tied to a tree, his hands bound high above his head. Across from him were a woman and two girls hanging from a branch, all three kicking and screaming in vain. *No one was going to be saving them,* I thought, as I tucked myself into a hiding place. The jungle was safe; the jungle would keep me from all the men with guns on the beach.

I noticed that their uniforms were grey in coloring, and faded after constant wear and wash. The elements had bleached them to a dull contrast, with their red sun flag flying in the background, gleaming white, despite the gray all around us. I wasn't much of a historian, but they had to be Japanese. I couldn't fathom how I was seeing this, or why, from their boots to their guns, everything they owned looked decades old. That was when I took it in.

This was sometime around World War II and the men before me were the Japanese Imperial Army invading some Asian country. "What the fuck?" I muttered, sinking deeper into the tree, seeking a hiding place that I didn't think would stand up much to their bullets. Ancient weapons or not, a gun was quite effective at killing people.

I continued watching the scene casually, almost as if I had been sitting inside a movie theater, not in the middle of an invasion. I was glued into the screen before me. An officer-looking type holding a long sword was pointing at the man who'd first had red eyes. Now black, his eyes were quickly filling with dark pools of tears as he screamed back at the man. *He has normal eyes now*; I thought from my hiding spot.

The officer pointed to the woman and children hanging from the branches, their tiny forms still swaying and fighting for oxygen. He then directed one of his men to light a torch.

The red-eyed man screamed like a wild beast thrashing against his restraints, the bonds holding tight as the man with the torch touched the woman's feet first. Hungry flames shot up her, devouring her in seconds, followed by the two little girls. Their anguish was deep and beyond heinous, only matched by the red-eyed man attached to the tree. His screams were louder than any of the bullets that had been fired today.

The man kicked and screamed, pulling from the tree, when the bindings flew apart suddenly, and he fell forward with a force, landing in the dirt below him. He was on his feet though, quickly overtaking the officer in a blind rage.

He beat the man to the ground and then gave chase to the now-fleeing solider who had used the torch. Red-eye caught him, savagely bringing him down to the ground. A small skirmish broke between the two, and red-eye jammed both his thumbs into the man's eyes, sending blood all over them both. I turned my head, fighting the urge to vomit again.

The red-eyed man let loose a wounded howl and he went back to the officer, taking his sword, and begun hacking deep ridges into his body, all the while screaming. When he was finished, he threw his sword down into the red sand. I tracked the red-eyed man's movements until he ran into the jungle on the other side of the clearing, before I dared risking coming from my hiding spot.

Even as I was twenty feet away from the man's family, I could still see their forms hanging from the branches burning. I smelled their flesh as it roasted, mixing in with the black smoke.

I stopped before them with my heart beating, when the woman turned her charred face to me, "Run, run... you can't escape; you can't undo," she screamed in broken English.

The two little girls chimed in their voices as well. "Can't escape, can't destroy," they giggled without lips.

I fell back, trying to avoid their curses and shrieks. I crawled, my eyes never leaving them; I was afraid they would come down from their burning places and take me with them.

I kept going back until I hit something that felt hard. I turned, seeing a boot. I looked up seeing the young Japanese soldier who had his eyes gouged out, pointing out over the ocean. I followed his fingers to see an infinite number of explosions off in the distance. The explosions were erupting into beautiful mushroom clouds of death; I read somewhere once that when nuclear bombs went off, if you lived long enough to see the flare from the bombs, then you feel the blast first.

Which is what I considered as the aftereffect came slamming towards me, lifting me off my feet. I screamed, but my voice was snuffed out as the wave of heat hit me…å

I blinked, and I was back in the factory with the stunned red-eyed man above me. Both of our faces utterly bewildered.

The red-eyed man fell off me and moved back, whether from the wound to his chest or from the experience, I couldn't tell. We had shared a moment with more intimacy than most people's sex life; it wasn't something to be shared, I realized. It was horrific; a surreal nightmare I was still reeling from. That had been his family, and they were all gone now. Hesitantly, I got to my feet as the red-eyed man appeared lost. His eyes no longer blazed red, but rather dimmed to a soft glow. *Was that him in the forest, his family that had died? It had to be.*

As I made it to my feet, I never let my own eyes leave him. It was only a matter of time before he snapped out his trance and when he did, something terrible was going to happen to me. You aren't supposed to see people's demons; some things were supposed to stay hidden.

I tucked the purple blade gingerly back into my belt. Both blades possessed a tremendous amount of power, though I wasn't going to get the time to figure out their uses at this current moment. I pulled the blue blade from my belt once more; this time I visualized the exact moment in time when my family had been truly safe.

A time when everything was how it should be, not how things are now. As I placed the cold steel to my lips, I kept the image of my family in my head and blew into the holes of the blade.

Same as before, I was dematerialized into thousands of pieces, stretching into the shadows of the rooms.

The last image that I saw of the factory was the red-eyed man finally coming back into the chamber.

His face went from bewilderment to madness, and I knew in that instant, even before I began my quest to gain more power from him over the coming years, that he was the enemy. He was someone that would be coming for me as long as I drew breath.

I remember the last images of him on the beach and the animalistic way he had torn into both the soldiers. I shuddered at the thought, somewhere in the loose bits I now occupied. The sensation didn't last long. When I came back together, I was standing inside my modest living room.

Most of the furniture was hand-me-down, and the floor was littered with the toys of my kids. I had made it back; something wasn't right, though. The house was empty, with no sounds of my children playing; no music from my wife singing in the late summer air. Instead, endless silence stretched from me out over what seemed like miles. I called out for my wife and got no response. In my panic, I began to wander the house in search of my family.

Feeling lost and alone, I went to my living room and lay on the couch. I sifted through the events of the day. So many things had happened, I did not know where to begin.

My stomach decided to lead the way first and followed it all the way to my kitchen. When I entered, I blinked, shaking my head in surprise. The contents of the house were littered before me. Everything, from food items to clothing, had been meticulously rendered into uselessness.

I searched my memory, wondering what the kitchen had looked like before everything changed. I froze, remembering this was as it had been before my family and I had left. I had tried to make an inventory of our house and take what we needed, but the yellow cloud had swept across the world as if it was alive and sought vengeance.

I ran to the calendar taped to the fridge. My girls had always done a great job of keeping the schedule up to date every morning, making a ritual out of it. Sure enough, the calendar was marked "April 24th,

2015." It was the exact time that we had left the house, just as soon as the yellow cloud appeared over the neighborhood.

I sprung up to the blinds, pulling them open, to see the outside world covered in the yellow dust. Everything was melting away under the toxic cloud; even the house, from what I could tell, was about to fall in from the dust.

My family wasn't here because they had already died; I had missed them by days. I looked around, smelling the food goods, which were now rotting, and the state of dust finding its way in, despite the precautions my wife and I had made for the house.

We had hoped that by the time we made it out to her mother's place in the west, the storm would have depleted, and we would have been able to come home—my home, or what was left of it—looked like it had been days since I left. I hadn't gone back in time; I was just back to where I started. And there, their bodies still lay on the floor, where I had left them, now very nearly melted to the bone as the dust continued its onslaught.

"No, no, this isn't supposed to be happening," I shouted, swallowing the bitter taste that was forming in my mouth. I slid to the floor, my back knocking over the rotten food on the way to the ground. I looked at the blue blade in my hand and pictured the moment with my family again.

I blew much slower than I had the first time in front of the red-eyed man, wondering what might have been the reason my flight ended up back at the house after their deaths, instead of back to the *when*, like I had wanted.

I broke down into the shadows of the room, coming back an instant later in my living room. Once the dizziness of the travel wore off, I stumbled my way into the kitchen and saw the place where my body weight had crushed the food I was lying on. Still the same place, still the same time. "Fuck!" I yelled, punching my fist into the wall. The drywall crumbled around me and pinged off the ground, sending an echo into the empty house. I pulled the blue blade out and angrily blew into its holes, trying to play a different song.

Ten times, I blew into the blade once more, each time ending up in various parts of the house. I would picture different moments of my life, like picture frames of my memories. It was all to no avail; nothing was bringing me back to the *when* that the memories had occurred, only back to the *where*. It was all useless, like counting the grains of sand on a beach while the tide pulled all around you.

That was when I tried the calendar, thinking perhaps I could use that as a guideline. A witness in time for where I wanted to go, I would be able to head back to the *when*.

I pictured a memory of my family at the local fair, because that had been on my youngest daughter's birthday. I could never forget the date. It did not work. I ended up at the festival, almost dying from the radiation of the yellow plague before I teleported back to the house.

In my fury, I tore the cabinets of my kitchen down, ripped into the furniture that my wife and I had spent years collecting. My rage lasted for what felt like hours, in a blood-fouled rampage.

I yanked the blue blade from my pocket, the weight feeling oddly light in my hands. I needed to learn how to use this tool; I thought back to the song that the purple blade had produced when I used it, compared to the red-eyed man.

Maybe, he used a different pitch or tone... Who am I kidding? I don't even know the differences myself. That... red-eyed son of a bitch is going to pay for this. I grunted while kicking over a chair in my house. He had set me up, he'd let me take his blades only to give me false hope.

As the dining chair smashed into the wall, the shadows danced underneath it in the dying light of the day. I figured I would only have a few more hours in the house before the gas started caving in. It was only a matter of time. I could transport anywhere in the world, but I would never be able to outrun this plague.

I took my life back into my hands; I wasn't going to die in a festering yellow death with no one to hear my screams as my flesh melted away. Pulling the blue blade free from my pockets once more, I played the only melody that made sense. It wasn't flashy, and it wasn't going to be downloaded to anyone's music player anytime soon.

I ended up back at the factory, the trip taxing my senses less. I was becoming used to the magic of the blade. I looked around, pulling both blades out and preparing for an attack from that red-eyed son of a bitch. I couldn't detect anyone's presence, and mostly all I could hear was the sound of slowly dying machines from the ever-increasing assault of the yellow plague outside.

I felt confident that I was alone. Still, that didn't mean I'd lower my guard. I looked around the main room at the workstations, and scribbled on one of the desks were words that said" "I do not know who you are. That was brave, but a stupid thing you did. Be seeing you real soon." I read it, imagining a slow dagger from within slicing its way up my back. I had pissed off someone with a power that I couldn't comprehend.

He wasn't here, and all traces I had of finding him were now gone. I slumped to the floor, feeling defeated in every sense of the word. I jammed the little blue blade into the ground; the blade barely pierced the tile floor of the factory. *Look at this shit; it's not even good for cutting. What use do I have for such a device?*

My fist shot out to the blade, punching it, sending it flying across the room. As the hilt hit the wall, I heard a click. Out from the blade shot out an image of the world; it was cast in a blue light showing Earth. I stepped towards the light, blinking, I wasn't sure what exactly it was. It looked like a visual of the entire Earth, only an Earth covered in a massive yellow cloud, enveloping the world in the hologram.

When I pressed my fingers against the blue and yellow world, it moved with mine and I swirled the interface until I came to my state. The cloud wasn't as dark yellow over the area I thought myself to be in, yet I could tell it would soon be covered like the rest of the world.

Soon everything would fade to yellow, I thought.

Frustrated, I spun the planet and pulled my hands out from the image; in response, the room filled with thousands of Earths. I gasped, my eyes looking around the room. All around me were an infinite number of Earths. I couldn't even count the sheer amount of them; it had to number well over a million, just from what I could take in. All tiny little blue planets; some looked like the one I was on now, others were dry with no water, and even more were smoldering rocks of fire.

"What the hell—what is this?" I muttered, searching for my voice in what I realized was an infinite universe of planets of which I could never fathom the depth. My eyes tracked along the planets until I fixed on one not too far from the yellowing world I was on. It held a tiny red light glowing in the center of its mass.

I walked towards that world and took it into my hand, the world getting larger in my palms. I could see a small Earth that looked like my own, and looking from the top to bottom, I could see no difference. I pushed my fingers to the edge of the planet, zooming in deeper into its image, until I saw a mountain pass. The pass was littered with weapons of war, twisted in a violent cataclysm.

I pushed my fingers slowly forward, searching for the red light I had seen, until I came to the source. The source of the mysterious red light was none other than the red-eyed man, casually strolling through the carnage as if he were walking in the park. Not a care in the world, not a sniffle in the breeze that was made up of smoke.

I felt a movement in the pit of my stomach, it wasn't out of fear; it felt more like jealousy. *How could he be so calm, how come red got to act like nothing bad had happened, despite what I had seen on that beach?*

I looked at the blue blade lying on the ground; I was going to have to chase after this man. *He must know some way to roll back time. He must know something. I can stop all of this.* My world was ending, and with an event that could not be explained—a man had made shadows choke a woman. *None of it made sense, and the senseless had to yield sense at some point—it had to.*

I was holding on to a fool's hope, based on the idea that a stranger who had nearly killed me was going to be somehow able to help me. I picked the blade up and imagined the hillside near the man. I thought of its graying grass, withered away from the poisoning of war, of the soft footsteps the man was making into the ground as he walked so calmly.

I blew into the blade, and I broke apart into the shadows again, just in time as I saw the yellow clouds finally seep through the walls. I had avoided the death I should have been due; I was going to fix it somehow.

As I floated across the vastness of space, I saw my yellow planet melt away like ice cream in the hot sun. Stars and planets twisted and folded around me and my speed began to increase until I entered a white void. For as far as my eyes could see, space was empty, and I was lost in nothingness, without form or void.

I remained in the void until a black speck appeared in the distance; my broken form stretched to the hole at a blinding speed until I reached it and came out into another universe. I flew past what looked like the planet Saturn, only this Saturn was beyond massive. It easily would dwarf the entirety of my universe and then would have some to spare.

As I passed the other planets in the solar system, they appeared to look the same as my own, only bigger. When I came to the "Earth," I gasped at the size of it and wondered how any man on that planet could ever have seen it all. Its green forests stretched as far as I could see. Its oceans were beyond imagination.

I came down onto the planet and once again formed up from the shadows. I patted myself down once I was on solid ground, making sure I hadn't left anything in that strange white room.

I considered the sky, feeling the weight of being one of the smallest things in existence. I was a flea—no, a microscopic germ—lost in an ocean of possibilities I had stumbled upon unknowingly. I looked down at the ground and vomited. I tried to keep my voice down as I fought vertigo, in addition to the feeling of hopelessness.

When I finished, I wiped my hands into the dirt on the ground around me and pulled out both the purple blade and blue blade. I was ready to attack the red-eyed man once more; this time I was going to catch him.

I followed the path I had seen the red-eyed man creep along earlier. I came to the top of a hillside and was astonished by the mayhem below. Down from me was the aftermath of a great battle. Thousands and thousands of bodies lay before the hill I was on. The earth was a bleached red in the sun-drenched dirt; mixed in with crimson-colored steel, blinding in its reflection of the sun.

I pulled down my gas mask as I saw buzzards circling overhead. I could tell they were about to feast for a very long time. I made my way down the hillside, stepping over the corpses. The sheer amount of them became alarming to me; the bodies were torn in such ways I couldn't differentiate one man from the other. A meat-grinding of men, slaughtered like sheep.

I felt a wave of nausea hit and my legs began to wobble. *There was no way I would be able to find the man through all of this,* I thought as I started to run through the bodies, trying to escape the endless sea of them that was spoiling around me.

I felt like the most arrogant, pompous asshole there was, to think I could follow that man through all that lay in front of me. I jerked wildly, trying to see my way out of the storm of bodies that screamed to me from the ground, their last dying moments frozen forever on their faces; all shame that could have been had in life was now gone.

I started to drown in the gore, a sea of blood hitting me in waves over and over. My legs gave out, and I fell hard into the soft exposed tissue of someone's back. Blood smeared across my mask, and I was thankful once again I had found the mask. Its simple rubber pieces were protecting me from more than I had ever imagined possible.

All around me, I could hear the voices of the dead; I was living their nightmares in a field of death, and I felt myself peeing. A human being was just not meant to see as much death as I had in the last few hours. I was lost, and all around me was the army of the dead, eager to take me down with them.

I fumbled for the blue blade in my pocket and looked into the distance as I placed the blade up against my mouth, trying my best not to smell. I played the blade and teleported off as far as the horizon.

And still, I was in the army of the dead. I repeated the process six more times before I finally saw the end of the bodies. In the distance were massive machines of war, or what looked like the metal bodies of some machine-god. I vomited and pressed the blade against my mouth once more, and felt myself turn into a shadow. I came back on the top of the machines, my feet shaking from the journey. My stomach was in knots; it was all too much for me.

I stepped past the massive death machines and walked up the steep hill behind them. I couldn't look behind me; there was nothing to see, and if anyone had ever happened to find themselves among this necropolis, they would say God had left the world. God had let it burn into a crater of war.

I ascended the hill soon reaching its summit. Once I was on top, I looked out before me and saw only rolling green mounds in the distance. No indication of my mysterious red-eyed man.

I activated the map on the blue blade once again, and the red light flashed, shown on the map, a blinking dot not too far off in the distance. It blew my mind how he was moving so quickly, how he had made it through the death. I shuddered at the thought, not sure if it was the cold or just a bad feeling that made me afraid.

I blew into the blade, playing my song on that hillside, until I came to where the dot had been.

All I found was a dying man; he looked no different from the military men I had discovered in the field. A shallow cut dotted his neck, leading down his throat, and was obscured by his blood. I searched the man and found a canteen and a letter addressed to a young woman.

In the letter, it spoke of how the young man was going to take part in a huge battle, but one that was necessary to save the world. It stated he would be home, no matter what. I had looked at the human form before me, laid out on the ground like a trophy, and I understood something at that moment. This young man had survived the epic battle, making him the lone survivor. He had most likely been on his way home; he would have been showered with praise and worshiped as a hero. But he would never get to give his letter to his love now. I folded the letter and stuck it back into the man's pocket, while taking a sip from his canteen.

I thought about both the young man and the woman I had found back on my planet. Both had been the last remainders in an unfortunate situation, but had the chance to turn things around. This young man—maybe he could have saved his planet like that woman had claimed to do on mine. *So perhaps that red-eyed bastard was targeting heroes of sorts, on every planet.*

This was a lead, something I could use to find that evil man. I capped the canteen and tucked it into my pocket, knowing it wasn't going to be easy finding him after all.

I pulled out the blue blade and activated the giant blue map of the cosmos, searching for that elusive red dot in the vastness of space. I would find my red-eyed man on multiple planets, eventually. But each time, he would always be one step ahead, one hero in the dust to taunt me. As the bodies mounted, I became less wary of my prey and became to understand him better. Our cat and mouse game would last for years, but I never ceased to chase him, even though he always moved ahead of me.

I continued my search, for years, following the red-eyed man, and every time he was a step ahead of me. I learned that to many, he was known as a man in shadows, a red-eyed devil. And his legend was accurate; no one lived long enough to tell much about him. I was always either minutes or seconds too late to capture him. In my despair, an idea came forth as to how to capture this man. On every planet, the story was always the same, it was always an Earth. I learned I was not alone, that other worlds existed with life. Just like my own planet, my own reality. I cared little for that—I only wanted the reality with my family, one I had to keep learning. I had learned from other people on my travels that the man was working jobs.

As to exactly why he was killing the heroes of doomed planets, I could not ascertain the meaning behind that. However, I did figure out his pattern. It appeared my adversary only showed himself on planets on the very edge of either changing their ways or being lost forever. I had seen this since, from war-torn worlds to peaceful worlds, where a politician of some substance had won and was bringing peace to his planet. Or a world where radiation caused by some asshole's weapon had killed everyone.

Regardless of the scenario, it was always the same. The hero of those planets was his target. From there, I was able to piece together that he wouldn't appear to every doomed planet until certain criteria had been met. First: It took a hero to rise in the world for the man in shadows to show up.

Second: The red-eyed man somehow knew the exact future of that hero, usually because he was the one to end their life. They never stood a chance, every time; he just always seemed to know, no matter what the hero did.

Third: He would not intervene in whatever was causing the end on those planets; he would just kill that person. Usually though, the very death of that person was enough.

Lastly: I had witnessed him once following a man for a week, only for that man to do something that had changed his faith, of sorts. Which prompted the man in shadows to follow a new person; I hadn't quite figured that reason yet. What that target had done to alter the interest of my quarry I was unsure, but it was something I imagined made him no longer the hero.

An idea formed, one which would require me to have patience and would end with me getting my prize: my family. I began to stop following him; instead, I started looking to other places in the universe. I needed something that would cause the end of a world.

Not only that, I needed a world not already ending. I had no idea how the man knew when a world was supposed to end. That only left me with the option of engineering an apocalypse on my own. I searched for months for planets dying on their own. Every time, though, shadows would show up and the process would be repeated all over again.

It wasn't working, until I came to a planet draped in a darkness that seemed endless. All around, spirits and apparitions floated by. All manner of those who had died and those who were dying tortured my ears with their cries. It was a world dipped in a sea of black. Layered with walls and all kinds of darkness. I thought the world was fruitless, already gone, until I found a dying man, his mind broken and shattered, but he did tell me something I could use.

"Memories are the truest terror in this world. Over time, all wounds will heal, or you will move on from them, but memories will set out each day to never arrive in time to help us. A memory can be your downfall as you chase it to the end."

I looked at the man, puzzled by his words.

The man pointed to a small box a few feet away from him. It was nondescript, save for a thin purple paint decorating the outside and a few minor chips in the paint. Confused, I looked at the man, needing an explanation for the unknown.

The man nodded once more to the box, and I knew what he meant. Something bad was inside that box, something that would kill me if I gave it a chance. I turned back to the old man as the light left his eyes. *This planet is already dead and gone; I would have to find a new place. Continue to take my time and set my trap.*

I activated the blue hologram and looked for a planet that would suit my needs. I was going to have to do a lot of killing, I thought. I was going to have to do a lot of watching. I found a planet; it was like my own. I blew into the blade, and I felt myself become shadows. I was becoming death; I was going to be a man who would be reunited with my family.

I came to the planet; it was in a relatively peaceful state, as mine had been before the plague had turned it into a yellow death trap. I remembered in the early days, as I scoped out the planet for a worthy target, I hid away in the shadows, watching a great deal of people from afar.

I spent three weeks in a city called Charlotte inside the state of North Carolina. Atop my lofty shack, I watched. And as I watched, despair ran my heart into the ground. I began to doubt my plan; holes became evident in my plot and I wondered if I had any chance of ever capturing him.

It was a long shot, becoming more farfetched by every minute. I happened to glance down and saw a man coming out of a local ice cream shop with his daughter. Even from a distance, I could see the happiness inside them; I could almost feel it. *Perfect.* I smiled and let the words ring power back into my plan. I knew it was just a hope; I now had a chance. A real person had showed up. A good person. Finally, it was my best shot.

I followed the man and what I assumed was his young daughter to their apartment duplex. They lived in a good neighborhood; it wasn't too expensive, it showed the man was well off, but modest enough. I made a mental note as I waited on the roof of the house outside until nightfall.

Once I saw all the lights go out in the apartment, I began my plan, moving in to gain more information about him. I made my way into the building using the blue blade—I could see inside a dark hallway from my ledge. Travel was now easy for me with the blade. I found his door and teleported into his apartment. I looked at the man's pictures on the walls, the general state of his happiness. *Everything is modest with this man; he is someone who loves his family very much. It wasn't that I needed a family man, I needed a genuinely heroic person. This guy might be the type. Or he could be some scumbag—it was hard to tell with anyone.* I needed more proof.

As I gazed at a picture on the stairwell, I didn't hear the tiny footsteps of a girl; I didn't listen to the young lady, until I heard her gasp. She stared me down in a state of total bewilderment, a keen eye of innocence that only children knew how to show. Kids could give a stare that did more than any words about something wrong; such as a man in a gas mask inside a young girl's house.

I saw the sleep inside the girl's eyes disappear and her understanding that I was real and shouldn't be in her home.

She started to yell, and I crossed the distance between us, snatching her mouth closed with my hands. She screamed, muffled, into my hands as I took her to the ground. I tightened my grip over her face which easily covered her mouth and nose. She kicked and jerked, and I risked looking up to see if the noise had awakened the man. I felt her tiny hands thrashing against my form; it was like a fish fighting back as a bear tried to eat the fish. She lacked the size or strength to get out.

My heart pounded in my chest as I pressed harder, trying to get her to be quiet. I whispered, "Please, little girl; please be quiet." The girl responded by digging her fingernails into my hands. My grip loosed, and the girl kicked up hard into my groin. I fell forward as her tiny body slipped under mine and she ran back to her room. I heard the shriek as she called out for help.

I stood up, mustering my body before it was too late. I heard the clatter of my pockets as something fell out. No time to pick it up, no time to stop now. My whole plan was about to be ruined because I couldn't handle a little girl. The girl reached the door at the end of the hallway before I did, her voice low even as she coughed and tried to scream. I must have hurt her windpipe when I was holding her mouth. *I must kill her*, I thought. *I don't want to, but she will scream, and the entire plan could be ruined. She has to die.*

I busted in the door, knocking the girl over. She fell back, hitting her head against her bed. I was breathing hard, and I wasn't aware how much I was repeating, "I'm sorry, I am so sorry."

I kept wishing for the girl to stay down as I watched her beaten form on the ground. Her eyes fluttered, and she looked at me, her piercing blue eyes as bright as any ocean I had ever seen. She had a determination I had seen in many—in fact, it was mostly the look I saw in heroes who fell to the red-eyed man. Some would keep that look, the "you can't stop me" look, even when they faced death.

This small girl was no different; in fact, I knew what I needed to do even before my heart accepted the answer. I moved forward, still repeating, "I'm sorry." I snatched the girl's throat again as she kicked and kicked. She landed a blow in my groin again; her punch was lacking the strength necessary to hurt me this time and I managed to hold on. She dug her fingernails into my fingers, cutting them deep, spilling my blood on her and the floor. It was all pointless, though; she had no power.

Swearing, I smacked her head against the bed rail repeatedly until I heard a crack. Her body spasmed once, twice, and ceased to move. I stopped my breath, sucking in the smell of death as I dropped the girl to the ground like a sack of potatoes. Which was fitting for her, cast aside as casually as a vegetable; I felt sick as I kept repeating, "I'm sorry."

I stopped my never-ending string of words and took notice of my surroundings again. I was inside the girl's bedroom, and the house was quiet—a little bit too silent. The noise should have woken up that red-headed man. On cue, I heard the slow steps of someone sneaking on the staircase, doing their best to be faint as they walked down. What the average person didn't realize was what sounds muted to them isn't how it sounds to someone else from a distance. Learning how to sneak up on a man without any noise is a skill that must be practiced. To be truly quiet, you have to be quiet—there was no other way to explain it. You have to be like wind captured in a glass; invisible to all, unheard by even a mouse.

I pulled the purple blade from my waistband and positioned myself at an angle from the opened bedroom door. If it was the father, he had no way of knowing that I was inside the room—at least, not without having to step inside.

I could hear his breathing, the speed steadily increasing. He was scared and was afraid to come in. I kept my blade, ready to lash out at the man at a given moment. I held my breath and waited for him to make the first move, and when my breath finally came ready to pop, the man stepped through the threshold of his daughter's bedroom.

Ignoring everything else in the room, the man beelined for his dead daughter stretched out on the floor. I sprang from my hiding spot, stabbing the blade into his back and catching him by surprise. The blade went in deep, and the man had a second to cry out before its effects took hold. I pulled the knife out and checked the man's eyes. Sure enough, they were swimming in deep pools of blue; he was lost under my spell.

I had learned from my travels how to use both my blades quite extensively. I pressed the blade to my mouth and started spinning my tune; this was the delicate part. Using the knife, I could show the man a paradise equivalent to his wildest dreams meeting the Playboy Mansion. Or I could flay his dreams based on his worst nightmares. Right now, I was having him imagine himself inside his bed. I found *less is more* when it came to brainwashing.

Next, I was able to pick my way through his mind, seeing the web of his memories and every person he'd ever touched. Everything he'd ever loved. Desires, pains, hopes, and dreams. I was the last shrink in a world full of chaos. Once I had gathered every bit of information about the man, I prepared my plan. It was going to take some time. It seemed that he was truly a family man; his thoughts were mostly about his wife and child.

He was a computer guy, opinion of himself a little high, overall carefree with great potential to become a hero. I wiped my brow as I played the flute, seeing deeper inside his mind. As I played, though, I failed once more to notice something I should have observed before. The purple box given to me by an old man dying on some planet far away was glowing inside the living room.

The flashing light was seemingly harmless as I forced the man to walk back to his bedroom; I ignored it, believing it to be so—I still hadn't figured out how to use the box. I would just have to try something else. Once inside, I was able to ensnare his wife under my spell as well—like the man, she failed to realize how much noise she made while sneaking around upstairs with a hammer.

I played the last bit of my blade, trying to erase the memories of me being in their home. I wasn't sure what I would do about the daughter. *The best thing,* I thought, *is to delete her real memory from their heads. Treat her as if she was nothing more than a photograph on a wall. This is the worst thing I've ever done,* I thought, though I knew I was making the right choice. Killing her was one thing, but to take away the memory of love—that is monstrous. Only, if they couldn't remember her, I had done nothing wrong.

I was going to be able to fix all of this soon. I started to purge these people's memories, when the shining light from the box burst forward with radiation that I could see even from upstairs.

I covered my eyes, pulling down my mask as I ran towards the light, hoping that I had not somehow messed up my plan after everything I had done, everything for my family. I ran into the living room, the light burning through even my mask lens. I squinted as a form appeared from the box. It was circling in a ray of millions of colors. It took a shape I could not fathom.

I gripped my purple blade, readying my attack against the unknown, when I heard a voice inside my head.

Like sand, your memories fall through your fingers, So lonely,

When an island can't see why the sand lies across him,
When 'missing' doesn't have a blind date to lose,
even Death reminisces over the dead.

When there's nothing to be,
nothing can fill what I'm missing,
there's no emptiness for a mind to have feared.

The distance is too far for an echo!
And too dark for the eloquent thought to travel.
Though the memory thus fades into the wind.

You are grains of sand, slipping through my fingers.
Your memories will never be whole again.

The message of the voice caused my fingers to vibrate, and I almost dropped the blade. Suddenly the colorful form disappeared, shooting into thousands of pieces, and flew all around me into the outside world. I gasped, feeling like someone had just gone inside me, a dagger inside my windpipe cutting all the way down to my chest. I felt exposed and naked before the world.

My knees buckled and I fell, walloping the ground. As I sweated, and vomit once again charged its way up my throat, I looked to the top of the staircase, seeing an empty spot. I wasn't sure who that voice was, or what the overall message of its words were. Something made me feel like I should leave that place as soon as possible. The purple box radiated with one final blast before disappearing into colors, just like the thing inside had. I reached into my pocket and pulled out the blue blade. A quick twirl and I was on the outside of the apartment complex again.

A frigid realization came over me: the full weight of what exactly I had unleashed wouldn't become apparent for a while. I would succeed in my goal; I had managed to create the world ending event, just not in a way where I would have any control.

In horror, I stood dumbfounded as the city around me tore and crumbled into pieces and the streets ran rivers of bodies and blood. I closed my eyes, not wanting to see what I had done. I ended up forcing my eyes open at the flashing lights and screams I heard overhead. I felt like I was in a war zone. The city was a crumbling house of cards. The citizens, twinkles of tinder to the great flame of doom.

As my hell on this Earth was unleashed, I saw James—I now knew everything about the man—the father who's daughter I had stolen, same as mine was stolen from me. He stood alone, overlooking the annihilation of everything that made any sense in his world. He was a brave man, I decided at that moment. Somehow able to face the darkness of the world; he was looking towards something directly across from him. For a moment, I wondered if it was me he had found, when I saw his eyes tracking up to his wife.

From this close, I could see her skin crawling as if something had invaded the inside. She was standing at the edge. I sucked in my breath, knowing what was going to come next. She was muttering, "Memories, memories leave me be. Memories, memories take me as thou made my offspring. Memories, kill my husband, get him to suffer." She continued as I watched the horror on James' face turn to pure and utter terror. His wife spoke one final sentence before she jumped to her death on the pavement below: "Your fault."

He screamed, and the rest of the world did not stop. His wife would soon become nothing but a horrible memory. One that I was sure he would never be able to live down. I wondered, though, what she meant by it being his fault. He had done nothing wrong. I had searched his mind; he would have jumped off that building to save his wife if he could have. I looked at his building; people below were leaning in its direction. My spot across the road wouldn't be secure for long; I would need to move soon.

I turned, leaving James for my safety; I hoped I hadn't ruined this plan. This many deviations made me nervous—it wasn't my style to play fast and loose. This operation had taken enough effort. In the back of my mind, though, I'd set forth to make my plan into a reality. I had replaced some of James' memories. Just enough to tide him over until I could sort this mess out.

That put me in the perfect position to do what needed to be done; I could correct the oversights of tonight when next I saw James. Turn that man into a hero, bring the man in shadows and then capture that elusive red-eye. I just needed to get control of the situation again.

However, this, this apocalypse around me was unforeseen. I was going to have to move quickly to help James. Quickly to help myself. I whirled my blue blade and transported myself to a better location, watching the circus play out below me. I could see thousands of what appeared to be ordinary people. Only these regular people were blank, covered in a loss that I could not understand. They were all heading to James' duplex. I wondered why that might be, when I patted my pockets in reflex—I had left the purple box inside the apartment. I assumed it had gone completely when I saw the sparks coming from it. I remembered now that it had still been there as I left. Smaller, but still there. *Why hadn't I picked it up?*

I swore at my stupidity. There was no way I was going to make it through all of that. I bided my time in the apartment adjacent to James', and felt the pressure from the army inside his home.

It was like being stuck in a vacuum, judging by the level of noise, and everything swirling and heading for one man's living room. I stayed above James' duplex. I saw black smoke rising from inside his apartment. I had tested out the powers of the purple blade before, even if I hadn't been around, and it would project what I wanted him to see. I was confident that part of my plan would work. It had to; I just had to get that box back. Leaving it open and uncontrolled spelled bad for me.

As the people entered James' place, I saw him stumbling on the inside. I waited; I wanted to see if any people followed James. Hours passed, and I could hear noises from James place. Soon, it was days passing, I fell asleep at one point, the harsh sun beating down on my tattered clothes. I stayed hiding on the roof as the world around me grew silent. When I was sure that James was alone, I decided to follow. There was a moment of time when I had lost track of him from earlier. Again I assured myself that it wasn't a worry. He was still alive, somehow hiding inside of his home like a coward.

Besides James being a good man, I'd picked him because he wasn't the type to go out of his way to be a hero. Which made him predictable, made him comfortable. I had tested my knife; I had run through my plan. There were a few setbacks, but I could handle them.

Using the blue blade, I was able to teleport inside James' apartment. Once I made it inside, I found him unconscious, his body gnarled and burnt like an animal in a slaughterhouse.

His forehead burned and was covered with sweat; I had no real experience in medical needs. I fumbled, dragging him out of the kitchen. His dead weight was made all the worse from his smell. He felt like death, a living corpse I had found, when by all rights he should have been dead.

I set the wounded man on the ground and looked at his hand. He was going to die quickly, from what I could tell; I breathed hard. My rage was building; I had gone through all this effort just to lose this man. That wasn't going to happen. I wasn't going to give up so easily. A whole world was turning into a shitstorm around me; I wasn't going to be the primary cause of it.

I felt in a way that somewhere, that red-eyed monster was laughing at me; he would find it funny, my constant failure in capturing him. I pulled the blue blade from my pocket. I dug through James' house until I found a computer in his office. The power was still on—that was surprising. As I typed, searching for a local hospital, I felt a cold shiver run its wet hands down my body over and over. I had to stop multiple times to check and see if I was alone.

I soon found a hospital in the local area. I whirled the blue blade, and I turned into shadows, flying towards the pictures I'd found in the search. Inside the hospital, I took my time in the abandoned tomb-like structure, looking through various medical products. Once I found everything I needed, I left the hospital. And again, the entire time I was there, a strange feeling never left as if I was being watched.

Back inside James' house, I found him on the floor, coughing and climbing his way to the door. I had to admire his bravery, and the man just didn't seem to want to quit. Only, he wasn't the only one that would not stop, no matter the situation. Over the next couple of days, I nursed James back into health, kept him from becoming infected and dying when I needed him most.

Each night I would lay him down and use the purple blade, repairing his memories the way that I saw fit, erasing every image of myself from his mind. Instead, I carefully built a lie that he and I had known each other for several years. It was easy, pretending to be something you are not; human relationships are nothing more than triggered emotions based on situational responses.

I decided to leave the memories of his daughter, and even left him with his wife's final moments. Seeing what had transpired between them had sickened me to the core. No poor man should have had to kill his own wife. James had a mission, though; he was going to help me save this planet.

We were going to hunt the most dangerous prey in the entire universe. My biggest problem was not James, though. I couldn't find my purple box and all the while I couldn't help but feel uneasy. Like I was being eyed by something big, something dangerous. Every day, James and I were alone in his place, with no trace of the people I had seen the night I dropped the box. For that matter, no evidence of anyone else in the city. It was as if the whole city had simply stopped. A fragment in time.

After another few days, I left James alone on the ground in the kitchen, erasing the memories of him and me together. As I cleaned the apartment one last time, I saw movement coming from the young girl's room. I had become accustomed to the strange aberrations that seemed to stalk the world now. Still, though, the freaks had a way of scaring me, nonetheless. They just weren't human. Without the blue blade, the things would have caught me a couple of times. I would study them up close later, I noted. They did their job; the city was empty. That was all that mattered.

"Destroy the world, let James save the world. Lure the big man in, save your family. Keep to the plan," I stated as I took the blue blade from my pocket and slowly made my way to the girl's room.

The room smelled of dry blood and little girl's soap; which was a much more pleasant smell in the background, rather than her decaying form inside the fridge. I still wasn't sure how that had happened, I hadn't had any time to find out what the creatures were made of, or what exactly they were doing here.

I tiptoed inside the darkness of the girl's room when I saw the young lady who I had murdered only a few days ago.

She stood perfectly still, her eyes transfixed on me, not blinking. I stood facing towards her, afraid to move. I was holding my breath, keeping as still as possible. She had managed to frighten me to the point that I could not move. I felt stuck in place from her powerful gaze.

I walked backward out of the room, feeling her eyes inside my head as I made my way out to Jim. He was on the ground of the kitchen, and I felt a steady increasing thump in my heart. I needed to get out of here, before whatever that thing was in that girl's room decided to come after me.

I pulled on my mask, feeling safe in its rubber confines, leaving me feeling like I was somehow protected from that demon girl's stare. She just wasn't a natural part of this world, and something felt wrong. I took one last look at James, not sure if my plan had any real chance of success now. My whole plan depended on whether I could turn this now broken man into a hero; even more challenging was to capture that elusive son of a bitch and hopefully undo everything that he had caused. The death of that young girl and the man almost dead inside his kitchen was his fault. It wasn't mine.

She floated closer, and I flinched back, afraid of her eyes. I hadn't found a way to deal with those things yet. Though iron from James memories looked promising. I needed to find some. Sparing one last glance at James, I pulled my mask up, placing the blue blade to my mouth. I pictured the next building over, and I blew into the blade. I left that house, the girl tracking me the whole way. I flinched when she appeared near me, and I blew into the edge, this time a lot further away. I had lost her, as I stood in an empty park, near a soccer field.

I could go back and get James—that girl though, I had a feeling she would still be there. I just needed to figure out how to deal with her. *The plan would work, the plan would always work.* I went to blow into the blue blade again, but as I pressed the cold foreign metal to my mouth, nothing came. Stunned, I tried repeatedly, trying the process again and again until I was all out of breath. I looked at the blade; its coloring was changing from an icy blue to a faint azure, borderline white. Frustrated, I threw the blade to the ground, and upon impact the blade shattered.

"Son-of-a-bitch!" I cursed into the open park. I had no idea where I was, where James' house was. *Why have an address when I had the blade?* The blades must have run on some kind of power source. I had used both blades considerably in the years since I had acquired them. I swore more, echoing the calls of an angry lion losing its meal. I would just have to trust my plan; it would work soon enough.

As the sun set over the city, I looked around me. Things were in the windows. I was not alone. I moved out of the park, heading deeper into the city. I just had to get back to James. The game was set, the pieces were in play, and I was ready to do the impossible in the name of love. All the pieces had their tools, and all the pieces were at play…

I pulled my hands away from the man before me. We had known each other for twenty years. *Twenty years, his name was Wilson,* I thought. He had killed my daughter. I felt nothing at this, as the last of his memories flowed into my head. *After all, what was a daughter?*

Chapter 60

As I leaned over Wilson's body, in shock and still taking it in, further memories of his continued to flood into my mind...

Benny and I drove for three miles, weaving in and out of the city's obscurities. The time it took was unknown to me; all I could get off my mind was how the plan had gone wrong.

Twenty years of losing your loved ones, twenty years of constant scares and absolutely no form of any genuine human contact. I'd always figured that would make a person a lot harder. I thought that Jim was a lot tougher. I held the purple dagger in my lap; I'd looked at it many times a day. With all the power it granted me, I still elected to leave the hero to have somewhat free will at the end. It was just hard to control people who were capable of abstract thought. That's why it worked better on Benny—he was too far gone to think.

I had managed to get to James early on, way back when this had all occurred. I had planted the idea that he had known me during his whole life. It wasn't that hard; all I had to do was plant the image of me over someone else he had known.

Which still wasn't that easy. A nerd like James always had only a few friends. His type always had close friends though, which made it all too exhausting. I was eventually able to seamlessly integrate into his life, yet it might have just been thrown into a fire from the start. In the end, he still didn't do what I needed him to do. All I needed was for him to kill. Ignore that big heart of his, just to lay waste to beings that didn't even exist.

My throat filled with spit and bitter anger, every time I thought of

James. I wanted to picture the flash of his eyes closing repeatedly as he ended. *All he had to do was kill the ghosts and save the girl. That's the basic plot to every hero journey ever made.* In the end, though, my plan didn't work. That never happens; that wasn't supposed to happen.

I breathed in deep, controlling my anger as Benny drove.

I looked at my side mirror, catching my reflection; my hair was turning a light gray in patches. When had that started happening? I was getting older every day, my crusade no closer than it was twenty years ago. I had been trying to save my family for so long now that I didn't even know if it was possible anymore, or if it was even worth it.

I had taken the lives of so many people to get where I was, told too many lies and tales just to get what I wanted. And what I wanted was my vengeance. I had waited for an eternity; scratching, dangling the bait to attract the attention of the shark.

Was it worth it, though? I looked at my hands, flexing the knuckles, and feeling them pop from my movements. I had lost the blue knife twenty years ago; I had lost my chances of ever tracking my quarry. I had to plan, after being marooned on this planet. It had been the opportunity that got me here; there would be an opportunity again, I had figured. I was a murderer, yes, I knew that, but it could all be undone. All I had to do was catch that shadow, to tighten my hands around him again and end him.

No ocean of blood was too much, no graves of stars were cost too high. To lose one's everything, to lose everything that I had… that is something guys like James would never understand.

Guys like James are weak, weak in the mind, weak in the head, unlike me. I am strong. I can adapt and overcome, yes, I can, and I will find a way to catch the elusive man, the most elusive of men, and I will work out the way to return my family. I will do whatever it takes, no matter whom or what gets in my way. I squeezed my fingers together, feeling the power return to my limbs.

Yes, that is what I am going to do, I am going to find a way. I thought of my children, I thought of my wife. *My lovely, beautiful woman; I am going to get her back and soon, she will have to forgive me—*

"Hey boss, where we heading?" asked Benny as he looked at me nervously and back towards the road. His eyes were flickering over the pavement as the massive army of my ghosts circled behind us.

"Head for a tall building—that one off in the distance," I said, pointing to one of the larger buildings still intact here and in the next few states.

"You sure? I mean we can—" Benny started to speak.

"Be quiet and drive," I snapped at Benny. I had given him enough free will, and he had shown me the error of my ways by causing Jim and that girl to grow closer together.

That was the one thing that jeopardized the entire plan, and I should have taken care of her in the first place. No matter, though, the new scheme was simple. If the man in shadows only appeared at the end of the world, then I was going to kill every thing on this planet until he appeared. I would be the bait this time, not someone else. I would be the hero and wait for him.

Once he was here, then I would make my move. I would get back my family, and none of this would matter. The power that he posed, I had often wondered in my many years of planning where exactly he had gotten it from, and whom or what had granted him this power.

What force would give rise to a man like that? I thought about the time back on the island. He had lost his family as well, which meant that he and I should have at least understood each other in that regard.

As I sat and thought, Benny made it to the tower. Its massive structure was only equaled by another tower opposite it. Both buildings were covered in vines and littered with shattered glass. However, it was the perfect place to plan my next move.

We arrived at the building, and I glided up the stairs with no fear of infrastructure failure, no fear of anything that was going to go "boo." *I am the scariest thing in the darkness; I am the reason for a night light.* I found the office at the very back, at the very top. The inside was covered with mold on the ground, and the whole room reeked.

I donned my gas mask and within seconds, the smell wasn't as bad. I was able to think clearer when all senses were dulled, safe from this filthy world. I sat down in the rotting remains of a chair and shifted through the holes in my plan.

I had summoned the ghost children to attack us at the cabin—I had taken control of the children weeks before; all in preparation for the assault. The hardest part had been hiding the children from that damn girl Holly's senses. She was always suspecting something. That was why I gave the ghost boy Joey power—instead of giving him raw power such as the girl Holly had, I gave the boy powers of blocking. He had a shield that stretched like a dome over everything, only allowing what could be seen and felt by what I had told the boy should be done. I even used the blade to make everyone docile and trusting—*and hadn't it worked! None of them suspected a thing.*

That was why little Joey seemed so dull and with no personality. I had to give the boy so many memories, but not enough to be able to remember who or what he was. Every night, I would have Kim bring him to my office. I would pull back any memories of his old life he'd started to regain.

So, when Jim was knocked out, I swooped in and altered his memories just enough. I implanted the idea that he had to rescue Kim, that he had to save her no matter what. The biggest kicker was that when he saved Kim from the ghosts, he would have to kill the demons, including Kim.

With her dead, along with the ghost of his daughter, Jim would start actively hunting the ghosts to extinction. I would help him in that process by killing all the other ghosts around the world, or subjecting them to my will, if need be. Eventually, the numbers would bring shadows here.

The hardest part was altering James' memories. I just had to knock him out to do it. His daughter was always around, and for my dagger to work, I need to have a physical touch. Not to mention that its power seemed to be leaving. I wasn't sure why, but it took longer to implant what I wanted using the blade now. It didn't affect passive feelings as well as it used to. James was too suspicious the whole time. I should have tightened my hold on him when I had the chance. To make matters worse, I had to turn off everything that would lead Jim away from Kim.

What I didn't see coming was Jim somehow ignoring everything I had planned in my mind. He had done something heroic, I suppose, setting all those… things free. But, it wasn't as brave as him destroying all the ghosts on the planet. *After all, they'd destroyed the world. Why set them free?*

I thought deeper, with anger growing inside my chest, *the plan should have worked.* The red-eyed man should have appeared and would have killed Jim, a martyr for all injustice in this world, and my army of ghosts would have been enough to overpower the shadow man.

I had to make the plan so complicated in the first place to maintain the illusion of free will with the hero. After all, no one could save the world if they were a slave inside their mind. I popped my fingers while sitting in the chair, letting all my hate flow through me. When I stood up with the answer, my plan would have worked overtime; it just didn't have enough kindling, enough wood for the fire.

I left the moldy room and walked down the hallway, finding Kim and Benny awaiting me in what appeared to be an old employee's lounge. Benny didn't even look up from his sitting position. Drugs and smoke had long since rotted what little brain Benny had. I'd promised the man his brother's body back in return for his services. He didn't question anything, just constantly demonstrated how useless he was.

Kim however, she kept her eyes glued to the floor. I knew what she was thinking; about the tragedy that this world had torn her husband and only child away from her. I couldn't control Christina as well as

I liked, she was too strong willed. And Rob, the crippled shit had a brain—go figure. Both helped keep me prepared and able to carry out my many operations over the years. They made it possible for me to find Jim and to recruit more ghosts unwillingly.

As for Kim, I had brought back her son. It didn't matter what state he was in, ghost or alive. She finally had someone who could relate to, despite flesh and blood no longer existing between the two of them. If she had her child, I could get her to do anything I wanted. Even betraying and lying to an innocent man, by all accounts.

Innocent was a stretch with Jim. He was an animal in every sense of the word. I had looked in his head and seen the sins that he had committed throughout his life. Jim was gone now; he had a good shot at finally ending my long fast for my family.

I looked at Kim and Benny, just two of my other tools. Not the best, or the sharpest, but exactly what I needed to bring that shadow back into my life.

I spoke quickly and deliberately: "You two are not to leave this building under any circumstances. I will be having the army search out all other humans besides those in this room. And then those humans will all be killed. Humanity will die very soon. Any questions?"

Neither spoke, so I turned, getting ready to send my army of ghosts onto the world.

"Wait, Wilson, when can I get my brother back?" Benny asked. I turned back towards Benny, my anger growing at his audacity to ask me such a question.

"You're part of the problem; you and your brother had one job. Kill Jim's daughter; get rid of her so the plan could be easily carried out. Instead, you bring them closer together. Forcing me to use one of my strongest ghosts! Your niece, who turned out to be as useless as her uncle, also failed. My answer is no, Benny. Your brother will not be coming back today, or, for that matter, any time soon," I snarled

Benny cast his eyes to the ground like the dog he was. I wanted nothing more than to kill him at that moment, to tear his head off with my bare hands. I considered unleashing another torture on his mind. I never enjoyed doing that to a man, but it motivated people in such interesting ways. I stuffed that feeling down for now; some bombs were just meant to go off at a particular time. That one, however, wasn't ready yet. The long exposure to horror and the subsequent unwinding of my sanity due to the horror could wait. Soon, this would all be over.

I smoothed down my clothes, a tick I caught myself doing more often as the days wore on. I looked at Benny and Kim. They were both poor lost souls, latching onto anything that was holding out a bone, like dogs. I was here to give these dogs a purpose; I was here to help these people.

"What's happened, has happened and can't be undone. Unforeseen holes always pop up in a plan."

I paused, letting my words sink into the group. The next part was the most important and I needed everyone to perform one last task for me. I continued, making sure to hit every syllable and word with one-hundred-percent clarity.

"I will be sending out the ghosts for one last mission: to kill everything that is alive on this planet; everything else outside of this room. It will be worth it, though, a reckoning that can be only completed with the death of everyone." I turned from the two and stared off into the distance as the sun was setting over the scrawl of a ghost city.

"To kill everyone is to give everyone that died unjustly the chance at life. To murder the world, to snatch the last flicker from the candle is to give a bonfire in return..."

And those are the memories of my friend Wilson, I thought as they quickly disappeared, and I left his body in the dusty room. My walk was strained as I headed to the doorway, out of this broken room I was in.

Chapter 61

Each floor I passed on the way out of the second tower was covered in dust, littered with the remains of the years. A monument of metal with not a soul in its confines. At the bottom floor, a young woman and child met me.

She was younger looking now; I still recognized her from earlier, with darker black hair, fewer lines at her corners. *Her name is Kim*; I thought to myself, *I had given her my name.* Not sure what to say to her, I avoided her and went around towards the doors.

"This morning, you made a promise; will you still stand by it?" she asked as I made my way to the door.

I turned back to her, the blue line shared between the two of us still visible. The young child next to her had sandy blond hair and the same slim build as his mother. He had no line, but his eyes were black like Wilson's. *So what if there's two fewer ghosts? I had no other plan for the others.* I nodded my head towards Kim; she nodded back taking the young boy's hand, and they disappeared.

Turning back to the doors, I wrapped myself tighter. I had taken Wilson's coat before leaving. It was getting colder outside, and I was afraid that the winter would only keep getting colder. Outside, my army of ghosts all stood before me. Tiny and Kyle looked calm and apprehensive; in fact, all my comrades looked eager for something.

I felt something hot on my legs and boots. I looked down at the tattered remains of my jeans; blood dripped on them from my gnarled hand. The power I had used to hold the blood in was fading fast. Worse was the very air I was breathing was noxious; a poison of fumes and gray snow fell all around us. All of this probably from the littered remains of the other building, a fitting end to everything.

I looked at the huge crowd before me, some connected through blue lines, some just... blank, like they had no idea where and what they were. That made us all the lost, the shades of who we were. I could feel power gathered from my connected ghosts and I drew on it, like the drawing of a blade. When it was finished, there was no more blood coming out of my arm.

I looked up, and there were thousands of strangers all staring at me, all absent and long faced. Some round, some on all fours, some in the air, all staring right at me. I wondered why they looked at me. I tried talking to some as I passed through their ranks; no one responded. And the whole time, I noticed that a large majority of them had this weird blue line sprouting from them. It was peculiar.

A harsh wind swept over me as I wandered amongst the quiet, as I was calling them now. *Maybe they didn't understand what I was saying; maybe I didn't understand what I was saying.*

Every few steps, my eyes would burn from something floating in the air and my chest ached, causing me to pause, coughing, until yellow came out of my mouth, mixed in with this murky brown.

I wander far from the broken remains of some huge building. I imagined it must have been built for giant men. What a strange place it was to be littered with so much metal and scraps of twisted rubble amongst splotches of red. A world composed entirely of gray and cold. I made it to the top floor of a building during my wandering. It seemed warm enough—I was very cold.

Inside a room, there was a wooden box frame, and a small wooden chair was overlooking a balcony. I sat down in the chair, feeling strangely tired, and I kept getting all these feelings like I needed something, as I sat. My middle section of my body was rumbling, and my throat felt like I had swallowed glass. I was having trouble knowing the names of everything. One second, something would come, the next, I would forget what I had been thinking. Everything was floating.

My head felt rattled, shaking in this frozen planet.

I kept thinking I should move from the chair and the open window. It was hard for me; I wasn't sure what I was or what even the window was. I noticed after a while that things didn't stay in my head, I would have to keep concentrating on dust, as everything else was so scattered.

Now in that room alone, I was disoriented, lost inside my mind. I wasn't sure if it was bad or good. *Why had I come into this room in the first place? Why did my body shake?* I felt this burning along my skin. An icy dragon dancing all over me, scaring me like shadows running over a frozen lake. *Why did it have to be so cold—what is the cold?* So I sang a song, the only song that I understood in the cold:

What makes a wounded man dance?
What makes that man smile?
Can he smile?
Will there be light kept in your heart for the wounded?
Will you stand by as a gun is in his grip, becoming lighter and lighter
Until all that is left are his lingering thoughts on the wall?

You don't have to be a jailer to lock away a man's heart.

Without love his heart will dangle into the darkness, only bait for the real monsters in life.

With all the monsters that await in the darkness and angels always a breath too late; he will want to die.

And yet puddles become deeper, darker, endless drops in a sea of darkness; only forlornness will exist.

Everywhere is a lonely place to die for the wounded man, if he's never had love.

It matters not the scars that strike his body or the terror in his heart.

Make that wounded man smile again, show him the light, take him to dance.

Show him the embrace of a warm hug, a kiss on his lips for the start of the days, or until the end of days.
Show him it's more natural to die, but even harder to live.
In whatever way love is a verb, caring is easy if the heart is open,
My, you should watch those legs move to the beat of love.

I sang to no one, as my words danced into the day.

Chapter 62

I pondered each trail of dust that gathered inside my mind when a voice spoke up from behind me.

"Hello, Jim," said someone who had a ring over the "J" sound; it sounded very different from my voice. Naturally, I latched onto his voice. It had been so long since I'd heard anything, even the sounds in my head sounded mumbled, deformed. Nothing that I could hold on to.

I spun in my splintered chair to see a man dressed in neat black trousers and a long coat that came almost to his knees. He had a black tie, a black matching hat, dark hair, and cinnamon-colored skin. I felt like I had seen him before; I felt words coming back to me as I looked at him. Yes… words, things that could describe my world around me. My body shook as I looked at him. Images of flashy dull grays and crystals of red fiery pain lashed all over me. *The more I could describe, the worse it felt. I shouldn't be able to understand words; this was awful, a retched thing to understand pain.*

My eyes tracked down to his eyes; they were a dark shade of red, glowing crimson. Despite his appearance before me, he still had a glow about him that I couldn't place, like someone who was completely at ease, and the cold seemed to not affect him in the slightest.

"Who are you, mister?" I asked the man as he leaned against the wall next to me, crossing his arms and legs.

"I had a name once. A long time ago, I had a family just like you," he said, ignoring my question.

I thought about what he said; *I had a family? I wonder what happened to them and why can't I remember them?* "I had a family?" I asked, perplexed at the very notion, the very idea throwing up waves inside my head and leaving nothing known.

"Yes, you had a family. This will be a lot easier if you remember—here." The man spoke and stepped towards me, brandishing a long purple dagger from under his suit jacket. I saw dozens of strange blades when he removed the knife, all different sizes and colors. None looked pleasant.

I was more concerned about him using that long blade on me; it had a wicked look about it that didn't scream "playing nice" time. I stood up, knocking the chair over. "Look, mister, I don't want any trouble—"

"It's no trouble at all, James," the man said, plunging the dagger into my head. My eyes couldn't track the movement as the blade went hilt-deep into me. I flinched, and I was thrown into a roller coaster, my mind spinning into a vortex of colors. I was shown an image of a small baby being placed into the arms of a mother.

She had the same angular features as me, and a man next to her had a mop top of red hair. I was jerked again and shown the life of that baby; his love of computers, learning, all his awkwardness of life leading up to his adult life.

That boy grew up to be a successful person, married to a beautiful blonde girl who looked like the very image of an angel on a cloud. Together, the couple managed to make a beautiful baby. And by God, was she beautiful. She had her mother's hair, but the deep blue eyes of her father.

An image of the three at a shining park was shown next. The father twirling the girl around with his hands and the mother giggling in the background; I could tell that it was the happiest time in the man's life.

Then, things... things went down into the dark below; I was spun further along the man's life. I saw his wife jumping from a building, his hand being bitten off by himself, his daughter dying. The images moved faster and faster until I vomited. I heard his voice, somewhere in the pictures, the voice of the man with red eyes, the man in shadows, the man from Wilson's memories. The man from the bar, so long ago.

"Do you remember now, Jim? Do you know now?" he asked as I drifted along in the darkness, a depth blacker than a planet with no sun.

"Yes, I remember," I answered to the night.

I knew what my name was now. My name was James, and I was a father and a husband. I had lost everything I had in my life, becoming a monster in the process of gaining my revenge. I started to weep in the darkness; the one thing I never wanted in this wasteland of life was to be made to remember it.

I closed my lids for a long time, swimming in the gloom of my eyes. When I opened them, I was in a room, with the walls and ceiling sun-dried yellow from many years of not being kept up.

I lifted my head, seeing a balcony at the end of an opened section of the room. Turning my face, I could see a knocked-over wooden chair and the wicked smile of a madman was looking right back at me.

"Welcome back, James. How was your trip?" he asked, smiling wide.

"Memory lane was fan-fucking-tastic. Thank you for that," I responded angrily, but knowing of my current state, I had a better chance of flying to the moon than beating this guy. I thought about calling my army of ghosts, but what was the point? If it weren't him driving me mad right now, it would be some other terror instead. "What do you want, devil?" I asked the man.

"Devil? What is this, a medieval witch hunt? Please, Jim, I thought better of you," he stated.

I stood up slowly; something was burning in my stomach. I couldn't get the images out of my head. "Are they real?" I asked.

"Did you say something, Jim? You really need to speak up," he said mockingly.

I cleared my throat before speaking. "Is everything you shown me true? Did all that happen?" I asked, feeling sicker as the words came from my mouth.

"Would it make you feel any better, knowing the truth?" The man in shadows sighed. "Here, take a seat before you pass out. I will try and explain everything. We have time... well, you know what will need to happen," Shadows said, pulling the chair up to me.

I sat down. I still felt like an endless pit had been opened inside my stomach.

"Rough day huh, Jim?" Shadows asked, a hint of concern in his voice.

I turned my head and gave him a long look. "Just get on with it already," I grunted.

"Okay, grumpy. Well, for starters, yes, the images you saw of Wilson just now are correct. And before you ask, my dagger here can change what people know—show them things, anything the wielder wants them to see. It can also control you, within limits. Wilson was in possession, as you know, of two of my daggers," he said gesturing with the one in his hand.

I faced forward, looking out over the balcony. The sun was starting to come up in the distance as a light rain began to fall. It all felt familiar, like him and I had been doing this for a very long time. Hearing his story, the pieces adding into place. *Listening to him helped; you can only sink so deep into an ocean before you hit bottom, and this was just part of the sinking,* I thought.

"So, yes, Wilson killed your daughter. It was an accident, of course; the poor delusional fool thought he could bring back the dead. The painful truth of life is simple: enjoy your time with your loved ones while you can, but you can never change what is; change will only just change again. And there is nothing more to it, nothing more than the endless waves all around us," Shadows informed me.

"Were you the man that planted that letter, long ago? The man in the bar?" I asked.

"Yes," he responded.

I shuddered, continuing on. "I... figured as much. That always bugged me. I suppose you could explain what happened and why you did that, huh?"

"I needed to get more information as to why Wilson liked you so much; see how much he knew."

I thought about his words. "You could have just asked."

"Yes, I suppose," he said nonchalantly.

I clenched my fist, grinding my teeth as I pinched my words. "Can—you tell me why on Earth you gave him the option of being able to do what he did to everyone here—what he did to my daughter!"

"There is madness in us all; Wilson chose to take a weapon from a being he did not understand. To that end, Wilson broke that weapon on accident. The weapon had the power to weaponize memories, the most abundant source of power on any planet with anything that is self-aware. What you have been seeing, what you have been fighting against for all these years, were just memories, flashes of your mind. Ghosts, like you thought, and in a sense, that is all memories are—ghosts of what we know and remember." Shadows let the words die in the air. Then he continued. "It is my job to watch first and act accordingly at the right time. Those are the rules," he said bluntly.

"Yeah well, who wrote the rules on living anyways? I sure as hell did not. You're telling me that a man killed this entire planet because he couldn't stand being without his family—no, you're telling me that he did this all on accident because an eight-year-old little girl scared a man in the dark? Why didn't you stop him! If you knew exactly what he was doing, you could have easily killed him," I replied stubbornly.

The man in shadows cleared his throat as well, taking his time to be deliberate. "Yes, that is exactly what I am telling you. I can't tell you everything now, but there are only two constants in this. Two universal truths. No matter your species, or what dimension you're in, all things living are entitled to two things: a life and death. I had no idea what Wilson was doing until it had already begun," Shadows said.

I remained quiet, continuing to stare at the balcony. I wasn't sure what hurt most, the fact that Wilson had killed my daughter—twice—or that it was all because he wanted to bring back his family. I hated Wilson with everything I had. I did, and it was just hard when—I didn't want to finish my thought; it had been too much sorrow for one day.

"So that you know, this isn't the way things were supposed to go. Everything went downhill fast for you," he said, pulling out an old rusted pan out of his jacket. "I thought you would like this back. You did a lot with an iron skillet. Shocking, really—you had such a connection to that iron tub of yours that you turned iron into a source that could kill memories." He smirked, looking at my old iron pan.

"You keep saying that. How the hell were things supposed to go, asshole?" I blew the words from my mouth.

"You were working on a video game, a video game that you spent most of your nights working on in a modest office. Well, one day, that game would have been finished, and the amazing thing is that your game would have inspired another mind, that would change the world. Your world was to have an end in peace; it was to prosper for many generations. You were supposed to help save this planet. The moment Wilson picked you, the time that he decided to follow you home was the moment that both of your destinies changed. Wilson was, in fact, the hero of this planet once he changed everything. He introduced a virus on an otherwise clean planet. An unending cancer on this Earth, spreading endlessly. You're now the last remaining living thing, besides the birds and the bees. I am sorry—truly I am,"

Shadows said somberly.

He looked off into the window beyond, before speaking. "It saddens me deeply to come into a story like this. It's like reading part of a book and someone switching it out while you're reading it, never knowing what was supposed to be said. That is life, though, a series of moments that may be chronological. Most of the time they're not so, as far as we can tell. Every story is always being told only from a certain point. I am sorry to say, Jim, that your story never got to have its point beyond just one thing: you got to have love in your life at least. Though, having that love lost may not have been worth it in the end." He sighed, looking back at me.

"How would you even know what it's like to have lost a family?" I declared.

"I had a family once; I loved them very much. But, that—that is my story, another tale for another time. We were all fathers. It seemed we were both willing to turn into monsters to get our families back." His red eyes drilled holes into mine.

His words hit me hard; *I was the last man on Earth. Not only that, he was implying that I was some villain. That I had lost everything in my life, for no other reason than it just happened.* "So, Wilson picked me? Lucky fucking me, they should throw me a party. Tell you what? Keep your apology and shove it. Why not just let me rule my mound of mud?" I shouted.

The man in shadows stepped around the front of my chair and knelt until we were both eye level.

"This is all a part of the balance, Jim. Like I said, I am sorry for what happened. I know what it's like... I know what it's like to lose everything that you hold dear inside your life, only for it all to end, snuffed out like the flame of a candle. Wilson sought to gain my power—to turn back the wheels of time. That isn't a power that I have, but what I do have is knowledge, access to those who control the balance. You have nothing here for you, Jim." He stood and pulled another item from inside his coat and threw it into my lap.

It was a noose, already tied, and already fitted for my size. "You can sit here and wail in a self-pity party until the end of your days. That won't be long, though, I assure you. That wound on your arm can only be held in by their power for so much longer. You're slipping; memories such as what you call the ghosts, are driven by them. If you have no new strong memories to share, well, eventually, you will die. That is what that nitwit failed to understand when he took the memory box. Its power will eventually kill the user, period. Unless that user can keep making more memories. The ghosts only appeared to people because they had memories of something robust enough to either attract other memories or create new ones," he said, stepping behind me again.

I followed him with my gaze as he stopped at the adjacent wall, facing it. "Are you saying Holly was only a memory I was keeping alive in my mind?" I asked weakly.

"No, I am saying that she was there, from the very beginning. You were feeding her, keeping her alive. She only remained because you continued, Jim. All the ghosts will turn as your wife did with time. Turn into shades of themselves, until they finally fade away. Their bones are gone, their memories burnt like the reels from a movie. Eventually, this world was going to die. Everything was doomed the moment that man teleported into your home. Life serves to cycle to death, just as death cycles to life. There is no changing that," Shadows stated, swinging round in front of me again.

"Come with me, Jim; there is no reason to die here," he pleaded, looking at the wall like he was searching for a hidden answer within its confines.

"And what are you offering me... eternal damnation in a fiery pit?" I quipped.

The man in shadows sighed a very long breath, rubbing the top of his head. "Once again, I am not the Devil—the Devil would be jealous of the number of souls that I have come across, the things I've done."

Shadows looked at the wall, his mind somewhere in an endless stream. "My time in this job—it is ending. I need a replacement. For soon, I will be rejoining my family."

Rejoining, did he mean that? After all, he was the one who had said death could not be undone. "You will get your family back—but how?" I stammered.

"That is a question I can't answer either—I will have to show you. Come with me through the door." He gestured, taking a blue knife out of his coat; he stabbed the knife to the hilt through the weakened walls, tracing a door in its crumbling rock. True to statement, a blue door formed before him. I could see light coming from the door, but I couldn't see what was making the light, from my vantage point.

If he could be with his family, I thought. "What will happen if I come with you?" I asked.

"Lots will," he answered.

"Will—will any more die?" I hesitantly asked.

"An untold amount will, yes, I assure you—if the answer to us being reunited with our families is out there. If there is something else than the black and white of the galaxy, you stand a better chance of finding it by coming with me than staying here," he stated.

I wanted to come with him; I wanted to hold my girls once more in my arms. I couldn't leave the chair. I thought of Holly, my lighthouse when I was lost in the most raging seas. She wouldn't have wanted me to kill everyone just for her. Holly wouldn't have wanted me to have done what I did to Wilson, or to Benny. She would have wanted forgiveness. Maybe that was why I kept her memories; she was my conscience. I felt their deaths on my mind; I felt everyone who I had ever hurt, both the living and the dead. Their memories were cemented inside me for the rest of my days. I looked at the rope, and I knew my answer.

"I've come to believe that there are things that cannot be changed, like air is needed to make fire. I cannot leave this place any more than the moths can leave a flame once they see its light. I can have no more blood on my hands. My memories of this place keep me here," I stated, facing the balcony.

"What a shame, James, you would have been magnificent at this job," the man in shadows said.

I waved him on, still facing forward, knowing what I had to do to set things right. I waited a long time in the silence of the room. It was oddly peaceful; everything felt right at that moment. I stood up, taking the rope with me to the balcony overlooking the ruins of my city.

Down below me were memories, memories that had taken the shape of every form there is. Tall, broad, short, black, white, male, female, the young and the old. All fragments of a bigger picture than what they realized; all were searching for the meaning of what was in their heads, unable to move on from this place. They were ghosts of the mind, ghosts of everything that I could remember.

I tied the rope to the railing on the balcony; I hoped I had gotten the knot tight enough. I stepped up on to the railing, thousands of eyes looked upon me: center of the stage for the end of the world. I was the final punchline of the entirety of humanity; the last man on Earth would die without anyone to watch.

To my wife, thank you for the joy you gave me in our union. I am truly sorry for the way it went for our daughter. To both Holly and Molly, Daddy is the one to be blamed, not you, kiddos. I guess there is a heart after all in this ugly armadillo, I joked to myself. Facing my demise would be grossly mundane if I ended it on a sad note.

Might as well go out with my head held high. "My name is James, I was a computer guy all my life. I was the best in the world at solving problems. I had a loving wife and a beautiful daughter in every sense of the word. They were mine, and I was theirs. My name is James. I don't want to remember anymore. I am a ghost of the man I used to be. I—we are the ghosts of what we used to be."

I looked over the edge. Seeing all the ghosts below me, I had hoped to not become one, but I already had. I lifted my right leg and let it hang over the railing. The ledge no longer felt so wide.

Before I could jump, a giggle came from behind me. A father could never forget the noise of his children.

I turned my head fast, a large smile on my face. It had to be her. "Holly?"

About the Author

Jonathan Blazer is an Air force veteran, having served six years overseas. Mr. Blazer, born in Montgomery Alabama, has spent more time traveling and writing on the road than living at home. He holds a Bachelors of History from the University of Maryland, and is the author of a Psychological Horror Novel; "Out of the Night." He currently resides in Seattle, Washington working as a Systems Administrator. Mr. Blazer spends his time training for a thru-hike of the Appalachian Trail while writing his second novel.

CPSIA information can be obtained
at www.ICGtesting.com
Printed in the USA
LVHW091622101119
636890LV00001B/98/P